The Paris Review Book

of Heartbreak, Madness, Sex, Love, Betrayal,

Outsiders, Intoxication, War, Whimsy, Horrors,

God, Death, Dinner, Baseball, Travels,

The Art of Writing, and Everything

Else in the World Since 1953

THE PARIS REVIEW BOOK

of Heartbreak, Madness, Sex, Love, Betrayal,

Outsiders, Intoxication, War, Whimsy, Horrors,

God, Death, Dinner, Baseball, Travels,

The Art of Writing, and Everything

Else in the World Since 1953

❊

By the Editors of The Paris Review

WITH AN INTRODUCTION BY

GEORGE PLIMPTON

PICADOR · NEW YORK

THE PARIS REVIEW BOOK OF HEARTBREAK, MADNESS, SEX, LOVE, BETRAYAL, OUTSIDERS, INTOXICATION, WAR, WHIMSY, HORRORS, GOD, DEATH, DINNER, BASEBALL, TRAVELS, THE ART OF WRITING, AND EVERYTHING ELSE IN THE WORLD SINCE 1953. Copyright © 2003 by The Paris Review. All rights reserved. Printed in the United States of America. No part of this book may be used or reproduced in any manner whatsoever without written permission except in the case of brief quotations embodied in critical articles or reviews. For information, address Picador, 175 Fifth Avenue, New York, N.Y. 10010.

www.picadorusa.com

Picador® is a U.S. registered trademark and is used by St. Martin's Press under license from Pan Books Limited.

For information on Picador Reading Group Guides, as well as ordering, please contact the Trade Marketing department at St. Martin's Press.
Phone: 1-800-221-7945 extension 763
Fax: 212-677-7456
E-mail: trademarketing@stmartins.com

Designed by Kathryn Parise

LIBRARY OF CONGRESS CATALOGING-IN-PUBLICATION DATA AVAILABLE UPON REQUEST

ISBN 0-312-42238-5 (hc)
ISBN 0-312-42239-3 (pbk)
EAN 978-0312-42239-4

First Picador Paperback Edition: September 2004

10 9 8 7 6 5 4 3 2 1

Contents

✤

SEX

LOVE

BETRAYAL

WHIMSY

HORRORS

GOD

DEATH

DINNER

BASEBALL

TRAVELS

THE ART OF WRITING

Introduction

✠

The magazine from which the contents of this anthology have been gathered has been around for a long time. It is celebrating its fiftieth anniversary, a rare thing indeed since literary magazines enjoy rather butterfly-like existences, fading when both the enthusiasm of their editors and the number of subscribers flags.

The first issue of *The Paris Review* was published in the spring of 1953. At the time Paris was a lively center of literary activity, inexpensive, a postwar period with many young American writers there on the GI Bill of Rights. It was in this kind of culture dish atmosphere that *The Paris Review* was conceived by the novelist Peter Matthiessen, the late novelist Harold L. Humes, Donald Hall, who became its first poetry editor, William Pène du Bois, the art editor, and the undersigned, who has stuck with it since its beginnings. An introductory essay by William Styron stated the *Review*'s aims—to feature fiction and poetry rather than criticism. A noted decision was made to bypass the critics and interview the authors themselves to inquire of the creative process. A much remarked upon interview with E.M. Forster appeared in the first issue, dealing in part with why he (the most eminent writer in the English language at the time) had not written a novel since 1924. The ensuing series on the craft of writing, over two hundred and fifty interviews with novelists and poets, has been referred to by admirers as the DNA of literature. The present volume includes a number of excerpts from the series.

The *Review*'s half century of production has seen the early work published of a pantheon of writers and poets—William Styron, Evan S. Connell, Philip Roth, Nadine Gordimer, James Salter, Rick Bass, T. Coraghessan Boyle, Richard Ford, Mona Simpson, Jeffrey Eugenides, David Foster Wallace, Rick Moody, among the fiction writers, too many to list of the many hundreds of poets selected. The nonfiction material (in addition to the interviews on craft) has been extensive— reminiscences, articles, photographic essays, a series entitled "The Man in the Back Row Has a Question." As one can imagine, the source material from which to draw the contents for such an anthology as this is vast.

One way of judging a magazine is by what is called "shelf life"—a statistic that the most popular magazine editors don't enjoy very much. Their contributors have to be satisfied by not thinking of such things. On the other hand, a literary magazine, a quarterly like *The Paris Review,* has certain advantages. It doesn't arrive so often as to startle a subscriber with its frequency of appearance. It tends to be an anthology in itself, its contents worthy of more than a passing glance. So rather than being consigned to a wastepaper basket, it is set up on a shelf until eventually it becomes a collector's item. Old copies of the *Review* in the days before paper was treated with a preservative are handled with reverence, as if carved jade, so that its owner can turn its parchment-brown pages to study an early poem by a poet now hoary with distinction.

What has made it possible for this publication with its considerable shelf life to reach such a lofty plateau—a fiftieth anniversary? The answer lies, of course, in the large number of editors and writers who have seen fit to sustain what they thought was a good idea in the first place. Many come first as readers—often interns fresh from their university studies. Over 20,000 manuscripts come in annually, all read with diligent care and in hopes that perhaps *this one* will spring apart from the others and get passed on to the editors. In the homey clutter of the *Review*'s small office, the readers work in its basement— a worn blue carpet, stuffingless armchairs to disguise its semblance of a boiler room with its overhead pipes, electric meters clicking on a wall. Some stay on to become editors and give years rather than a summer to the *Review*.

Those who have come to the magazine for a short period, and even those who háve remained with editorial positions, rarely have had the time to browse through all the contents in the issues that line the office shelves. Fifty years' worth! But that, of course, has been the procedure for those who put together this anthology. One of the particular pleasures for the undersigned has been the number of times in the process of selection they would exclaim their wonder and delight at what they'd come across. It is hard to imagine that the contents herein will not produce a similar reaction in the reader.

—George Plimpton

Letter to an Editor

Dear—:

The preface which you all wanted me to write, and which I wanted to write, and finally wrote, came back to me from Paris today so marvelously changed and re-worded that it seemed hardly mine. Actually, you know, it shouldn't be mine. Prefaces are usually communal enterprises and they have a stern dull quality of group effort about them—of Manifesto, Proclamation of Aims, of "Where We Stand"—of editors huddled together in the smoke-laden, red-eyed hours of early morning, pruning and balancing syntax, juggling terms and, because each editor is an individual with different ideas, often compromising away all those careless personal words that make an individualistic statement exciting, or at least interesting. Prefaces, I'll admit, are a bore and consequently, more often than not, go unread. The one I sent you, so balanced and well-mannered and so dull—I could hardly read it myself when I finished it—when it came back to me with your emendations and corrections I couldn't read it at all. This, I realize, is the fault of neither or none of us; it's inevitable that what Truth I mumble to you at Lipp's over a beer, or that Ideal we are perfectly agreed upon at the casual hour of 2 A.M. becomes powerfully open to criticism as soon as it's cast in a printed form which, like a piece of sculpture, allows us to walk all around that Truth or Ideal and examine it front, side, and behind, and for minutes on end. Everyone starts hacking off an arm, a leg, an ear—and you end up with a lump.

At any rate, I'd like to go over briefly a few of the things you questioned; we'll still no doubt disagree, but that's probably for the better. There are magazines, you know, where a questioning word amounts to dishonesty, and disagreement means defection.

First, I said, "Literarily speaking, we live in what has been described as the Age of Criticism. Full of articles on Kafka and James, on Melville, or whatever writer is in momentary ascendancy; laden with terms like *architectonic, Zeitgeist,* and *dichotomous,* the literary magazines seem today on the verge of doing away with literature, not with any philistine bludgeon but by smothering it under the weight of learned chatter." (Perfect beginning for a preface, you may note; regard the arch rhythms, the way it fairly looks down the nose at the reader.)

All right, then I said, "There is little wonder" (always a nice oblique phrase to use in a preface) "that, faced with Oedipus and Myth in Charlotte Brontë, with meter in Pope and darkness in Dante, we put aside our current quarterly with its two short poems, its one intellectualized short story, in deference to *Life,* which brings us at least 'The Old Man and the Sea.'" This, of course, as you remember, was only by way of getting to the first brave part of the Manifesto: that THE PARIS REVIEW would strive to give predominant space to the fiction and poetry of both established and new writers, rather than to people who use words like *Zeitgeist.* Now in rebuttal, one of you has written that it is not always editorial policy that brings such a disproportion of critical manuscripts across the editors' desks, pointing out that "in our schools and colleges all the emphasis is on analysis and organization of ideas, not creation." The result is that we have critics, not creators, and you go on to suggest that, since this is the natural state of things, we should not be too haughty in stating our intention of having more fiction and poetry in THE PARIS REVIEW.

To this I can only say: *d'accord.* Let's by all means leave out the lordly tone and merely say: dear reader, THE PARIS REVIEW *hopes* to emphasize creative work—fiction and poetry—not to the exclusion of criticism, but with the aim in mind of merely removing criticism from the dominating place it holds in most literary magazines and putting it pretty much where it belongs, i.e., somewhere near the back of the book. O.K.? But as for *Zeitgeist,* which you accuse me of denouncing unnecessarily, I still don't like it, perhaps because, complying with the traditional explanation of intolerance, I am ignorant of what it means. I hope one of you will help me out.

Among the other points I tried to make was one which involved THE PARIS REVIEW having no axe to grind. In this we're pretty much in agreement, I believe, although one of you mentioned the fact that in the first number of *The Exile* there were "powerful blasts" by Pound, among others, which added considerably to the interest of the magazine. True, perhaps. But is it because we're sissies that we plan to beat no drum for anything; is it only because we're wan imitations of our predecessors—those who came out bravely for anything they felt deeply enough was worth coming out bravely for? I don't think so. I think that if we have no axes to grind, no drums to beat, it's because it seems to us—for the moment, at least—that the axes have all been ground, the drumheads burst with beating. This attitude does not necessarily make us—as some of the Older Boys have called us—the Silent Generation (the fact of THE PARIS REVIEW belies that), or the Scared Generation, either, content to lie around in one palsied, unprotesting mass. It's not so much a matter of protest now, but of waiting; perhaps, if we have to be categorized at all, we might be called the Waiting Generation— people who feel and write and observe, and wait and wait and wait. And go on writing. I think THE PARIS REVIEW should welcome these people into its pages—the good writers and good poets, the non-drumbeaters and non-axe-grinders. So long as they're good.

Finally, and along these lines, I was taken pretty much to task by one of you for making the perhaps too general statement that there are signs in the air that this generation can and will produce literature equal to that of any in the past. Well, I suppose that is another Ringing Assertion, but it's a writer's statement, almost necessarily, and not a critic's. A critic nowadays will set up straw-men, saying that Mailer had Ahab in mind when he created Sergeant Croft, that Jim Jones thought of Hamlet when he came up with his bedevilled Private Prewitt, stating further, however, that neither of these young men have created figures worthy of Melville or Shakespeare; they do this, or they leap to the opposite pole and cry out that no one writing today even *tries* to create figures of the tragic stature of Lear. For a writer, God forbid either course. I still maintain that the times get precisely the literature that they deserve, and that if the writing of this period is gloomy the gloom is not so much inherent in the literature as in the times. The writer's duty is to keep on writing, creating memorable Pvt. Prewitts and Sgt. Crofts, and to hell with Ahab. Perhaps the critics are right: this generation may not produce literature equal to that of any past generation—who cares? The writer will be dead before anyone can judge him—but he *must* go on writing, reflecting disorder, defeat, despair, should that be all he sees at the moment, but ever searching for the elusive love, joy, and hope—qualities which, as in the act of life itself, are best when they have to be struggled for, and are not commonly come by with much ease, either by a critic's formula or by a critic's yearning. If he does not think one way or another, that he can create literature worthy of himself and of his place, at this particular moment in history, in his society, then he'd better pawn his Underwood, or become a critic.

    Ever faithfully yours,

—Bill Styron

HEARTBREAK

Lorrie Moore

⌗

Terrific Mother

Although she had been around them her whole life, it was when she reached thirty-five that holding babies seemed to make her nervous—just at the beginning, a twinge of stage fright swinging up from the gut. "Adrienne, would you like to hold the baby? Would you mind?" Always these words from a woman her age looking kind and beseeching—a former friend, she was losing her friends to babble and beseech—and Adrienne would force herself to breathe deep. Holding a baby was no longer natural—she was no longer natural—but a test of womanliness and earthly skills. She was being observed. People looked to see how she would do it. She had entered a puritanical decade, a demographic moment—whatever it was—when the best compliment you could get was: You would make a terrific mother. The wolf whistle of the nineties.

So when she was at the Spearsons' Labor Day picnic, and when Sally Spearson had handed her the baby, Adrienne had burbled at it as she would a pet, had jostled the child gently, made clicking noises with her tongue, affectionately cooing, "Hello punkinhead, hello my little punkinhead," had reached to shoo a fly away and, amidst the smells of old grass and the fatty crackle of the barbecue, lost her balance when the picnic bench, dowels rotting in the joints, wobbled and began to topple her—the bench! The wobbly picnic bench was toppling her! And when she fell backward, spraining her spine—in the slowed quickness of this flipping world she saw the clayey clouds, some frozen faces, one lone star like the nose of a jet—and when the

baby's head hit the stone retaining wall of the Spearsons' newly terraced yard and bled fatally into the brain, Adrienne went home
shortly thereafter, after the hospital and the police reports, and did
not leave her attic apartment for seven months, and there were fears,
deep fears for her, on the part of Martin Porter, the man she had been
dating, and on the part of almost everyone, including Sally Spearson
who phoned tearfully to say that she forgave her, that Adrienne might
never come out.

Those months were dark and cavernous with mourning. Martin
Porter usually visited her bringing a pepper cheese or a Casbah cous-
cous cup; he had become her only friend. He was divorced and
worked as a research economist, though he looked more like a Scottish lumberjack—graying hair, red-flecked beard, a favorite flannel
shirt in green and gold. He was getting ready to take a trip abroad.
"We could get married," he suggested. That way, he said, Adrienne
could accompany him to northern Italy, to a villa in the Alps set up for
scholars and academic conferences. She could be a spouse. They
gave spouses studios to work in. Some studios had pianos. Some had
desks or potter's wheels. "You can do whatever you want." He was
finishing the second draft of a study of first-world imperialism's im-
pact on third-world monetary systems. "You could paint. Or not. You
could not paint."
    She looked at him closely, hungrily, then turned away. She still felt
clumsy and big, a beefy killer in a cage, in need of the thinning prison
food. "You love me, don't you," she said. She had spent the better
part of seven months napping in a leotard, an electric fan blowing at
her, her left ear catching the wind, capturing it there in her head, like
the sad sea in a shell. She felt clammy and doomed. "Or do you just
feel sorry for me?" She swatted at a small swarm of gnats that had appeared suddenly out of an abandoned can of Coke.
    "I don't feel sorry for you."
    "You don't?"
    "I *feel* for you. I've grown to love you. We're grownups here. One
grows to do things." He was a practical man. He often referred to the
annual departmental cocktail party as "standing around getting paid."
    "I don't think, Martin, that we can get married."

"Of course we can get married." He unbuttoned his cuffs as if to roll up his sleeves.

"You don't understand. Normal life is no longer possible for me. I've stepped off all the normal paths and am living in the bushes. I'm a bushwoman now. I don't feel that I can have the normal things. Marriage is a normal thing. You need the normal courtship, the normal proposal." She couldn't think what else. Water burned her eyes. She waved a hand dismissively, and it passed through her field of vision like something murderous and huge.

"Normal courtship, normal proposal," Martin said. He took off his shirt and pants and shoes. He lay on the bed in just his socks and underwear and pressed the length of his body against her. "I'm going to marry you, whether you like it or not." He took her face into his hands and looked longingly at her mouth. "I'm going to marry you till you puke."

They were met at Malpensa by a driver who spoke little English but who held up a sign that said VILLA HIRSCHBORN, and when Adrienne and Martin approached him, he nodded and said, "Hello, *buon giorno.* Signor Porter?" The drive to the villa took two hours, uphill and down, through the countryside and several small villages, but it wasn't until the driver pulled up to the precipitous hill he called *La Madre Vertiginoso,* and the villa's iron gates somehow opened automatically then closed behind them, it wasn't until then, winding up the drive past the spectacular gardens and the sunny vineyard and the terraces of the stucco outbuildings, that it occurred to Adrienne that Martin's being invited here was a great honor. He had won this *thing,* and he got to live here for a month.

"Does this feel like a honeymoon?" she asked him.

"A what? Oh, a honeymoon. Yes." He turned and patted her thigh indifferently.

He was jet-lagged. That was it. She smoothed her skirt, which was wrinkled and damp. "Yes, I can see us growing old together," she said, squeezing his hand. "In the next few weeks, in fact." If she ever got married again, she would do it properly. The awkward ceremony, the embarrassing relatives, the cumbersome, ecologically unsound gifts. She and Martin had simply gone to City Hall, and then asked their family and friends not to send presents but to donate money to Greenpeace. Now, however, as they slowed before the squashed-nosed stone lions at the entrance of the villa, its perfect border of forget-me-nots and yews, its sparkling glass door, Adrienne gasped. *Whales,* she thought quickly. *Whales* got my crystal.

The upstairs "Principessa" room, which they were ushered into by a graceful, bilingual butler named Carlo, was elegant and huge—a piano, a large bed, dressers stenciled with festoons of fruit. There was maid service twice a day, said Carlo. There were sugar wafers, towels, mineral water and mints. There was dinner at eight, breakfast until nine. When Carlo bowed and departed, Martin kicked off his shoes and sank into the ancient, tapestried chaise. "I've heard these 'fake' quattrocento paintings on the wall are fake for tax purposes only," he whispered. "If you know what I mean."

"Really," said Adrienne. She felt like one of the workers taking over the Winter Palace. Her own voice sounded booming. "You know, Mussolini was captured around here. Think about it."

Martin looked puzzled. "What do you mean?"

"That he was around here. That they captured him. I don't know. I was reading the little book on it. Leave me alone." She flopped down on the bed. Martin was changing already. He'd been better when they were just dating, with the pepper cheese. She let her face fall deep into the pillow, her mouth hanging open like a dog's, and then she slept until six, dreaming that a baby was in her arms but that it turned into a stack of plates, which she had to juggle, tossing them into the air.

A loud sound awoke her. A falling suitcase. Everyone had to dress for dinner, and Martin was yanking things out, groaning his way into a jacket and tie. Adrienne got up, bathed and put on pantyhose which, because it had been months since she had done so, twisted around her leg like the stripe on a barber pole.

"You're walking as if you'd torn a ligament," said Martin, locking the door to their room, as they were leaving.

Adrienne pulled at the knees of the hose, but couldn't make them work. "Tell me you like my skirt, Martin, or I'm going to have to go back in and never come out again."

"I like your skirt. It's great. You're great. I'm great," he said, like a conjugation. He took her arm and they limped their way down the curved staircase (Was it sweeping? Yes! It was sweeping!) to the dining room, where Carlo ushered them in to find their places at the table. The seating arrangement at the tables would change nightly, Carlo said in a clipped Italian accent, "to assist the cross-pollination of ideas."

"Excuse me?" said Adrienne.

There were about thirty-five people, all of them middle aged, with the academic's strange, mixed expression of merriment and weariness. "A cross between flirtation and a fender bender," Martin had described it once. Adrienne's place was at the opposite side of the room from him, between a historian writing a book on a monk named Jaocim de Flore and a musicologist who had devoted his life to a quest for "the earnest andante." Everyone sat in elaborate wooden chairs, the backs of which were carved with gargoylish heads that poked up from behind either shoulder of the sitter, like a warning.

"De Flore," said Adrienne, at a loss, turning from her carpaccio to the monk man. "Doesn't that mean 'of the flower'?" She had recently learned that *disaster* meant "bad star" and she was looking for an opportunity to brandish and bronze this tidbit in conversation.

The monk man looked at her. "Are you one of the spouses?"

"Yes," she said. She looked down then back up. "But then so is my husband."

"You're not a screenwriter, are you?"

"No," she said. "I'm a painter. Actually more of a printmaker. Actually, more of a—right now I'm in transition."

He nodded and dug back into his food. "I'm always afraid they're going to start letting *screenwriters* in here."

There was an arugula salad, and osso bucco for the main course. She turned now to the musicologist. "So you usually find them insincere? The andantes?" She looked quickly out over the other heads to give Martin a fake and girlish wave.

"It's the use of the minor seventh," sniffed the musicologist. "So fraudulent and replete."

"If the food wasn't so good, I'd leave now," she said to Martin. They were lying in bed, in their carpeted skating rink of a room. It could be weeks, she knew, before they'd have sex here. "*So fraudulent and re-plete,*" she said in a high nasal voice the likes of which Martin had heard only once before, in a departmental meeting chaired by an embittered, interim chair who did imitations of colleagues not in the room. "Can you even use the word *replete* like that?"

"As soon as you get settled in your studio, you'll feel better," said Martin, beginning to fade. He groped under the covers to find her hand and clasp it.

"I want a divorce," whispered Adrienne.

"I'm not giving you one," he said, bringing her hand up to his chest and placing it there, like a medallion, like a necklace of sleep, and then he began softly to snore, the quietest of radiators.

They were given bagged lunches and told to work well. Martin's studio was a modern glass cube in the middle of one of the gardens. Adrienne's was a musty stone hut twenty minutes farther up the hill and out onto the wooded headland, along a dirt path where small darting lizards sunned. She unlocked the door with the key she had been given, went in, and immediately sat down and ate the entire bagged lunch—quickly, compulsively, though it was only nine-thirty in the morning. Two apples, some cheese, and a jam sandwich. "A jelly bread," she said aloud, holding up the sandwich, scrutinizing it under the light.

She set her sketch pad on the work table and began a morning full of killing spiders and drawing their squashed and tragic bodies. The spiders were star shaped, hairy, and scuttling like crabs. They were fallen stars. Bad stars. They were earth's animal-try at heaven. Often she had to step on them twice—they were large and ran fast. Stepping on them once usually just made them run faster.

It was the careless universe's work she was performing, death itchy, and about like a cop. Her personal fund of mercy for the living was going to get used up in dinner conversation at the villa. She had no compassion to spare, only a pencil and a shoe.

"Art *trouvé?*" said Martin, toweling himself dry from his shower, as they dressed for the evening cocktail hour.

"Spider *trouvé,*" she said. "A delicate, aboriginal dish." Martin let out a howling laugh that alarmed her. She looked at him, then looked down at her shoes. He needed her. Tomorrow she would have to go down into town and find a pair of sexy Italian sandals that showed the cleavage of her toes. She would have to take him dancing. They would have to hold each other and lead each other back to love or they'd go nuts here. They'd grow mocking and arch and violent. One of them would stick a foot out, and the other would trip. That sort of thing.

At dinner she sat next to a medievalist who had just finished his sixth book on *The Canterbury Tales.*

"Sixth," repeated Adrienne.

"There's a lot there," he said defensively.

"I'm sure," she said.

"I read deep," he added. "I read hard."

"How nice for you."

He looked at her narrowly. "Of course, *you* probably think I should write a book about Cat Stevens." She nodded neutrally. "I see," he said.

For dessert Carlo was bringing in a white chocolate torte, and she decided to spend most of the coffee and dessert time talking about it. Desserts like these are born, not made, she would say. She was already practicing, rehearsing for courses. "I mean," she said to the Swedish physicist on her left, "until today, my feeling about white chocolate, was: Why? What was the point? You might as well have been eating goddamn *wax.*" She had her elbow on the table, her hand up near her face, and she looked anxiously past the physicist to smile at Martin at the other end of the long table. She waved her fingers in the air like bug legs.

"Yes, of course," said the physicist, frowning. "You must be— well, are you one of the *spouses?*"

She began in the mornings to gather with some of the other spouses— they were going to have little tank tops printed up—in the music room for exercise. This way she could avoid hearing words like *Heidegger-ian* and *ideological* at breakfast; it always felt too early in the morning for those words. The women pushed back the damask sofas, and cleared a space on the rug where all of them could do little hip and thigh exercises, led by the wife of the Swedish physicist. Up, down, up down.

"I guess this relaxes you," said the white-haired woman next to her.

"Bourbon relaxes you," said Adrienne. "This carves you."

"Bourbon carves you," said a redhead from Brazil.

"You have to go visit this person down in the village," whispered the white-haired woman. She wore a Spalding sporting goods T-shirt.

"What person?"

"Yes, what person?" asked the blonde.

The white-haired woman stopped and handed both of them a card from the pocket of her shorts. "She's an American masseuse. A couple of us have started going. She takes lire or dollars, doesn't matter. You have to phone a couple days ahead."

Adrienne stuck the card in her waistband. "Thanks," she said, and resumed moving her leg up and down like a toll gate.

For dinner there was *tachino a la scala*. "I wonder how you make this?" Adrienne said aloud.

"My dear," said the French historian on her left. "You must never ask. Only wonder." He then went on to disparage sub-altered intellectualism and dormant tropes.

"Yes," said Adrienne, "dishes like these do have about them a kind of *omnihistorical reality*. At least it seems like that to me." She turned quickly.

To her right sat a cultural anthropologist who had just come back from China where she had studied the infanticide.

"Yes," said Adrienne. "The infanticide."

"They are on the edge of something horrific there. It is the whole future, our future as well, and something terrible is going to happen to them. One feels it."

"How awful," said Adrienne. She could not do the mechanical work of eating, of knife and fork, up and down. She let her knife and fork rest against each other on the plate.

"A woman has to apply for a license to have a baby. Everything is bribes and rations. We went for hikes up into the mountains, and we didn't see a single bird, a single animal. Everything, over the years, has been eaten."

Adrienne felt a light weight on the inside of her arm vanish and return, vanish and return, like the history of something, like the story of all things. "Where are you from ordinarily?" asked Adrienne. She couldn't place the accent.

"Munich," said the woman. "Land of *Oktoberfest*." She dug into her food in an exasperated way then turned back toward Adrienne to smile a little formally. "I grew up watching all these grown people in green felt throwing up in the street."

Adrienne smiled back. This was how she would learn about the world, in sentences at meals; other people's distillations amidst her own vague pain, dumb with itself. This, for her, would be knowledge—a shifting to hear, an emptying of her arms, other people's experiences walking through the bare rooms of her brain, looking for a place to sit.

"Me?" she too often said, "I'm just a dropout from Sue Bennet College." And people would nod politely and only sometimes ask, "Where's that?"

The next morning in her room she sat by the phone and stared. Martin had gone to his studio; his book was going fantastically well, he said, which gave Adrienne a sick, abandoned feeling—of being unhappy and unsupportive—which made her think she was not even one of the spouses. Who was she? The opposite of a mother. The opposite of a spouse.

She was Spider Woman.

She picked up the phone, got an outside line, dialed the number of the masseuse on the card.

"*Pronto*," said the voice on the other end.

"Yes, hello, *per favore, parle anglese?*"

"Oh, yes," said the voice. "I'm from Minnesota."

"No kidding," said Adrienne. She lay back and searched the ceiling for talk. "I once subscribed to a haunted-house newsletter published in Minnesota," she said.

"Yes," said the voice a little impatiently. "Minnesota is full of haunted-house newsletters."

"I once lived in a haunted house," said Adrienne. "In college. Me and five roommates."

The masseuse cleared her throat confidentially. "Yes. I was once called on to cast the demons from a haunted house. But how can I help you today?"

Adrienne said, "You were?"

"Were? Oh, the house, yes. When I got there, all the place needed was to be cleaned. So I cleaned it. Washed the dishes and dusted."

"Yup," said Adrienne. "Our house was haunted that way, too."

There was a strange silence in which Adrienne, feeling something tense and moist in the room, began to fiddle with the bagged lunch on the bed, nervously pulling open the sandwiches, sensing that, if she turned just then, the phone cradled in her neck, the baby would be there, behind her, a little older now, a toddler, walked toward her in a ghostly way by her own dead parents, a nativity scene corrupted by error and dream.

"How can I help you today?" the masseuse asked again, firmly.

Help? Adrienne wondered abstractly, and remembered how in certain countries, instead of a tooth fairy, there were such things as tooth spiders. How the tooth spider could steal your children, mix them up, bring you a changeling child, a child that was changed.

"I'd like to make an appointment for Thursday," she said. "If possible. Please."

For dinner there was *vongole in umido,* the rubbery, wine-steamed meat prompting commentary about mollusk versus crustacean anatomy. Adrienne sighed and chewed. Over cocktails there had been a long discussion of peptides and rabbit tests.

"Now lobsters, you know, have what is called a hemi-penis," said the man next to her. He was a marine biologist, an epidemiologist, or an anthropologist. She'd forgotten which.

"Hemi-penis." Adrienne scanned the room a little frantically.

"Yes." He grinned. "Not a term one particularly wants to hear in an intimate moment, of course."

"No," said Adrienne, smiling back. She paused. "Are you one of the spouses?"

Someone on his right grabbed his arm, and he now turned in that direction to say why yes he did know Professor so-and-so . . . and wasn't she in Brussels last year giving a paper at the hermeneutics conference?

There came *castagne al porto* and coffee. The woman to Adrienne's left finally turned to her, placing the cup down on the saucer with a sharp clink.

"You know, the chef has AIDS," said the woman.

Adrienne froze a little in her chair. "No, I didn't know." Who was this woman?

"How does that make you feel?"

"Pardon me?"

"How does that make you feel?" She enunciated slowly, like a reading teacher.

"I'm not sure," said Adrienne, scowling at her chestnuts. "Certainly worried for us if we should lose him."

The woman smiled. "Very interesting." She reached underneath the table for her purse and said, "Actually, the chef doesn't have AIDS—at least not that I'm aware of. I'm just taking a kind of survey to test people's reactions to AIDS, homosexuality and general notions of contagion. I'm a sociologist. It's part of my research. I just arrived this afternoon. My name is Marie-Claire."

Adrienne turned back to the hemi-penis man. "Do you think the people here are mean?" she asked.

He smiled at her in a fatherly way. "Of course," he said. There was a long silence with some chewing in it. "But the place *is* pretty as a postcard."

"Yeah, well," said Adrienne, "I never send those kinds of postcards. No matter where I am I always send the kind with the little cat jokes on them."

He placed his hand briefly on her shoulder. "We'll find you some cat jokes." He scanned the room in a bemused way and then looked at his watch.

She had bonded in a state of emergency, like an infant bird. But perhaps it would be soothing, this marriage. Perhaps it would be like a nice warm bath. A nice warm bath in a tub flying off a roof.

At night she and Martin seemed almost like husband and wife, spooned against each other in a forgetful sort of love—a cold, still heaven through which a word or touch might explode like a moon, then disappear, unremembered. She moved her arms to place them around him, and he felt so big there, huge, filling her arms.

•

The white-haired woman who had given her the masseuse card was named Kate Spalding, the wife of the monk man, and in the morning she asked Adrienne to go jogging. They met by the lions, Kate once more sporting a Spalding T-shirt, and then they headed out over the gravel, toward the gardens. "It's pretty as a postcard here, isn't it?" said Kate. Out across the lake the mountains seemed to preside over the minutiae of the terra cotta villages nestled below. It was May and the Alps were losing their snowy caps, nurses letting their hair down. The air was warming. Anything could happen.

Adrienne sighed. "But do you think people have *sex* here?"

Kate smiled. "You mean casual sex? Among the guests?"

Adrienne felt annoyed. "*Casual* sex? No, I don't mean *casual* sex. I'm talking about difficult, randomly profound, Sears and Roebuck sex. I'm talking marital."

Kate laughed in a sharp, barking sort of way, which for some reason hurt Adrienne's feelings.

Adrienne tugged on her socks. "I don't believe in casual sex." She paused. "I believe in casual marriage."

"Don't look at me," said Kate. "I married my husband because I was deeply in love with him."

"Yeah, well," said Adrienne. "I married my husband because I thought it would be a great way to meet guys."

Kate smiled now in a real way. Her white hair was grandmotherly, but her face was youthful and tan, and her teeth shone generous and wet, the creamy incisors curved as cashews.

"I'd tried the whole single thing but it just wasn't working," Adrienne added, running in place.

Kate stepped close and massaged Adrienne's neck. Her skin was lined and papery. "You haven't been to see Ilke from Minnesota yet, have you?"

Adrienne feigned perturbance. "Do I seem that tense, that lost, that . . ." and here she let her arms splay spastically. "I'm going tomorrow."

"He was a beautiful child, didn't you think?" In bed Martin held her until he rolled away, clasped her hand and fell asleep. At least there was that: a husband sleeping next to a wife, a nice husband sleeping close. It meant something to her. She could see how through the years it would gather power, its socially sanctioned animal comfort, its night life a dreamy dance about love. She lay awake and remembered when her father had at last grown so senile and ill that her mother could no longer sleep in the same bed with him—the mess, the smell—and had had to move him, diapered and rank, to the guest room next door. Her mother had cried, to say this farewell to a husband. To at last lose him like this, banished and set aside like a dead man, never to sleep with him again: she had wept like a baby. His actual death she took less hard. At the funeral she was grim and dry and invited everyone over for a quiet, elegant tea. By the time two years had passed, and she herself was diagnosed with cancer, her sense of humor had returned a little. "The silent killer," she would say, with a wink. "The *silent killer*." She got a kick out of repeating it, though no one knew what to say in response, and at the very end she kept clutching the nurses' hems to ask, "Why is no one visiting me?" No one lived that close, explained Adrienne. No one lived that close to anyone.

Adrienne set her spoon down. "Isn't this soup *interesting?*" she said to no one in particular. "*Zup-pa mari-ta-ta!*" Marriage soup. She decided it was perhaps a little like marriage itself: a good idea that, like all ideas, lived awkwardly on earth.

"You're not a poetess, I hope," said the English geologist next to her. "We had a poetess here last month, and things got a bit dodgy here for the rest of us."

"Really." After the soup there was risotto with squid ink.

"Yes. She kept referring to insects as 'God's typos' and then she kept us all after dinner one evening so she could read from her poems, which seemed to consist primarily of the repeating line, 'The hairy kiwi of his balls.'"

"Hairy kiwi," repeated Adrienne, searching the phrase for a sincere andante. She had written a poem once herself. It had been called "Garbage Night in the Fog" and was about a long sad walk she'd taken once on garbage night.

The geologist smirked a little at the risotto, waiting for Adrienne to say something more, but she was now watching Martin at the other table. He was sitting next to the sociologist she'd sat next to the previous night, and as Adrienne watched she saw Martin glance, in a sickened way, from the sociologist, back to his plate, then back to the sociologist. "The *cook?*" he said loudly, then dropped his fork and pushed his chair from the table.

The sociologist was frowning. "You flunk," she said.

"I'm going to see this masseuse tomorrow." Martin was on his back on the bed, and Adrienne was straddling his hips, usually one of their favorite ways to converse. One of the Mandy Patinkin tapes she'd brought was playing on the cassette player.

"The masseuse. Yes, I've heard," said Martin.

"You have?"

"Sure, they were talking about it at dinner last night."

"Who was?" She was already feeling possessive, alone.

"Oh, one of them," said Martin, smiling and waving his hand dismissively.

"Them," said Adrienne coldly. "You mean one of the spouses, don't you. Why are all the spouses here women? Why don't the women scholars have spouses?"

"Some of them do, I think. They're just not here."

"Where are they?"

"Could you move," he said irritably, "you're sitting on my groin."

"Fine," she said and climbed off.

The next morning she made her way down past the conical evergreens of the terraced hill—so like the grounds of a palace, the palace of a moody princess named Sophia or Giovanna—ten minutes down the winding path to the locked gate to the village. It had rained in the night, and snails, golden and mauve, decorated the stone steps, sometimes dead center, causing Adrienne an occasional quick turn of the ankle. A dance step, she thought. Modern and bent-kneed. Very Martha Graham. *Don't kill us. We'll kill you.* At the top of the final stairs to the gate she pressed the buzzer that opened it electronically, and then dashed down to get out in time. YOU HAVE THIRTY SECONDS, said the sign. TRENTA MINUTI SECONDI USCIRE. PRESTO! One needed a key to get back in from the village, and she clutched it like a charm.

She had to follow the Via San Carlo to Corso Magenta, past a hazelnut gelato shop and a bakery with wreaths of braided bread and muffins cut like birds. She pressed herself up against the buildings to let the cars pass. She looked at her card. The masseuse was above a *farmacia,* she'd been told, and she saw it now, a little sign that said, MASSAGGIO DELLA VITA. She pushed on the outer door and went up.

Upstairs through an open doorway, she entered a room lined with books: books on vegetarianism, books on healing, books on juice. A cockatiel, white with a red dot like a Hindu wife's, was perched atop a picture frame. The picture was of Lake Como or Garda, though when you blinked it could also be a skull, a fissure through the center like a reef.

"Adrienne," said a smiling woman in a purple peasant dress. She had big, frosted hair and a wide, happy face that contained many shades of pink. She stepped forward and shook Adrienne's hand. "I'm Ilke."

"Yes," said Adrienne.

The cockatiel suddenly flew from its perch to land on Ilke's shoulder. It pecked at her big hair, then stared at Adrienne, accusingly.

Ilke's eyes moved quickly between Adrienne's own, a quick read, a radar scan. She then looked at her watch. "You can go into the back room now, and I'll be with you shortly. You can take off all your clothes, also any jewelry—watches, or rings. But if you want you can leave your underwear on. Whatever you prefer."

"What do most people do?" Adrienne swallowed in a difficult, conspicuous way.

Ilke smiled. "Some do it one way; some the other."

"All right," Adrienne said and clutched her pocketbook. She stared at the cockatiel. "I just wouldn't want to rock the boat."

She stepped carefully toward the back room Ilke had indicated, and pushed past the heavy curtain. Inside was a large alcove, windowless and dark, with one small bluish light coming from the corner. In the center was a table with a newly creased flannel sheet. Speakers were built into the bottom of the table, and out of them came the sound of eery choral music, wordless *oohs* and *aahs* in minor tones, with a percussive sibilant chant beneath it that sounded to Adrienne like "Jesus is best, Jesus is best," though perhaps it was

"Cheese, I suspect." Overhead hung a mobile of white stars, crescent moons and doves. On the blue walls were more clouds and snowflakes. It was a child's room, a baby's room, everything trying hard to be harmless and sweet.

Adrienne removed all her clothes, her earrings, her watch, her rings. She had already grown used to the ring Martin had given her, and so it saddened and exhilarated her to take it off, a quick glimpse into the landscape of adultery. Her other ring was a smokey quartz, which a palm reader in Milwaukee—a man dressed like a gym teacher and set up at a card table in a German restaurant—had told her to buy and wear on her right index finger for power.

"What kind of power?" she had asked.

"The kind that's real," he said. "What you've got here," he said, waving around her left hand, pointing at the thin silver and turquoise she was wearing, "is squat."

"I like a palm reader who dresses you," she said later to Martin in the car on their way home. This was before the incident at the Spearson picnic, and things seemed not impossible then; she had wanted Martin to fall in love with her. "A guy who looks like Mike Ditka, but who picks out jewelry for you."

"A guy who tells you you're sensitive, and that you will soon receive cash from someone wearing glasses. Where does he come up with this stuff?"

"You don't think I'm sensitive."

"I mean the money and glasses thing," he said. "And that gloomy bit about how they'll think you're a goner, but you're going to come through and live to see the world go through a radical physical change."

"That was gloomy," she agreed. There was a lot of silence and looking at the night-lit highway lines, the fireflies hitting the windshield and smearing, all phosphorescent gold, as if the car were flying through stars. "It must be hard," she said, "for someone like you to go out on a date with someone like me."

"Why do you say that?" he'd asked.

She climbed up on the table, stripped of ornament and the power of ornament, and slipped between the flannel sheets. For a second she felt numb and scared, naked in a strange room, more naked even than in a doctor's office, where you kept your jewelry on, like an odalisque. But it felt new to do this, to lead the body to this, the body with its dog's obedience, its dog's desire to please. She lay there waiting, watching the mobile moons turn slowly, half-revolutions, while from the speakers beneath the table came a new sound, an electronic, synthesized version of Brahms's lullaby. An infant. She was to become an infant again. Perhaps she would become the Spearsons' boy. He had been a beautiful baby.

Ilke came in quietly and appeared so suddenly behind Adrienne's head, it gave her a start.

"Move back toward me," whispered Ilke, "move back toward me," and Adrienne shifted until she could feel the crown of her head grazing Ilke's belly. The cockatiel whooshed in and perched on a nearby chair.

"Are you a little tense?" she said. She pressed both her thumbs at the center of Adrienne's forehead. Ilke's hands were strong, small, bony. Leathered claws. The harder she pressed the better it felt to Adrienne, all of her difficult thoughts unknotting and traveling out, up into Ilke's thumbs.

"Breathe deeply," said Ilke. "You cannot breathe deeply without it relaxing you."

Adrienne pushed her stomach in and out.

"You are from the Villa Hirschborn, aren't you?" Ilke's voice was a knowing smile.

"Ehuh."

"I thought so," said Ilke. "People are very tense up there. Rigid as boards." Ilke's hands moved down off Adrienne's forehead, along her eyebrows to her cheeks, which she squeezed repeatedly, in little circles, as if to break the weaker capillaries. She took hold of Adrienne's head and pulled. There was a dull, cracking sound. Then she pressed her knuckles along Adrienne's neck. "Do you know why?"

Adrienne grunted.

"It is because they are over educated and can no longer converse with their own mothers. It makes them a little crazy. They have literally lost their mother tongue. So they come to me. I am their mother, and they don't have to speak at all."

"Of course they *pay* you."

"Of course."

Adrienne suddenly fell into a long falling—of pleasure, of surrender, of glazed-eyed dying, a piece of heat set free in a room. Ilke rubbed Adrienne's earlobes, knuckled her scalp like a hairdresser, pulled at her neck and fingers and arms, as if they were jammed things. Adrienne would become a baby, join all the babies, in heaven where they lived.

Ilke began to massage sandalwood oil into Adrienne's arms, pressing down, polishing, ironing, looking, at a quick glimpse, like one of Degas's laundresses. Adrienne shut her eyes again and listened to the music, which had switched from synthetic lullabies to the contrapuntal sounds of a flute and a thunderstorm. With these hands upon her, she felt a little forgiven and began to think generally of forgiveness, how much of it was required in life: to forgive everyone, yourself, the people you loved, and then wait to be forgiven by them. Where was all this forgiveness supposed to come from? Where was this great inexhaustible supply?

"Where are you?" whispered Ilke. "You are somewhere very far."

Adrienne wasn't sure. Where was she? In her own head, like a dream; in the bellows of her lungs. What was she? Perhaps a child. Perhaps a corpse. Perhaps a fern in the forest in the storm; a singing bird. The sheets were folded back. The hands were all over her now. Perhaps she was under the table with the music, or in a musty corner of her own hip. She felt Ilke rub oil into her chest, between her breasts, out along the ribs, and circularly on the abdomen. "There is something stuck here," Ilke said. "Something not working." Then she pulled the covers back up. "Are you cold?" she asked, and though Adrienne didn't answer, Ilke brought another blanket, mysteriously heated, and laid it across Adrienne. "There," said Ilke. She lifted the blanket so that only her feet were exposed. She rubbed oil into her soles, the toes, something squeezed out of Adrienne, like an olive. She felt as if she would cry. She felt like the baby Jesus. The grown Jesus. *The poor will always be with us.* The dead Jesus. Cheese is the best. Cheese is the best.

At her desk in the outer room, Ilke wanted money. Thirty-five thousand lire. "I can give it to you for thirty thousand, if you decide to come on a regular basis. Would you like to come on a regular basis?" asked Ilke.

Adrienne was fumbling with her wallet. She sat down in the wicker rocker near the desk. "Yes," she said. "Of course."

Ilke had put on reading glasses and now opened up her appointment book to survey the upcoming weeks. She flipped a page, then flipped it back. She looked out over her glasses at Adrienne. "How often would you like to come?"

"Every day," said Adrienne.

"*Every day?*"

Ilke's hoot worried Adrienne. "Every *other* day?" Adrienne peeped hopefully. Perhaps the massage had bewitched her, ruined her. Perhaps she had fallen in love.

Ilke looked back at her book and shrugged. "Every other day," she repeated slowly as a way of holding the conversation still while she checked her schedule. "How about at two o'clock?"

"Monday, Wednesday and Friday?"

"Perhaps we can occasionally arrange a Saturday."

"Okay. Fine." Adrienne placed the money on the desk and stood up. Ilke walked her to the door and thrust her hand out formally. Her face had changed from its earlier pinks to a strange and shiny orange.

"Thank you," said Adrienne. She shook Ilke's hand, but then leaned forward and kissed her cheek; she would kiss the business out of this. "Good-bye," she said. She stepped gingerly down the stairs; she had not entirely returned to her body yet. She had to go slow. She felt a little like she had just seen God, but also a little like she had just seen a hooker. Outside she walked carefully back toward the villa, but first stopped at the gelato shop for a small dish of hazelnut ice cream. It was smooth, toasty, buttery, like a beautiful liqueur, and she thought how different it was from America, where so much of the ice cream now looked like babies had attacked it with their cookies.

"Well, Martin, it's been nice knowing you," Adrienne said smiling. She reached out to shake his hand with one of hers and pat him on the back with the other. "You've been a good sport. I hope there will be no hard feelings."

"You've just come back from your massage," he said a little numbly. "How was it?"

"As you would say, 'Relaxing.' As I would say—well, I wouldn't say."

Martin led her to the bed. "Kiss and tell," he said.

"I'll just kiss," she said, kissing.

"I'll settle," he said. But then she stopped and went into the bathroom to shower for dinner.

At dinner there was *zuppa alla paesana* and then *salsicce alla griglia con spinaci*. For the first time since they'd arrived, she was seated near Martin, who was catercorner to her left. He was seated next to another economist and was speaking heatedly with him about a book on labor division and economic policy. "But Wilkander ripped that theory off from Boyer!" Martin let his spoon splash violently into his *zuppa* before a waiter came and removed the bowl.

"Let us just say," said the other man calmly, "that it was a sort of homage."

"If that's 'homage,'" said Martin, fidgeting with his fork, "I'd like to do a little 'homage' on the Chase Manhattan Bank."

"I think it was felt that there was sufficient looseness there to warrant further explication."

"Right. And one's twin sibling is simply an explication of the text."

"Why not," smiled the other economist, who was calm, probably a supply-sider.

Poor Martin, thought Adrienne. Poor Keynesian Martin, poor Marxist Martin, perspiring and red. "Left of Lenin?!" she had heard him exclaiming the other day to an agriculturalist. "Left of *Lenin?!* Left of the Lennon Sisters, you mean!" Poor godless, raised-an-atheist-in-Ohio Martin. "On Christmas," he'd said to her once, "we used to go down to The Science Store and worship the Bunsen burners."

She would have to find just the right blouse, just the right perfume, greet him on the chaise lounge with a bare shoulder and a purring, "Hello, Mister Man." Take him down by the lake near the Sfondrata chapel and get him laid. Hire somebody. She turned to the scholar next to her, who had just arrived this morning.

"Did you have a good flight?" she asked. Her own small talk at dinner no longer shamed her.

"Flight is the word," he said. "I needed to flee my department, my bills, my ailing car. Come to a place that would take care of me."

"This is it, I guess. Though they won't fix your car. Won't even discuss it, I've found."

"I'm on a Guggenheim," he said.

"How nice!" She thought of the museum in New York, and of a pair of earrings she had bought in the gift shop there but had never worn because they always looked broken, even though that was the way they were supposed to look.

". . . but I neglected to ask the foundation for enough money. I didn't realize what you could ask for. I didn't ask for the same amount everyone else did, and so I received substantially less."

Adrienne was sympathetic. "So instead of a regular Guggenheim, you got a little Guggenheim."

"Yes," he said.

"A Guggenheimy," she said.

He smiled in a troubled sort of way. "Right."

"So now you have to live in Guggenheimy town."

He stopped pushing at a sausage with his fork. "Yes. I heard there would be wit here."

She tried to make her lips curl, like his.

"Sorry," he said. "I was just kidding."

"Jet lag," she said.

"Yes."

"Jetty laggy." She smiled at him. "Baby talk. We love it." She paused. "Last week of course we weren't like this. You've arrived a little late."

He was a beautiful baby. In the dark there was thumping, like tom-toms, and a piccolo high above it. She couldn't look, because when she looked, it shocked her, another woman's hands all over her. She just kept her eyes closed, and concentrated on surrender, on the restful invalidity of it. Sometimes she concentrated on being where Ilke's hands were—at her feet, at the small of her back.

"Your parents are no longer living, are they?" Ilke said in the dark.

"No."

"Did they die young?"

"Medium. They died medium. I was a menopausal, afterthought child."

"Do you want to know what I feel in you?"

"All right."

"I feel a great and deep gentleness. But I also feel that you have been dishonored."

"Dishonored?" So Japanese. Adrienne liked the sound of it.

"Yes. You have a deeply held fear. Right here." Ilke's hand went just under Adrienne's ribcage.

Adrienne breathed deeply, in and out. "I killed a baby," she whispered.

"Yes, we have all killed a baby—there is a baby in all of us. That is why people come to me, to be reunited with it."

"No, I've killed a real one."

Ilke was very quiet and then she said, "You can do the side-lying now. You can put this pillow under your head; this other one between your knees." Adrienne rolled awkwardly onto her side. Finally Ilke said, "This country, its pope, its church, makes murderers of women. You must not let it do that to you. Move back toward me. That's it."

That's not *it*, thought Adrienne, in this temporary dissolve, seeing death and birth, seeing the beginning and then the end, how they were the same quiet black, same nothing ever after: everyone's life appeared in the world like a movie in a room. First dark, then light, then dark again. But it was all staggered so that somewhere there was always light.

That's not it. That's not it, she thought. But thank you.

When Adrienne left that afternoon, seeking sugar in one of the shops, she moved slowly, blinded by the angle of the afternoon light but also believing she saw Martin coming toward her in the narrow street, approaching like the lumbering logger he sometimes seemed to be. Her squinted gaze, however, failed to catch his, and he veered suddenly left into a *calle*. By the time she reached the corner, he had disappeared entirely. How strange, she thought. She had felt close to something, to him, and then suddenly not. She climbed the path back up toward the villa and went and knocked on the door of his studio, but he wasn't there.

"You smell good," she greeted Martin. It was some time later and she had just returned to the room to find him there. "Did you just take a bath?"

"A little while ago," he said.

She curled up to him, teasingly. "Not a shower? A bath? Did you put some scented bath salts in it?"

"I took a very masculine bath," said Martin.

She sniffed him again. "What scent did you use?"

"A manly scent," he said. "Rock. I took a rock-scented bath."

"Did you take a bubble bath?" She cocked her head to one side.

He smiled. "Yes, but I, uh, made my own bubbles."

"You did?" She squeezed his biceps.

"Yeah. I hammered the water with my fist."

She walked over to the cassette player and put a cassette in. She looked over at Martin, who looked suddenly unhappy. "This music annoys you, doesn't it?"

Martin squirmed. "It's just—why can't he sing any one song all the way through?"

She thought about this. "Because he's Mr. Medleyhead?"

"You didn't bring anything else?"

"No."

She went back and sat next to Martin, in silence, smelling the scent of him, as if it were odd.

For dinner there was *vitello alla salvia,* baby peas and a pasta made with caviar. "Nipping it in the bud," sighed Adrienne. "An early frost." A fat, elderly man arriving late pulled his chair out onto her foot, then sat down on it. She shrieked.

"Oh, dear, I'm sorry," said the man, lifting himself up as best he could.

"It's okay," said Adrienne. "I'm sure it's okay."

But the next morning, at exercises, Adrienne studied it closely during the leg lifts. The big toe was swollen and blue, and the nail had been loosened and set back at an odd and unhinged angle. "You're going to lose your toenail," said Kate.

"Great," said Adrienne.

"That happened to me once, during my first marriage. My husband dropped a dictionary on my foot. One of those subconscious things."

"You were married before?"

"Oh, yes," she sighed. "I had one of those rehearsal marriages, you know, where you're a feminist and train a guy, and then some *other* feminist comes along and *gets* the guy."

"I don't know." Adrienne scowled. "I think there's something wrong with the words *feminist* and *gets the guy* being in the same sentence."

"Yes, well—"

"Were you upset?"

"Of course. But then, I'd been doing everything. I'd insisted on separate finances, on being totally self-supporting. I was working. I was doing the child care. I paid for the house, I cooked it, I cleaned it. I found myself shouting, "This is feminism? Thank you, Betty!""

"But now you're with someone else."

"Pre-taught. Self-cleaning. Batteries included."

"Someone else trained him, and you stole him."

Kate smiled. "Of course. What, am I crazy?"

"What happened to the toe?"

"The nail came off. And the one that grew back was wavy and dark and used to scare the children."

"Oh," said Adrienne.

"Why would someone publish six books on Chaucer?" Adrienne was watching Martin dress. She was also smoking a cigarette. One of the strange things about the villa was that the smokers had all quit smoking, and the non-smokers had taken it up. People were getting in touch with their alternative centers. Bequeathed cigarettes abounded. Cartons were appearing outside people's doors.

"You have to understand academic publishing," said Martin. "No one reads these books. Everyone just agrees to publish everyone else's. It's one big circle jerk. It's a giant economic agreement. When you think about it, it probably violates the Sherman Act."

"A circle jerk?" she said uncertainly. The cigarette was making her dizzy.

"Yeah," said Martin, reknotting his tie.

"But six books on Chaucer? Why not, say, a Cat Stevens book?"

"Don't look at me," he said. "I'm in the circle."

She sighed. "Then I shall sing to you. Mood music." She made up a romantic, Asian-sounding tune and danced around the room with her cigarette, in a floating, wing-limbed way. "This is my Hopi dance," she said. "So full of hope."

Then it was time to go to dinner.

The cockatiel now seemed used to Adrienne and would whistle twice, then fly into the back room, perch quickly on the picture frame and wait with her for Ilke. Adrienne closed her eyes and breathed deeply, the flannel sheet pulled up under her arms, tightly, like a sarong.

Ilke's face appeared overhead in the dark, as if she were a mother just checking, peering into a crib. "How are you today?"

Adrienne opened her eyes to see that Ilke was wearing a pin that said: SAY A PRAYER. PET A ROCK.

Say a Prayer. "Good," said Adrienne. "I'm good." Pet a Rock.

Ilke ran her fingers through Adrienne's hair, humming faintly.

"What is this music today?" Adrienne asked. Like Martin, she too had grown weary of the Mandy Patinkin tapes, all that unshackled exuberance.

"Crickets and elk," Ilke whispered.

"Crickets and elk."

"Crickets and elk and a little harp."

Ilke began to move around the table, pulling on Adrienne's limbs and pressing deep into her tendons. "I'm doing choreographed massage today," Ilke said. "That's why I'm wearing this dress."

Adrienne hadn't noticed the dress. Instead, with the lights now low, except for the illuminated clouds on the side wall, she felt herself sinking into the pools of death deep in her bones, the dark wells of loneliness, failure, blame. "You may turn over now," she heard Ilke say. And she struggled a little in the flannel sheets to do so, twisting in them, until Ilke helped her, as if she were a nurse and Adrienne someone old and sick—a stroke victim, that's what it was. She had become a stroke victim. Then lowering her face into the toweled cheek plates the brace on the table offered up to her (the cradle, Ilke called it), Adrienne began quietly to cry, the deep touching of her body, melting her down to some equation of animal sadness, shoe leather and brine. She began to understand why people would want to live in these dusky nether zones, the meltdown brought on by sleep or drink or this. It seemed truer, more familiar to the soul than was the busy complicated flash that was normal life. Ilke's arms leaned into her, her breasts brushing softly against Adrienne's head, which now felt connected to the rest of her only by filaments and strands. The body suddenly seemed a tumor on the brain, a mere means of conveyance, a wagon; the mind's go-cart taken apart, laid in pieces on this table. "You have a knot here in your trapezius," Ilke said, kneading Adrienne's shoulder. "I can feel the belly of the knot right here," she said, pressing hard, bruising her shoulder a little, and then easing up. "Let go," she said. "Let go all the way, of everything."

"I might die," said Adrienne. Something surged in the music and she missed what Ilke said in reply, though it sounded a little like "Changes are good." Though perhaps it was "Chances aren't good." Ilke pulled Adrienne's toes, milking even the injured one, with its loose nail and leaky underskin, and then she left Adrienne there in the dark, in the music, though Adrienne felt it was she who was leaving, like a person dying, like a train pulling away. She felt the rage loosened from her back, floating aimlessly around in her, the rage that did not know at what or whom to rage though it continued to rage.

She awoke to Ilke's rocking her gently. "Adrienne, get up. I have another client soon."

"I must have fallen asleep," said Adrienne. "I'm sorry."

She got up slowly, got dressed, and went out into the outer room; the cockatiel whooshed out with her, grazing her head.

"I feel like I've just been strafed," she said, clutching her hair.

Ilke frowned.

"Your bird. I mean, by your bird. In there—" she pointed back toward the massage room—"*that* was great." She reached into her purse to pay. Ilke had moved the wicker chair to the other side of the room so that there was no longer any place to sit down or linger. "You want lire or dollars?" she asked and was a little taken aback when Ilke said rather firmly, "I'd prefer lire."

Ilke was bored with her. That was it. Adrienne was having a religious experience, but Ilke—Ilke was just being social. Adrienne held out the money and Ilke plucked it from her hand, then opened the outside door and leaned to give Adrienne the rushed bum's kiss—left, right—and then closed the door behind her.

Adrienne was in a fog, her legs noodly, her eyes unaccustomed to the light. Outside, in front of the *farmacia*, if she wasn't careful, she was going to get hit by a car. How could Ilke just send people out into the busy street like that, ducks for the kill, fatted calves, a farewell to arms? Her body felt doughy, muddy. This was good, she supposed. Decomposition. She stepped slowly, carefully, her Martha Graham step, along the narrow walk between the street and the stores. And when she turned the corner to head back up toward the path to the Villa Hirschborn, there stood Martin, her husband, rounding a corner and heading her way.

"Hi!" she said, so pleased suddenly to meet him like this, away from what she now referred to as "the compound." "Are you going to the *farmacia?*" she asked.

"Uh, yes," said Martin. He leaned to kiss her cheek.

"Want some company?"

He looked a little blank, as if he needed to be alone. Perhaps he was going to buy condoms.

"Oh, never mind," she said gaily. "I'll see you later, up at the compound, before dinner."

"Great," he said, and took her hand, took two steps away, and then let her hand go, gently, midair.

She walked away, toward a small park—il Giardino Leonardo—out past the station for the vaporetti. Near a particularly exuberant rhododendron sat a short, dark woman with a bright turquoise bandanna knotted around her neck. She had set up a table with a sign: CHIROMANTE: TAROT E FACCIA. Adrienne sat down opposite her in the empty chair. "Americano," she said.

"I do faces, palms or cards," the woman with the blue scarf said.

Adrienne looked at her own hands. She didn't want to have her face read. She lived like that already. It happened all the time at the villa, people trying to read your face—freezing your brain with stoney looks and remarks made malicious with obscurity, so that you couldn't read *their* faces, while they were busy reading yours. It all made her feel creepy, like a lonely head on a poster somewhere.

"The cards are the best," said the woman. "Ten thousand lire."

"Okay," said Adrienne. She was still looking at the netting of her open hands, the dried riverbed of life just sitting there. "The cards."

The woman swept up the cards, and dealt half of them out, every which way in a kind of swastika. Then without glancing at them, she leaned forward boldly and said to Adrienne, "You are sexually unsatisfied. Am I right?"

"Is that what the cards say?"

"In a general way. You have to take the whole deck and interpret."

"What does this card say?" asked Adrienne, pointing to one with some naked corpses leaping from coffins.

"Any one card doesn't say anything. It's the whole feeling of them." She quickly dealt out the remainder of the deck on top of the other cards. "You are looking for a guide, some kind of guide, because the man you are with does not make you happy. Am I right?"

"Maybe," said Adrienne, who was already reaching for her purse to pay the ten thousand lire so that she could leave.

"I am right," said the woman, taking the money and handing Adrienne a small, smudged business card. "Stop by tomorrow. Come to my shop. I have a powder."

Adrienne wandered back out of the park, past a group of tourists climbing out of a bus, back toward the Villa Hirschborn—through the gate, which she opened with her key, and up the long stone staircase to the top of the promontory. Instead of going back to the villa, she headed out through the woods toward her studio, toward the dead tufts of spiders she had memorialized in her grief. She decided to take a different path, not the one toward the studio, but one that led farther up the hill, a steeper grade, toward an open meadow at the top, with a small Roman ruin at its edge—a corner of the hill's original fortress still stood there. But in the middle of the meadow, something came over her—a balmy wind, or the heat from the uphill hike, and she took off all her clothes, lay down in the grass and stared around at the dusky sky. To either side of her the spokes of tree branches crisscrossed upward in a kind of cat's cradle. More directly overhead she studied the silver speck of a jet, the metallic head of its white stream like the tip of a thermometer. There were a hundred people inside this head of a pin, thought Adrienne. Or was it, perhaps, just the head of a pin? When was something truly small, and when was it a matter of dis-

tance? The branches of the trees seemed to encroach inward and rotate a little to the left, a little to the right, like something mechanical,
and as she began to drift off, she saw the beautiful Spearson baby, cooing in a clown hat, she saw Martin furiously swimming in a pool, she
saw the strewn beads of her own fertility, all the eggs within her, leap
away like a box of tapioca off a cliff. It seemed to her that everything
she had ever needed to know in her life she had known at one time or
another, but she just hadn't known all those things at once, at the same
time, at a single moment. They were scattered through, and she had
had to leave and forget one in order to get to another. A shadow fell
across her, inside her, and she could feel herself retreat to that place in
her bones where death was and you greeted it like an acquaintance in a
room; you said hello and were then ready for whatever was next—
which might be a guide, the guide that might be sent to you, the guide
to lead you back out into your life again.

Someone was shaking her gently. She flickered slightly awake to
see the pale, ethereal face of a strange older woman leaning over,
peering down at her as if Adrienne were something odd in the bottom
of a tea cup. The woman was dressed all in white—white shorts,
white cardigan, white scarf around her head. The guide.

"Are you—the guide?" whispered Adrienne.

"Yes, my dear," the woman said in a faintly English voice that
sounded like the good witch of the north.

"You are?" Adrienne asked.

"Yes," said the woman. "And I've brought the group up here to
view the old fort, but I was a little worried that you might not like all
of us traipsing past here while you were, well—are you all right?"

Adrienne was more awake now and sat up to see at the end of the
meadow the group of tourists she'd previously seen below in the
town, getting off the bus.

"Yes, thank you," mumbled Adrienne. She lay back down to think
about this, hiding herself in the walls of grass, like a child hoping to
trick the facts. "Oh, my god," she finally said, and groped about to
her left to find her clothes and clutch them, panicked, to her belly.
She breathed deeply, then put them on, lying as flat to the ground as
she could, hard to glimpse, a snake getting back inside its skin, a
change, perhaps, of reptilian heart. Then she stood, zipped her

pants, secured her belt buckle and, squaring her shoulders, walked bravely past the bus and the tourists who, though they tried not to stare at her, did stare.

By this time everyone in the villa was privately doing imitations of everyone else. "Martin, you should announce who you're doing before you do it," said Adrienne, dressing for dinner. "I can't really tell."

"Cube-steak yuppies!" Martin ranted at the ceiling. "Legends in their own mind! Rumors in their own room!"

"Yourself. You're doing yourself." She straightened his collar and tried to be wifely.

For dinner there was *cioppino* and *insalata mista* and *pesce con pignoli*, a thin piece of fish like a leaf. From everywhere around the dining room scraps of dialogue—rhetorical barbed wire, indignant and arcane—floated over toward her: "As an aesthetician, you can't not be interested in the sublime!" or "Why, that's the most facile thing I've ever heard!" or "Good grief, tell him about the Peasants' Revolt, would you?" But no one spoke to her directly. She had no subject, not really, not one she liked, except perhaps movies and movie stars. Martin was at a far table, his back toward her, listening to the monk man. At times like these, she thought, it was probably a good idea to carry a small hand puppet.

She made her fingers flap in her lap.

Finally, one of the people next to her turned and introduced himself. His face was poppy-seeded with whiskers, and he seemed to be looking down, watching his own mouth move. When she asked him how he liked it here so far, she received a fairly brief history of the Ottoman Empire. She nodded and smiled, and at the end he rubbed his dark beard, looked at her compassionately, and said, "We are not good advertisements for this life. Are we?"

"There *are* a lot of dingdongs here," she admitted. He looked a little hurt, so she added, "But I like that about a place. I do."

When after dinner she went for an evening walk with Martin, she tried to strike up a conversation about celebrities and movie stars. "I keep thinking about Princess Caroline's husband being killed," she said.

Martin was silent.

"That poor family," said Adrienne. "There's been so much tragedy."

Martin glared at her. "Yes," he said facetiously. "That poor, cursed family. I keep thinking, what can I do to help? What can I do? And I think, and I think, and I think so much I'm helpless. I throw up my hands and end up doing nothing. I'm helpless!" He began to walk faster, ahead of her, down into the village. Adrienne began to run to keep up. Marriage, she thought, it's an institution, all right.

Near the main piazza, under a streetlamp, the CHIROMANTE: TAROT E FACCIA had set up her table again. When she saw Adrienne, she called out, "Give me your birthday, signora, and your husband's birthday, and I will do your charts to tell you whether the two of you are compatible! Or—" She paused to study Martin skeptically as he rushed past. "Or, I can just tell you right now."

"Have you been to this woman before?" he asked, slowing down. Adrienne grabbed Martin's arm and started to lead him away.

"I needed a change of scenery."

Now he stopped. "Well," he said sympathetically, calmer after some exercise, "who could blame you." Adrienne took his hand, feeling a grateful, marital love—alone, in Italy, at night, in May. Was there any love that wasn't at bottom a grateful one? The moonlight glittered off the lake like electric fish, like a school of ice.

"What are you doing?" Adrienne asked Ilke the next afternoon. The lamps were particularly low, though there was a spotlight directed onto a picture of Ilke's mother, which she had placed on an end table, for the month, in honor of Mother's Day. The mother looked ghostly, like a sacrifice. What if Ilke were truly a witch? What if fluids and hairs and nails were being collected as offerings in memory of her mother?

"I'm fluffing your aura," she said. "It is very dark today, burned down to a shadowy rim." She was manipulating Adrienne's toes and Adrienne suddenly had a horror-movie vision of Ilke with jars of collected toe juice in a closet for Satan, who, it would be revealed, *was* Ilke's mother. Perhaps Ilke would lean over suddenly and bite Adrienne's shoulder, drink her blood. How could Adrienne control these thoughts? She felt her aura fluff like the fur of a screeching cat. She imagined herself, for the first time, never coming here again. Good-bye. Farewell. It would be a brief affair, a little nothing; a chat on the porch at a party.

Fortunately, there were other things to keep Adrienne busy.

She had begun spray-painting the spiders and the results were interesting. She could see herself explaining to a dealer back home that the work represented the spider web of solitude—a vibration at the periphery reverberates inward (experiential, deafening) and the spider rushes out from the center to devour the gong, the gonger and the gong. Gone. She could see the dealer taking her phone number and writing it down on an extremely loose scrap of paper.

And there was the occasional after-dinner sing-song, scholars and spouses gathered around the piano in various states of inebriation and forgetfulness. "Okay, that may be how you learned it, Harold, but that's *not* how it goes."

There was also the Asparagus Festival, which, at Carlo's suggestion, she and Kate Spalding in one of her T-shirts—*all right already with the T-shirts, Kate*—decided to attend. They took a hydrofoil across the lake and climbed a steep road up toward a church square. The road was long and tiring and Adrienne began to refer to it as the Asparagus Death Walk.

"Maybe there isn't really a festival," she suggested, gasping for breath, but Kate kept walking, ahead of her.

Adrienne sighed. Off in the trees were the ratchety cheeping of birds and the competing, hourly chimes of two churches, followed later by the single off-tone of the half hour. When she and Kate finally reached the Asparagus Festival, it turned out to be only a little ceremony where a few people bid very high prices for clutches of asparagus described as "*bello, bello,*" the proceeds from which went to the local church.

"I used to grow asparagus," said Kate on their walk back down. They were taking a different route this time, and the lake and its ochre villages spread out before them, peaceful and far away. Along the road wildflowers grew in a pallet of pastels, like soaps.

"I could never grow asparagus," said Adrienne. As a child her favorite food had been "asparagus with holiday sauce." "I did grow a carrot once, though. But it was so small I just put it in a scrapbook."

"Are you still seeing Ilke?"

"This week, at any rate. How about you?"

"She's booked solid. I couldn't get another appointment. All the scholars, you know, are paying her regular visits."

"Really?"

"Oh, yes," said Kate very knowingly. "They're tense as dimes." Already Adrienne could smell the fumes of the Fiats and the ferries and delivery vans, the Asparagus Festival far away.

"Tense as dimes?"

Back at the villa, Adrienne waited for Martin, and when he came in, smelling of sandalwood, all the little deaths in her bones told her this: he was seeing the masseuse.

She sniffed the sweet parabola of his neck and stepped back. "I want to know how long have you've been getting massages. Don't lie to me," she said slowly, her voice hard as a spike. Anxiety shrank his face: his mouth caved in, his eyes grew beady and scared.

"What makes you think I've been getting—" he started to say. "Well, just once or twice."

She leaped away from him and began pacing furiously about the room, touching the furniture, not looking at him. "How could you?" she asked. "You know what my going there has meant to me! How could you not tell me?" She picked up a book on the dressing table—*Industrial Relations Systems*—and slammed it back down. "How could you horn in on this experience? How could you be so furtive and untruthful?"

"I am terribly sorry," he said.

"Yeah, well, so am I," said Adrienne. "And when we get home, I want a divorce." She could see it now, the empty apartment, the bad eggplant parmigiana, all the Halloweens she would answer the doorbell, a boozy divorcee frightening the little children with too much enthusiasm for their costumes. "I feel so fucking *dishonored!*" Nothing around her seemed able to hold steady; nothing held.

Martin was silent and she was silent and then he began to speak, in a beseeching way, there it was the beseech again, rumbling at the edge of her life like a truck. "We are both so lonely here," he said. "But I have only been waiting for you. That is all I have done for the last eight months. To try not to let things intrude, to let you take your time, to make sure you ate something, to buy the goddamn Spearsons a new picnic bench, to bring you to a place where anything at all might happen, where you might even leave me, but at least come back into life at last—"

"You did?"

"Did what?"

"You bought the Spearsons a new *picnic bench?*"

"Yes, I did."

She thought about this. "Didn't they think you were being hostile?"

"Oh . . . I think, yes, they probably thought it was hostile."

And the more Adrienne thought about it, about the poor bereaved Spearsons, and about Martin and all the ways he tried to show her he was on her side, whatever that meant, how it was both the hope and shame of him that he was always doing his best, the more she felt foolish, deprived of reasons. Her rage flapped awkwardly away like a duck. She felt as she had when her cold, fierce parents had at last grown sick and old, stick boned and saggy, protected by infirmity the way cuteness protected a baby, or should, it should protect a baby, and she had been left with her rage—vestigial girlhood rage—inappropriate and intact. She would hug her parents good-bye, the gentle, emptied sacks of them, and think, where did you go?

Time, Adrienne thought. What a racket.

Martin had suddenly begun to cry. He sat at the bed's edge and curled inward, his soft, furry face in his great hard hands, his head falling downward into the bright plaid of his shirt.

She felt dizzy and turned away, toward the window. A fog had drifted in, and in the evening light the sky and the lake seemed a singular blue, like a Monet. "I've never seen you cry," she said.

"Well, I cry," he said. "I can even cry at the sports page if the games are too close. Look at me, Adrienne. You never really look at me."

But she could only continue to stare out the window, touching her fingers to the shutters and frame. She felt far away, as if she were back home, walking through the neighborhood at dinnertime: when the cats sounded like babies and the babies sounded like birds, and the fathers were home from work, their children in their arms gumming the language, air shaping their flowery throats into a park of singing. Through the windows wafted the smell of cooking food.

"We are with each other now," Martin was saying. "And in the different ways it means, we must try to make a life."

Out over the Sfondrata chapel tower, where the fog had broken, she thought she saw a single star, like the distant nose of a jet; there were people in the clayey clouds. She turned, and for a moment it seemed they were all there in Martin's eyes, all the absolving dead in residence in his face, the angel of the dead baby shining like a blazing creature, and she went to him, to protect and encircle him, seeking the heart's best trick, *oh, terrific heart.* "Please, forgive me," she said.

And he whispered, "Of course. It is the only thing. Of course."

Jonathan Galassi

Elms

to a teacher

Your "yet-to-be-dismantled" elms are few,
and by the time you read this may be gone.
In my own childhood we had one or two
that framed the lawn before the hurricane,
trees that were far too noble to survive
a time like ours, too slender or sublime.
Something in us wouldn't let them live.

Or was it only that they'd served their time?
"The size of our abidance" wasn't theirs,
the way it can't be yours. That is a trait
of nature, as it is a trait of ours
to see in something passing something great:
our backwardlookingness that makes a tree
the genius of the place it cannot be.

Issue 80, 1981

Bernard Cooper

✠

The Fine Art of Sighing

You feel a gradual welling up of pleasure, or boredom, or melancholy. Whatever the emotion, it's more abundant than you ever dreamed. You can no more contain it than your hands can cup a lake. And so you surrender and suck the air. Your esophagus opens, diaphragm expands. Poised at the crest of an exhalation, your body is about to be unburdened, second by second, cell by cell. A kettle hisses. A balloon deflates. Your shoulders fall like two ripe pears, muscles slack at last.

My mother stared out the kitchen window, ashes from her cigarette dribbling into the sink. A sentry guarding her solitude, she'd turned her back on the rest of the house. I'd tiptoe across the linoleum and make my lunch without making a sound. Sometimes I saw her back expand, then heard her let loose one plummeting note, a sigh so long and weary it might have been her last. Beyond our backyard, above telephone poles and apartment buildings, rose the brown horizon of the city; across it glided an occasional bird, or the blimp that advertised Goodyear tires. She might have been drifting into the distance, or lamenting her separation from it. She might have been wishing she were somewhere else, or wishing she could be happy where she was, a middle-aged housewife dreaming at her sink.

My father's sighs were more melodic. What began as a somber sigh could abruptly change pitch, turn gusty and loose, and suggest by its very transformation that what begins in sorrow might end in relief. He could prolong the rounded vowel of oy, or let it ricochet like an echo, as if he were shouting in a tunnel or a cave. Where my mother sighed from ineffable sadness, my father sighed at simple things: the coldness of a drink, the softness of a pillow, or an itch that my mother, following the frantic map of his words, finally found on his back and scratched.

A friend of mine once mentioned that I was given to long and ponderous sighs. Once I became aware of this habit, I heard my father's sighs in my own and knew for a moment his small satisfactions. At other times, I felt my mother's restlessness and wished I could leave my body with my breath, or be happy in the body my breath left behind.

It's a reflex and a legacy, this soulful species of breathing. Listen closely: my ancestors lungs are pumping like bellows, men towing boats along the banks of the Volga, women lugging baskets of rye bread and pike. At the end of each day, they lift their weary arms in a toast; as thanks for the heat and sting of vodka, their *a-h-hs* condense in the cold Russian air.

At any given moment, there must be thousands of people sighing. A man in Milwaukee heaves and shivers and blesses the head of the second wife who's not too shy to lick his toes. A judge in Munich groans with pleasure after tasting again the silky bratwurst she ate as a child. Every day, meaningful sighs are expelled from schoolchildren, driving instructors, forensic experts, certified public accountants, and dental hygienists, just to name a few. The sighs of widows and widowers alone must account for a significant portion of the carbon dioxide released into the atmosphere. Every time a girdle is removed, a foot is submerged in a tub of warm water, or a restroom is reached on a desolate road . . . you'd think the sheer velocity of it would create mistrals, siroccos, hurricanes; arrows should be swarming over satellite maps, weathermen talking a mile a minute, ties flapping from their necks like flags.

Before I learned that Venetian prisoners were led across it to their execution, I imagined that the Bridge of Sighs was a feat of invisible engineering, a structure vaulting above the earth, the girders and trusses, the stay ropes and cables, the counterweights and safety rails connecting one human breath to the next.

Issue 135, 1995

Heather McHugh

Intensive Care

*

As if intensity were a virtue we say
good and. Good and drunk. Good and dead.
What plural means is everything
that multiplying greatens, as if two
were more like ninetynine than one,
or one were more like zero than
like anything. As if
you loved me, you will leave me.

**

You (are the man who) made
roadmaps to the ovaries
upon his dinner napkin.
I('m the woman who) always forgot
where she was—in a state,
in a sentence. Absently stirring
my alphabet soup, I remember
childhood's clean white calendar
and blueprint of the heart.

***

As if friends were to be saved
we are friends. We talk to ourselves,
go home at the same time.
As if beds were to be made
not born in, as if love
were just heredity
we know the worst, we fear
the known. Today we were bad
and together; tonight
we'll be good and alone.

Issue 80, 1981

Raymond Carver

Careful

After a lot of talking—what his wife, Inez, called *assessment*—Lloyd moved out of the house and into his own place. He had two rooms and a bath on the top floor of a three-story house. Inside the rooms, the roof slanted down sharply. If he walked around, he had to duck his head. He had to stoop to look from his windows and be careful getting in and out of bed. There were two keys. One key let him into the house itself. Then he climbed some stairs that passed through the house to a landing. He went up another flight of stairs to the door of his room and used the other key on that lock.

Once, when he was coming back to his place in the afternoon, carrying a sack with three bottles of André champagne and some lunch meat, he stopped on the landing and looked into his landlady's living room. He saw the old woman lying on her back on the carpet. She seemed to be asleep. Then it occurred to him she might be dead. But the TV was going, so he chose to think she was asleep. He didn't know what to make of it. He moved the sack from one arm to the other. It was then that the woman gave a little cough, brought her hand to her side, and went back to being quiet and still again. Lloyd continued on up the stairs and unlocked his door. Later that day, toward evening, as he looked from his kitchen window, he saw the old woman down in the yard, wearing a straw hat and holding her hand against her side. She was using a little watering can on some pansies.

In his kitchen, he had a combination refrigerator and stove. The refrigerator and stove was a tiny affair wedged into a space between the sink and the wall. He had to bend over, almost get down on his knees, to get anything out of the refrigerator. But it was all right because he didn't keep much in there, anyway—except fruit juice, lunch meat, and champagne. The stove had two burners. Now and then he heated water in a saucepan and made instant coffee. But some days he didn't drink any coffee. He forgot, or else he just didn't feel like coffee. One morning he woke up and promptly fell to eating crumb doughnuts and drinking champagne. There'd been a time, some years back, when he would have laughed at having a breakfast like this. Now, there didn't seem to be anything very unusual about it. In fact, he hadn't thought anything about it until he was in bed and trying to recall the things he'd done that day, starting with when he'd gotten up that morning. At first, he couldn't remember anything noteworthy. Then he remembered eating those doughnuts and drinking champagne. There was a time when he would have considered this a mildly crazy thing to do, something to tell friends about. Then, the more he thought about it, the more he could see it didn't matter much one way or the other. He'd had doughnuts and champagne for breakfast. So what?

In his furnished rooms, he also had a dinette set, a little sofa, an old easy chair, and a TV set that stood on a coffee table. He wasn't paying the electricity here, it wasn't even his TV, so sometimes he left the set on all day and all night. But he kept the volume down unless he saw there was something he wanted to watch. He did not have a telephone, which was fine with him. He didn't want a telephone. There was a bedroom with a double bed, a nightstand, and a chest of drawers. A bathroom gave off from the bedroom.

The one time Inez came to visit, it was eleven o'clock in the morning. He'd been in his new place for two weeks, and he'd been wondering if she were going to drop by. But he was trying to do something about his drinking, too, so he was glad to be alone. He'd made that much clear—being alone was the thing he needed most. The day she came, he was on the sofa, in his pajamas, hitting his fist against the right side of his head. Just before he could hit himself again, he heard voices downstairs on the landing. He could make out his wife's voice. The sound was like the murmur of voices from a faraway crowd, but he knew it was Inez and somehow knew the visit was an important one. He gave his head another jolt with his fist, then got to his feet.

He'd awakened that morning and found that his ear had stopped up with wax. He couldn't hear anything clearly, and he seemed to have lost his sense of balance, his equilibrium, in the process. For the last hour he'd been on the sofa, working frustratedly on his ear, now and again slamming his head with his fist. Once in a while he'd massage the gristly underpart of his ear, or else tug at his lobe. Then he'd dig furiously in his ear with his little finger and open his mouth, simulating yawns. But he'd tried everything he could think of, and he was nearing the end of his rope. He could hear the voices below break off their murmuring. He pounded his head a good one and finished the glass of champagne. He turned off the TV and carried the glass to the sink. He picked up the open bottle of champagne from the drainboard and took it into the bathroom where he put it behind the stool. Then he went to answer the door.

"Hi, Lloyd," Inez said. She didn't smile. She stood in the doorway in a bright spring outfit. He hadn't seen these clothes before. She was holding a canvas handbag that had sunflowers stitched onto its sides. He hadn't seen the handbag before, either.

"I didn't think you heard me," she said. "I thought you might be gone or something. But the woman downstairs—what's her name? Mrs. Matthews—she thought you were up here."

"I heard you," Lloyd said. "But just barely." He hitched his pajamas and ran a hand through his hair. "Actually, I'm in one hell of a shape. Come on in."

"It's eleven o'clock," she said. She came inside and shut the door behind her. She acted as if she hadn't heard him. Maybe she hadn't.

"I know what time it is," he said. "I've been up for a long time. I've been up since eight. I watched part of the *Today* show. But just now I'm about to go crazy with something. My ear's plugged up. You remember that other time it happened? We were living in that place near the Chinese takeout joint. Where the kids found that bulldog dragging its chain? I had to go to the doctor then and have my ears flushed out. I know you remember. You drove me and we had to wait a long time. Well, it's like that now. I mean it's that bad. Only I can't go to a doctor this morning. I don't have a doctor, for one thing. I'm about to go nuts, Inez. I feel like I want to cut off my head or something."

He sat down at one end of the sofa, and she sat down at the other end. But it was a small sofa, and they were still sitting close to each other. They were so close he could have put out his hand and touched her knee. But he didn't. She glanced around the room and then fixed her eyes on him again. He knew he hadn't shaved and that his hair stood up. But she was his wife, and she knew everything there was to know about him.

"What have you tried?" she said. She looked in her purse and brought up a cigarette. "I mean, what have you done for it so far?"

"What'd you say?" He turned the left side of his head to her. "Inez, I swear, I'm not exaggerating. This thing is driving me crazy. When I talk, I feel like I'm talking inside a barrel. My head rumbles. And I can't hear good, either. When *you* talk, it sounds like you're talking through a lead pipe."

"Do you have any Q-tips, or else Wesson oil?" Inez said.

"Honey, this is serious," he said. "I don't have any Q-tips or Wesson oil. Are you kidding?"

"If we had some Wesson oil, I could heat it and put some of that in your ear. My mother used to do that," she said. "It might soften things up in there."

He shook his head. His head felt full and like it was awash with fluid. It felt like it had when he used to swim near the bottom of the municipal pool and come up with his ears filled with water. But back then it'd been easy to clear the water out. All he had to do was fill his lungs with air, close his mouth and clamp down on his nose. Then he'd blow out his cheeks and force air into his head. His ears would pop, and for a few seconds he'd have the pleasant sensation of water running out of his head and dripping onto his shoulders. Then he'd heave himself out of the pool.

Inez finished her cigarette and put it out. "Lloyd, we have things to talk about. But I guess we'll have to take things one at a time. Go sit in the chair. Not *that* chair, the chair in the kitchen! So we can have some light on the situation."

He whacked his head once more. Then he went over to sit on a dinette chair. She moved over and stood behind him. She touched his hair with her fingers. Then she moved the hair away from his ears. He reached for her hand, but she drew it away.

"Which ear did you say it was?" she said.

"The right ear," he said. "The right one."

"First," she said, "you have to sit here and not move. I'll find a hairpin and some tissue paper. I'll try to get in there with that. Maybe it'll do the trick."

He was alarmed at the prospect of her putting a hairpin inside his ear. He said something to that effect.

"What?" she said. "Christ, I can't hear you, either. Maybe this is catching."

"When I was a kid, in school," Lloyd said, "we had this health teacher. She was like a nurse, too. She said we should never put anything smaller than an elbow into our ear." He vaguely remembered a wall chart showing a massive diagram of the ear, along with an intricate system of canals, passageways, and walls.

"Well, your nurse was never faced with this exact problem," Inez said. "Anyway, we need to try *something*. We'll try this first. If it doesn't work, we'll try something else. That's life, isn't it?"

"Does that have a hidden meaning or something?" Lloyd said.

"It means just what I said. But you're free to think as you please. I mean, it's a free country," she said. "Now, let me get fixed up with what I need. You just sit there."

She went through her purse, but she didn't find what she was looking for. Finally, she emptied the purse out onto the sofa. "No hairpins," she said. "Damn." But it was as if she were saying the words from another room. In a way, it was almost as if he'd imagined her saying them. There'd been a time, long ago, when they used to feel they had ESP when it came to what the other one was thinking. They could finish sentences that the other had started.

She picked up some nail clippers, worked for a minute, and then he saw the device separate in her fingers and part of it swing away from the other part. A nail file protruded from the clippers. It looked to him as if she were holding a small dagger.

"You're going to put that in my ear?" he said.

"Maybe you have a better idea," she said. "It's this, or else I don't know what. Maybe you have a pencil? You want me to use that? Or maybe you have a screwdriver around," she said and laughed. "Don't worry. Listen, Lloyd, I won't hurt you. I said I'd be careful. I'll wrap some tissue around the end of this. It'll be all right. I'll be careful, like

I said. You just stay where you are, and I'll get some tissues for this. I'll make a swab."

She went into the bathroom. She was gone for a time. He stayed where he was on the dinette chair. He began thinking of things he ought to say to her. He wanted to tell her he was limiting himself to champagne and champagne only. He wanted to tell her he was tapering off the champagne, too. It was only a matter of time now. But when she came back into the room, he couldn't say anything. He didn't know where to start. But she didn't look at him, anyway. She fished a cigarette from the heap of things she'd emptied onto the sofa cushion. She lit the cigarette with her lighter and went to stand by the window that faced onto the street. She said something, but he couldn't make out the words. When she stopped talking, he didn't ask her what it was she'd said. Whatever it was, he knew he didn't want her to say it again. She put out the cigarette. But she went on standing at the window, leaning forward, the slope of the roof just inches from her head.

"Inez," he said.

She turned and came over to him. He could see tissue on the point of the nail file.

"Turn your head to the side and keep it that way," she said. "That's right. Sit still now and don't move. Don't move," she said again.

"Be careful," he said. "For Christ's sake."

She didn't answer him.

"Please, please," he said. Then he didn't say any more. He was afraid. He closed his eyes and held his breath as he felt the nail file turn past the inner part of his ear and begin its probe. He was sure his heart would stop beating. Then she went a little farther and began turning the blade back and forth, working at whatever it was in there. Inside his ear, he heard a squeaking sound.

"Ouch!" he said.

"Did I hurt you?" She took the nail file out of his ear and moved back a step. "Does anything feel different, Lloyd?"

He brought his hands up to his ears and lowered his head.

"It's just the same," he said.

She looked at him and bit her lips.

"Let me go to the bathroom," he said. "Before we go any farther, I have to go to the bathroom."

"Go ahead," Inez said. "I think I'll go downstairs and see if your landlady has any Wesson oil, or anything like that. She might even have some Q-tips. I don't know why I didn't think of that before. Of asking her."

"That's a good idea," he said. "I'll go to the bathroom."

She stopped at the door and looked at him, and then she opened the door and went out. He crossed the living room, went into his bedroom, and opened the bathroom door. He reached down behind the stool and brought up the bottle of champagne. He took a long drink. It was warm, but it went right down. He took some more. In the beginning, he'd really thought he could continue drinking if he limited himself to champagne. But in no time he found he was drinking three or four bottles a day. He knew he'd have to deal with this pretty soon. But first, he'd have to get his hearing back. One thing at a time, just like she'd said. He finished off the rest of the champagne and put the empty bottle in its place behind the stool. Then he ran water and brushed his teeth. After he'd used the towel, he went back into the other room.

Inez had returned and was at the stove heating something in a little pan. She glanced in his direction, but didn't say anything at first. He looked past her shoulder and out the window. A bird flew from the branch of one tree to another and preened its feathers. But if it made any kind of bird noise, he didn't hear it.

She said something that he didn't catch.

"Say again," he said.

She shook her head and turned back to the stove. But then she turned again and said, loud enough and slow enough so he could hear it: "I found your stash in the bathroom."

"I'm trying to cut back," he said.

She said something else. "What?" he said. "What'd you say?" He really hadn't heard her.

"We'll talk later," she said. "We have things to discuss, Lloyd. Money is one thing. But there are other things, too. First we have to see about this ear." She put her finger into the pan and then took the pan off the stove. "I'll let it cool for a minute," she said. "It's too hot right now. Sit down. Put this towel around your shoulders."

He did as he was told. He sat on the chair and put the towel around his neck and shoulders. Then he hit the side of his head with his fist.

"Goddamn it," he said.

She didn't look up. She put her finger into the pan once more, testing. Then she poured the liquid from the pan into his plastic glass. She picked up the glass and came over to him.

"Don't be scared," she said. "It's just some of your landlady's baby oil, that's all it is. I told her what was wrong, and she thought this might help. No guarantees," Inez said. "But maybe this'll loosen things up in there. She said it used to happen to her husband. She said this one time she saw a piece of wax fall out of his ear, and it was like a big plug of something. It was ear wax was what it was. She said try this. And she didn't have any Q-tips. I can't understand that, her not having any Q-tips. That part really surprises me."

"Okay," he said. "All right. I'm willing to try anything. Inez, if I had to go on like this, I think I'd rather be dead. You know? I mean it, Inez."

"Tilt your head all the way to the side now," she said. "Don't move. I'll pour this in until your ear fills up, then I'll stopper it with this dishrag. And you just sit there for ten minutes, say. Then we'll see. If this doesn't do it, well, I don't have any other suggestions. I just don't know what to do then."

"This'll work," he said. "If this doesn't do it, I'll find a gun and shoot myself. I'm serious. That's what I feel like doing, anyway."

He turned his head to the side and let it hang down. He looked at the things in the room from this new perspective. But it wasn't any different from the old way of looking, except that everything was on its side.

"Farther," she said. He held onto the chair for balance and lowered his head even more. All of the objects in his vision, all of the objects in his life, it seemed, were at the far end of this room. He could feel the warm liquid pour into his ear. Then she brought the dishrag up and held it there. In a little while, she began to massage the area around his ear. She pressed into the soft part of the flesh between his jaw and skull. She moved her fingers to the area over his ear and began to work the tips of her fingers back and forth. After a while, he didn't know how long he'd been sitting there. It could have been ten minutes. It could have been longer. He was still holding onto the chair. Now and then, as her fingers pressed the side of his head, he could feel the warm oil she'd poured in there wash back and forth in the canals inside his ear. When she pressed a certain way, he imagined he could hear, inside his head, a soft, swishing sound.

"Sit up straight," Inez said. He sat up and pressed the heel of his hand against his head while the liquid poured out of his ear. She caught it in the towel. Then she wiped the outside of his ear.

Inez was breathing through her nose. Lloyd heard the sound her breath made as it came and went. He heard a car pass on the street outside the house and, at the back of the house, down below his kitchen window, the clear *snick-snick* of pruning shears.

"Well?" Inez said. She waited with her hands on her hips, frowning.

"I can hear you," he said. "I'm all right! I mean I can *hear*. It doesn't sound like you're talking underwater anymore. It's fine now. It's okay. God, I thought for a while I was going to go crazy. But I feel fine now. I can hear everything. Listen, honey, I'll make coffee. There's some juice, too."

"I have to go," she said. "I'm late for something. But I'll come back. We'll go out for lunch sometime. We need to talk."

"I just can't sleep on this side of my head, is all," he went on. He followed her into the living room. She lit a cigarette. "That's what happened. I slept all night on this side of my head, and my ear plugged up. I think I'll be all right as long as I don't forget and sleep on this side of my head. If I'm careful. You know what I'm saying? If I can just sleep on my back, or else on my left side."

She didn't look at him.

"Not forever, of course not, I know that. I couldn't do that. I couldn't do it the rest of my life. But for a while, anyway. Just my left side, or else flat on my back."

But even as he said this he began to feel afraid of the night that was coming. He began to fear the moment he would begin to make his preparations for bed and what might happen afterwards. That time was hours away, but already he was afraid. What if, in the middle of the night, he accidentally turned onto his right side, and the weight of his head pressing into the pillow were to seal the wax again into the dark canals of his ear? What if he woke up then, unable to hear, the ceiling inches from his head?

"Good God," he said. "Jesus, this is awful. Inez, I just had something like a terrible nightmare. Inez, where do you have to go?"

"I told you," she said, as she put everything back into her purse and made ready to leave. She looked at her watch. "I'm late for something." She went to the door. But at the door she turned and said something else to him. He didn't listen. He didn't want to. He watched her lips move until she said what she had to say. When she'd finished, she said, "Good-bye." Then she opened the door and closed it behind her.

He went into the bedroom to dress. But in a minute he hurried out, wearing only his trousers, and went to the door. He opened it and stood there, listening. On the landing below, he heard Inez thank Mrs. Matthews for the oil. He heard the old woman say, "You're welcome." And then he heard her draw a connection between her late husband and himself. He heard her say, "Leave me your number. I'll call if something happens. You never know."

"I hope you don't have to," Inez said. "But I'll give it to you, anyway. Do you have something to write it down with?"

Lloyd heard Mrs. Matthews open a drawer and rummage through it. Then her old woman's voice said, "Okay."

Inez gave her their telephone number at home. "Thanks," she said.

"It was nice meeting you," Mrs. Matthews said.

He listened as Inez went on down the stairs and opened the front door. Then he heard it close. He waited until he heard her start their car and drive away. Then he shut the door and went back into the bedroom to finish dressing.

After he'd put on his shoes and tied the laces, he lay down on the bed and pulled the covers up to his chin. He let his arms rest under the covers at his side. He closed his eyes and pretended it was night and pretended he was going to fall asleep. Then he brought his arms up and crossed them over his chest to see how this position would suit him. He kept his eyes closed, trying it out. All right, he thought. Okay. If he didn't want that ear to plug up again, he'd have to sleep on his back, that was all. He knew he could do it. He just couldn't forget, even in his sleep, and turn onto the wrong side. Four or five hours sleep a night was all he needed anyway. He'd manage. Worse things could happen to a man. In a way, it was a challenge. But he was up to it. He knew he was. In a minute, he threw back the covers and got up.

He still had the better part of the day ahead of him. He went into the kitchen, bent down in front of the little refrigerator, and took out a fresh bottle of champagne. He worked the plastic cork out of the bottle as carefully as he could, but there was still the festive *pop* of champagne being opened. He rinsed the baby oil out of his glass, then poured it full of champagne. He took the glass over to the sofa and sat down. He put the glass on the coffee table. Up went his feet onto the coffee table, next to the champagne. He leaned back. But after a time, he began to worry some more about the night that was coming on. What if, despite all his efforts, the wax decided to plug his other ear? He closed his eyes and shook his head. Pretty soon, he got up and went into the bedroom. He undressed and put his pajamas back on. Then he moved back into the living room. He sat down on the sofa once more, and once more put his feet up. He reached over and turned the TV on. He adjusted the volume. He knew he couldn't keep from worrying about what might happen when he went to bed. It was just something he'd have to learn to live with. In a way, this whole business reminded him of the thing with the doughnuts and champagne. It was not that remarkable at all, if you thought about it. He took some champagne. But it didn't taste right. He ran his tongue over his lips, then wiped his mouth on his sleeve. He looked and saw a film of oil on the champagne.

He got up and carried the glass to the sink where he poured it into the drain. He took the bottle of champagne into the living room and made himself comfortable on the sofa. He held the bottle by its neck as he drank. He'd never before drunk straight from the bottle, but it didn't seem that much out of the ordinary. He decided that even if he were to fall asleep sitting up on the sofa in the middle of the afternoon, it wouldn't be any more strange than somebody having to lie on his back for hours at a time. He lowered his head to peer out the window. Judging from the angle of the sunlight, and the shadows that had entered the room, he guessed it was about three o'clock.

Joseph Brodsky

⌖

To Urania

I.K.

Everything has its limit, including sorrow.
A windowpane stalls a stare; nor does a grill abandon
a leaf. One may rattle the keys, gurgling down a swallow.
Loneliness cubes a man at random.
A camel sniffs at the rail with a resentful nostril;
a perspective cuts emptiness deep and even.
And what is space anyway if not the
body's absence at every given
point? That's why Urania's older than sister Clio!
In daylight or with the soot-rich lantern,
you see the globe's pate free of any bio,
you see she hides nothing, unlike the latter.
There they are, blueberry-laden forests,
rivers where the folk with bare hands catch sturgeon
or the towns in whose soggy phonebooks
you are starring no longer. Further eastward, surge on
brown mountain ranges; wild mares carousing
in tall sedge; the cheekbones get yellower
as they turn numerous. And still further east, steam
    dreadnoughts or cruisers,
and the expanse grows blue like laced underwear.

Issue 103, 1987

MADNESS

Zelda Fitzgerald

✠

from Zelda: A Worksheet

[Dear Scott,] It's ghastly losing your mind and not being able to see clearly, literally or figuratively—and knowing that you can't think and that nothing is right, not even your comprehension of concrete things like how old you are or what you look like.

Where are all my things? I used to always have dozens of things and now there doesn't seem to be any clothes or anything personal in my trunk—I'd love the gramophone.

What a disgraceful mess—but if it stops our drinking it is worth it, because then you can finish your novel and write a play and we can live somewhere and can have a house with a room to paint and write like we had, with friends for Scottie and there will be Sundays and Mondays again which are different from each other and there will be Christmas and winter fires and pleasant things to think of when you're going to sleep—and my life won't lie up the back-stairs of music-halls and yours won't keep trailing down the gutters of Paris—if it will only work, and I can keep sane and not a bitter maniac—

Dear Scott,

I have not the slightest indication of what your intentions are towards me. After five months of suffering and misery and isolation, at least the pathological side of my illness has disappeared. For the rest, I am a woman of thirty and, it seems to me, entitled to some voice in decisions concerning me. I have had enough and it is simply wasting my time and ruining my health keeping up the absurd pretense that a

lesion in the head is curable. Will you make the necessary arrangements that I leave here and seek some satisfactory life for myself or
shall I write to Daddy that he should come over? . . . I believe three
months is the usual limit of these sorts of struggles and I have no intention of any longer internment. If you want an idea of what it's like,
you might pass up your next tennis game.

Malcolm Lowry

⌖

from Lunar Caustic

IV

Sweltering, delirious night telescoped into foetid day: day into
night: he realised it was twilight though he had thought it dawn.
Someone sat on his bed with a hand on his pulse, and forcing his eyes
open he saw a wavering white form which divided into three, became
two and finally came into focus as a man in a white gown.

The man—a doctor?—dropped Plantagenet's wrist. "You've certainly got the shakes," he said.

"Shakes, yes." The quivering of his body was such that, after his
initial surprise, it impeded his speech, "Well, what's wrong with
me?" He tried to rise on his elbow which, jumping, did not hold him;
he sank or fell back with a groan.

"Alcohol . . . And perhaps other things. Judging from your remarks in the last few days I'd say it's about as bad as you suspect."

"What did I say?"

The doctor smiled slightly. "You said, 'hullo, father, return to the
presexual revives the necessity for nutrition.' Sounds as though you
once read a little book."

"Oh Christ! Oh God! Oh Jesus!"

"You made some fine giveaways." The doctor shook his head,
"But let's be concrete. Who is Ruth? And the six Cantabs?"

"Bill Plantagenet and his Seven Hot Cantabs," he corrected and
continued with nervous rapidity, "We went a treat in Cambridge, at

the May Balls, or at the Footlights Club. We were all right with our first records, too, we took that seriously. But when we got over here we just broke up." He grasped the doctor's arm. "I couldn't seem to hold the boys together at all. Damn it, I don't know just what didn't happen. Of course there were complications about unions, income taxes, head taxes, a price on our heads—"

"You're British, of course?"

"God knows where they all are now. The bull fiddle's fighting in Spain, and the saxophone section—and it's all my damn irresponsible bloody fault too." He put his head down, burying it under the pillow. "In a way I lost my contract, I lost my band, I lost Ruth." He sat up, shaking, looking at the doctor furtively, yet with a certain rebelliousness. "I've been playing in dives. But it's my hands, my hands, look—" he held them out, shaking. "They're not big enough for a real pianist, I can't stretch over an octave on a piano. On a guitar I fake all the time."

The doctor shook his head. "You didn't leave Ruth because your hands couldn't stretch an octave," he said. "And where is Ruth? I assume she's your wife."

"I don't know. I don't care. Hell with her! She only brought me back as a sort of souvenir from Europe. Perhaps it was America I was in love with. You know, you people get sentimental over England from time to time with your guff about sweetest Shakespeare. Well, this was the other way round. Only it was Eddie Lang and Joe Venuti and the death of Bix . . . What about a drink? And I wanted to see where Melville lived. You'll never know how disappointed I was not to find any whalers in New Bedford."

The doctor rose and stood looking down at him. "I'll send you a paraldehyde and splash. Perhaps it was your heart you couldn't make stretch an octave."

"Please don't go!" He tried to sit up, grasping the doctor's arm. "I've got to tell you—"

"Try it here for a few days, you'd better," the doctor said not unkindly. He disengaged his arm, and wiped his forehead, sighing. "It won't do you any harm. Where did you get those muscles?"

"Muscles," said Plantagenet, his teeth chattering. "Yes. I suppose so. That's weight lifting. And I once took a freighter to the Orient,

came back full of lions, one day I'd like to tell you about the lions. After that I read Melville instead. Four years ago I held the Cambridge
record for the two-arm press; matter of fact, the only weight I can't
lift—"

He managed to stagger to his feet, feeling the hospital tilt under
him like a ship . . . Still trembling violently he walked to the high
barred windows that gave on the East River. Heat haze hung over the
waterfront. He looked down, his knees knocking together, at the wet
grass below, and the broken coal barge. Amidships where the hull
had split, a mass of wet iron balanced. He glanced away—the tangled
object had become a sailor sprawled broken on the deck in brown,
shining oil-skins.

From the steel scaffolding that shored up the powerhouse, a pulley
dropped a loop of rope; he saw a man hanging by the neck from this;
it was the drummer of his band—but the vision faded instantly.

Staring out at the river his agony was like a great lidless eye.

Darkness was falling; through the clearing haze the stars came out.
Over the broken horizon the Scorpion was crawling. There was the
red, dying sun, Antares. To the southeast, the Retreat of the Howling
Dog appeared. The stars taking their places were wounds opening in
his being, multiple duplications of that agony, of that eye. The constellations might have been monstrosities in the delirium of God. Disaster seemed smeared over the whole universe. It was as if he were
living in the preexistence of some unimaginable catastrophe, and he
steadied himself a moment against the sill, feeling the doomed earth itself stagger in its heaving spastic flight toward the Hercules Butterfly.

"I'se bin here just up to almos' exactly let me see, men, seventeen
days and a half exac." Battle was tap dancing behind him.

"Dat guy talks wif his feet."

"Yes sah," said Battle, whirling around, "I do that thing, Man!"

"He comes from Louisiana; he knocked that old engineer's tooth
out," said Garry beside him.

"Now I catch Jersey Blues," Battle said. "I'se got fifteen customers." He skipped off.

—He was conscious that time was passing, that he was getting
"better." The periodic, shuddering metamorphoses his mind projected upon almost every object, bad as they were, were no longer so

atrociously vivid. Moreover he had at first forgotten for long periods that he was able to get out when he wished. Now he forgot more rarely. He was only a drunk, he thought. Though he had pretended for awhile that he was not, that he was mad with the full dignity of madness. The man who thought himself a ship. And time was passing; only his sense of it had become subject to a curious prorogation. He didn't know whether it was the fifth or the sixth day that found him still staring out of the window at twilight, with Garry and Mr. Kalowsky by his side like old faithful friends. The powerhouse no longer was a foreign place. The wharves, the motorboats, the poverty grass, he had received into his mind now, together with the old coal barge, to which Garry often turned.

"It was condemned," he would say. "One day it collapsed and fell apart."

Garry looked at Bill wildly, grasping his arm. "The houses of Pompeii were fallen!" His voice dropped to a whisper. "And you'd see a house suddenly fall in, *collapse*; and the melted rock and the hot mud poured down; people ran down to the boat. But it was collapsed." Looking up he added breathlessly, "Gold rings and boxes of money and strange tables and they dug down the side of the great mountain."

"Yes suh, man," Battle danced. "He's de ole man of the mountain. He track along wit a horse and ban'. Put a jiggle in his tail as you pass him by—" he danced away singing, "De biggest turtle I ever see, he twice de size of you and me."

Kalowsky stood quietly watching, pursing his lips continually in and out like a dying fish. What was that film Plantagenet had seen once, where the shark went on swallowing the live fish, even after it was dead?

Garry clutched Bill's arm again. "Listen. What do you think will be left of this building in a few years? *I'll* tell you. They'd still find the brick buildings but there wouldn't be any beds, only a rusty frame, and the radiator, you would touch it and it would fall to pieces. All that would be left of the piano would be the keys; all the rest would rot. And the floor." Garry paused, considering. "And one of us sat on it and the whole thing fell down, collapsed. We went out the door where the fire escape was and it fell off, seven stories off, it fell down."

But what had really begun to make things a bit more tolerable for him was this very comradeship of his two friends. Sometimes he even tricked himself into imagining that a kind of purpose united them. Part of the truth was that like new boys in a hostile school, like sailors on their first long voyage on a miserable ship, like soldiers in a prison camp, they were drawn together in a doleful world where their daydreams mingled, and finding expression, jostled irresponsibly, yet with an underlying irreducible logic, around the subject of homecoming. Yet with them "home" was never mentioned, save very obliquely by Garry. Plantagenet sometimes suspected the true nature of that miraculous day they looked to when their troubles would all be ended, but he couldn't give it away. Meanwhile it masqueraded before them in the hues of various dawns—never mind what was going to happen in its practical noontide.

As a matter of fact, with one part of his mind, he was seriously convinced that Mr. Kalowsky and Garry were at least as sane as he: he felt too that he would be able to convince the doctor, when he saw him again, that an injustice had been committed, which never would otherwise have come to light.

But trying to explain their whole situation to himself his mind seemed to flicker senselessly between extremities of insincerities. For with another part of his mind he felt the encroachment of a chilling fear, eclipsing all other feelings, that the thing they wanted was coming for him alone, before he was ready for it; it was a fear worse than the fear that when money was low one would have to stop drinking; it was compounded of harrowed longing and hatred, of fathomless compunctions, and of a paradoxical remorse, as it were in advance, for his failure to attempt finally something he was not now going to have time for, to face the world honestly; it was the shadow of a city of dreadful night without splendour that fell on his soul; and how darkly it fell whenever a ship passed!

Issue 29, 1963

Barbara Hamby

⚏

Delirium

Just before I fainted in the restaurant that evening,
    I was telling you a story about a madman
    I saw earlier in the day
as I walked home from my ballet class
    just off the Piazza Santa Maria del Carmine.
After crossing the bridge of Santa Trinità,
    looking in at the Ghirlandaio frescoes
    of the Sassetti family,
then wondering how many women there were
    who were young and rich enough
to wear the see-through lace cowboy shirts
    in the Gianni Versace windows
    on the Via Tornabuoni,
at the intersection of the Via de Calzaioli
    and the Via del Corso,
I walked into the hullabaloo being drummed up
    by a bearded man who was stalking back and forth,
    screaming something in Italian, of course,
    and waving his arms in the air.
But when he turned he would reach down with one hand,
    clamp his crotch,
    and then pull his body around
as though his hips were a bad dog
    and his genitals a leash he was yanking.

After each turn he'd continue stalking and flailing,
    until time to turn again.
So I am trying to explain this and our pizza comes,
    and I saw off a bite, but it is too hot,
so what do I do but swallow it, and it's too hot,
    and I think, it's too hot,
and my voice decelerates as if it is a recording
    on a slowly melting tape and the scene
    in the restaurant begins to recede:
in the far distance I see the bearded man ranting
    on the street,
then, nearer but retreating quickly, you
    and the long corridor of the restaurant,
then it's as if I am falling into a cavity behind me,
    one that is always there, though I've learned to ignore it,
but I'm falling now, first through a riot of red rooms,
    then gold, green, blue and darker
    until I finally drift into the black room
    where my mind can rest.
I wake up in the kitchen, lying on a wooden bench,
    with you and the waiter staring at me.
"I'm fine," I say, though it's as if I am pulling
    my mind up from a deep well.
The waiter brings me a bowl of soup,
    which I don't want, but it doesn't matter because
the lights go out and a man at the next table says,
    "*Primo quella signora ed ora la luce,*"
which means, first that woman and now the light,
    and it's so dark that I can't see myself or you,
and I feel as if I'm turning and a mad voice
    rises from my stomach
and cries where are we anyway, and who, and what, and why?

Issue 134, 1995

Susan Mitchell

❖

Autobiography

Who am I who speaks to you?

Though that's not it exactly. Try this. What behind
the eyes had looked out so central, so
solid was no longer
in its sours and saccharines, its careful
modulations, not even

a shadow of its   For a long time I watched

the unbraiding into thinner and thinnest   the way clouds
tall stalks of something in a field through which wind
the tassles untassling

I was behind where I stood and up ahead looking back.

Though that's not it exactly.

And how did I feel about all this? I said
that is not the question most likely
to succeed, but even so I'll take it the way

male and female are conveniences, rough categories, the make-do.

Is precision a better way? As soon as they asked me
which was more enjoyable I lost the taste
of myself. Though to call who I am
Tiresias would limit
the story. It was as if the one
talking were now a handful of crystals
absorbing the rays of the sun, a spectrum
out there in space, all the colors of the rainbow
primal and urgent, tensed, arched over

and also looking down into a stream
where flowed and wavered the reds, the yellows, green

I don't want to get lost in explaining. The colors
were doing what I was, a correlative
for anger, joy, fear, wonder, eagerness and more, all the
    emotions

so I could look at them, taking my time, naming each one.

And that was it, folks.

Anonymous as hundreds of girls at an air show.

Think flicker and fluid and flow, and all of it
seething and reaching out for
attention the way serpents coupling and uncoupling and

no particular reason why one at any given moment
reigns supreme, all of it up
for grabs, so to speak. Oh, did I forget to say

there was no enclosure, no frame?

I was placed in understanding, and from looking

so long inside, as if at the sun, I was
blinded and had to grope at
my body to know for sure, man or woman
and the shock: was this splitting or growing, adding
or subtracting? I yearned open and where
branch had been, declivity, cleft as if

pulled inside out by desire.

Is it wholeness I want?

Or fission? Frisson of, its
frequency, its pitch?

Bobbie Ann Mason

⚭

Do You Know What It Means
to Miss New Orleans?

In the airport limousine on the way into New Orleans, the driver says, "See that cemetery we're passing? In New Orleans, no one is buried underground—dig five feet and you hit water. New Orleans is below sea level. So people are buried in vaults, above ground."

In the dark, the shapes of the vaults stand out like rows of playhouses.

"Nobody has a basement either," says the driver.

"That would make my job a lot easier," says Sherry Williams, the lone passenger, vaguely. A city virtually on the ocean, yet below sea level, is a contradiction that hardly registers with her.

"How's that?"

"I'm an archaeologist. I dig up the past."

Sherry has not seen her old friend, Marlene Ballew, in ten years. Not since college. When Marlene wrote, suggesting the reunion in New Orleans, Sherry realized that it was finally time to see her again, and she felt guilty that she had waited so long. They had drifted apart after Marlene had been institutionalized for a series of nervous breakdowns. In the bleak hospital, Marlene cheerfully made paper flowers and painted watercolors of government intrigue—Watergate scenes. The last time Sherry saw her, Marlene recited poetry, screeching and cackling like all three witches in *Macbeth*, poems that no one would have thought Marlene knew, like "Kubla Khan" and "Leda and the Swan." When she forgot words, she supplied others without missing a beat. Sherry felt that Marlene was a lost person, no longer reachable.

She left Kentucky, going away to graduate school in New York and returning to Kentucky only once, when her mother died.

In her letter, Marlene said she was cured. She was married, with a
two-year-old child and a splendid home on Irvine Road in Lexington.
She wrote, "I'm so calm now, you wouldn't believe it. Having kids
changes you. It's something to do with hormones. I'm okay now. Really, I'm fine." Marlene's husband was going to New Orleans on business, and Marlene was going along. She invited Sherry to come. "I
know it sounds ridiculous—you're too far away. But I keep thinking
of how we always talked of going to Mardi Gras but never did. Mardi
Gras is over, but maybe it's not too late to have a reunion."

Marlene comes at her like a gust of wind, her arms open wide. Her
hair, which used to be long and straight, is cut short, with springy little curls. It is the wrong style for her baby-fine hair, but on Marlene it
looks fashionably extreme, like something on a model in *Vogue*. When
they embrace in the hotel room, Sherry feels Marlene's small, fragile
frame, plump now, and breaks into tears. Marlene, ignoring the tears,
cries out, "Tell all! Do you still put beer on your hair? Is *Get Smart*
still your favorite show? I still think you look like Ninety-Nine. Tell
me all about the males you've had affairs with. I want to know EVERY-
THING."

Sherry has forgotten that Marlene always called men "males," an
impersonal word, and it brings back memories: the way Marlene
sometimes jerks herself into an uncharacteristically prim, upright
posture when she catches herself slumping; her flamboyant behavior
in public; the way she craves luxuries, like this hotel room. They are
sharing the room. Ed, Marlene's husband, is attending a convention
at a hotel in the French Quarter, but that hotel was filled and Marlene
insisted on being with Sherry at the Hyatt. Marlene says, "I stayed
with him last night, and I couldn't sleep for all the jazz bands."

They exchange news quickly. Only the highlights of the past ten
years seem relevant, and they leave out most things, hurrying along to
the present.

"Did you want to marry him?" Marlene, cross-legged on one of
the beds and smoking a skinny brown cigarette, is referring to
Sherry's recent lover.

"No. It was all wrong. He wanted to have children right away, but

I didn't want to give up my career. Anybody who marries me will have to traipse around while I dig up old tools and pots." She laughs apologetically. "Imagine discussing that so rationally. People used to just get married without asking any questions like that."

"Tools and pots," says Marlene with a laugh. "Pools and tots."

Sherry is so thirsty after the martini on the plane that she is gulping a soft drink from the machine down the corridor. Then she says, "But I'm afraid I'm never going to find the right man. I'm too demanding."

This is a point she wants to make for Marlene's sake. She is aware that she wants Marlene to think she has in some way failed at something, because Sherry always seemed to be the successful one—her 3.8 average in college, her teaching career—while Marlene suffered one disappointment after another. She yawns, to shift the subject. "I'm trying to remember that guy we both went out with in the same week. Sam? Eddie? That guy who handed us both the exact same line?"

"His name was Bill Harrison."

"What did he say? Some trite image, like 'Your skin is like velvet,' or 'You have lips like roses.' What was it?"

Marlene says, "He said, 'Your eyes are deep, like resonant pools of amber.' Whatever those are."

"What garbage! How on earth did you remember that?"

Marlene shrugs. "Some things just stick to my brain."

The next morning at breakfast in the hotel courtyard, Marlene talks proudly about her daughter, Shannon. The night before, Marlene showed Sherry a picture of the child, a blonde toddler in a pinafore with the word ME on it.

"I should have brought you something for your baby," Sherry says apologetically. "A present."

"Having a baby was the hardest thing I ever did," says Marlene. "They say you don't remember the pain, but you can. What I can't remember is the pain of being crazy. I know I went through some awful times. I hurt people. I hurt myself. I almost killed myself once or twice—not deliberately, just out of craziness. Just being a show-off, really." She shudders. "I lost a whole chunk of my life."

"In your letter, you said you're fine," says Sherry carefully. "Are you? Are you really?"

Marlene nods, her coffee cup in her face. Her thin, penciled eyebrows are like the faint outlines of birds in a seascape. She says, "Before Shannon was born, I went through some depression, and afterward it was worse, so I knew I needed something. I'm taking lithium. There are some side effects, but it keeps me under control."

"What side effects?"

"Oh, nothing serious. Except I gain weight like crazy!" She laughs, looking at her plate. "All these calories."

When she signals the waiter for more coffee, making a sharp click with her fingers, it hits Sherry that Marlene drinks coffee now. She is dressed in white, with lace on her blouse, and despite her added weight she looks light enough to blow away.

"I have to stay away from palm readers and psychics," Marlene says suddenly. "It's all the energy they radiate. I get worked up and then I flip out."

In New Orleans, the sight of palm trees is startling. In upstate New York, there was still snow on the ground. Sherry strolls with Marlene through the French Quarter. On Bourbon Street, Marlene gleefully points out odd items in stores—coffee cups made in the shape of breasts, purple pasties with long tassels, T-shirts with shockingly obscene messages. Marlene plays with the idea of getting a T-shirt for Ed. Her laughter flies down the street. On lace-work balconies, women are drying their hair and men are drinking whiskey from bottles in brown bags. Sherry and Marlene stop for chicory coffee and beignets at a café on Jackson Square. A small Dixieland group is performing in the street.

"I'm glad we finally got together here, even if it isn't Mardi Gras," Marlene says, smiling. The sun lights up her hair and makes it look like the light coming through a tree in the spring, when the leaves are just emerging.

"I'm glad, too."

"Don't you go back to Kentucky anymore?"

"Not since Mother died. I didn't want to see my father. There are too many hard feelings. I didn't even want to see Kentucky again." Sherry brushes a crumb off the table. "I never think about it."

"You've lost your accent."

"I have a confession to make. All those years, I was afraid to get in touch with you again because I felt guilty. I have plenty of reasons to be bitter about my father, but none for losing touch with you." Sherry sips her coffee. "I should have been a better friend."

"You had your work to think of. That's your strength," Marlene says warmly. "You were always so brilliant. I read an article of yours in a journal and it made me so proud. I recognized you in it! It reminded me of that paper you wrote for me once for history." Marlene breaks off into laughter.

At Marlene's urging, Sherry tells about her current work. In the small upstate town where she lives now, she has discovered evidence that a substantial Indian culture was there four hundred years before. The culture has not been documented. It was always said there weren't any Indians there—that the Indians used that land for their hunting grounds and their settlements were farther south, nearer the river.

"But I've been around talking to the farmers and I've seen some things they've found in their fields. Arrowheads and pottery fragments and utensils. You wouldn't believe all the stuff they've collected. Bushel baskets full. And they never said anything. But they've known all along there were Indians there."

"The farmers would know," Marlene says, nodding.

She snaps her fingers for a refill of coffee, and the waiter fills both cups. Marlene puts sugar in her coffee, saying, "I shouldn't eat all this sugar." She folds the empty sugar packet in half, then folds it over again and creases it. "Did you see how rude that waiter was? He won't get a tip from me."

On the street, a white-faced harlequin is creeping up behind people, tapping on their shoulders and pantomiming a conversation. People are laughing. Marlene says, "That's how I feel sometimes, sneaking up on strangers, trying to make them listen, but no words come out."

The musicians are playing "Do You Know What It Means to Miss New Orleans?" Sherry sings along, but she cannot remember the words beyond the title. The bizarre clutter of the street scene has strange echoes of the past, as though the whole psychedelic era had found its place and come to rest in New Orleans.

Idly, Sherry says, "Have you noticed that in all the songs about this city, they pronounce it New Or-LEENS, to make it rhyme? Nothing rhymes with New OR-le-ans. 'Way Down Yonder in New Or-LEENS' is another one."

"However you pronounce it, I could really learn to love this city," Marlene says, her voice rising clear and joyful above the music.

"I'm surprised to realize how familiar New Orleans is, through its music. I've always heard about Bourbon Street. Rampart Street. Papa Joe's." Sherry is groping for this familiarity. There is nothing really familiar about New Orleans, a place where people are buried above ground. The stuffed Aunt Jemimas propped in the doorways of shops are depressing. Sherry feels as remote from the black cultural heritage of this city as she feels from her old friend Marlene.

Marlene's husband Ed is tall and heavy-set, with capped front teeth that have the artificial look of guitar picks. Sherry is drinking Hurricanes with Marlene and Ed at a revolving rooftop restaurant. Marlene has a flirtatious way with her husband, as though she doesn't take him seriously. She gives him looks of disbelief, teasing him, drawing him out. Ed has an old-fashioned manner of hovering over Marlene and Sherry, the way older men might have done when they were college girls, ten years ago. In some men, these quaint manners might still be charming, forgivable, but Sherry has the feeling that Ed is forcing them, extending his protectiveness of an unstable wife to her friend.

The restaurant revolves slowly, so that they can see the whole city spread out around them—the bright, green-lighted dome of a tall building, some glass towers, the distant lights fading into the horizon of darkness, and in the foreground, the Louisiana Superdome, like a mushroom growing in the dark. Its lights are out. They are on a turntable, rotating slowly, but the effect is deceptive. Sherry feels they are sitting still, and the wall with the scenes is moving.

Ed is a sales representative for an air-conditioning firm. He is still wearing his name tag from the convention he is attending. He explains to Sherry the advantages of one air-cooling system over another. When the Superdome rolls by, he describes its complex cooling system. Marlene looks at him blankly.

"Talk about a contract," Ed says, returning her gaze. "If I'd had that contract, we'd be on easy street today."

Marlene says, "Sherry, tell Ed about your Indian discoveries. Oh, Ed, this is so exciting."

"Oh, nothing's really materialized yet." Embarrassed, Sherry explains her project briefly. "Nobody thought the Iroquois Indians lived there, but I think I can document it and I hope to make a lot of new discoveries about their culture."

"That's great," says Ed. "I always thought the Indians got a bad break. They need somebody to take an interest."

Marlene sometimes looks at her husband the way Nancy Reagan looked at Ronald Reagan during the campaign, but then the look fades and she seems sad. Sherry wonders about mixing Hurricanes and lithium. A Hurricane has three shots of rum in it.

When Marlene is in the restroom, Ed leans over to Sherry and says confidentially, "That little baby has meant a world of difference to Marlene. She worships her."

"She needed someone to care for." Sherry had been the one to take care of Marlene. Now Ed is taking care of her. "We drifted apart," she says distractedly. "Marlene was my best friend, but I couldn't handle it."

Ed shakes his head. "It hasn't been easy, let me tell you. But she's all right. Having that baby was the best thing that ever happened to her."

By the time Marlene returns, Sherry's head is whirling. The absurdity of sitting with Ed and Marlene on this lazy Susan in the sky hits her. They could be gods on Olympus, feasting. She half-expects Marlene to recite "Kubla Khan." When she sits down, the flames from the candles light up Marlene's face, and in this lighting Sherry sees the lines around her friend's eyes.

In the hotel elevator, Marlene presses her forehead against the glass back and looks down on the center courtyard, framed by twenty-seven stories of balconies. The sound of Dixieland jazz floats up. They walk along the corridor of the twentieth floor, hugging the wall, away from the low edge of the balcony. In the room, the maid has turned their bedcovers down and left weather reports and gold-wrapped chocolates on their pillows. The tooth fairy was here. Sherry waits for Marlene to talk about Ed, but Marlene sprawls wearily on the bed, the chocolates spilling from her hand.

"It's my turn to confess," she says, sitting up. "I knew I'd have to be drunk to do it."

"What is it, Marlene?"

Marlene's eyes are closed, and her eyeshadow has settled on the creases of her eyelids, making sharp blue lines. Marlene sits up and fusses with the paper on a chocolate. "Do you remember when those guys in the art department said we were lesbians?"

"Vaguely. I remember you said somebody thought that."

"It wasn't just one opinion—it was dozens of people. That whole art department believed it."

"I just remember hearing a rumor. I didn't think anything of it."

"I shouldn't eat all this sugar," Marlene says, biting on the chocolate. "At first what they said made me angry, but then I believed it was true. I realized they were saying something obvious."

"You never said much about it."

"I didn't know how to tell you. But it really affected me," Marlene says. "I don't even know how to tell you now."

"What did you feel?"

"I always loved you. Didn't you know that?"

"I loved you too, Marlene, and I always cared about you. What was wrong with that?"

"I always admired you—and when that came up, I got to thinking about what it meant." Marlene pauses. "I thought it was right that you went away. I didn't try to find you. I thought you made the right decision then. You were so smart and you were going to make something out of yourself. You didn't need me, hanging along, depending on you. I would have ruined your career."

"That's stupid, Marlene!" Sherry staggers to the bathroom. She draws some water and takes a drink, then brushes her teeth up and down with ferocity. She's sad that Marlene harbored these feelings, angry at what they have done to her.

"You imagined all that, Marlene," she says, returning. "There was nothing to it. What did your analysts make of it?"

Marlene shrugs. "They can analyze me till they're blue in the face, but it makes no difference. I'm a manic-depressive, and that's all chemical. So they don't even try to understand me. They just write the prescriptions." She punches the pillow and places it behind her head, against the headboard. "Aren't they saying homosexuality is genetic nowadays? That's chemistry, isn't it? You should know. You're a scientist."

Sherry begins undressing. She is very tired, and the Hurricane is still whirling. She wishes she could find the eye of the hurricane, a place to rest. She says, "Even if it were true, it's not the disgrace now that it was then."

In the middle of the night, Sherry hears Marlene throwing up in the bathroom. Half awake and confused, Sherry recalls Marlene's hysteria once when she took her to the hospital, Marlene claiming loudly that a CIA agent had given her LSD as an experiment. She said she wasn't insane. It was only an acid flashback, she said. By that time Sherry had learned to recognize the signs—the dislocation, the breathlessness, the endless talk.

The light from the bathroom makes a triangle on the wall. In the corridor, someone's door slams.

Marlene, seeing Sherry awake, says, "I think I've got food poisoning."

"Should I call Ed?"

"No. Please don't." Marlene tries to light a cigarette, then clutches her stomach. "It was that gumbo yesterday at lunch. It had oysters in it."

Marlene disappears into the bathroom again. Sherry feels cold. She reaches for her robe. It occurs to her that vomiting is like flipping out. Both are involuntary expressions, inner explosions. She feels a wave of panic.

"It'll pass," says Marlene, returning to bed. "I've had it before, from fish sticks in Denver. Never order fish that far inland! You're okay, aren't you? You didn't have the gumbo."

In the morning, Sherry brings Marlene orange juice and toast from the courtyard. Marlene drinks the orange juice but cannot eat the toast.

"I won't die," she says, trying to smile. "It will do me good to go on a diet."

"You need fluids," says Sherry.

"This is silly. Let me tell you what I want you to do. I want you to go out sightseeing. No sense wasting your trip."

"I don't want to leave you here like this."

"Take that trolley car out through the city. They say it's a lovely ride. You can see the real New Orleans."

"I'm not really that much of a tourist. I should stay here with you."

"You've got to go. You came all the way from New York. You can't miss this opportunity. I want you to go and tell me what it's like."

"Don't you want me to call Ed?"

"No. I'll be okay. I just have to get this out of my system."

"Are you sure?"

Marlene sits up on the edge of the bed and reaches for her purse. "I'm ordering you to leave me here," she says sternly. "You don't have to take care of me."

On the St. Charles trolley, which curves across the city, Sherry sits across from two young couples with knapsacks. One of the two girls has a tiny baby in a yellow playsuit. The boy next to her is reading aloud from the guidebook, while jiggling the baby by the hand, in rhythm with the trolley. Actually, Sherry is glad to be alone for a while. Marlene's confession recolors Sherry's memories, something like reevaluating shards of pottery in the light of a new theory. Bits and pieces, fraught with new meaning, float forth: scenes of Marlene's worshipful regard, the way Marlene liked the same artists Sherry did, even the way she had bothered to find an article of hers in some obscure journal.

A tourist information clerk told Sherry to get off six blocks past Napoleon Street at the Garden District, where there were quaint shops in old Victorian houses. But there is some mistake. There are no shops, although there are plenty of old houses. Undecided where to get off, Sherry rides past Loyola and Tulane, side by side across from a park. An avenue of palm trees, lined up as perfectly as tenpins, stands perpendicular to St. Charles. The trolley lurches gently along, and Sherry, tense, resists its motion. The mansions begin to change to small frame houses. The people on the seats facing hers are consulting their guidebook and talking with the driver. They look alarmed. When they suddenly decide to get off, Sherry follows them.

"Do you know where we are?" Sherry asks the girl with the baby. She seems too young to have a child.

Smiling widely, the girl says, "We were going to make the complete circuit, but the driver says you can't; you have to get off and get back on again."

"I'm with you then," Sherry says. "I don't want to get stranded at the end of the line."

She waits for the return trolley with the group on a grassy median. They are from Ohio, and it's their spring break. The baby's mother sets the baby on the grass and changes its diaper. When his mother says, "He's been so good on this trip," Sherry tries to imagine what her student days would have been like if she, or Marlene, had had a baby. Students nowadays seemed so normal, so much less desperate, than when she and Marlene were students. For a moment, she wonders if Marlene's craziness was just the craziness of their generation.

One of the boys crosses the street to a gas station and brings back Cokes.

"Please take this one," he says to Sherry, handing her a can. "I can share one with my wife."

Sherry accepts the drink gratefully. The sun is high and she feels sweat stains under her arms.

"Hey! Have you been to Brennan's?" the boy asks. "We went to Brennan's for breakfast. It was incredible. We had about five courses."

His wife, the baby's mother, says, "We had champagne, and dessert. And omelets."

"I had crepes," says the other girl, who is sitting cross-legged in the grass, looking in the mirror of a compact. She is having trouble with her contact lens.

A trolley comes by, but they are in no hurry. The girl is still fussing over her contact lens, and the boy with blond curls is busy repacking his knapsack. The baby's father is holding the baby and singing it a song about panda bears. Sherry stays with the little group, drinking her Coke while the sun beats down on her head.

In the evening, Marlene is still shaky, but she feels well enough to go to the French Quarter with Sherry. Ed is attending his convention banquet. Sherry eats shrimp Creole, but Marlene sips tea. They talk about young people today, based on Sherry's report of the kids on the trolley. There is something loving and nostalgic about the way

Marlene talks about old times, even about her breakdowns. "I was cuckoo!" she says. "But I didn't care. I thought I knew everything behind the whole Watergate conspiracy, and I would have testified if they had only sent me a subpoena." She laughs. "I thought the salvation of the whole country was up to me and Martha Mitchell."

After ordering coffee, Sherry says, "I've been thinking about last night. I don't know what to say, Marlene. We've gone our separate ways. How can I make it up to you?"

"Don't think about it," Marlene says.

In the dark, they cross Jackson Square Park and go up the steps to the river. They stroll up the wooden walk, past couples on benches, to see the steamer *Natchez*, which has a bright red paddle wheel. They stand there and gaze at the lights of a gift shop on the upper deck. A tour bus drives up then to the waterfront and turns around. Marlene and Sherry return to the wooden walk.

"Are you happy with Ed?" Sherry asks suddenly, in the wrong tone, one of disapproval. "I had to ask."

Marlene laughs. She is having trouble with her spike heels on the boardwalk. "Oh, sure. He's not my ideal, but he's good to me. I wish you could get to know him."

Marlene turns to face the river. A helicopter is flying low, its sound coming closer, with a searchlight playing down over the water.

"They're looking for something," Marlene says.

The helicopter passes, its searchlight sweeping the water like paint from a spray can.

"I have to confess one more thing, Marlene. I was always afraid to see you again, because I was afraid if I got around you, you'd flip out again. I thought I was a bad influence because I always took charge, and I was afraid of what you might do when you were out of control. I was afraid you'd do something . . . violent."

"Oh, stop it!" Marlene cries. "Your guilt is making me sick. You keep seeing me as I was then, as if you were the one who had grown up and I was still a child. Don't you think I've changed too?" Marlene's voice carries across the water. "I don't blame you." More quietly, she says, "I can forgive us both for the way we were then."

"I'm sorry." Sherry doesn't know what to say.

Marlene says, "Something's lost. Maybe a boat."

Upriver, beyond the bridge, the helicopter turns around and returns, its searchlight playing closer to the bank near them. On the water are occasional dark spots. Marlene and Sherry watch while the searchlight rides the water downstream. In the distance, at the bend, toward the Gulf, they see another searchlight.

"Somebody's boat must have overturned," says Marlene.

The wind is coming off the river. The helicopter is winking downstream, turning around, returning. A man and woman behind Sherry and Marlene are having an intense conversation, something about a promise to get some concert tickets. Marlene is insisting a boat is lost, but Sherry feels it is obvious that a person must have jumped off the bridge.

"Look, Marlene," Sherry says suddenly, as she sees the moon rising above a cloud. "Look how the moon is turned on its side down here. The waning moon looks lopsided. It's fading from the top instead of the side. In the North, it fades from the side, but it looks distorted down here because we're closer to the equator. We're seeing the moon from a different angle down here." She pauses, wondering. "Or is it this way in Kentucky too?"

Marlene looks skeptically at the moon. "I don't know. I never really thought about it." Her voice is flat, like the squashed moon.

"I wish I could remember," Sherry says, blinking back tears. "I can't remember how the moon looked in Kentucky."

Robert Stone

❊

The Ascent of Mount Carmel

Ten miles to the south, the road on which they drove turned inland, crossed the mountains on the spine of Baja, and ran for thirty miles within sight of the Sea of Cortez. At the final curve of its eastward loop, a dirt track led from the highway toward the shore, ending at a well-appointed fishing resort called Benson's Marina. At Benson's there was a large, comfortable ranch house in the Sonoran style, a few fast powerboats rigged for big game fishing and a small airstrip. Benson ran a pair of light aircraft for long distance transportation and fish spotting.

In the early hours of the morning, their car turned into Benson's and pulled up beside his dock. Walker had slept; a light cokey sleep, full of theatrical nightmares that had his sons in them.

The woman on the seat beside him was an actress named Lu Anne Bourgeois whom he had not seen for ten years. Nearly that long before, he had written a screenplay for her based on Kate Chopin's *The Awakening*. It was being filmed now, near the hotel from which they had come. They were both long married to other, absent people.

That night, at the hotel, there had been a party at which bad things had been said and Walker had been knocked down. They had driven to Benson's pursuing the illusion of escape.

Lu Anne walked straight to the lighted pier and stood next to the fuel pumps, looking out across the gulf. Walker climbed from the car and asked the driver to park it out of the way. In the shadow of the boathouse, he had some more cocaine. The drug made him feel jittery and cold in the stiff ocean wind. Lu Anne had a bottle of scotch in her tote bag, so he had a drink from it.

After a few minutes, Benson's son Enrique came out looking sleepy and suspicious. He was a Eurasian, the son of a Texas promoter who had realized his dreams and a Mexican-born Chinese woman. When he recognized Lu Anne he smiled.

"You two want to go to Cabo again?" he asked. At the beginning of shooting, Lu Anne's husband had been with her and the two of them had flown to Cabo San Lucas. Benson had mistaken Walker for Lu Anne's husband. As the two men shook hands, Walker watched him realize his mistake.

"No," Lu Anne said. "We want to go to Villa Carmel."

He was looking down at the ground in embarrassment, an unworldly young man.

"I don't know, ma'am. There's a *chubasco* over the mountains. I have to get the weather."

"Of course," Lu Anne said.

The youth stood with them for a minute or so and then went back inside the main house.

"We should go back," Walker said.

She shook her head.

"They can't shoot without you," Walker told her, taking another slug from the bottle. "You should be back at work tomorrow. And I should be gone."

Lu Anne kept looking out to sea.

"I don't think I want to go back to work tomorrow. And I don't want you to go."

"It's senseless," Walker said.

He looked anxiously into her eyes, seeing there what he had feared to see. She had married her psychiatrist in an absurd futile gesture of hope. She worked, although not often; she was a wife and a mother. Still mad, he thought. Otherwise she would not be there beside him. "I don't know why you want to go to Villa Carmel. What's there?"

She smiled at him quickly, surprised him.

"Wait until you see."

"Weren't we near there once?" Walker asked. "You were shooting somewhere in the Sierra. A long time ago."

"We were miles away. We were shooting a Mexican setting of *Death Harvest* in Benjamin Constant."

"Was it Benjamin Constant?" Walker asked. "Or was it Benjamin Hill?"

"It was way the other side of Monte Carmel. Villa Carmel is on this side. The Pacific side."

"Why do you want to go there?"

"The reason . . ." she began and paused. "The reason is a pretty reason. You'll have to trust me." She took hold of his hand. "Do you?"

"Well," Walker said, "we're out here together in this storm of stuff. What have I got to lose?"

"We'll see," Lu Anne said.

Young Benson came back with his map case and climbed to the small room above the boathouse that was his operations shack. He was sporting the leather jacket and white silk scarf it pleased him to wear aloft. When he turned on the lights, an English language weather report crackled over the transmitter. Walker and Lu Anne on the pier below could not make it out.

She looked through her tote bag and came up with a white bank envelope filled with bills and handed it to Walker.

"What's this?"

"To pay him."

He started to protest. She turned away. "My party," she said.

Climbing the wooden stairs to Benson's office, he put the envelope beside his wallet, still stuffed with his winnings from Santa Anita. Both of them had so much money, he thought. It was so convenient.

"How's the weather?" he asked young Benson when he was in the office.

"*Garay!*" young Benson said, looking wide eyed at him. "Man, what a shiner you got!"

Walker put a hand to his swollen face.

"Is it real?" the young pilot asked. Walker looked at him in blank uncomprehension.

"I thought it might not be real," the youth explained. "I thought maybe it was fake."

"Ah," Walker said. "It's real. An accident. A misstep."

"Yeah," Benson said, "well let's see. Reckon I can get you all over there. We might have a problem coming back. When you need to be back?"

"I don't know. Can you wait for us?"

"That's expensive," the young man said uncertainly. "If the *chubasco* settles in we might get stuck."

"When can we leave?"

"When it's light," Benson said.

Walker took five hundred-dollar bills out of the envelope.

"Take us over for the day. If we're not back by sunset tomorrow we'll throw in a few hundred more."

"Three hundred for the day, if I wait. Five hundred if I have to wait overnight."

"Good," Walker said. He gave the youth five hundred. "Hold it on deposit."

She was waiting for him at the foot of the steps.

"Will he take us?"

"He'll take us at first light. He says the weather might keep us over there. Is there a hotel in Villa Carmel?"

She did not answer him. He looked at the sky; it was clear and lightening faintly. The moon was down. The autumn constellations showed Venus was in Taurus, the morning star.

He asked her if she knew what it meant because it was the sort of thing she knew. Again she failed to answer him.

After a while she pointed to their driver, who was asleep behind the wheel of his parked limousine.

"Pay him," she said. "Pay him and send him back."

"You're sure?"

"Gordon, I'm going to Monte Carmel. Do you want to be with me or not?"

He went over and woke up the driver and paid him and watched the car's tail lights bounce over the road between Benson's and the highway.

"Why there?" he asked her.

He thought, to his annoyance, that she would ignore his question again.

"Because there's a shrine there," she said. "And I require its blessedness."

"That'll be lost on me," Walker said.

She looked at him with a knowing, kindly condescension.

There was light above the Gulf of California, gray-white at first, then turning to crimson. It spread with all the breathtaking alacrity of tropical mornings. Walker found its freshening power wearisome. He was a little afraid of it.

Morn be sudden, he thought. Eve be soon.

Benson came out of his office and clattered down the steps to the dock, sweeping his scarf dashingly behind him in the wind.

"Let's go, folks."

"Is it a Christian shrine?" Walker asked. "I mean," he suggested, "they don't sacrifice virgins there?"

"Never virgins," Lu Anne said. "They sacrifice cocksmen there. And ritual whores."

"If you could give me a hand with the aircraft, mister," young Benson said over his shoulder as they fell in behind him, "I would appreciate it a whole lot."

Benson hauled open the hangar's sliding door and moved the wheel blocks aside. Then he and Walker guided the aircraft out of the hangar and into position. By the time they were ready to board the morning was in full possession. The disc of the sun was still below the Gulf but the morning kites were up against layers of blue and the lizard cries of unseen desert birds sounded in the brush until the engine's roar shut them out of hearing.

"She's a real sparkler," Benson said when they were airborne. Walker, who had been sniffing cocaine from his hand, looked at the youth blankly again. Was he referring to Lu Anne, buckled into the seat behind him?

Benson never took his eyes from the cockpit windshield.

"I mean the day is," he explained. "I mean you wouldn't know there was bad weather so close."

"Yes," Walker said. "I mean no. I mean we'll never get enough of it."

A few minutes out, they could see the peaks of the coast on the eastern shore of the Gulf and the sun rising over them. The whole sea spread out beneath them, glowing in its red rock confines, a desert ocean, a sea for signs and miracles.

He turned to look at Lu Anne and saw her crying happily. The sight encouraged him to a referential joke.

"Was there ever misery loftier than ours?" he shouted over the engine.

She shook her head, denying it.

"Everybody O.K.?" Benson asked.

"Everybody will have to do," Walker told him.

Within the hour they were landed on a basic grass airstrip in the heart of a narrow valley rimmed with verdant mountains. The air was damp and windless. A knot of round-faced, round-shouldered Indian children watched them walk to the corrugated iron hangar that served the field. A herd of goats were nibbling away at the borders of a strip. Through a distant stand of ramon trees, Walker could make out the whitewashed buildings of town—the dome and bell tower of a church, rooftops with bright laundry, a cement structure with art deco curves surmounted with antennas. Villa Carmel.

While Benson did his paperwork, a middle-aged Indian with a seraphic smile approached Walker to inquire whether a taxi was desired. Lu Anne was out in the sun, shielding her eyes, squinting up at the ridge line of the green mountains to the east.

Walker directed the man who had approached him to telephone for a car and within ten minutes it arrived, a well-maintained Volkswagen minibus with three rows of seats crowded into it. He bought a bottle of mineral water at the hangar stand and they climbed aboard.

They drove into the center of Villa Carmel with two other passengers—Benson and an American in a straw sombrero who had been lounging about the hangar and who never glanced at them. In the course of the brief ride, Walker underwent a peculiar experience. He was examining what he took to be his own face in the rearview mirror, when he realized that the roseate, self-indulgent features he had been ruefully studying were not his own but those of the man in the seat in front of him. His own, when he brought them into his line of sight, looked like a damaged shoulder of beef. The odd sense of having mistaken his own face remained with him for some time thereafter.

When they pulled into the little ceiba-shaded square of Villa Carmel, Benson and the American got out and the driver looked questioningly toward Lu Anne and Walker.

"Tell him the shrine," Lu Anne said.

Walker tried the words he knew for shrine—*la capilla, el templo*. The elderly driver shrugged and smiled. His smile was that of the man at the airport, a part of the local Indian language.

"Monte Carmel," Lu Anne said firmly. "*Queremos ir ahi.*"

Without another word, the driver shifted gears and then circled the square, heading back the way they had come.

They drove again past the airstrip and followed the indifferently surfaced road into the mountains. As they gained distance they were able to turn and see that the town of Villa Carmel itself stood on the top of a wooded mesa. The higher their minibus climbed along the escarpment, the deeper the green valleys were that fell away beside the road. They passed a waterfall that descended sheerly from a piñon grove to a sunless pool below. Vultures on outstretched motionless wings glided up from the depths of the barrancas, riding updrafts as the sun warmed the mountain air.

When they were almost at the top of the ridge, the minibus pulled over and halted at the beginning of a dirt track. They could see across the next valley, which was not wild like the one from which they ascended but rich with cultivation. A railroad track ran across its center. There were towns, strung out along a paved highway. Miles beyond another range of mountains rose, to match the range on which they stood.

"We've been here," Walker said to Lu Anne. "Haven't we?" He got out of the bus and walked to a cliffside. "We stayed in that valley, at a hot springs there. You were working in these hills. Or else," he said, nodding across the valley, "in those."

Her attention was fixed on a winding rocky pathway that led up a hillside on their right, toward the very top of the hill. Walker saw her question the driver and the driver, smiling as ever, shake his head. He walked back to the bus.

"Is he saying," Lu Anne asked, "that he can't drive up there?"

Walker spoke with the driver and determined that, indeed, the man was cheerfully declining to take them farther.

"He says he can't make it up there," Walker told Lu Anne. "He says the bus wouldn't go up."

Looking the track over, Walker saw that it appeared to be little more than a goat trail, hardly a road at all.

"Pay him," Lu Anne said.

He had nothing smaller than a twenty. Shamefacedly he put it in the driver's hand. The driver responded with no more than his customary smile.

"I want him to come back this evening," Lu Anne said.

When Walker suggested this to the driver, the driver said that it would be dangerous for them to spend the day in the mountains alone. There were bad people from the cities, he said, who came on the highway and did evil things.

"We won't be near the highway," Lu Anne said.

So Walker asked the man to return before sundown and the man smiled and drove away. Walker suspected they would never see him again.

Lu Anne walked across the road to the foot of the path.

"Hey, bo," she said. "Don't you know we're going up?"

Walker knew. He fell into step with her.

"The next hill," he said to her when they had gone a way, "that never was a thing that troubled me."

"No," Lu Anne said.

"I was always hot for the next hill. Next horizon. Whatever there was. That's why I came along now."

He paused, looked around and took a pinch. It was very wasteful. When he had satisfied himself, he took a drink of bottled water. Lu Anne took some cocaine from him.

"Yes," she said. "You're Walker."

"They don't call me Walker for nothing," Walker said. "It's a specialty."

"Of what does it consist?" Lu Anne asked.

"Well," he said, "there's the road. And there's one."

"And how does one approach the road?"

"One steps off confidently. One in front of the other. Hay foot, straw foot. Briskly."

"Oh," Lu Anne said, "that's you, Gordon. That's your style all right." She linked arms with him. "Tell us more."

"Well," he said, "there are things to know."

"I knew there would be. Tell."

"There's to and fro. There's back and forth. There's up. Likewise down. There's taking care of your feet."

"And the small rain," Lu Anne said.

"And mud. And gravel and sand. And shit. And wet rot and dry rot. And going over fences."

"Can you look back?"

"Never back. You can look down. You have to see where you're going."

"But is there a place for art?" Lu Anne asked with a troubled frown. "It's all so functional."

"There's whistling. That's the principal art. The right tunes in the right places. Whatever gets you through the afternoon."

"How sad," Lu Anne said. They walked on, winding upward along the hillside. "How sublime."

"The road is never sublime," Walker told her. "The road is pedestrian."

When they had walked for half an hour, they could see both valleys—the plains to the east, and the forested barranca through which they had come.

They stopped to drink the rest of their water and take more of the drug. The road over which they had driven ran close to the summit; the top of Monte Carmel was only a quarter mile or so above them.

"Your road is mine, Walker," she told him.

"Right," he said. He glanced at her; she was clutching the collar of the army shirt she had thrown on. Her eyes were bright with pain.

"It was always me for you."

"I knew that," he said. He was thinking that, of course, they would never have lasted three months together by the day. Arrivals, departures, fond absences and dying falls were all there had ever been to it. Bird songs and word games, highs and high romance. "We weren't free."

"Oh, baby," she said, "there ain't no free."

"Only," Walker said, "the comforts of philosophy."

"Which in your case," Lu Anne said, "is me."

Walker laughed and so did she.

"Likewise the consolations of religion," Lu Anne said, "which is why we are out here . . ."

"Under the great vault of heaven," Walker suggested.

"Under the great vault," she repeated, "of heaven." She stopped and began to cry. She knelt in the dust, her eyes upturned in absurd rapture, doing the virgin's prayer. Walker was appalled. He bent to her.

"Can't you help me?" she asked.

"I would die for you," he said. It was true, he thought, but not really helpful. He was the kind of lover that Edna Pontellier was a mother. At the same moment he realized that his life was in danger and that he might well, as he had earlier suspected, have come to Mexico to die. His heart beat fearfully. His sides ached.

"I don't require dying for," Lu Anne said. He considered that she deceived herself. Weeping, she looked childlike and stricken, but even in his recollection she had never been more beautiful. She had grown so thin in the course of the film that her face had contracted to its essential lines which were strong and noble, lit by her eyes with intelligence and generosity and madness. The philosophy whose comforts she represented was Juggernaut.

He knelt breathless beside her and realized that he was happy. That was why he had come, to be with her in harm's way and be happy.

She looked into his face and touched his hair. "Poor fish," she said. "I was always there for you."

"Well," Walker said, "here I am."

"Too late."

She raised her eyes again.

"And nothing up there, eh? No succor? No bananas?"

He helped her to her feet.

"Who knows?" Walker said. "Maybe."

"Maybe, eh?"

She stayed where she was; Walker was above her on the trail, which grew steeper as it ascended.

"Do you know why I was an actress?" she asked him.

"Why?"

A sudden luminous smile crossed her face. He could not imagine what force could drive such a smile through tears and regret.

"You'll see," she said and took him by the hand. She climbed with strong sure steps. Just short of the crest, she released his hand and fell to her knees.

"This is the way we go up," she said. He watched her struggle up the last rise, one knee before the other. When he tried to help her, she thrust his hand away.

"This is how the Bretons pray," she told him. "The Bretons pray like anything."

So it was on her knees that she mounted the top of the hill. Walker went on before her, to find a featureless building of the local stone with a thatched roof. Over the door, a wooden sign rattled on the unimpeded wind of the mountaintop, lettered to read *Seguridad Nacional*. There was a noxious smell in the thin air.

He stood panting before the building, and he realized at once when he had seen it last and why the landscape to the east had seemed so familiar. Ten or perhaps twelve years before, he had come down from Guadalajara by limousine to visit her on the set of a Traven remake. The unit had been based on the Constancia Hot Springs in the cultivated valley to the east. He had worked many Mexican locations and sometimes confused them in memory, but he remembered it quite well now, seeing the homely building with its sign. The unit's laborers had thrown it up in a day or two.

Lu Anne crawled over the coarse yellow grass of the hilltop on her knees. A long slow roll of the thunder echoed along the mountain range. An enormous bank of storm clouds was drifting toward them from the coast.

"This is a holy place," Lu Anne said. "Sacred to me."

"This is the police post from that Traven picture," Walker told her. "It isn't anything or anywhere. It's fake."

"It's holy ground," she told him. "The earth is bleeding here."

Walker went around behind the building; the ground there was muddy and stinking. He found an empty wooden trough with a litter of corn cobs around it. There was a barred window through which he could see stacked ears of maize and heaped grain sacks.

He went back to where Lu Anne was kneeling.

"For God's sake, Lu Anne! It's a fucking corn crib on a pig farm."

Lu Anne leaned forward in her kneeling posture and pressed her forehead into the dirt.

Walker laughed.

"Oh, wow," he cried. "I mean, remember the ceremony they had? The governor of the state came out? They were going to make it a film museum." He stalked about in manic high spirits. "It was going to be a showplace of cinema, right? For the whole hemisphere, as I recall. Second only to Paris, a rival collection. Oh Christ, that's rich."

Lu Anne raised her head, filled her hands with dry earth and pressed them against her breasts.

"A film museum," Walker shouted. "On top of a hill in the middle of a desert in the middle of a jungle. Funny? Oh my word."

He lay down in the spiky desert grass.

"So everybody went away," Walker crowed, "and they turned it into a pig farm." He rested his head on his arm.

He lay crying with laughter, fighting for breath at the edge of exhaustion, shielding his eyes against his forearm. When the first lightning flash lit up the corners of his vision he had a sense of lost time, as though he might have been unconscious for some seconds or asleep. He raised his head and saw Lu Anne standing naked over him. He scurried backwards, trying to gain his feet. A great thunderclap echoed in all the hollows of their hill.

"What have you done to me, Walker?"

There was such rage in her eyes, he could not meet them. He looked down and saw that her feet were covered in blood. Streaks of it laced her calves, knees to ankles. When he looked up she showed him that her palms were gouged and there was a streak of blood across her left side.

"I was your sister Eve," she said. "It was my birthday. Look at my hands."

She held them palms out, fingers splayed. The blood ran down her wrists and onto the yellow grass. When he backed away, rising to one knee, he saw a little clutter of blood-stained flint shards beside the pile of her clothes.

He turned to her about to speak and saw the lightning flash behind her. The earth shook under him like a scaffold. He saw her raised up, as though she hung suspended between the trembling earth and the storm. Her hair was wild, her body sheathed in light. Her eyes blazed amethyst.

"Forgive me," Walker said.

She stretched forth her bloody hand on an arm that was serpentine and unnatural. She smeared his face with blood.

"I was your sister Eve," Lu Anne said. "I was your actress. I lived and breathed you. I enacted and I took forms. Whatever was thought right, however I was counseled. In my secret life I was your secret lover."

Propped on one knee, Walker reached out his own hand to touch her but she was too far away. The lightning flashed again, lighting the black sky beneath which Lu Anne stood suspended.

"I never failed you. Other people begged me, Walker, and they got no mercy out of me. My men got no mercy. My children got none. Only you. Do you see my secret eyes?"

"Yes," Walker said.

"Whose are they like?"

"I don't know," he said.

"Only truth here. It's a holy place."

"It's not a place," Walker said. "You're bleeding and you're going to be cold." He stood up and took off his windbreaker to cover her but she remained beyond his reach. "It's nowhere."

"Gordon, Gordon," she said, "your road is mine. I own the ground you stand on. This is the place I want you."

"There's nothing here," he said. He looked around him at the stone, the bare hilltop. "It never was a place."

"Panic, Gordon? Ask me if I know about panic. I'm the one that breathed in the boneyard. I've had the Long Friends since I was sweet sixteen." The Long Friends were creatures of her delusion. He had never quite determined what they looked like. He thought of them as old women, smelling of mildew and sachet.

"I can't choose the music I hear, whether it's good music or bad. I'm your actress, Gordon, this is mine. I know every rock and thorn and stump of this old mountain. I may be with you somewhere else and all the time we're really here. Did you think of that?"

"No," Walker said.

"Don't be afraid, Gordon. Look at me. Whose eyes?"

He only stared at her, holding his windbreaker.

"Gordon," she said, "you cannot be so blind."

"Mine," he said.

"They are your eyes," she told him. "I'm your actress, that's right. I'm wires and mirrors. See me dangle and flash all shiny and hung up there? At the end of your road? Mister what-did-you-say-your-name-is Walker? See that, huh?"

"Yes, I see."

"Yes? Hey, that's love, man."

"So it is," Walker said.

She cupped a hand beside her ear. "You say it is?"

"I said it was, yes."

"Well you goddam right it is, honey."

Walker was compelled to admit that it was and it would never do either of them the slightest bit of good.

"Why me I wonder?"

"Why?" She looked at him thoughtfully. "Oh la." She shrugged. "One day many years ago I think you said something wonderful and you looked wonderful saying it. I mean, I should think it would have been something like that, don't you?"

"But you don't happen to remember what?"

"Oh, you know me, Gordon. I don't listen to the words awfully well. I'm always checking delivery and watching the gestures. Anyway," she said, marking a line with her finger between his eyes and hers, "it's the eyes. Down home they say you shoot a deer you see your lover in his eyes. A bear the same, they say. It's a little like that, eh? Hunting and recognition. A light in the eyes and you're caught. So I was. So I remain."

"If a hart do lack a hind," Walker said, "let him seek out Rosalind."

She smiled distantly. The lightning flashed again, farther away. "What good times we have on our mountain," she said. "Poetry and music." She closed her eyes and passed her bloody hands before her face, going into character. "If the cat will after kind, so be sure will Rosalind."

Walker took a deep breath.

"But it never worked out."

"Things don't work out, Gordon. They just be."

Walker stared at his friend. "You're all lights," he said. He was seeing her all lights, sparkles, pinwheels.

"Oh yes," she said cheerfully. "Didn't you see? Didn't you?" She shook her head in wonder. "How funny you are."

"I never did," he said.

"This is the mountain where you see the things you never saw. There are eighty-two thousand colors here, Gordon. I've been your mirror. Now I'll be more. And you'll be my mirror."

"More and a mirror," Walker said. "How about that?"

"Gordon, Gordon," she said delightedly, "your two favorite things. More and mirrors."

"It's a kind of cocaine image, isn't it?"

"No, my love, my life. It's the end of the road. It's through the looking glass. Because there's only one love, my love. It's all the same one."

"I'm not going to make it," he told her. "I can't keep it together."

With her lissome arms and her long painterly fingers she wove him a design, resting elbow on forearm, the fingers spread in an arcane gesture.

"All is forgiven, Gordon. Mustn't be afraid. I'm your momma. I'm your bride. There's only one love."

"I've heard the theory advanced," Walker said.

"Have you? It's all true, baby. Only one love and we'll fall in it."

"O.K.," Walker said.

"O.K.!" she cried. "Aw-right!" She stepped toward him; he still saw her against the sky and the storm. "So you might as well come with me, don't you think?"

"On that theory," Walker admitted, "I might as well."

Her limitless arms embraced him. He went to her. She pursed her lips, briskly business, and took the wad of cocaine and the Quaalude box from his pocket.

"Put your toys away," she said. She flung them over her shoulder into the dry brush. "We don't take out our toys when we fall in love. We'll be our toys when we fall in love. We'll be our own little horses."

He looked over her shoulder to where she had tossed the drug.

She frowned at him and pulled at his collar.

"And we take our clothes off. We don't require clothes."

Walker took off his windbreaker. As she was unbuttoning his shirt it began to rain. He shivered. He watched her unbuckle his trousers, smearing blood across them.

"I know there's a reason," he said, "that we don't require clothes but I can't remember what it is."

She looked up at him with the same sly wink she had flashed heavenward on the climb.

"Gordon," she sighed, "don't be such an old schoolteacher."

He watched her blood seep into his clothes as she undressed him. He could not believe how much of it there was.

"Rain," he said to her.

"We'll pray," she answered. "And then we'll sleep."

He looked up into the storm and saw the black sky whirling.

"No!" he shouted. "No you don't."

His pants fell down about his ankles as he started to run. He kicked them off, bent to pick them up and ran off dragging them behind him. Lu Anne stayed where she was, watching him sadly. He ran to where she had left her own clothes and scooped them up. The clothes and the sharp stones around them were covered with blood.

The door of the building looked massive but half of it came off in his hand when he pulled at the latch. Behind it, about four feet inside the building, the owners of the grain had built a serious door, secured with a rusty padlock. Walker huddled in the sheltered space between the broken false door and the true one.

Outside, Lu Anne stood in the hard tropical rain and shook her hair. The rain washed the blood from her wounds and cleaned the grass around her.

"Lu Anne," he called. "Come inside."

She stopped whirling her hair in the rain and looked at him laughing, like a child.

"You come out."

He picked up his windbreaker and went after her. He was wearing his shoes and socks and a pair of bloodstained jockey shorts.

"Come on, Lu," he said. "Chrissakes."

He advanced on her holding the bloody jacket like a matador advancing on a bull. When he came near, she picked up a stone and held it menacingly over her shoulder.

"You better stay away from me, Walker."

"You are so fucking crazy," Walker told Lu Anne. "I mean you *are*, man. You're batshit."

She threw the stone not overhand but sidearm and very forcefully. It passed close to his bruised right cheekbone, a very near miss.

"Fuck you," he said. He turned his back on her but at once thought better of it. He began to back toward the shelter with the windbreaker still out before his face, the better to intercept stones. When he was back in his shelter he discovered the whiskey in Lu Anne's tote bag.

"Hot ziggity," he whispered to himself. He took two long swallows and displayed the bottle to Lu Anne.

"Lookit this, Lu Anne," he shouted. "You gonna come in here and have a drink or stay out there and bleed holy Catholic blood."

He watched her pick her way daintily over the sharp stones toward his shelter.

"I'll have just a little bit," she said. "A short one."

Walker was wary of attack.

"You won't hit me with a rock, will you?"

"Don't be silly," she said.

"You almost took the side of my head off just now."

"It was a reflex, Gordon. You presented an alarming spectacle."

"Panic in the face of death," Walker admitted. "Obliteration phobia."

"You were washed in the blood," Lu Anne told him. "You'll never get *there* again." She reached for the bottle he was cradling. "I thought I was offered a drink earlier."

Walker watched her help herself to several belts.

"What was going to happen?" he asked her.

"I guess we were going to die. What's wrong with that?"

"Living is better than dying. Morally. Don't you think?"

"I think we had permission. We may never have it again."

Walker took the bottle from her and drank.

"We'll begin from here," Walker said. "We'll mark time from this mountain."

"Who will, Gordon? You and me?"

"Absolutely," Walker burbled happily. "Baptism! Renewal! Rebirth!"

Lu Anne pointed through the rain toward the road they had climbed. "It'll all be down from here, Gordon."

"Christ," Walker said, "you threw my coke away. I had at least six grams left."

"Takes the edge off baptism, renewal and rebirth, doesn't it? When you're out of coke?"

"We should have some now," Walker said petulantly. "Now we have something to celebrate."

"Screw you," Lu Anne said. "Live! Breathe in, breathe out. Tick tock! Hickory Dickory. You get off on this shit, brother, it's yours. And you may have my piece."

Walker took up some of their blood stained clothing and placed it over Lu Anne's wounds to staunch the bleeding. The rain increased, sounding like a small stampede in the thatch overhead.

"What about your kids?" Walker said.

Lu Anne was looking at the rain. She bit her lip and rubbed her eyes.

"Goddam you, Gordon! What about your kids?"

"I asked you first," Walker said. "And I told you about mine."

"Mine, they've never seen me crazy. They never would. They'd remember me as something very ornate and mysterious. They'd always love me. I'd be fallen in love, the way we nearly were just now."

Walker yawned. "Asleep in the deep."

He arranged his windbreaker and his duck trousers to cover them as thoroughly as possible.

"Yeah," Lu Anne said and sighed. "Yeah, yeah."

They settled back against the mud and straw.

"Things are crawling on us," Walker said sleepily.

"Coke bugs," Lu Anne told him.

For some time they slept, stirring by turns, talking in their dreams. When Walker awakened, he was covered in sweat and bone weary. He kicked the false door aside. The sky was clear. He sat up and saw the yellow grass and the wildflowers of the hilltop glistening with lacy coronets of moisture. On his knees, he crept past Lu Anne and went outside. The *chubasco* had passed over them. The wall of low gray-black clouds was withdrawing over the valley to the east, shadowing its broad fields. An adjoining hill stood half in the light and half in the storm's gloom. Its rocky peak was arched with a bright rainbow.

Walker examined his nakedness. His arms, torso and legs were streaked with Lu Anne's blood; his shorts dyed roseate with it.

"Sweet Christ," he said. There was no water anywhere.

When he heard her whimper he went inside and helped her stand. She was half covered with bloody rags and her hair matted with blood but her stigmatic wounds were superficial for all their oozing forth. She had been making her hands bleed as much as possible, the way a child might.

She came outside, shielding her eyes with her forearm.

"How's your Spanish?" Walker asked her.

"I can't speak Spanish. I thought you could. Anyway what's it matter?"

"Sooner or later we're going to have to explain ourselves and it's going to be really difficult."

"Difficult in any language," Lu Anne said. "Almost impossible."

"How do you think I'd make out thumbing?"

"Well," she said, "you don't seem to be injured but you're covered with blood. Only people with a lot of tolerance for conflict would pick you up. Of course I'd pick you up."

"We'd better have a drink," Walker said.

"Oh my land," Lu Anne said, when Walker had given her some whiskey, "look at the rainbow!"

"Why did you have to throw my cocaine away," Walker demanded. "Now I can't function."

"It's right back there somewhere," she said, indicating the brush around the stone house. "You can probably find it."

"It's water soluble," Walker told her. "Christ."

"I have never been at such close quarters with a rainbow," Lu Anne said. "What a marvel!"

"You know what I bet?" Walker said. "I bet it's a sign from God." He went to the shelter where they had lain and sorted through their clothes. There was not a garment unsoiled with Lu Anne's blood. "God's telling us we're really fucked up."

Lu Anne watched the rainbow fade and wept.

"What now?" Walker demanded. "More signs and wonders?" He held up his bloody trousers for examination. "I might as well put them on," he said. "They must be better than nothing."

"Gordon," Lu Anne said.

Walker paused in the act of putting on his trousers and straightened up. "Yes, my love?"

She came over and put her arms around him and leaned her face against his shoulder.

"I know it must all mean something, Gordon, because it hurts so much."

Walker smoothed her matted hair.

"That's not true," he told her. "It's illogical."

"Gordon, I think there's a mercy. I think there must be."

"Well," Walker said, "maybe you're right." He let her go and began pulling on his trousers. "Who knows?"

"Don't humor me," Lu Anne insisted. "Do you believe or not?"

"I suppose if you don't like my answer I'll get hit with a rock."

She balanced on tiptoe, jigging impatiently. "Please say, Gordon."

Walker buckled his belt.

"Mercy? In a pig's asshole."

"Oh, dear," Lu Anne said. She walked away from him toward a rock against which he had left the whiskey and helped herself to a drink. When she had finished the drink, she froze with the bottle upraised, staring into the distance.

"Did you mention a pig's asshole?" she asked him. "Because I think I see one at this very moment. In fact I see several."

Walker went and stood beside her. On a lower slope, great evil tusked half-wild pigs were clustered under a live oak, rooting for oakballs. A barrel size hog looked up at them briefly, then returned to its foraging.

"Isn't that strange, Gordon? I mean you had just mentioned a pig's asshole and at that very moment I happened to look in that direction and there were all those old razorbacks. Isn't that remarkable?"

Walker had been following her with her faded bloodstained army shirt. "It's a miracle," he said. He hung the shirt around her shoulders and took hold of one of her arms. "The Gadarene swine."

Dull-eyed, she began walking down the hill. Walker started after her. She tripped and got to her feet again. He followed faster, waving the shirt.

"Lu Anne," he shouted, "those animals are dangerous."

She stopped and let him come abreast of her. When he moved to cover her with her shirt, she turned on him, fists clenched.

"Who do you think it was," she screamed, "that breathed in the graveyard? Who was bound in the tomb?"

Walker stayed where he was, watching her, ready to jump.

"You don't think that filthy tomb person with the shit for eyes, you don't think he saw who I was? Answer me," she screamed. "Answer me! Answer me Walker goddam it!"

Walker only stared at her.

She threw her head back and howled, waving her fists in the air.

"For God's sake, Lu Anne."

"Talk to me about Gadarene swine? Who do you think it was bound in fetters and chains? Where do you think I came by these?" She pointed around her, at things invisible to him. "Don't you torment me! Torment me not, Walker!"

"C'mon," he said. "I was joking."

Her lip rolled back in a snarl. He looked away. She turned her back on him and went to a place beside the house where the mud was deep and there was a pile of seed husks, head high.

"Jesus," she cried. "Son of the Most High God. I adjure thee by God, that thou torment me not."

"Amen," Walker said.

She clasped her hands and looked at the last wisps of rainbow. "I adjure thee, Son of the Most High God. I adjure thee. Torment me not." She buried her face and hands in the pile of chaff. After a moment, she got up and went up to Walker. She seemed restored in some measure and he was not afraid of her.

"You're a child of God, Walker," she said. "Same as me."

"Of course," Walker said.

"That's right," Lu Anne said. "Isn't it right?"

"Yes," Walker said. "Right."

"But you can't take the unclean spirit out of a woman, can you, brother?"

She touched his lips with her fingertips, then brought her hand down, put it on his shoulder and looked at the sky. "Ah, Christ," she said, "it's dreadful. It's dreadful we have spirits and can't keep them clean."

"Well," Walker said. "You're right there."

"No one can take it out. Man, I have watched and I have prayed. And I've had help, Walker."

"Yes," Walker said. "I know."

"If you don't believe me," Lu Anne said, "just ask me my name."

"What's your name, Lu Anne?"

"My name is Legion," she said. "For we are many."

For a minute or so she let him hold her.

"Is it all right now?" he asked.

"It's not all right," she said. "But the worst is over."

He was delighted with the reasonableness of her answer. He went to get himself a drink. When he returned Lu Anne was lying in the stack of seed husks.

"Well," he said, "that looks comfortable."

"Oh, yes," she said, "very comfortable."

He lay down beside her in the warm sun and buried his arms in the seeds.

"Downright primal."

"Primal is right," Lu Anne said. She laughed at him and shook her head. "You don't know what this pile is do you? Do you? Because you're a city boy."

She sat in the pile, sweeping aside the seed husks with a rowing motion until the manure it covered was exposed and she sat naked in a mix of mud and droppings, swarming with tiny pale creatures that fled the light.

"There it is," she told Walker. "The pigshit at the end of the rainbow. Didn't you always know it was there?"

"You'll get an infection," Walker said. He was astonished at what Lu Anne had revealed to him. "You're cut."

"Out here waiting to be claimed, Gordon. Ain't it mystical? How about a drink, man?"

When he bent to offer her the bottle she pulled him down into the pile beside her.

"I had a feeling you'd do that," he said. "I thought . . ."

"Stop explaining," Lu Anne told him. "Just shut up and groove on your pigshit. You earned it."

"I guess it must work something like an orgone box," Walker suggested.

"Walker," Lu Anne said, "when will it cease, the incessant din of your goddam speculation? Will only death suffice to shut your cotton-picking mouth?"

"Sorry," Walker said.

"Merciful heavens! Show the man a pile of shit and he'll tell you how it works." She made a wad of mud and pig manure and threw it in his face. "There, baby. There's your orgone. Have an orgone-ism."

She watched Walker attempt to brush the manure from his eyes.

"Wasn't that therapeutic?" she asked. "Now you get the blessing." She reached out and rubbed the stuff on his forehead in the form of a cross. "In the name of pigshit and pigshit and pigshit. Amen. Let us reflect in this holy season on the transience of being and all the stuff we done wrong. Let's have Brother Walker here give us only a tiny sampling of the countless words at his command to tell us how we're doing."

"Not well."

"Yeah, we are," Lu Anne told him. "We're going with the flow. This is where the flow goes."

"I wondered," Walker said.

SEX

Donald Barthelme

⚹

Alice

twirling around on my piano stool my head begins to swim my head begins to swim twirling around on my piano stool twirling around on my piano stool a dizzy spell eventuates twirling around on my piano stool I begin to feel dizzy twirling around on my piano stool

I want to fornicate with Alice but my wife Regine would be in-sulted Alice's husband Buck would be insulted my child Hans would be insulted my answering service would be insulted tingle of insult running through this calm loving healthy productive tightly-knit

the hinder portion scalding-house good eating Curve B in addition to the usual baths and ablutions military police sumptuousness of the washhouse risking misstatements kept distances iris to iris queen of holes damp, hairy legs note of anger chanting and shouting konk sense of "mold" on the "muff" sense of "talk" on the "surface" konk^2 all sorts of chemical girl who delivered the letter give it a bone plummy bare legs saturated in every belief and ignorance rational living private client bad bosom uncertain workmen mutton-tugger obedience to the rules of the logical system Lord Muck hot tears harmonica rascal

can you produce chaos? Alice asked certainly I can produce chaos I said I produced chaos she regarded the chaos chaos is handsome and attractive she said and more durable than regret I said and more nourishing than regret she said

I want to fornicate with Alice but it is a doomed project fornicating with Alice there are obstacles impediments preclusions estoppels I will exhaust them for you what a gas see cruel deprivements SECTION SEVEN moral ambiguities SECTION NINETEEN Alice's thighs are like SECTION TWENTY-ONE

I am an OB I obstetricate ladies from predicaments holding the bucket I carry a device connected by radio to my answering service bleeps when I am wanted can't even go to the films now for fear of bleeping during filmic highpoints can I in conscience *turn off* while fornicating with Alice?

Alice is married to Buck I am married to Regine Buck is my friend Regine is my wife regret is battologized in SECTIONS SIX THROUGH TWELVE and the actual intercourse intrudes somewhere in SECTION FORTY-THREE

I maintain an air of serenity which is spurious I manage this by limping my limp artful creation not an abject limp (Quasimodo) but a proud limp (Byron) I move slowly solemnly through the world miming a stiff leg this enables me to endure the gaze of strangers the hatred of pediatricians

we discuss discuss and discuss important considerations swarm and dither

for example in what house can I fornicate with Alice? in my house with Hans pounding on the bedroom door in her house with Buck shedding his sheepskin coat in the kitchen in some temporary rented house what joy

can Alice fornicate without her Malachi record playing? will Buck miss the Malachi record which Alice will have taken to the rented house? will Buck kneel before the rows and rows of records in his own house running a finger along the spines looking for the Malachi record? poignant poignant

can Buck the honest architect with his acres of projects his mobs
of draughtsmen the alarm bell which goes off in his office whenever
the government decides to renovate a few blocks of blight can Buck
object if I decide to renovate Alice?

and what of the boil on my ass the right buttock can I lounge in the
bed in the rented house in such a way that Alice will not see will not
start away from in fear terror revulsion

and what of rugs should I rug the rented house and what of cups
what of leaning on an elbow in the Hertz Rent-All bed having forni-
cated with Alice and desiring a cup of black and what of the soap
powder dish towels such a cup implies and what of a decent respect
for the opinions of mankind and what of the hammer throw

I was a heavy man with the hammer once should there be a spare
hammer for spare moments?

Alice's thighs are like great golden varnished wooden oars I assume I haven't seen them

chaos is tasty AND USEFUL TOO

colored clothes paper handkerchiefs super cartoons bit of fresh
the Pope's mule inmission do such poor work together in various
Poujadist manifestations deep-toned blacks waivers play to the gas
Zentralbibliothek Zurich her bare ass with a Teddy bear blatty string
kept in a state of suspended tension by a weight cut from the backs of
alligators

you can do it too it's as easy as it looks

there is no game for that particular player white and violet over
hedge and ditch clutching airbrush still single but wearing a ring the
dry a better "feel" in use pretended to be doing it quite unconsciously
fishes hammering long largish legs damp fine water dancer, strains of

music, expenses of the flight Swiss emotion transparent thin alkaline and very slippery fluid danger for white rats little country telephone booths brut insults brought by mouth famous incidents

in bed regarding Alice's stomach it will be a handsome one I'm sure but will it not also resemble some others?

or would it be possible in the rented house to dispense with a bed to have only a mattress on the floor with all the values that attach to that or perhaps only a pair of blankets or perhaps only the skin of some slow-moving animal such as the slug the armadillo or perhaps only a pile of read newspapers

wise Alice tells you things you hadn't heard before in the world in Paris she recognizes the Ritz from the Babar books oh yes that's where the elephants stay

or would it be possible to use other people's houses at hours when these houses were empty would that be erotic? could love be made in doorways under hedges under the sprinting chestnut tree? can Alice forego her Malachi record so that Buck kneeling before the rows of records in his empty deserted abandoned and pace-setting house fingering the galore of spines there would *find* the Malachi record with little peeps of gree peeps of gree good for Buck!

shit

Magritte

what is good about Alice is first she likes chaos what is good about Alice is second she is a friend of Tom

SECTION NINETEEN TOM plaster thrashing gumbo of explanations grease on the Tinguely new plays sentimental songs sudden torrential rains carbon projects evidence of eroticism conflict between zones skin, ambiguous movements baked on the blue table 3 mm. a stone had broken my windshield hurricane damage impulsive behav-

ior knees folded back lines on his tongue with a Magic Marker gape
orange tips ligamenta lata old men buried upright delights of everyone's life uninteresting variations pygmy owl assume the quadrupedal
position in which the intestines sink forward measurement of kegs
other sciences megapod nursemaid said very studied, hostile things
she had long been saving up breakfast dream wonderful loftiness
trank red clover uterine spasms guided by reason black envelopes
highly esteemed archers wet leg critical menials making gestures
chocolate ice pink and green marble weight of the shoes I was howling in the kitchen Tom was howling in the hall white and violet over
hedge and ditch clutching oolfoo quiet street suburban in flavor
quiet crowd only slightly restive as reports of the letters from Japan
circulate

I am whispering to my child Hans my child Hans is whispering to
me Hans whispers that I am faced with a problem in ethics the systems of the axiologicalists he whispers the systems of the deontologi-
calists but I am not privy to these systems I whisper try the New
School he whispers the small device in my coat pocket goes bleep!

nights of ethics at the New School

is this "middle life"? can I hurry on to "old age"? I see Alice walking away from me carrying an A & P shopping bag the shopping bag
is full of haunting melodies grid coordinates great expectations
French ticklers magic marks

nights of ethics at the New School "good" and "bad" as terms with
only an emotive meaning I like the Walrus best Alice whispered he ate
more than the Carpenter though the instructor whispered then I like
the Carpenter best Alice whispered but he ate as many as he could get
the instructor whispered

yellow brick wall visible from rear bedroom window of the rented
house

I see Alice walking away from me carrying a Primary Structure

MOVEMENT OF ALICE'S ZIPPER located at the rear of Alice's dress running from the neckhole to the bumhole yes I know that the first is an attribute of the dress the second an attribute of the girl but I have located it for you in some rough way the zipper you could find it in the dark

a few crones are standing about next to them are some louts the crones and louts are talking about the movement of Alice's zipper

rap Alice on the rump standing in the rented bedroom I have a roller and a bucket of white paint requires a second coat perhaps a third who knows a fourth and fifth I sit on the floor next to the paint bucket regarding the yellow brick wall visible there a subway token on the floor I pick it up drop it into the paint bucket slow circles on the surface of the white paint

insurance?

confess that for many years I myself took no other measures, followed obediently in the footsteps of my teachers, copied the procedures I observed painted animals, frisky inventions, thwarted patrons, most great hospitals and clinics, gray gauzes transparent plastic containers Presidential dining room about 45 cm. coquetry and flirtation knit games beautiful tension beaten metal catch-penny devices impersonal panic Klinger's nude in tree tickling nose of bear with long branch or wand unbutton his boots fairly broad duct, highly elastic walls peerless piece "racing" Dr. Haacke has poppy-show pulled me down on the bed and started two ceiling-high trees astonishing and little-known remark of Balzac's welter this field of honor financial difficulties what sort of figure did these men cut?

Alice's husband Buck calls me will I gather with him for a game of golf? I accept but on the shoe shelf I cannot find the correct shoes distractedness stupidity weak memory! I am boring myself what should the punishment be I am forbidden to pick my nose forevermore

Buck is rushing toward me carrying pieces of carbon paper big as bedsheets what is he hinting at? duplicity

bleep! it is the tipped uterus from Carson City calling

SECTION FORTY-THREE then I began chewing upon Alice's long and heavy breasts first one then the other the nipples brightened freshened then I turned her on her stomach and rubbed her back first slow then fast first the shoulders then the buttocks

possible attitudes found in books 1) I don't know what's happening to me 2) what does it mean? 3) seized with the deepest sadness, I know not why 4) I am lost, my head whirls, I know not where I am 5) I lose myself 6) I ask you, what have I come to? 7) I no longer know where I am, what is this country? 8) had I fallen from the skies, I could not be more giddy 9) a mixture of pleasure and confusion, that is my state 10) where am I, and when will this end? 11) what shall I do? I do not know where I am

but I do know where I am I am on West Eleventh Street shot with lust I speak to Alice on the street she is carrying a shopping bag I attempt to see what is in the shopping bag but she conceals it we turn to savor rising over the Women's House of Detention a particularly choice bit of "sisters" statistics on the longevity of life angelism straight as a loon's leg conceals her face behind *pneumatiques* hurled unopened scream the place down tuck mathematical models six hours in the confessional psychological comparisons scream the place down Mars yellow plights make micefeet of old cowboy airs cornflakes people pointing to the sea overboots nasal contact 7 cm. prune the audience dense car correctly identify chemical junk blooms of iron wonderful loftiness sentient populations

Issue 43,.1968

S.X. Rosenstock

❖

Rimininny!

And they read no more that day.
—Dante

If you can't fuck me while I read, fuck off.
You're not the best of what's been thought or said,
Not yet. But youth, with genius, is enough.

Ménage à trois is greatness, not rebuff,
If you gain art from what art's represented.
If you can't fuck me while I read, fuck off.

I want you, and I want a paragraph
Of lengthy James; he does go on. My love,
Can you? I shouldn't praise his length? Enough

Of him? The body of work's living proof
We're all rare forms, and living . . . in the dead.
If you can't *A Little Tour in France* me while I read,
   fuck off.

I signal lusts by *title*, not handkerchief,
Since I'm the sex of all that I have read;
Sometimes I write this sex. Kiss me enough,

And well enough, that I may bear the snub
That reading's not a *sexual preference*.
If you can't fuck me while I read, fuck off,
Or rave how *I'm* a work of art enough.

Issue 138, 1996

John Updike

Two Cunts in Paris

Although stone nudes are everywhere—some crammed
two to a column, supple caryatids,
and others mooning in the Tuileries—
the part that makes them women is the last
revelation allowed to art; the male
equipment, less concealable, is seen
since ancient items: a triune bunch of fruit.

Courbet's oil, *L'Origine du monde,* was owned
by Madame Jacques Lacan and through some tax
shenanigans became the Musée d'Orsay's.
Go see it there. Beneath the pubic bush—
a matted Rorschach blot—between blanched thighs
of a fat and bridal docility,
a curved and rosy closure says, "*Ici!*"

We sense a voyeur's boast. The *Ding an sich,*
self-knowledgeless, a centimeter long
as sculpted, in *terre cuite,* in fine detail
of labia and perineum, exists
in the Musée des Arts Décoratifs,
by Claudion (Claude Michel *dit*.) A girl
all young and naked, with perfected limbs

and bundled, banded hair, uplifts her legs
to hold upon her ankles a tousled dog
yapping in an excitement forever frozen:
caught in the impeccably molded clay
his canine agitation and the girl's,
the dark slits of her smile and half-shut eyes
one with the eyelike slot she lets us see.

Called *La Gimblette* ("ring-biscuit"—a low pun?),
this piece of the eternal feminine,
a doll of femaleness whose vulval facts
are set in place with a watchmaker's care,
provides a measure of how far art falls
of a Creator's providence, which gives
His creatures, all, the homely means to spawn.

William T. Vollmann

⚜

from The Art of Fiction CLXIII

VOLLMANN

I think that the time has just about come for me to slack off a little bit, try to enjoy life and also paint more watercolors of girls with no clothes on.

INTERVIEWER

Sounds pleasant.

VOLLMANN

One of the things that I had to do occasionally while I was collecting information for that prostitute story, "Ladies and Red Lights" from *The Rainbow Stories,* was sit in a corner and pull down my pants and masturbate. I would pretend to do this while I was asking the prostitutes questions. Because otherwise, they were utterly afraid of me and utterly miserable, thinking I was a cop.

INTERVIEWER

Not the most comforting sight though.

VOLLMANN

Perhaps not. But I have no problem like that anymore—what helps me now are the watercolors. I paint nudes of them, and I can chat with them while I paint them. They feel really sorry for me because they look at the watercolors, which are not a hundred percent figurative, and they think that they are really atrocious. So they just imagine that I am a total loser. They open up to me, and I give them money and they give me all kinds of things.

INTERVIEWER

It's clear that parts of *Butterfly Stories* have to be fictional, but still I wonder, did you have unprotected sex with that many prostitutes? Why take those risks?

VOLLMANN

Well, I wouldn't mind finding some other way. When I was writing *Angels, Rainbow Stories* and the other stories, that sort of thing wasn't particularly interesting to me—getting involved with all the prostitutes that way. But I kept thinking when I first began writing that my female characters were very weak and unconvincing. What is the best way to really improve that? I thought, Well, the best way is to have relationships with a lot of different women. What's the best way to do *that?* It's to pick up whores.

INTERVIEWER

Has this worked?

VOLLMANN

I don't know, but I feel that I have created some really good characters. Also, I often feel lonely. It's been really nice for me to have all of these women who really, I truly believe, care about me. I care about them. I keep in touch with them. I help them out, they help me out; they pay my rent because I can write about them. I do pictures of them, I give them pictures; I paint them myself. It works pretty well.

INTERVIEWER

It seems to me you'd learn a whole lot about how prostitutes think and are, and not necessarily that much about more conventional women.

VOLLMANN

Right. Well, I have been able to sleep around with some of them, too.

INTERVIEWER

Well, good. I'm glad to hear that.

Louis Begley

❇

from The Art of Fiction CLXXII

INTERVIEWER

I don't know writers who write about sex better than you do.

BEGLEY

Thank you. I enjoy doing it.

INTERVIEWER

I think the frankness of it is what makes it so sexy.

BEGLEY

It could be. I agree that those scenes are good. I'm not ashamed to admit that occasionally I've found myself aroused by my own descriptions of sex.

Vladimir Nabokov

✠

from The Art of Fiction XL

INTERVIEWER

Your sense of the immorality of the relationship between Humbert Humbert and Lolita is very strong. In Hollywood and New York, however, relationships are frequent between men of forty and girls very little older than Lolita. They marry—to no particular public outrage; rather, public cooing.

NABOKOV

No, it is not *my* sense of the immorality of the Humbert Humbert-Lolita relationship that is strong; it is Humbert's sense. *He* cares, I do not. *I* do not give a damn for public morals, in America or elsewhere. And, anyway, cases of men in their forties marrying girls in their teens or early twenties have no bearing on Lolita whatever. Humbert was fond of "little girls"—not simply "young girls." Nymphets are girl-children, not starlets and "sex kittens." Lolita was twelve, not eighteen, when Humbert met her. You may remember that by the time she is fourteen, he refers to her as his "aging mistress."

Issue 41, 1967

Richard Howard

⚸

With a Potpourri from Down Under

Anything but rotten, such flowers are ill
named, remaining exempt from the compost fate
   by a decorum of fatigue, keeping still
      the power to generate
a world of their own, long since over the hill,

   or of ours. Inhale them and you can recall
—what? Whatever is recoverable just
   and only just for having been, after all,
      forgotten. Closer—you must
put your nose right into the powdery ball

   of bloom to get the good of it, past the blue
of unrecognizeable gentians, past wild
   roses tamed to mild rose, even past a few
      patently dead leaves reconciled
by dust with the livid petals. There. Now you

   have it, strong for all the insistent pastels
(as if life were forged by Marie Laurencin—
   or death, for that matter), now you have the smells
      of a room we first met in:
two kittens, pot, and the pungence that wells

up out of the ampoules of amyl nitrite
apparently used, *chez* Tom, instead of *sauce*
        béchamel. That was a foregone appetite,
                though it makes less of a loss
if you couple the lovemaking our first night

        with a myth instead of with a person—me,
yourself, whoever in between: we become
        creators when we have a past. So make free
                with the odors coming from
this irresponsible present: breathe deeply,

        and a bed in Vermont will be unmade; stir
the wan remains and you will have invented
        closets in Florence which were
                identically scented,
clearings in Hawaii heretofore a blur—

        I know. I've tried it, slipping habit's traces
by a quick whiff myself, gaining from partial
        immersion the totally risen graces
                of going down into all
the intimate reek, the must of dark places.

        Now you take over. Each garden is a grave,
I grant you, but there are resurrections here:
        our senses make us giants in what time we have
                (Proust's law)—use yours then, my dear,
on a gift that savors of more than we can save.

Issue 79, 1981

Anthony Hecht

✠

Le Jet d'Eau

after Baudelaire

My dear, your lids are weary;
Lower them, rest your eyes—
As though some languid pleasure
Wrought on you by surprise.
The tattling courtyard fountain
Repeats this night's excess
In fervent, ceaseless tremors
Of murmur and caress.

   A spray of petaled brilliance
      That uprears
   In gladness as the Moon
      Goddess appears
   Falls like an opulent glistening
      Of tears.

Even thus, your soul's arousal,
Primed by the body's joys,
Ascends in quenchless cravings
To vast, enchanted skies,
And then brims over, dying
In swoons, faint and inert,

And drains to the silent, waiting
Dark basin of my heart.

  A spray of petaled brilliance
      That uprears
  In gladness as the Moon-
      Goddess appears
  Falls like an opulent glistening
      Of tears.

You, whom the night makes radiant,
How amorous to lie, spent,
Against your breasts and listen
To the fountain's soft lament.
O Moon, melodious waters,
Wind-haunted trees in leaf,
Your melancholy mirrors
My ardors and their grief.

  A spray of petaled brilliance
      That uprears
  In gladness as the Moon-
      Goddess appears
  Falls like an opulent glistening
      Of tears.

Issue 148, 1998

Rick Moody

✠

from The Ring of Brightest Angels
Around Heaven

II

Everyone in New York City does not go to sex clubs. Above Fifty-seventh Street on the East Side they march to and from hired cars as if the subway and its content were television fictions. There is the guy with the private life up here, with the call girl problem or the fucking-boys-in-a-motel-in-the-Bronx problem. There is the ragged teenager whose ambition is to throw off his or her Upper East Side address, the kid who takes the limo to the shooting gallery on Lexington and 125th, but truly this Upper East Side is a separate city, where only the occasional skirmish with the New York of this story takes place. The Upper East Side has its loneliness, it has its isolation, it has its lost opportunities, its disintegrating families, it has its murder and its addiction and its adultery and homosexuality sure, but all this is *cushioned*. Disconsolation drifts out of the Upper East Side, in some river of chance, drifts neglected like waste, until it lands somewhere else.

So another friend I knew from that time, Toni Gardner, went to a club called Wendy's. Saturday nights in the meat packing district. In the same space as the Ruin. A club for women. *Private sex parties.* They had auctions. You could *auction yourself*. There was a line of those willing to be auctioned. It snaked back to the black plywood bar. A lot of people wanted to participate. If you were willing to wait for a while, you could know your value.

The auctioneer, a woman in her forties, specialized in a certain stage patter ironically imitative of the classic auction house style. The Christie's and Sotheby's style. She was well-dressed and knowledge-able and articulate about the artifacts at hand. Her argot was full of hyperbolic folderol, jokes and salacious commentary, and it was de-livered at an unintelligible pace. She enabled, through the blur of her rhetoric, a host of ritual couplings all based upon principles of chance and economics. On the other hand, maybe she was like the country auctioneer, sending off the calf to be made veal: *Woman of the age of twenty-five, hair the color of cinnamon, eyes an arctic blue, height and weight, well, she's of a certain size—she's in tip-top physical condition—note the breasts, fountains of maternity, which I can only describe to you by falling into the use of those old metaphors—perfect fruits—and an ass to die for, yeah to die for—yes, this dyke can sing, I can promise you that—in these black jeans, well she will do whatever transports you, this young dyke of twenty-five—I can promise you, and let's start with an opening bid of a hundred and fifty dollars for the eve-ning; do I hear a hundred and fifty, yeah, one seventy-five, who will pay one seventy-five for this auburn beauty from the country, from the . . . from the state of Maine, that's right—never visited these precincts be-fore and ready to be broken on the rack of your choice, fresh from the un-forgiving and dramatic coasts of Maine—unwise in the ways of Manhattan—do I hear one seventy-five, one ninety, do I have one ninety, two hundred dollars—she assures me she can take a dildo all the way to its rubberized base, two twenty-five, do I hear, two thirty—a bot-tom, yeah, she's a bottom of compliance such as you have never experi-enced, SOLD! YES! SOLD!* And so on until the obscure and almost unlit cavern rocked with the dynamics of ownership. Her voice now a whisper in the microphone, devoid of affect, the words delivered without feeling at all, just the words, a perfect simulacrum of auction slang and then you were owned. You were owned.

Toni was from the Upper East Side by way of the suburbs—she had never been to Maine at all—and she got out of that neighborhood as soon as she could. Took the bus down Fifth Avenue and only went back for holidays. I met her at Rutgers. When she auctioned herself after a few drinks, I was with her. She'd had a hard time persuading them to let me in. They quizzed you out front if you were a guy. If there was a moment's hesitation in your responses you were gone. *Are you a fag?* If you even quarreled with the usage, you were alone walking past empty warehouses. Way, way West. No cabs. No buses. No subways.

Back then, Wendy's was just coming into prominence as an event. It was making a transition from a prior location, where it had simply been a bar, and the flyers were getting more and more aggressive: *Wendy's, the dungeon of destiny for discerning dykes.* Or: *Wendy's, Cruising, Dancing, Humiliation.* Toni had recently stumbled into the new room in the back, the one with the vinyl bed in it, and she often found bodies writhing there, including, once, the body of a composition professor we'd had at Rutgers. *She gave the stupidest assignments.* Wendy's sprouted these new rooms, like a starfish regrowing itself. Private rooms down this long, gaslit corridor. Like the steam tunnels under the Rutgers campus. Tunnels like architectural diagrams for the uterine and fallopian insides of the customers. Wendy's was a mystery. You could never tell if the pool table would be there, if the cages would be there, if the bartender who was alluring last week still had her shift. The specifics came and went. Including the pertinent information. Wendy's operated on Saturday nights, as it had once operated only on Thursdays; it changed locations. It had a phone. It didn't. It had live music. It didn't. Sometimes it was in the meat-packing district and sometimes it was gone altogether.

Likewise being auctioned that night were the services of a first-rate dominatrix, who would demonstrate her gifts on the premises, later in the evening. A tattooist and scarification expert also auctioned some work. One of the bartenders auctioned herself. We were supposed to use *play money*, simulated legal tender bills, but this counterfeiting diluted the effect of the transaction. Therefore a subterranean market existed that featured real cash. Toni got into this long unruly line— she was soon to be the beauty from Maine, the cinnamon-haired beauty—after we'd sat there a while, excitably. And it wasn't so strange that she did it, really. The auction wasn't that far, say, from a *coming out party* back in Montclair, where Toni had lived as a kid.

Things weren't going well for her professionally. She didn't really know what she wanted to do; she had spent a couple of years talking in therapy about *vocational choice anxiety*. And she had flipped a car in Long Island visiting her parents' summer house. She owed them a lot of money for it. She'd moved out of the Upper East Side after being engaged to a nice boy with a legal practice. Toni auctioned herself to slip these binds. She did it for fun, an amnesiac fun.

She danced in a go-go cage, beside the auctioneer, dressed in black jeans and a tank top; she made sure to sport her tattoos, and she affected an insouciant look, as if daring a bidder. This was *the* look among the lots at Wendy's auction—a look that mixed subject and object, *sub* and *dom*—and therefore not terribly novel. Toni didn't garner the highest price. That went to a woman in a sort of librarian costume who seemed to weep nervously as a pair of anxious bidders competed aggressively for her. She brought a thousand dollars for the night.

The music was speed metal. Speed metal with girl singers. The place shook with it. Toni danced. At last, the bidding was completed. Two hundred and fifty dollars. A scattered and diffident applause. The crowd parted a little bit, and in a movie slow motion the employees of Wendy's, the handlers, waved Toni over, waved her over to the edge of the stage, waving like construction flagmen, where *two* women were waiting for her. Two women had bid together for her. A consortium. They were fucking cheap, was Toni's first feeling, she explained to me later. *They were fucking cheap, they couldn't even afford to buy their own slave for the evening—they had to go in on one.* No way was she going with them. No way. They were cheap.

But then Toni began to warm to the idea a little. She was charmed, it turned out, by their garishness. By the ugly complexities they presented. She hated them at first and in her disdain she started to like them. At the bar. As she stepped from the stage, Toni took one hand from each of them—from Doris and Marlene—and they repaired to the bar. One of her owners was a good lesbian and one was a bad lesbian. The good lesbian was Doris, and she came from Bernardsville, New Jersey, but she didn't go to Rutgers like Toni Gardner did. *She went to Princeton.* Doris's parents were disappointed when she made clear her object choice to them, when Doris told her parents that *she was in love with a woman.* But they were supportive. (Her mom was especially supportive because she was in therapy with Dr. Bernice Neptcong, who had an office right in Princeton.) They supported her efforts to find a loving, caring relationship.

Unfortunately, Toni told me, Doris didn't want a loving, caring relationship exactly, or perhaps these terms were simply more elastic to
her than might be supposed by Bernice Neptcong. To Doris loving
and caring always seemed to have a certain amount of trouble attached
to them. Love and trouble were really identical to her. So Doris formed
an attachment with Marlene, the bad lesbian. Marlene was a tall, exotic sex worker—Marlene was not her real name—who had platinum
blond hair and coffee-colored skin, who slept with men at a reasonably successful escort agency and who came home at night aggrieved
by her profession. She drank a lot. She dabbled with harder drugs.

Marlene's cheekbones were like the sharp side of an all-purpose
stainless-steel survival jackknife and her eyes narrowed to reflect disappointment and loss, which, when combined with her biceps, her
violent and toned physique, made for a compelling female beauty.
Doris, on the other hand, looked like an Ivy League intellectual. She
had thick black glasses and she shaved the back of her head. She wore
maroon velveteen bell bottoms and had a navel ring, frequently infected. She was a little older than her clothes suggested.

Marlene and Doris, Toni realized, didn't have much to say to each
other. Toni didn't know, yet, that Marlene had just come back from a
hard day at an escort agency where she had to fuck a whole bunch of
strangers, guys for whom deceit was a simple fact of their day, who
wove deceit and its responsibilities into their schedule like deceit was
just another calendar appointment. And she didn't know that Doris
also hated her job at the women's magazine where she worked on the
copy desk—she aspired to write articles for *Camera Obscura*. Toni
thought Marlene was the harder of the two. Marlene was like a teakettle almost boiled off. Anything could upset her, it seemed, any little
stray remark. But in truth Doris was harder. Doris was detached and
skeptical and full of calcified antipathies.

Their apartment was in the Clinton section of Manhattan, also
called Hell's Kitchen, where Jorge Ruiz lived. On the night that Toni
was auctioned off to Marlene and Doris, Jorge, as I have said, was arguing with a pre-op transsexual, Crystal, about whether to buy crack
cocaine from the guy on Forty-third Street who was out to chisel
them. At that very moment, while Jorge was just lifting the hem of
Crystal's cheap synthetic miniskirt and pulling delicately on the mesh

of her white fishnet stockings, Doris, Marlene and Toni were throwing light switches a couple of blocks away.

It was a small one-bedroom and it was draped in leather items, in stuff from the Pink Pussycat or the Pleasure Chest. There was restraining gear, and they even had a gynecologist's exam table with houseplants on it. The table had stirrups and everything. There was another decorating strain, too: Bernardsville chic: It was a kind of homely, countervailing sensibility. Doris hadn't been able to shake it yet, though she was in her thirties. She had a few museum posters, Monet's years at Giverny or the Treasures of Egypt, and some handsome black Ikea furniture and a lovely imitation Persian area rug made in Belgium. Her parents helped her to buy these. Doris and Marlene also had one of those little yapping dogs, a corgi or something, named Bernice Neptcong, M.D. Doris would say, *Get out of the way, Bernice Neptcong.* The dog was vicious. An attack rat.

Marlene had clamps, Toni told me. She liked to have you apply the clamps to her nipples and then, also, to her labia, though the best part, Marlene said, and Toni repeated to me, *I'm telling you—the best part is when they come off.* She also used clothespins, because you could take a little of the spring out of them, bend them back and forth a few times, and they didn't hurt quite as much. The three of them had already had enough drinks to loosen up—it was almost three in the morning—so their clothes were off in a hurry. They'd barely turned the dead bolts. Except that Marlene had this idea about donning other clothes. Once she had her clothes off, she was striding, like some carnivorous game animal, across the room toward the closet. She had a closet full of garments of the diligent bondage fantast. So they took off their clothes and they put on these leather chaps in which their asses were exposed. Shredded T-shirts through which the edges of leather brassieres or the slope of a breast were evident. On Toni, the costume was kind of large. She was normally in the petite range. Doris made her own selections wearily, as though this part of the proceedings were as new as selecting the temperature for a load of laundry.

Marlene had Doris and Toni attach the clamps to her body. She whispered brusquely. They observed a clinical, professional silence as they did it—because the procedure involved pain and had the so-

briety of pain. Toni performed her role intently as though the process were curative or therapeutic and because she didn't know Doris
and Marlene well enough to chatter anyway. Toni hadn't told them
anything—they knew nothing about her except her nakedness, the
shape of her tattoos: the Ghost Rider skull on her shoulder blade,
the Minnie Mouse on her ass.

Though now they knew that she liked novelty. Toni went down on
Marlene. It was pretty hard to avoid the clothespins in that posture,
but brushing against them turned out to be part of the point. Marlene
let the breath of God pass from her lips. She seemed a little dizzy, and
the region that was clamped became enlarged. It must have hurt like
shit, Toni told me, *because those things were on there pretty well and
she was grinding up against me and they were getting caught in my
hair or I was pushing them aside and she was just moaning in that way
people do, moaning like this was the straight vanilla thing*. This went
on for a while and finished with Marlene producing a formidable
strap-on dildo from a Doc Martens shoe box under the bed. Marlene
reached and shoved the box back under the bed. A ripple of pain
seemed to overtake her as she did so, and she huffed once with it, as
though this were a brisk sort of exercise.

Marlene arranged the dildo harness *over* her clamps, organizing
these hazards disinterestedly. They might as well have been curlers.
She stood. She stepped out of the leather chaps and into the black ly-
cra harness with a real weariness. A couple of clothespins sprung
loose and she let them go. Then she guided the dildo through the
hole in the harness. Its pinkish, Caucasian color was ridiculous. She
had a large bottle of Astroglide already waiting on the floor beside the
bed, and she told Doris to lean over and grab it, and then, while Toni
was doing busy work on her breasts, fingerpainting them, she lubri-
cated her lover's ass and vagina both, as though she were baby-oiling
an infant—with just this detachment—and bid Doris kneel at the edge
of the bed. Marlene, standing, fucked Doris in the ass, while Toni got
around the side and fondled Doris's clitoris. Toni was doing the same
to herself. *It was like jazz-dancing*; Toni told me, *it was all these moves
and steps like that bitch in Montclair, Mrs. Beatty, tried to ram into my
head when I was in Jazzercise on Mondays and Wednesdays when Mom
was doing the day-care center thing*. But the fact was: Toni liked it. It

was thrilling the way the last reel of a film is thrilling. You just want to
see it all played out.

Doris on the other hand seemed to be walking through it a little
bit. *Penetration, you know, isn't always the coolest thing among
women,* Toni said. Doris held clumps of Toni's cinnamon hair in her
hands as she, Doris, was being fucked by Marlene. She gently tousled
Toni's hair, mumbling slightly, with a kind of sexual agitation that
had a little sadness in it too. The amazing thing, though, was that
Marlene was getting the whole dildo up into Doris, *grinding up into
her with those fucking clamps and clothespins all over her!* Finally,
though, Doris seemed to have enough of it, and she pulled the fac-
simile out of her ass with a sigh, reaching behind her; looking behind
her in this vulnerable way and then pulling the thing out of her, she
stood and pushed Marlene down on the bed, masturbating the rubber
dick attached to Marlene, as though it could feel, pulling the condom
off it, yes condom, and jerking it off, grinding against her lover's hips
until Marlene seemed to be in some thrall of shuddering and pain,
kissing Doris on the mouth, reaching up to gently kiss her goodnight.
Oh God, Marlene said, as Doris knelt to remove the clamps one by
one, first the nipple clamps, and the skin underneath was bruised
with red rings around it. Even on Marlene's dark skin you could see
the welts rising. And then the clothespins from her labia. Marlene fingered the damage in an inebriate swoon. *Oh God.* Toni and Doris
stood around her, around the foot of the bed. Marlene probed with
her long dark stalks for the evidence of the clothespins. Then she lay
back on the bed. Rolled away on her side. Doris wiped her hands on
the comforter at the foot of the bed, almost as if that simulated thing,
the simulated dick, had ejaculated onto her, as if she'd had Marlene's
very semen upon her.

And then she turned her attentions to Toni. She said something
that Toni didn't hear, the two of them angling around one another
like wrestlers now, angling as if to grasp one another, and then the
words became clear, their quaintness, Doris wanted to be held, *really,*
Toni told me. *Believe it or not, she just wanted to be held,* so the two of
them were hugging, and Toni really felt like she was Doris's dad or
something, holding her, and then this paternal kindness or whatever
it was gave way to another set of roles, another set of styles. They

were lying on the bed next to Marlene who was in some narcotic semi-consciousness, and they were facing one another head to foot, going down on each other, because the just holding each other part was okay, but it led elsewhere right then. They were unclothed now, the pile of fantasy gear sitting atop their street clothes like an upper layer of sediment. Doris tasted musty to Toni, as though forgotten in all the rush to arrange things, and Toni felt badly for her. So pity became a component in this secondary tangle of erotics. Pity in there too, like yet another partner, an unwanted partner. Toni's first and only instance of transportation that evening was a little ripple, really, and she made more noise with it than it required. She faked it. *By then, there really wasn't anything going on that was doing it for me, so I faked it,* she told me. Doris in the meantime was having the revelation of the shy. All the contentment in the world seemed to come out of some locked basement and crowd around her. There was sentiment everywhere; the world was her damp handkerchief, her multi-volume diary. It was the kind of orgasm, to Toni, that was promised by the good-natured phonies who wrote sex manuals. *Loving as Lesbians (By and For and How To).* Or, *The Gay Woman: A Manual for Lovers and Friends.* Come out of your cellar cabinets of shame, *womyn*, and *celebrate!* Know the community of love!

—Wow, Doris said, Oh God. Wow. Oh.

—Mm, Toni said.

Now they lay beside one another in the light of a single bedside lamp.

—Don't worry about her, Doris said. Out cold. Once she's out you could jump on the mattress and she wouldn't notice.

Toni smiled nervously.

—You want to spend the night?

—Can we all fit on here?

They could, sure, though Toni wasn't totally convinced she wanted to spend the night. She was kind of hoping they couldn't all fit. She kind of wanted to go back to her own bed and sort through the fleeting recollections of the evening: dancing in the cage, putting on the bondage gear, fitting a clamp onto another woman's nipple, the exponential complications of a threesome. She felt overtaxed, like she'd sat through a double feature in the front row. She was cranky, short-tempered. It didn't make any difference. Toni was worried about hurting Doris's feelings for some reason, for some stupid girl reason. So she stayed. Soon all three women were arranged in the enormous bed. Marlene's lungs wheezed like an old bellows. Doris, on the other hand, was a light sleeper. Toni was between the two of them and she couldn't get comfortable all night—the gravitational yank of those bodies was too much for her. And Doris kept throwing a leg over her, pinning her, as though Toni were there for good.

A diner on Ninth Avenue. After a silent and hungover breakfast, the three of them made another date for the Thursday following. *Would you want to come visit us again?* Marlene said. And Marlene did indeed seem to want to try it again. But there was another part of her— Toni told me over the weekend, when she and I went to a bar on First Avenue called simply *Bar*—there was another part of Marlene that was suspicious somehow, evidently suspicious, that the two of them, Toni and Doris, had been *fucking around without her.* Taking advantage of her intermittent consciousness. She must have had some infrared surveillance device, Toni thought, some unconscious sensor watching out for her interests. Or else she was just keenly attuned to the inevitability of heartache. *Rejection sensitivity.* So what if Doris and Toni *were* doing it? It was part of the problem of three people. *You really gotta trust each other,* Toni told me. *Cause there's always two on and one off.* But Marlene couldn't withstand the implications, and as the thought took root, it sent forth these poisonous boughs.

That was no surprise. The picture of Marlene got worse as Toni learned about it. Marlene flew into a rage if the place, if the apartment in Clinton, was not swept clean; if the dog, Bernice Neptcong (a male) had not been walked; if the pictures were crooked, if Doris happened to show any interest, conversational or otherwise, in any male who didn't wear dresses and have breasts; if, for even a moment, Marlene had the sensation that Doris was preoccupied with another woman. Or sometimes Marlene flew into a rage just out of fatigue, just out of daily confusion. And when Marlene flew into a rage, *she sometimes beat Doris.* This is what Toni found out before the second date ever took place, when she met Doris for a drink, because Doris called her at work and said, *I have to talk to you. Let's meet at this bar on St.*

Mark's. It's important. Her voice was hushed as if even the security on her work phone had somehow been breached.

This fact of battery seemed to slip almost casually from Doris and Marlene to Toni and Doris and then to Toni and me, the enormity of it almost routine or incidental at first, as if it were not about people at all, as if there were not bruises on Doris's china features, as if it were about a way that people lived in New York City, an awful way that people lived in New York City, where woman beat their children in public, and men beat one another on the subways. Toni told me and I said nothing because this beating was a vacuum, a lifelessness that I couldn't really adjust to at first, and then I passed it on, passed on that silence to someone else, who in turn passed it on, the idea that good people, principled women, occasionally beat one another out of confusion and sadness and loss and thereby put the purple, the hematoma, in the flag that hung over city hall.

Bruises had appeared all over Doris. She frequently wore sunglasses. She spoke of falling down stairs and walking into doors. It was getting difficult at the office, as it had been difficult at offices in the past. *I've been fired from jobs before,* Doris said, her hands trembling as she lit a cigarette. Her voice was dull and methodical; she smelled clean, obsessively clean, to Toni; her skin was the palest white, the color of gallery walls.

—I can't lose another job because of her. I'm not functioning as it is. You know? It's getting embarrassing. I'm tired of going through it . . . It's humiliating and it's really tiring too. I'm tired of living like this. There's this dull way things go around and around again and I'm almost thirty-two years old and I don't want to live like this anymore.

Doris would veer off in another direction, onto another subject, and then she would come back to it. And then another refrain emerged. *She asked Toni if she knew anywhere they could cop some cocaine.* They were drinking and having the conversation that veered from the tragic to the mundane, from battery to discussions of rock-and-roll bands, and then suddenly Doris was trying to procure. No delicate way to announce it, like there was no delicate way to say that you have been beaten by your lover and that you haven't exactly done anything about it yet. Doris said, *Do you know where we could pick up?* And since Toni lived in the East Village she did know where to buy drugs, though she was no regular customer, she knew where, because you passed it every day. Wasn't terribly complicated. So they walked down Twelfth Street and copped some rock from the first cluster of dangerous-looking boys they saw. That simple. The boys took their twenty dollars and came back a little later with the vials, the vials with their little red plastic caps. Doris and Toni smoked it together in a basement stairwell.

Then the complaints were spilling from Doris's mouth in long, artificial strings. How had she assumed this role, this victim role? What *king of mystery was there in her family of origin?* Where could blame be settled so that her burden would be lighter? She was victimized by Marlene. Marlene pulled all the strings. She was thinking back to her parents' *concept of child-rearing and its hidden language of coercion.* Doris was powerless. She needed to *share her truth.* To set *boundaries.* The passions of battery were stirred way down in the unconscious, in the history of the species, not up where Doris or anyone could control them. She didn't know if she could shake it. She wanted to leave but she didn't know if she could. There was something operatic about Doris not walking the dog and then getting hit. There were all kinds of hatred between Doris and Marlene. Marlene was systematically trying to *murder* Doris. Doris had actually woke to find Marlene holding a pillow over her head as she slept, she had found Marlene tampering with jars of prescription medication that she had in a cabinet—*I have these attacks of nerves,* Doris said. Marlene couldn't handle, in the end, that Doris's family had money and that hers did not, the differences between the classes were too much for her, though Doris herself felt she understood the misery that Marlene had come from. She could see how Marlene's childhood in the city was just a long story of deprivation. She could see how her life had been devoid of any model for affection. *But she didn't have to murder her for it.* She didn't have to buy a gun, which was what Marlene was talking about doing, ostensibly to defend them from the fucking creeps in Hell's Kitchen, *fucking creeps.* And then just as suddenly, Doris was in love again. She had not exhausted all of her love for Marlene. Marlene was radiant when she was happy, she had a smile that would stop at nothing. When she was happy, her face seemed to open and to reply *yes* to everything, to the abandoned buildings, to the crack dealers, to the repulsive men who paid her. Her face said *yes,* and it was clear how revolutionary and dangerous was the *yes* of a woman who was *grabbing the world by its dick and yanking.* Marlene happy, Doris said, was as dangerous as a souped-up automatic weapon. But then on the other hand she was dangerous when she wasn't happy and that was where all the trouble started. Marlene was dangerous. She was just thinking out loud. Marlene was dangerous. (Toni was telling me in the bar.) And that was when Doris began to think about what she might do about the problem. There was no longer any way around it.

They went to Wendy's together, the next Saturday. All three of them. For a minute, everything seemed to be going all right. There was a new room where a woman in thigh-high boots and black leather gloves was throwing darts. There was another auction, and the three of them discussed buying a fourth woman. They were particularly fond of a little girl in a white party dress who shivered and grimaced like a child abandoned in a department store. This little girl would have waited among the men's shirts for weeks for the mother who would never return.

But they didn't have enough cash between them really to pay for the girl, who was a hot item. Top dollar for this girl. They were back at the Clinton apartment; it was only 12:30. The dog was walked, the apartment was clean. The three of them were there in the apartment, and already the process of unclothing themselves seemed ritualized. Something had gone out of it. Toni knew she was just chasing kicks, and it didn't make her feel that good. Marlene seemed intent on being the passive recipient of whatever fucking was going to take place that night. She had a tableau in mind; it was theatrical. She was actively arranging for her passivity. Through some superhuman effort, Doris managed to keep the whole thing together for a time. She strapped on the pink dildo and fucked Marlene in the missionary position, but both of them seemed sad and distant, and Toni lay around drinking beer and lending a hand now and then. The air was hot and still. The heat was a malevolent force in the apartment. By the time they climbed under a lone sheet, the three of them were covered in the sweat of exertion and also the sweat of connections not entirely made. They were each a little drunk.

When Toni awoke, the sun was muffled in humidity. They had coffee, and she wondered if Doris was imagining the whole thing. New York City was quiet, it was Sunday morning, people were absorbed with that newspaper, and no ill feeling would spill onto the streets of the city until noon. Vice was canceled for a time out of respect for a few regular churchgoers. When Toni went home, when she called me later to go for a drink, she had a feeling this auction vogue had run its course now. She could go on to other things. *Sex just isn't that important,* she said. *You can get into it for a while and then you can get into something else.* She was thinking about maybe going back out to Long Island for the summer.

But that night Doris called again. She had to see Toni right away. Right away. She was a mess. *I've broken my wrist,* she said. *My wrist is in a sling.* Doris couldn't go to work the next day, looking like one of those women who, in dark sunglasses, stands by her man, who limps slightly and walks very slowly. Her wrist in a sling. Something about the night before. Marlene had just flipped out. She was coming at Doris with a lamp, one of those halogen lamps. She was going to break a fucking halogen lamp over Doris's head. They had been kissing while she slept, Marlene cried, Doris and Toni had been fucking without her. *And we hadn't!* Doris said, as if Toni needed to be conscripted into her version of the story. *And I told her that!* And Marlene started bringing up crazy stuff. Stuff that happened months ago. Why was Doris leaving early for the office on a Tuesday in March? If she actually went to the gynecologist in April did she have any proof? Marlene was bringing up things that never happened, totally imagining things. So Doris did what she had never done before. *She took a swing at Marlene.* Hit her in the arm and broke her own wrist. Just like that. Broke it like it was the tiny limb on a sapling. Marlene didn't have anything more than a bruise, but Doris's arm was broken and now Marlene wasn't talking to her anymore. Marlene was shattering furniture in the apartment. Marlene was silent and implacable and breaking things. Oh it was horrible, it was horrible, New York was horrible, and life was horrible, full of compromises—she was crying now—and other people controlled you, people you would never know, never even know their middle names or what their vices were, the stuff they never told you, the real pornography of sensitivity, the pornography of love and affection, the pornography of plain old bliss . . . You never knew anything and you passed into old age knowing nothing except the color of some *fucking bathtub toy from your childhood. Let's go get high,* Doris said. *I want to get high. I just want to get high.*

Doris made this plan. She told Toni. Their anniversary was coming up. She and Marlene had been together two years. She would make a plan to spend the day with Marlene. It involved taking Marlene to see a play. The theater. *Shakespeare in the Park.* Yep. In New York you could work your way past the homeless people in midtown and the homeless guys sleeping in the park and the guys who were auctioning off their tragedies, their TB, their KS, their HIV, their veteran status, for alms, and you could go see these plays in the park. *Shakespeare in the Park.* Anyone could go. And though Marlene had little formal education, Shakespeare moved her—all those old tragedies with their sins of pride and their purgations. She especially liked strong women characters. Lady Macbeth and Cleopatra. So they were seeing *Lear* and Doris knew she was a Reagan or Goneril; sharper than serpent's teeth, Toni told me, because at that very moment the other part of the plan was taking effect. Because Doris was leaving. Doris was leaving. Doris was springing it on Marlene. And Toni was agreeing. Out of pity.

So Toni and a team of illegal aliens broke into Doris's and Marlene's apartment, fed the dog, Bernice Neptcong, with fresh steak, actually feeding the dog steak like in some PG-13 heist movie, because the dog, raised by Marlene, would fasten its jaws onto any intruder, and they didn't want to have to kill it, and while the dog was eating the steak, a fine cut, I would imagine lean, lean, lean, Toni was directing this team of illegal aliens who had no real interest in the haste or deceit involved in their work because they just needed the work; Toni was directing them to what she believed was Doris's furniture and CDs and books and sexually explicit videos and pictures of Monet's years at Giverny and was putting them into an unmarked, rented van that was double-parked in front of the Korean deli below. It was too bad that it had to be on their anniversary, Toni told me, but Doris couldn't think of another way to shake her, another day, another perfect time and place. Or maybe the cruelty that was involved in this plan was very much on Doris's mind, for the two years of cruelty she had received, and this was the best way to work it out, the most perfect way to make her point, a point thematically coherent and consistent, like a play itself, a point with the coincidences and destinies of a play.

I guess I have to admit here, too, that as a friend of Toni's I served as an accomplice to this crime. I served as a lookout, just in case Marlene or one of her friends (though she didn't have many friends) might have some synergistic understanding of what was going on, some sudden impulsive need to go see if Bernice Neptcong, M.D., had enough water in all this heat. Shamefully, I stood on the street as the Hispanic guys, their faces twisted into the solemn, sensitive gazes of funeral parlor employees, carried the furniture out of the apartment at a trot.

Finally, there was an intermission at *Lear,* between the third and fourth acts and Doris told Marlene, giving her an affectionate little peck on the cheek, that she had to go to the bathroom. Doris's lips were not thin lips, as I might have imagined, the lips of preppy women from Bernardsville. No, through some strange genetic twist, she had been given the broad, full lips of a lover, and even at the beginning Marlene had adored these lips, Toni believed, had adored kissing Doris. So Doris's lips were now descending on Marlene's razor cheeks, and Marlene, as a matter of course, was pretending not to care entirely, though inside perhaps, where things were all tangled up, there was some interior paroxysm of joy or gladness at the bounty of love, though this paroxysm was smothered by the cool of New York. Then Doris gave her a little hug. She was wearing a black tank top and black jeans, and Marlene was, too, Marlene was wearing almost the same thing, and Doris gave her a little squeeze, and said she had to go to the *comfort station.* She laughed and said it, *comfort station.*

And then she took off. She was sobbing like a baby, sobbing like that girl left in the department store, sobbing in a way that can't be ameliorated by the stuff in this world, no matter how much good happens. But by the time she met another friend, Debby, over by *Tavern on the Green,* by the time she met Debby she had settled down a little bit. Debby had borrowed a car, a black Toyota Celica with plastic wrap in the rear windows from where they had been shattered, and they were driving straight to Newark airport, where Doris was catching a flight to New Orleans to stay with some cousins for a couple of weeks.

Elsewhere, with crack timing, the illegal aliens and Toni were driving Doris's stuff to mini-storage over in the west teens, just above the meat-packing district.

Marlene in the meantime was sitting on the blanket under the trees. Just a regular old blanket from the apartment, nothing special. And she was eating a cheap piece of cheddar cheese on a Triscuit and watching the edges of the audience fray as people came and went, and thinking what a great breeze, what a killer breeze and then wondering, when the play had begun again, where Doris was, but just wondering briefly, not giving it that much thought, and then watching some of the play and getting concerned, packing things up as if she was going to leave, wondering if leaving was the right thing to do, if staying put was maybe better, because if Doris was lost—as she was often lost, a little absent-minded—it would be better if one of them weren't moving and then getting pissed off, really pissed off, *fuck,* and getting up and blocking somebody's fucking view of RAIN RAIN RAIN or some such passage and sitting back down and then getting worried because the rage that Marlene felt was in part worry, rage blanketing worry based on experience, some experience of loss, and so she was getting up and walking fast, now, purposefully, in a way you might have found scary if you were watching her, walking fast toward the Portosans, or whatever brand they had installed over on the other side of the field where everyone was sitting, and looking at the line of people there, unable to ask any of the women there, the overdressed women, the society chicks who had read *Shakespeare in college,* if they had seen a woman in black jeans, suddenly unable to do it somehow, unable to do it, shy or something, and then wandering around the Portosans, in the woods, the woods of Central goddamn Park, wandering, past Tavern on the Green and back to the play, hearing applause, not paying any attention to it, seeing a dozen women who looked like Doris, looked exactly like her until you got up close, until you could see up close that they had one birthmark that Doris didn't have, or they held one opinion that was not Doris's, or that they were fucking boys instead of girls, although otherwise they *were* Doris, seeing them and working upstream to the spot where she and Doris had sat and not finding her, in the dark now, getting dark, worried, concerned, enraged, yeah, murderously enraged, worried. Doris's headless, raped body in the Ramble, raped by some fucking pervert, worried, and then walking out of the park, empty now, followed by cops on horses, not cops that you would ask to help you, though, they were no help, cops, gangsters attached at the waist to horses, so worried, walking back toward the apartment down Eighth Avenue, down through the sleaze, down Eighth Avenue, walking automatically, not thinking at all, not feeling, just thinking the worst, but in a disembodied way, permitting the worst just to swim in her wherever it would—Doris's headless body. Doris's headless body, her jeans and her breasts and then no head, just bones and tubing and pink gelatinous stuff, and then turning up the street and fitting the key in the lock that was broken anyway, and checking the mail just because *Doris liked to get mail*, checking the mail just for Doris, and climbing up the poorly lit and warped steps to the third floor and fitting the key in the door, not knowing right then how time was stretching out in this moment, not knowing how long it was taking to turn that key because she was imagining the worst but in a detached way, in a way while she was planning to go to Wendy's that night, or in a way while she was thinking about her job and almost crying with how much she hated it and how the guys thought they could just do anything . . . and regretting all the trouble with Doris, regretting it and not being able to explain it, not even being able to admit it exactly, imagining trouble but not seeing the real trouble that lay right in front her. And then turning the handle and seeing the blankness, the emptiness in that space.

The apartment was just about cleaned out.

Doris on her way to New Orleans; she was having a drink on the plane. And then she was in the Big Easy. The second day there she went to Mobile. To the Gulf Coast. The sun was high, and it was humid and the water was a fabulous blue. It was nothing like New York City. When you were in Mobile, New York City just didn't exist at all, it was somebody's fever dream. And then she called Toni that night, because she hadn't left Toni the number, knowing that Marlene would call Toni wanting to know if she was a part of it, if she was responsible for it, wanting the number, wanting revenge, and sure enough Toni said she had called weeping, hysterical, *How could you do this to me how could you do this to me how could you do this to me* *how could any human being do this to another human being?* but Toni had the machine on and had gone to stay with Debby who also had her machine screening. Marlene's hoarse, throaty screams. Beyond the frequency that telecommunications could handle. Marlene's shrill recognitions drifting out over New York.

Actually, by the time Doris was in Mobile, Marlene was already dead. Doris was on the plane when it happened. The exact moment was lost to her; she felt no shiver of symbiosis. She felt no paranormal sadness. She was over Tuscaloosa. Or she was at the baggage check when Marlene hanged herself. All of this is fucking *true*, I can tell you that. Marlene hanged herself. Doris abandoned her girlfriend at a performance of Shakespeare in the Park and then flew to New Orleans— and this is what Marlene did afterwards. She hanged herself with rope she got at a hardware store right next to the Best Western on Eighth Avenue. She left a crumpled twenty on the counter. The guy in the store didn't even notice when she overlooked her change. When Marlene did it she was alone, and she wasn't discussing it with anyone. She had to make sure the bar in the closet was sturdy enough. She would have to really make her mind up once and for all, because it was pretty low, that bar and hanging yourself in there would take a lot of work. Marlene left no note, as Doris had left no note explaining her own disappearance. She used the handcuffs in their apartment, which once had bound her and Doris together while they made love, to cuff herself behind the back, and another set on her ankles. She put the ankle cuffs on first, then the handcuffs, and then she put her head through a slipknot. A regular old slipknot. And then she threw herself off balance and gasped as she fell over, stumbling to her side, kicking around the boots on the floor of the half-empty closet, kicking over boots and bondage gear and the other stuff Doris had left her, wanting to get up again, but all tangled and having trouble getting up, desperate to get up now, weeping, but not getting up. The energy to do so dissipated. Shocked in the last second, terrified, and then resigned, powerless. Her last breath spread in an even film in the still air of the apartment. She settled down to room temperature.

The closet door was open. The dog paid no attention. He had been fondled and loved that afternoon by Toni and the guys from

Ecuador. He'd eaten steak. But then when Marlene was dead Bernice Neptcong, the dog, became somehow uncomfortable. He went and sniffed at the long dark legs half-folded awkwardly under Marlene. And then he curled up by one ankle for the long wait. When they found her days later, when the neighbors complained, Bernice was shivering and hungry, but he struck out blindly nonetheless at the super, the police—these interlopers in the drama of neglect—baring his teeth, protecting the lost lives that had prized him. This was his kingdom now.

Three weeks later Doris was walking down Eighth Street late at night. The streets were empty. She was on her way to Avenue D. Ten days back in the city. She had tried to get in touch with Toni, but it wasn't turning out exactly as she'd hoped. She hoped that Toni would be around when she got back. In New Orleans the unspeakable drama of her predicament created a space between her and her cousins. She found this space again in Princeton. She was more alone than ever before, though she had fled from Marlene to escape loneliness, though she had opposed loneliness with what strength she had. Death mocked all this stuff. These weeks made clear the overpressure of fate. She'd taken too much time off from her job. She didn't really have anywhere to stay. She certainly wasn't going back to the apartment. And Toni wouldn't see her. So she had come to this address in the East Village. She had come by herself, feeling nauseated and lost, for the dull thrill of carelessness.

In the bakery on Eighth and D, Doris waited in line like everyone else. The woman in front of her actually bought some bread to go with her heroin—it was a demonstration loaf of stale Italian—but Doris wasn't here for bread. She was here for a dime bag. In front of her in line was Jorge Ruiz. His clothes were shabby. Throughout his transaction, he never once raised his eyes. Neither did Doris. She wouldn't have recognized him anyway; she wouldn't have known how close their lives were; she wouldn't have seen anything, lost in the flow of her own disgrace.

Toni Morrison

⚜

from The Art of Fiction CXXXIV

INTERVIEWER

Why do writers have such a hard time writing about sex?

MORRISON

Sex is difficult to write about because it's just not sexy enough. The only way to write about it is not to write much. Let the reader bring his own sexuality into the text. A writer I usually admire has written about sex in the most off-putting way. There is just too much information. If you start saying "the curve of . . ." you soon sound like a gynecologist. Only Joyce could get away with that. He said all those forbidden words. He said *cunt*, and that was shocking. The forbidden word can be provocative. But after a while it becomes monotonous rather than arousing. Less is always better.

Margaret Atwood

✠

from The Art of Fiction CXXI

INTERVIEWER

Is sex easy to write about?

ATWOOD

If by "sex" you mean just the sex act—"the earth moved" stuff—well, I don't think I write those scenes much. They can so quickly become comic or pretentious or overly metaphoric. "Her breasts were like apples," that sort of thing. But "sex" is not just which part of whose body was where. It's the relationship between the participants, the furniture in the room or the leaves on the tree, what gets said before and after, the emotions—act of love, act of lust, act of hate. Act of indifference, act of violence, act of despair, act of manipulation, act of hope? Those things have to be part of it.

Striptease has become less interesting since they did away with the costumes. It's become Newtonian. The movement of bodies through space, period. It can get boring.

Issue 117, 1990

Mordecai Richler

✠

A Liberal Education

J oyce phoned him at the office. Before she could get a word out, he
said, "If you ask me, almost all of Doug's problems can be traced to
that bloody school."

"Would you rather that he was educated as you were?"

Mortimer had been to Upper Canada College. "I don't see why
not."

"Full of repressions and establishment lies."

Establishment. Camp. WASP. She had all the bloody modish words.
"Well I—"

"We'll discuss it later. Just please please don't be late for the rehearsal."

Mortimer had only been invited to the rehearsal for the Christmas
play because he was in publishing and Dr. Booker, the founder,
wanted Oriole to do a book about Beatrice Webb House. Drama was
taught at the school by a Miss Lilian Tanner, who had formerly been
with Joan Littlewood's bouncy group. A tall, willowy young lady,
Miss Tanner wore her long black hair loose, a CND button riding her
scrappy bosom. She assured Mortimer he was a most welcome visitor
to her modest little workshop. Mortimer curled into a seat in the rear
of the auditorium, trying to appear as unobtrusive as possible. He
was only half-attentive to begin with, reconciled to an afternoon of te-
dium larded with cuteness.

"We have a visitor this afternoon, class," Miss Tanner began
sweetly, "Mr. Mortimer Griffin of Oriole Press."

Curly-haired heads, gorgeous pig-tailed heads, whipped around; everybody giggly.

"Now all together, class . . ."

"GOOD AFTERNOON, MR. GRIFFIN."

Mortimer waved, unaccountably elated.

"Settle down now," Miss Tanner demanded, rapping her ruler against the desk. "Settle down, I said."

The class came to order.

"Now this play that we are going to perform for the Christmas concert was written by . . . class?"

"A marquis!"

"Bang on!" Miss Tanner smiled, flushed with old-fashioned pride in her charges, and then she pointed her ruler at a rosy-cheeked boy. "What's a marquis, Tony?"

"What hangs outside the Royal Court Theatre."

"No, no, darling."

There were titters all around. Mortimer laughed himself, covering his mouth with his hand.

"That's a marquee. This is a marquis. A—"

A little girl bobbed up, waving her arms. Golden head, red ribbons. "A French nobleman!"

"Righty-ho! And what do we know about him . . . class?"

A boy began to jump up and down. Miss Tanner pointed her ruler at him.

"They put him in prison."

"Yes. Anybody know why?"

Everybody began to call out at once.

"Order! Order!" Miss Tanner demanded. "Whatever will Mr. Griffin think of us?"

Giggles again.

"You have a go, Harriet. Why was the marquis put in prison?"

"Because he was absolutely super."

"Mmm . . ."

"*And such a truth-teller.*"

"Yes. Any other reasons . . . Gerald?"

"Because the puritans were scared of him."

"Correct. And what else do we know about the marquis?"

"Me, me!"

"No, me, Miss. Please!"

"Eeney-meeney-miney-mo," Miss Tanner said, waving her ruler, "catch a bigot by the toe . . . Frances!"

"That he was the freest spirit what ever lived."

"*Who* ever lived. Who, dear. And who said that?"

"Apollinaire."

"Jolly good. Anything else . . . Doug?"

"Um, he cut through the banality of everyday life."

"Indeed he did. And who said that?"

"Jean Genet."

"No."

"Hugh Hefner," another voice cried.

"Dear me, that's not even warm."

"Simone de Beauvoir."

"Right. And who is she?"

"A writer."

"Good. Very good. Anybody know anything else about the marquis?"

"He was in the Bastille and then in another place called Charenton."

"Yes. All together, class . . . Charenton."

"CHARENTON."

"Anything else?"

Frances jumped up again. "I know. Please, Miss Tanner. Please, me."

"Go ahead, darling."

"He had a very, very, very big member."

"Yes indeed. And—"

But now Frances' elder brother, Jimmy, leaped to his feet, interrupting. "Like Mummy's new friend," he said.

Shrieks. Laughter. Miss Tanner's face reddened, for the first time she stamped her foot. "Now I don't like that, Jimmy. I don't like that one bit."

"Sorry, Miss Tanner."

"That's tittle-tattle, isn't it?"

"Yes, Miss Tanner."

"We mustn't tittle-tattle on one another here."

". . . sorry . . ."

"And now," Miss Tanner said, stepping up to the black-board, "can anyone give me another word for member?"

"COCK," came a little girl's shout, and Miss Tanner wrote it down.

"Beezer."

"PWICK."

"Male organ."

"PENIS."

"Hard-on."

Miss Tanner looked dubious. She frowned. "Not always," she said, and she didn't write it down.

"FUCKING-MACHINE."

"*Putz.*"

"You're being sectarian again, Monty," Miss Tanner said, some-what irritated.

"Joy-stick."

A pause.

"Anybody else?" Miss Tanner asked.

"Hot rod."

"Mmm. Dodgey," Miss Tanner said, but she wrote it down on the black-board, adding a question mark. "Anybody else?"

"Yes," a squeaky voice cried, now that her back was turned.

"Teakettle."

Miss Tanner whirled around, outraged. "*Who said that?*" she demanded.

Silence.

"Well, I never. I want to know who said that. *Immediately.*"

No answer.

"Very well, then. No rehearsal," she said, sitting down and tapping her foot. "We are simply going to sit here and sit here and sit here until who ever said that owns up."

Nothing.

"I'm sorry about this fuck-up, Mr. Griffin. It's most embarrassing."

Mortimer shrugged.

"I'm waiting, class."

Finally a fat squinting boy came tearfully to his feet. "It was me, Miss Tanner," he said in a small voice. "I said teakettle."

"Would you be good enough to tell us why, Reggie?"

". . . when my nanny . . . I mean my little brother's nanny, um, takes us, ah, out . . ."

"Speak up, please."

"When my nanny takes me, um, us . . . to Fortnum's for tea, well before I sit down she always asks us do we, do . . ." Reggie's head hung low; he paused, swallowing his tears, ". . . do I have to water my teakettle."

"Well. Well, well. I see," Miss Tanner said severely. "Class, can anyone tell me what Reggie's nanny is?"

"A prude!"

"Repressed!"

"Victorian!"

"All together now."

"REGGIE'S NANNY IS A DRY CUNT!"

"She is against . . . class?"

"Life-force."

"And?"

"Pleasure!"

"RIGHT. *And truth-sayers.* Remember that. Because it's sexually repressed bitches like Reggie's nanny who put truth-sayers like the marquis in prison."

The class was enormously impressed.

"May I sit down now?" Reggie asked.

"Sit down, what?"

"Sit down, please, Miss Tanner?"

"Yes, Reggie. You may sit down."

At which point Mortimer slipped out of the rear exit of the auditorium, without waiting to see a run-through of the play, without even finding out what play they were doing.

"Excuse me, beg your pardon," Mortimer muttered, leading Joyce and Agnes Laura Ryerson to their seats in the Beatrice Webb auditorium, which was gaily tricked out with reams of colored ribbons, balloons, and mistletoe for the Christmas play. A rosy-cheeked boy skipped across the stage waving a placard which read: PHILOSOPHY IN THE BEDROOM. He was followed by a giggly, plump ten-year-old girl with another placard: DIALOGUE THE FOURTH.

Mortimer focused on the stage, where four nude ten-year-olds (two boys, two girls) were frolicking on an enormous bed. The effect was comic, making Mortimer recall an old *Saturday Evening Post* cover by Norman Rockwell which had a freckled little girl sitting at her mother's dressing table, the gap between her teeth showing as she puckered her lips to try on her mother's lipstick.

The boy playing Dolmance said, "I see but one way to terminate this ridiculous ceremony: look here, Chevalier, we are educating this pretty girl, we are teaching her all a little girl of her age should know and, the better to instruct her, we join—we join—we join—"

"Some practice to theory," the prompter hissed.

"—some practice to theory. She must have a tableau dressed for her: it must feature a prick—"

"Louder, please," a parent behind Mortimer called out.

"—a prick discharging, that's where presently we are; would you like to serve as a model?"

The Chevalier de Mirvel, played by a big black West Indian boy whom the audience desperately wanted to do well, responded, biting back his laughter, "Surely, the proposal is too flattering to refuse, and Mademoiselle has the charms that will quickly guarantee the desired lesson's effects."

Madame de Saint-Ange, a gawky child, all ribs and knees it seemed, squealed, "Then let's go on: to work!"

Which was when they fell to wrestling on the bed, the Chevalier de Mirvel, to judge by his laughter, being the most ticklish of the four.

"Oh, indeed," Eugenie hollered, " 'tis too much, you abuse my inexperience to such a degree . . ."

The West Indian boy kissed Eugenie.

"Smack, smack," Dolmance called out, for Miss Tanner had encouraged them to improvise.

"Here comes the mushy stuff," Madame de Saint-Ange pitched in, alienating herself from her part. She was, after all, only playing Madame de Saint-Ange. For real, as Miss Tanner had explained, she was Judy Faversham.

"Oh, God!" the West Indian boy hollered. "What fresh, what sweet attractions!"

Agnes Laura Ryerson's face went the color of ashes. Behind Mortimer, a man demanded gruffly of his wife, "When does Gerald come on stage?"

"Quiet, James."

Yet another father voiced his displeasure. "There aren't enough parts."

"It's a classic, Cyril."

"All the same, it's a school play. There should be more parts. It's jolly unfair to the other children."

Mortimer's attention was gripped by the free-for-all on stage. Puzzling over the nude, goose-pimply children entwined on the bed, he wondered, the Chevalier de Mirvel aside, which leg, what ribcage, belonged to whom. Dolmance squealed: "I have seen girls younger than this sustain still more massy pricks: with courage and patience life's greatest obstacles are surmounted—"

"Here come the clichés," the man behind Mortimer said, groaning.

"—'Tis madness to think one must have a child deflowered by only very small pricks. I hold the contrary view, that a virgin shoud be delivered to none but the vastest engines to be had . . ."

Suddenly the stage lights dimmed and the bed was abandoned to the Chevalier de Mirvel and Eugenie. Secondary lights brightened and behind the free-floating gauze that formed the rear bedroom wall there magically loomed the boys and girls of the second form, Doug's form, cupids as it were, humming a nervy, bouncy tune and carrying flickering, star-shaped lights. There was enthusiastic applause and only one harsh cry of "Derivative!" from the man behind Mortimer, as the kids filed onstage and formed a circle round the bed, where the Chevalier de Mirvel and Eugenie still tussled. Then, taking the audience completely by surprise, a fairy godmother, wearing a tall pointed hat, all sparkly and wound round and round in shimmering blue chiffon, was suspended in midair over the bed. The fairy godmother was none other than Mr. Yasha Krashinsky, who taught Expressive Movement at Beatrice Webb House.

Deafening applause greeted the rotund, dangling Yasha Krashinsky, a touching measure of support, as it was widely known that he had soon to appear at Old Bailey, charged with importuning outside Covent Garden. While the second form choir hummed, Yasha Krashinsky chanted: "Le Chevalier de Mirvel is wilting. Our fair Eugenie is fading fast. They will only make it, grownups, if you believe in the cure-all powers of the orgasm. Grownups, do you believe in the orgasm?"

"Yes!"

The pitch of the humming heightened. Yasha Krashinsky chanted: "The young virgin and her lover cannot hear you. Louder, grownups. Do you believe in the orgasm?"

"YES! YES! YES!"

Blackness on stage. The throbbing of drums. Squeals from the bed. One of the boys from the second form choir took a step forward, raised his arms aloft, and shouted: "Hip! Hip!"

"HURRAH!" returned the choir.

"Hip! Hip!"

"HURRAH!"

A spotlight picked out the fairy godmother, Yasha Krashinsky, as he was lowered with a clunk onstage, and poured a flask of red paint into a bucket.

"EUGENIE IS A WOMAN NOW," the choir sang to the tune of "Pomp and Circumstance." "EUGENIE IS A WOMAN NOW."

Once the play was done, the children skipped off to the dining hall, where choc-ices, a conjurer, and a Popeye cartoon show awaited them. The adults remained in the auditorium, where they were served *vin rosé* and cheese squares. Dr. Booker, Yasha Krashinsky, and finally Miss Lilian Tanner mounted the stage to shouts of bravo, and the meeting was called to order. Mortimer was immensely encouraged to discover that he was not alone in being rather put off by the Beatrice Webb House production of *Philosophy in the Bedroom*. He was in a minority, a reactionary minority, but he was not alone. As the meeting progressed beyond niceties, Mortimer was heartened to see other parents come to the boil. The play was not the issue. It was, however, symptomatic of what some parents felt had come to ail the school.

Francis Wharton, the enlightened TV producer, began by saying he had always voted socialist; he deplored censorship in any shape or form, on either side of the so-called Iron Curtain; Victorian double standards were anathema to him; but all the same he thought it a bit much that just because his thirteen-year-old daughter was the only girl in the fifth form to stop at petting—

"Shame," somebody called out.

—*heavy petting*—

The objector shrugged, unimpressed.

—was no reason for her to come home with a scarlet T for Tease painted on her bosom.

This brought Lady Gillian Horsham, the Oxfam organizer, to her feet. Lady Horsham wished for more colored neighbors in Lowndes Square. She had, she said, found the play on the twee side here and there, but, on balance, most imaginative.

"Yes, yes," Dr. Booker interrupted bitingly, "but?"

Lady Horsham explained that her daughter, also in the fifth form, but not so cripplingly inhibited as the previous speaker's child—

"Hear! Hear!"

—had already been to the London Clinic to be fitted with a diaphragm.

"That's the stuff!"

"Good girl!"

But, she continued, but, wasn't it all rather premature? Not, mind you, that she was a prude. But, as they were all socialists, it seemed to her irresponsible that while their sisters in Africa and India were in such desperate need of diaphragms—

"Not germane," somebody hollered.

Yes, it was germane, Lady Horsham continued. But look at it another way, if you must. Parents were already overburdened with spiraling fees, the cost of summer and winter uniforms, hockey sticks, cricket bats, and whatnot. Was it fair that they should now also have to fork out for new diaphragms each term as, let's face it, these were growing girls? Couldn't the girls of the fifth form, without psychological damage—

"Your question, please?"

—without risk, practice *coitus interruptus?*

"Spoil-sport!"

"Reactionary!"

Dr. Booker beamed at his people, gesturing for silence. "If I may make a positive point, there is no reason why the tuck shop co-op, which already sells uniforms the girls have outgrown to younger students, could not also dispose of diaphragms that have begun to pinch, *so long as the transaction was not tarnished by the profit motive.*"

Next to speak up, Tony Latham, the outspoken Labour backbencher, explained that while it certainly did not trouble him personally that his boy masturbated daily, immediately following the Little Fibber Bra commercials on ITV, it was quite another matter when his parents, up from the country, were visiting. Latham's parents, it was necessary to understand, were the product of a more inhibited, censorious age: it distressed them, rather, to see their only grandchild playing with himself on the carpet, while they were taking tea.

"Your question, Mr. Latham?"

Could it be put to Yasha Krashinsky, overworked as he is, that he keep the boys for five minutes after Expressive Movement class, and have them masturbate before they come home?

"But I do," Yasha put in touchily. "I do, my dear chap."

Other, more uncompromisingly radical parents now demanded their say. There could be no backsliding at Beatrice Webb House. "You begin," a lady said, "by forbidding masturbation in certain rooms or outside prescribed hours and next thing you know the children, our children, are driven back into locked toilets to seek their pleasure, and still worse have developed a sense of guilt about auto-stimulation."

"Or," another mother said, looking directly at Lady Horsham, "you allow one greedy-guts in the fourth form to hold on to her precious little hymen and next thing out goes fucking in the afternoon."

Some compromises were grudgingly agreed to. Diaphragms, for instance, would be made optional until a girl reached the sixth form. On the other hand, Dr. Booker absolutely refused to stream girls into classes of those who did and those who didn't. It would be heartless, he said feelingly, to stamp a girl of twelve frigid for the rest of her life.

Some, if not all, late developers might grow up to surpass seemingly more avid girls in sexual appetite.

There followed a long and heated discussion on the play, its larger meanings within meanings, and then a debate on Beatrice Webb House finances, co-op shares, and needs and plans for the future. Dr. Booker received a standing ovation at the end.

LOVE

David Foster Wallace

Little Expressionless Animals

It's 1976. The sky is low and full of clouds. The grey clouds are bulbous and wrinkled and shiny. The sky looks cerebral. Under the sky is a field, in the wind. A pale highway runs beside the field. Lots of cars go by. One of the cars stops by the side of the highway. Two small children are brought out of the car by a young woman with a loose face. A man at the wheel of the car stares straight ahead. The children are silent and have very white skin. The woman carries a grocery bag full of something heavy. Her face hangs loose over the bag. She brings the bag and the white children to a wooden fencepost, by the field, by the highway. The children's hands, which are small, are placed on the wooden post. The woman tells the children to touch the post until the car returns. She gets in the car and the car leaves. There is a cow in the field near the fence. The children touch the post. The wind blows. Lots of cars go by. They stay that way all day.

It's 1970. A woman with red hair sits several rows from a movie theater's screen. A child in a dress sits beside her. A cartoon has begun. The child's eyes enter the cartoon. Behind the woman is darkness. A man sits behind the woman. He leans forward. His hands enter the woman's hair. He plays with the woman's hair, in the darkness. The cartoon's reflected light makes faces in the audience flicker: the woman's

Note: This is fiction and where real proper names are used here, they denote only objects of public perception and record, not persons alive or deceased.

eyes are bright with fear. She sits absolutely still. The man plays with her red hair. The child does not look over at the woman. The theater's cartoons, previews of coming attractions, and feature presentation last almost three hours.

Alex Trebek goes around the *JEOPARDY!* studio wearing a button that says PAT SAJAK LOOKS LIKE A BADGER. He and Sajak play racquetball every Thursday.

It's 1986. California's night sky hangs bright and silent as an empty palace. Little white sequins make slow lines on streets far away under Faye's warm apartment.

Faye Goddard and Julie Smith lie in Faye's bed. They take turns lying on each other. They have sex. Faye's cries ring out like money against her penthouse apartment's walls of glass.

Faye and Julie cool each other down with wet towels. They stand naked at a glass wall and look at Los Angeles. Little bits of Los Angeles wink on and off, as light gets in the way of other light.

Julie and Faye lie in bed, as lovers. They compliment each other's bodies. They complain against the brevity of the night. They examine and reexamine, with a sort of unhappy enthusiasm, the little ignorances that necessarily, Julie says, line the path to any real connection between persons. Faye says she had liked Julie long before she knew that Julie liked her.

They go together to the *O.E.D.* to examine the entry for the word "like."

They hold each other. Julie is very white, her hair prickly-short. The room's darkness is pocked with little bits of Los Angeles, at night, through glass. The dark drifts down around them and fits like a gardener's glove. It is incredibly romantic.

On 12 March 1988 it rains. Faye Goddard watches the freeway outside her mother's office window first darken and then shine with rain. Dee Goddard sits on the edge of her desk in stocking feet and looks out the window too. *JEOPARDY!*'s director stands with the show's public relations coordinator. The key grip and cue-card lady huddle over some notes. Alex Trebek sits alone near the door in a canvas director's chair, drinking a can of soda. The room is reflected in the dark window.

"We need to know what you told her so we can know whether she'll come," Dee says.

"What we have here Faye is a twenty-minutes-tops type of thing," says the director, looking at the watch on the underside of her wrist. "Then we're going to be in for at least another hour's set-up and studio time. Or we're short a slot, meaning satellite and mailing overruns."

"Not to mention a boy who's half-catatonic with terror and general neurosis right this very minute," Muffy deMott, the P.R. coordinator, says softly. "Last I saw he was fetal on the floor outside Makeup."

Faye closes her eyes.

"My husband is watching him," says the director.

"Thank you ever so much, Janet," Dee Goddard says to the director. She looks down at her clipboard. "All the others for the four slots are here?"

"Everybody who's signed up. Most we've ever had. Plus a rather scary retired WAC who's not even tentatively slotted til late April. Says she can't wait any longer to get at Julie."

"But no Julie," says Muffy deMott.

Dee squints at her clipboard. "So how many is that altogether, then?"

"Nine," Faye says softly. She feels at the sides of her hair.

"We got nine," says the director; "enough for at least the full four slots with a turn-around of two per slot." The rain on the aluminum roof of the Merv Griffin Enterprises building makes a sound in this room, like the frying of distant meat.

"And I'm sure they're primed," Faye says. She looks at the backs of her hands, in her lap. "What with Janet assuming the poor kid will bump her. Your new mystery data guru."

"Don't confuse the difference between me, on one hand, and what I'm told to do," says the director.

"He won't bump her," the key grip says, shaking her head. She's chewing gum, stimulating a little worm of muscle at her temple.

Alex Trebek belches quietly, his hand to his mouth. Everyone looks at him.

Dee says, "Alex, perhaps you'd put the new contestants in the booth for now, tell them we may or may not be experiencing a slight delay. Thank them for their patience."

Alex rises, straightens his tie. His soda can rings out against the metal bottom of a wastebasket.

"A good host and all that," Dee smiles kindly.

"Gotcha."

Alex leaves the door open. The sun breaks through the clouds outside. Palm trees drip and concrete glistens. Cars sheen by, their wipers on Sporadic. Janet Goddard, the director, looks down, pretends to study whatever she's holding. Faye knows that sudden sunlight makes her feel unattractive.

In the window Faye sees Dee's outline check its own watch with a tiny motion. "Questions all lined up?" the outline asks.

"Easily four slots' worth," says the key grip; "categories set, all monitors on the board check. Joan's nailing down the sequence now."

"That's my job," Faye says.

"Your job," the director hisses, "is to tell Mommy here where your spooky little girlfriend could possibly be."

"Alex'll need all the cards at the podium very soon," Dee tells the grip.

"Is what your job is today." Janet stares at Faye's back.

Faye Goddard gives her ex-stepfather's wife Janet Goddard the finger, in the window. "One of those for every animal question," she says.

The director rises, calls Faye a bitch who looks like a praying mantis, and leaves through the open door, closing it.

"Bitch," Faye says.

Dee complains with a weak smile that she seems simply to be surrounded by bitches. Muffy deMott laughs, takes a seat in Alex's chair. Dee eases off the desk. A splinter snags and snaps on a panty-ho. She assumes a sort of crouch next to her daughter, who is in the desk chair, at the window, her bare feet resting on the sill. Dee's knees crackle.

"If she's not coming," Dee says softly, "just tell me. Just so I can get a jump on fixing it with Merv. Baby."

It is true that Faye can see her mother's bright-faint image in the window. Here is her mother's middle-aged face, the immaculately colored and styled red hair, the sore-looking wrinkles that triangulate around her mouth and nose, trap and accumulate base and makeup as the face moves through the day. Dee's eyes are cigarette-red, supported by deep circles, pouches of dark blood. Dee is pretty except for the circles. This year Faye has been able to see the dark bags just starting to bulge out beneath her own eyes, which are her father's, dark brown and slightly thyroidic. Faye can smell Dee's breath. She cannot tell whether her mother has had anything to drink.

Faye Goddard is twenty-six; her mother is fifty.

Julie Smith is twenty.

Dee squeezes Faye's arm with a thin hand that's cold, from the office.

Faye rubs at her nose. "She's not going to come, she told me. You'll have to bag it."

The key grip leaps for a ringing phone.

"I lied," says Faye.

"My girl," Dee pats the arm she's squeezed.

"I sure didn't hear anything," says Muffy deMott.

"Good," the grip is saying. "Get her into Makeup." She looks over at Dee. "You want her in Makeup?"

"You did good," Dee tells Faye, indicating the closed door.

"I don't think Mr. Griffin is well," says the cue-card lady.

"He and the boy deserve each other. We can throw in the WAC. We can call *her* General Neurosis."

Dee uses a thin hand to bring Faye's face close to her own. She kisses her gently. Their lips fit perfectly, Faye thinks suddenly. She shivers, in the air conditioning.

"*JEOPARDY!* QUEEN DETHRONED AFTER THREE-YEAR REIGN"
—Headline, *Variety*, 13 March 1988

"Let's all be there," says the television.

"Where else would I be?" asks Dee Goddard, in her chair, in her office, at night, in 1987.

"We bring good things to life," says the television.

"So did I," says Dee. "I did that. Just once."

Dee sits in her office at Merv Griffin Enterprises every weeknight and kills a tinkling pitcher of wet weak martinis. Her office walls are covered with store-bought aphorisms. Humpty Dumpty was pushed. When the going gets tough the tough go shopping. Also autographed photos. Dee and Bob Barker, when she wrote for *Truth or Conse-quences*. Merv Griffin, giving her a plaque. Dee and Faye between Wink Martindale and Chuck Barris at a banquet.

Dee uses her remote matte-panel to switch from NBC to MTV, on cable. Consumptive-looking boys in makeup play guitars that look more like jets or weapons than guitars.

"Does your husband still look at you the way he used to?" asks the television.

"Safe to say not," Dee says drily, drinking.

"She drinks too much," Julie Smith says to Faye.

"It's for the pain," Faye says, watching.

Julie looks through the remote viewer in Faye's office. "For killing the pain, or feeding it?"

Faye smiles.

Julie shakes her head. "It's mean to watch her like this."

"You deserve a break today," says the television. "Milk likes you. The more you hear, the better we sound. Aren't you hungry for a flame-broiled Whopper?"

"No I am not hungry for a flame-broiled Whopper," says Dee, sitting up straight in her chair. "No I am not hungry for it." Her glass falls out of her hand.

"It was nice what she said about you, though." Julie is looking at the side of Faye's face. "About bringing one good thing to life."

Faye smiles as she watches the viewer. "Did you hear about what Alex did today? Sajak says he and Alex are now at war. Alex got in the engineer's booth and played with the Applause sign all through *The Wheel*'s third slot. The audience was like applauding when people lost turns and stuff. Sajak says he's going to get him."

"So you don't forget," says the television. "Look at all you get."

"Wow," says Dee. She sleeps in her chair.

Faye and Julie sit on thin towels, in 1987, at the edge of the surf, nude, on a nude beach, south of Los Angeles, just past dawn. The sun is behind them. The early Pacific is a lilac cube. The women's feet are washed and abandoned by a weak surf. The sky's color is kind of grotesque.

Julie has told Faye that she believes lovers go through three different stages in getting really to know one another. First they exchange anecdotes and inclinations. Then each tells the other what she believes. Then each observes the relation between what the other believes and what she in fact *does*.

Julie and Faye are exchanging anecdotes and inclinations for the twentieth straight month. Julie tells Faye that she, Julie, best likes: contemporary poetry, unkind women, words with univocal definitions, faces whose expressions change by the second, an obscure and limited-edition Canadian encyclopedia called *LaPlace's Guide to Total Data*, the gentle smell of powder that issues from the makeup compacts of older ladies, and the *O.E.D.*

"The encyclopedia turned out lucrative, I guess you'd have to say."

Julie sniffs air that smells yeasty. "It got to be just what the teachers tell you. The encyclopedia was my friend."

"As a child, you mean?" Faye touches Julie's arm.

"Men would just appear, one after the other. I felt so sorry for my mother. These blank, silent men, and she'd hook up with one after the other, and they'd move in. And not one single one could love my brother."

"Come here."

"Sometimes things would be ugly. I remember her leading a really ugly life. But she'd lock us in rooms when things got bad, to get us out of the way of it." Julie smiles to herself. "At first sometimes I remember she'd give me a straightedge and a pencil. To amuse myself. I could amuse myself with a straightedge for hours."

"I always liked straightedges, too."

"It makes worlds. I could make worlds out of lines. A sort of jagged magic. I'd spend all day. My brother watched."

There are no gulls on this beach at dawn. It's quiet. The tide is going out.

"But we had a set of these *LaPlace's Data Guides*. Her second husband sold them to salesmen who went door to door. I kept a few in every room she locked us in. They did, really and truly, become my friends. I got to be able to feel lines of consistency and inconsistency in them. I got to know them really well." Julie looks at Faye. "I won't apologize if that sounds stupid or dramatic."

"It doesn't sound stupid. It's no fun to be a kid with a damaged brother and a mother with an ugly life and to be lonely. Not to mention locked up."

"See, though, it was *him* they were locking up. I was there to watch him."

"An autistic brother cannot be decent company for somebody, no matter how much you loved him, is all I mean," Faye says, making an angle in the wet sand with her toe.

"Taking care of him took incredible amounts of time. He wasn't company, though; you're right. But I got so I wanted him with me. He got to be my job. I got so I associated him with my identity or something. My right to take up space. I wasn't even eight."

"I can't believe you don't hate her," Faye says.

"None of the men with her could stand to have him around. Even the ones who tried couldn't stand it after a while. He'd just stare and flap his arms. And they'd say sometimes when they looked in my mother's eyes they'd see him looking out." Julie shakes some sand out of her short hair. "Except he was bright. He was totally inside himself, but he was bright. He could stare at the same thing for hours and not be bored. And it turned out he could read. He read very slowly and never out loud. I don't know what the words seemed like to him." Julie looks at Faye. "I pretty much taught us both to read, with the encyclopedia. Early. The illustrations really helped."

"I can't believe you don't hate her."

Julie throws a pebble. "Except I don't, Faye."

"She abandoned you by a road because some guy told her to."

Julie looks at the divot where the pebble was. The divot melts. "She really loved this man who was with her." She shakes her head. "He made her leave *him*. I think she left me to look out for him. I'm thankful for that. If I'd been without him right then I don't think there would have been any me left."

"Babe."

"I'd have been in hospitals all this time, instead of him."

"What, like he'd have been instantly unautistic if you weren't there to watch him?"

Among things Julie Smith dislikes most are: greeting cards, adoptive parents who adopt without first looking inside themselves and evaluating their capacity to love, the smell of sulphur, John Updike, insects with antennae, and animals in general.

"What about kind women?"

"But insects are maybe the worst. Even if the insect stops moving, the antennae still wave around. The antennae never stop waving around. I can't stand that."

"I love you, Julie."

"I love you too, Faye."

"I couldn't believe I could ever love a woman like this."

Julie shakes her head at the Pacific. "Don't make me sad."

Faye watches a small antennaeless bug skate on legs thin as hairs across the glassy surface of a tidal pool. She clears her throat.

"OK," she says. "This is the only line on an American football field of which there is only one."

Julie laughs. "What is the fifty."

"This, the only month of the year without a national holiday, is named for the Roman emperor who. . . ."

"What is August."

The sun gets higher; the blood goes out of the blue water.

The women move down to stay in the waves' reach.

"The ocean looks like a big blue dog to me, sometimes," Faye says, looking. Julie puts an arm around Faye's bare shoulders.

" 'We loved her like a daughter,' said *JEOPARDY!* public relations coordinator Muffy deMott. 'We'll be sorry to see her go. Nobody's ever influenced a game show like Ms. Smith influenced *JEOPARDY!*' "

—Article, *Variety*, 13 March 1988

Weak waves hang, snap, slide. White fingers spill onto the beach and melt into the sand. Faye can see dark sand lighten beneath them as the water inside gets tugged back out with the retreating tide.

The beach settles and hisses as it pales. Faye is looking at the side of Julie Smith's face. Julie has the best skin Faye's ever seen on anyone anywhere. It's not just that it's so clear it's flawed, or that here in low sun off water it's the color of a good blush wine; it has the texture of something truly alive, an elastic softness, like a ripe sheath, a pod. It is vulnerable and has depth. It's stretched shiny and tight only over Julie's high curved cheekbones; the bones make her cheeks hollow, her eyes deep-set. The outlines of her face are like clefs, almost Slavic. Everything about her is sort of permeable: even the slim dark gap between her two front teeth seems a kind of slot, some recessive invitation. Julie has used the teeth and their gap to stimulate Faye with a gentle deftness Faye would not have believed.

Julie has looked up. "Why, though?"

Faye looks blankly, shakes her head.

"Poetry, you were talking about," Julie smiles, touching Faye's cheek.

Faye lights a cigarette in the wind. "I've just never liked it. It beats around bushes. Even when I like it it's nothing more than a really oblique way of saying the obvious, it seems like."

Julie grins. Her front teeth have a gap. "Olé," she says. "But consider how very, very few of us have the equipment to deal with the obvious."

Faye laughs. She wets a finger and makes a scoreboard-mark in the air. They both laugh. An anomalous wave breaks big in the surf. Faye's finger tastes like smoke and salt.

Pat Sajak and Alex Trebek and Bert Convy sit around, in slacks and loosened neckties, in the Merv Griffin Entertainment executive lounge, in the morning, watching a tape of last year's World Series. On the lounge's giant screen a batter flails at a low pitch.

"That was low," Trebek says.

Bert Convy, who is soaking his contact lenses, squints at the replay.

Trebek sits up straight. "Name the best low-ball hitter of all time."

"Joe Pepitone," Sajak says without hesitation.

Trebek looks incredulous. "Joe Pepitone?"

"Willie Stargell was a great low-ball hitter," says Convy. The other two men ignore him.

"Reggie Jackson was great," Sajak muses.

"Still is," Trebek says, feeling absently at the pulse in his own wrist.

A game show host has a fairly easy professional life. All five of a week's slots can be shot in one long day. Usually one hard week a month is spent on performance work at the studio. The rest of the host's time is his own. Bert Convy makes the rounds of car shows and mall openings and *Love Boat* episodes and is a millionaire several times over. Pat Sajak plays phenomenal racquetball, and gardens. No one is exactly sure what Alex Trebek does with his time.

There's a hit. Sajak throws a can of soda at the screen. Trebek and Convy laugh.

Sajak looks over at Bert Convy. "How's that tooth, Bert?"

Convy's hand strays to his mouth. "Still discolored," he says grimly.

Trebek looks up. "You've got a discolored tooth?"

Convy feels at a bared canine. "A temporary thing. Already clearing up." He narrows his eyes at Alex Trebek. "Just don't tell Merv about it."

Trebek looks around, as if to see who Convy is talking to. "Me? This guy right here? Do I look like that sort of person?"

"You look like a game show host."

Trebek smiles broadly. "Probably because of my perfect and beautiful and flawless teeth."

"Bastard," mutters Convy.

Sajak tells them to both pipe down.

The dynamics of the connection between Faye Goddard and Julie Smith tend, those around them find, to resist clear articulation. Faye is twenty-six and has worked Research on the *JEOPARDY!* staff for the past forty months. Julie is twenty, has foster parents in La Jolla, and has retained her *JEOPARDY!* championship through over seven hundred market-dominating slots.

Forty months ago game-show production mogul Merv Griffin decided to bring the popular game *JEOPARDY!* back from syndicated oblivion, to retire Art Flemming in favor of the waxily handsome, fairly distinguished, and surprisingly intelligent Alex Trebek, the former model who'd made his bones in the game show industry hosting the short-lived *High Rollers* for Barris/NBC. Dee Goddard, who'd written for shows as old as *Truth or Consequences* and *Name That Tune*, had worked Promotion/Distribution on *The Joker's Wild*, and had finally produced the commercially shaky but critically acclaimed *Gambit*, was hired by MGE as the new *JEOPARDY!*'s production executive. A period of disordered tension followed by Griffin's decision to name Janet Lerner Goddard—forty-eight, winner of two Clios, but also the wife of Dee's former husband—as director of the revised show; and in fact Dee is persuaded to stay only when Merv Griffin's executive assistant puts in a personal call to New York, where Faye Goddard, having left Bryn Mawr in 1982 with a degree in library science, is doing an editorial stint at *Puzzle* magazine. Merv's right-hand man offers to put Faye on staff at *JEOPARDY!* as Category-/Question-researcher.

Faye works for her mother.

Summer, 1985, Faye has been on the *JEOPARDY!* team maybe four months when a soft-spoken and weirdly pretty young woman comes in off the freeway with a dirty jean jacket, a backpack, and a *Times* classified ad detailing an MGE contestant search. The girl says she wants *JEOPARDY!*; she's been told she has a head for data. Faye interviews her and is mildly intrigued. The girl gets a solid but by no means spectacular score on a CBE general knowledge quiz, this particular version of which turns out to feature an important zoology section. Julie Smith barely makes it into an audition round.

In a taped audition round, flanked by a swarthy Shriner from Encino and a twig-thin Redding librarian with a towering blonde wig, Julie takes the game by a wide margin, but has trouble speaking clearly into her microphone, as well as difficulty with the quirky and distinctive *JEOPARDY!* inversion by which the host "asks" the answer and a contestant must supply the appropriate question. Faye gives Julie an audition score of three out of five. Usually only fives and fours are to be called back. But Alex Trebek, who spends at least part of his free time haunting audition rounds, likes the girl, even after she turns down his invitation for a cola at the MGE commissary; and Dee Goddard and Muffy deMott pick Julie out for special mention from among eighteen other prospectives on the audition tape; and no one on the staff of a program still in its stressful initial struggle to break back into a respectable market share has anything against hauntingly attractive young female contestants. Etc. Julie Smith is called back for insertion into the contestant rotation sometime in early September, 1985.

JEOPARDY! slots forty-six through fifty are shot on 17 September. Ms. Julie Smith of Los Angeles first appears in the forty-sixth slot. No one can quite remember who the reigning champion was at that time.

Palindromes, Musical Astrology, The Eighteenth Century, Famous Edwards, The Bible, Fashion History, States of Mind, Sports Without Balls.

Julie runs the board in both rounds. Every question. Never been done before, even under Flemming. The other two contestants, slack and grey, have to be helped off-stage. Julie wins $22,500, every buck on the board, in half an hour. She earns no more in this first match only because a flustered Alex Trebek declares the Final Jeopardy wagering round moot, Julie Smith having no incentive to bet any of her winnings against opponents' scores of $0 and $-400, respectively. A wide-eyed and grinning Trebek doffs a pretend cap to a blank-faced Julie as electric bongos rattle to the running of the closing credits.

Ten minutes later Faye Goddard locates a missing Julie Smith in a remote section of the contestants' dressing area. (Returning contestants are required to change clothes between each slot, conducing to the illusion that they've 'come back again tomorrow.') It's time for *JEOPARDY!* slot forty-seven. A crown to defend and all that. Julie sits staring at herself in a harsh makeup mirror framed with glowing bulbs, her face loose and expressionless. She has trouble reacting to stimuli. Faye has to get her a wet cloth and talk her through dressing and practically carry her upstairs to the set.

Faye is in the engineer's booth, trying to communicate to her mother her doubts about whether the strange new champion can make it through another televised round, when Janet Goddard calmly directs her attention to the monitor. Julie is eating slot forty-seven and spitting it out in little pieces. Lady Bird Johnson's real first name turns out to be Claudia. The Florida city that produces more Havana cigars than all of Cuba is revealed to be Tampa. Julie's finger abuses the buzzer. She is on Alex's answers with the appropriate questions before he can even end-punctuate his clues. The first-round board is taken. Janet cuts to commercial. Julie sits at her little desk, staring out at a hushed studio audience.

Faye and Dee watch Julie as the red lights light and Trebek's face falls into the worn creases of a professional smile. Something happens to Julie Smith when the red lights light. Just a something. The girl who gets a three-score and who stares with no expression is elsewhere. Every concavity in that person now seems to have come convex. The camera lingers on her. It seems to ogle. Often Julie appears on-screen while Trebek is still reading a clue. Her face, on-screen, gives off an odd lambent UHF flicker; her expression, distantly serene, radiates a sort of oneness with the board's data.

Trebek manipulates the knot of his tie. Faye knows he feels the something, the odd, focused flux in the game's flow. The studio audience gasps and whispers as Julie supplies the Latin name for the common radish.

"No one knows the Latin word for radish," Faye says to Dee. "That's one of those deadly ones I put in on purpose in every game."

The other two contestants' postures deteriorate. Someone in the audience loudly calls Julie's name.

Trebek, who has never before had an audience get away from him, gets more and more flustered. He uses forty expensive seconds relating a tired anecdote involving a Dodgers game he saw with Dan Rather. The audience hoots impatiently for the game to continue.

"Bad feeling, here," Faye whispers. Dee ignores her, bends to the monitor.

Janet signals Alex for a break. Moist and upstaged, Alex promises America that he'll be right back, that he's eager to inquire on-air about the tremendous Ms. Smith and the even more tremendous personal sacrifices she must have made to have absorbed so much data at such a tender age.

JEOPARDY! breaks for a Triscuit advertisement. Faye and Dee stare at the monitor in horror. The studio audience is transfixed as Julie Smith's face crumples like a Kleenex in a pocket. She begins silently to weep. Tears move down the clefs of her cheeks and drip into her mike, where for some reason they hiss faintly. Janet, in the booth, is at a loss. Faye is sent for a cold compress but can't make the set in time.

The lights light. America watches Julie Smith murder every question on the Double Jeopardy board, her face and vinyl jacket slickered with tears. Trebek, suddenly and leguminously cool, pretends he notices nothing, though he never asks (and never in hundreds of slots does he ask) Julie Smith any of the promised personal questions.

The game unfolds. Faye watches a new, third Julie respond to answer after answer. Julie's face dries, hardens. She is looking at Trebek with eyes narrowed to the width of paper-cuts.

In Final Jeopardy, her opponents again cashless, Julie coolly overrides Trebek's moot-motion and bets her entire twenty-two-five on the fact that the first part of Peking Man discovered was a fragment of jaw. She ends with $45,000. Alex pretends to genuflect. The audience applauds. There are bongos. And in a closing moment that Faye Goddard owns, captured in a color-still that hangs over her iron desk, Julie Smith, on television, calmly and deliberately gives Alex Trebek the finger.

A nation goes wild. The switchboards at MGE and NBC begin jangled two-day symphonies. Pat Sajak sends three dozen long-stemmed reds to Julie's dressing table. The market share for the last segment of *JEOPARDY!* slot forty-seven is a fifty—on a par with Super Bowls and assassinations. This is 24 September 1985.

"My favorite word," says Alex Trebek, "is *moist*. It is my favorite word, especially when used in combination with my second-favorite word, which is *loincloth*." He looks at the doctor. "I'm just associating. Is it OK if I just associate?"

Alex Trebek's psychiatrist says nothing.

"A dream," says Trebek. "I have this recurring dream where I'm standing outside the window of a restaurant, watching a chef flip pancakes. Except it turns out they're not pancakes—they're faces. I'm watching a guy in a chef's hat flip faces with a spatula."

The psychiatrist makes a church steeple with his fingers and contemplates the steeple.

"I think I'm just tired," says Trebek. "I think I'm just bone-weary. I'm tired of the taste of my teeth in my mouth. I'm tired of everything. My job sucks string. I want to go back to modelling. My cheek muscles ache, from having to smile all the time. All this hair spray is starting to attract midges. I can't go outdoors at night anymore."

"This girl you work with," says the doctor.

"And Convy reveals today that he's getting a discolored tooth," Trebek says. "Tell me *that* augurs well, why don't you."

"This contestant you talk about all the time."

"She lost," Trebek says, rubbing the bridge of his nose. "She lost yesterday. Don't you read papers, ever? She lost to her own brother, after Janet and Merv's exec snuck the damaged little bastard in with a rigged five-audition and a board just crawling with animal questions."

The psychiatrist hikes his eyebrows a little. They are black and angled, almost hinged.

"Queer story behind that," Trebek says, feeling at his wrist for his pulse. "I got it fourth-hand, but still. Parents abandoned the children, as kids. There was the girl and her brother. Lunt. Can you imagine a champion named Lunt? Lunt was autistic. He and the girl got abandoned out in the middle of nowhere somewhere. Grisly. She was adopted and the brother was institutionalized. In a state institution. This hopelessly autistic kid, who it turns out he's got the whole *LaPlace's Data Guide* memorized. They both like memorized this thing, as kids. And I thought *I* had a rotten childhood, boy." Trebek shakes his head. "But he got put away, and the girl got adopted by some people in La Jolla who were not, from the sense I get, princes among men. She ran away. She got on the show. She kicked ass. She was fair and a good sport and took no crapola. She used her prize money to pay these staggering bills for Lunt's autism. Moved him to a private hospital in the desert that was supposed to specialize in sort of . . . *yanking* people outside themselves. Into the world." Trebek takes a breath.

"And I guess they yanked him OK," he says, "at least to where he could talk. Though he still hides his head under his arm whenever things get tense. Plus he's weird-looking. And but he comes and bumps her off with this torrent of zoology data." Trebek plays with a cufflink. "And she's gone."

"You said in our last hour together that you thought you loved her."

"She's a lesbian," Trebek says flatly. "She's a lesbian through and through. I think she's one of those political lesbians. You know that kind? The kind with the anger? She looks at men like they're unsightly stains on the air. Plus she's involved with our ditz of a head researcher, which if you don't think the F.C.C. took a dim view of *that* little liaison you've got another. . . ."

"Free-associate," orders the doctor.

"Image association?"

"I have no problem with that."

"I invited the girl for coffee, or a Tab, years ago, right at the start, in the commissary, and she gave me this haunting but also hunting smile. Told me she could never imbibe caffeine with a man who wore a digital watch. The hell she says. She gave me the finger on national television. She's practically got a crewcut. Sometimes she looks like a vampire. Once, in the contestant booth, the contestant booth is where we keep all the contestants for all the slots, once one of the lights in the booth was flickering, they're fluorescent lights, and she said to get her the hell out of that booth, that flickering fluorescence made her feel like she was in a nightmare. And there *was* a sort of nightmary quality to that light, I remember. It was like there was a pulse in the neon. Like blood. Everybody in the booth got nervous." Trebek strokes his mustache. "Odd girl. Something odd about her. When she smiled things got bright, too focused. It took the fun out of it, somehow.

"I love her, I think," Trebek says. "She has a way with a piece of data. To see her with an answer. . . . Is there such a thing as an intellectual caress? I think of us together: seas part, stars shine spotlights. . . ."

"And this researcher she's involved with?"

"Nice enough girl. A thick, friendly girl. Not fantastically bright. A little emotional. Has this adoration-versus-loathing thing with her mother." Trebek ponders. "My opinion: Faye is like the sort of girl who's constantly surfing on her emotions. You know? Not really in control of where they take her, but not quite ever wiping out, yet, either. A psychic surfer. But scary-looking, for so young. These black, bulging, buggy eyes. Perfectly round and black. Impressive breasts, though."

"Mother-conflicts?"

"Faye's mother is one very tense production exec. Spends far too much time obsessing about not obsessing about the fact that our director is her ex-husband's wife."

"A woman?"

"Janet Lerner Goddard. Worst director I've ever worked with. Dee hates her. Janet likes to play with Dee's head; it's a head that admittedly tends to be full of gin. Janet likes to put little trinkety reminders of Dee's ex in Dee's mailbox at the office. Old bills, tieclips. She plays with Dee's mind. Dee's obsessing herself into stasis. She's barely able to even function at work anymore."

"Image associated with this person?"

"You know those ultra-modern rifles, where the mechanisms of aiming far outnumber those of firing? Dee's like that. God am I scared of being like that."

The psychiatrist thinks they have done all they can for today. He shows Trebek the door.

"I also really like the word *bedizen*," Trebek says.

In those first fall weeks of 1985, a public that grows with each Nielsen sweep discerns only two areas of even potential competitive vulnerability in Ms. Julie Smith of Los Angeles. One has to do with animals. Julie is simply unable to respond to clues about animals. In her fourth slot, categories in Double Jeopardy include Marsupials and Zoological Songs, and an eidetic pharmacist from Westwood pushes Julie all the way to Final Jeopardy before she crushes him with a bold bet on Eva Braun's shoe-size.

In her fifth slot (and what is, according to the game's publicized rules, to be her last—if a winner she'll be retired as a five-time champion), Julie goes up against a spectacularly fat Berkeley mailman who claims to be a cofounder of the California chapter of MENSA. The third contestant is a neurasthenic (but gorgeous—Alex keeps straightening his tie) Fullerton stenographer who wipes her lips compulsively on the sleeve of her blouse. The stenographer quickly accumulates a negative score, and becomes hysterically anxious during the second commercial break, convinced by the skunked, vengeful and whispering mailman that she will have to pay *JEOPARDY!* the nine hundred dollars she's down before they will let her leave the set. Faye dashes out during Off-Air; the woman cannot seem to be reassured. She keeps looking wildly at the exits as Faye runs off-stage and the red lights light.

A bell initiates Double Jeopardy. Julie, refusing to meet the audience's eye, begins pausing a bit before she responds to Alex. She leaves openings. Only the mailman capitalizes. Julie stays ahead of him. Faye watches the stenographer, who is clearly keeping it together only through enormous exercise of will. The mailman closes on Julie. Julie assumes a look of distaste and runs the board for several minutes, down to the very last answer, Ancient Rome for a Thousand: author of *De Oratore* who was executed by Octavian in 43 B.C. Julie's finger hovers over the buzzer; she looks to the stenographer. The mailman's eyes are closed in data-search. The stenographer's head snaps up. She looks wildly at Julie and buzzes in with Who is Tully. There is a silence. Trebek looks at his index card. He shakes his head. The stenographer goes to -$1900 and seems to suffer something resembling a petit mal seizure.

Faye watches Julie Smith buzz in now and whisper to her mike that, though Alex was doubtless looking for the question Who is Cicero, in point of fact one Marcus Tullius Cicero, 106–43 B.C., was known variously as both Cicero *and* Tully. Just as Augustus's less common appellation is Octavian, she points out, indicating the card in the host's hand. Trebek looks at the card. Faye flies to the Resource Room. The verdict takes only seconds. The stenographer gets the credit and the cash. Out of the emotional red, she hugs Julie on-camera. The mailman fingers his lapels. Julie smiles a really magnificent smile. Alex, genuinely moved, declaims briefly on the spirit of good clean competition he's proud to have witnessed here today. Final Jeopardy sees Julie effect the utter annihilation of the mailman, who is under the impression that the first literature in India was written by Kipling. The slot pulls down a sixty-five share. Hardly anyone notices Julie's and the stenographer's exchange of phone numbers as the bongos play. Faye gets a tongue-lashing from Muffy deMott on the inestimable importance of researching all possible questions to a given answer. The shot of Julie buzzing in with the correction makes the "Newsmakers" column of *Newsweek*.

That night Merv Griffin's executive assistant calls an emergency policy meeting of the whole staff. MGE's best minds take counsel. Alex is sent out for coffee and Cokes.

Griffin murmurs to his right-hand man. His man has a shiny face and a black toupee. The man nods, rises:

"Can't let her go. Too good. Too hot. She's become the whole show. Look at these figures." He brandishes figures.

"Rules, though," says the director. "Five slots, retire undefeated, come back for Champion's Tourney, in April. Annual event. Tradition. Art Flemming. Fairness to whole contestant pool. An ethics type of thing."

Griffin whispers into his shiny man's ear. Again the man rises.

"Balls in a trough," the shiny man says to the director. "The girl's magic. Figures do not lie. The Triscuit people have offered to double the price on thirty-second spots, long as she stays." He smiles with his mouth but not his eyes, Faye sees. "Shoot, Janet, we could just call this the Julia Smith Show and still make mints."

"Julie," says Faye.

"Right."

Griffin whispers up at his man.

"Need Merv mention we should all see substantial salary and benefit incentives at work here?" says the shiny man, flipping a watch-fob. "A chance here to be industry heroes. Heroines. MGE a Camelot. You, all of you, knights." Looks around. "Scratch that. Queens. Entertainment Amazons."

"You don't get rid of a sixty share without a fight," says Dee, who's seated next to Faye, sipping at what looks to Faye a little too much like water. The director whispers something in Muffy deMott's ear.

There's a silence. Griffin rises to stand with his man. "I've seen the tapes, and I'm impressed as I've never been impressed before. She's like some lens, a filter for that great unorganized force that some in the industry have spent their whole lives trying to locate and focus." This is Merv Griffin saying this. Eyes around the table are lowered. "What is that force?" Merv asks quietly. Looks around. He and his man sit back down.

Alex Trebek returns in shirtsleeves, with refreshments.

Griffin whispers and the shiny man rises. "Merv posits that this force, ladies, gentleman, is the capacity of facts to transcend their internal factual limitations and become, in and of themselves, meaning, feeling. This girl not only kicks facts in the ass. This girl informs trivia with import. She makes it human, something with the power to emote, evoke, cathart. She gives the game the simultaneous transparency and mystery all of us in the industry have groped for, for decades. A sort of union of contestantorial head, heart, gut, buzzer-finger. She is, or can become, the game show incarnate. She is mystery."

"What, like a cult thing?" Alex Trebek asks, opening a can of soda at arm's length.

Merv Griffin gives Trebek a cold stare.

Merv's man's face gleams. "See that window?" he says. "That's where the rules go. Out the window." Feels at his nose. "Does your conscientious entertainer retain—and here I say think about all the implications of 'retention,' here—" looking at Janet, "I mean does he cling blindly to rules for their own sake when the very goal and purpose and *idea* of those rules walks right in off the street and into the hearts of every Triscuit consumer in the free world?"

"Safe to say not," Dee says drily.

The man: "So here's the scoop. She stays till she's bumped. We cannot and will not give her any help on-air. Off-air she gets anything within what Merv defines as reason. We get her to play a little ball, go easy on the board when strategy allows, give the other players a bit of a shot. We tell her we want to play ball. DeMott here is one of our carrots."

Muffy deMott wipes her mouth on a commissary napkin. "I'm a carrot?"

"If the girl plays ball, then you, deMott, you start in on helping the kid shelter her income. Tell her we'll give her shelter through MGE. Take her from the seventy bracket to something more like a twenty. Capisce? She's got to play ball, with a carrot like that."

"She sends all her money to a hospital her brother's in," Faye says softly, next to her mother.

"Hospital?" Merv Griffin asks. "What hospital?"

Faye looks at Griffin. "All she told me was her brother was in Arizona in a hospital because he has trouble living in the world."

"The world?" Griffin asks. He looks at his man.

Griffin's man touches his wig carefully, looks at Muffy. "Get on that, deMott," he says. "This hospitalized-brother thing. If it's good P.R., see that it's P.'d. Take the girl aside. Fill her in. Tell her about the rules and the window. Tell her she's here as long as she can hang." A significant pause. "Tell her Merv might want to do lunch, at some point."

Muffy looks at Faye. "All right."

Merv Griffin glances at his watch. Everyone is instantly up. Papers are shuffled.

"Dee," Merv says from his chair, absently fingering a canine tooth. "You and your daughter stay for a moment, please."

Idaho, Coins, Truffaut, Patron Saints, Historical Cocktails, Animals, Winter Sports, 1879, The French Revolution, Botanical Songs, The Talmud, 'Nuts to You.'

One contestant, slot two-eighty-seven, 4 December 1986, is a bespectacled teenage boy with a smear of acne and a shallow chest in a faded Mozart T-shirt; he claims on-air to have revised the Western solar calendar into complete isomorphism with the atomic clocks at the U.S. Bureau of Time Measurement in Washington. He eyes Julie beadily. Any and all of his winnings, he says, will go toward realizing his father's fantasy. His father's fantasy turns out to be a spa, in the back yard of the family's Orange County home, with an elephant on permanent duty on each side of the spa, spouting.

"God am I tired," Alex intones to Faye over a soda and handkerchief at the third commercial break. Past Alex, Faye sees Julie, at her little desk, looking out at the studio audience. People in the audience vie for her attention.

The boy's hopes for elephants are dashed in Final Jeopardy. He claims shrilly that the Islamic week specifies no particular sabbath.

"Friday," Julie whispers.

Alex cues bongos, asks the audience to consider the fact that Californians never ("*never*," he emphasizes) seem to face east.

"Just the facts on the brother who can't live in the world, is all I want," Merv Griffin says, pushing at his cuticles with a paperclip. Dee makes soft sounds of assent.

"The kid's autistic," Faye says. "I can't really see why you'd want data on an autistic person."

Merv continues to address himself to Dee. "What's wrong with him exactly. Are there different degrees of autisticness. Can he talk. What's his prognosis. Would he excite pathos. Does he look too much like the girl. And et cetera."

"We want total data on Smith's brother," iterates the gleaming face of Merv's man.

"Why?"

Dee looks at the empty glass in her hand.

"The potential point," Merv murmurs, "is can the brother do with a datum what she can do with a datum." He switches the paper-clip to his left hand. "Does the fact that he has as Faye here put it trouble being in the world, together with what have to be impressive genetics, by association," he breathes, "add up to mystery-status? Game-show-incarnation?" He works a cuticle. "Can he do what she can do?"

"Imagine the possibilities," says the shiny man. "We're looking way down the road on this thing. A climax type of deal, right? Antigone-thing. If she's going to get bumped sometime, we obviously want a bumper with the same kind of draw. The brother's expensive hospitalization at the sister's selfless expense is already great P.R."

"Is he mystery, I want to know," says Merv.

"He's *autistic*," Faye says, staring bug-eyed. "Meaning they're like trying to teach him just to talk coherently. How not to go into convulsions whenever somebody looks at him. You're thinking about maybe trying to put him on the air?"

Merv's man stands at the dark office window. "Imagine sustaining the mystery beyond the individual girl herself, is what Merv means. The mystery of total data, that mystery made a sort of antic, ontic self-perpetuation. We're talking fact sustaining feeling, right through the change that inevitably attends all feeling, Faye."

"We're thinking perpetuation, is what we're thinking," says Merv. "Every thumb over at Triscuit is up, on this one."

Dee's posture keeps deteriorating as they stand there.

"Remember, ladies," Merv's man says from the window. "You're

either part of the solution, or you're part of the precipitate." He guf-
faws. Griffin slaps his knee.

Nine months later Faye is back in the office of Griffin's man. The man
has different hair. He says:

"I say two words to you, Faye. I say F.C.C., and I say separate
apartments. We do not I repeat do not need even a whiff of scandal.
We do not need a *Sixty-Four-Thousand-Dollar-Question*-type-scandal
kind of deal. Am I right? So I say to you F.C.C., and separate pads.

"You do good research, Faye. We treasure you here. I've personally heard Merv use the word 'treasure' in connection with your
name."

"I don't give her any answers," Faye says. The man nods vigorously.

Faye looks at the man. "She doesn't need them."

"All I'm saying to you is let's make our dirty linen a private matter," says the shiny man. "Treasure or no. So I say keep your lovely
glass apartment, that I hear so much about."

That first year, ratings slip a bit, as they always do. They level out at
incredible. MGE stock splits three times in nine months. Alex buys a
car so expensive he's afraid to drive it. He takes the bus to work. Dee
and the cue-card lady acquire property in the canyons. Faye explores
IRA's with the help of Muffy deMott. Julie moves to a bungalow in
Burbank, continues to live on fruit and seeds, and sends everything
after her minimal, post-shelter taxes to the Palo Verde Psychiatric
Hospital in Tucson. She turns down a *People* cover. Faye explains to
the *People* people that Julie is basically a private person.

It quickly gets to the point where Julie can't go out anywhere without some sort of disguise. Faye helps her select a mustache and explains to her about not too much glue.

Extrapolation from LAX Airport flight-plan data yields a scenario in
which Merv Griffin's shiny man, *JEOPARDY!* director Janet Goddard,
and a Mr. Mel Goddard, who works subsidiary rights at Screen
Gems, board the shiny man's new Piper Cub on the afternoon of 17
September 1987, fly non-stop to Tucson, Arizona, and enjoy a three-

day stay among flying ants and black spiders and unimaginable traffic and several sizzling, carbonated summer monsoons.

"Dethroning Ms. Smith after 700-plus victories last night was one 'Mr. Lunt' of Arizona, a young man whose habit of hiding his head under his arm at crucial moments detracted not at all from the virtuosity with which he worked a buzzer and board that had, for years, been the champion's own."

                                    —Article, *Variety*, 13 March 1988

WHAT NEXT FOR SMITH?

                                    —Headline, *Variety*, 14 March 1988

Los Angeles at noon today in 1987 is really hot. A mailman in mailman-shorts and wool knee-socks sits eating his lunch in the black guts of an open mailbox. Air shimmers over the concrete like fuel. Sunglasses ride every face in sight.

Faye and Julie are walking around West L.A. Faye wears a bathing suit and rubber thongs. Her thongs squeak and slap.

"You did *what*?" Faye says. "You did what for a living before you saw our ad?"

"A psychology professor at UCLA was doing tests on the output of human saliva in response to different stimuli. I was a professional subject."

"You were a professional salivator?"

"It paid me, Faye. I was seventeen. I'd had to hitch from La Jolla. I had no money, no place to stay. I ate seeds."

"What, he'd like ring bells or wave chocolate at you and see if you'd drool?"

Julie laughs, gap-toothed, in mustache and sunglasses, her short spiked hair hidden under a safari hat. "Not exactly."

"So what, then?"

Faye's thongs squeak and slap.

"Your shoes sound like sex," Julie says.

"I'm going to marry that girl," Alex Trebek tells his psychiatrist, who's manipulating a plastic disc, trying to get a BB in the mouth of a clown.

•

Dee Goddard and Muffy deMott sit in Dee's office, overlooking the freeway, today, at noon, in the air conditioning, with a pitcher of martinis, watching the *All New Newlywed Game*.

"It's the *All New Newlywed Game*!" says the television.

"Weak show," says Dee. "All they do on this show is humiliate newlyweds. A series of low gags."

"I like this show," Muffy says, reaching for the pitcher that's refrigerating in front of the air conditioner. "It's people's own fault if they're going to let Bob Eubanks embarrass them on national daytime just for a dryer or a skimobile."

"Cheap show. Mel got a look at their books once. A really . . . a really chintzy operation." Dee jiggles a lemon twist.

Bob Eubanks's head fills the screen.

"Jesus will you look at the size of the head on that guy."

"Youthful-looking, though," Muffy muses. "He never seems to age. I wonder how he does it."

"He's traded his soul for his face. He worships bright knives. He makes sacrifices to dark masters on behalf of his face."

Muffy looks at Dee.

"Actually he's got a wife who's about twelve, is how he does it," Dee says.

"Nice girl, though. She brought brandied peaches to the NBC potluck last year? Was that the one?"

"A special grand prize chosen just for you," says the television.

Dee leans forward. "Will you just look at that head. His forehead simply *dominates* the whole shot. They must need a special lens."

"I sort of like him. He's sort of funny."

"I'm just glad he's on the inside of the set, and I'm on the outside, and I can turn him off whenever I want."

Muffy holds her drink up to the window's light and looks at it. "And of course you never lie there awake considering the possibility that it's the other way around."

Dee crosses her ankles under her chair. "Dear child, we are in this business precisely to make sure that that is *not* a possibility."

They both laugh.

"You hear stories, though," Muffy says. "About these lonely or somehow disturbed people who've had only the TV all their lives, their parents or whoever started them right off by plunking them down in front of the set, and as they get older the TV comes to be their whole emotional world, it's all they have, and it becomes in a way their whole way of defining themselves as existents, with a distinct identity, that they're outside the set, and everything else is inside the set." She sips.

"Stay right where you are," says the television.

"And then you hear about how every once in a while one of them gets on TV somehow. By accident," says Muffy.

"There's a shot of them in the crowd at a ball game, or they're interviewed on the street about a referendum or something, and they go home and plunk down in front of the set, and all of a sudden they look and they're *inside* of the set." Muffy pushes her glasses up. "And sometimes you hear about how it drives them mad, sometimes."

"There ought to be special insurance for that or something," Dee says, tinkling the ice in the pitcher.

"Maybe that's an idea."

Dee looks around. "You seen the vermouth around here anyplace?"

Julie and Faye walk past a stucco house the color of Pepto-Bismol. A VW bus is backing out of the driveway. It sings the high sad song of the Volkswagen-in-Reverse. Faye wipes her forehead with her arm. She feels moist and sticky. She feels like something hot in a plastic bag.

"But so I don't know what to tell them," she says.

"Being involved with a woman doesn't automatically make you a lesbian," says Julie.

"It doesn't make me Marie Osmond, either, though."

Julie laughs. "A cross you'll have to bear." She takes Faye's hand.

Julie and Faye take walks a lot. Faye drives over to Julie's place and helps her into her disguise. Julie wears a mustache and hat, Bermuda shorts, a Hawaiian shirt, and a Nikon.

"Except what if I am a lesbian?" Faye asks. She looks at a small child methodically punching a mild-faced father in the back of the thigh while the father buys Häagen-Dazs from a vendor. "I mean,

what if I am a lesbian, and people ask me why I'm a lesbian?" Faye re-
leases Julie's hand to pinch sweat off her upper lip. "What do I say if
they ask me why?"

"You anticipate a whole lot of people questioning you about your
sexuality?" Julie asks. "Or are there particular people you're worried
about?"

Faye doesn't say anything.

Julie looks at her. "I can't believe you really even care."

"Maybe I do. What questions I care about aren't really your business. You're why I might be a lesbian; I'm just asking you to tell me
what I can say."

Julie shrugs. "Say whatever you want." She has to keep straightening her mustache, from the heat. "Say lesbianism is simply one kind
of response to Otherness. Say the whole point of love is to try to get
your fingers through the holes in the lover's mask. To get some kind
of hold on the mask, and who cares how you do it."

"I don't want to hear mask-theories, Julie," Faye says. "I want to
hear what I should really tell people."

"Why don't you just tell me which people you're so worried
about."

Faye doesn't say anything. A very large man walks by, his face red
as steak, his cowboy boots new, a huge tin star pinned to the lapel of
his business suit.

Julie starts to smile.

"Don't smile," says Faye.

They walk in silence. The sky is clear and spread way out. It shines
in its own sun, glassy as aftershave.

Julie smiles to herself under her hat. The smile's cold. "You know
what's fun, if you want to have fun," she says, "is to make up explanations. Give people reasons, if they want reasons. Anything you want.
Make reasons up. It'll surprise you: the more improbable the reason,
the more satisfied people will be."

"That's fun?"

"I guarantee you it's more fun than twirling with worry over the
whole thing."

"Julie?" Faye says suddenly. "What about if you lose, sometime?

Do we stay together? Or does our being together depend on the show?"

A woman in terri-cloth shorts is giving Julie a pretty brazen look. Julie looks away, in her hat.

"Here's one," she says. "If people ask, you can give them this one. You fall totally in love with a man who tells you he's totally in love with you, too. He's older. He's important, in terms of business. You give him all of yourself. He goes to France, on important business. He won't let you come. You wait for days and don't hear from him. You call him, in France, and a woman's voice says a French hello on the phone, and you hear the man's electric shaver in the background. A couple days later you get a hasty French postcard he'd mailed on his first day there. It says: 'Scenery is here. Wish you were beautiful.' You reel into lesbianism, from the pain."

Faye looks at the curved side of Julie's face, deep skin of a perfect white grape.

Julie says, "Tell them this man who broke your heart quickly assumed in your memory the aspects of a political cartoon: enormous head, tiny body, all unflattering features exaggerated."

"I can tell them all men everywhere look that way to me now."

"Give them this one. You meet a boy, at your East Coast college. A popular and beautiful and above all—and this is what attracts you most—a terribly *serious* boy. A boy who goes to the library and gets out a copy of *Gray's Anatomy*, researches the precise location and neurology of the female clitoris—simply, you're convinced, to allow him to give you pleasure. He plays your clitoris, your whole body, like a fine instrument. You fall for the boy completely. The intensity of your love creates what you call an organic situation: a body can't walk without legs; legs can't walk without a body. He becomes your body."

"But pretty soon he gets tired of my body."

"No, he gets obsessed with your body. He establishes control over your own perception of your body. He makes you diet, or gain weight. He makes you exercise. He supervises your haircuts, your makeovers. Your body can't make a move without him. You get muscular, from the exercise. Your clothes get tighter and tighter. He traces your changing outline on huge sheets of butcher's paper and hangs them in his room, in a sort of evolutionary progression. Your friends think you're nuts. You lose all your friends. You become more and more dependent on the boy and the boy's circle of friends. He's introduced you to all his friends. He made you turn slowly around while he introduced you, so they could see you from every conceivable angle."

"I'm miserable with him."

"No, you're deliriously happy. But there's not much you, at the precise moment you're feeling most complete."

"He makes me lift weights while he watches. He has barbells in his room."

"Your love," says Julie, "springs from your incompleteness, but also reduces you to another's prosthetic attachment, calcified by the Medusa's gaze of his need."

"I told you I didn't want abstractions about this stuff," Faye says impatiently.

Julie walks, silent, with a distant frown of concentration. Faye sees a big butterfly beat incongruously at the smoke-black window of a long limousine. The limousine is at a red light. Now the butterfly falls away from the window. It drifts aimlessly to the pavement and lies there, bright.

"He makes you lift weights, in his room, at night, while he sits and watches," Julie says quietly. "Pretty soon you're lifting weights nude while he watches from his chair. You begin to be uneasy. For the first time you taste something like degradation in your mouth. The degradation tastes like tea. Night after night it goes. Your mouth tastes like tea when he eventually starts going outside, to the window, to the outside of the window at night, to watch you lift weights nude."

"I feel horrible when he watches through the window."

"Plus, eventually, his friends. It turns out he starts inviting all his friends over at night to watch through the window with him as you lift weights. You're able to make out the outlines of all the faces of his friends. You can see them through your own reflection in the black glass. The faces are rigid with fascination. The faces remind you of the carved faces of pumpkins. As you look you see a tongue come out of one of the faces and touch the window. You can't tell whether it's the beautiful serious boy's tongue or not."

"I reel into lesbianism, from the pain."

"You still love him, though."

Faye's thongs slap. She wipes her forehead and considers.

"I'm in love with a guy and we get engaged and I start going over to his parents' house with him for dinner. One night I'm setting the table and I hear his father in the living room laughingly tell the guy that the penalty for bigamy is two wives. And the guy laughs too."

An electronics shop pulls alongside them. Faye sees a commercial behind the big window, reflected in the fly's-eye prism of about thirty televisions. Alan Alda holds up a product between his thumb and forefinger. Smiles at it.

"You're in love with a man," says Julie, "who insists that he can love you only when you're standing in the *exact center* of whatever room you're in."

Pat Sajak plants lettuce in the garden of his Bel Air home. Bert Convy boards his Lear, bound for an Indianapolis Motor Home Expo.

"A dream," says Alex Trebek. "I have this dream where I'm sitting in a chair on a little hill in the middle of a field. The field, which is verdant and clovered, is covered with rabbits. They sit and look at me. There must be a million rabbits in that field. They all sit and look at me. Some of them lower their little heads to eat clover. But their eyes never leave me. They sit there and look at me, a million bunny rabbits, and I look back."

"Uncle," says Patricia ("Patty-Jo") Lunt, stout and loose-faced behind the cash register of the Holiday Inn Restaurant at the Holiday Inn, Interstate 70, Ashtabula, Ohio:

"Uncle uncle uncle uncle."

"No," says Faye. "I meet a man in the park. We're both walking. The man's got a tiny puppy, the cutest and most beautiful puppy I've ever seen. The puppy's on a little leash. When I meet the man the puppy wags its tail so hard that it loses its little balance. The man lets me play with the puppy. I scratch its stomach and it licks my hand. The man has a picnic lunch in a hamper. We spend all day in the park, with the puppy. By sundown I'm totally in love with the man with the puppy. I stay the night with him. I let him inside me. I'm in love. I start to see the man and the puppy whenever I close my eyes.

"I have a date with the man in the park a couple days later. This time he's got a different puppy with him, another beautiful puppy that wags its tail and licks my hand, and the man's hand. The man says it's the first puppy's brother."

"Oh, Faye."

"And but this goes on, me meeting the man in the park, him having a different puppy every time, and the man is so warm and loving and attentive toward both me and the puppies that soon I'm totally in love. I'm totally in love on the morning I follow the man to work, just to surprise him, like with a juice and danish, and I follow him and discover that he's actually a professional cosmetics researcher who performs product experiments on puppies, and kills them, and dissects them, and that before he experiments on each puppy he takes it to the park, and walks it, and uses the beautiful puppies to attract women, who he seduces."

"You're so crushed and revolted you become a lesbian," says Julie.

Pat Sajak comes close to skunking Alex Trebek in three straight games of racquetball. In the health club's locker room Trebek feels at his pulse and complains of fatigue, distraction, difficulty sleeping, odors of camphor and lime. Sajak recommends gardening, for relaxation.

"I need you to articulate for me the dynamics of this connection between Faye Goddard and Julie Smith," Merv Griffin tells his shiny executive. His man stands at the office window, watching cars move by on the Hollywood Freeway, in the sun. The cars glitter.

"You and your mother happen to go to the movies," Faye says. She and Julie stand wiping themselves in the shade of a leather shop's awning. "You're a child. The movie is *Son of Flubber*, from Disney. It lasts pretty much the whole afternoon." She gathers her hair at the back of her neck and lifts it. "After the movie's over and you and your mother are outside, on the sidewalk, in the light, your mother breaks down. She has to be restrained by the ticket man, she's so hysterical. She tears at her beautiful fiery hair that you've always admired and wished you could have had, too. She's totally hysterical. It turns out a man in the theater behind you was playing with your mother's hair all through the movie. He was touching her hair in a sexual way. She was horrified and repulsed, but didn't make a sound, the whole time, I guess for fear that you, the child, would discover that a strange man in the dark was touching your mother in a sexual way. She breaks down on the sidewalk. Her husband has to come. She spends a year on antidepressants. Then she drinks.

"Years later her husband, your stepfather, leaves her for a woman. The woman has the same background, career interests, and general sort of appearance as your mother. Your mother gets obsessed with whatever slight differences between herself and the woman caused your stepfather to leave her for the woman. She drinks. The woman plays off her emotions, like the insecure and basically shitty human being she is, by dressing as much like your mother as possible, putting little mementos of your stepfather in your mother's mailbox, coloring her hair the same shade of red as your mother does. You all work together in the same tiny but terrifyingly powerful industry. It's a tiny and sordid and claustrophobic little community, where no one can get away from the nests they've fouled. You reel into confusion. You meet this very unique and funny and sad and one-of-a-kind person."

"The rain in Spain," director Janet Goddard says to a huge adolescent boy so plump and pale and vacant that he looks like a snowman. "I need you to say 'The rain in Spain' without having your head under your arm.

"Pretend it's a game," she says.

It's true that, the evening before Julie Smith's brother will beat Julie Smith on her seven-hundred-and-forty-first *JEOPARDY!* slot, Faye tells Julie about what Merv Griffin's man and the director have done. The two women stand clothed at Faye's glass wall and watch distant mountains become Hershey kisses in an expanding system of shadow.

Faye tells Julie that it's because the folks over at MGE have such respect and admiration for Julie that they want to exercise careful control over the choice of who replaces her. That to MGE Julie is the mystery of the game show incarnate, and that the staff is understandably willing to do pretty much anything at all in the hopes of hanging onto that power of mystery and incarnation through the inevitability of change, loss. Then she says that that was all just the shiny executive's bullshit, what she just said.

Julie asks Faye why Faye has not told her before now what is going to happen.

Faye asks Julie why Julie sends all her sheltered winnings to her brother's doctors, but will not talk to her brother.

Julie isn't the one who cries.

Julie asks whether there will be animal questions tomorrow.

There will be lots and lots of animal questions tomorrow. The director has personally compiled tomorrow's categories and answers. Faye's been temporarily assigned to help the key grip try to repair a defectively lit *E* in the set's giant *JEOPARDY!* logo.

Faye asks why Julie likes to make up pretend reasons for being a lesbian. She thinks Julie is really a lesbian because she hates animals, somehow. Faye says she does not understand this. She cries, at the glass wall.

Julie lays her hands flat on the clean glass.

Faye asks Julie whether Julie's brother can beat her.

Julie says that there is no way her brother can beat her, and that deep down in the silence of himself her brother knows it. Julie says that she will always know every fact her brother knows, plus one.

Through the window of the Makeup Room, Faye can see a grey paste of clouds moving back over the sun. There are tiny flecks of rain on the little window.

Faye tells the makeup lady she'll take over. Julie's in the makeup chair, in a spring blouse and faded cotton skirt, and sandals. Her legs are crossed, her hair spiked with mousse. Her eyes, calm and bright and not at all bored, are fixed on a point just below her own chin in the lit mirror. A very small kind smile for Faye.

"You're late I love you," Faye whispers.

She applies base.

"Here's one," Julie says.

Faye blends the border of the base into the soft hollows under Julie's jaw.

"Here's one," says Julie. "To hold in reserve. For when you're really on the spot. They'll eat it up."

"You're not going to get bumped. He's too terrified to stand up, even. I had to step over him on the way down here."

Julie shakes her head. "Tell them you were eight. Your brother was silent and five. Tell them your mother's face hung tired from her head, that first men and then she herself made her ugly. That her face just hung there with love for a blank silent man who left you touching wood forever by the side of the road. Tell them how you were left, by your mother, by a field of dry grass. Tell them the field and the sky and the highway were the color of old laundry. Tell them you touched a post all day, your hand and a broken baby's bright-white hand, waiting for what had always come back, every single time, before."

Faye applies powder.

"Tell them there was a cow." Julie swallows. "It was in the field, near where you held the fence. Tell them the cow stood there all day, chewing at something it had swallowed long ago, and looking at you. Tell them how the cow's face had no expression on it. How it stood there all day, looking at you with a big face that had no expression." Julie breathes. "How it almost made you need to scream. The wind sounds like screams. Stand there touching wood all day with a baby who is silence embodied. Who can, you know, stand there forever, waiting for the only car it knows, and not once have to understand. A cow watches you, standing, the same way it watches anything."

A towelette takes the excess powder. Julie blots her lipstick on the blotter Faye holds out.

"Tell them that, even now, you cannot stand animals, because animals' faces have no expression. Not even the possibility of it. Tell them to look, really to look, into the face of an animal, sometime."

Faye runs a gentle pick through Julie's moist spiked hair.

Julie looks at Faye in a mirror bordered with bulbs. "Then tell them to look closely at men's faces. Tell them to stand perfectly still, for a time, and to look into the face of a man. A man's face has nothing on it. Look closely. Tell them to look. And not at what the faces do—men's faces never stop moving—they're like antennae. But all the faces do is move through different configurations of blankness."

Faye looks for Julie's eyes in the mirror.

Julie says, "Tell them there are no holes for your fingers in the masks of men. Tell them how could you ever even hope to love what you can't grab onto."

Julie turns her makeup chair and looks up at Faye. "That's when I love you, if I love you," she whispers, running a finger down her white powdered cheek, reaching to trace a line of white onto Faye's own face. "Is when your face moves into expression. Try to look out from yourself, different, all the time. Tell people that you know your face is least pretty at rest."

She keeps her fingers on Faye's face. Faye closes her eyes against tears. When she opens them they're shiny. Julie is still looking at her. She's smiling a wonderful smile. Way past twenty. She takes Faye's hands.

"You asked me once how poems informed me," she says. Almost a whisper—her microphone-voice. "And you asked whether we, us, depended on the game, to even be. Baby?" lifting Faye's face with one finger under the chin. "Remember? Remember the ocean? Our dawn ocean, that we loved? We loved it because it was like us, Faye. That ocean was *obvious*. We were looking at something obvious, the whole time." She pinches a nipple, too softly for Faye even to feel. "Oceans are only oceans when they move," Julie whispers. "Waves are what keep oceans from just being very big puddles. They're just waves. And every wave in the ocean is finally going to meet what it moves toward, and break. The whole thing we looked at, the whole time you asked, was *obvious*. It was obvious and a poem because it was us. See things like that, Faye. Your own face, changing expression. A wave, breaking on a rock, giving up its shape in a gesture that *expresses* that shape. See?"

It wasn't at the beach that Faye had asked about the future. It was in Los Angeles. And what about the anomalous wave that came out of nowhere and broke on itself.

Julie is looking at Faye. "See?"

Faye's eyes are open. They get wide. "You don't like my face at rest?"

The set is powder blue. The giant *JEOPARDY!* logo is lowered. Its *E* flickers a palsied fluorescent flicker. Julie turns her head from the sick letter. Alex has a flower in his lapel. The three contestants' names appear in projected cursive before their desks. Alex blows Julie the traditional kiss. Pat Sajak gives Faye a thumbs-up from stage-opposite. He gestures. Faye looks around the curtain and sees a banana peel on the pale blue carpet, carefully placed in the tape-marked path Alex takes every day from his podium to the board full of answers. Dee Goddard and Muffy deMott and Merv Griffin's shiny man hunch over monitors in the director's booth. Janet Goddard arranges a shot of a pale round boy who dwarfs his little desk. The third contestant, in the middle, feels at his makeup a little. Faye smells powder. She watches Sajak rub his hands together. The red lights light. Alex raises his arms in greeting. There is no digital watch on his wrist.

The director, in her booth, with her headset, says something to camera two.

Julie and the audience look at each other.

Issue 106, 1988

Rosanna Warren

⌖

Cyprian

Phi Beta Kappa poem
Yale, 2000

We could almost see her
where she is said to have risen in the bay
from sea foam and the blood of Ouranos' sliced genitals
tossed out of heaven.

We could almost see
how she must have sat on the long arm of rock
that half-cradled the bay
and how she combed seaweed out of her hair with a
    scallop shell

before rising in a commotion of salt light and doves'
    wings
to terrorize the earth.
Squinting, we could almost believe
as we could almost see

inland, at Paphos, her temple erect
on the ruined marble floor paving
amid column chunks and cringing olive trees
as the horizon trembled in haze

and distant mountains tried in their softness to resemble
    the female body.
But it was inside
that shed of a museum across the spongy road, our eyes
maladjusted to dimness, that

she appeared, I think: if it is in
the sudden intake of breath, the fluttered pulse, that she
    registers:
not as one would have imagined,
no body at all, no womanliness,

not Greek, not even human as a god should be,
but that uncarven black vertical basalt thrust
into consciousness
throbbed in the room alone,

just a rock
on a pedestal, a terrible rock
they worshipped epochs ago before the Greeks
gave her a name a story a shape:

a rock in the dark for which we had paid in Cypriot coins,
for which we still clutched
small paper tickets, damp in our palms.
When I have fought you

most, when we have lain
separate in the puzzle of sheets
until dawn flushed away clots of night, and still we lay apart:
she was there, she presided—

she of many names;
sea-goddess; foam-goddess; heavenly
Ourania crowned, braceleted and beringed in gold and
    gems;
Melaina the black one; Skotia, dark one;

Killer of Men; Gravedigger; She-Upon-the-Graves;
Pasiphaessa the Far-Shining;
and she to whom we sacrificed,
Aphrodite Apostrophia,

She Who Turns Herself Away.

Ted Hughes

from The Art of Poetry LXXI

Could you talk a bit more about Sylvia?

Sylvia and I met because she was curious about my group of friends
at university and I was curious about her. I was working in London
but I used to go back up to Cambridge at weekends. Half a dozen or
so of us made a poetic gang. Our main cooperative activity was drinking in the Anchor and our main common interest, apart from fellow
feeling and mutual attraction, was Irish, Scottish and Welsh traditional songs—folk songs and broadsheet ballads. We sang a lot.
Recorded folk song was rare in those days. Our poetic interests were
more mutually understood than talked about. But we did print a
broadsheet of literary comment. In one issue, one of our group, our
Welshman, Dan Huws, demolished a poem that Sylvia had published, "Caryatids." He later became a close friend of hers, wrote a
beautiful elegy when she died. That attack attracted her attention.
Also, she had met one of our group, Lucas Myers, an American, who
was an especially close friend of mine. Luke was very dark and
skinny. He could be incredibly wild. Just what you hoped for from
Tennessee. His poems were startling to us—Hart Crane, Wallace
Stevens vocabulary, zany. He interested Sylvia. In her journals she
records the occasional dream in which Luke appears unmistakably.
When we published a magazine full of our own poems, the only issue

of *St. Botolph's,* and launched it at a big dance party, Sylvia came to see what the rest of us looked like. Up to that point I'd never set eyes on her. I'd heard plenty about her from an English girlfriend who shared supervisions with her. There she suddenly was, raving Luke's verses at Luke and my verses at me. Once I got to know her and read her poems, I saw straight off that she was a genius of some kind. Quite suddenly we were completely committed to each other and to each other's writing. The year before, I had started writing again, after the years of the devastation of university. I'd just written what have become some of my more anthologized pieces—"The Thought Fox," the Jaguar poems, "Wind." I see now that when we met, my writing, like hers, left its old path and started to circle and search. To me, of course, she was not only herself: she was America and American literature in person. I don't know what I was to her. Apart from the more monumental classics—Tolstoy, Dostoyevsky and so on—my background reading was utterly different from hers. But our minds soon became two parts of one operation. We dreamed a lot of shared or complementary dreams. Our telepathy was intrusive.

Jeanette Winterson

✸

from The Art of Fiction CL

WINTERSON

I think men can really get in the way when you are trying to sort your
life out and get on with it. Because they just take up so much space.
I'm not under any illusions that I could have been where I am now in
literary terms if I had been heterosexual. I really believe I would not
be. Because—and this has gotten me into huge trouble before, but I
suppose I may as well get into trouble again—I can't find a model, a
female literary model who did the work she wanted to do and led an
ordinary heterosexual life and had children. Where is she? I am no
fool, I mean I looked at this at the time. I don't think people's sexuality is really that fixed. I had various boys at various times as well as
various girls. There was a part of me which instinctively knew that in
order to be able to pursue my life, which was going to be hard enough
anyway, I would be much better off, either on my own or with a
woman. A man would simply get in the way, and I would have to use
up energy that I didn't have to spare. I do believe that to be the case.
It probably wouldn't be the case now, say, if I changed to a new partner, because I am sufficiently established. But I do think that when
you are young and you are trying to make your way in the world it really is an issue.

Women who have tried to push it aside as an issue say things like,
"Well, I won't even think about having children until I am forty."
Then of course they are completely knackered. It seems to me diffi-
cult enough to have children when you have got all the energy of be-

ing twenty-one. Some of the people I know who had children quite late, pushing forty, are exhausted. They are not the women they were twenty years ago, and they can't manage not to have any sleep for two years. So by pushing the problem into the future you don't solve it. The issue of how women are going to live with men and bring up children and perhaps do the work they want to do has in no way been honestly addressed. It is simply being made into a problem that you have when you're forty instead of when you are twenty.

Issue 145, 1997

Edmund White

※

from The Art of Fiction CV

INTERVIEWER
Do you see the range, the reactions, the emotions in heterosexual love and homosexual love to be approximately similar?

WHITE
I think there is an equally complex gamut but the two experiences are not coincident. You can't say all the things a straight woman goes through in her courtship, marriage and divorce are the same as a gay man experiences in meeting another man, living with him and breaking up with him. They're not the same emotions, they don't occur in the same sequence nor do they have the same social repercussions. But there are enough similarities to permit us to speak to each other. When a straight man breaks up with his girlfriend, the break is often decisive; it's very hard for them to move from the end of their affair into an ongoing friendship. However, I would say that many—if not most—gay men who break up continue to be best friends. And they may even continue to live together. They may enter into a period of rivalry during which each of them tries to meet somebody new first. When that phase wears out their friendship gets mellower and better. This is something which seems unthinkable to most straight people; they don't know how we can do it, but there is a great deal of comradeship that lies under the discourse of homosexual love. There is a discourse of gay friendship, and then there is a kind of male-male

friendship which straight men know about, and there is also a discourse of love which straight men have with women. The idea that those discourses can come together in one relationship, and that when the love ends the friendship can continue, astonishes many outsiders.

Kenneth Koch

✠

To the French Language

I needed to find you and, once having found you, to keep you
You who could make me a physical Larousse
Of everyday living, you who would present me to Gilberte
And Anna and Sonia, you by whom I could be a surrealist
And a dadaist and almost a fake of Racine and of Molière.
   I was hiding
The heavenly dolor you planted in my heart:
That I would never completely have you.
I wanted to take you with me on long vacations
Always giving you so many kisses, *ma française*—
Across rocky mountains, valleys, and lakes
And I wanted it to be as if
Nous faisions ce voyage pour l'éternité
Et non pas uniquement pour la brève durée d'une année
   boursière en France.
Those days, and that idea, are gone.
A little hotel on the rue de Fleurus
Was bursting with you.
And one April morning, when I woke up, I had you
Stuck to the tip of my tongue like a Christmas sticker
I walked out into the street, it was Fleurus
And said hello which came out Bonjour Madame
I walked to the crèmerie four doors away and sat down.
I was lifted up by you. I knew I couldn't be anything to you

But an aspiring lover. Sans ego. It was the best relationship
Of relationships sans ego, that I've ever had.
I know you love flattery and are so good at it that one can
    hardly believe
What you are saying when it is expressed in you.
But I have loved you. That's no flattering statement
But the truth. And still love you, though now I'm not in love
    with you.
The woman who first said this to me nearly broke my heart,
But I don't think I'm breaking yours, because it's a *coeur*
In the first place and, for another thing, it beats under *le soleil*
On a *jeudi* or *vendredi matin* and besides you're not listening
    to me
At least not as you did on the days
I sat around in Aix-en-Provence's cafés waiting for you
To spark a conversation—about nothing in particular. I was on
    stage
At all times, and you were the script and the audience
Even when the theater had no people in it, you were there.

Issue 158, 2001

Charlie Smith

✠

Los Dos Rancheros

I can see the moon like a bullet sunk in the clouds' body
and it seems to me the worst has happened. *Nothing
really touches me*, she says and begins to express her contempt.
For a second everything gets transparent. At my café breakfast
I sweat profusely and attempt to comfort
the silverware and consider the water, shimmering
in its glass like precious liquid crystal, to be my friend.
When the government cars go by, the big black-curtained cars
containing dignitaries who will one day beg God to save them,
I get up from my seat and stand on the steps looking at the sky
trying not to think of how what was between us—whatever
you call this corybantic—turned up dead this morning,
but it's no use. Now everything refers to it,
including the young man in the Los Dos Rancheros Restaurant
dreaming Puebla or Ixatlan back into shape, who
jabs one song after another into the jukebox
hard like a man jabbing his finger into the face
of someone impossible to convince, who halfway to his table
stops to throw his head back and laugh with a sound
like a grease fire smothering. I walk out into the
charmlessly evicerating street
where everyone is doing the best he can to keep the dark
from climbing over his back. *Take your hands off me*,
a woman screams and throws herself out of a car.

Even in sleep, the blind newsseller says, *my life is confusion.*
From here I plot a course that will take me into an area
in which I am respected and praised for leaving her.
You can look me up, she's saying into the phone when I return,
I am the one who fell in love with the captain and lost her honor
not to mention her fortune and now I live
this retired life, that is to say this life of routine
and memory in which I am without hope. Says this
and gives me a look. Quietly the strangulations begin again.
What do you think? That nothing can kill the world, not even
     love?

Issue 155, 2000

Michael Cunningham

❖

Pearls

Angela. I love what you left behind. Your scent, melony, yet sharp and immaculate as yogurt. Your diaphragm, placed, according to the promise, in my nightstand drawer as a token of fidelity. And the pearls. The pearls.

I started finding them this evening, just after I got home. I'd expected a note. To be frank, I'd expected a present. You are such a maniac for gifts. So I entered the apartment in double-edged anticipation: dreading your absence, but looking forward to the surprise you'd planned, the particular way you had chosen to make yourself remembered. Of course, I found nothing at first, and read it symbolically. Leaving no remembrances was a way of saying "forget me." I felt greedy, and abashed. If I didn't deserve nothing you wouldn't have left me nothing, right? Stomach creeping, I went to the bathroom to wash my face. And there found the first pearl.

It lay in the basin, such a match for the white enamel that it looked like part of the fixture. I picked it up and rolled it between my thumb and finger. Recognized it: one of the cheap imitations from that ultra-long strand of yours, those impossibly opalescent pellets that reached, unwound, from your neck to your ankles. The sight of it made my blood jump. It carried such an image of you, naked, belted at the waist by pearls which bit lightly into your flesh, emphasizing its softness and its resiliency. I saw no design behind a pearl in my sink, was sufficiently slow-witted to chalk it up to accident. How does one accidently lose a single pearl? I scrubbed my face and went to the kitchen to mix a drink.

The second pearl lay in the tumbler I took from the cabinet. Immediately, I saw your mind, ticking off my particular traffic patterns, and your hand, paint-smeared and raw, holding a pearl. My apartment was full of pearls. Beautiful. You are simple and wily as a geisha.

As of bedtime, I have found seventy-three of them. At the outset, I giddily ransacked the place like a kid hunting Easter eggs, snatching up all the easy ones. The ones in kitchen cabinets, all the prizes in wine goblets and coffee cups, and then those from the living room: a pearl in each plant, pearls in the bookshelves, a row of pearls balanced on the molding over the door. Did you intend that as an arch for me to pass unwittingly under? Of course you did. You intend everything you do.

I uncovered a few of the trickier ones, those behind paintings and the ones in light fixtures. Then I decided to knock off. I wanted to draw out the process, to know for another day or two that vestiges of you remained hidden around me. The pearls I did find I heaped in the center of the bed: gleaming there, they looked unutterably womanish. Are pearls considered emblems for the clitoris? I ask, because I suspect you'd know.

I went to bed early, in your honor, and, washing myself, found three more: one in the bathtub faucet (very clever), one in the soap dish, and the one that dolloped out of my toothpaste tube (how did you ever get it in there?). This brings the total to seventy-six. I must be nearing the end of the strand.

My thoughts and devotions to you, sweetheart. Is it as damp and wind-bitten as we imagined? Don't worry. Six months isn't long. Meanwhile, I wait for you, here in my pearl-studded flat.

Morning. I found a couple more right off, in the pockets of my robe. And the one in the coffee. That one presented itself in an especially lovely way. I had scooped the grounds into a filter, and poured water through, then found a pearl, lodged among the scum like a treasure left by the tide on a dirty beach. Beautiful. I'm afraid the one in the toaster was not quite such a good idea. It melted, and released some kind of smoke I suspect may have been poisonous. At first I thought it was the toast burning, and extracted it, to find another

pearl, heated to a teardrop, clinging to the crust. You can't imagine
the smell. Do you suppose they use gasoline somehow in the production of synthetic pearls?

At any rate, I am stirred and delighted. Have you found the present
I hid in your suitcase? It was the warmest I could find. The clerk said
nothing is as warm as Irish wool. And to me, even the name "Yale"
sounds cold. If I were assigned that word in charades, I would opt for
"sounds like," and pantomime a gale: neck-snapping wind, snow
blown into needles. I hated giving you up to that, that cold breathy
"Y" and that long "a," slippery as ice. Remember that it will be good
for your painting. I considered calling you this morning, but decided
to honor our pact. Instead I sat in the apartment, in the robe you gave
me, and practiced sending scenic telepagrams: you and I together,
several years from now, on an island off Canada, a luminous place imbued with that pale gray northern light, sharing kitchen and bedroom
but maintaining separate studios, where our paintings prosper like
crops. Did you receive the image? After trying to send that, I must admit that I worked on a few private ones, things not suited to cross-
country transmissions. Those hips and thighs of yours. That dense
overripe jungle. Your bigness makes me swell. I love you more for not
being pretty, for the gaunt determination of your face and the grim-
ness of your mouth. You are cold and luscious as the moon. Your images engaged me so that I was late getting off for class, ran out of the
apartment unshaven, with a pearl in each jacket pocket and, as I realized halfway down the stairs, too late to do anything about it, a pearl
in my left shoe.

My classes shlumped along as usual. How is it possible for undergraduates to produce such rigid, unfeeling lines? They are not unfeeling people. But I couldn't draw anything so dead if I tried. There's
not a half-dozen like you per generation. Your sense of volume, those
delicate, bottomless grays. And you always know just where to cut.
My favorite is still the velvety little mouse-colored painting, slashed
across by that seething comet's tail of green. I'd associated limpid
green with hospital corridors. Only you could have given that color
teeth.

Don't lose your bite, angel. Watch out for the enemy: the infernal

Five Sections. Five sections of drawing and mixed media, undergraduate division, can dull you like a diet of oily, overcooked food. If you hadn't turned up at this cow college, and made my life opalescent, I might be dead by now of indigestion.

I dodged a departmental meeting (subject: the strain exerted on our limited budget by the indiscriminate use of paper clips, when staples are just as effective at a fraction of the cost), to get home and find some more pearls. In an hour, I located two dozen of them. If painting doesn't pan out for you, you might be able to work this new-found ability into some sort of career. Who but a genius would have thought to conceal pearls not only among the slats of a venetian blind but in the pleats of the curtain as well, to produce a double, clattering rain. They fell, as designed, at my feet.

It is now late evening, and you haven't broken the pact. To be quite frank, I'm a little surprised. I'd expected a phone call by now, promise or none. You are so blamed strong.

By the way, those pearls in the shower drain have clogged things up terribly. I can't see them, of course, but know they must be there, because when I try to use the shower, my rinse water starts burbling back up at me, faithful as bad luck. The drain worked fine before you left. I've got the plumber coming a week from Tuesday, which is the soonest he could make it. Plumbers do a better business these days than most painters.

I tried to do some painting after dinner, but it wouldn't go. Paint still keeps flattening out on me. My colors turn murky, and I can't put the depth into them. That's never happened to you, has it? The world in your eyes has always been a place deep and frightening as your own body, eminently worth painting. That's why Yale wanted you so. To be honest, I envy you your newness. To be excruciatingly honest, I envy you your talent. I am proud to have been a teacher of yours. Note the phraseology there: I could just as easily have called myself "your teacher," as in *proud to have been your teacher,* and ridden the implication that I was the only one. But I know there have been others.

Including the pearl in the toaster, I have now got a hundred and twenty-three of them. Laid end to end, they would surely reach, in a dotted line, from my bed clear out the front door. Eleven o'clock my time, and you still haven't called. I've thought of doing it myself, but damn if I'm going to break the pact. I'm the one who's got to stay in Oklahoma, teaching the unteachable. I'm the one whose pinks aspire to be clean and shocking as a gash cut in the side of a living salmon, and whose pinks keep turning out unsurprising as mud. Damn if I'll break the pact and call.

Morning number two. I slept in my clothes, with the pearls beside me. A dragon guarding treasure. I am just a bit of a dragon, aren't I? I'm not pretty, and I'm not quite what anyone would call young anymore. I'm no twenty-two-year-old whiz cutting the wind in New Haven, that's for sure. I make breakfast, and find no pearls. That sounds like a line you might use in describing a stymied housewife, doesn't it? The opening to her story: *Betty Barnett cooked oyster stew for her family every Friday for thirty years, and never once found a pearl.* I brew empty coffee, toast bread.

All my pockets have been picked clean. I shouldn't have been so greedy. I should never have agreed to your lunatic pact. Why no phone calls? Why an embargo on letters? You do insist on your tests, don't you? Been in school too long, you want my honest opinion. Geography may not buckle under testing, but people do. So in four months' time, we find out whether our ideas of one another are strong enough to withstand separation. The knowledge could be useful someday, I'll admit. Meantime, I have your diaphragm, one hundred and twenty-three of your pearls, and my own five daily sections. Today I teach them savagely, yelling at every student for failing to draw the way you do. You're going to put this penny-ante college on the map, you know that? *No*, shrieks the art instructor. *Fill the page just this way. Run the figure slightly off, dip her foot into space the paper doesn't occupy.* Do it the Angela Feinstein way. Thus the Angela Feinstein school is established, unbeknownst to its students.

Tonight, I call. You are not in. I know it is unbalanced, but can't stop the thought: you are with somebody. A high-blown Yale painter, whose pinks are legend. Who invites you up to his place, to look at his pinks. Diaphragms are available in any drugstore. Aren't they? I know so little of women's mechanics. I don't even know where you get a diaphragm.

I eat a bowl of Grapenuts for dinner, and you know what comes tumbling out of the box along with the cereal. Do you know what I do with it? Swallow it like a pill. I go directly to my studio and begin painting, as though I expected the drug to have an effect. Nothing unusual moves my hand.

A day, a night, another day. I have called you three more times, and am afraid of calling again. Afraid of finding you in, and afraid of not finding you. More pearls have surfaced: inside the receiver of my telephone, tucked into underwear I haven't worn in years, taped to the bottom of the drawer in which I keep my journal. Is there anything of mine you haven't touched? I put the pearls together on the floor, arranged them in an oval, and they made a necklace of impossible length. You went out and bought extras, didn't you? Now I've got them all. I have checked the apartment as thoroughly as I would if I were a spy, searching for hidden microphones. Found things I didn't know I had. But now you are contained. I have made a full assessment of your leavings. I can fit them into a shoebox, and close the lid.

Next morning. You've got me. You are too smart for me. I didn't check the ice, did I? It couldn't have been better choreographed. As you probably know, from the radio signals these pearls undoubtedly send off the moment they reach unfettered air, I had a girl up last night. A girl, not a woman. One of my undergraduates, who is a damn sight more graceful than her name. Her name is Tilly. I had Tilly over because I thought I might expire from loneliness and rancor, and because you haven't answered your phone four times running. The seduction I staged was a masterpiece of self-mortification: Vivaldi on the stereo, hearty slaps of cologne on my jowls and belly. And worse than that: my whole life's story, with appropriate deletions. I must have talked at Tilly for an hour and a half. I was out of control. Tilly, bless her, listened all the way, sipping delicately at the club soda she'd requested in lieu of the wine offered by her exploiter. Said exploiter drank generously of said wine. And kept talking.

I had reached a particularly awkward stretch in my story, the complicated part about my own unwillingness to quit Oklahoma, and the

subsequent battle it engendered between you and me (your accusations of chicken-heartedness, my own fear of failure, my fear of success); Tilly concentrated, or feigned concentration, with her glass of
soda held close to her face, the rim pressed thoughtfully against her
cheek. I told her I was terrified of every painter more acclaimed than
I. I demonstrated what that sort of terror can do with the painting
process: made an explosion in the air with my hands. And at that moment, the ice in Tilly's soda had melted sufficiently to release you-
know-what. It floated lazily to the top, among limpid bubbles. Tilly
didn't notice it. She thought I was staring, benumbed, at her face.

Do I need to tell you that I felt like something from Edgar Allan
Poe? That you might just as well have risen up out of that glass yourself, hovered like smoke over Tilly's left shoulder, and mouthed the
words "chicken-heart" at me while Tilly sipped blissfully away? Of
course, I sent her home. Of course, she was offended. And, for the
next three months, I will face her wounded eyes and tensed shoulders
every Monday, Wednesday and Friday at one-thirty.

What do you want from me? I can't abide the fact that, somewhere
in my apartment, there've got to be more pearls. You must have
dropped them into the heating vents, the bowels of the air conditioner; I'm sure they watch me as I sleep. I didn't know when we took
each other on that something like this could happen. That I could feel
so invaded, and so isolated. Today I wrap your diaphragm in brown
paper and mail it to you. Your basic symbolic communication. Men
and women deprived of telephone contact must, in this late age, resort to pictograms. I wait ardently for your reply.

And it arrives, eight days later. Ten feet of jeweler's string. Just what
do you mean by this? When I saw the envelope, I thought you had
broken down and written. But no, all it contained was the string. I'm
supposed to make a strand for you, eh? Keep your pearls in order?
Guard the flame? Thanks, but no. I acknowledge the fact that I have
flunked the test. I do not have your kind of stuff. I require comforts.
Letters, phone calls. Quiet mornings and evenings, earned dinners,
manageable work. I reserve the right to find solace in a new pair of
shoes.

And I am a fearful man. I dread the blinding light, the hunger for pain I see in you people who disappear into paint. So spare me, please. When you come back, if you come back, do not telephone, and do not stop by. I've been thinking of switching apartments, to stop myself from sleepwalking, groping for pearls.

Classes, meetings, classes again. My days measure themselves off into orderly segments. I am benign in the classroom, paternal; the students think I am responding to their growth, and like me better. Even Tilly has relaxed her shoulders inching downward, as I frown over her work, absorbed in it, suggesting hair-line changes. She really is quite lovely, cool and golden limbed. And she has begun settling into the notion that I, as an artist, am entitled to fits of rudeness, lapses of taste. In a week or more, I can probably ask her out again.

I have been wearing the jeweler's string wound around my ankle, so tightly that it interferes with the flow of blood. My left foot is usually numb and tingling. If I'm beginning to walk with a limp, though, no one around here has mentioned it yet.

A.R. Ammons

Everything

*found on the back of an envelope from
Helen Vendler, 1.28.1981*

You came one day and
as usual in such matters
significance filled everything—
your eyes, the things you
knew, the way you turned,
leaned, stood, or sat,
this way or that: when
you left, the area around here rose
a tilted tide, and everything that
offers desolation drained away.

BETRAYAL

Lucille Clifton

⌖

Lorena

Woman cuts off husband's penis,
later throws it from car window.
                    —News Report

it lay in my palm soft and trembled
as a new bird and i thought about
authority and how it always insisted
on itself, how it was master
of the man, how it measured him, never
was ignored or denied, and how it promised
there would be sweetness if it was obeyed
just like the saints do, like the angels
and i opened the window and held out my
uncupped hand; i swear to god
i thought it could fly

Marilyn Hacker

⬭

Migraine Sonnets

It's a long way from the bedroom to the kitchen
when all the thought in back of thought is loss.
How wide the dark rooms are you walk across
with a glass of water and a migraine
tablet. Sweat of hard dreams: unforgiven
silences, missed opportunities.
The night progresses like chronic disease,
symptom by symptom, sentences without pardon.
It's only half past two, you realize.
Five windows are still lit across the street.
You wonder: Did you tell as many lies
as it now appears were told to you?
And if you told them, how did you not know
they were lies? Did you know, and then forget?

There were lies. Did you know, and then forget
if there was a lie in the peach orchard? There was the lie
a saxophone riffed on a storm-thick summer sky,
there was the lie on a postcard, there was the lie thought
and suggested, there was the lie stretched taut
across the Atlantic, there was the lie that lay
slack in the blue lap of a September day,
there was the lie in bed, there was the lie that caught
its breath when it came, there was the lie that wept.

There was the lie that read the newspaper.
There was the lie that fell asleep, its clear
face relaxing back to the face of a child.
There was the lie you held while you both slept.
A lie hung framed in the doorway, growing wild.
The face framed in the doorframe is a wild
card now, mouth could eat silence, mouth could speak
the indigestible. Eyes, oh tourmaline, a crack
in the glass, break the glass. Down a green-tiled
corridor double doors open. Who was wheeled
through, hallucinating on a gurney, weak
with relief as muscle and nerve flickered awake,
while a dreamed face framed in a doorframe opened and smiled?
Precisely no one's home. No dog will come
to lay his jowls across bent knees and drool
and smile the black-gummed smile he shares with wolves.
The empty doorframe frames an empty room
whose dim fluorescence is perpetual.
The double doors close back upon themselves.

The double doors close back upon themselves
The watcher from the woods rejoins the pack:
shadows on branches' steely lacework, black
on black, dark ornaments, dark wooden shelves.
Fever-wolves, guardians a lamp dissolves
in pitiless logic, as an insomniac
waits to hear the long night crack and break
into contaminated rusty halves.
This is the ninety-seventh (count) night watch in
the underbrush of hours closed on you since
a lie split open like a rotten fruit.
A metal band around your head begins
to tighten; pain shutters your eyes like too much light.
It's a long way from the bedroom to the kitchen.

Issue 159, 2001

Jonathan Franzen

✠

Chez Lambert

St. Jude: that prosperous midwestern gerontocracy, that patron saint of the really desperate. The big houses and big cars here filled up only on holidays. Rain pasted yellow leaves to cars parked in blue handicapped slots. Teflon knees and Teflon hips were flexed on fairways; roomy walking shoes went squoosh, squoosh on the ramps and people movers at the airport.

Nobody laughed at seniors in St. Jude. Whole economies, whole cohorts, depended on them. The installers and maintainers of home-security systems, the wielders of feather dusters and complicated vacuums, the actuaries and fund managers, the brokers and tellers, the sellers of sphagnum moss and nonfat cottage cheese and nonalcoholic beer and aluminum stools for sitting in the bathtub with, the suppliers of chicken cordon bleu or veal Parmesan and salad and dessert and a fluorescently lit function room at $13.95 a head for Saturday night bridge clubs, the sitters who knitted while their charges dozed under afghans, the muscular LPNs who changed diapers in the night, the social workers who recommended the hiring of the LPNs, the statisticians who collated data on prostate cancer and memory and aging, the orthopedists and cardiologists and oncologists and their nurses, receptionists and bloodworkers, the pharmacists and opticians, the performers of routine maintenance on American-made sedans with inconceivably low odometer readings, the blue-uniformed carriers of Colonial-handicrafts catalogues and pension checks, the bookers of tours and cruises and flights to Florida, the projectionists of PG-rated movies at theaters with Twilight Specials, the drafters of wills and the executors of irrevocable trusts, the radio patrolmen who responded to home-security false alarms and wrote tickets for violating minimum-speed postings on expressways, the elected state officials who resisted property-tax reassessment, the elected national representatives who kept the entitlements flowing, the clergy who moved down corridors saying prayers at bedsides, the embalmers and cremators, the organists and florists, the drivers of ambulances and hearses, the engravers of marble markers and the operators of gas-powered Weed Whackers who swept across the cemeteries in their pollen masks and protective goggles and who once in a long while suffered third-degree burns over half their bodies when the motors strapped to their backs caught fire.

The madness of an invading system of high pressure. You could feel it: something terrible was going to happen. The sun low in the sky, a mockery, a lust gone cold. Gust after gust of entropy. Trees restless, temperatures falling, the whole northern religion of things coming to an end. No children in the yards here. Shadows and light on yellowing zoysia. The old swamp white oak rained acorns on a house with no mortgage. Storm windows shuddered in the empty bedrooms. Distantly the drone and hiccup of the clothes dryer, the moan of a leaf blower, the smell of apples, the smell of the gasoline with which Alfred Lambert had cleaned the brush from his morning painting of the porch furniture. At three o'clock the fear set in. He'd awakened in the great blue chair in which he'd been sleeping since lunch. He'd had his nap and there would be no local news until five o'clock. Two empty hours were a sinus in which infections raged. He struggled to his feet and stood by the Ping-Pong table, listening in vain for Enid.

Ringing throughout the house was an alarm bell that no one but Alfred and Enid could hear directly. It was the alarm bell of anxiety. We should imagine it as one of those big cast-iron dishes with an electric clapper that sends schoolchildren into the street in fire drills, and we should imagine it ringing for so many hours that the Lamberts no longer heard the message of "bell ringing" but, as with any sound that continues for so long that you have the leisure to learn its component sounds (as with any word you stare at until it resolves itself into a string of dead letters), instead heard a clapper going ping-ping-ping-ping-ping against a metallic resonator, not a pure tone but a granular sequence of percussions with a keening overlay of overtones; ringing for so many days that it simply blended into the background except at certain early-morning hours when one or the other of them awoke in a sweat and realized that a bell had been ringing in their head for as long as they could remember; ringing for so many months that the sound had given way to a kind of metasound whose rise and fall was not the beating of compression waves but the much, much slower waxing and waning of their *consciousness* of the sound. Which consciousness was particularly acute when the weather itself was in an anxious mood. Then Enid and Alfred—she on her knees in the dining room opening drawers, he surveying the disastrous Ping-Pong table—each felt near to exploding with anxiety.

The anxiety of coupons, in a drawer containing boxes of candles in designer colors, also utensils of pewter and silver in flannel bags. Overlaying these accessories for the dinner parties that Enid no longer gave was a stratum of furtiveness and chaos, because these dining-room drawers often presented themselves as havens for whatever Enid had in hand when Alfred was raging and she had to cover up her operations, get them out of sight at whatever cost. There were coupons bundled in a rubber band, and she was realizing that their expiration dates (often jauntily circled in red ink by the manufacturer, a reminder to act quickly while the discount opportunity lasted) lay months and even years in the past: that these hundred-odd coupons, whose total face value exceeded $60 (potentially $120 at the supermarket on Watson Road that doubled coupons), and which she had clipped months *before* their expiration, had all gone bad. Tilex, sixty cents off. Excedrin PM, a dollar off. The dates were not even *close*. The dates were *historical*. The alarm bell had been ringing for *years*.

She pushed the coupons back in among the candles and shut the drawer. She was looking for a letter that had come by registered mail some weeks ago. She had stashed it somewhere quickly because Alfred had heard the mailman ring the bell and shouted, "Enid! Enid!" but had not heard her shout, "Al, I'm getting it!" and he had continued to shout, "Enid!" coming closer and closer, and she had disposed of the envelope, presumably somewhere within fifteen feet of the

front door, because the sender was The Axon Group, 24 East Industrial Serpentine, Schwenkville, PA, and some weeks or perhaps
months earlier she had received a certified letter from Axon that for
reasons known better to her than (thankfully) to Alfred she had been
too anxious to open immediately, and so it had disappeared, which
was no doubt why Axon had sent a second, registered letter subsequently, and this entire circumstance was something she preferred to
keep from Alfred, because he got so darned anxious and was impossible to deal with, especially regarding the situation with Axon (which,
thankfully, he knew almost nothing about), and so she had stashed
the second letter as well before Alfred had emerged from the basement bellowing like a piece of earth-moving equipment, "There's
somebody at the door!" and she'd fairly screamed, "The mailman!
The mailman!" and he'd shaken his head at the complexity of it all.

She felt sure that her own head would clear if only she didn't have
to wonder, every five minutes, what Alfred was up to. It seemed to her
that he had become somewhat depressed, and that he ought, therefore, to try to take an interest in life. She encouraged him to take up
his metallurgy again, but he looked at her as if she'd lost her mind.
(She didn't understand what was so wrong with a friendly suggestion
like that; she didn't understand why he had to be so *negative*.) She
asked whether there wasn't some work he could do in the yard. He
said his legs hurt. She reminded him that the husbands of her friends
all had hobbies (David Schumpert his stained glass, Kirby Root his
intricate chalets for nesting purple finches, Chuck Meisner his plaster
casts of great monuments of the ancient world), but Alfred acted as if
she were trying to distract him from some great labor of his, and what
was that labor? Repainting the wicker furniture? He'd been repainting the love seat since Labor Day. She seemed to recall that the last
time he'd painted the furniture it had taken him only a few hours to
do the love seat. But he went to his workshop morning after morning,
and after three weeks she ventured in to see how he was doing, and
the only thing he'd painted was the legs. After three weeks! And he'd
clearly missed a spot on one of the legs! He seemed to wish that she
would go away. He said that the brush had gotten dried out, that that
was what was taking so long. He said that scraping wicker was like
trying to peel a blueberry. He said there were crickets. She felt a

shortness of breath then, but perhaps it was only the smell of gasoline and the dampness of the workshop that smelled like urine (but could not possibly be urine). She fled upstairs to look for the letters from Axon.

Six days a week several pounds of mail came through the slot in the front door, and since nothing incidental was allowed to pile up on the main floor—since the fiction of living in this house was that no one lived here—Enid faced a substantial tactical challenge. She did not think of herself as a guerrilla, but a guerrilla was what she was. By day she ferried material from depot to depot, often just a step ahead of the governing force. By night, beneath a charming but too-dim sconce at a too-small table in the breakfast nook, she staged various actions: paid bills, balanced checkbooks, attempted to decipher Medicare co-payment records and make sense of a threatening Third Notice from a medical lab which demanded immediate payment of $0.22 while simultaneously showing an account balance of $0.00 carried forward and thus indicating that she owed nothing and in any case offering no address and naming no entity to which remittance might be made. It would happen that the First and Second Notices were underground somewhere, and because of the constraints under which Enid waged her campaign she had only the dimmest sense of where those other Notices might be on any given evening. She might suspect perhaps the family-room closet, but the governing force, in the person of Alfred, would be watching a network news-magazine at a volume thunderous enough to keep him awake, and he had every light in the family room burning, and there was a non-negligible possibility that if she opened the closet door a cascade of catalogues and *House Beautiful*s and miscellaneous Merrill Lynch statements would come toppling and sliding out, incurring Alfred's wrath. There was also the possibility that the Notices would not be there, since the governing force staged random raids on her depots, threatening to "pitch" the whole lot of it if she didn't take care of it, but she was too busy dodging these raids ever quite to take care of it, and in the succession of forced migrations and deportations any lingering semblance of order was lost, and so the random Nordstrom's shopping bag that was camped behind a dust ruffle with one of its plastic handles semidetached would contain the whole shuffled pathos of a refugee existence—nonconsecutive issues of *Good Housekeeping*, black-and-white snapshots of Enid in the 1940s, brown recipes on high-acid paper that called for wilted lettuce, the current month's telephone and gas bills, the detailed First Notice from the medical lab instructing copayers to ignore subsequent billings for less than fifty cents, a complimentary cruise-ship photo of Enid and Alfred wearing leis and sipping beverages from hollow coconuts, and the only extant copies of two of their children's birth certificates, for example.

Although Enid's ostensible foe was Alfred, what made her a guerrilla was the house that occupied them both. They had always aimed high in decorating it, and its furnishings were of the kind that no more brooked domestic clutter than a hotel lobby would. As without in prosperous St. Jude, so within chez Lambert. There was furniture by Ethan Allen. Spode and Waterford in the breakfront. The obligatory ficus, the inevitable Norfolk pine. Copies of *Architectural Digest* fanned on a glass-topped coffee table. Touristic plunder—enamelware from China, a Viennese music box that Enid out of a sense of duty and mercy every so often wound up and raised the lid of. The tune was "Strangers in the Night."

It's to their credit, I think, that both Lamberts were hopelessly ill-equipped to manage such a house; that something in each of them rebelled at the sterility. Alfred's cries of rage on discovering evidence of incursions—a Nordstrom's bag surprised in broad daylight on the basement stairs, nearly precipitating a tumble—were the cries of a government that could no longer govern. It was finance that betrayed him first. He developed a knack for making his printing calculator spit columns of meaningless eight-digit figures, and after he devoted the better part of an afternoon to figuring the cleaning woman's social-security payments five different times and came up with four different numbers and finally just accepted the one number ($635.78) that he'd managed to come up with twice (the correct figure was $70.00), Enid staged a nighttime raid on his filing cabinet and relieved it of all tax files, which might have improved household efficiency had the files not found their way into a Nordstrom's bag with some misleadingly ancient *Good Housekeeping*s concealing the more germane documents underneath, which casualty of war led to the cleaning woman's filling out the forms herself, with Enid merely writing the checks and Alfred shaking his head at the complexity of it all.

It's the fate of most Ping-Pong tables in home basements eventually to serve the ends of other, more desperate games. When Alfred retired he appropriated the eastern end of the table for his banking and correspondence. At the western end was the portable color TV on which he'd intended to watch the local news while sitting in his great blue chair but which was now fully engulfed by *Good Housekeeping*s and the seasonal candy tins and baroque but cheaply made candleholders that Enid never quite found time to transport to the Nearly New consignment shop. The Ping-Pong table was the one field on which the civil war raged openly. At the eastern end Alfred's calculator was ambushed by floral-print pot holders and souvenir coasters from the Epcot Center and a device for pitting cherries that Enid had owned for thirty years and never used; while he, in turn, at the western end, for absolutely no reason that Enid could ever fathom, ripped to pieces a wreath made of pine cones and spray-painted filberts and Brazil nuts.

To the east of the Ping-Pong table lay the workshop that housed his metallurgical lab, the industry underpinning the seamless prosperity of the house above. This workshop was now home to a colony of mute, dust-colored crickets that clustered and roiled in various corners. There was something fetal about these crickets, something provisional. When you surprised them they scattered like a handful of dropped marbles, some of them misfiring at crazy angles, others toppling over with the weight of their own copious protoplasm, which had the color and texture of pus. They popped all too easily, and cleanup took more than one Kleenex. The Lamberts had many afflictions that they believed to be outsized, extraordinary, unheard-of—unmentionable—and the crickets were one of them.

The gray dust of evil spells and the enchanted cobwebs of a place that time had forgotten cloaked the thick insulating bricks of the electric arc furnace, the Hellmann's Real Mayonnaise jars filled with exotic rhodium, with sinister cadmium, with stalwart bismuth, the handprinted labels browned and blasted by the leakage of vapors from nearby glass-stoppered bottles of sulfuric acid and aqua regia, and the quad-ruled notebooks with cracked leather spines in which the latest entry in Alfred's hand dated from that time, nearly twenty years ago, before the spell was cast, before the betrayal. Something as daily and friendly as a pencil still occupied the random spot on the workbench where Alfred had laid it in a different decade; the passage of so many years imbued the pencil with a kind of enmity. Worse than a palace in ruins is a palace abandoned and decaying and untouched: if it were ruined it could be forgotten. A ceramic crucible of something metallurgical still sat inside the furnace. Asbestos mitts hung from a nail beneath two certificates of U.S. patents, the frames warped and sprung by dampness. On the hood of a binocular microscope with an oil-immersion lens lay big chips of peeled paint from the ceiling. The only dust-free objects in the room were a wicker love seat on a dropcloth, a can of Rustoleum and some brushes, and a couple of YUBAN coffee cans which despite increasingly irrefutable olfactory evidence Enid chose not to believe were filling up with her husband's urine, because what earthly reason could he have, in a house with two and a half bathrooms, for peeing in a YUBAN can?

Until he retired, Alfred had slept in an armchair that was black. Between his naps he read *Time* magazine or watched *60 Minutes* or golf. On weeknights he paged through the contents of his briefcase with a trembling hand. The chair was made of leather that you could smell the cow in.

His new chair, the great blue one to the west of the Ping-Pong table, was built for sleeping and sleeping only. It was overstuffed, vaguely gubernatorial. It smelled like the inside of a Lexus. Like something modern and medical and impermeable that you could wipe the smell of death off easily, with a damp cloth, before the next person sat down to die in it.

The chair was the only major purchase Alfred ever made without Enid's approval. I see him at sixty-seven, a retired mechanical engineer walking the aisles of one of those midwestern furniture stores that only people who consider bargains immoral go to. I see him passing up lesser chairs—chairs with frivolous levers, chairs that don't seem important enough. For his entire working life he has taken naps in chairs subordinate to Enid's color schemes, and now he has received nearly five thousand dollars in retirement gifts. He has come to the store to spend the better part of this on a chair that celebrates, through its stature and costliness, the only activity in which he is truly himself. After a lifetime of providing for others, he needs even more than deep comfort and unlimited sleep: he needs public recognition of this need. Unfortunately, he fails to consider that monuments built for eternity are seldom comfortable for short-term accommodation. The chair he selects is outsized in the way of professional basketball shoes. I see his fingers trembling as they trace the multiple redundancy of the stitching. It's a lifetime chair—a mechanical engineer's chair, a chair designed to function under extraordinary stress, a chair with plenty of margin for error. On the minus side it's so much larger than any person who'd sit in it—is at once so yielding and so magnificent—that it forces its occupant into the postures of a sleeping child. In the coming years he won't settle into this chair so much as get lost in it.

When Alfred went to China to see Chinese mechanical engineers, Enid went along and the two of them visited a rug factory to buy a rug for their family room. They were still unaccustomed to spending money on themselves, and so they chose one of the least expensive rugs. It had a design from the *Book of Changes* in blue wool on a field of beige. The blue of the chair Alfred brought into the house a few years later vaguely matched the blue of the rug's design, and Enid, who was strict about matching, suffered the chair's arrival.

Soon, though, Alfred's hands began to spill decaffeinated coffee on the rug's beige expanses, and wild grandchildren from the Rocky Mountains left berries and crayons underfoot, and Enid began to feel that the rug was a mistake. It seemed to her that in trying to save money in life she had made many mistakes like this. She reached the point of thinking it would have been better to buy no rug than to buy this rug. Finally, as Alfred went to sleep in his chair, she grew bolder. Her own mother had left her a tiny inheritance years ago, and she had made certain investments. Interest had been added to principal, certain stocks had performed rather well, and now she had an income of her own. She reconceived the family room in greens and yellows. She ordered fabrics. A paperhanger came, and Alfred, who was napping temporarily in the dining room, leaped to his feet like a man with a bad dream.

"You're redecorating *again?*"

"It's my own money," Enid said. "This is how I'm spending it."

"And what about the money *I* spent? What about the work *I* did?"

This argument had been effective in the past—it was, you might say, the constitutional basis of the tyranny's legitimacy—but it didn't work now. "That rug is nearly ten years old, and we'll never get the coffee stains out," Enid answered.

Alfred gestured at his blue chair, which under the paperhanger's plastic dropcloths looked like something you might deliver to a power station on a flatbed truck. He was trembling with incredulity, unable to believe that Enid could have forgotten this crushing refutation of her arguments, this overwhelming impediment to her plans; it was as if all the unfreedom and impossibility in which he'd spent his seven decades of life were embodied in this four-year-old but (because of its high quality) essentially brand-new chair. He was grinning, his face aglow with the awful perfection of his logic.

"*And what about the chair, then?*" he said. "*What about the chair?*"

Enid looked at the chair. Her expression was merely pained, no more. "I never liked that chair."

This was probably the most terrible thing she could have said to Alfred. The chair was the only sign he'd ever given of having a personal vision of the future. Enid's words filled him with such sorrow— he felt such pity for the chair, such solidarity with it, such astonished grief at its betrayal—that he pulled off the dropcloth and sank into its leather arms and fell asleep.

(This is one way of recognizing a place of enchantment: a suspiciously high incidence of narcolepsy.)

When it became clear that both the rug and Alfred's chair had to go, the rug was easily shed. Enid advertised in the free local paper and netted a nervous bird of a woman who was still making mistakes and whose fifties came out of her purse in a disorderly roll that she unpeeled and flattened with shaking fingers.

But the chair? The chair was a monument and a symbol and could not be parted from Alfred. It could only be relocated, and so it went into the basement and Alfred followed. And so in the house of the Lamberts, as in St. Jude, as in the country as a whole, life came to be lived underground.

•

Enid could hear him upstairs now, opening and closing drawers. In the streaklessly clean windows of the dining room was chaos. The berserk wind, the negating shadows. Now, of course, she had control of the upper floors. Now, when it was far too late.

Alfred stood in the master bedroom wondering why the drawers of his dresser were open, who had opened them, whether he had opened them himself. He could not help blaming Enid for his confusion. For witnessing it into existence. For existing, herself, as a person who could have opened these drawers.

"Al? What are you doing?"

He turned to the doorway where she'd appeared. He began a sentence: "I am—" but when he was taken by surprise, every sentence was an adventure in the woods; as soon as he could no longer see the light of the clearing from which he'd entered, it would come to him sickeningly that the crumbs he'd dropped for bearings had been eaten by birds, silent deft darting things that he couldn't quite see in the darkness but which were so numerous and swarming in their hunger that it seemed as if *they* were the darkness, as if the darkness weren't uniform, weren't an absence of light but a teeming and corpuscular thing, and indeed when as a studious teenager he'd encountered the word *crepuscular* in *McKay's Treasury of English Verse,* the corpuscles of biology had bled into his understanding of the word, so that for his entire adult life he'd seen in twilight a corpuscularity, as of the graininess of the high-speed film necessary for photography under conditions of low ambient light, as of a kind of sinister decay; and hence the panic of a man betrayed deep in the woods whose darkness was the darkness of starlings blotting out the sunset or black ants storming a dead opossum, a darkness that didn't just exist but actively *consumed* the bearings he had sensibly established for himself, lest he be lost; but in the instant of realizing he was lost, time became marvelously slow and he discovered hitherto unguessed eternities in the space between one word and the next, or rather he became trapped in that space between words and could only stand and watch as time sped on without him, the mindless part of him crashing on out of sight blindly through the woods while he, trapped, the grown-up Al, watched in considerable but oddly impersonal suspense to see if the panic-stricken little boy Freddie might, despite no longer knowing where he was or at what point he'd entered the woods of this sentence, still be fortunate enough to blunder into a clearing where Enid was waiting for him, unaware of any woods—"packing my suitcase," he heard himself say. This sounded right. Verb, possessive, noun. Here was a suitcase in front of him, an important confirmation. He'd betrayed nothing.

But Enid had spoken again. The audiologist had said he was mildly impaired. He frowned at her, not following.

"It's *Thursday*," she said, louder. "We're not going till *Saturday*."

"Saturday!" he echoed.

She berated him then, and for a while the crepuscular birds retreated, but outside the wind had blown the sun out, and it was getting very cold.

Issue 139, 1996

Joanna Scott

✣

You Must Relax!

What our grandmother keeps in her walk-in closet: pastel silks in pink and blue and peach, crepe de chine, chiffon, mousseline de soie, tulle, satin ribbons, boleros, corsets, hats with feathers, hats with cloth flowers, cloches, a beaded cap, tunics, hobble skirts, gray wool suits, evening dresses and dressing gowns.

Lately, Granny Madge has taken to locking herself in her closet. She sits on a metal folding chair for hours, counting aloud in a low, monotonous voice. While she counts we know that she is recalling those important moments that she would rather forget—it is her punishment to remember, she says. St. Paul de Vence, for instance, 1923, a garden party, a stone wall and morning glories wet with dew, slippery slate steps. She remembers exactly what she wore that day: her lemony silk dress and straw hat shaped like a chanterelle. Her husband wore gabardine. Her little boy Lou, our papa, wore knickers and a peasant blouse. Lou, his fists the size of apricots. He insisted on carrying the trifle himself though his arms couldn't reach entirely around the width of the glass bowl. Layers of wine-soaked sponge biscuits, ratafia cakes, whipped cream, fresh raspberries. He staggered beneath the weight. Still, such challenges are important to children. Madge believed, so she let him carry the bowl, guided him by the shoulders up the steps to the terrace, the brim of her hat covering Lou in shadow, his face pinched in a knot of concentration, reddening as he neared the trellis canopy. His mother didn't notice his diminishing strength or his gasps, though, because as she climbed the final steps she heard a familiar voice coming from the far corner of the terrace. She couldn't make out what it was saying but she recognized that voice. Five years had passed since she'd heard it last. If a century had passed she still would have known it instantly.

In an attempt to avoid the meeting she backed down a step, away from the terrace, fell off balance and stumbled. She jostled Lou ever so lightly, reason enough for him to give up his impossible effort. He let his arms go limp as he mounted the top step, and the bowl—a punch bowl that was an heirloom two generations old, glass engraved with an intricate floral design on the island of Murillo—the bowl, the trifle, the candied violets slipped from the little boy's arms and crashed onto the terrace.

The next awful minutes are like a photograph in our grand-mother's mind, a scene removed from time, coated with resin. She re-members: the embarrassed glances directed at her from three sides, the top of her son's bowed head, the splattered trifle that looked like the eviscerated carcass of a large rabbit, white fur and bruised, pur-plish tissue, the puddle of raspberry blood already coagulating. In her memory she stands apart, watches herself as though she were an-other guest, sees a woman, mesmerized, sees a boy with eyes squeezed shut trying to will away the accident and make time go back-ward, sees, then, a middle-aged man come toward her.

He'd grown a beard, a black, patchy chin-beard; he'd put on weight so his face had lost its slender, oval shape, and he wore a mon-ocle as though he were an intellectual when in fact he was nothing but a showman, a pretender who flaunted knowledge, exploited knowl-edge, used knowledge as an alchemist uses chemistry. Perhaps the five years since she'd seen him last, since she'd renounced him in an attempt to claim her self-respect again, had matured her so thor-oughly that she could judge with critical detachment the doctor who had once entranced her. Or was it that he had changed, had lost his confident manner, had replaced homeopathic promises with insin-cerity? The doctor three years earlier had seemed a wise man, almost a prophet; in his place, Madge saw a hypocrite.

He walked across the terrace toward her, the one animated figure in the frozen picture, moved as steadily as a flame burning down the stem of a matchstick. He squatted in front of the shattered bowl and began picking out fragments of glass as though this would somehow help, carefully removed one sliver after another, and arranged the pieces in a pile at his side.

Finally Lou opened his eyes, saw that his wish hadn't come true, time hadn't reversed itself, he'd failed miserably, and even worse, no one reproached him. They were too full of pity to reproach him—he may not have understood much about adults but he understood that they were pitying him. And now a bearded man knelt before him, a grown man on his knees; nothing Lou had done had ever produced such dramatic consequences. He looked up at his mother, not quite believing that he was responsible, looked back at the man, looked at his mother, saw an unfamiliar expression (and our grandmother, in her memory, sees everything now through her son's confusion), looked at the faces of strangers, looked at the man's hands again, then closed his eyes because he couldn't bear it anymore and began to scream.

His screams demanded action. There were brooms to be fetched, dustpans to be filled, Madge's husband, who had dallied at the bottom of the steps with the host and only now appeared, needed an explanation, Madge needed reassurance ("No doubt it would have been delicious, Madame Whitcombe"), the boy needed a biscuit, the doctor needed a towel. For some reason the hostess handed the towel to Madge first, so she was obligated to pass it to the doctor, who deliberately grabbed her hand along with the cloth, held her even when she tried to pull away, held her for so long and gazed at her with such offensive intimacy that for a second time a hush fell across the terrace, the guests stared, our grandmother blushed. It was a more fatal accident than a ruined trifle, this inopportune joining of hands.

Lou had taken refuge by his mother, stood underneath her outstretched arm, and the image of the three—the woman, the doctor, the boy in between—provided all the proof that anyone who ever had suspicions could have wanted. And they did have suspicions, Madge knew. Five years earlier people had whispered about her frequent consultations with the doctor, had wondered why her husband allowed her to go to Nice without an escort. But jealousy was as foreign to her husband as the French language had been to Madge during her first year abroad. She had learned French, though, had been forced to learn it, since her husband's touring agency kept him away for weeks at a time, and none of her neighbors spoke English. And now her husband would be forced to learn a new language: the language of jealousy. Not because the doctor looked at his wife with such ferocious interest; not because they continued to hold hands long after the interval proper for a greeting. While others saw proof, her husband would have a revelation: the woman, the doctor, the boy. As unarguable as simple addition. The boy, with his coxcomb of black hair and his large, wide-set brown eyes, his low forehead, his impish, pointed chin, was the obvious sum of two parts.

The doctor had damned Madge forever, had intended as much, she believed. Surely he must have known that she and her husband would be at this garden party. Four years ago he'd moved his practice from Nice to London, was now on his way to Lake Como for a holiday, had obviously delayed the last leg of the trip so he could be here, so he could see Madge, lovely Madge, "as beautiful as ever," he murmured, and finally released her.

She wiped her palm, wet from perspiration, on the side of her dress, gave him a polite if strained nod and pushed her son around the broken bowl and away from the stranger who was his natural father. Though everyone else knew the truth, even her husband—yes, her husband knew best of all—her son must never know.

And with nothing more to watch but much to discuss, the guests regrouped into neat patterns of colors that seemed to Madge both haphazard and carefully designed, like tinted glass in a kaleidoscope. While they didn't talk about her directly, through the next hour the men smiled at her with oblique amusement; and the women kept glancing from husband to wife to doctor, their eyes drawn by some irresistible force. The force of scandal. In private parlors and bedrooms gossip would flow from these people, her gentle Catholic friends, gossip would take the place of the trifle as their dessert, gossip would enrage, fatten, delight them, would give their insignificant lives meaning. Not only had the doctor calmed Madge's fraught American nerves five years earlier, not only had he given her back her peace of mind, he'd given her a bastard son as well. Not just a son. A son with Jewish blood. He'd given a Jewish baby to a Protestant adulteress—mixed blood, no good would come of the boy, he'd suffer for his mother's shame, and wasn't it more than coincidence that he'd dropped the precious glass bowl, a trial run for future catastrophes, the first act of many acts of violence to follow? Who could blame the doctor? He was just a man, with a man's instincts, a man's vulnerabilities.

Other women in the village had traveled to Nice by themselves to consult the famous doctor; other women had let him touch them as no one but their husbands should have touched them. But only Madge had borne his child. She knew what they would say about her behind her back; she knew that these self-proclaimed libertarians made pets of Jews, even on occasion made love to them. They wouldn't condemn her for love. But there was the question of purity. She had brought an impure child into the world, and though they could forgive him, they would never forgive her. She didn't have to rely on malicious confidantes to know what her friends were thinking. They would satisfy their hunger, would obscure the actual object of their prejudice by directing their thrilling, rapacious hatred at her.

Was our grandmother making unfair assumptions about these people? No fingers had been pointed, after all; no accusations had been made. To some observers this gathering might have held no secrets—once the trifle had been cleared up the guests resumed their separate conversations, mingled, told jokes, ate and drank and eventually dispersed. A garden party like any other garden party. This was one interpretation, and probably a few uninformed guests believed it. Maybe most of them believed it and hardly gave Madge a second thought. But the guest with the most at stake learned at this party that he'd been betrayed by his wife. Though her husband would never confront her directly, from that day on he would begin to withdraw behind a silent, brooding mask, would pretend that he no longer cared about her or Lou until he drove himself to despair with the lie.

They forced themselves to linger at the party. Madge's husband wandered around the rim of the terrace, admired the roses and foxglove and held out his empty glass whenever the waiter came by with an open bottle of champagne. Madge strolled from group to group, nodded politely when opinions were exchanged, brushed her fingers through her son's hair, caressed his cheek, kept him close to her, ostentatiously displayed her love for her son. Whatever her friends said about her, they couldn't deny that she loved her son.

After a suitable length of time the family departed, managing a discreet exit. Yet even as they descended the slate steps Madge sensed, and perhaps her husband sensed as well, that they would never appear together in public again.

Our grandmother is sitting in the dark. She used to spend her days in the living room playing solitaire or staring out the window. Now she just sits in the dark in the closet and counts aloud, higher and higher.

Once in a while she stops counting and listens. Or she remembers listening, though it is almost the same thing. She remembers listening for the sounds of footsteps, cowbells, a dog's bark, anything that would destroy the illusion of solitude. She spent the summer of 1923 roving the hills with her son, gathering dandelion leaves and sorrel for salads that would never be made, nettles for stews, rosehips for syrups. After a rain she would forage in the pine groves for puffballs the size of turnips full of brown, powdery spores. And boleti, satanic boleti with spongy red caps. She would set the deadly mushrooms on the windowsill out of her son's reach, and when they had withered and shriveled she would throw them out and pick more. That summer she enjoyed a rare freedom, though at the time such freedom seemed a trap. No matter how far she walked she never reached a place satisfactorily remote, where she could have screamed as loud as she pleased, where she could have spit and danced naked. She was afraid, perpetually afraid of being discovered, afraid most of all of being discovered by the one who always accompanied her: her son.

Our father still speaks of these days as the finest of his childhood. No lessons to study, no obligations, nothing to do but leap over logs and bathe in shallow creeks, throw pebbles at fish, pet the whiskered muzzles of ponies, catch toads and grasshoppers. Ordinarily his mother was a grave and didactic presence, an unrelenting moral supervisor. *Energy, application, painstaking patience and persistence.* These were the words Madge used to repeat to her son. But that summer she acted as though idleness were the sole objective. The sun burnt Lou until he was "as crisp as a pygmy, and wasn't he just as illiterate and wild!" or so Aunt Sarah—Madge's sister—declared when she arrived in St. Paul de Vence to take charge. Someone had to take charge while the man of the house was off charting next year's tour through Greece, preoccupied with the difficult arrangements to be made, hotels to be booked, coaches to be hired, so busy that he didn't even have time to write to his wife. In his absence, the usually orderly household deteriorated. Weeks before Aunt Sarah arrived Madge had dismissed the cook, and she didn't even notice when spiders began spinning their webs across the doorways. Her son's mop of hair became so dense with tangles that she would simply pat her hands over the top without brushing it, bills remained sealed, and one afternoon she lifted the cloth from the bird-cage and discovered her neglected pair of canaries motionless on the floor of the cage. In their nest she found a cluster of speckled eggs.

That same day she wrote a long letter to her husband and addressed it to the pension where he was staying in Athens. She put her son to bed early and prepared supper for herself—a piece of chèvre, day-old bread, a fennel bulb, claret and boleti in cream. She ate three poisonous mushroom caps, laid down her spoon, and waited.

Rather, she continued to wait. She had been waiting all summer, and the stomach cramps at first were an exhilarating commencement: something was about to happen. She retired to her bedroom, propped herself up on her pillows and opened a book about gardening. But the drawings on the page made her nauseous, as though the sensation of taste were located in her eyes, the illustrations nothing but wormy, putrid pieces of food. Mushrooms in cream.

She hurried to the toilet, pulled her dress up and her bloomers down, shat a thin, bluish liquid, rolled over onto her knees and vomited. So this was life revealed: filthy, stinking, nothing noble about it, only pain and shit and bile. She retched again. Life leaked out, spilled, dripped, abandoned her. Madge had broken the trust, so life renounced its loyalties, left her hollow, or nearly so, and stuporous, drenched in sweat.

She managed to crawl back to her bed and almost immediately fell into a heavy slumber, only to wake an hour later for the second exodus: pain and shit and bile. But still enough life remained to keep the vital organs working, and though when she returned to bed the second time she felt sure she was dying, she woke at noon the following day to find that she hadn't died. And it was a good thing, wasn't it? With the cook gone someone had to prepare meals for her son. Her poor boy. Better for a boy to have an imperfect mama than no mama at all, she told herself as she ran her finger along the curved ridge of his spine. Her sweet child must have crawled into bed with her early in the morning, had forced himself to lie absolutely still so he wouldn't wake her and had fallen asleep.

Her joints throbbed, her brain seemed squeezed in a vise, but she managed to push herself to her feet. Downstairs in the kitchen she patched together a meal for her son of sliced peaches and eggs. Not until she had set his plate on the table did she notice the leftovers. A skin had formed on the cream; an inky brown leaked from the remaining mushrooms, and the color had spread like cracks in ice. Her son could have climbed up on the chair and helped himself. She might have poisoned her own son, her only child, might have even, in her despair, left the pan of mushrooms out for him—a mad-woman's attempt to destroy the witness. She was insane, clearly, and if anyone had been checking on her these last weeks they would have surely committed her to an asylum, locked her away out of reach of the boy, restrained her so she could do no harm to anyone.

She let the eggs grow rubbery and cold and her son sleep while she wrote to her sister, who was married to an antique dealer and lived in Sussex, inviting her to visit. Then she poured the mushrooms into a square of cheesecloth folded to triple thickness, dropped the bundle into a burlap sack, and because she couldn't think how else to get rid of it she buried the sack in the vegetable garden.

Granny Madge didn't stay in Provence long enough to find out whether new mushrooms ever sprouted; a week after Aunt Sarah arrived Madge's letter to her husband was returned unopened, along with a note from the owner of the Athens pension informing her that her husband had never arrived, had never even landed in Piraeus. It appeared that Madge's husband had boarded a ship bound for Greece in Naples but had disappeared en route. Whether he had fallen or had been pushed, no one knew. The captain had filed a report with the police in Piraeus, and he would keep the gentleman's trunk in his possession until further notice.

Madge traveled with her son to Piraeus to claim her husband's belongings; from Greece they took a steamer back to New York. She wore black tulle over her head and had her meals delivered to her cabin. She hardly touched the food. By then, a month and a half since she'd last seen her husband, she knew that though she was a widow her family of two would soon be joined by a third: before he had set out for Greece, her husband had made certain that he left something of himself behind.

She gave birth to a second son the following winter. She soon tired of the city and by spring she had made up her mind to move upstate. She chose Spragton as her home simply by closing her eyes and placing her finger on a map.

Our grandmother is sitting in the closet in the dark. She inhales deeply, holds the darkness in her lungs as a child might hold water in his mouth. To us, the closet smells like an elderly woman—a particular combination of perfumes and old fabrics, the smell as unique as a thumbprint, slightly stale but not unpleasant. To Granny Madge, however, the closet smells of money. Whatever she wears, her wealth is obvious, she can't help it and would prefer to disguise the truth, though that would mean additional purchases, more money spent on new clothes that weren't so conspicuously dear, more money converted into less distinguished goods. Not that she was ever a spendthrift. Just the opposite. From the start she thought of her wardrobe as an investment—she spared no expense in the early years, and she's been rewarded with high returns.

Still, she wishes that her affluence weren't so apparent. Even strangers recognize the smell that clings to her. In the lightless closet she tries to differentiate between the smell of wealth and her own scent, but the air is saturated with purchases, articles that have only increased in value over time and that someday will be dispersed among the rest of us. Yes, she invested wisely—she knows that to her heirs, everything stems from this.

She exhales, inhales through her mouth with short, choppy gulps. She wonders whether she could choose not to breathe, could willfully close out the offensive smell, could hold her breath and still keep counting. It is comforting, but not comforting enough, to follow a sequence.

We are all proud of our grandmother. It wasn't with money—not entirely—that she gained influence. And her looks didn't "melt any hearts," as one ancient and slightly drunken Spragton dignitary had recently said to her in a fit of nostalgia. Her slight, girlish figure and tightly-wound chignon would have served another woman better, a woman who was less severe than our grandmother, less demanding. No, Margaret Whitcombe conquered Spragton by doing what she does so well—by counting aloud one wintry afternoon five decades ago.

Between 1900 and 1930 the population of Spragton increased by seventy percent. Our grandmother was lucky to arrive when the town still welcomed strangers, and if our family would never enjoy the status of families descended from the original settlers, Granny Madge did manage to become one of the town's most influential leaders. A widow, mother of two small children, a woman of independent means, not nearly as demure as she should have been, even tyrannical at times, without important connections and, evidently, with no intention of remarrying—who would have predicted in those early months that she would rise to such heights?

Of course she didn't have to start from scratch. On top of her inheritance she had money from her husband's life insurance policy. She had an original Paul Poiret dress. And she had two disarming sons, Lou a would-be lady's man even at the age of five, our Uncle Harry a sanguine infant who rarely fussed, a mother's dream. Whatever doubts the people of Spragton had about our grandmother, her devotion to her sons was undeniable. With a family to support, Madge's aggressive manner could be excused, could even be admired. Still, she needn't have been so suspicious, really—no one would have tried to take advantage of her. Spragton was made up of plain, trustworthy people, neighbors who prided themselves on their honesty. Fair and square, no one surreptitiously jacked the price or tried to undersell a competitor, no one disguised terms with legal jargon, no one inflated the worth of services. Naive ethics, perhaps, but intentionally naive—greed was considered not an intrinsic human trait but an aberration: both the cheat and the customer who believed himself cheated were unnatural, especially the latter, since in this economy based on trust no one had to worry. Or so the typical Spragton businessman believed. No one dared to cheat, no one dared to complain. Each small business was like a windmill, an intelligible source of power driven by an unpredictable, external element. Blades turned with an easy whir and hum or did not turn at all, depending on the weather. The essential thing was to invest your money well.

At first the board members of the major bank in town treated our grandmother warily. She had enough money to cause trouble, enough to know the pleasures of wealth, enough to want more. They would, they assumed, have to reckon with her. But once they had decided that her apparent ambition was nothing but pronounced maternal instinct, their doubts gave way to affectionate concern, though not yet to respect. Margaret Whitcombe had to win their respect.

"Affectionately Yours." With this, Velma Bartholomew, wife of Murrian, Chairman of the Board, signed the invitation. And she meant it, too, for Velma was a woman brimming with affection, a woman so adroitly officious that she gave the impression of belonging to whomever she was addressing, even in conversation poised her body in such a way—her back slightly arched, chin raised, eyes lowered—that she seemed on the verge of falling into the arms of whomever stood opposite.

At the Bartholomews' home one afternoon over fifty years ago, our grandmother stood opposite Velma, endured the gushing praise of this person she hardly knew, wearing all the while the distracted look of a mother who, with much reluctance, has left her young children in a stranger's care.

It was a small party, given in honor of those newcomers who hadn't arrived in Spragton looking for handouts. Among them, Madge was particularly deserving, by common vote the bravest pilgrim of them all—everyone wanted to do something for her, though in the three months since she'd been in town she had made it clear that she would accept nothing for free. Unfortunate, the men agreed, that the widow was so testy.

Since she refused to hire an accountant to manage her finances, Murrian Bartholomew had to deal with her himself, though he relied on his wife to soften her hard edges, and he kept their meetings brief. Along with the others he felt great sympathy for the young widow. But when it came to business she had shown herself to be unyielding and unrelenting, nimble, potentially vicious, "a witch, to tell the truth," he had confessed to the bank's vice-president once while Madge sat outside his office. And she had overheard—not every word

but enough to understand from then on the precise nature of Spragton's affection.

Poor widow, devoted mother, witch. Give her a glass of punch and
let the wives take charge, let her prove that she can hold her own
where she belongs, a lady among ladies. So Murrian privately reasoned that day at his party, and he led the men into his library. Here,
away from their wives, the old guard could begin campaigning, which
was the purpose of this party or of any of Murrian Bartholomew's
parties. His fellow board members plied new, would-be investors first
with bourbon, then with promises, assuring their interested listeners
that whatever else was said about this northern outpost, the business-
men of Spragton never ran afoul. Fair and square. If Spragton had a
motto, this would have been it: fair and square.

Though from the adjacent room Madge couldn't make out the particular negotiations taking place in the library, she had a talent for in-
tuiting essences. She would have preferred to hear Murrian's sales
pitch directly rather than through Velma. But resentment is useless
for a woman, our grandmother believed. She thought it better to
conform than to protest, better to take what she could given the re-
striction, better to maintain her dignity. With energy, application,
painstaking patience and persistence, a woman could do well for herself. Quite well. A woman could pose a formidable challenge.

Velma was admiring Madge's very handsome if somewhat passé
beaded cap, when she interrupted to introduce her mother-in-law,
"Lady Bart," a small, stooped old woman who obviously had meant
to sneak past but now had to submit to her daughter-in-law's smothering embrace.

"Isn't she sweet," Velma said, smiling with such affection that her
lips curled back to reveal gums the color of peat. "She'd fit on a
spoon. Wouldn't you like to eat her for dessert!"

Lady Bart, the infamously fretful Lady Bart, four foot three inches
high, seventy-nine years old, was, Madge would soon understand, the
key to her own reputation. It took her only a few minutes to see the
possibilities contained in this irascible miniature, who looked even
smaller than she was because of her bent posture, but whose eyes
were huge and seemed to grow larger as she raised her head, the
knotty brown irises like liquid spilled on white cloth.

"Catholic, Missus?" Lady Bart wasted no time, and though Velma encouraged her with a nervous giggle to ignore the question, Madge was quick to reply.

"No, as a matter of fact."

She had the distinct sensation that the old woman was trying to frighten her, trying to make herself appear as monstrous as possible. But Madge felt instead a similar fascination to what she had once felt watching the rolling eyes of an unbroken colt that was tied securely in its box stall, felt, too, that she were facing a distorted reflection of herself, perhaps a reflection of what she would become. She didn't recoil, and the old woman, realizing that this stranger was more resistant than most, softened.

"That's all right," she said with a shrug. "All roads lead to God."

From then until Lady Bart's death the following month the old woman and the young widow were committed friends; and by the end of the night Murrian Bartholomew no longer considered our grandmother a witch. On the contrary, he believed her to be the cleverest woman he'd ever met, a woman who managed to succeed where dozens of doctors, preachers, herbalists and apothecaries had failed. Our grandmother, against all odds, gave sleep back to Lady Bart.

"She hasn't been well," Velma explained intrusively, stroked the old woman's gray tendrils of hair, smiled at her with affection.

But Lady Bart's story was her own to tell, and she pushed away Velma's hands impatiently. "They think I'm . . ." she said, tapping her temple with her forefinger. "Haven't slept for six months. Six months!" Clearly the old woman considered insomnia her unique talent. What had begun as a sickness had become a triumph—it wasn't that she had lost the ability to sleep, but she had conquered the need, and she never felt as alive, she confessed later, as she did in the lost hours of the night. While the rest of the world slept, Lady Bart kept watch. If she didn't keep watch, who would know how much time had actually passed, or that time had passed at all?

"Can't trust clocks," she warned, taking Madge by the elbow, leading her away while Velma stared after the pair with astonishment and not a little anger. But Madge didn't notice Velma's anger. Tiny Lady Bart demanded her full attention. With a voice that sounded like toast being crumbled and fingers clenched so tightly around her arm that the next day she had bruises above her elbow, the old woman didn't give Madge a chance to hesitate.

In the front hall they took seats at one end of the long deacon's bench, Lady Bart chattering all the while about her remarkable ability. Six months. She hadn't slept for six months, and if Madge didn't believe her there were others who would testify that since July Lady Bart hadn't even dozed. She might have reclined now and then, she might have shut her eyes and folded her hands across her chest, but her senses remained awake. Always alert, always listening.

She had heard the clock in the hall toll every hour of every day for the past six months, she had sat through every dusk, midnight and dawn, had listened to rain, to sleet, to branches scratching the windowpane, had finally, after eight decades of ignorance, learned to live and would continue to live, defying sleep, defying death, emancipated, as she put it, from the tyranny of the body. She had rooted out the fear of death and so would not die from fear, which was why most people died—from the unspeakable terror of departure, an exhausting terror that, in fact, shortens life, Lady Bart explained, her lips pursed, stretching the wrinkled skin of her face. Whatever we believe, whatever we think, whatever we attempt, we die—so why live in fear? Fear is blasphemous; through fear, the coward argues with God. Why bother arguing? Purge yourself of fear, and you'll live twice as long or longer, you'll live as long as God wants you to live. St. Narcissus died at the age of one hundred and sixty-five. St. Anthony at one hundred and five, the Hermit Paul at one hundred and thirteen, and St. Simon, the Virgin's nephew, at the age of one hundred and seven and only then because he was martyred. Most people kill themselves gradually, a whiskey in one hand, the supposedly rejuvenating serum of a heifer in the other, both poison, both shocks to the system.

Lady Bart believed that sleep was a shock to the system, the devil's work. How had she come to this conclusion? The problem, our grandmother reasoned, lay at the center of her logic. The old woman believed it her duty to prolong life but worried that if she relaxed for a moment life would be taken from her. Fear, this same blasphemous fear, was the inspiring force behind Lady Bart's insomnia. Afraid to lose control, afraid to sleep, she had disguised her fear as courage and considered herself more noble than others because of her efforts.

Even as Lady Bart prattled on, Madge devised a plan. She listened politely to the old woman's sermon on the near immortality of the terrestrial envelope and then proposed the wager that would mark the beginning of the end for Lady Bart: our grandmother boasted that she could cure any insomniac. If Lady Bart agreed to follow her instructions she would, before the hour was up, be fast asleep.

Madge had never tried the mesmeric cure on anyone, nor had she given it much thought in the years since the doctor of Nice had massaged her own neck with his relentlessly seductive fingers. But "progressive relaxation" was as dependable as a tested recipe. If she failed she would leave Spragton and never return, she said—a vow made impulsively and dishonestly. If our grandmother had failed, she would have readily gone back on her word and stayed put. It was useless to try to escape, she knew by then. No matter what, she would dig in her heels and make Spragton her home. She would never run away again.

"You think you can do it?" The old woman gave a short laugh, more like the cough of a small, sickly dog. "You think you can put out the light in here?" She tapped her forehead. "Try! Go ahead, try!" What wicked pleasure Lady Bart took in the dare; how proud she was, this thin, inexhaustible woman who wanted to live forever. But if, as she claimed, she had conquered the need for sleep, the idea still tempted her. Madge tempted, and that afternoon Lady Bart began the slow withdrawal that for six months she had successfully forestalled.

Crafty Ulysses stopped the flow of blood with special incantations; the French physician Corvisart treated the Empress Josephine with pills of breadcrumbs. Somewhere between these extremes of magic and delusion lies the science, or art, of hypnosis. The doctor—our grandfather—had been developing his own peculiar method when Madge was referred to him. Instead of treating his patients with drugs or sending them to costly spas, he believed "progressive relaxation" to be the most effective cure for nervous collapse. "You Must Relax!" became his byword and eventually the title of his book that received international attention. But Madge went to him in the early days of his practice, when he still called his treatments experiments. Madge was one of his most successful experiments. He groped (literally, in the final sessions, with the lights off, her blouse unbuttoned) and evolved a method "to quiet the nerve-muscle system, including what is commonly called 'the mind.'"

Obedient, cynical, but vaguely hopeful, Lady Bart followed Madge's instructions, put her feet up on the bench and leaned back until her head rested against our grandmother's thigh. The aim, Madge explained, was "to cease contracting each and every muscle"—the doctor's exact words, and as she repeated them she heard his voice, a disembodied voice, ingeniously persuasive. As she massaged the old woman's scalp she repeated what she heard.

"Trust me. Keep your legs uncrossed and close your eyes gradually, bend your left arm at the elbow, let your hand fall limply from the wrist, now bend your hands backward, now forward, press your wrists against the bench, bend your neck, wrinkle your forehead, frown. Trust me. You are beginning to learn clearly what you must not do. You must relax, but first you must feel the tension, cultivate the muscle sense, understand what the slightest movement entails in order to lie still. Now try to lie still, do as I say, trust me. You don't trust me. If you trusted me you wouldn't blink, keep your eyes closed tightly and breathe when I tell you to breathe, breathe in time with the numbers and keep your eyes shut tightly. Two, three, four—you'd sleep if you trusted me, you don't trust me yet, don't speak, considerable energy is wasted in unnecessary speech, let it go, my dear, let it go. Five, six, seven. See how very simple it is. If you trusted me . . . do you trust me yet? Do you feel the slow spreading outward from the center? The body yearns to expand and finally to dissolve. Let it go. Trust me."

How long it took, Madge couldn't say—maybe thirty minutes, maybe two hours. But the old woman had fallen asleep long before Granny Madge reached one thousand. She stopped counting, searched the oily, lined face for any stirring, but the lips were pressed together, the jaw set willfully, as though sleep were her decision and our grandmother merely an onlooker. But even with this illusion of self-determination Lady Bart would from now on be dependent upon Madge as Madge had once been dependent upon the doctor, deceived by him into believing that she could not fall asleep without him, could not, therefore, exist without him.

What a fool she'd been, but never, never again. She was in control this time, the purveyor of mesmeric freedom. She waited contentedly for someone from the party to venture into the hall and find the two women, the sleepless old matriarch at last asleep, her head resting on Madge's lap.

"It's nothing short of a miracle!" This was what they said, and our grandmother became a legend in Spragton, earning on a single afternoon respect that would last through her lifetime. But as if she had been granted one wish, only one, and had spent it on Lady Bart, our grandmother couldn't repeat the cure on anyone else. She tried, for years she tried.

Lately, she's been trying it on her own stubborn self, counting in bed, counting in the bath, counting in her closet with the door shut, the light off. We hear it day and night: the deep breaths and then the monotonous counting, the tedious ascents from one. We know better than to interrupt.

Beth Gylys

Marriage Song

They have affairs. They rarely stop to think
until they're begging for a second chance.
We love and learn we sometimes need a drink.

Impatient with his life, he quipped, "We blink
we're forty: with wives, kids, retirement plans."
They have affairs. It isn't what we think.

He saw this woman at the skating rink,
watching their sons play hockey from the stands.
He fought the urge to ask her for a drink.

She wore those stretchy pants, a long faux mink,
slid next to him and said, "Hi, my name's Nance."
He wanted her right there. He couldn't think.

They fucked in hotel rooms, designer pink,
drank cheap champagne. He signed her underpants.
They fucked and ordered something else to drink.

His wife broke all the dishes in the sink,
took both the kids and flew first-class to France.
They have affairs—it's never what they think.
We sigh and shake our heads. We have a drink.

Issue 149, 1998

Louise Erdrich

✣

The Beet Queen

Long before they planted beets in Argus and built the highways, there was a railroad. Along the track, which crossed the Dakota-Minnesota border and stretched on east to Minneapolis, everything that made the town arrived. All that diminished the town departed by that route too. On a cold spring morning in 1932 the train brought both an addition and a subtraction. They came by freight. By the time they reached Argus their lips were violet and their feet were so numb that, when they jumped out of the boxcar, they stumbled and scraped their palms and knees through the cinders.

The boy was a tall fourteen, hunched with his sudden growth and very pale. His mouth was sweetly curved, his skin fine and girlish. His sister was only eleven years old, but already she was so short and ordinary that it was obvious she would be this way all her life. Her name was as square and practical as the rest of her: Mary. She brushed her coat off and stood in the watery wind. Between the buildings there was only more bare horizon for her to see, and from time to time men crossing it. Wheat was the big crop then, and this topsoil was so newly tilled that it hadn't all blown off yet, the way it had in Kansas. In fact, times were generally much better in eastern North Dakota than in most places, which is why Karl and Mary Lavelle had come there on the train. Their mother's sister, Fritzie, lived on the eastern edge of town. She ran a butcher shop with her husband.

The two Lavelles put their hands up their sleeves and started walking. Once they began to move they felt warmer although they'd been traveling all night and the chill had reached in deep. They walked east, down the dirt and planking of the broad main street, reading the signs on each false-front clapboard store they passed, even reading the gilt letters in the window of the brick bank. None of these places was a butcher shop. Abruptly, the stores stopped and a string of houses, weathered gray or peeling gray, with dogs tied to their porch railings, began.

Small trees were planted in the yards of a few of these houses and one tree, weak, a scratch of light against the gray of everything else, tossed in a film of blossoms. Mary trudged solidly forward, hardly glancing at it, but Karl stopped. The tree drew him with its delicate perfume. His cheeks went pink, he stretched his arms out like a sleep-walker, and in one long transfixed motion he floated to the tree and buried his face in the white petals.

Turning to look for Karl, Mary was frightened by how far back he had fallen and how still he was, his face pressed in the flowers. She shouted, but he did not seem to hear her and only stood, strange and stock-still, among the branches. He did not move even when the dog in the yard lunged against its rope and bawled. He did not notice when the door to the house opened and a woman scrambled out. She shouted at Karl too, but he paid her no mind and so she untied her dog. Large and anxious, it flew forward in great bounds. And then, either to protect himself or to seize the blooms, Karl reached out and tore a branch from the tree.

It was such a large branch, from such a small tree, that blight would attack the scar where it was pulled off. The leaves would fall away later that summer and the sap would sink into the roots. The next spring, when Mary passed it on some errand, she saw that it bore no blossoms and remembered how, when the dog jumped for Karl, he struck out with the branch and the petals dropped around the dog's fierce out-stretched body in a sudden snow. Then he yelled, "Run!" and Mary ran east, toward Aunt Fritzie. But Karl ran back to the boxcar and the train.

So that's how I came to Argus. I was the girl in the stiff coat. After I ran blind and came to a halt, shocked not to find Karl behind me, I looked up to watch for him and heard the train whistle long and shrill.

That was when I realized Karl had jumped back on the same boxcar and was now hunched in straw, watching out the opened door. The only difference would be the fragrant stick blooming in his hand. I saw the train pulled like a string of black beads over the horizon, as I have seen it so many times since. When it was out of sight, I stared down at my feet. I was afraid. It was not that with Karl gone I had no one to protect me, but just the opposite. With no one to protect and look out for, I was weak. Karl was taller than me but spindly, older of course, but fearful. He suffered from fevers that kept him in a stuporous dream state and was sensitive to loud sounds, harsh lights. My mother called him delicate, but I was the opposite. I was the one who begged rotten apples from the grocery store and stole whey from the back stoop of the creamery in Minneapolis, where we were living the winter after my father died.

This story starts then, because before that and without the year 1929, our family would probably have gone on living comfortably and even have prospered on the Minnesota land that Theodor Lavelle broke and plowed and where he brought his bride, Adelaide, to live. But because that farm was lost, bankrupt like so many around it, our family was scattered to chance. After the foreclosure, my father worked as day labor on other farms in Minnesota. I don't even remember where we were living the day that word came. I only remember that my mother's hair was plaited in two red crooked braids and that she fell, full length, across the floor at the news. It was a common grain-loading accident, and Theodor Lavelle had smothered in oats. After that we moved to a rooming house in the Cities, where my mother thought that, with her figure and good looks, she could find work in a fashionable store. She didn't know, when we moved, that she was pregnant. In a surprisingly short amount of time we were desperate.

I didn't know how badly off we were until my mother stole six heavy, elaborately molded silver spoons from our landlady, who was kind or at least harbored no grudge against us, and whom my mother counted as a friend. Adelaide gave no explanation for the spoons, but she probably did not know I had discovered them in her pocket. Days later, they were gone and Karl and I owned thick overcoats. Also, our shelf was loaded with green bananas. For several weeks we drank quarts of buttermilk and ate buttered toast with thick jam. It was not long after that, I believe, that the baby was ready to be born.

One afternoon my mother sent us downstairs to the landlady. This woman was stout and so dull that I've forgotten her name although I recall vivid details of all else that happened at that time. It was a cold late-winter afternoon. We stared into the glass-faced cabinet where the silver stirrup cups and painted plates were locked after the theft. The outlines of our faces stared back at us like ghosts. From time to time Karl and I heard someone groan upstairs. It was our mother, of course, but we never let on as much. Once something heavy hit the floor directly above our heads. Both of us looked up at the ceiling and threw out our arms involuntarily, as if to catch it. I don't know what went through Karl's mind, but I thought it was the baby, born heavy as lead, dropping straight through the clouds and my mother's body. Because Adelaide insisted that the child would come from heaven although it was obviously growing inside of her, I had a confused idea of the process of birth. At any rate, no explanation I could dream up accounted for the groans, or for the long scream that tore through the air, turned Karl's face white, and caused him to slump forward in the chair.

I had given up on reviving Karl each time he fainted. By that time I trusted that he'd come to by himself, and he always did, looking soft and dazed and somehow refreshed. The most I ever did was support his head until his eyes blinked open. "It's born," he said when he came around, "let's go upstairs."

But as if I knew already that our disaster had been accomplished in that cry, I would not budge. Karl argued and made a case for at least going up the stairs, if not through the actual door, but I sat firm and he had all but given up when the landlady came back downstairs and told us, first, that we now had a baby brother, and, second, that she had found one of her grandmother's silver spoons under the mattress and that she wasn't going to ask how it got there, but would only say we had two weeks to get out.

The woman probably had a good enough heart. She fed us before she sent us upstairs. I suppose she wasn't rich herself, could not be bothered with our problems, and besides that, she felt betrayed by

Adelaide. Still, I blame the landlady in some measure for what my mother said that night, in her sleep.

I was sitting in a chair beside Adelaide's bed, in lamp light, holding the baby in a light wool blanket. Karl was curled in a spidery ball at Adelaide's feet. She was sleeping hard, her hair spread wild and bright across the pillows. Her face was sallow and ancient with what she had been through, but after she spoke I had no pity.

"We should let it die," she mumbled. Her lips were pale, frozen in a dream. I would have shaken her awake but the baby was nestled hard against me.

She quieted momentarily, then she turned on her side and gave me a long earnest look.

"We could bury it out back in the lot," she whispered, "that weedy place."

"Mama, wake up," I urged, but she kept speaking.

"I won't have any milk. I'm too thin."

I stopped listening. I looked down at the baby. His face was round, bruised blue, and his eyelids were swollen almost shut. He looked frail, but when he stirred I put my little finger in his mouth, as I had seen women do to quiet their babies, and his suck was eager.

"He's hungry," I said urgently, "wake up and feed him."

But Adelaide rolled over and turned her face to the wall.

Milk came flooding into Adelaide's breasts, more than the baby could drink at first. She had to feed him. Milk leaked out in dark patches on her pale-blue shirtwaists. She moved heavily, burdened by the ache. She did not completely ignore the baby. She cut her skirts up for diapers, sewed a layette from her nightgown, but at the same time she only grudgingly cared for his basic needs, and often left him to howl. Sometimes he cried such a long time that the landlady came puffing upstairs to see what was wrong. I think she was troubled to see us in such desperation, because she silently brought up food left by the boarders who paid for meals. Nevertheless, she did not change her decision. When the two weeks were up, we still had to move.

Spring was faintly in the air the day we went out looking for a new place. The clouds were high and warm. All of the everyday clothes Adelaide owned had been cut up for the baby, so she had nothing but her fine things, lace and silk, good cashmere. She wore a black coat, a pale green dress trimmed in cream lace, and delicate string gloves. Her beautiful hair was pinned back in a strict knot. We walked down the brick sidewalks looking for signs in windows, for rooming houses of the cheapest kind, barracks, or hotels. We found nothing, and finally sat down to rest on a bench bolted to the side of a store. In those times, the streets of towns were much kindlier. No one minded the destitute gathering strength, taking a load off, discussing their downfall in the world.

"We can't go back to Fritzie," Adelaide said, "I couldn't bear to live with Pete."

"We have nowhere else," I sensibly told her, "unless you sell your heirlooms."

Adelaide gave me a warning look and put her hand to the brooch at her throat. I stopped. She was attached to the few precious treasures she often showed us—the complicated garnet necklace, the onyx mourning brooch, the ring with the good yellow diamond. I supposed that she wouldn't sell them even to save us. Our hardship had beaten her and she was weak, but in her weakness she was also stubborn. We sat on the store's bench for perhaps half an hour, then Karl noticed something like music in the air.

"Mama," he begged, "Mama, can we go? It's a fair!"

As always with Karl, she began by saying no, but that was just a formality and both of them knew it. In no time, he had wheedled and charmed her into going.

The Orphan's Picnic, a fair held to benefit the orphans of Saint Jerome's after the long winter, was taking place just a few streets over at the city fairground. We saw the banner blazing cheerful red, stretched across the entrance, bearing the seal of the patron saint of loneliness. Plank booths were set up in the long, brown winter grass. Cowled nuns switched busily between the scapular and holy medal counters, or stood poised behind racks of rosaries, shoeboxes full of holy cards, tiny carved statuettes of saints, and common toys. We swept into the excitement, looked over the grab bags, games of chance, displays of candy and religious wares. Adelaide stopped at a secular booth that sold jingling hardware, and pulled a whole dollar from her purse.

"I'll take that," she said to the vendor, pointing. He lifted a pearl-handled jacknife from his case and Mama gave it to Karl. Then she pointed at a bead necklace, silver and gold.

"I don't want it," I said to Adelaide.

Her face reddened, but after a slight hesitation she bought the necklace anyway. Then she had Karl fasten it around her throat. She put the baby in my arms.

"Here, Miss Damp Blanket," she said.

Karl laughed and took her hand. Meandering from booth to booth, we finally came to the grandstand, and at once Karl began to pull her toward the seats, drawn by the excitement. I had to stumble along behind them. Bills littered the ground. Posters were pasted up the sides of trees and the splintery walls. Adelaide picked up one of the smaller papers.

THE GREAT OMAR, it said, AERONAUT EXTRAORDINAIRE. APPEARING HERE AT NOON. Below the words there was a picture of a man—sleek, mustachioed, yellow scarf whipping in a breeze.

"Please," Karl said, "please!"

And so we joined the gaping crowd.

The plane dipped, rolled, buzzed, glided above us and I was no more impressed than if it had been some sort of insect. I did not crane my neck or gasp, thrilled, like the rest of them. I looked down at the baby and watched his face. He was just emerging from the newborn's endless sleep and from time to time now he stared fathomlessly into my eyes. I stared back. Looking into his face that day, I found a different arrangement of myself—bolder, quick as light, ill-tempered. He frowned at me, unafraid, unaware that he was helpless, only troubled at the loud drone of the biplane as it landed and taxied toward us on the field.

Thinking back now, I can't believe that I had no premonition of what power The Great Omar had over us. I hardly glanced when he jumped from the plane and I did not applaud his sweeping bows and pronouncements. I hardly knew when he offered rides to those who dared. I believe he charged a dollar or two for the privilege. I did not notice. I was hardly prepared for what came next.

"Here!" my mother called, holding her purse up in the sun.

Then without a backwards look, without a word, with no warning

and no hesitation, she elbowed through the crowd collected at the
base of the grandstand and stepped into the cleared space around the
pilot. That was when I looked at The Great Omar for the first time,
but, as I was so astonished at my mother, I can hardly recall any detail
of his appearance. The general impression he gave was dashing, like
his posters. The yellow scarf whipped out and certainly he had some
sort of moustache. I believe he wore a grease-stained white sweater,
perhaps a loose coverall. He was slender and dark, much smaller in
relation to his plane than the poster showed, and older. After he
helped my mother into the passenger's cockpit and jumped in behind
the controls, he pulled a pair of green goggles down over his face.
And then there was a startling, endless moment, as they prepared for
the takeoff.

"Clear prop!"

The propeller made a wind. The plane lurched forward, lifted
over the low trees, gained height. The Great Omar circled the field in
a low swoop and I saw my mother's long red crinkly hair spring from
its tight knot and float free in an arc that seemed to reach out and tangle around his shoulders.

Karl stared in stricken fascination at the sky, and said nothing as
The Great Omar began his stunts and droning passes. I did not
watch. Again, I fixed my gaze on the face of my little brother and concentrated on his features, blind to the possibilities of Adelaide's sudden liftoff. I only wanted her to come back down before the plane
smashed.

The crowd thinned. People drifted away, but I did not notice. By
the time I looked into the sky The Great Omar was flying steadily
away from the fairgrounds with my mother. Soon the plane was only
a white dot, then it blended into the pale blue sky and vanished.

I shook Karl's arm but he pulled away from me and vaulted to the
edge of the grandstand. "Take me!" he screamed, leaning over the
rail. He stared at the sky, poised as if he'd throw himself into it.

Satisfaction. That was the first thing I felt after Adelaide flew off.
For once she had played no favorites between Karl and me, but left us
both. So there was some compensation in what she did. Karl threw
his head in his hands and began to sob into his heavy wool sleeves.
Only then did I feel frightened.

Below the grandstand, the crowd moved in patternless waves. Over us the clouds spread into a thin sheet that covered the sky like muslin. We watched the dusk collect in the corners of the field. Nuns began to pack away their rosaries and prayer books. Colored lights went on in the little nonreligious booths. Karl slapped his arms, stamped his feet, blew on his fingers. He was more sensitive to cold than I. Huddling around the baby kept me warm.

The baby woke, very hungry, and I was helpless to comfort him. He sucked so hard that my finger was white and puckered, and then he screamed. People gathered around us there. Women held out their arms, but I did not give the baby to any of them. I did not trust them. I did not trust the man who sat down beside me, either, and spoke softly. He was a young man with a hard-boned, sad, unshaven face. What I remember most about him was the sadness. He wanted to take the baby back to his wife so she could feed him. She had a new baby of her own, he said, and enough milk for two.

"I am waiting," I said, "for our own mother."

"When is she coming back?" asked the young man.

I could not answer. The sad man waited with open arms. Karl sat mute on one side of me, gazing into the dark sky. Behind and before, large interfering ladies counseled and conferred.

"Give him the baby, dear."

"Don't be stubborn."

"Let him take the baby home."

"No," I said to every order and suggestion. I even kicked hard when one woman tried to take my brother from my arms. They grew discouraged, or simply indifferent after a time, and went off. It was not the ladies who convinced me, finally, but the baby himself. He did not let up screaming. The longer he cried, the longer the sad man sat beside me, the weaker my resistance was, until finally I could barely hold my own tears back.

"I'm coming with you then," I told the young man. "I'll bring the baby back here when he's fed."

"No," cried Karl, coming out of his stupor suddenly, "you can't leave me alone!"

He grabbed my arm so fervently that the baby slipped, and then the young man caught me, as if to help, but instead he scooped the baby to himself.

"I'll take care of him," he said, and turned away.

I tried to wrench from Karl's grip, but like my mother he was strongest when he was weak, and I could not break free. I saw the man walk into the shadows. I heard the baby's wail fade. I finally sat down beside Karl and let the cold sink into me.

One hour passed. Another hour. When the colored lights went out and the moon came up, diffused behind the sheets of clouds, I knew the young man wasn't coming back. And yet, because he looked too sad to do any harm to anyone, I was more afraid for Karl and myself. We were the ones who were thoroughly lost. I stood up. Karl stood with me. Without a word we walked down the empty streets to our old rooming house. We had no key but Karl displayed one unexpected talent. He took the thin-bladed knife that Adelaide had given him, and picked the lock.

Once we stood in the cold room, the sudden presence of our mother's clothing dismayed us. The room was filled with the faint perfume of the dried flowers that she scattered in her trunk, the rich scent of the clove-studded orange she hung in the closet and the lavender oil she rubbed into her skin at night. The sweetness of her breath seemed to linger, the rustle of her silk underskirt, the quick sound of her heels. Our longing buried us. We sank down on her bed and cried, wrapped in her quilt, clutching each other. When that was done, however, I acquired a brain of ice.

I washed my face off in the basin, then I roused Karl and told him we were going to Aunt Fritzie's. He acquiesced, suffering again in a dumb lethargy. We ate all there was to eat in the room, two cold pancakes, and packed what we owned in a small cardboard suitcase. Karl carried that. I carried the quilt. The last thing I did was reach far back in my mother's drawer and pull out her small round keepsake box. It was covered in blue velvet and tightly locked.

"We might need to sell these things," I told Karl. He hesitated but then, with a hard look, he took the box.

We slipped out before sunrise and walked to the train station. In the weedy yards there were men who knew each boxcar's destination.

We found the car we wanted and climbed in. There was hay in one corner. We spread the quilt over it and rolled up together, curled tight, with our heads on the suitcase and Adelaide's blue velvet box between us in Karl's breast pocket. We clung to the thought of the treasures inside of it.

We spent a day and a night on that train while it switched and braked and rumbled on an agonizingly complex route to Argus. We did not dare jump off for a drink of water or to scavenge food. The one time we did try this the train started up so quickly that we were hardly able to catch the side rungs again. We lost our suitcase and the quilt because we took the wrong car, farther back, and that night we did not sleep at all for the cold. Karl was too miserable even to argue with me when I told him it was my turn to hold Adelaide's box. I put it in the bodice of my jumper. It did not keep me warm, but even so, the sparkle of the diamond when I shut my eyes, the patterns of garnets that whirled in the dark air, gave me something. My mind hardened, faceted and gleaming like a magic stone, and I saw my mother clearly.

She was still in the plane, flying close to the pulsing stars, when suddenly Omar noticed that the fuel was getting low. He did not love Adelaide at first sight, or even care what happened to her. He had to save himself. Somehow he had to lighten his load. So he set his controls. He stood up in his cockpit. Then in one sudden motion he plucked my mother out of her seat like a doll and dropped her overboard.

All night she fell through the awful cold. Her coat flapped open and her pale green dress wrapped tightly around her legs. He red hair flowed straight upward like a flame. She was a candle that gave no warmth. My heart froze. I had no love for her. That is why, by morning, I allowed her to hit the earth.

By the time we saw the sign on the brick station, I was dull again, a block of sullen cold. Still, it hurt when I jumped, scraping my cold knees and the heels of my hands. The pain sharpened me enough to read signs in windows and rack my mind for just where Aunt Fritzie's shop was. It had been years since we visited.

Karl was older, and I probably should not hold myself accountable for losing him too. But I didn't call him. I didn't run after him. I couldn't stand how his face glowed in the blossoms' reflected light, pink and radiant, so like the way he sat beneath our mother's stroking hand.

When I stopped running, I realized I was alone and now more truly lost than any of my family, since all I had done from the first was to try and hold them close while death, panic, chance, and ardor each took them their separate ways.

Hot tears came up suddenly behind my eyes and my ears burned. I ached to cry, hard, but I knew that was useless and so I walked. I walked carefully, looking at everything around me, and it was lucky I did this because I'd run past the butcher shop and, suddenly, there it was, set back from the road down a short dirt drive. A white pig was painted on the side, and inside the pig, the lettering "Kozka's Meats." I walked toward it between rows of tiny fir trees. The place looked both shabby and prosperous, as though Fritzie and Pete were too busy with customers to care for outward appearances. I stood on the broad front stoop and noticed everything I could, the way a beggar does. A rack of elk horns was nailed overhead. I walked beneath them.

The entryway was dark, my heart was in my throat. And then, what I saw was quite natural, understandable, although it was not real.

Again, the dog leapt toward Karl and blossoms from his stick fell. Except that they fell around me in the entrance to the store. I smelled the petals melting on my coat, tasted their thin sweetness in my mouth. I had no time to wonder how this could be happening because they disappeared as suddenly as they'd come when I told my name to the man behind the glass counter.

This man, tall and fat with a pale brown moustache and an old blue denim cap on his head, was Uncle Pete. His eyes were round, mild, exactly the same light brown as his hair. His smile was slow, sweet for a butcher, and always hopeful. He did not recognize me even after I told him who I was. Finally his eyes widened and he called out for Fritzie.

"Your sister's girl! She's here!" he shouted down the hall.

I told him I was alone, that I had come in on the boxcar, and he lifted me up in his arms. He carried me back to the kitchen where Aunt Fritzie was frying a sausage for my cousin, the beautiful Sita, who sat at the table and stared at me with narrowed eyes while I tried to tell Fritzie and Pete just how I'd come to walk into their front door out of nowhere.

They stared at me with friendly suspicion, thinking that I'd run away. But when I told them about The Great Omar, and how Adelaide held up her purse, and how Omar helped her into the plane, their faces turned grim.

"Sita, go polish the glass out front," said Aunt Fritzie. Sita slid unwillingly out of her chair. "Now," Fritzie said. Uncle Pete sat down heavily. The ends of his moustache went into his mouth, he pressed his thumbs together under his chin, and turned to me. "Go on, tell the rest," he said, and so I told all of the rest, and when I had finished I saw that I had also drunk a glass of milk and eaten a sausage. By then I could hardly sit upright. Uncle Pete took me in his strong arms and I remember sagging against him, then nothing. I slept that day and all night and did not wake until the next morning. Sleep robbed me as profoundly as being awake had, for when I finally woke I had no memory of where I was and how I'd got there. I lay still for what seemed like a long while, trying to place the objects in the room.

This was the room where I would sleep for the rest of my childhood, or what passed for childhood anyway, since after that train journey I was not a child. It was a pleasant room, and before me it belonged entirely to cousin Sita. The paneling was warm-stained pine. Most of the space was taken up by a tall oak dresser with fancy curlicues and many drawers. A small sheet of polished tin hung on the door and served as a mirror. Through that door, as I was trying to understand my surroundings, walked Sita herself, tall and perfect with a blond braid that reached to her waist.

"So you're finally awake." She sat down on the edge of my trundle bed and folded her arms over her small new breasts. She was a year older than me. Since I'd seen her last, she had grown suddenly, like Karl, but her growth had not thinned her into an awkward bony creature. She was now a slim female of utter grace.

I realized I was staring too long at her, and then the whole series of events came flooding back and I turned away. Sita grinned. She looked down at me, her strong white teeth shining, and she stroked the blond braid that hung down over one shoulder.

"Where's Auntie Adelaide?" she asked.

I did not answer.

"Where's Auntie Adelaide?" she asked, again. "How come you came here? Where'd she go? Where's Karl?"

"I don't know."

I suppose I thought the misery of my answer would quiet Sita but that was before I knew her. It only fueled more questions.

"How come Auntie left you alone? Where's Karl? What's this?"

She took the blue velvet box from my pile of clothes and shook it casually next to her ear.

"What's in it?"

For the moment at least, I bested her by snatching the box with an angry swiftness she did not expect. I rolled from the bed, bundled my clothes into my arms, and walked out of the room. The one door open in the hallway was the bathroom, a large smoky room of many uses that soon became my haven since it was the only door I could bolt against my cousin.

Every day for weeks after I arrived in Argus, I woke up thinking I was back on the farm with my mother and father and that none of this had happened. I always managed to believe this until I opened my eyes. Then I saw the dark swirls in the pine and Sita's arm hanging off the bed above me. I smelled the air, peppery and warm from the sausage makers. I heard the rhythmical whine of meat saws, slicers, the rippling beat of fans. Aunt Fritzie was smoking her sharp Viceroys in the bathroom. Uncle Pete was outside feeding the big white German shepherd that was kept in the shop at night to guard the canvas bags of money.

Every morning I got up, put on one of Sita's hand-me-down pink dresses, and went out to the kitchen to wait for Uncle Pete. I cooked breakfast. That I made fried eggs and a good cup of coffee at age eleven was a source of wonder to my aunt and uncle, and an outrage to Sita. That's why I did it every morning, with a finesse that got more casual until it became a habit to have me there.

From the first I made myself essential. I did this because I had to, because I had nothing else to offer. The day after I arrived in Argus and woke up to Sita's calculating smile I also tried to offer what I thought was treasure, the blue velvet box that held Adelaide's heirlooms.

I did it in as grand a manner as I could, with Sita for a witness and with Pete and Fritzie sitting at the kitchen table. That morning, I walked in with my hair combed wet and laid the box between the two of them. I looked at Sita as I spoke.

"This should pay my way."

Fritzie looked at me. She had my mother's features sharpened one notch past beauty. Her skin was rough and her short curled hair was yellow, bleached pale, not golden. Fritzie's eyes were a swimming, crazy shade of blue that startled customers. She ate heartily, but her constant smoking kept her string-bean thin and sallow.

"You don't have to pay us," said Fritzie, "Pete, tell her. She doesn't have to pay us. Sit down, shut up, and eat."

Fritzie spoke like that, joking and blunt. Pete was slower. "Come. Sit down and forget about the money," he said. "You never know about your mother . . ." he added in an earnest voice that trailed away when he looked at Aunt Fritzie. Things had a way of evaporating under her eyes, vanishing, getting sucked up into the blue heat of her stare. Even Sita had nothing to say.

"I want to give you this," I said. "I insist."

"She insists," exclaimed Aunt Fritzie. Her smile had a rakish flourish because one tooth was chipped in front. "Don't insist," she said. "Eat."

But I would not sit down. I took a knife from the butter plate and started to pry the lock up.

"Here now," said Fritzie. "Pete, help her."

So Pete got up slowly and fetched a screwdriver from the top of the icebox and sat down and jammed the end underneath the lock.

"Let her open it," said Fritzie, when the lock popped up. So Pete pushed the little round box across the table.

"I bet it's empty," Sita said. She took a big chance saying that, but it paid off in spades and aces between us growing up, because I lifted the lid a moment later and what she said was true. There was nothing of value in the box.

Stick pins. A few thick metal buttons off a coat. And a ticket describing the necklace of tiny garnets, pawned for practically nothing in Minneapolis.

There was silence. Even Fritzie was at a loss. Sita nearly buzzed off her chair in triumph but held her tongue, that is until later, when she would crow. Pete put his hand on his head in deep vexation. I stood quietly, stunned.

What is dark is light and bad news brings slow gain, I told myself. I could see a pattern to all of what happened, a pattern that suggested completion in years to come. The baby was lifted up while my mother was dashed to earth. Karl rode west and I ran east. It is opposites that finally meet.

Issue 95, 1985

OUTSIDERS

✠

Jonathan Lethem

❈

Tugboat Syndrome

Context is everything. Dress me up and see. I'm a carnival barker, an auctioneer, a downtown performance artist, a speaker in tongues, a senator drunk on filibuster. My mouth won't quit, though mostly I whisper or subvocalize like I'm reading aloud, my Adam's apple bobbing, jaw muscle beating like a miniature heart under my cheek, the noise suppressed, the words escaping silently, mere ghosts of themselves, husks empty of breath and tone. In this diminished form the words rush out of the cornucopia of my brain to course over the surface of the world, tickling reality like fingers on piano keys. Caressing, nudging. They're an invisible army on a peacekeeping mission, a peaceable horde. They mean no harm. They placate, interpret, massage. Everywhere they're smoothing down imperfections, putting hairs in place, putting ducks in a row, replacing divots. Counting and polishing the silver. Patting old ladies gently on the behind, eliciting a giggle. Only—here's the rub—when they find too much perfection, when the surface is already buffed smooth, the ducks already orderly, the old ladies complacent, then my little army rebels, breaks into the stores. Reality needs a prick here and there, the carpet needs a flaw. My words begin plucking at threads nervously, seeking purchase, a weak point, a vulnerable ear. That's when it comes, the urge to shout in the church, the nursery, the crowded movie house. It's an itch at first. Inconsequential. But that itch is soon a torrent behind a straining dam. Noah's flood. That itch is my whole life.

Here it comes now. Cover your ears. Build an ark. I've got Tourette's.

"Eat me!" I scream.

I grew up in the library of St. Vincent's Home for Boys in downtown
Brooklyn, on a street which serves as the off-ramp to the Brooklyn
Bridge. There the Home faced eight lanes of traffic, lined by Brooklyn's central sorting annex for the post office, a building that hummed
and blinked all through the night, its gates groaning open to admit
trucks bearing mountains of those mysterious items called letters; by
the Burton Trade School for Automechanics, where hardened students attempting to set their lives dully straight spilled out twice a day
for sandwich-and-beer breaks, overwhelming the cramped bodega
next door; by a granite bust of Lafayette, indicating his point of entry
into the Battle of Brooklyn; by a car lot surrounded by a high fence
topped with wide curls of barbed wire and wind-whipped fluorescent flags, and by a red-brick Quaker meetinghouse that had presumably been there when the rest was farmland. In short, this jumble of
stuff at the clotted entrance to the ancient, battered borough was offi-
cially Nowhere, a place strenuously ignored in passing through to
Somewhere Else. Until rescued by Frank Minna I lived, as I said, in
the library.

I set out to read every book in that tomblike library, every miserable
dead donation ever indexed and forgotten there—a mark of my profound fear and boredom at St. Vincent's as well as an early sign of
my Tourettic compulsions for counting, processing and inspection.
Huddled there in the windowsill, turning dry pages and watching
dust motes pinball through beams of sunlight, I sought signs of my
odd dawning self in Theodore Dreiser, Kenneth Roberts, J.B.
Priestley and back issues of *Popular Mechanics* and failed, couldn't
find the language of myself. I was closer on Saturday mornings—
Daffy Duck especially gave me something, if I could bear to imagine
growing up a dynamited, beak-shattered duck. Art Carney on *The
Honeymooners* gave me something too, in the way he jerked his
neck, when we were allowed to stay up to see him. But it was Minna

who brought me the language, Minna and Court Street that let me speak.

We four were selected because we were the four white boys at St. Vincent's. I was surely undersold goods, a twitcher and nosepicker retrieved from the library instead of the schoolyard, probably a retard, certainly a regrettable, inferior offering. Mr. Kassel was a teacher who knew Frank Minna from the neighborhood, and his invitation to Minna to borrow us for the afternoon was a first glimpse of the halo of favors and favoritism that extended around Minna—"knowing somebody" as a life condition. Minna was our exact reverse, we who knew no one and benefited nothing from it when we did.

Minna had asked for white boys to suit his clients' presumed prejudice—and his own certain ones. But he didn't show any particular tenderness that first day, a sweltering August weekday afternoon after classes, streets like black chewing gum, slow-creeping cars like badly projected science-class slides in the haze. Though he seemed a man to us, Minna was probably twenty-five. He was gangly except for a tiny potbelly in his pocket-T, and his hair was combed into a smooth pompadour, a Brooklyn hairstyle that stood outside time, projecting from some distant Frank Sinatra past. He opened the rear of his dented, graffitied van and told us to get inside, then slammed and padlocked the doors without explanation, without asking our names.

We four gaped at one another, giddy and astonished at this escape, not knowing what it meant, not really needing to know. The others, Tony, Gilbert and Danny, were willing to be grouped with me, to pretend I fit with them, if that was what it took to be plucked up by the outside world and seated in the dark on a dirty steel truckbed vibrating its way to somewhere that wasn't St. Vincent's. Of course I was vibrating too, vibrating before Minna rounded us up, vibrating inside always and straining to keep it from showing. I didn't kiss the other three boys, but I wanted to. Instead I made a kissing, chirping sound, like a bird's peep, over and over: "Chrip, chrip, chrip."

Tony told me to shut the fuck up, but his heart wasn't in it, not this day, in the midst of life's unfolding mystery. For Tony, especially, this was his destiny coming to find him. He saw more in Minna from the first because he'd prepared himself to see it. Tony Vermonte was famous at St. Vincent's for the confidence he exuded, confidence that a mistake had been made, that he didn't belong in the Home. He was Italian, better than the rest of us, who didn't know what we were. His father was either a mobster or a cop—Tony saw no contradiction in this, so we didn't either. The Italians would return for him, in one guise or another, and that was what he'd taken Minna for.

Tony was famous for other things as well. He had lived outside the Home and then come back. A Quaker family had taken Tony in, intending to give him a permanent home. He'd announced his contempt even as he packed his clothes: They weren't Italian. Still, he lived with them for a few months. They installed him at Brooklyn Friends, a private school a few blocks away, and on his way home most days he'd come and hang on the St. Vincent's fence and tell stories of the private-school girls he'd felt up and sometimes penetrated, the faggy private-school boys who swam and played soccer but were easily humiliated in fistfights. Then one day his foster parents found prodigious Tony in bed with one girl too many: their own sixteen-year-old daughter. Or so the story went; there was only one source. Anyway, he was reinstalled at St. Vincent's, where he fell easily into his old routine of beating up and befriending me on alternating afternoons.

Gilbert Coney was Tony's right hand, a stocky boy just passing for tough—he would have beamed at you for calling him a thug. But he was tolerant of me, and we had a couple of secrets. On a Home for Boys visit to the Museum of Natural History, Gilbert and I had split from the group and returned to the room dominated by an enormous plastic blue whale suspended from the ceiling, which had been the focus of the official visit. But underneath the whale was a gallery of murky dioramas of undersea life, lit so you had to press close to the glass to find the wonders tucked deep in the corners. In one a sperm whale fought a giant squid. In another a killer whale pierced a floor of ice. Gilbert and I wandered hypnotized, and when a class of third graders was led away we found we had the giant hall to ourselves. Gilbert showed me his discovery: a small brass door beside the penguin diorama had been left unlocked. When he opened it we saw that it led both behind and into the penguin scene.

"Get in, Lionel," said Gilbert.

If I'd not wanted to, it would have been bullying, but I wanted to desperately. Every minute the hall remained empty was precious. The lip of the doorway was knee-high. I clambered in and opened the flap in the ocean-blue painted boards that made the side wall of the diorama, then slipped into the picture. The ocean floor was a smooth bowl of painted plaster. I scooted down the grade on my bended knees, looking out at a flabbergasted Gilbert on the other side of the glass. Swimming penguins were mounted on rods extending straight from the far wall, and others were suspended in the plastic waves of ocean surface that now made a low ceiling over my head. I caressed the nearest penguin, one mounted low, shown diving in pursuit of a fish, patted its head, stroked its gullet as though helping it swallow a dry pill. Gilbert guffawed, thinking I was performing comedy for him, when in fact I'd been overwhelmed by a tender, touchy impulse toward the stiff, poignant penguin. Now it became imperative that I touch *all* the penguins, or all I could, anyway—some were inaccessible to me, on the other side of the barrier of the ocean's surface, standing on ice floes. Shuffling on my knees I made the rounds, affectionately tagging each swimming bird before I made my escape back through the brass door. Gilbert was impressed, I could tell. I was now a kid who'd do anything, do crazy things. He was right and wrong, of course—once I'd touched the first penguin I had no choice.

Somehow this led to a series of confidences. I was crazy but also easily intimidated, which made me Gilbert's idea of a safe repository for his crazy feelings. Gilbert was a precocious masturbator, and looking for some triangulation between his own experiments and schoolyard lore. Did I do it? How often? One hand or two? Close my eyes? Ever rub against the mattress? I took his inquiries seriously, but I didn't really have the information he needed, not yet. My stupidity made Gilbert grouchy at first, and he spent a week or two glowering to let me know what galactic measures of pain awaited if I ratted him out. Then he came back, more urgent than ever. Try it and I'll watch, he said. It's not so hard. I obeyed, as I had in the museum, but the results weren't as good. I couldn't treat myself with the tenderness I'd lavished on the penguins, at least not in front of Gilbert. He became grouchy again, and after two or three go-arounds the subject was permanently dropped.

Tourette's teaches you what people will ignore and forget, teaches you to see the mechanism people employ to tuck away the incongruous, the disruptive—it teaches you because you're the one lobbing the incongruous and disruptive their way. Once I sat on a bus a few rows ahead of a man with a belching tic—long, groaning, almost vomitous-sounding noises, the kind a fifth grader learns to make by swallowing a bellyful of air, then forgets by high school when charming girls becomes more vital than freaking them out. This man's compulsion was terribly specific: he sat at the back of the bus, and only when every head faced forward did he give out with his digestive simulacra. Then, every sixth or seventh time, he'd mix in a messy farting sound. He was a miserable-looking black man in his sixties. Despite the peek-a-boo brilliance of his timing, it was clear to anyone he was the source, and so the other riders coughed reprovingly, quit giving him the satisfaction of looking. Of course, our not glancing back freed him to run together great uninterrupted phrases of his ripest noise. To all but me he was just an antisocial jerk fishing for attention. But I saw that it was unmistakably a compulsion, a tic—Tourette's—and I knew those other passengers would barely recall it a few minutes after stepping off to their destinations. Despite how that maniacal croaking filled the auditorium of the bus, the concertgoers were plainly engaged in the task of forgetting the music. Consensual reality is both fragile and elastic, and it heals like the skin of a bubble. The belching man ruptured it so quickly and completely that I could watch the wound instantly seal.

Similarly, I doubt the other boys directly recalled my bouts of kissing. That tic was too much for us all. Nine months or so after touching the penguins I had begun to overflow with reaching, tapping, grabbing and kissing urges. Those compulsions emerged first, while language was still trapped like a roiling ocean under a calm floe of ice, the way I'd been trapped in the underwater half of the penguin display. I'd be-

gun reaching for door frames, kneeling to grab at skittering loosened
sneaker laces (a recent fashion among the toughest boys at St. Vincent's, unfortunately for me), incessantly tapping the metal-pipe legs
of the schoolroom desks and chairs and, worst, grabbing and kissing
my fellow boys. I grew terrified of myself then and burrowed deeper
into the library, but I was forced out for classes or meals. Then it
would happen. I'd lunge at someone and kiss their cheek or neck or
forehead, whatever I hit. After, compulsion expelled, I could try to explain, defend myself or flee. I kissed Greg Toon and Edwin Torres,
whose eyes I'd never dared meet. I kissed Leshawn Montrose, who'd
broken Mr. Voccaro's arm with a chair. I kissed Tony Vermonte and
Gilbert Coney and tried to kiss Danny Fantl. I kissed my own counter-
parts, other invisible boys working the margins at St. Vincent's. "It's a
game!" I'd say, pleadingly. "It's a game." Since the most inexplicable
things in our lives were games, with their ancient embedded rituals,
British Bulldog, Ringolevio and Scully, it seemed possible I might persuade them this was another one, the Kissing Game. Just as important,
I might persuade myself. "It's a game," I'd say desperately, as tears of
pain ran down my face. Leshawn Montrose cracked my head against a
porcelain water fountain; Greg Toon and Edwin Torres generously
only shucked me off onto the floor. Tony Vermonte twisted my arm
behind my back and forced me against a wall. "It's a game," I
breathed. He released me and shook his head, full of contempt and
pity. Danny Fantl saw my move coming and faked me out, then vanished down a stairwell. Gilbert stood and glared, deeply unnerved due
to our private history. "A game," I reassured him.

Meantime beneath that frozen shell a sea of language was reaching
full boil. It became harder and harder not to notice that when a television pitchman said *to last the rest of a lifetime* my brain went *to rest the
lust of a loaftomb,* that when I heard "Alfred Hitchcock" I silently
replied "Altered Houseclock," that when I sat reading Booth Tark-
ington in the library, my throat and jaw worked behind my clenched
lips, desperately fitting the syllables of the prose to the rhythms of
"Rapper's Delight," which was then playing every fifteen or twenty
minutes out on the yard.

•

I found other outlets, other obsessions. The pale thirteen-year-old Mr. Kassel pulled out of the library and offered to Minna was prone to floor-tapping, whistling, tongue clicking, rapid head turns and wall stroking, anything but the direct utterances for which my Tourette's brain most yearned. Language bubbled inside me now but it felt too dangerous to let out. Speech was intention, and I couldn't let anyone else or myself know how intentional my craziness felt. Pratfalls, antics, those were accidental lunacy, and so forgivable. Practically speaking, it was one thing to stroke Leshawn Montrose's arm, or even to kiss him, another entirely to walk up and call him Shefawn Mongoose or Fuckyou Moonprose. So, though I collected words, treasured them like a drooling sadistic captor, melting them down, filing off their edges, before release I translated them into physical performance, manic choreography.

My body was an overwound watch spring, one which could easily drive a vast factory mechanism like the one in *Modern Times,* which we watched that year in the basement of the Brooklyn Public Library on Fourth Avenue. I took Chaplin as a model: obviously blazing with aggression, he'd managed to keep his trap shut and so had skirted danger and been regarded as cute. I needn't exactly strain for a motto: silence, golden, get it? Got it. Hone your timing instead, burnish those physical routines, your idiot wall stroking and lace chasing, until they're funny in a flickering black-and-white way, until your enemies don policemen's caps and begin tripping over themselves, until doe-eyed women swoon. So I kept my tongue wound in my teeth, ignored the pulsing in my cheek, the throbbing in my gullet, persistently swallowed language back like vomit. It burned as hotly.

We rode a mile or two before Minna's van halted, engine guttering to a stop. Then he let us out of the back and we found ourselves in a gated warehouse yard under the shadow of the Brooklyn-Queens Expressway, in a ruined industrial zone. Minna led us to a large truck, a detached twelve-wheel trailer with no cab in evidence, then rolled up the back to reveal a load of identical cardboard crates, a hundred, two hundred, maybe more.

"Couple you boys get up inside," said Minna distractedly. Tony and Danny had the guile to immediately leap into the truck, where they could work shaded from the sun. "You're just gonna run this stuff inside, that's all. Hand shit off, move it up to the front of the truck, get it in. Straight shot, you got it?" He pointed to the warehouse. We all nodded, and I peeped. It went unnoticed.

Minna opened the big panel doors of the warehouse and showed us where to set the crates. We started quickly, then wilted in the heat. Tony and Danny massed the crates at the lip of the truck while Gilbert and I made the first dozen runs, then the older boys ceded their advantage and began to help us drag them across the blazing yard. Minna never touched a crate; he spent the whole time in the office of the warehouse, a cluttered room full of desks, file cabinets, tacked-up notes and pornographic calendars and a stacked tower of orange traffic cones, visible to us through an interior window, smoking cigarettes and jawing on the telephone, apparently not listening for replies. Every time I glanced through the window his mouth was moving, but the door was closed, and he was inaudible behind the glass. At some point another man appeared, from where I wasn't sure, and stood in the yard wiping his forehead as though he were the one laboring. Minna came out, the two stepped inside the office, the other man disappeared. We moved the last of the crates inside, Minna rolled the gate of the truck and locked the warehouse, pointed us back to his van, but paused before shutting us into the back.

"Hot day, huh?" he said, looking at us directly for what might have been the first time.

Bathed in sweat, we nodded, afraid to speak.

"You monkeys thirsty? Because personally I'm dying out here."

Minna drove us to Smith Street, a few blocks from St. Vincent's, and pulled over in front of a bodega, then bought us pop-top cans of Miller, and sat with us in the back of the van, drinking. It was my first beer.

"Names," said Minna, pointing at Tony, our obvious leader. We said our first names, starting with Tony. Minna didn't offer his own, only drained his beer and nodded. I began tapping the truck panel beside me.

Physical exertion over, astonishment at our deliverance from St. Vincent's receding, my symptoms found their opening again.

"You probably ought to know, Lionel's a freak," said Tony, his voice vibrant with self-regard. He jerked his thumb in my direction.

"Yeah, well, you're all freaks, if you don't mind me pointing it out," said Minna. "No parents—or am I mixed up?"

Silence.

"Finish your beer," said Minna, tossing his can past us, into the back of the van.

And that was the end of our first job for Frank Minna.

But Minna rounded us up again the next week, brought us to that same desolate yard, and this time he was friendlier. The task was identical, almost to the number of boxes, and we performed it in the same trepidatious silence. I felt a violent hatred burning off Tony in my and Gilbert's direction, as though he thought we were in the process of screwing up his Italian rescue. Danny was exempt and oblivious. Still, we'd begun to function as a team—demanding physical work contained its own truths, and we explored them despite ourselves.

Over beers Minna said, "You like this work?"

One of us said *sure*.

"You know what you're doing?" Minna grinned at us, waiting. The question was confusing. "You know what kind of work this is?"

"What, moving boxes?" said Tony.

"Right, moving. Moving work. That's what you call it when you work for me. Here, look." He stood to get into his pocket, pulled out a roll of twenties and a small stack of white cards. He stared at the roll for a minute, then peeled off four twenties and handed one to each of us. It was my first twenty dollars. Then he offered us each a card. It read: *L & L Movers. Gerard & Frank Minna*. And a phone number.

"You're Gerard or Frank?" said Tony.

"Minna, Frank." Like *Bond, James*. He ran his hand through his hair. "So you're a moving company, get it? Doing moving work." This seemed a very important point: that we call it *moving*. I couldn't imagine what else to call it.

"Who's Gerard?" said Tony. Gilbert and I, even Danny, watched Minna carefully. Tony was questioning him on behalf of us all.

"My brother."

"Older or younger?"

"Older."

Tony thought for a minute. "Who's L & L?"

"Just the name, L & L. Two Ls. Name of the company."

"Yeah, but what's it mean?"

"What do you need it to mean, Fruitloop—Living Loud? Loving Ladies? Laughing at you Losers?"

"What, it doesn't mean anything?" said Tony.

"I didn't say that, did I?"

"Least Lonely," I suggested.

"There you go," said Minna, waving his can of beer at me. "L & L Movers, Least Lonely."

Tony, Danny and Gilbert all stared at me, uncertain how I'd gained this freshet of approval.

"Liking Lionel," I heard myself say.

"Minna, that's an Italian name?" said Tony. This was on his own behalf, obviously. It was time to get to the point. The rest of us could all go fuck ourselves.

"What are you, the census?" said Minna. "Cub reporter? What's your full name, Jimmy Olsen?"

"Lois Lane," I said.

"Tony Vermonte," said Tony, ignoring me.

"Vermont-ee," repeated Minna. "That's what, like a New England thing, right? You a Red Sox fan?"

"Yankees," said Tony, confused and defensive. The Yankees were champions now, the Red Sox their hapless, eternal victims, vanquished most recently by Bucky Dent's famous home run. We'd all watched it on television.

"Luckylent," I said, remembering. "Duckybent."

Minna erupted with laughter. "Yeah, Ducky fucking Bent! That's good. Don't look now, it's Ducky Bent."

"Lexluthor," I said, reaching out to touch Minna's shoulder. He only stared at my hand, didn't move away. "Lunchy-looper, Laughyluck—"

"All right, Loopy," said Minna. "Enough already."

"Loopylip—" I was desperate for a way to stop. My hand went on tapping Minna's shoulder.

"Let it go," said Minna, and now he returned my shoulder taps, once, hard. "Don't tug the boat."

•

To tugboat was to try Minna's patience. Any time you pushed your luck, said too much, overstayed a welcome or overestimated the usefulness of a given method or approach you were guilty of having tugged the boat. *Tugboating* was most of all a dysfunction of wits and storytellers, and a universal one: anybody who thought themselves funny would likely tug a boat here or there. Knowing when a joke or verbal gambit was right at its limit, quitting before the boat had been tugged, that was art.

Years before the word *Tourette's* was familiar to any of us, Minna had me diagnosed: Terminal Tugboater.

Distributing eighty dollars and those four business cards was all Minna had to do to instate the four of us as the junior staff of L & L Movers. Twenty dollars and a beer remained our usual pay. Minna would gather us sporadically, on a day's notice, or no notice at all—the latter possibility became incentive, once we'd begun high school, for us to return to St. Vincent's directly after classes and lounge in the schoolyard, pretending not to listen for the distinctive grumble of his van's motor. The jobs varied enormously. We'd load merchandise, like the cartons in the trailer, in and out of storefront basement grates all up and down Court Street, borderline shady activity that it seemed wholesalers ought to be handling themselves, transactions sealed with a shared cigar in the back of the shop. Or we'd bustle apartment loads of furniture in and out of brownstone walk-ups, legitimate moving jobs, where fretting couples worried we weren't old or expert enought to handle their belongings—Minna would hush them, remind them of the cost of distractions: "The meter's running." We put sofas through third-story windows with a makeshift cinch and pulley, Tony and Minna on the roof, Gilbert and Danny in the window to receive, me on the ground with the guide ropes. A massive factory building under the Manhattan Bridge, owned by an important unseen friend of Minna's, had been damaged in a fire, and we moved the inhabitants for free, as some sort of settlement or concession. The terms were obscure, but Minna was terrifically urgent about it, seething at any delay—the only meter running now was Minna's credibility with his friend-client. Once we emptied an entire electronics showroom into Minna's truck, pulling unboxed stereos off shelves and out of window displays, disconnecting the wires from lit, blinking amplifiers, eventually even taking the phone off the desk—it would have seemed a sort of brazen burglary had Minna not been standing on the sidewalk in front, drinking beer and telling jokes with the man who'd unpadlocked the shop gates for us as we filed past with the goods. Everywhere Minna connived and cajoled and dropped names, winking at us to make us complicit, and everywhere Minna's clients stared at us boys, some wondering if we'd palm a valuable when they weren't looking, some trying to figure the angle, perhaps hoping to catch a hint of disloyalty, an edge over Minna they'd save for when they needed it. We palmed nothing, revealed no disloyalty. Instead we stared back, tried to make them flinch. And we listened, gathered information. Minna was teaching us, when he meant to and when he didn't.

It changed us as a group. We developed a certain collective ego, a presence apart at the Home. We grew less embattled from within, more from without: non-white boys sensed in our privilege a hint of their future deprivations and punished us for it. Age had begun to heighten those distinctions anyway. So Tony, Gilbert, Danny and myself smoothed out our old antipathies and circled the wagons. We stuck up for one another, at the Home and at Sarah J. Hale, our local high school.

There at Sarah J.: the St. Vincent's Boys were disguised, blended with the larger population, a pretty rough crowd despite their presumably having parents and siblings and telephones and bedroom doors with locks and a thousand other unimaginable advantages. There we mixed with girls for the first time—what mixing was possible with the brutal, strapping black girls of Sarah J., gangs of whom laid afterschool ambushes for any white boy daring enough to have flirted, even made eye-contact, with one inside the building. The girls were claimed by boyfriends too sophisticated to bother with school, who rode by for them at lunch hour in cars throbbing with amplified basslines and sometimes boasting bullet-riddled doors, and their only use for us was as a dartboard for throwing lit cigarette butts. Yes, relations between the sexes were strained at Sarah J., and I doubt any of us four, even Tony, so much as copped a feel from the girls we were schooled with there.

Minna's Court Street was the old Brooklyn, a placid ageless surface alive underneath with talk, with deals and casual insults, a neighborhood political machine with pizzeria and butcher-shop bosses and unwritten rules everywhere. All was talk except for what mattered most, which were unspoken understandings. The barbershop, where he took us for identical haircuts that cost three dollars each, except even that fee was waived for Minna—no one had to wonder why the price of a haircut hadn't gone up since 1966, nor why six old barbers were working out of the same ancient storefront; the barbershop was a retirement home, a social club and front for a backroom poker game. The barbers were taken care of because this was Brooklyn, where people *looked out*. Why would the prices go up, when nobody walked in who wasn't part of this conspiracy, this trust?—though if you spoke of it you'd surely meet with confused denials, or laughter and a too-hard cuff on the cheek. Another exemplary mystery was the "arcade," a giant storefront containing three pinball machines and six or seven video games, Asteroids, Frogger, Centipede, and a cashier who'd change dollars to quarters and accept hundred-dollar bills folded into lists of numbers, names of horses and football teams. The curb in front of the arcade was lined with Vespas. They sat without anything more than a bicycle lock for protection, a taunt to vandals. A block away, on Smith, they would have been stripped, but here they were pristine, a curbside showroom. It didn't need explaining—this was Court Street. And Court Street, where it passed through Carroll Gardens and Cobble Hill, was the only Brooklyn, really—north was Brooklyn Heights, secretly a part of Manhattan, south was the harbor, and the rest, everything east of the Gowanus Canal, apart from small outposts of civilization in Park Slope and Windsor Terrace, was an unspeakable barbarian tumult.

Sometimes he needed just one of us. He'd appear at the Home in his Impala instead of the van, request someone specific, then spirit them away to the bruised consternation of those left behind. Tony was in and out of Minna's graces, his ambition and pride costing him as much as he won, but he was unmistakably our leader and Minna's right hand. He wore his private errands with Minna like Purple Hearts, but refused to report on their content to the rest of us. Danny, athletic, silent and tall, became Minna's greyhound, sent on private deliveries and rendezvous, and given early driving lessons in a vacant Red Hook lot, as though Minna were grooming him for work as an international spy, or Kato for a new Green Hornet. Gilbert, all bullish determination, was pegged for the grunt work, sitting in double-parked cars, repairing a load of ruptured cartons with strapping tape, and repainting the van, whose graffitied exterior some of Minna's neighbors had apparently found objectionable. And I was an extra set of eyes and ears and opinions. Minna would drag me along to backrooms and offices and barbershop negotiations, then debrief me afterwards. What did I think of that guy? Shitting or not? A moron or retard? A shark or a mook? Minna encouraged me to have a take on everything, and to spit it out, as though he thought my verbal disgorgings were only commentary not yet anchored to subject matter. And he adored my echolalia. He thought I was doing impressions.

Needless to say, it wasn't commentary and impressions, but my verbal Tourette's flowering at last. Like Court Street, I seethed behind the scenes with language and conspiracies, inversions of logic, sudden jerks and jabs of insult. Now Minna had begun to draw me out. With his encouragement I freed myself to ape the rhythm of his overheard dialogues, his complaints and endearments, his for-the-sake-of arguments. And Minna loved my effect on his clients and associates, the way I'd unnerve them, disrupt some schmooze with an utterance, a head jerk, a husky *"eatme!"* I was his special effect, a running joke embodied. They'd look up startled and he'd wave his hand knowingly, counting money, not even bothering to look at me. "Don't mind him, he can't help it," he'd say. "Kid's shot out of a cannon." Or: "He likes to get a little nutty sometimes." Then he'd wink at me, acknowledge our conspiracy. I was evidence of life's unpredictability and rudeness and poignancy, a scale model of his own nutty heart. In this way Minna licensed my speech, and speech, it turned out, liberated me from the overflowing disaster of my Tourettic self, turned out to be the tic that satisfied where others didn't, the scratch that briefly stilled the itch.

"You ever listen to yourself, Lionel?" Minna would say later, shaking his head. "You really are shot out of a fucking cannon."

"*Scott Out Of The Canyon!* I don't know why, I just—*fuckitup!*—I just can't stop."

"You're a freak show, that's why. Human freak show, and it's free. Free to the public."

"Freefreak!" I tapped his shoulder.

"That's what I said: a free human freak show."

"Makes you think you're Italian?" said Minna one day, as we all rode together in his Impala.

"What do I look like to you?" said Tony.

"I was thinking maybe Greek," said Minna. "I used to know this Greek guy went around knocking up the Italian girls down Union Street, until a couple their older brothers took him out under the bridge. You remind me of him, you know? Got that dusky tinge. I'd say half Greek. Or maybe Puerto Rican."

"Fuck you."

"Probably know all your parents. We're not talking the international jet set here—bunch of teen mothers, probably live in a five-mile radius, need to know the goddamn truth."

We learned to negotiate the labyrinth of Minna's weird prejudices blind, and blindly. Hippies, for instance, were dangerous and odd, also sort of sad in their utopian wrongness. ("Your parents must of been hippies," he'd tell me. "That's why you came out the superfreak you are.") Homosexual men were harmless reminders of the impulse Minna was sure lurked in all of us—and "half a fag," was more shameful than a whole one. Certain baseball players were half a fag. So were most rock stars and anyone who'd been in the Armed Services but not in a war. The Arabic population of Atlantic Avenue was as unfathomable as the Indian tribes that had held our land before Columbus. "Classic" minorities—Irish, Jews, Poles, Italians, Greeks and Puerto Ricans were the clay of life itself, funny in their essence, while blacks and Asians of all types were soberly snubbed, unfunny. But bone-stupidity, mental illness and familial or sexual anxiety—

these were the bolts of electricity that made the clay walk, the animating forces that rendered human life amusing. It was a form of racism, not respect, that restricted blacks and Asians from ever being stupid like a Mick or Polack. If you weren't funny you didn't quite exist. And it was usually better to be fully stupid, impotent, lazy, greedy or freakish than to seek to dodge your destiny, or layer it underneath pathetic guises of vanity or calm.

Though Gerard Minna's name was printed on the business card, we met him only twice, and never on a moving job. The first time was Christmas day, at Minna's mother's apartment.

Carlotta Minna was an *old stove*. That was the Brooklyn term for it, according to Minna. She was a cook who worked in her own apartment, making plates of sautéed squid and stuffed peppers and jars of tripe soup which were purchased at her door by a constant parade of buyers, mostly neighborhood women with too much housework and single men, young or elderly, bocce players who'd take her plates to the park with them, racing bettors who'd eat her food standing up outside the OTB, butchers and contractors who'd sit on crates in the backs of their shops and wolf her cutlets, folding them with their fingers like waffles. She truly worked an old stove, too, a tiny enamel four-burner that was crusted with ancient sauces and on which three or four pots invariably bubbled. The whole kitchen glowed with heat like a kiln. Mrs. Minna herself seemed to have been baked, her whole face dark and furrowed like the edges of an overdone calzone. We never arrived without nudging aside some buyers from her door, nor without packing off with plateloads of food. When we were in her presence Minna bubbled himself, with talk, all directed at his mother, banking cheery insults off anyone else in the apartment, delivery boys, customers known and unknown, tasting everything she had cooking and making suggestions on every dish, poking and pinching every raw ingredient or ball of unfinished dough and also his mother herself, her earlobes and chin, wiping flour off her dark arms with his open hand. And she never once uttered a word.

That Christmas Minna had us all up to his mother's to eat at her table, first nudging aside sauce-glazed stirring spoons and baby-food jars of spices to clear spots for our plates. Minna stood at the stove, sampling her broth, and Mrs. Minna hovered over us as we devoured her meatballs, running her floury fingers over the backs of our chairs, then gently touching our heads, the napes of our necks. We pretended not to notice, ashamed to show that we drank in her nurturance as eagerly as her meat sauce. We splashed, gobbled, kneed one another under the table. Privately, I polished the handle of my spoon, quietly aping the motions of her fingers on my nape, and fought not to twist in my seat and jump at her. All the while she went on caressing with hands that would have horrified us if we'd looked close.

Minna spotted her and said, "This is exciting for you, Ma? I got all of motherless Brooklyn up here for you. Merry Christmas."

Minna's mother only produced a sort of high, keening sigh. We stuck to the food.

"*Motherless Brooklyn,*" repeated a voice we didn't know.

It was Minna's brother, Gerard. He'd come in without our noticing. A fleshier, taller Minna. His eyes and hair were as dark, his mouth as wry, lips deep-indented at the corners. He wore a brown-and-tan leather coat, which he left buttoned, his hands pushed into the fake patch pockets.

"So this is your little moving company," he said.

"Hey, Gerard," said Minna.

"Christmas, Frank," said Gerard Minna absently, not looking at his brother. Instead he was making short work of the four of us, his hard gaze snapping us each in two like bolt cutters on inferior padlocks. It didn't take long before he was done with us forever—that was how it felt.

"Yeah, Christmas to you," said Minna. "Where you been?"

"Upstate," said Gerard.

"What, with Ralph and them?" I detected something new in Minna's voice, a yearning, sycophantic strain.

"More or less."

"What, just for the holidays you're gonna go talkative on me? Between you and Ma it's like the Cloisters up here."

"I brought you a present." He handed Minna a white legal envelope, stuffed fat. Minna began to tear at the end, and Gerard said in a voice low and full of ancient sibling authority: "Put it away."

Now we understood we'd all been staring. All except Mrs. Minna, who was at her stove, piling together a cornucopic holiday plate for her older son.

"Make it to go, Mother."

She moaned again, closed her eyes.

"I'll be back," said Gerard. He put his hands on her, much as Minna did. "I've got a few people to see today. I'll be back tonight. Enjoy your little orphan party."

He took the foil-wrapped plate and was gone.

Minna said: "What're you staring at? Eat your food!" He stuffed the white envelope into his jacket. Then he cuffed us, the bulging gold ring on his middle finger clipping our crowns in the same place his mother had fondled.

One day in April, five months after that Christmas meal, Minna drove up with all his windows thoroughly smashed, the van transformed into a blinding crystalline sculpture, a mirrorball on wheels, reflecting the sun. It was plainly the work of a man with a hammer or crowbar and no fear of interruption. Minna appeared not to have noticed; he ferried us out to a job without mentioning it. On our way back to the Home, as we rumbled over the cobblestones of Hoyt Street, Tony nodded at the windshield, which sagged in its frame like a beaded curtain, and said: "So what happened?"

"What happened to what?" It was a Minna game, forcing us to be literal when we'd been trained by him to talk in glances, in three-corner shots.

"Somebody fucked up your van."

Minna shrugged, excessively casual. "I parked it on that block of Pacific Street."

We didn't know what he was talking about.

"These guys around that block had this thing about how I was uglifying the neighborhood." A few weeks after Gilbert's paint job the van had been covered again with graffiti, vast ballooning font and an overlay of stringy tags. Something made Minna's van a born target, the flat battered sides like a windowless subway car, a homely public surface crying for spray paint where private cars were inviolate. "They told me not to park it around there anymore."

Minna lifted both hands from the wheel to gesture his indifference. We weren't totally convinced.

"Someone's sending a message," said Tony.

"What's that?" said Minna.

"I just said it's a message," said Tony.

"Yeah, but what are you trying to say?" said Minna.

"*Fuckitmessage,*" I suggested impulsively.

"You know what I mean," said Tony defiantly, ignoring me.

"Yeah, maybe," said Minna. "But put it in your own words." I could feel his anger unfolding, smooth as a fresh deck of cards.

"*Put it in your fuckitall!*" I was like a toddler devising a tantrum to keep his parents from fighting.

But Minna wasn't distractable. "Quiet, Freakshow," he said, never taking his eyes from Tony. "Tell me what you said," he told Tony again.

"Nothing," said Tony. "Damn." He was backpedaling.

Minna pulled the van to the curb at a fire hydrant on the corner of Bergen and Hoyt. Outside, a couple of black men sat on a stoop, drinking from a bag. They squinted at us.

"Tell me what you said," Minna insisted.

He and Tony stared at one another, and the rest of us melted back. I swallowed away a few variations.

"Just, you know, somebody's sending you a message." Tony smirked.

This clearly infuriated Minna. He and Tony suddenly spoke a private language in which *message* signified heavily. "You think you know a thing," he said.

"All I'm saying is I can see what they did to your truck, Frank." Tony scuffed his feet in the layer of tiny cubes of safety glass that had peeled away from the limp window and lay scattered on the floor of the van.

"That's not all you said, Dickweed."

Dickweed: it was different from any insult Minna had bestowed on us before. Bitter as it sounded—*dickweed*. Our little organization was losing its innocence, although I couldn't have explained how or why.

"I can't help what I see," said Tony. "Somebody put a hit on your windows."

"Think you're a regular little wiseguy, don't you?"

Tony stared at him.

"You want to be Scarface?"

Tony didn't give his answer, but we knew what it was. *Scarface* had opened a month before and Al Pacino was ascendant, a personal colossus astride Tony's world, blocking out the sky.

"See, the thing about Scarface," said Minna, "is before he got to be Scarface he was *Scabface*. Nobody ever considers that. You have to want to be Scabface first."

For a second I thought Minna was going to hit Tony, damage his face to make the point. Tony seemed to be waiting for it too. Then Minna's fury leaked away.

"Out," he said. He waved his hand, a Caesar gesturing to the heavens through the roof of his refitted postal van.

"What?" said Tony. "Right here?"

"Out," he said again, equably. "Walk home, you muffin asses."

We sat gaping, though his meaning was clear enough. We weren't more than five or six blocks from the Home, anyway. But we hadn't been paid, hadn't gone for beers or slices or a bag of hot, clingy zeppole. I could taste the disappointment—the flavor of powdered sugar's absence. Tony slid open the door, dislodging more glass, and we obediently filed out of the van and onto the sidewalk, into the day's glare, the suddenly formless afternoon.

Minna drove off, leaving us there to bob together awkwardly before the drinkers on the stoop. They shook their heads at us, stupid-looking white boys a block from the projects. But we were in no danger there, nor were we dangerous ourselves. There was something so primally humiliating in our ejection that Hoyt Street itself seemed to ridicule us, the humble row of brownstones and sleeping bodegas. We were inexcusable to ourselves. Others clotted street corners, not us, not anymore. We rode with Minna. The effect was deliberate: Minna knew the value of the gift he'd withdrawn.

"*Muffin ass,*" I said forcefully, measuring the shape of the words in my mouth, auditioning them for tic-richness. Then I sneezed, induced by the sunlight.

Gilbert and Danny looked at me with disgust, Tony with something worse.

"Shut up," he said. There was cold fury in his teeth-clenched smile.

"Tellmetodoit, muffinass," I croaked.

"Be quiet now," warned Tony. He plucked a piece of wood from the gutter and took a step towards me.

Gilbert and Danny drifted away from us warily. I would have followed them, but Tony had me cornered against a parked car. The men on the stoop stretched back on their elbows, slurped their malt liquor thoughtfully.

"*Dickweed*," I said. I tried to mask it in another sneeze, which made something in my neck pop. I twitched and spoke again. "*Dickweed! Dicketywood!*" I was trapped in a loop of self, stuck refining a verbal tic to free myself from its grip. Certainly I didn't mean to be defying Tony. Yet *dickweed* was the name Minna had called him, and I was throwing it in his face.

Tony held the stick he'd found, a discarded scrap of lattice with clumps of plaster stuck to it. I stared, anticipating my own pain like I'd anticipated Tony's, at Minna's hand, a minute before. Instead Tony moved close, stick at his side, and grabbed my collar.

"Open your mouth again," he said.

I grabbed Tony back, my hands exploring the neck of his T-shirt, fingers running inside it like an anxious, fumbling lover. Then, struggling not to speak, I pursed my lips, jerked my head to the side and kissed his knuckles where they gripped my collar.

Gilbert and Danny had started up Hoyt Street in the direction of the Home. "C'mon, Tony," said Gilbert, tilting his head. Tony ignored them. He scraped his stick in the gutter and came up with a smear of dog shit, mustard yellow and pungent.

"Open," he said.

Gilbert and Danny slinked away, heads bowed. The street was brightly, absurdly empty. Nobody but the men on the stoop, impassive witnesses. I jerked my head as Tony jabbed with his stick, and he only managed to paint my cheek. I could smell it though, powdered sugar's opposite, married to my face.

"*Eat me!*" I shouted. Falling back against the car behind me, I turned my head again and again, twitching away, enshrining the moment in ticceography. The stain followed me, adamant, on fire.

Our witnesses crinkled their paper bags, offered ruminative sighs.

Tony dropped his stick and turned away. He'd disgusted himself, couldn't meet my eye. About to speak, he thought better of it, instead jogged to catch Gilbert and Danny as they shrugged away up Hoyt Street, leaving the scene.

We didn't see Minna again until five weeks later, Sunday morning at the Home's yard, late May. He had his brother Gerard with him; it was the second time we'd laid eyes on him.

None of us had seen Frank in the intervening weeks, though I know the others, like myself, had each wandered down Court Street, nosed at a few of his usual haunts, the barbershop, the arcade. He wasn't in them. It meant nothing, it meant everything. He might never reappear, but if he turned up and didn't speak of it we wouldn't think twice. We didn't speak of it to one another, but a pensiveness hung over us, tinged with orphan's melancholy, our resignation to permanent injury. A part of each of us still stood astonished on the corner of Hoyt and Bergen, where we'd been ejected from Minna's van.

A horn honked, the Impala's, not the van's. Then the brothers got out and came to the cyclone fence and waited for us to gather. Tony and Danny were playing basketball, Gilbert ardently picking his nose on the sidelines. That's how I picture it, anyway. I wasn't in the yard when they drove up. Gilbert had to come inside and pull me out of the library, to which I'd mostly retreated since Tony's attack. I was wedged into a windowsill seat when Gilbert found me, immersed in a novel by Allen Drury.

Frank and Gerard were dressed too warmly for that morning, Frank in his bomber jacket, Gerard in his patchwork leather coat. The back seat of the Impala was loaded with shopping bags packed with what looked like Frank's clothes and a pair of old leather suitcases. They stood at the fence, Frank bouncing nervously on his toes, Gerard hanging on the mesh, fingers dangling through, doing nothing to conceal his impatience with his brother, an impatience shading into disgust.

Frank smirked, raised his eyebrows, shook his head. Danny held his basketball between forearm and hip; Minna nodded at it, mimed a set shot, dropped his hand at the wrist and made a delicate *o* with his mouth to signify the *swish* that would result.

Then, idiotically, he bounced a pretend pass to Gerard. His brother didn't seem to notice. Minna shook his head, then wheeled, aimed two trigger fingers through the fence, and grit his teeth for *rat-tat-tat,* a little imaginary schoolyard massacre. We could only gape. It was as though somebody had taken Minna's voice away. And Minna *was* his voice—didn't he know? His eyes said yes, he did. They looked panicked, like they'd been caged in the body of a mime.

Gerard gazed off emptily into the yard, ignoring the show. Minna made a few more faces, wincing, chuckling silently, shaking off some invisible annoyance by twitching his cheek. I fought to keep from mirroring him.

Then he cleared his throat. "I'm, ah, going out of town for a while," he said at last.

We waited for more. Minna just nodded and squinted and grinned his close-mouthed grin at us as though he were acknowledging applause.

"Upstate?" said Tony.

Minna coughed in his fist. "Oh yeah. Place my brother goes. He thinks we ought to get a little country air."

"When are you coming back?" said Tony.

"Ah, coming back," said Minna. "You got an unknown there, Scarface. Unknown factors."

We must have gaped at him, because he added, "I wouldn't wait underwater, if that's what you had in mind."

We were in our second year of high school. Till now I'd counted my future in afternoons, but with Minna leaving, a door of years swung open. And Minna wouldn't be there to tell us what to think of Minna's not being there, to give it a name.

"All right, Frank," said Gerard, turning his back to the fence. "Motherless Brooklyn appreciates your support. I think we better get on the road."

"My brother's in a hurry," said Frank. "He's seeing ghosts everywhere."

"Yeah, I'm looking right at one," said Gerard, though in fact he wasn't looking at anyone, only the car.

Minna tilted his head at us, at his brother, to say *you know*. And *sorry*.

Then he pulled a book out of his pocket, a small paperback. I don't think I'd ever seen a book in his hands before. "Here," he said to me. He dropped it on the pavement and nudged it under the fence with the toe of his shoe. "Take a look," he said. "Turns out you're not the only freak in the show."

I picked it up. *Understanding Tourette's Syndrome* was the title. It was the first time I'd seen the words.

"Meaning to get that to you," he said. "But I've been sort of busy."

I reached for him through the fence and tapped his shoulder, once, twice, let my hand fall, then raised it again and let fly a staccato burst of Tourettic caresses.

"Eatme, Minnaweed," I said under my breath.

"You're a laugh and a half, Freakshow," said Minna, his face completely grim.

"Great," said Gerard, taking Minna by the arm. "Let's get out of here."

Tony had been searching every day after school, I suspect. It was three days later that he found it and led us others there, to the edge of the Brooklyn-Queens Expressway at the end of Baltic. The van was diminished, sagged to its rims, tires melted. The explosion had cleared the windows of their crumbled panes of safety glass, which now lay in a spilled penumbra of grains on the sidewalk and street, together with flakes of traumatized paint and smudges of ash, a photographic map of force. The panels of the truck were layered, graffiti still evident in bone-white outline, all else, Gilbert's shoddy coat of enamel and the manufacturer's ancient green, now chalky black, and delicate like sunburned skin. It was like an X ray of the van that had been before.

We circled it, strangely reverent, afraid to touch, and then I ran away, toward Court Street, before anything could come out of my mouth.

Truman Capote

✠

from The Art of Fiction XVII

Did you have much encouragement in those early days and by whom?

Good Lord! I'm afraid you've let yourself in for quite a saga. The answer is a snake's nest of nos and a few yesses. You see, not altogether but by and large my childhood was spent in parts of the country and among peoples unprovided with any semblance of a cultural attitude. Which was probably not a bad thing, in the long view. It toughened rather too soon to swim against the current . . . indeed, in some areas I developed the muscles of a veritable barracuda, especially in the art of dealing with one's enemies, an art no less necessary than knowing how to appreciate one's friends.

But to go back. Naturally in the milieu aforesaid, I was thought somewhat *eccentric,* which was fair enough, and *stupid,* which I suitably resented. Still, I despised school . . . or schools, for I was always changing from one to another . . . and year after year failed the simplest subjects out of loathing and boredom. I played hooky at least twice a week and was always running away from home. Once I ran away with a friend who lived across the street . . . a girl much older than myself who in later life achieved a certain fame. Because she murdered a half-dozen people and was electrocuted at Sing Sing. Someone wrote a book about her. They called her the Lonely Hearts Killer. But there, I'm wandering again. Well, finally, I guess I was around twelve, the principal at the school I was attending paid a call on my family, and told them that in his opinion, and in the opinion of the faculty, I was "subnormal." He thought it would be the sensible, the humane action to send me to some special school equipped to handle backward brats. Whatever they may have privately felt, my family as a whole took offical umbrage, and in an effort to prove I wasn't subnormal pronto packed me off to a psychiatric study clinic at a university in the east where I had my I.Q. inspected. I enjoyed it thoroughly and—guess what?—came home a genius, so proclaimed by science. I don't know who was the more appalled: my former teachers, who refused to believe it, or my family, who didn't want to believe it—they'd just hoped to be told I was a nice normal boy. Ha ha! But as for me, I was exceedingly pleased—went around staring at myself in mirrors and sucking in my cheeks and thinking over in my mind, my lad, you and Flaubert . . . or de Maupassant or Mansfield or Proust or Chekhov or Wolfe, whoever was the idol of the moment.

Charles Simic

Against Winter

The truth is dark under your eyelids.
What are you going to do about it?
The birds are silent; there's no one to ask.
All day long you'll squint at the gray sky.
When the wind blows you'll shiver like straw.

A meek little lamb you grew your wool
Till they came after you with huge shears.
Flies hovered over your open mouth,
Then they, too, flew off like the leaves,
The bare branches reached after them in vain.

Winter coming. Like the last heroic soldier
Of a defeated army, you'll stay at your post,
Head bared to the first snowflake.
Till a neighbor comes to yell at you,
You're crazier than the weather, Charlie.

Adrienne Rich

Thirty-three

Piece by piece I seem
to re-enter the world: I first began

a small, fixed dot, I still can see
that old myself, a darkblue thumbtack

pushed into the scene,
a hard little head protruding

from the pointillist's buzz and bloom.
After a time the dot

begins to ooze. Certain heats
melt it.
     Now I was hurriedly

blurring into ranges
of burnt red, burning green,

whole biographies swam up and
swallowed me like Jonah—

Jonah! I was Wittgenstein,
Mary Wollstonecraft, the soul

of Louis Jouvet, dead
in a blown-up photograph.

Till, wolfed almost to shreds,
I learned to make myself

unappetizing. Scaly as a dry bulb
thrown into a cellar

I used myself, let nothing use me.
Like being on a private dole,

sometimes more like cutting bricks in Egypt.
What life was there, was mine,

now and again to lay
one hand on a warm brick

and touch the sun's ghost
with economical joy.

Such much for those days. Soon
practise may make me middling-perfect, I'll

dare inhabit the world
trenchant in motion as an eel, solid

as a cabbage-head. I have invitations:
a curl of mist steams upward

from the fields, visible as my breath,
houses along a road stand waiting

like old women knitting, breathless
to tell their tales.

Issue 31, 1964

Jorge Luis Borges

⬦

Funes the Memorious

I remember him (I have no right to utter this sacred verb, only one man on earth had that right and he is dead) with a dark passion flower in his hand, seeing it as no one has ever seen it, though he might look at it from the twilight of dawn till that of evening, a whole lifetime. I remember him, with his face taciturn and Indian-like and singularly *remote,* behind the cigarette. I remember (I think) his angular, leather-braiding hands. I remember near those hands a maté gourd bearing the Uruguayan coat of arms; I remember a yellow screen with a vague lake landscape in the window of his house. I clearly remember his voice: the slow, resentful, nasal voice of the old-time dweller of the suburbs, without the Italian sibilants we have today. I never saw him more than three times; the last was in 1887 . . . I find it very satisfactory that all those who knew him should write about him; my testimony will perhaps be the shortest and no doubt the poorest, but not the most impartial in the volume you will edit. My deplorable status as an Argentine will prevent me from indulging in a dithyramb, an obligatory genre in Uruguay whenever the subject is an Uruguayan. *Highbrow, city slicker, dude*: Funes never spoke these injurious words, but I am sufficiently certain I represented for him those misfortunes. Pedro Leandro Ipuche has written that Funes was a precursor of the supermen, "a vernacular and rustic Zarathustra"; I shall not debate the point, but one should not forget that he was also a kid from Fray Bentos, with certain incurable limitations.

My first memory of Funes is very perspicuous. I can see him on an afternoon in March or February of the year 1884. My father, that year, had taken me to spend the summer in Fray Bentos. I was returning from the San Francisco ranch with my cousin Bernardo Haedo. We were singing as we rode along and being on horseback was not the only circumstance determining my happiness. After a sultry day, an enormous slate-colored storm had hidden the sky. It was urged on by southern wind, the trees were already going wild; I was afraid (I was hopeful) that the elemental rain would take us by surprise in the open. We were running a kind of race with the storm. We entered an alleyway that sank down between two very high brick sidewalks. It had suddenly got dark; I heard some rapid and almost secret footsteps up above; I raised my eyes and saw a boy running along the narrow and broken path as if it were a narrow and broken wall. I remember his baggy gaucho trousers, his rope-soled shoes. I remember the cigarette in his hard face, against the now limitless storm cloud. Bernardo cried to him unexpectedly: "What time is it, Ireneo?" Without consulting the sky, without stopping, he replied: "It's four minutes to eight, young Bernardo Juan Francisco." His voice was shrill, mocking.

I am so unperceptive that the dialogue I have just related would not have attracted my attention had it not been stressed by my cousin, who (I believe) was prompted by a certain local pride and the desire to show that he was indifferent to the other's tripartite reply.

He told me the fellow in the alleyway was one Ireneo Funes, known for certain peculiarities such as avoiding contact with people and always knowing what time it was, like a clock. He added that he was the son of the ironing woman in town, María Clementina Funes, and that some people said his father was a doctor at the meat packers, an Englishman by the name of O'Connor, and others that he was a horse tamer or scout from the Salto district. He lived with his mother, around the corner from the Laureles house.

During the years eighty-five and eighty-six we spent the summer in Montevideo. In eighty-seven I returned to Fray Bentos. I asked, as was natural, about all my acquaintances and, finally, about the "chronometrical" Funes. I was told he had been thrown by a half-tamed horse on the San Francisco ranch and was left hopelessly paralyzed. I remember the sensation of uneasy magic the news produced in me: the only time I had seen him, we were returning from San

Francisco on horseback and he was running along a high place; this fact, told me by my cousin Bernardo, had much of the quality of a dream made up of previous elements. I was told he never moved from his cot, with his eyes fixed on the fig tree in the back or on a spider web. In the afternoons, he would let himself be brought out to the window. He carried his pride to the point of acting as if the blow that had felled him were beneficial . . . Twice I saw him behind the iron grating of the window, which harshly emphasized his condition as a perpetual prisoner: once, motionless, with his eyes closed; another time, again motionless, absorbed in the contemplation of a fragrant sprig of santonica.

Not without a certain vaingloriousness, I had begun at that time my methodical study of Latin. My valise contained the *De Viris Illustribus* of Lhomond, Quicherat's *Thesaurus*, the commentaries of Julius Caesar and an odd volume of Pliny's *Historia Naturalis*, which then exceeded (and still exceeds) my moderate virtues as a Latinist. Everything becomes public in a small town; Ireneo, in his house on the outskirts, did not take long to learn of the arrival of these anomalous books. He sent me a flowery and ceremonious letter in which he recalled our encounter, unfortunately brief, "on the seventh day of February of the year 1884," praised the glorious services my uncle Gregorio Haedo, deceased that same year, "had rendered to our two nations in the valiant battle of Ituzaingó" and requested the loan of any one of my volumes, accompanied by a dictionary "for the proper intelligence of the original text, for I am as yet ignorant of Latin." He promised to return them to me in good condition, almost immediately. His handwriting was perfect, very sharply outlined; his orthography, of the type favored by Andrés Bello: *i* for *y*, *j* for *g*. At first I naturally feared a joke. My cousins assured me that was not the case, that these were peculiarities of Ireneo. I did not know whether to attribute to insolence, ignorance or stupidity the idea that the arduous Latin tongue should require no other instrument than a dictionary; to disillusion him fully, I sent him the *Gradus ad Parnassum* of Quicherat and the work by Pliny.

On the fourteenth of February, I received a telegram from Buenos Aires saying I should return immediately, because my father was "not at all well." May God forgive me; the prestige of being the recipient of an urgent telegram, the desire to communicate to all Fray Bentos the contradiction between the negative form of the message and the peremptory adverb, the temptation to dramatize my suffering, affecting a virile stoicism, perhaps distracted me from all possibility of real sorrow. When I packed my valise, I noticed the *Gradus* and the first volume of the *Historia Naturalis* were missing. The *Saturn* was sailing the next day, in the morning; that night, after supper, I headed towards Funes's house. I was astonished to find the evening no less oppressive than the day had been.

At the respectable little house, Funes's mother opened the door for me.

She told me Ireneo was in the back room and I should not be surprised to find him in the dark, because he knew how to pass the idle hours without lighting the candle. I crossed the tile patio, the little passageway; I reached the second patio. There was a grape arbor; the darkness seemed complete to me. I suddenly heard Ireneo's high-pitched, mocking voice. His voice was speaking in Latin; his voice (which came from the darkness) was articulating with morose delight a speech or prayer or incantation. The Roman syllables resounded in the earthen patio; my fear took them to be indecipherable, interminable; afterwards, in the enormous dialogue of that night, I learned they formed the first paragraph of the twenty-fourth chapter of the seventh book of the *Historia Naturalis*. The subject of that chapter is memory; the last words were *ut nihil non iisdem verbis redderetur auditum*.

Without the slightest change of voice, Ireneo told me to come in. He was on his cot, smoking. It seems to me I did not see his face until dawn; I believe I recall the intermittent glow of his cigarette. The room smelled vaguely of dampness. I sat down; I repeated the story about the telegram and my father's illness.

I now arrive at the most difficult point in my story. This story (it is well the reader know it by now) has no other plot than that dialogue which took place half a century ago. I shall not try to reproduce the words, which are now irrecoverable. I prefer to summarize with veracity the many things Ireneo told me. The indirect style is remote and weak; I know I am sacrificing the efficacy of my narrative; my readers should imagine for themselves the hesitant periods which overwhelmed me that night.

Ireneo began by enumerating, in Latin and in Spanish, the cases of prodigious memory recorded in the *Historia Naturalis:* Cyrus, king of the Persians, who could call every soldier in his armies by name; Mithridates Eupator, who administered the law in the twenty-two languages of his empire; Simonides, inventor of the science of mnemonics; Metrodorus, who practiced the art of faithfully repeating what he had heard only once. In obvious good faith, Ireneo was amazed that such cases be considered amazing. He told me that before that rainy afternoon when the blue-gray horse threw him, he had been what all humans are: blind, deaf, addlebrained, absentminded. (I tried to remind him of his exact perception of time, his memory for proper names; he paid no attention to me.) For nineteen years he had lived as one in a dream: he looked without seeing, listened without hearing, forgetting everything, almost everything. When he fell, he became unconscious; when he came out, the present was almost intolerable in its richness and sharpness, as were his most distant and trivial memories. Somewhat later he learned that he was paralyzed. The fact scarcely interested him. He reasoned (he felt) that his immobility was a minimum price to pay. Now his perception and his memory were infallible.

We, at one glance, can perceive three glasses on a table; Funes, all the leaves and tendrils and fruit that make up a grape vine. He knew by heart the forms of the southern clouds at dawn on the 30th of April, 1882, and could compare them in his memory with the mottled streaks on a book in Spanish binding he had only seen once and with the outlines of the foam raised by an oar in the Río Negro the night before the Quebracho uprising. These memories were not simple ones; each visual image was linked to muscular sensations, thermal sensations, etc. He could reconstruct all his dreams, all his half-dreams. Two or three times he had reconstructed a whole day; he never hesitated, but each reconstruction had required a whole day. He told me: "I alone have more memories than all mankind has probably had since the world has been the world." And again: "My dreams are like you people's waking hours." And again, toward dawn: "My memory, sir, is like a garbage heap." A circle drawn on a blackboard, a right triangle, a lozenge—all these are forms we can fully and intuitively grasp; Ireneo could do the same with the stormy mane of a pony, with a herd of cattle on a hill, with the changing fire and its innumerable ashes, with the many faces of a dead man throughout a long wake. I don't know how many stars he could see in the sky.

These things he told me; neither then nor later have I ever placed them in doubt. In those days there were no cinemas or phonographs; nevertheless, it is odd and even incredible that no one ever performed an experiment with Funes. The truth is that we live out our lives putting off all that can be put off; perhaps we all know deep down that we are immortal and that sooner or later all men will do and know all things.

Out of the darkness, Funes's voice went on talking to me.

He told me that in 1886 he had invented an original system of numbering and that in a very few days he had gone beyond the twenty-four-thousand mark. He had not written it down, since anything he thought of once would never be lost to him. His first stimulus was, I think, his discomfort at the fact that the famous thirty-three gauchos of Uruguayan history should require two signs and two words, in place of a single word and a single sign. He then applied this absurd principle to the other numbers. In place of seven thousand thirteen, he would say (for example) *Máximo Pérez;* in place of seven thousand fourteen, *The Railroad;* other numbers were *Luis Melián Lafinur, Olimar, Sulphur, the reins, the whale, the gas, the caldron, Napoleon, Augustín de Vedia.* In place of five hundred, he would say *nine.* Each word had a particular sign, a kind of mark; the last in the series were very complicated . . . I tried to explain to him that this rhapsody of incoherent terms was precisely the opposite of a system of numbers. I told him that saying 365 meant saying three hundreds, six tens, five ones, an analysis which is not found in the "numbers" *The Negro Timoteo* or *meat blanket.* Funes did not understand me or refused to understand me.

Locke, in the seventeenth century, postulated (and rejected) an impossible language in which each individual thing, each stone, each bird and each branch, would have its own name; Funes once projected an analogous language, but discarded it because it seemed too general to him, too ambiguous. In fact, Funes once remembered not only every leaf of every tree of every wood, but also every one of the times he had perceived or imagined it. He decided to reduce each of his past days to some seventy thousand memories, which would then be defined by means of ciphers. He was dissuaded from this by two considerations: his awareness that the task was interminable, his awareness that it was useless. He thought that by the hour of his death he would not even have finished classifying all the memories of his childhood.

The two projects I have indicated (an infinite vocabulary for the natural series of numbers, a useless mental catalogue of all the images of his memory) are senseless, but they betray a certain stammering grandeur. They permit us to glimpse or infer the nature of Funes's vertiginous world. He was, let us not forget, almost incapable of ideas of a general, Platonic sort. Not only was it difficult for him to comprehend that the generic symbol *dog* embraces so many unlike individuals of diverse size and form; it bothered him that the dog at 3:14 (seen from the side) should have the same name as the dog at 3:15 (seen from the front). His own face in the mirror, his own hands, surprised him every time he saw them. Swift relates that the emperor of Lilliput could discern the movement of the minute hand; Funes could continuously discern the tranquil advances of corruption, of decay, of fatigue. He could note the progress of death, of dampness. He was the solitary and lucid spectator of a multiform, instantaneous and almost intolerably precise world. Babylon, London and New York have overwhelmed with their ferocious splendor the imaginations of men; no one, in their populous towers or their urgent avenues, has felt the heat and pressure of a reality as indefatigable as that which day and night converged upon the hapless Ireneo, in his poor South American suburb. It was very difficult for him to sleep. To sleep is to turn one's mind from the world; Funes, lying on his back on his cot in the shadows, could imagine every crevice and every molding in the sharply defined houses surrounding him. (I repeat that the least important of his memories was more minute and more vivid than our perception of physical pleasure or physical torment.) Towards the east, along a stretch not yet divided into blocks, there were new houses, unknown to Funes. He imagined them to be black, compact, made of homogeneous darkness; in that direction he would turn his face in order to sleep. He would also imagine himself at the bottom of the river, rocked and annihilated by the current.

With no effort, he had learned English, French, Portuguese and Latin. I suspect, however, that he was not very capable of thought. To think is to forget differences, generalize, make abstractions. In the teeming world of Funes, there were only details, almost immediate in their presence.

The wary light of dawn entered the earthen patio.

Then I saw the face belonging to the voice that had spoken all night long. Ireneo was nineteen years old; he had been born in 1868; he seemed to me as monumental as bronze, more ancient than Egypt, older than the prophecies and the pyramids. I thought that each of my words (that each of my movements) would persist in his implacable memory; I was benumbed by the fear of multiplying useless gestures.

Ireneo Funes died in 1889, of congestion of the lungs.

—translated by J.E.I.

Issue 28, 1962

Alice Munro

✣

Spaceships Have Landed

Eunie Morgan's house was the third one past Monk's. It was the
last house on the road. Around midnight, Eunie's mother said,
she had heard the screen door close. She heard the screen door and
thought nothing of it. She thought of course that Eunie had gone out
to the toilet. Even in 1953 the Morgans had no indoor plumbing.

Of course none of them went as far as the toilet, late at night. Eunie
and the old woman squatted on the grass. The old man watered the
spirea at the far end of the porch.

Then I must have gone to sleep, Eunie's mother said, but I woke
up later on, and I thought that I never heard her come in.

She went downstairs and walked around in the house. Eunie's
room was behind the kitchen, but she might be sleeping anywhere on
a hot night. She might be on the couch in the front room or stretched
out on the hall floor to get the breeze between the doors. She might
have gone out on the porch where there was a decent car seat that her
father, years ago, had found discarded farther down the road. Her
mother could not find her anywhere. The kitchen clock said twenty
past two.

Eunie's mother went back upstairs and shook Eunie's father till he
woke up.

"Eunie's not down there," she said.

"Where is she then?" said her husband, as if it was up to her to
know. She had to shake him and shake him, to keep him from going

back to sleep. He had a great indifference to news, a reluctance to listen to what anybody said, even when he was awake.

"Get up, get up," she said. "We got to find her." Finally he obeyed her, sat up, pulled on his trousers and his boots. "Get your flashlight," she told him, and with him behind her she went down the stairs again, out onto the porch, down into the yard. It was his job to shine the flashlight—she told him where. She directed him along the path to the toilet, which stood in a clump of lilacs and currant bushes at the back of the property. They poked the light inside the building and found nothing. Then they peered in among the sturdy lilac trunks—these were practically trees—and along the path—almost lost now—that led through a sagging section of the wire fence to the wild growth along the river bank. Nothing there. Nobody.

Back through the vegetable garden they went, lighting up the dusted potato plants and the rhubarb that was now grandly gone to seed. The old man lifted a great rhubarb leaf with his boot, and shone the light under that.

His wife asked whether he had gone crazy.

She recalled that Eunie used to walk in her sleep. But that was years ago.

She spotted something glinting at the corner of the house, like knives or a man in armour.

"There. There," she said. "Shine it there. What's that?"

It was only Eunie's bicycle, that she rode to work every day.

Then the mother called Eunie's name. She called it at the back and the front of the house; plum trees grew as high as the house in front and there was no sidewalk, just a dirt path between them. Their trunks crowded in like watchers, crooked black animals. When she waited for an answer she heard the gulp of a frog, close, as if it sat in those branches. Morgan's place was the last on this road, last of the houses with their backs to the river. Half a mile farther on, the road ended up in a field too marshy for any use, with weedy poplars growing up through the willow-bushes and elderberries. In the other direction, it met the road from town, then crossed the river and climbed the hill to the chicken farm. On the river flats lay the old fairgrounds, some grandstands abandoned since before the War, when the fair here was taken over by the big fair at Walley. The racetrack oval was still marked out in the grass.

This was where the town set out to be, over a hundred years ago. Mills and hostelries were here. But the river floods persuaded people to move to higher ground. House plots remained on the map, and roads laid out, but only the one row of houses where people lived who were too poor or in some way too stubborn to change—or, at the other extreme, too temporary in their living arrangements to object to the invasion of the water.

They gave up—Eunie's parents did. They sat down in the kitchen without any light on. It was between three and four o'clock. It must have seemed as if they were waiting for Eunie to come and tell them what to do. It was Eunie who was in charge in that house and they probably could hardly imagine a time when it had been otherwise. Nineteen years ago she had literally burst into their lives. Mrs. Morgan had thought she was having the change and getting stout—she was stout enough already that it did not make much difference. She thought the commotion in her stomach was what people called indigestion. She knew how people got children, she was not a dunce—it was just that she had gone on so long without any such thing happening. One day in the post office she had to ask for a chair, she was weak and overcome by cramps. Then her water broke, she was hustled over to the hospital, and Eunie popped out with a full head of white hair. She made her claim to attention from the moment of her birth.

One whole summer Eunie and Rhea played together. They never thought of their activity as play, but playing was what they called it, to satisfy other people. It was the most serious part of their lives. What they did the rest of the time seemed frivolous, forgettable. When they cut from Eunie's yard down to the riverbank they became different people. Each of them was called Tom. The Two Toms. A Tom was a noun to them, not just a name. It was not male or female. It meant somebody exceptionally brave and clever but not always lucky, and—just barely—indestructible. The Toms had a battle which could never end, and this was with the Bannershees. (Perhaps Rhea and Eunie had heard of banshees.) The Bannershees lurked along the river and could take the form of robbers or Germans or skeletons. Their tricks and propensities were endless. They laid traps and lay in ambush and tortured the children they had stolen. Sometimes Eunie and Rhea got some real children—the McKays who lived briefly in one of the river houses—and persuaded them to let themselves be tied up and thrashed with cattails. But the McKays could not or would not submit themselves to the plot, and they soon cried or escaped and went home, so that it was just the Toms again.

The Toms built a city of mud by the riverbank. It was walled with stones against the Bannershees' attack and contained a royal palace, a swimming pool, a flag. But then the Toms took a journey and the Bannershees leveled it all. (Of course Eunie and Rhea had to change themselves, often, into Bannershees.) A new leader appeared, a Bannershee queen; her name was Joylinda, and her schemes were diabolical. She had poisoned the blackberries growing on the bank, and the Toms had eaten some, being careless and hungry after their journey. They lay writhing and sweating down among the juicy weeds when the poison struck. They pressed their bellies into mud that was slightly soft and warm like just-made fudge. They felt their innards shrivel and they were shaking in every limb, but they had to get up and stagger about, looking for an antidote. They tried chewing sword grass—which true to its name could slice your skin—they smeared their mouths with mud, and considered biting into a live frog if they could catch one, but decided at last it was chokecherries that would save them from death. They ate a cluster of the tiny chokecherries and the skin inside their mouths puckered desperately, so that they had to run to the river to drink the water. They threw themselves down on it, where it was all silty among the waterlilies and you couldn't see the bottom. They drank and drank it, while the bluebottles flew straight as arrows over their heads. They were saved.

Emerging from this world in the late afternoon, they found themselves in Eunie's yard where her parents would be working still, or again, hoeing or hilling or weeding their vegetables. They would lie down in the shade of the house, exhausted as if they had swum lakes or climbed mountains. They smelled of the river, of the wild garlic and mint they had squashed underfoot, of the hot rank grass and the foul mud where the drain emptied. Sometimes Eunie would go into the house and get them something to eat—slices of bread with corn syrup or molasses. She never had to ask if she could do this. She always kept the bigger piece for herself.

They were not friends in the way that Rhea would understand being friends later on. They never tried to please or comfort each other. They did not share secrets, except for the game, and even that was not a secret because they let others take part. But they never let the others be Toms. So maybe that was what they shared, in their intense and daily collaboration. The nature, the danger, of being Toms.

Eunie never seemed subject to her parents or even connected to them in the way of other children. Rhea was struck by the way Eunie ruled her own life, the careless power she had in the house. When Rhea said that she had to be home at a certain time, or that she had to do chores or change her clothes, Eunie was affronted, disbelieving. Every decision Eunie made must have been on her own. When she was fifteen she stopped going to school and got a job in the glove factory. Rhea could imagine her coming home and announcing to her parents what she had done. No, not even announcing it—it would come out in an offhand way, maybe when she started getting home later in the afternoon. Now that she was earning money, she bought a bicycle. She bought a radio and listened to it in her room late at night. Perhaps her parents would hear shots ring out then, vehicles roaring through the streets. She might tell them things she had heard—the news of crimes and accidents, hurricanes, avalanches. Rhea didn't think they would pay much attention. They were busy and their life was eventful, though the events in it were seasonal and had to do with the vegetables which they sold in town to earn their living. The vegetables, the raspberries, the rhubarb. They hadn't time for much else.

While Eunie was still in school Rhea was riding her bicycle, so they never walked together although they took the same route. When Rhea rode past Eunie, Eunie was in the habit of shouting out something challenging, disparaging. Hi ho, Silver! And now, when Eunie had a bicycle, Rhea had started walking—there was a notion at the high school that any girl who rode a bicycle, after grade nine, looked gawky and ridiculous. Eunie would dismount and walk along beside Rhea, as if she was doing her a favor.

It was not a favor at all—Rhea did not want her. Eunie had always been a peculiar sight, tall for her age, with sharp, narrow shoulders, a whitish-blond crest of fuzzy hair sticking up at the crown of her head, a cocksure expression and a long, heavy jaw. That jaw gave a thickness to the lower part of her face that seemed reflected in the phlegmy growl of her voice. When she was younger none of that had mattered—her own conviction, that everything about her was proper had daunted many. But now she was five feet nine or ten, drab and mannish in her slacks and bandannas, with big feet in what looked like men's shoes, a hectoring voice and an ungainly walk—she had gone right from being a child to being a character. And she spoke to Rhea with a proprietary air that grated, asking her if she wasn't tired of going to school, or if her bike was broken and her father couldn't afford to get it fixed. When Rhea got a permanent, Eunie wanted to know what had happened to her hair. All this she thought she could do because she and Rhea lived on the same side of town and had played together, in an era that seemed to Rhea so distant and discardable. The worst thing was when Eunie launched into accounts that Rhea found both boring and infuriating, of murders and disasters and freakish events that she had heard about on the radio. Rhea was infuriated because she could not get Eunie to tell her whether these things had really happened, or even to make that distinction—as far as Rhea could tell—to herself.

Was that on the news, Eunie? Was it a story? Were there people acting it out in front of a microphone or was it reporting? Eunie! Was it real or was it a play?

It was Rhea, never Eunie, who would get frazzled by these questions. Eunie would just get on her bicycle and ride away.

"Toodeley oodeley oo! See you in the Zoo!"

Eunie's job suited her, surely. The glove factory occupied the second and third floors of a building on the main street, and in the warm weather when the windows were open you could hear not only the sewing machines but the loud jokes, the quarrels and insults, the famous rough language of the women who worked there. They were supposed to be of a lower class than waitresses, much lower than store clerks. They worked longer hours and made less money, but that didn't make them humble. Far from it. They came jostling and joking down the stairs and burst out on to the street. They yelled at cars, in which there were people they knew, and people they didn't know. They spread disorder as if they had every right.

People close to the bottom, like Eunie Morgan, or right at the top, like Billy Doud, showed a similar carelessness, a blunted understanding.

During her last year at high school, Rhea got a job, too. She worked in the shoe store on Saturday afternoons. Billy Doud came into the store, in early spring, and said he wanted to buy a pair of rubber boots, like the ones hanging up outside.

He took off his shoes and displayed his feet in fine black socks. Rhea told him that it would be better to wear woolen socks, work socks, inside rubber boots, so that his feet wouldn't slide around. He asked if they sold such socks and said he would buy a pair of those too, if Rhea would bring them. Then he asked her if she would put the wool socks on his feet.

That was all a ploy, he told her later. He didn't need either one, boots or socks.

His feet were long and white and perfectly sweet-smelling. A scent of lovely soap arose, a whiff of talcum. He leaned back in the chair, tall and pale, cool and clean—he himself might have been carved of soap. A high curved forehead, temples already bare, hair with a glint of tinsel, sleepy ivory eyelids. He was through college at last, he was twenty-four years old and home to learn the piano-factory business.

"That's sweet of you," he said, and asked her to go to a dance that night, the opening dance of the season in the Walley Pavilion.

After that they went to the dance in Walley every Saturday night. They didn't go out together during the week, because Billy had to get up early and go to the factory and learn the business—from his mother, known as the Tartar, and Rhea had to do some housekeeping for her father and brothers. Her mother was in the hospital, in Hamilton.

"There goes your heartthrob," girls would say, if Billy drove by the school when they were out playing volleyball, or passed on the street, and in truth Rhea's heart did throb—at the sight of him, his bright hatless hair, his negligent but surely powerful hands on the wheel. But also at the thought of herself suddenly singled out, so unexpectedly chosen, with the glow of a prizewinner—or a prize—about her now, a grace formerly hidden. Older women she didn't even know would smile at her on the street; girls wearing engagement rings spoke to her by name, and in the mornings she would wake up with the sense that she had been given a great present, but that her mind had boxed it away overnight, and she could not for a moment remember what it was.

Billy brought her honor everywhere but at home. That was not un-expected—home, as Rhea knew it, was where they cut you down to size. Her younger brothers would imitate Billy offering their father a cigarette. *Have a Pall Mall, Mr. Sellers.* They would flourish in front of him an imaginary package of ready-mades. The unctuous voice, the complacent gesture, made Billy Doud seem asinine. *Putty,* was what they called him, first *Silly Billy,* then *Silly Putty,* then *Putty* by itself.

"You quit tormenting your sister," Rhea's father said. Then he took it up himself, with a business-like question.

"You aim to keep on at the shoe store?"

Rhea said, "Why?"

"Oh. I was just thinking. You might need it."

"What for?"

"To support that fellow. Once his old lady's dead and he runs the business into the ground."

And all the time Billy Doud said how much he admired Rhea's fa-ther. Men like your father, he said. Who work so hard. Just to get along. And never expect any different. And are so decent, and even-tempered, and kindhearted. The world owes a lot to men like that.

They would leave the dance around midnight and drive in the two cars to the parking spot, at the end of a dirt road on the bluffs above Lake Huron. Billy kept the radio on, low. He always had the radio on, even though he might be telling Rhea some complicated story. His stories had to do with his life at college, with parties and practical jokes and dire escapades sometimes involving the police. They al-ways had to do with drinking. Once somebody who was drunk vom-ited out a car window, and so noxious was the drink he had taken that the paint was destroyed all down the side of the car. The characters in these stories were not known to Rhea, except for Wayne. Girls' names

cropped up occasionally, and then she might have to interrupt. She
had seen Billy Doud home from college, over the years, with girls
whose looks, or clothes, whose jaunty or fragile airs, she had been
greatly taken with, and now she had to ask him, was Claire the one
with the little hat that had a veil, and the purple gloves? In church?
Which one had the long red hair and the camel's hair coat? Who wore
velvet boots with mouton tops?

Usually Billy was not able to remember, and if he did go on to tell
her more about these girls, what he had to say might not be complimentary.

When they parked, and sometimes even while they drove, Billy put
an arm around Rhea's shoulders and squeezed her. A promise. There
were promises also during their dances. He was not too proud to nuz-
zle her cheek then or drop a row of kisses on her hair. The kisses he
gave her in the car were quicker, and the speed, the rhythm of them,
the little smacks they might be served up with, informed her that they
were jokes, or partly jokes. He tapped his fingers on her, on her knees
and just at the top of her breasts, murmuring appreciatively and then
scolding himself, or scolding Rhea, saying that he had to keep the lid
on her.

"You're quite the baddy," he said. He pressed his lips tightly
against hers as if it was his job to keep both their mouths shut.

"How you entice me," he said, in a voice not his own, the voice of
some sleek and languishing movie actor, and slipped his hand between her legs, touched the skin above her stocking—then jumped
and laughed, as if she was too hot there, or too cold.

"Wonder how old Wayne is getting on?" he said.

The rule was that after a time either he or Wayne would sound a
blast on the car horn, and then the other one had to answer. This
game—Rhea did not understand that it was a contest, or at any rate
what kind of a contest it was—came eventually to take up more and
more of his attention. "What do you think?" he would say, peering
into the night at the dark shape of Wayne's car. "What do you think,
should I give the boy the horn?"

On the drive back to Carstairs, to the bootlegger's, Rhea would
feel like crying, for no reason, and her arms, her legs would feel heavy
and useless. Left alone, she would probably have fallen fast asleep,

but she couldn't stay alone because Lucille—Wayne's girl—was afraid of the dark, and when Billy and Wayne went into Monk's Rhea had to keep Lucille company.

Lucille was a thin, fair-haired girl with a finicky stomach, irregular periods and sensitive skin. The vagaries of her body fascinated her, and she treated it as if it was a balky valuable pet. She always carried baby oil in her purse and patted it onto her face which would have been savaged, a little while ago, by Wayne's bristles. The car smelled of baby oil and there was another smell under that, like bread dough.

"I'm going to make him shave once we get married," she said to Rhea. "Right before."

Billy Doud had told Rhea that Wayne had told him he had stuck to Lucille all this time, and was going to marry her, because she would make a good wife. He said that she wasn't the prettiest girl in the world, and she certainly wasn't the smartest, and for that reason he would always feel secure in the marriage. She wouldn't have a lot of bargaining power, he said. And she wasn't used to having a lot of money.

"Some people might say that was taking a cynical approach," Billy had said. "But others might say, realistic. A minister's son does have to be realistic, he's got to make his own way in life. Anyway, Wayne is Wayne."

"Wayne is Wayne," he had repeated with solemn pleasure.

"So how about you?" said Lucille. "Are you getting used to it?"

"Oh, yes," Rhea said.

"They say it's better without gloves on. I guess I'll find out once I'm married."

Rhea was too embarrassed to admit not having understood at once what they were talking about.

Lucille said that once she was married she would be using sponges and jelly. Rhea thought that sounded like a dessert, but she did not laugh, because she knew Lucille would take such a joke as an insult. Lucille began to talk about the conflict that was raging around her wedding, about whether the bridesmaids should wear picture hats or wreaths of rosebuds. Lucille had wanted rosebuds, and she thought it was all arranged, and then Wayne's sister had got a permanent that turned out badly. Now she wanted a hat to cover it up.

"She isn't a friend even, she's only in the wedding because of being his sister, and I couldn't leave her out. She's a selfish person."

Wayne's sister's selfishness had made Lucille break out in hives.

Something had changed in Rhea since she had turned out to be so lucky and had been smiled at, accepted by people like Lucille, shown what respect was owing to her by becoming Billy Doud's girl. It was a matter of getting *inside*, of being entirely and gratefully normal, of living within the life of the town. Rhea used to see the town of Carstairs from outside, as if it had a mysterious personality hidden from all the other people who lived inside it. For instance, one day in winter, looking by chance out the back window of the library in the town hall, she saw a team of horses pulling a load of grain sacks on the municipal weigh scales. Snow was falling. The horses were heavy workhorses, which were growing rare now, except that some farmers used them in winter, on the roads that were not ploughed. The big grain sacks, the heavy obedient animals, the snow, made Rhea think suddenly that the town was muffled in great distances, in snow-choked air, and that the life in it was a timeless ritual. And another day, a mildly overcast day in late fall, when she was walking home from school, heading out of town, she saw the dust blowing and it seemed to blow from over-worked, half-hopeless farms into stores where there were bolts of old dried cloth, and into dim rooms over the stores and into the barbershop with its stubborn thick-leaved nameless window plant, and the dentist's office with the little plush-lined drawers where he kept the false teeth. A place of waiting, of loneliness, unfinished gestures. These feelings or visions didn't come so much from what she could see before her as they did from books that she had got to read from that same library—Russian stories and *Winesburg, Ohio*. She might have been embarrassed by that fact, if she had thought about it. She was brought up to be embarrassed by any reliance on books, or any kind of stretching or blurring of the facts. She was brought up not to be a fool. So she was happy, now that she was turning out not to be that—she was happy to be waiting for her boyfriend Billy Doud outside the bootlegger's, with an engaged girl, Lucille, and to be talking about wedding hats. It was just that she felt cut off. She and Lucille had rolled down the car windows for air, and outside was the night with the river washing out of sight, at its lowest now, among the large white stones, and the frogs and crickets singing, the dirt roads faintly, faintly shining, on their way to nowhere, and the falling-down grandstand in the old fairgrounds sticking up like a crazy skeletal tower, in the dark. She was cut off from all of that. Blindfolded and cut off. Why?

Rhea was sitting in the bootlegger's house—Monk's—a bare, narrow wooden house soiled halfway up the walls by the periodic flooding of the river. Billy Doud was playing cards at one end of the big table. Rhea was seated in a rocking chair, over in a corner by the coal-oil stove, out of the way.

Ordinarily Rhea wouldn't have been inside this house at all. She would have been sitting outside with Lucille, in either Wayne's car or Billy's. Billy and Wayne would go in for one drink, promising to be out in half an hour. (This promise was not to be taken seriously.) But on this night—it was early in August—Lucille was at home sick, Billy and Rhea had gone to the dance in Walley by themselves and afterward they hadn't parked, they had driven directly across country to Monk's. Monk's was on the edge of Carstairs, where Billy and Rhea lived. Billy lived in town, Rhea lived on the chicken farm, just up over the bridge from this row of houses along the river.

When Billy saw Wayne's car parked outside Monk's he greeted it as if it had been Wayne himself. "Ho-ho-ho! Wayne-the-boy!" he cried. "Beat us to it!" He gave Rhea's shoulder a squeeze. "In we go," he said. "You too."

Mrs. Monk opened the back door to them, and Billy said, "See—I brought a neighbor of yours." Mrs. Monk looked at Rhea as if Rhea had been a stone on the road. Billy Doud had odd ideas about people. He lumped them together, if they were poor—what he would call poor—or *working class.* (Rhea knew that term only from books.) He lumped Rhea in with the Monks because she lived up the hill on the chicken farm—not understanding that her family didn't consider themselves neighbors to the people in these houses, or that her father would never in his life have sat down to drink there.

Rhea had met Mrs. Monk on the road to town, but Mrs. Monk never spoke. Her dark, graying hair was coiled up at the back of her head, and she didn't wear makeup. She had kept a slender figure, as not many women did in Carstairs. Her clothes were neat and plain, not particularly youthful but not what Rhea thought of as house-wifely. She wore a checked skirt tonight and a short-sleeved yellow blouse. Her expression was always the same—not hostile, but grave and preoccupied, as if she had a familiar weight of griefs and worries.

She led Billy and Rhea into this room in the middle of the house. The men sitting at the table did not look up or take any notice of Billy until he pulled out a chair. There might have been some sort of rule about this. All ignored Rhea. Mrs. Monk lifted something out of the rocking chair and made a gesture for her to sit down.

"Get you a Coca-Cola?" she said.

The crinoline under Rhea's lime-green dance dress made a noise like crackling straw as she sat down. She laughed apologetically, but Mrs. Monk had already turned away. The only person who took any notice of the noise was Wayne, who was just coming into the room from the front hall. He raised his black eyebrows in a comradely but incriminating way. She never knew whether Wayne liked her or not. Even when he danced with her, at the Walley Pavilion (he and Billy did an obligatory, one-time-a-night, exchange of partners) he held her as if she was a package he was barely responsible for. He was a lifeless dancer.

He and Billy hadn't greeted each other as they usually did, with a growl and a punch in the air. They were cautious and reserved in front of these older men.

Besides Dint Mason and the man who sold pots and pans, Rhea knew Mr. Martin from the dry cleaners and Mr. Boles the undertaker. Some of the others had familiar faces and some didn't. None of these men would be exactly in disgrace for coming here—Monk's was not a disgraceful place. Yet it left a slight stain. It was mentioned as if it explained something. Even if a man flourished. *He goes to Monk's.*

Mrs. Monk brought Rhea a Coca-Cola without a glass. It was not cold.

What Mrs. Monk had removed from the chair, to let Rhea sit down, was a pile of clothes that had been dampened and rolled up for ironing. So, ironing went on here, ordinary housekeeping. Pie crust might be rolled out on that table. Meals were cooked—there was the woodstove, cold and spread with newspapers now, the coal-oil stove serving for summer. There was a smell of coal-oil and damp plaster. Flood stains on the wallpaper. Barren tidiness, dark green blinds pulled down to the window sills. A tin curtain in one corner, probably concealing an old dumbwaiter.

Mrs. Monk was to Rhea the most interesting person in the room. Her legs were bare, but she wore high heels. They were tapping all the time on the floorboards. Around the table, back and forth from the sideboard where the whiskey bottles were (and where she would pause, to write things down on a pad of paper—Rhea's Coca-Cola, the broken glass). Tap-tap-tap down the back hall to some supply base from which she returned with a clutch of beer bottles in each hand. She was watchful as a deaf-mute, and as silent, catching every signal around the table, responding obediently, unsmilingly, to every demand. This brought to Rhea's mind the rumors there were, about Mrs. Monk, and she thought of another sort of signal a man might make. Mrs. Monk would lay aside her apron, she would precede him out of the room into the front hall, where there must be a stairway, leading to the bedrooms. The other men, including her husband, would pretend not to notice. She would mount the stairs without looking back, letting the man follow with his eyes on her neat buttocks in her schoolteacher's skirt. Then on a waiting bed she arranges herself without the least hesitation or enthusiasm. This indifferent readiness, this cool accommodation, the notion of such a quick and driven and bought and paid-for encounter was to Rhea shamefully exciting.

To be so flattened and used and hardly to know who was doing it to you, to take it all in with that secret capability, over and over again.

She thought of Wayne coming out of the front hall just as she and Billy were being brought into the room. She thought, what if he was coming from up there? (Later, he told her that he had been using the phone—phoning Lucille, as he had promised. Later she came to believe those rumors were false.)

Wayne had raised his hand to her across the room, meaning, was she thirsty? He brought her another bottle of Coca-Cola and slid down to the floor beside her. "Sit down before I fall down," he said.

She understood from the first sip, or maybe from the first sniff, or even before that, that there was something else in her drink besides Coca-Cola. She thought that she would not drink all, or even half, of it. She would just take a little drink now and then, to show Wayne that he had not flummoxed her.

"Is that all right?" said Wayne, "Is that the kind of drink you like?"

"It's fine," Rhea said. "I like all kinds of drinks."

"All kinds? That's good. You sound like the right kind of girl for Billy Doud."

"Does he drink a lot?" Rhea said. "Billy?"

"Put it this way," said Wayne. "Is the Pope Jewish? No. Wait. Was Jesus Catholic? No. Continue. I would not want to give you the wrong impression. Nor do I want to get clinical about this. Is Billy a drunk? Is he an alcoholic? Is he an assoholic? I mean an asshole-oholic? No, I got that wrong too. I forgot who I was talking to. Excuse please. Eliminate. Solly."

He said all this in two strange voices—one artificially high, sing-song, one gruff and serious. Rhea didn't think that she had ever heard him say so much before, in any kind of voice. It was Billy who talked, usually. Wayne said a word now and then, an unimportant word that seemed important because of the tone in which he said it. And yet this tone was often quite empty, quite neutral, the look on this face blank. That made people nervous. There was a sense of contempt be-ing held in check. Rhea had seen Billy try to stretch a story, twist it, change its tone—all in order to get Waynes's grunt of approval, his absolving bark of laughter.

"You must not come to the conclusion that I don't like Billy," said Wayne. "No. No. I would never want you to think that."

"But you don't like him," Rhea said with satisfaction. "You don't at all." The satisfaction came from the fact that she was talking back to Wayne. She was looking him in the eye. No more than that. For he had made her nervous, too. He was one of those people who make far more of an impression than their size, or their looks, or anything about them, warrants. He was not very tall, and his compact body might have been pudgy in childhood—it might get pudgy again. He had a square face, rather pale except for the bluish shadow of the beard that wounded Lucille. His black hair was very straight and fine, and often flopped over his forehead.

"Don't I?" he said with surprise. "Do I not? How could that be? When Billy is such a lovely person? Look at him over there, drinking and playing cards with the common people. Don't you find him nice? Or do you ever think it's a little strange when anybody can be so nice all the time? *All the time.* There's only one time I've known him to slip up, and that's when you get him talking about some of his old girl-friends. Don't tell me you haven't noticed that."

He had his hand on the leg of Rhea's chair. He was rocking her.

She laughed, giddy from the rocking or perhaps because he had hit on the truth. According to Billy the girl with the veil and the purple gloves had a breath tainted by cigarette smoking, and another girl used vile language when she got drunk, and one of them had a skin infection, a *fungus*, under her arms. Billy had told Rhea all these things regretfully, but when he mentioned the fungus he broke into a giggle. Unwillingly, maliciously, he giggled.

"He does rake those poor girls over the coals." Wayne said. "The hairy legs. The hal-it-os-is. Doesn't it ever make you nervous? But then you're so nice and clean. I bet you shave your legs every night." He ran his hand down her leg, which by good luck she had shaved before going to the dance. "Or do you put that stuff on them, it melts the hair away? What is that stuff called?"

"Neet," Rhea said.

"Neet! That's the stuff. Only doesn't it have kind of a bad smell? A little moldy or like yeast or something? Yeast. Isn't that another thing girls get? Am I embarrassing you? I should be a gentleman and get you another drink. If I can stand and walk I'll get you another drink."

"This has not got hardly any whiskey in it," he said, of the next Coca-Cola he brought her. "This won't hurt you." She thought that the first statement was probably a lie, but the second was certainly true. Nothing could hurt her. And nothing was lost on her. She did not think that Wayne had any good intentions. Nevertheless, she was enjoying herself. All the bafflement, the fogged-in feeling she had, when she was with Billy, had burned away. She felt like laughing at everything that Wayne said, or that she herself said. She felt safe.

"This is a funny house," she said.

"How is it funny?" said Wayne. "Just how is this house funny? You're the one that's funny."

Rhea looked down at this wagging black head and laughed, because he reminded her of some kind of dog. He was clever but there was a stubbornness about him that was close to stupidity. There was a dog's stubbornness and some misery too, about the way he kept bumping his head against her knee now, and jerking it back to shake the black hair out of his eyes.

She explained to him, with many interruptions during which she had to laugh at the possibility of explaining, that what was funny was the tin curtain in the corner of the room. She said that she thought there was a dumbwaiter behind it that went up and down from the cellar.

"We could curl up on the shelf," Wayne said. "Want to try it? We could get Billy to let down the rope."

She looked again for Billy's white shirt. So far as she knew he hadn't turned around to look at her once since he sat down. Wayne was sitting directly in front of her now, so that if Billy did turn around he wouldn't be able to see that her shoe was dangling from one toe and Wayne was flicking his fingers against the sole of her foot.

She said that she would have to go to the bathroom first.

"I will escort you," Wayne said.

He grabbed her legs to help himself up. Rhea said, "You're drunk."

"I'm not the only one."

The Monks' house had a toilet, in fact a bathroom, off the back hall. The bathtub was full of cases of beer—not cooling, just stored there. The toilet flushed properly. Rhea had been afraid it wouldn't, because it looked as if it hadn't, for the last person.

She looked at her face in the mirror over the sink and spoke to it with recklessness and approval. "Let him," she said. *"Let him."* She turned off the light and stepped into the dark hall. Hands took charge of her at once, and she was guided and propelled out the back door. Up against the wall of the house, she and Wayne were pushing and grabbing and kissing each other. She had the idea of herself, at this juncture, being opened and squeezed, opened and squeezed shut, like an accordion. She was getting a warning, too—something in the distance, not connected with what she and Wayne were doing. A troop of demons in the distance, trying to make themselves understood.

The Monks' dog had come up silently and was nosing in between them. Wayne knew its name.

"Get down, Rory! Get down, Rory!" he said as he yanked at Rhea's crinoline.

The warning was from her stomach, which was being shoved so tightly against the wall. The back door opened, Wayne said something clearly into her ear—she would never know which of these things happened first—and she was suddenly released and began to vomit. She had no intention of vomiting until she started. Then she went down on her hands and knees and vomited until her stomach felt wrung out like a poor rotten rag. When she finished she was shivering as if a fever had hit her, and her dance dress and crinoline were wet where the vomit had splattered.

Somebody else, not Wayne, pulled her up and wiped her face with the hem of the dress.

"Keep your mouth closed and breathe through your nose," Mrs. Monk said. "You get out of here," she said, either to Wayne or to Rory. She gave all of them their orders in the same voice, without sympathy and without blame. She pulled Rhea around the house to her husband's truck and half hoisted her into it.

Rhea said, "Billy."

"I'll tell your Billy. I'll say you got tired. Don't try to talk."

"I'm through throwing up," Rhea said.

"You never know," said Mrs. Monk, backing the truck out on to the road. She drove Rhea up the hill and into her own yard without saying anything more. When she had turned the truck around and stopped she said, "Watch out when you're stepping down. It's a bigger step than a car."

Rhea got herself into the house, used the bathroom without closing the door, kicked off her shoes in the kitchen, climbed the stairs, wadded up her dress and crinoline and pushed them far under the bed.

•

Rhea's father got up early, to gather the eggs and get ready to go to Hamilton, as he did every second Sunday. The boys were going with him—they could ride in the back of the truck. Rhea was not going, because there wouldn't be room in front. Her father was taking Mrs. Corey, whose husband was in the same hospital as Rhea's mother. When he took Mrs. Corey with him he always put on a shirt and a tie, because they might go into a restaurant on the way home.

He came and knocked on Rhea's door to tell her they were leaving.

"If you find time heavy you can clean the eggs on the table," he said.

He walked to the head of the stairs, then came back.

He called through her door. "Drink lots and lots of water."

Rhea wanted to scream at them all to get out of the house. She had things to consider, things inside her head that could not get free because of the pressure of the people in the house. That was what was causing her to have such a headache. After she had heard the truck's noise die away along the road she got out of bed carefully, downstairs, took three aspirins, drank as much water as she could hold, and measured coffee into the pot without looking down.

The eggs were on the table, in six-quart baskets. There were smears of hen-dirt and bits of straw stuck to them, waiting to be rubbed off with steel wool.

What things? Words, above all. The words that Wayne had said to her just as Mrs. Monk came out the back door.

I'd like to fuck you if you weren't so ugly.

She got dressed, and when the coffee was ready she poured a cup and went outside, out to the side porch which was in deep morning shade. The aspirins had started to work, and now instead of the headache she had a space in her head, a clear precarious space with a light buzz around it.

She was not ugly. She knew she was not ugly.

How can you ever be sure, that you are not ugly.

But if she was ugly, would Billy Doud have gone out with her in the first place?

Billy Doud prided himself on being kind.

But Wayne was very drunk when he said that.

Drunkards speak truth.

It was a good thing she was not going to see her mother that day. If she ever wormed out of Rhea what was the matter—and Rhea could never be certain that she would not do that—then her mother would want Wayne chastised. She would be capable of phoning his father the minister. The word *fuck* was what would incense her, more than the word *ugly*. She would miss the point entirely.

Rhea's father's reaction would be more complicated. He would blame Billy, for taking her into a place like Monk's. Billy, Billy's sort of friends. He would be angry about the *fuck* part but really he would be ashamed of Rhea. He would be forever ashamed that a man had called her ugly.

You cannot let your parents anywhere near your real humiliations.

She knew she was not ugly.

How could she know she was not ugly?

She did not think about Billy and Wayne, or about what this might mean between them. She was not as yet very interested in other people.

She did think that when Wayne said those words he used his real voice.

She did not want to go back inside the house. She didn't want to have to look at the baskets full of dirty eggs. She started walking down the lane, wincing in the sunlight, lowering her head between one island of shade and the next. Each tree was different there and each was a milestone, when she used to ask her mother how far she could go to meet her father, coming home from town. As far as the hawthorn tree, as far as the beech tree, as far as the maple. He would stop and let Rhea ride on the running board.

A car hooted from the road. Somebody who knew her, or just a man going by? She wanted to get out of sight, so she cut across the field that the chickens had picked clean and paved slick with their droppings. In one of the trees at the far side of this field her brothers had built a tree house. It was just a platform, with boards nailed to the tree trunk to climb. Rhea did that, she climbed up and sat on the platform. She saw that her brothers had cut windows in the leafy branches, for spying. She could look down on the road, and presently she saw a few cars bringing country children into town to the early Sunday school at the Baptist church. The people in the cars couldn't see here.

Billy or Wayne wouldn't be able to see her, if by any chance they should come looking, with explanations or accusations or apologies.

In another direction, she could see flashes of the river and a part of the old fairgrounds. It was easy from there to make out where the racetrack used to go round, in the long grass.

She saw a person walking, following the racetrack. It was Eunie Morgan, and she was wearing her pajamas. She was walking along the racetrack, in light-colored, pale pink pajamas, at about half-past nine in the morning. She followed the track until it veered off, going down to where the riverbank path used to be. The bushes hid her.

Eunie Morgan with her white hair sticking up, her hair and her pajamas catching the light. Like an angel in feathers. But walking in her usual awkward, assertive way—body tilted forward, arms swinging free. Rhea didn't know what Eunie could be doing there. She didn't know anything about Eunie's disappearance. The sight of Eunie seemed both strange and natural to her.

She remembered how, on hot summer days, she used to think that Eunie's hair looked like a snowball or like threads of ice preserved from winter, and she would want to mash her face against it, to get cool.

She remembered the hot grass and garlic and the jumping-out-of-your-skin feeling, when they were turning into Toms.

She went back to the house and phoned Wayne. She counted on his being home and the rest of his family in church.

"I want to ask you something and not on the phone," she said. "Dad and the boys went to Hamilton."

When Wayne got there she was on the porch, cleaning eggs.

"I want to know what you meant," she said.

"By what?" said Wayne.

Rhea looked up at him, and kept looking, with an egg in one hand and a piece of steel wool in the other.

"I was drunk," Wayne said. "You're not ugly."

Rhea said, "I know I'm not."

"I feel awful."

"Not for that," said Rhea.

"I was drunk. It was a joke."

Rhea said, "You don't want to get married to Lucille."

He leaned into the railing. She thought maybe he was going to be sick. But he got over that and tried his raising of the eyebrows, his discouraging smile.

"Oh, really? No kidding? So what advice do you have for me?"

"Write a note," said Rhea, just as if he had asked seriously. "Get in your car. Drive to Calgary."

"Just like that."

"If you want, I'll ride with you to Toronto. You can drop me there and I'll stay at the Y and get a job."

All this astonished Rhea, as it came out, almost as much as it did Wayne. But she couldn't go back on any of it.

"Did you ever look at a map?" Wayne said. "You don't go through Toronto on the way to Calgary. You go across at Sarnia and up through the States to Winnipeg. Then Calgary."

"Drop me off in Winnipeg then, that's better."

"One question. Have you had a sanity test recently?"

"No."

When Rhea saw her, Eunie was on her way home. It was a surprise to Eunie to find the riverbank path not clear as she was expecting it it be, but all grown up with brambles. When she pushed out into her own yard she had scratches and smears of blood on her arms and forehead, and bits of leaves caught in her hair. One side of her face was dirty, too, from resting on the ground.

In the kitchen Eunie found her mother and her father and her Aunt Muriel Martin, and Norman Slater, the Chief of Police, and Billy Doud. After her mother had phoned her Aunt Muriel, her father had stirred himself, and said that he was going to phone Mr. Doud. He had worked in Doud's when he was young, and remembered how Mr. Doud, Billy's father, was always sent for in an emergency.

"You mean the one that's dead," said Eunie's mother. "What if you get *her*?" But he phoned anyway, and got Billy, who hadn't been to bed.

Aunt Muriel Martin had phoned the chief of police. He said he would be down as soon as he got dressed and ate his breakfast. This took him some time. He disliked anything puzzling or disruptive, anything that might force him to make decisions which could be criticized later or result in his looking like a fool. Of all the people in the kitchen, he might have been the happiest to see Eunie home safe, and to hear her story. It was right out of his jurisdiction. There was nothing to be followed up, nobody to be charged.

Eunie said that three children had come up to her, in her own yard, in the middle of the night. They said that they had something to show her. "What's that?" she said. She asked them what they were doing up so late at night. She didn't recall what they answered.

She found herself being borne along by them, without ever having said that she would go. They took her out through the gap in the fence at the corner of the yard and along the path by the riverbank. She was surprised to find the path so well opened up—she had the idea that it must be all overgrown, now that she didn't go that way anymore.

It was two boys and a girl who took her. They looked about nine or ten or eleven years old, and they all wore the same sort of outfit—a kind of seersucker sunsuit with a bib in front and straps over the shoulders. So fresh and clean, as if just off the ironing board. The hair of these children was straight, light brown and shiny. How could she tell at night what color their hair was and that their sunsuits were made of seersucker? When she came out of the house she hadn't brought the flashlight. They must have brought some kind of light with them—that was her impression.

They took her along the path and out onto the old fairgrounds. They took her to their tent. But it seemed to her that she didn't see that tent once from the outside. She was just suddenly inside it, and she saw that it was white, very high, and shivering like the sails on a boat; also it was lit up, and again she had no idea where the light was coming from. And a certain part of this tent, or building or whatever it was, seemed to be made of glass. Yes. Green glass, a very light green, as if panels of it were slid in between the sails. Possibly to a glass floor, because she was walking in her bare feet on something cool and smooth—not grass at all, and certainly not gravel.

(Later on, in the newspaper, there was a drawing, an artist's conception, of something like a sailboat in a saucer. But flying saucer was not what Eunie called it—she called it a tent, at least when she was talking about it immediately afterwards. Also she said nothing about what appeared in print later, in a book of such stories, concerning the capture and investigation of her body, the sampling of her blood and fluids, the possibility that one of her secret eggs had been spirited away, that fertilization might have taken place in an alien dimension—subtle or explosive, at any rate indescribable, mating, that sucked Eunie's genes into the lifestream of the invaders.)

She was set down in a seat she hadn't noticed, she couldn't say if it was a plain chair or a throne, and these children began to weave a veil around her. It was like mosquito netting or some such stuff, light but strong. All three of them moved continuously winding or weaving it around her, never bumping into each other. She did not ask one question. All possible questions, such as, "What do you think you're doing?" or "How did you get here?" or "Where are the grown-ups?" had just slipped off some place where she couldn't reach them. It was not that she was scared. She was opposite of scared, or uncomfortable. It was so pleasant, she couldn't describe it. (When she tried to, she said, "I was just as happy as a cow in clover.") And also everything had got to seem perfectly normal. You wouldn't ask questions, anymore than you would ask, "What is that teapot doing here?" when you were sitting in an ordinary room.

When she woke up there was nothing around her, nothing over her. She was lying in the hot sunlight, well on in the morning. In the fairgrounds, on the hard earth.

"Wonderful," said Billy Doud several times as he watched and listened to Eunie. He smelled of beer but seemed sober and very attentive. More than attentive—you might say, enchanted. Eunie's singular revelations, her dirty flushed face and her thickened, somewhat arrogant voice, appeared to wrap Billy Doud in delight. *Wonderful.*

His love—Billy Doud's kind of love—sprang up to meet a need that Eunie wouldn't know anything about.

Aunt Muriel said it was time to phone the newspapers.

Eunie's mother said, "Won't Bill Proctor be in church?" She was speaking of the editor of the Carstairs *Argus.*

"Bill Proctor can cool his heels," Aunt Muriel said. "I'm phoning *The London Free Press!*"

She did that, but she did not get to talk to the right person, only to some sort of caretaker, because of its being Sunday. "They'll be sorry!" she said. "I'm going to go over their heads right to *The Toronto Star!*"

She had taken charge of the story. Eunie let her. Eunie was satisfied. When she was not speaking, and when it seemed nobody was looking at her, she sat still, with a look of satisfaction and indifference on her face. She did not ask that anybody take charge of *her,* try to protect her, with seriousness and kindness, through what lay ahead. But Billy Doud had already made a vow to do that.

Eunie had some fame, for a while. Reporters came. A book writer came. A photographer took pictures of the fairgrounds, and of the racetracks, which was supposed to be the mark left by the spaceship. There was also a picture of the grandstand, and a caption that said it had been knocked down in the course of the landing.

Interest in this sort of story reached a peak years ago, then slowly dwindled.

"Who knows what happened," Rhea's father said, in a letter that he wrote to Calgary.

"One sure thing is, Eunie Morgan never made a cent out of it."

He was writing this letter to Rhea. Soon after they got to Calgary, Wayne and Rhea were married. You had to be married then, to get an apartment together—at least in Calgary—and they had discovered that they did not want to live separately. That would continue to be the way they felt most of the time, though they would discuss it— living separately—and threaten it, and give it a couple of brief tries.

Wayne left the paper and went into television. For years you might see him on the late news, sometimes in rain or snow on Parliament Hill, delivering some rumor or piece of information. Later he traveled to foreign cities and did the same thing there, and still later he got to be one of the people who sit indoors and discuss what the news means and who is telling lies.

(Eunie became very fond of television but she never saw Wayne, because she hated it when people just talked—she always switched at once to something happening.)

Back in Carstairs on a brief visit, and wandering in the cemetery, looking to see who has moved in since her last inspection, Rhea spots Lucille Flagg's name on a stone. But it is all right—Lucille isn't dead.

Her husband is, and Lucille has had her own name and date of birth cut on the stone along with his, ahead of time. A lot of people do this, because the cost of stonecutting is always going up.

Rhea remembers the hats and rosebuds, and feels a tenderness for Lucille that cannot ever be returned.

At this time Rhea and Wayne have lived together for far more than half their lives. They have had three children, and between them, counting everything, five times as many lovers. And now abruptly, surprisingly, all this turbulence and fruitfulness and uncertain but lively expectation has receded and she knows they are beginning to be old. There in the cemetery she says out loud, "I can't get used to it."

They look up the Douds, who are friends of theirs in a way, and together the two couples drive out to where the old fairgrounds used to be.

Rhea says the same thing there.

The river houses all gone. The Morgans' house, the Monks' house—everything gone of that first mistaken settlement. The land is now a floodplain, under the control of the Peregrine River Authority. Nothing can be built there anymore. A spacious parkland, a shorn and civilized riverbank—nothing left but a few of the same old trees standing around, their leaves still green but weighed down by a diffuse golden moisture that is in the air on this September afternoon not many years before the end of the century.

"I can't get used to it," says Rhea.

They are white-haired now, all four of them. Rhea is a thin and darting sort of woman, whose lively and cajoling ways have come in handy teaching English as a second language. Wayne is thin, too, with a fine white beard and a mild manner. When he's not appearing on television he might remind you of a Tibetan monk. In front of the camera he turns caustic, even brutal.

The Douds are big people, stately and fresh-faced, with a cushioning of wholesome fat.

Billy Doud smiles at Rhea's vehemence, and looks around with distracted approval.

"Time marches on," he says.

He pats his wife on her broad back, responding to a low grumble that the others haven't heard. He tells her they'll be going home in a minute, she won't miss the show she watches every afternoon.

•

Rhea's father was right about Eunie not making any money out of her experiences, and he was right too in what he had predicted about Billy Doud. After Billy's mother died, problems multiplied and Billy sold out. Soon the people who had bought the factory from him sold out in their turn and the plant was closed down. There were no more pianos made in Carstairs. Billy went to Toronto and got a job, which Rhea's father said had something to do with schizophrenics or drug addicts or Christianity.

In fact, Billy was working at halfway houses and group homes, and Wayne and Rhea knew this. Billy had kept up the friendship. He had also kept up his special friendship with Eunie. He hired her to look after his sister Bea when Bea began drinking a little too much to look after herself. (Billy was not drinking at all anymore.)

When Bea died, Billy inherited the house and made it over into a home for old people and disabled people who were not so old or disabled that they needed to be in bed. He meant to make it a place where they could get comfort and kindness and little treats and entertainments. He came back to Carstairs and settled in to run it.

He asked Eunie Morgan to marry him.

"I wouldn't want for there to be anything going on, or anything," Eunie said.

"Oh, my dear!" said Billy. "Oh, my dear, dear Eunie!"

INTOXICATION

Jay McInerney

⌘

It's Six A.M., Do You Know
Where You Are?

You are not the kind of guy who would be at a place like this at this time of the morning. But you are here, and you cannot say that the terrain is entirely unfamiliar, although the details are a little fuzzy. You are at a nightclub talking to a girl with a shaved head. The club is either the Bimbo Box or the Lizard Lounge. It might all come a little clearer if you could slip into the bathroom and do a little more Bolivian Marching Powder. There is a small voice inside of you insisting that this epidemic lack of clarity is the result of too much of that already, but you are not yet willing to listen to that voice. The night has already turned on that imperceptible pivot where two A.M. changes to six A.M. You know that moment has come and gone, but you are not yet willing to concede that you have crossed the line beyond which all is gratuitous damage and the palsy of unravelled nerve endings. Somewhere back there it was possible to cut your losses, but you rode past that moment on a comet trail of white powder and now you are trying to hang onto that rush. Your brain at this moment is composed of brigades of tiny Bolivian soldiers. They are tired and muddy from their long march through the night. There are holes in their boots and they are hungry. They need to be fed. They need the Bolivian Marching Powder.

Something vaguely tribal about this scene—pendulous jewelry, face paint, ceremonial headgear and hairstyles. You feel that there is also a certain Latin theme, which is more than the fading buzz of marimbas in your brain.

You are leaning back against a post which may or may not be structural with regard to the building, but which feels essential for the maintenance of an upright position. The bald girl is saying this used to be a good place to come before the assholes discovered it. You do not want to be talking to this bald girl, or even listening to her, which is all you're doing, but you don't have your barge pole handy, and just at the moment you don't want to test the powers of speech or locomotion.

How did you get here? It was your friend, Tad Allagash, who powered you in here, and now he has disappeared. Tad is the kind of guy who certainly would be at a place like this at this time of the morning. He is either your best self or your worst self, you're not sure which. Earlier in the evening it seemed clear that he was your best self. You started on the Upper East Side with champagne and unlimited prospects, strictly observing the Allagash rule of perpetual motion: one drink per stop. Tad's mission in life is to have more fun than anyone else in New York City, and this involves a lot of moving around, since there is always the likelihood that you are missing something, that where you aren't is more fun than where you are. You are awed by this strict refusal to acknowledge any goal higher than the pursuit of pleasure. You want to be like that. You also think that he is shallow and dangerous. His friends are all rich and spoiled, like the cousin from Memphis you met earlier in the evening who would not accompany you below Fourteenth Street because he said he didn't have a lowlife visa. This cousin had a girlfriend with cheekbones to break your heart, and you knew she was the real thing when she absolutely refused to acknowledge your presence. She possessed secrets—about islands, about horses—which you would never know.

You have traveled from the meticulous to the slime. The girl with the shaved head has a scar tattooed on her scalp. It looks like a long, sutured gash. You tell her it is very realistic. She takes this as a compliment and thanks you. You meant as opposed to romantic. "I could use one of those right over my heart," you say.

"You want I can give you the name of the guy did it. You'd be surprised how cheap." You don't tell her that nothing would surprise you now. Her voice, for instance, which is like the New Jersey State Anthem played through an electric shaver.

The bald girl is emblematic of the problem. What the problem is is that for some reason you think you are going to meet the kind of girl who is not the kind of girl who would be at a place like this at this time of the morning. When you meet her you are going to tell her that what you really want is a house in the country with a garden. New York, the club scene, bald women—you're tired of all that. Your presence here is only a matter of conducting an experiment in limits, reminding yourself of what you aren't. You see yourself as the kind of guy who wakes up early on Sunday morning and steps out to pick up the *Times* and croissants. You take a cue from the Arts and Leisure section and decide to check out some exhibition—costumes of the Hapsburg Court at the Met, say, or Japanese lacquerware of the Muromachi period at the Asia Society. Maybe you will call that woman you met at the publishing party Friday night, the party you did not get sloppy drunk at, the woman who is an editor at a famous publishing house even though she looks like a fashion model. See if she wants to check out the exhibition and maybe do an early dinner. You will wait until eleven A.M. to call her, because she may not be an early riser, like you. She may have been out a little late, at a nightclub, say. It occurs to you that there is time for a couple of sets of tennis before the museum. You wonder if she plays, but then, of course she would.

When you meet the girl who wouldn't et cetera, you will tell her that you are slumming, visiting your own six A.M. Lower East Side of the soul on a lark, stepping nimbly between the piles of garbage to the marimba rhythms in your head.

On the other hand, any beautiful girl, specifically one with a full head of hair, would help you stave off this creeping sense of mortality. You remember the Bolivian Marching Powder and realize you're not down yet. First you have to get rid of this bald girl because she is doing bad things to your mood.

In the bathroom there are no doors on the stalls, which makes it tough to be discreet. But clearly, you are not the only person here to take on fuel. Lots of sniffling going on. The windows in here are blacked over, and for this you are profoundly grateful.

Hup, two. Three, four. The Bolivian soldiers are back on their feet. They are off and running in formation. Some of them are dancing, and you must do the same.

Just outside the door you spot her: tall, dark, and alone, half-hiding behind a pillar at the edge of the dance floor. You approach laterally, moving your stuff like a bad spade through the slalom of a synthesized conga rhythm. She jumps when you touch her shoulder.

"Dance?"

She looks at you as if you had just suggested instrumental rape. "I do not speak English," she says, when you ask again.

"Français?"

She shakes her head. Why is she looking at you that way, like there are tarantulas nesting in your eye sockets?

"You are by any chance from Bolivia? Or Peru?"

She is looking around for help now. Remembering a recent encounter with a young heiress's bodyguard at Danceteria—or was it New Berlin?—you back off, hands raised over your head.

The Bolivian soldiers are still on their feet, but they have stopped singing their marching song. You realize that we are at a crucial juncture with regard to morale. What we need is a good pep talk from Tad Allagash, but he is not to be found. You try to imagine what he would say. *Back on the horse. Now we're really going to have some fun.* Something like that. You suddenly realize that he has already slipped out with some rich hose queen. He is back at her place on Fifth Ave., and they are doing some of her off-the-boat-quality drugs. They are scooping it out of tall Ming vases and snorting it off of each other's naked bodies. You hate Tad Allagash.

Go home. Cut your losses.

Stay. Go for it.

You are a republic of voices tonight. Unfortunately, the republic is Italy. All these voices are waving their arms and screaming at each other. There's an *ex cathedra* riff coming down from the Vatican: *Repent. There's still time. Your body is the temple of the Lord and you have defiled it.* It is, after all, Sunday morning, and as long as you have any brain cells left there will always be this resonant patriarchal basso echoing down the marble vaults of your churchgoing childhood to remind you that this is the Lord's day. What you need is another overpriced drink to drown it out. But a search of pockets yields only a dollar bill and change. You paid ten to get in here. Panic is gaining on you.

You spot a girl at the edge of the dance floor who looks like your last chance for earthly salvation against the creeping judgment of Sunday morning. You know for a fact that if you go out into the morning alone, without even your sunglasses, which you have forgotten (because who, after all, plans on these travesties), that the harsh, angling light will turn you to flesh and bone. Mortality will pierce you through the retina. But there she is in her pegged pants, a kind of doo-wop retro ponytail pulled off to the side, great lungs, as eligible a candidate as you could hope to find this late in the game. The sexual equivalent of fast food.

She shrugs and nods when you ask her to dance. You like the way she moves, half-tempo, the oiled ellipses of her hips and shoulders. You get a little hip and ass contact. After the second song she says she's tired. She's on the edge of bolting when you ask her if she needs a little pick-me-up.

"You've got some blow?" she says.

"Monster," you say.

She takes your arm and leads you into the Ladies'. There's another guy in the stall beside yours so it's okay. After a couple of spoons she seems to like you just fine and you are feeling very likeable yourself. A couple more. This girl is all nose. When she leans forward for the spoon the front of her shirt falls open in a way you can't help noticing. You wonder if this is her way of thanking you.

Oh yes.

"I love drugs," she says, as you march towards the bar.

"It's something we have in common," you say.

"Have you ever noticed how all the good words start with D? D and L."

You try to think about this. You're not quite sure what she's driving at. The Bolivians are singing their marching song but you can't quite make out the words.

"You know? Drugs. Delight. Decadence."

"Debauchery," you say, catching the tune now.

"Dexedrine."

"Delectable. Deranged. Debilitated."

"And L. Lush and luscious."

"Languorous."

"Lazy."

"Libidinous."

"What's that?" she says.

"Horny."

"Oh," she says, and casts a long, arching look over your shoulder. Her eyes glaze in a way that reminds you precisely of the closing of a sandblasted glass shower door. You can see that the game is over, though you're not sure which rule you broke. Possibly she finds "H" words offensive. She is scanning the dance floor for a man with a compatible vocabulary. You have more: *down* and *depressed; lost* and *lonely*. It's not that you are really going to miss this girl who thinks that *decadence* and *dexedrine* are the high points of the language of the Kings James and Lear, but the touch of flesh, the sound of another human voice. . . . You know that there is a special purgatory waiting out there for you, a desperate half-sleep which is like a grease fire in the brain pan.

The girl half-waves as she disappears into the crowd. There is no sign of the other girl, the girl who would not be here. There is no sign of Tad Allagash. The Bolivians are mutinous. You can't stop the voices.

Here you are again.

All messed up and no place to go.

It is worse even than you expected, stepping out into the morning. The light is like a mother's reproach. The sidewalk sparkles cruelly. Visibility unlimited. The downtown warehouses look serene and rested in this beveled light. A cab passes uptown and you start to wave, then realize you have no money. The cab stops. You jog over and lean in the window.

"I guess I'll walk after all."

"Asshole." He leaves rubber.

You start north, holding your hand over your eyes. There is a bum sleeping on the sidewalk, swathed in garbage bags. He lifts his head as you pass. "God bless you and forgive your sins," he says. You wait for the cadge, but that's all he says. You wish he hadn't said it.

As you turn away, what is left of your olfactory equipment sends a message to your brain. The smell of fresh bread. Somewhere they are baking bread. You see bakery trucks loading in front of a loft building on the next block. You watch as bags of rolls are carried out onto the loading dock by a man with a tattooed forearm. This man is already at work, so that regular people will have fresh bread for their morning tables. The righteous people who sleep at night and eat eggs for breakfast. It is Sunday morning and you have not eaten since . . . when? Friday night. As you approach, the smell of the bread washes over you like a gentle rain. You inhale deeply, filling your lungs with it. Tears come to your eyes, and you are filled with such a rush of tenderness and pity that you stop beside a lamppost and hang on for support.

You remember another Sunday morning in your old apartment on Cornelia Street when you woke to the smell of bread from the bakery downstairs. There was the smell of bread every morning, but this is the one you remember. You turned to see your wife sleeping beside you. Her mouth was open and her hair fell down across the pillow to your shoulder. The tanned skin of her shoulder was the color of bread fresh from the oven. Slowly, and with a growing sense of exhilaration, you remembered who you were. You were the boy and she was the girl, your college sweetheart. You weren't famous yet, but you had the rent covered, you had your favorite restaurant where the waitresses knew your name and you could bring your own bottle of wine. It all seemed to be just the way you had pictured it when you had discussed plans for marriage and New York. The apartment with the pressed tin ceiling, the claw-footed bath, the windows that didn't quite fit the frame. It seemed almost as if you had wished for that very place. You leaned against your wife's shoulder. Later you would get up quietly, taking care not to wake her, and go downstairs for croissants and the Sunday *Times,* but for a long time you lay there breathing in the mingled scents of bread, hair and skin. You were in no hurry to get up. You knew it was a moment you wanted to savor. You didn't know how soon it would be over, that within a year she would go back to Michigan to file for divorce.

You approach the man on the loading dock. He stops working and watches you. You feel that there is something wrong with the way your legs are moving.

"Bread." This is what you say to him. You meant to say something more, but this is as much as you can get out.

"What was your first clue?" he says. He is a man who has served his country, you think, a man with a family somewhere outside the city. Small children. Pets. A garden.

"Could I have some? A roll or something?"

"Get out of here."

The man is about your size, except for the belly, which you don't have. "I'll trade you my jacket," you say. It is one hundred percent raw silk from Paul Stuart. You take it off, show him the label.

"You're crazy," the man says. Then he looks back into the warehouse. He picks up a bag of hard rolls and throws them at your feet. You hand him the jacket. He checks the label, sniffs the jacket, then tries it on.

You tear the bag open and the smell of warm dough rushes over you. The first bite sticks in your throat and you almost gag. You will have to go slowly. You will have to learn everything all over again.

Mary McCarthy

✠

from Edmund Wilson

The following sections were excerpted from an unpublished chapter of Mary McCarthy's "intellectual autobiography," in which she distills one of the most celebrated and powerhouse literary nuptials of the twentieth century. McCarthy died without knowing that her chapter on Wilson was rejected by The New Yorker *and subsequently lost in an office upheaval. She left no diaries or first drafts for posthumous publication, which cast this "lost chapter" as the only unpublished work in her voluminous oeuvre.*

Wilson and Peggy were already at Mary's, in an upstairs private dining room. Far from not drinking, he was ordering a second round of double Manhattans when I arrived. Naturally I took one, then a second, without saying that I had already had drinks with Fred. But if I had, it would have made no difference. Wilson was in a bibulous mood. And I learned why he had said no to drinks before lunch that day in the Union Square restaurant: he had had a colossal hangover, and the hair of the dog was not one of his weaknesses.

His habit, as I came to know, was to get thoroughly soused (which we were on our way to doing at Mary's), then sleep it off and turn over a new leaf the next day on arising. Bathed and shaved, clad in snowy linen—he wore BVDs—he emerged from his toilet reborn, or like a risen god. That he did not smoke probably helped. The glowing pink man we had taken to lunch was a resurrected Wilson, who had harried hell the night before. The boys, who had read *I Thought of Daisy*

(I had not), might have guessed that the respected critic was no teetotaler.

After the double manhattans, we drank dago red and finally B&B. This was a favorite potion with Wilson, which I never came to like; for me, the sweetness of the benedictine spoiled the taste of the brandy. All that liquor loosened my tongue, and I had what was called a talking jag. Since Wilson seemed interested, I told them the story of my life: Seattle, the flu, the death of my parents, Minneapolis, and certainly quite a bit of Uncle Myers, not omitting, I fear, the razor strop. . . . Then, somehow, we were at the Chelsea Hotel, on West 23rd Street. Possibly we had dropped in on Ben Stolberg, who was living there at the time. I was no longer very conscious of Margaret Marshall, but she was still one of the party. Fairly soon, I hope, I "passed out."

As I learned the next day, my inert form put them in a quandary. Neither Peggy nor Wilson knew where I lived. Ben Stolberg would not have known either. If they had tried looking in the phone book, they would not have found me—Philip and I had only recently moved in. Wilson, though no doubt very drunk, rose to the occasion. He took a room for himself—he was living in the country, near Stamford—and another for Margaret and me.

Opening an eye the morning after, I looked cautiously across to the next bed, having assessed that I was in a twin-bedded room. With an episode like the one with the man in the Brooks Brothers shirt behind me, I had reason to fear the worst. In the other bed, a yawning Margaret Marshall opened her eyes. There was no one else in the room, so far as I could see, and I guessed that we were in a hotel. I let a cry escape me, a loud groan or moan. It was the same awful certainty speaking that had just awakened me, like a voice in my ear. "Oh, God, oh, God, I've disgraced *Partisan Review*." In my slip, I cried hopelessly while she looked on. Wilson must have gone back to Stamford. At any rate, we did not see him that morning. Doubtless he had paid our bill.

Issue 27, 1962

Stanley Elkin

⁂

The Guest

On Sunday Bertie walked into an apartment building in St. Louis, a city where, in the past, he had changed trains, waited for buses, or thought about Klaff, and where, more recently, truckers dropped him, or traveling salesmen stopped their Pontiacs downtown just long enough for him to reach into the back seat for his trumpetcase and get out. In the hallway he stood before the brass, mailboxed wall seeking the name of his friend, his friends' friend really, and his friends' friend's wife. The girl had danced with him at parties in the college town, and one night—he imagined he must have been particularly pathetic, engagingly pathetic—she had kissed him. The man, of course, patronized him, asked him questions that would have been more vicious had they been less naïve. He remembered he rather enjoyed making his long, patient answers. Condescension always brought the truth out of him. It was more appealing than indifference anyway, and more necessary to him now. He supposed he didn't care for either of them, but he couldn't go further. He had to rest or he would die.

He found the name on the mailbox—Mr. and Mrs. Stephen Feldman—the girl's identity, as he might have guessed, swallowed up in the husband's. It was no way to treat women, he thought gallantly.

He started up the stairs. Turning the corner at the second landing he saw a man, moving cautiously downward, burdened by boxes and suitcases and loose bags. Only when they were on a level with each other did Bertie, through a momentary clearing in the boxes, recognize Stephen Feldman.

"Old man, old man," Bertie said.

"Just a minute," Feldman said, forcing a package aside with his chin. Bertie stood, half a staircase above him, leaning against the wall. He grinned in the shadows, conscious of his ridiculous fedora, his eye patch rakishly black against the soft whiteness of his face. Black-suited, tiny, white-fleshed, he posed above Feldman, dapper as a scholarly waiter in a restaurant. He waited until he was recognized.

"Bertie? Bertie? Let me get rid of this stuff. Give me a hand, will you?" Feldman said.

"Sure," Bertie said. "It's on my family crest. One hand washing the other. Here, wait a minute." He passed Feldman on the stairs and held the door for him. He followed him outside.

"Take the key from my pocket, Bertie, and open the trunk. It's the blue convertible."

Bertie put his hand in Feldman's pocket. "You've got nice thighs," he said. To irritate Feldman he pretended to try to force the house key into the trunk lock. Feldman stood impatiently behind him, bal-ancing his heavy burdens. "I've been to Dallas, lived in a palace," Bertie said over his shoulder. "There's this great Eskimo who blows down there. Would you believe he's cut the best side ever recorded of 'Mood Indigo'?" Bertie shook the key ring as if it were a castanet.

Feldman dumped his load on the hood of the car and took the keys from Bertie. He opened the trunk and started to throw things into it. "Going somewhere?" Bertie asked.

"Vacation," Feldman said.

"Oh," Bertie said.

Feldman looked toward the apartment house. "I've got to go up for another suitcase, Bertie."

"Sure," Bertie said.

He went up the stairs behind Feldman. About halfway up he stopped to catch his breath. Feldman watched him curiously. He pounded his chest with his tiny fist and grinned weakly. "*Mea culpa,*" he said. "Mea booze. Mea sluts. Mea pot. Me-o-mea."

"Come on," Feldman said.

They went inside and Bertie heard a toilet flushing. Through a hall, through an open door, he saw Norma, Feldman's wife, staring absently into the bowl. "If she moves them now you won't have to stop at God knows what kind of place along the road," Bertie said brightly.

Norma lifted a big suitcase easily in her big hands and came into the living room. She stopped when she saw Bertie. "Bertie! Stephen, it's Bertie."

"We bumped into each other in the hall," Stephen said. Bertie watched the two of them look at each other.

"You sure picked a time to come visiting, Bertie," Feldman said.

"We're leaving on our vacation, Bertie," Norma said.

"We're going up to New England for a couple of weeks," Feldman told him.

"We can chat for a little with Bertie, can't we Stephen, before we go?"

"Of course," Feldman said. He sat down and pulled the suitcase next to him.

"It's very lovely in New England." Bertie sat down and crossed his legs. "I don't get up there very regularly. Not my territory. I've found that when a man makes it in the Ivy League he tends to forget about old Bertie," he said sadly.

"What are you doing in St. Louis, Bertie?" Feldman's wife asked him.

"It's my midwestern swing," Bertie said. "I've been down south on the southern sponge. Opened up a whole new territory down there." He heard himself cackle.

"Who did you see, Bertie?" Norma asked him.

"You wouldn't know her. A cousin of Klaff's."

"Were you living with her?" Feldman asked.

Bertie shook his finger at him. The Feldmans stared glumly at each other. Stephen rubbed the plastic suitcase handle. In a moment, Bertie thought, he would probably say, "Gosh, Bertie, you should have written. You should have let us know." He should have written! Did the Fuller Brush man write? Who would be home? Who wouldn't be on vacation? They were commandos, the Fuller Brush man and he. He was tired, sick. He couldn't move on today. Would they kill him because of their lousy vacation?

Meanwhile the Feldmans weren't saying anything. They stared at each other openly, their large eyes in their large heads on their large necks largely. He thought he could wait them out. It was what he *should* do. It should have been the easiest thing in the world—to wait out the Feldmans, to stare them down. Who was he kidding? It wasn't his forte. He had no forte. *That* was his forte. He could already hear himself begin to speak.

"Sure," he said. "I almost married that girl. Klaff's lady cousin. The first thing she ever said to me was 'Bertie, they never build drug stores in the middle of the block. Always on corners.' It was the truth. Well, I thought, this was the woman for me. One time she came out of the ladies' john of a Greyhound bus station and she said, 'Bertie, have you ever noticed how public toilets often smell like bubble gum?' That's what it was like all the time. She had all these institutional insights. I was sure we could make it together. It didn't work out." He sighed.

Feldman stared at him but Norma was beginning to soften, Bertie thought. He wondered randomly what she would be like in bed. He looked coolly at her long legs, her wide shoulders. Like Klaff's cousin. Institutional.

"Bertie, how are your eyes now?" she asked.

"Oh," he said, "still seeing double." He smiled. "Two for one. It's all right when there's something to look at. Other times I use the patch."

Norma seemed sad.

"I have fun with it," he said. "It doesn't make any difference which eye I cover. I'm ambidextrous." He pulled the black elastic band from his forehead. Instantly there were two large Stephens, two large Normas. The four Feldmans like a troupe of Jewish acrobats. He felt surrounded. In the two living rooms his four hands fumbled with the two patches. He felt sick to his stomach. He closed one eye and hastily replaced the patch. "I shouldn't try that on an empty stomach," he said.

Feldman watched him narrowly. "Gee, Bertie," he said finally, "maybe we could drop you someplace."

It was out of the question. He couldn't get into a car again. "Do you go through Minneapolis, Minnesota?" he asked indifferently.

Feldman looked confused and Bertie liked him for a moment. "We were going to catch the turnpike up around Chicago, Bertie."

"Oh, Chicago," Bertie said. "I can't go back to Chicago yet."

Feldman nodded.

"Don't you know anybody else in St. Louis?" Norma asked.

"Klaff used to live across the river, but he's gone," Bertie said.

"Look, Bertie . . ." Feldman said.

"I'm fagged," Bertie said helplessly, "locked out."

"Bertie," Feldman said, "do you need any money? I could let you have twenty dollars."

Bertie put his hand out mechanically.

"This is stupid," Norma said suddenly. "Stay *here.*"

"Oh, well—"

"No, I mean it. Stay *here.* We'll be gone for two weeks. What difference does it make?"

Feldman looked at his wife for a moment and shrugged. "Sure," he said, "there's no reason you couldn't stay here. As a matter of fact you'd be doing us a favor. I forgot to cancel the newspaper, the milk. You'd keep the burglars off. They don't bother a place if it looks lived in." He put twenty dollars on the coffee table. "There might be something you need," he explained.

Bertie looked carefully at them both. They seemed to mean it. Feldman and his wife grinned at him steadily, relieved at how easily they had come off. He enjoyed the idea himself. At last he had a real patron, a real matron. "O.K.," he said.

"Then it's settled," Feldman said, rising.

"It's all right?" Bertie said.

"Certainly it's all right," Feldman said. "What harm could you do?"

"I'm harmless," Bertie said.

Feldman picked up the suitcase and led his wife toward the door. "Have a good time," Bertie said, following them. "I'll watch things for you. Rrgghh! Rrrgghhhfff!"

Feldman waved back at him as he went down the stairs. "Hey," Bertie called, leaning over the banister, "did I tell you about that crazy Klaff? You know what nutty Klaff did out at U.C.L.A.? He became a second-story man." They were already down the stairs.

Bertie went back into the house. Closing the door he pressed his back against it and turned his head slowly across his left shoulder. He imagined himself photographed from underneath. "Odd man in," he said. In a moment he bounded off the door and into the center of the living room. "I'll bet there's a lease," he thought. "I'll bet there's a regular lease that goes with this place." He considered this for a moment with an awed respect. He couldn't remember ever having been in a place where the tenants actually had to sign a lease. He walked into the dining room and turned on the chandelier lights. "Sure there's a lease," Bertie said. He hugged himself. "How the fallen are mighty," he said.

He remembered his need to rest. In the living room he lay down on the couch without taking off his shoes. He sat up and pulled them off but when he lay down again he was uneasy. He had gotten out of the habit, living the way he did, of sleeping without shoes. In his friends' leaseless basements the nights were cold and he wore them for warmth. He put the shoes on again, but found he wasn't tired anymore. It was a fact that dependence gave him energy. He was never so alert as when people did him favors. It was having to be on your own that made you tired.

"Certainly," Bertie said to the committee, "it's a scientific fact. We've suspected it for years, but until our researchers divided up the town of Bloomington, Indiana, we had no proof. What our people found in that community was that the orphans and bastards were all the time sleepy and run down, but that the housewives and folks on relief were wide awake, alert, raring to go. It's remarkable. We can't positively state the link yet, but we're fairly certain that it's something to do with dependency in league perhaps with a particularly virulent form of—ahem—gratitude. Ahem. Ahem."

As he lectured the committee he wandered around the apartment, touring from right to left. He crossed from the living room into the dining room and turned right into the kitchen and then right again into the small room Feldman used for his study. "Here's where all the magic happens," Bertie said, glancing at the contour chair near Feldman's desk. He went back into the kitchen. "Here's where all the magic happens," he said, looking at Norma's electric stove. He stepped into the dining room and continued on, passing Norma's paintings, of picturesque little side streets in Mexico, of picturesque little side streets in Italy, of picturesque little side streets in Puerto Rico, until he came to a door that led to the back sun parlor. He went through it and found himself in a room with an easel, with paints in sexy little tubes, with brushes, with palettes and turpentine and rags. "Here's where all the magic happens," Bertie said and walked around the room to another door. He opened it and was in the Feldmans' master bedroom. He looked at the bed. "Here's where all the magic happens," he said. Through a door at the other end of the room was another small hall. On the right was the toilet. He went in and flushed it. It was one of those toilets with instantly renewable tanks. He flushed it again. And again. "The only kind to have," he said out of the side of his mouth, imagining a rental agent. "I mean it's like this. Supposing the missus has diarrhea or something. You don't want to have to wait until the tank fills up. Or suppose you're sick. Or suppose you're giving a party and it's mixed company. Well it's just corny to whistle to cover the noise, you know what I mean? 'Sjust corny. On the other hand you flush it once, suppose you're not through, then what happens? There's the damn noise after the water goes down. What have you accomplished? This way"—he reached across and jiggled the little lever and then did it a second time, a third, a fourth—"you never have any embarrassing interim, what we in the trade call 'flush lag.'"

He came out of the bathroom and at the other end of the hall found another bedroom, smaller than the first. It was the guest bedroom and Bertie knew at once that he would never sleep in it, that he would sleep in the Feldmans' big bed.

"Nice place you got here," he said when he had finished the tour.

"Dooing de woh eet ees all I tink of, what I fahting foe," the man from the Underground said. "Here ees eet fahrproof, air-condition and safe from Nazis."

"Stay out of Volkswagens, kid," Bertie said.

Bertie went back into the living room. He wanted some music but it was a cardinal principle with him never to blow alone. He would drink alone, take drugs alone, but somehow the depths of depravity were for him represented by having to play jazz alone. He had a vision of himself in a cheap hotel room sitting on the edge of an iron bedstead. Crumpled packages of cigarettes were scattered throughout the room. Bottles of gin were on top of the Gideon Bible, the Western

Union blanks. His trumpet was in his lap. "Perfect," Bertie said. "Norma Feldman could come in and paint it in a picture." Bertie shuddered.

The phonograph was in the hall between the dining and living rooms. It was a big thing, with the AM and the FM and the short wave and the place where you plugged in the color television when it was perfected. He found records in Feldman's little room and went through them rapidly. "Ahmad Jamahl for Christ's sake." He took the record out of its sleeve and broke it across his knee. He stood up slowly and kicked the fragments of the broken recording into a neat pile.

He turned around and scooped up as many of Feldman's recordings as he could carry and brought them to the machine. He piled them on indiscriminately and listened with visible, professional discomfort. He listened to *The New World Symphony,* to Beethoven's Fifth, to *My Fair Lady,* the Kingston Trio. The more he listened the more he began to dislike the Feldmans. When he could stand it no longer he tore the playing arm viciously away from the record and looked around him. He saw the Feldmans' bookcase.

"I'll read," he said.

He took down the Marquis de Sade and Henry Miller and Ronald Firbank and turned the pages desultorily. Nothing happened. He tried reading aloud in front of a mirror. He went back to the bookcase and looked for *The Egg and I* and *Please Don't Eat the Daisies.* The prose of a certain kind of bright housewife always made Bertie erotic but the Feldmans owned neither book. He browsed Rachel Carson's *Silent Spring* with only mild lasciviousness.

He went into their bedroom and opened the closet. He found a pair of Norma's shoes and put them on. Although he was no fetishist he had often promised himself that if he ever had the opportunity he would see what it was like. He walked around the apartment in Norma's high heels. All that happened was that he got a pain in his calves.

In the kitchen he looked into the refrigerator. There were some frozen mixed vegatables in the freezer compartment.

"I'll starve first," Bertie said.

He found a Billie Holliday record and put it on the phonograph. He hoped that Klaff out in Los Angeles was at this moment being beaten with rubber hoses by the police. He looked up at the kitchen clock. "Nine," he said. "Only seven in L.A. They probably don't start beating them up until later."

"Talk Klaff," he snarled, "or we'll drag you into the Blood Room."

"Flake off, copper," Klaff said.

"That's enough of that, Klaff. Take that and that and that."

"Bird lives," Bertie screamed suddenly, invoking the dead Charlie Parker. It was his code cry.

"Mama may have," Billie Holliday wailed, "Papa may have, But God Bless the child who's got his own, who—oo—zz—"

"Who—oo—zz," Bertie wailed.

"Got his own," Billie said.

"I'll tell him when he comes in, William," Bertie said.

Bertie waited respectfully until Billie was finished and turned off the music.

He wondered why so many people felt that Norman Mailer was the greatest living American novelist.

He sat down on the Feldmans' coffee table and marveled at his being alone in so big and well furnished an apartment. The Feldmans were probably the most substantial people he knew. Feldman was the only one from the old crowd who might make it, he guessed. Of course he was Jewish and that helped. Some Jews swung pretty good but he always suspected that in the end they would hold out on you. But then who wouldn't, Bertie wondered. Kamikaze pilots, maybe. Anyway this was Bertie's special form of anti-semitism and he cherished it. Melvin Gimpel, for example, his old roommate. Every time Melvin tried to kill himself by sticking his head in the oven he left the kitchen window open. Bertie laughed, remembering the time he had found Gimpel on his knees with his head on the oven door, oddly like the witch in Hansel and Gretel. Bertie closed the window and shook Gimpel awake.

"Mel," he yelled, slapping him and laughing. "Mel."

"Bertie, go away. Leave me alone, I want to kill myself."

"Thank God," Bertie said. "Thank God I'm in time. When I found that window closed I thought it was all over."

"What, the window was closed? My God, was the window closed?"

"Melvin Gimpel is so simple.

Thinks his nipple is a pimple," Bertie recited.

Bertie hugged his knees, and then, again, felt a wave of the nauseous sickness he had experienced that morning. "It's foreshadow-
ing. One day as I am shoveling my walk I will collapse and die."

When the nausea left him he thought again about his situation. It
was odd, he thought, being alone in so big a place. He had friends
everywhere and made his way from place to place like an old time
slave on the Underground Railway. For all the pathos of the figure he
knew he deliberately cut, there were always people to do him favors,
give him money, beer, drugs, to nurse him back to his normal state of
semi-invalidism, girls to kiss him in the comforting way he liked. This
was probably the first time he had been alone in months. He felt like a
dog whose master has gone away for the weekend. Just then he heard
some people coming up the stairs and he growled experimentally. He
went down on his hands and knees and scampered to the door,
scratching it with his nails. "Rrrgghhf," he barked. "Rrgghhfff!" He
heard whoever it was fumbling to open a door on the floor below him.
He smiled. "Good dog," he said. "Good dog, goodog, gudug, gudug-
guduggudug."

He whined. He missed his master. A tear formed in the corner of
his left eye. He crawled to a full-length mirror in the bathroom.
"Ahh," he said. "Ahh." Seeing the patch across his eye he had an inspiration. "Here, Patch," he called. "Come on, Patch."

He romped after his own voice.

He moved beside Norma Feldman's easel in the sun parlor. He
lowered his body carefully, pushing himself slightly backwards with
his arms. He yawned. He touched his chest to the wooden floor. He
wagged his tail and then let himself fall heavily on one side. He pulled
his legs up under him and fell asleep.

When he awoke he was hungry. He went into the kitchen but he knew
nothing about cooking. He fingered the twenty dollars in his pocket
that Feldman had given him. He could order out. The light in the hall
where the phone and phone books were was not good, so he tore
"Restaurants" from the Yellow Pages and brought the sheets with
him into the living room. Only two places delivered after one A.M. It

was already one-thirty. He dialed the number of a pizza place closest to him. It was busy so he dialed the other number.

"Pal, bring over a big one, half shrimp, half mushroom. And two six-packs." He gave the address. The man explained that the truck had just gone out and that he shouldn't expect delivery for at least another hour and a half.

"Put it in a cab," Bertie said. "While Bird lives Bertie spends."

He took out another dozen or so records and piled them on the machine. He sat down on the couch and drummed his trumpetcase with his fingers. He opened the case and fit the mouthpiece to the body of the horn. He put the trumpet to his lips and experienced the unpleasant shock of cold metal he always felt. He still thought it strange that men could mouth metal this way, ludicrous that his own official attitude should be a kiss. He blew a few bars in accompaniment to the record and put the trumpet back in the case. He felt in the side pockets of the trumpetcase and took out two pair of dirty underwear, some handkerchiefs and three pair of socks. He unrolled one of the pairs of socks and saw with pleasure that the drug was still there. He took out the bottle of carbon tetrachloride. This was what he cleaned his instrument with. It was what he would use to kill himself when he had finally made the decision.

He held the bottle to the light. "If nothing turns up," he said, "I'll drink this. And to hell with the kitchen window."

The cab driver brought the pizza and Bertie gave him the twenty dollars.

"I can't change that," the driver said.

"Did I ask you to change it?" Bertie said.

"That's twenty bucks there."

"Bird lives. Easy come, easy go go go," Bertie said.

The driver started to thank him.

"Go." He closed the door.

He spread Norma Feldman's largest tablecloth over the dining room table and then he took some china and some sterling from the big breakfront and laid several place settings. He found champagne glasses.

Unwrapping the pizza, he carefully plucked all the mushrooms from it ("American mushrooms," he said. "Very square. No visions.") and laid them in a neat pile on the white linen. ("Many mushloom," he said.

"Mushloom crowd.") He poured some beer into a champagne glass.

He rose slowly from his chair.

"Gentlemen," he said, "to the absent Klaff. May the police in Los Angeles, California beat his lousy ass off." He drank all the beer in one gulp and tossed the glass behind him over his shoulder. He heard the glass shatter and then a soft sizzling sound. He turned around and saw that he had gotten one of Norma's paintings right in a picturesque side street. Beer dripped ignobly down a donkey's leg. "Goddamn," Bertie said appreciatively, "*action* painting."

He ate perhaps a quarter of the pizza and got up from the table, wiping the corner of his lips with a big linen napkin.

"Gentlemen," he said, "I propose that the ladies retire to the bedroom while we men enjoy our cigars and port and some good talk."

"I propose that we men retire to the bedroom and enjoy the ladies," he said in Gimpel's voice.

"Here, here," he said in Klaff's voice. "Here, here. Good talk. Good talk."

"If you will follow me, gentlemen," he said in his own voice. He began to walk around the apartment. "I have been often asked the story of my life. These requests usually follow a personal favor someone has done me, a supper shared, a bed made available, a ride in one of the several directions. Indeed, I have become a sort of troubadour who does not sing so much as whine for his supper. Most of you—"

"Whine is very good with supper," Gimpel said.

"Gimpel, my dear, why don't you run into the kitchen and play?" Bertie said coolly. "Many of you may know the humble beginnings, the sordid details, the dark Freudian patterns, and those of you who are my friends—"

Klaff belched.

"Those of you who are my *friends,* who do not run off to mix it up with the criminal element in the Far West, have often wondered what will ultimately happen to me, to 'Poor Bertie' as I am known in the trade."

Bertie unbuttoned his shirt and let it fall to the floor. He looked defenceless in his undershirt, his skin pale as something seen in moonlight.

"Why, you wonder, doesn't he do something about himself, pull himself up by his bootstraps? Why, for example, doesn't he get his eyes fixed? Well, I've tried."

He kicked off his shoes.

"You have all admired my bushy moustache. Do you remember that time two years ago I dropped out of sight for four months? Well let me tell you what happened that time."

He took off his black pants.

"I had been staying with Royal Randle, the distinguished philologist and drunk. You will recall that Royal with Klaff and Myers and Gimpel and myself once constituted a quintet known familiarly as 'The Irresponsibles.'" Bertie sighed. "You remember the promises: 'It won't make any difference, Bertie. It won't make any difference, Klaff. It won't make any difference, fellas.' He married the girl in the Muu Muu."

He was naked now except for his socks. He shivered once and folded his arms across his chest.

"Do you know why the girl in the Muu Muu married Randle?" He paused dramatically. "*To get at me, that's why*. The others she didn't care about. She knew even before I did what they were like. Even what Klaff was like. She knew they were corrupt, that they had it in them to sell me out, to settle down—that all anyone had to do was wave their deaths in front of them and they'd come running, that reason and fucking money and getting it steady would win again. But in me she recognized the real enemy, the last of the go-to-hell-goddamn-its. Maybe the first.

"They even took me with them on their honeymoon. At the time I thought it was a triumph for dependency, but it was just a trick, that's all *that* was. The minute they were married this girl in the Muu Muu was after Randle to do something about Bertie. And it wasn't 'Poor' Bertie this time. It was she who got me the appointment with the mayor. Do you know what His Honor said to me? 'Shave your moustache and I'll give you a job clerking in one of my supermarkets.' Christ, friends, do you know I *did* it? Well, I'm not made of stone. They had taken me on their honeymoon for God's sake."

Bertie paused.

"I worked in that supermarket *for three hours*. Clean shaved. My moustache sacrificed as an earnest to the mayor. Well I'm telling you you don't know what square *is* till you've worked in a supermarket for three hours. They pipe in Mantovani. *Mantovani!* I cleared out for four months to raise my bushy moustache again and to forget. What you see now isn't the original, you understand. It's all second growth, and believe me it's not the same."

Bertie drew aside the shower curtain and stepped into the tub. He paused with his hand on "Hot."

"But I tell you this, friends, I tell you this. That I would rather be a moustached bum than a clean-shaved clerk. I'll work. Sure I will. When they pay anarchists. When they subsidize the hip. When they give grants to throw bombs. When they shell out for gainsaying."

He pulled the curtain and turned on the faucet and the rush of water was like applause.

After his shower Bertie went into the second bedroom and carefully removed the spread from the cot. Then he punched the pillow and mussed the bed. "Very clever," he said. "It wouldn't do to let them think I *never* slept here." He had once realized with sudden clarity that he would never, so long as he lived, make a bed.

He went then into the other bedroom and ripped the spread from the big double bed. For some time, in fact since he had first seen it, Bertie had been thinking about this bed. It was the biggest bed he would ever sleep in. (He thought invariably in such terms. One cigarette in a pack would suddenly become distinguished in his mind as the best, or the worst, he would smoke that day. A homely act, such as tying his shoelaces, if it had occurred with unusual ease, would be remembered forever. This lent to his vision an oblique sadness, conscious as he was that he was forever encountering experiences which would never come his way again.)

He slipped his naked body between the sheets and had no sooner made himself comfortable than he became conscious of the phonograph, still playing in the little hall. He couldn't hear it very well. He thought about turning up the volume but he had read somewhere about neighbors. He got out of bed and went to the phonograph. He moved the heavy machine through the living room, pushing it with difficulty over the seamed, bare wooden floor, trailing deep scratches. "Remember not to walk barefoot over there," he thought. At one point one of the legs caught in a loop of the Feldmans' shag rug and

Bertie strained to free it, finally breaking the thick thread and producing an interesting pucker along one end of the rug, not unlike the pucker in raised theatrical curtains. At last he maneuvered the machine into the hall just outside the bedroom. He plugged it in. He went back for the Billie Holliday recording he had heard earlier and put it on the phonograph. By lifting the arm that held and steadied the records on the spindle and pulling it back, he fixed it so the record would play all night.

He got back into the bed.

"Ah," he said, "the *sanctum sanctorum*." He rolled over and over from one side of the bed to the other. He tucked his knees into his chest and went under the covers. "It makes you feel kind of small and insignificant," he said.

"Ladies and Gentlemen, this is Graham Macnamee speaking to you from the Cave of the Winds. I have made my way into the heart of this darkness to find my friend, Poor Bertie, who, as you know, entered the bed eight weeks ago. Bertie is with me now, and while there isn't enough light for me to be able to see his condition, his voice may tell us something about his physical state. Bertie, just what *is* the official record?"

"Well, Graham, some couples have been known to stick it out for seventy-five years. Of course your average is much less than that, but still—"

"Seventy-five years."

"Seventy-five, yes sir. It's amazing, isn't it, Graham, when you come to think? All that time in one bed."

"It certainly is," Graham Macnamee said. "Do you think you'll be able to go the distance, Bert?"

"Who, me? No, no. A lot of folks have misunderstood my purpose in coming here. I'm rather glad you've given me the opportunity to clear that up. Actually my work here is scientific. This isn't a stunt or anything like that. I'm here to learn."

"Can you tell us about it, Bert?"

"Graham, it's been a fascinating experience if you know what I mean, but frankly there are many things we still don't understand. *I* don't know why they do it. All that licit love, that regularity. Take the case of Stephen and Norma, for example. And incidentally, you don't

want to overlook the significance of that name *Norma*. Norma/Nor-
mal, you see?"

"Say, I never thought of that."

"Well, I'm trained to think like that, Graham. In my work you
have to."

"Say," Graham Macnamee said.

"Sure. Well the thing is this, buddy, when I first came into this bed
I felt the aura, know what I mean, the *power*. I think it's built into the
mattress or something."

"Say."

"Shut your face, Graham, and let me speak, will you please? Well,
anyway, you feel surrounded. Respectable. Love is made here, of
course, but it's not love as we know it. There are things that must remain mysteries until we have more facts. I mean Graham, checks
could be cashed in this bed, for Christ's sake, credit cards honored.
It's ideal for family reunions and high teas. Graham, it's the kind of
place you wouldn't be ashamed to take your mother."

"Go to sleep, Bert," Graham Macnamee said.

"Say," Bertie said.

Between the third and fourth day of his stay in the Feldmans' apartment Bertie became restless. He had not been outside the house since
the Sunday he had come, even to bring in the papers Feldman had
told him about. (Indeed, it was by counting the papers that he knew
how long he had been there, though he couldn't be sure since he
didn't know whether the Feldmans had taken the Sunday paper with
them.) He could see them on the back porch through the window of
Norma's sun parlor. With the bottles of milk they made a strange little pile. He was not after all a caretaker. He was a guest. Feldman
could bring in his own papers, drink his own damn milk. For the
same reasons he had determined not even to answer the phone when
it rang.

One evening he tried to call Klaff at the Los Angeles County Jail,
but the desk sergeant wouldn't get him. He wouldn't even take a message.

Although he had not been outside since Sunday, Bertie had only a
vague desire to go out. He weighed this against his real need to rest

and his genuine pleasure in being alone in so big an apartment. Like the man in the joke who does not leave his Miami hotel room because it is costing him thirty-five dollars a day, Bertie decided he had better remain inside.

With no money left he was reduced to eating the dry, cold remainder of the pizza, dividing it mathematically into a week's provisions like someone on a raft. (Bertie actually fancied himself, not on a raft perhaps, but set alone and drifting in, say, the *Queen Mary*.) To supplement this he opened some cans of soup he found in the pantry and drank the contents straight, without first heating it or even adding water.

Steadily he drank away at the Feldmans' not really large stock of liquor. The twelve cans of beer, of course, had been devoured by the second morning.

After the second full day in the apartment his voices began to desert him. It was only with difficulty that he could manage his imitations, and only for short lengths of time. The glorious discussions that had gone on long into the night were now out of the question. He found he could not do Gimpel's voice any more and even Klaff's was increasingly difficult and largely confined to his low, caressing obscenities. Mostly he talked with himself, although it was a real strain to keep up his end of the conversation and it always made him cry when he said how pathetic he was and asked himself where do you go from here. "Oh to be like Bird," he thought. "Not to have to be a bum. To ask, as it were, no quarter."

At various times during the day he would call out, "Bird lives," in seeming stunning triumph. But he didn't believe it.

He watched a lot of television. ("I'm getting ammunition," he said. "It's scientific.")

And twice a day he masturbated in the Feldmans' bed.

He settled gradually, then, into restlessness. He knew, of course, that he had it always in his power to bring himself back up to the heights he had known in those wonderful first two days. He was satisfied, however, not to use this power, and thought of himself as a kind of soldier, alone, in a foxhole, in enemy territory, at night, at a bad time in the war, with one bullet in his pistol. Oddly he derived more pride (and comfort, and a queer security) from this single bullet than others might from whole cases of ammunition. It was his *strategic* bullet, the one he would use to get the big one, turn the tide, make the difference. The Feldmans would be away two weeks. He would not waste his ammunition. Just as he divided the stale pizza, cherishing each piece as much for the satisfaction he took from possessing it during a time of emergency as for any sustenance it offered, so he enjoyed his knowledge that at any time he could recoup his vanishing spirits. He shared with the squares ("Use their own weapons to beat them, Bertie.") a special pride in adversity, in having to do without, in having to expose whatever was left of his character to the narrower straits. It was strange, Bertie thought seriously, it was the paradox of the world and an institutional insight that might have come right out of the mouth of that slut in Dallas, but the most peculiar aspect of the squares wasn't their lack of imagination or their bland bad taste, but their ability, like the wildest fanatics, like the furthest out of the furthest out, to cling to the illogical, finally untenable notion that they must *have* and *have* in order to live, at the same time that they realized that it was better not to have. What seemed so grand to Bertie, who admired all impossible positions, was that they believed both things with equal intensity, never suspecting for a moment any inconsistency. And here was Bertie, Bertie thought, here was Bertie, inside their capitol, on the slopes of their mountains, on their smooth shores, who believed neither of these propositions, who believed in not having and in not suffering too, who yet realized the very same pleasure they would in having and not using.

It was the strangest thing that would ever happen to him, he thought.

"Are you listening, Klaff, you second-story fink?" Bertie yelled. "Do you see how your old pal is developing what is called character?"

And so, master of himself for once, he resolved (feeling what someone taking a vow feels) not to use the last of his drugs until the strategic moment of strategic truth.

That was Wednesday evening. By Thursday morning he had decided to break his resolution. He had not yielded to temptation, had not lain fitfully awake all night (indeed, his resolution had given him the serenity to sleep well) in the sweaty throes of withdrawal. There had been no argument or rationalization, nor had he decided that he had reached his limit or that this was the strategic moment he had been waiting for. He yielded as he always yielded, spontaneously, suddenly, unexpectedly, as the result neither of whim nor calculation. His important decisions were almost always reached without his knowledge and Bertie was often as surprised as the next one to see what he was going to do, to see, indeed, that he was already doing it. (Once someone had asked him whether he believed in Free Will and Bertie, after considering this for a moment as it applied to himself, had answered, "Free? Hell, it's positively *loose*.")

Having discovered his new intention Bertie was eager to realize it. As often as he had taken drugs (he never called it anything but drugs, never used the cute or obscene names, never even said "dope;" to him it was always "drugs," medicine for his spirit), they were still a major treat for him. ("It's a rich man's game," he had once told Klaff, and then he had leaned back philosophically. "You know, Klaff, it's a good thing I'm poor. When I think of the snobbish ennui of your wealthy junkies, I realize that they don't know how to appreciate their blessings. God keep me humble, Klaff. Abstinence makes the heart grow fonder, a truer word was never spoken.") Nor did a drug ever lose its potency for him. If he graduated from one to another it was not in order to recover some fading jolt, but to experience a new and different one. He held in contempt all those who professed disenchantment with the drugs they had been raised on and frequently went back to rediscover the old pleasures of marijuana, as a sentimental father might chew some of his boy's bubble gum. "Loyalty, Gimpel," he exclaimed, "loyalty, do you know what *that* is?"

He would and did try anything, though currently his favorite was mescaline for the visions it induced. Despite what he considered his eclectic tastes in these things, however, there were one or two things he would not do. He never introduced any drug by hypodermic needle. This he found disgusting and, frankly, painful. (He often said he could stand anything but pain and was very proud of his clear, unpunctured skin. "Not a mark on me," he would say, waving his arms like a professional boxer.) The other thing he would not do was take his drugs in the presence of other users for he found the company of addicts offensive. He was not above what he called "seductions," however. A seduction for him was to find some girl and talk her into letting him share his drugs with her. Usually it ended in their lying naked in a bed together, both of them serene, absent of all desire and what Bertie called "unclean thoughts."

"You know," he would say to the girl beside him, "I think that if all the world's leaders would take drugs and lie down on the bed naked like this without any unclean thoughts, that the cause of world peace would be helped immeasurably. What do you think?"

"I think so too," she would say.

Once he knew he was going to take the drug Bertie made his preparations. He went first to his trumpetcase and took out the last small packet of powder. He opened it carefully, first closing all the windows so that no sudden draft could blow any of it away. This had once happened to a friend of his and Bertie had never forgotten the warning.

"I am not one on whom a lesson is lost," Bertie said.

"You're O.K., Bertie," a Voice said. "Go, save France."

He laid it on the Feldmans' coffee table and carefully spread the paper, exactly like the paper wrapper around a stick of chewing gum, looking almost lustfully at the soft, flat layer of ground white powder. He held out his hand to see how steady it was and although he was not really shaky he did not trust himself to lift the paper from the table. He brought a water tumbler from the Feldmans' kitchen and gently placed it upside down on top of the powder. He was not yet ready to take it. Bertie was a man who postponed his pleasures as long as he possibly could. He let candy dissolve in his mouth and played with the threads on his tangerine before eating the fruit. It was a weakness in his character perhaps, but he laid it lovingly at the feet of his poverty.

He decided to wait until sundown to take the drug, reasoning that when it wore off it would be early next morning and he would be ready for bed. Sleep was one of his pleasures, too, and he approved of regularity in small things, taking a real pride in being able to keep hours. To pass the time until sundown he looked for something to do. He found some tools and busied himself by taking Norma's steam iron apart. There was still time left and he took a canvas and painted a picture. Because he did not know how to draw he simply covered the canvas first with one color and then with another, applying layer after layer of the paint thickly. Each block of color he made somewhat smaller than the last so that the finished painting portrayed successive jagged margins of color. He stepped back and considered his work seriously.

"Well it has texture, Bertie," Hans Hofmann said.

"Bertie," the Voice said suddenly, "I don't like to interrupt when you're working, but it's sundown."

"So it is," he said, looking up.

He went back into the living room and removed the tumbler. Taking up the paper in his fingers and creasing it as if he were a cowboy rolling a cigarette, Bertie tilted his head far back and inhaled the powder deeply. This part was always uncomfortable for him.

"Ooo," he said, "the bubbles." He stuffed the last few grains up his nose with his fingers. "Waste not, want not," he said.

Bertie sat down to wait. After half an hour in which nothing happened he became uneasy. "It's been cut," he said. "Sure, depend upon friends to do you favors." He was referring to the fact that the drug had been a going-away present from friends in Oklahoma City. He decided to give it fifteen more minutes. "Nothing," he said at last, disappointed. "Nothing."

The powder, as it always did, left his throat scratchy, and there was a bitter taste in his mouth. His soft palate prickled. He seized the water tumbler from the coffee table and walked angrily into the kitchen. He ran the cold water. He gargled and spit in the sink. In a few minutes the bitter taste and the prickly sensation had subsided and he felt about as he had before he had taken the drug. He was conscious however of a peculiar smell, unpleasant, unfamiliar, nothing like the odor of rotting flowers he associated with the use of drugs. He opened a window and leaning out, breathed the fresh air. As soon as he came away from the window, however, the odor was overpowering. He went to see if he could smell it in the other rooms. When he had made his tour he realized that the stench *must* be coming from the kitchen. Holding his breath he came back to see if he could locate its source. The kitchen was almost as Norma had left it. Bertie, of course, had done no cooking and although there were some empty soup and beer cans in the sink he knew *they* couldn't be causing the odor. He shrugged. Then he noticed the partially closed door to Stephen's study.

"Of course," he said. "Whatever it is must be in there." He pushed the door open. In the middle of the floor were two blackish mounds that looked like dark sawdust. Bertie stepped back in surprise.

"Camel shit," he said. "My God, how did *that* get in here?" He went closer to investigate. "That's what it is all right." He had never seen it before but a friend had and had described it to him. This stuff fitted the description perfectly. He considered what to do.

"I can't leave it there," he said. He found a dustpan and a broom and propping the pan against the leg of Stephen's chair he began to sweep the stuff up. He was surprised at how remarkably gummy it seemed. When he finished he washed the spot on the floor with a foaming detergent and stepped gingerly to the back door. He lifted the lid of the garbage can and shoved the broom and the contents of the dustpan and the dustpan itself into the can.

He went into the bathroom and washed his hands.

In the living room he saw the Chinaman.

"Jesus," Bertie said breathlessly.

The Chinaman lowered his eyes in a shy, almost demure smile. He said nothing, but motioned Bertie to sit in the chair across from him. Bertie, too frightened to disobey, sat down.

He waited for the Chinaman to tell him what he wanted. When after an hour (Bertie heard the chime clock strike nine times and then ten times) the Chinaman still had not said anything, he began to feel a little calmer. "Maybe he was just tired," Bertie thought, "and came in to rest." He realized that perhaps he and the Chinaman had more in common than had at first appeared. He looked at the fellow in this new light and saw that he had been foolish to fear him. The Chinaman was small, smaller even than Bertie. In fact he was only two feet tall. Perhaps what made him seem larger was the fact that he was wrapped in wide, voluminous white silk robes. Bertie stared at the robes, fascinated by the delicate filigree trim up and down their length. To see this closer he stood up and walked tentatively toward the Chinaman. The Chinaman gazed steadily frontwards and Bertie, seeing no threat, continued toward him.

He leaned down over the Chinaman and grasping the delicate lacework between forefinger and thumb gently drew it toward his eye. "May I!?" Bertie said. "I know a good deal about this sort of thing."

The Chinaman lowered his eyes.

Bertie examined the weird symbols and designs and, although he did not understand them, recognized at once their cabalistic origin.

"Magnificent," Bertie said at last. "My God, the man-hours that must have gone into this. *The sheer craftsmanship!* That's really a terrific robe you've got there."

The Chinaman lowered his eyes still further.

Bertie sat down in his chair again. He heard the clock strike eleven and he smiled at the Chinaman. He was trying to be sympathetic, patient. He knew the fellow had his reasons for coming and that in due time they would be revealed, but he couldn't help being a little annoyed. First the failure of the drug and then the camel shit on the floor and now this. However, he remained very polite.

There was nothing else to do so Bertie concentrated on the Chinaman's face.

Then a strange thing happened.

He became aware, as he scrutinized the face, of some things he hadn't noticed before. First he realized that it was the oldest face he had ever seen. He knew that this face was old enough to have looked on Buddha's. It was only *faintly* yellow, really, and he understood with a sweeping insight that originally it must have been white, as it was largely still, a striking, flat white, naked as a sheet, bright as teeth, that its yellowness was the yellowness of fantastic age, of pages in ancient books. As soon as he perceived this he understood the origin and mystery of the races. All men had at first been white; their different tints were only the shades of their different wisdoms. "Of course," he thought. "Of course. It's beautiful. Beautiful."

The second thing he noticed was that the face seemed extraordinarily wise. The longer he stared at it the wiser it seemed. Clearly this was the wisest Chinaman, and thus the wisest man, in the history of the world. Now he was impatient for the Chinaman to speak, to tell him his secrets, but Bertie also understood that so long as he was impatient the Chinaman would *not* speak, that he must become serene, as serene as the Chinaman himself, or the Chinaman would go away. As this occurred to him the Chinaman smiled and Bertie knew he had been right.

Bertie was aware that if he just sat there, deliberately trying to become serene, nothing would happen. He decided that the best way to become serene was to ignore the Chinaman, to go on about his business as if the Chinaman weren't even there.

He stood up. "Am I getting warm?" Bertie asked.

The Chinaman lowered his eyes and smiled.

"Well, then," Bertie said, rubbing his hands, "let's see."

He went into the kitchen to see if there was anything he could do there to make him serene.

He washed out the empty cans of soup.

He strolled into the bedroom and made the bed. This took him an hour. (He heard the clock strike twelve and then one.)

He took a record off the machine and, starting from the center hole and working to the outer edge, counted all the ridges. (This took him fourteen seconds and he was pleased at how quickly and efficiently he worked.)

He found a suitcase in one of the closets and packed all of Norma's underwear into it.

He got a pail of water and some soap and washed all the walls in the small bedroom.

It was in the dining room, however, that he finally achieved serenity. He studied Norma's pictures of side streets throughout the world and with sudden insight understood what was wrong with them. He took some tubes of white paint and with a brush worked over the figures, painting back into the flesh all their original whiteness. He made the Mexicans white, the Negroes, feeling as he worked an immense satisfaction, the satisfaction not of the creator, nor even of the reformer, but of the restorer.

Swelling with serenity he went back into the living room and sat down in his chair.

For the first time the Chinaman met Bertie's gaze directly, and Bertie realized that something important was going to happen.

The Chinaman slowly, very slowly, began to open his mouth. Bertie watched the slow parting of the Chinaman's thin lips, the gleaming teeth, white and bright as fence pickets. Gradually the rest of the room darkened and the thinly padded chair on which Bertie sat grew incredibly soft. Bertie knew they had been transported somehow, that they were now in a sort of theater. The Chinaman was seated on a kind of raised platform. Meanwhile the mouth continued to open, slowly as an ancient drawbridge. Tiny as the Chinaman was the mouth seemed enormous. Bertie gazed into it, seeing nothing. At last, deep back in the mouth, Bertie saw a brief flashing, as of a small crystal on a dark rock suddenly illuminated by the sun. In a moment he saw it again, brighter now, longer sustained. Soon it was so bright that Bertie had to force himself to look at it. Then the mouth went black. Before he could protest the brightness was overwhelming again and he saw a cascade of what seemed like diamonds tumble out of the Chinaman's mouth. It was the Chinaman's tongue.

The tongue, twisting, turning over and over like magicians' silks pulled endlessly from a tube, continued to pour from the Chinaman's mouth.

Bertie saw that it had the same whiteness as the rest of his face and was studded with bright, beautiful jewels. On the tongue, long now as an unfurled scroll, were black, thick Chinese characters. It was the secret of life, the world, the universe. Bertie could barely see for the tears of gratitude in his eyes. Desperately he wiped the tears away with his fists. He looked back at the tongue and stared at the strange words, realizing that he could not read Chinese. He was sobbing helplessly now but he knew there was not much time. The presence of the Chinaman gave him courage and strength and he *forced* himself to read the Chinese. As he concentrated it became easier, the characters somehow re-forming, translating themselves into a sort of decipherable Chinesey script, like the words *chop suey* on the neon sign outside a Chinese restaurant. Bertie was breathless from his effort and the stunning glory of what was being revealed to him. Frequently he had to pause, punctuating his experience with queer little squeals.

"Oh," he said. "Oh. Oh."

Then it was over.

He was exhausted but his knowledge glowed in him like fire. "So *that's* it," was all he could say. "So *that's* it. So *that's* it."

Bertie saw that he was no longer in the theater. The Chinaman was gone and Bertie was back in the Feldmans' living room. He struggled for control of himself. He knew it was urgent that he tell someone what had happened to him. Desperately he pulled open his trumpetcase. Inside he had pasted sheets with the names, addresses and phone numbers of all his friends.

"Damn Klaff," he said angrily. "Damn second-story Klaff in his lousy jail."

He spotted Gimpel's name and the phone number of his boarding house in Cincinnati. He tore the sheet from where it was pasted inside the lid and rushed to the phone. He placed the call. "Life and death," he screamed at Gimpel's bewildered landlady, "life and death."

When Gimpel came to the phone Bertie began to tell him, coherently, but with obvious excitement, all that had happened. Gimpel was as excited as himself.

"Then the Chinaman opened his mouth and this tongue with writing on it came out."

"Yeah!" Gimpel said. "Yeah? Yeah?"

"Only it was in Chinese," Bertie shouted.

"Chinese," Gimpel said.

"But I could read it, Gimpel! *I could read it!*"

"I didn't know you could read Chinese," Gimpel said.

"It was the meaning of life."

"Yeah?" Gimpel said. "Yeah? What'd it say? What'd it say?"

"What?" Bertie said.

"What'd it say? What'd the Chink's tongue say was the meaning of life?"

"I forget," Bertie said and hung up.

He slept until two the next afternoon and when he awoke he felt as if he had been beaten up. His tongue was something that did not quite fit in his mouth, and throughout his body he experienced a looseness of the bones, as though his skeleton were a mobile put together by an amateur. He groaned dispiritedly, his eyes still closed. He knew he had to get up out of the bed and take a shower and shave and dress, that only by making extravagant demands on it would his body give him any service at all. "You *will* make the Death March," he warned it ruthlessly.

He opened his eyes and what he saw disgusted him and turned his stomach. His eye patch had come off during the night and now there

were two of everything. He saw one eye patch on one pillow and another eye patch on another pillow. Hastily he grabbed for it but he had
chosen the wrong pillow. He reached for the other eye patch and the
other pillow but somehow he had put out one of his illusory hands. It
did not occur to him to shut one eye. At last, by covering all visible
space, real or illusory, with all visible fingers, real or illusory—like
one dragging a river—he recovered the patch and pulled it quickly
over one of his heads.

He stood stunned in his hot shower and then shaved, cutting his
neck badly. He dressed. "Whan 'e iz through his toilette, *Monsieur*
will see how much better 'e feel," his valet said.

He doubted it and didn't answer.

In the dining room he tried not to look at Norma's paintings but
could not help noticing that many of her sunny side streets had,
overnight, become partial snow scenes. He had done that, he remembered, though he could not recall now exactly why. It seemed to have
something to do with a great anthropological discovery he had made
the night before.

He finished the last of the pizza, gagging on it briefly.

Considering the anguish of his body it suddenly occurred to him
that perhaps he was hooked. This momentarily appealed to his sense
of the dramatic, but then he realized that it would be a terrible thing
to have happen to him. He could not afford to be hooked and he knew
with a sense of calm sadness that his character could no more sustain
the responsibility of a steady drug habit than it could sustain the responsibility of any other kind of pattern.

"Oh what a miserable bastard I am," he said.

In near panic he considered leaving the Feldmans' apartment immediately but he knew that he was in no condition to travel.

"You wouldn't get to the corner," he said.

He felt massively sorry for himself. The more he considered it the
more certain it appeared that he was hooked. It was terrible. Where
would he get the money to buy the drugs? What would they do to his
already depleted physical resources?

"Oh what a miserable bastard I am," he said again.

To steady himself he took a bottle of Scotch from the shelf in the
pantry where Feldman kept it. Bertie did not like hard liquor. Though

he drank a lot, it was beer he drank, or when he could get them, the sweeter cordials. Scotch and bourbon had always seemed vaguely square to him. But he had already finished the few liqueurs that Feldman had, and now nothing was left but Scotch. He poured himself an enormous drink.

Sipping it calmed him (though his body still ached) and he considered what to do. If he *was* hooked the first thing was to tell his friends. Telling his friends his latest failure was something Bertie regarded as a sort of responsibility. Thus his rare letters to them usually brought Bertie's intimates—he laughed at the word—nothing but bad news. He would write that a mistress had given him up, and, with his talent for mimicry, set down her last long disappointed speech to him, in which she exposed in angry, honest language the hollowness of his character, his infinite weakness as a man, his vileness. When briefly he had turned to homosexuality to provide himself with funds, the first thing he did was write his friends about it. Or he wrote of being fired from bands when it was discovered how bad a trumpeter he really was. He spared neither himself nor his friends in his passionate self-denunciations.

Almost automatically, then, he went into Feldman's study and began to write to all the people he could think of. As he wrote he pulled heavily at the whiskey remaining in the bottle.

At first the letters were long, detailed accounts of symptoms and failures and dashed hopes, but as evening came on and he grew inarticulate he realized it was more important—and, indeed, added to the pathos of his situation—for him just to get the facts to them.

"Dear Klaff," he wrote at last, "I am hooked. I am at the bottom, Klaff. I don't know what to do." Or "Dear Randle, I'm hooked. Tell your wife. I honestly don't know where to turn."

And "Dear Myers, how are your wife and kids? Poor Bertie is hooked. He is thinking of suicide."

That one day he would have to kill himself he had known for a long time. It would happen, and even in the way he had imagined. One day he would simply drink the bottle of carbon tetrachloride. But he had been in no hurry. Now it seemed like something he might have to do before he had meant to, and, oddly, what he resented most was the idea of having to change his plans.

He imagined what people would say.

"I let him down, Klaff," Randle said.

"Everybody let him down," Klaff said.

"Everybody let him down," Bertie said. "Everybody let him down."

Weeping, he took a last drink from Feldman's bottle and stumbled into the living room where he passed out on the couch.

That night Bertie was awakened by a flashlight shining in his eyes. Bertie threw one arm across his face defensively and struggled to sit up. So clumsy were his efforts that whoever was holding the flashlight started to laugh.

"Stop that," Bertie said indignantly, and thought, "I have never been so indignant in the face of danger."

"You said they were out of town," a voice said. The voice did not come from behind the flashlight and Bertie wondered how many there might be.

"Jesus, I thought so. Nobody's answered the phone for days. I never seen a guy so plastered. He stinks."

"Kill him," the first voice said.

Bertie stopped struggling to get up.

"Kill him," the voice repeated.

"What is this?" Bertie said thickly. "What is this?"

"Come on, he's so drunk he's harmless," the second voice said.

"Kill him," the first voice said again.

"You kill him," the second voice said.

The first voice giggled.

They were playing with him, Bertie knew. Nobody who did not know him could want him dead.

"Turn on the lights," Bertie said.

"Screw that," the second voice said. "You just sit here in the dark, sonny, and you won't get hurt."

"We're wasting time," the first voice said.

A beam from a second flashlight suddenly intersected the beam from the first.

"Say," Bertie said nervously, "it looks like the opening of a super-market."

Bertie could hear them working in the dark, moving boxes, pulling drawers.

"Are you folks Negroes?" Bertie called. No one answered him. "I mean I dig Negroes, man—*men*. Miles. Jay Jay. Bird lives." Bertie heard a closet door open.

"You *are* robbing the place, right? I mean you're actually *stealing*, aren't you? This isn't just a social call. Maybe you know my friend Klaff?"

The men came back into the living room. From the sound of his footsteps Bertie knew one of them was carrying something heavy.

"I've got the TV," the first voice said.

"There are some valuable paintings in the dining room," Bertie said.

"Go see," the first voice said.

One of Norma's pictures suddenly popped out of the darkness as the man's light shone on it.

"Crap," the second voice said.

"You guys can't be all bad," Bertie said.

"Any furs?" It was a third voice and it startled Bertie. Someone flashed a light in Bertie's face. "Hey you," the voice repeated, "does your wife have any furs?"

"Wait a minute," Bertie said as though it were a fine point they must be made to understand, "you've got it wrong. This isn't *my* place. I'm just taking care of it while my friends are gone." The man laughed.

Now all three flashlights were playing over the apartment. Bertie hoped a beam might illuminate one of the intruders but this never happened. Then he realized he didn't want it to happen, that he was safe as long as he didn't see any of them. Suddenly a light caught one of the men behind the ear. "Watch that light. Watch that light," Bertie called out involuntarily.

"I found a trumpet," the second voice said.

"Hey, that's mine," Bertie said angrily. Without thinking he got up and grabbed for the trumpet. In the dark he was able to get his fingers around one of the pistons, but the man snatched it away from him easily. Another man pushed Bertie back down on the couch.

"Could you leave the carbon tetrachloride?" Bertie asked miserably.

In another ten minutes they were ready to go.

"Shouldn't we do something about the clown?" the third voice said.

"Nah," the second voice said.

They went out the front door.

Bertie sat in the darkness. "I'm drunk," he said after a while. "I'm hooked and drunk. It never happened. It's still the visions. The apartment is a vision. The darkness is. Everything."

In a few minutes he got up and wearily turned on the lights.

"Magicians," Bertie thought, seeing even in a first glance all they had taken. Lamps were gone, drapes. He walked through the apartment. The TV was gone. Suits were missing from the closets. Feldman's typewriter was gone. The champagne glasses. The silver. His trumpet was gone.

Bertie wept. He thought of phoning the police but then wondered what he could tell them. They had been in the apartment twenty minutes and he hadn't even gotten a look at their faces.

Then he shuddered, realizing the danger he had been in. "Thieves," he said. "Killers." But even as he said it he knew it was an exaggeration. He personally had never been in any danger. He had the fool's ancient protection, his old immunity against consequence.

He wondered what he could say to the Feldmans. They would be furious. Then, as he thought about it, he realized that this, too, was an exaggeration. They would not be furious. Like the thieves they would make allowances for him, as people always made allowances for him. They would forgive him and possibly even try to give him something toward the loss of his trumpet.

Bertie began to grow angry. They had no right to patronize him like that. If he was a clown it was because he had chosen to be. It was a way of life. Why couldn't they respect it? He should have been hit over the head like other men. How dare they forgive him? For a moment it was impossible for him to distinguish between the thieves and the Feldmans.

Then he had his idea. As soon as he thought of it he knew it would work. He looked around the apartment to see what he could take. There was some costume jewelry the thieves had thrown on the bed. Bertie scooped it up and stuffed it into his pockets.

He looked at the apartment one more time and then got the hell out of there. "Bird lives," he sang to himself as he raced down the stairs. "He lives and lives."

It was wonderful. How they would marvel. He couldn't get away with it. Even the Far West wasn't far enough. How they hounded you if you took something from them! He would be back, no question, and they would send him to jail, but first there would be the confrontation, maybe even in the apartment itself, Bertie in handcuffs, and the Feldmans staring at him, not understanding and angry at last, and something in their eyes like fear.

Issue 34, 1965

William Faulkner

✠

from The Art of Fiction XII

FAULKNER

My own experience has been that the tools I need for my trade are paper, tobacco, food, and a little whisky.

INTERVIEWER

Bourbon, you mean?

FAULKNER

No, I ain't that particular. Between scotch and nothing, I'll take scotch.

John Irving

from The Art of Fiction XCIII

INTERVIEWER

You've said that the reason both Hemingway and Fitzgerald wrote their best books in their twenties (they were twenty-seven when they wrote *The Sun Also Rises* and *The Great Gatsby*) is that they "pickled their brains." Do you really believe that?

IRVING

Yes, I really believe that. They should have gotten better as they got older; *I've* gotten better. We're not professional athletes; it's reasonable to assume that we'll get better as we mature—at least, until we start getting senile. Of course, some writers who write their best books early simply lose interest in writing; or they lose their concentration—probably because they want to do other things. But Hemingway and Fitzgerald really lived to write; their bodies and their brains betrayed them. I'm such an incapable drinker, I'm lucky. If I drink half a bottle of red wine with my dinner, I forget who I had dinner with—not to mention everything that I or anybody else said. If I drink more than half a bottle, I fall instantly asleep. But just think of what novelists do: fiction writing requires a kind of memory, a vigorous, invented memory. If I can forget who I had dinner with, what might I forget about my novel-in-progress? The irony is that drinking is especially dangerous to novelists; memory is vital to us. I'm not so down on drinking for writers from a moral point of view; but booze is clearly not good for writing *or* for driving cars. You know what

Lawrence said: "The novel is the highest example of subtle interrelatedness that man has discovered." I agree! And just consider for one second what drinking does to "subtle interrelatedness." Forget the "subtle"; "interrelatedness" is what makes novels work—without it, you have no narrative momentum; you have incoherent rambling. Drunks ramble; so do books by drunks.

Hunter S. Thompson

※

from The Art of Journalism I

INTERVIEWER

The drug culture. How do you write when you're under the influence?

THOMPSON

My theory for years has been to write fast and get through it. I usually write five pages a night and leave them out for my assistant to type in the morning.

INTERVIEWER

This, after a night of drinking and so forth?

THOMPSON

Oh yes, always, yes. I've found that there's only one thing that I can't work on and that's marijuana. Even acid I could work with. The only difference between the sane and the insane is that the sane have the power to lock up the insane. Either you function or you don't. Functionally insane? If you get paid for being crazy, if you can get paid for running amok and writing about it . . . I call that sane.

INTERVIEWER

Almost without exception writers we've interviewed over the years admit they cannot write under the influence of booze or drugs—or at the least what they've done has to be rewritten in the cool of the day. What's your comment about this?

THOMPSON

They lie. Or maybe you've been interviewing a very narrow spectrum of writers. It's like saying, "Almost without exception women we've interviewed over the years swear that they never indulge in sodomy"— without saying that you did all your interviews in a nunnery. Did you interview Coleridge? Did you interview Poe? Or Scott Fitzgerald? Or Mark Twain? Or Fred Exley? Did Faulkner tell you that what he was drinking all the time was really iced tea, not whiskey? Please. Who the fuck do you think wrote the Book of Revelation? A bunch of stone-sober clerics?

Issue 156, 2000

William Burroughs

⚜

from The Art of Fiction XXXVI

INTERVIEWER

The visions of drugs and the visions of art don't mix?

BURROUGHS

Never. The hallucinogens produce visionary states, sort of, but morphine and its derivatives decrease awareness of inner processes, thoughts and feelings. They are pain killers, pure and simple. They are absolutely contraindicated for creative work, and I include in the lot alcohol, morphine, barbiturates, tranquilizers—the whole spectrum of sedative drugs. As for visions and heroin, I had a hallucinatory period at the very beginning of addiction, for instance, a sense of moving at high speed through space, but as soon as addiction was established, I had no visions—vision—at all and very few dreams.

INTERVIEWER

Why did you stop taking drugs?

BURROUGHS

I was living in Tangier in 1957, and I had spent a month in a tiny room in the Casbah staring at the toe of my foot. The room had filled up with empty Eukodol cartons; I suddenly realized I was not doing *anything*. I was dying. I was just apt to be finished. So I flew to London and turned myself over to Dr. John Yerbury Dent for treatment. I'd heard of his success with the apomorphine treatment. Apomorphine is simply morphine boiled in hydrochloric acid; it's nonaddicting. What the apomorphine did was to regulate my metabolism. It's a metabolic regulator. It cured me physiologically. I'd already taken the cure once at Lexington, and although I was off drugs when I got out, there was a physiological residue. Apomorphine eliminated that. I've been trying to get people in this country interested in it, but without much luck. The vast majority—social workers, doctors—have the cop's mentality toward addiction. A probation officer in California wrote me recently to inquire about the apomorphine treatment. I'll answer him at length. I always answer letters like that.

Jim Carroll

✛

from The Basketball Diaries

SUMMER 1966

In ten minutes it will make four days about that I've been nodding on this ratty mattress up here in Headquarters. Haven't eaten except for three carrots and two Nestle's fruit and nut bars and both my fore-arms sore as shit with all the little specks of caked blood covering them. My two sets of gimmicks right alongside me in the slightly bloody water in the plastic cup on the crusty linoleum, probably used by every case of hepatitis in upper Manhattan by now. Totally zonked, and all the dope scraped or sniffed clean from the tiny cello-phane bags. Four days of temporary death gone by, no more bread, with its hundreds of nods and casual theories, soaky nostalgia (I could have got that for free walking along Fifth Ave. at noon), at any rate a thousand goofs, some still hazy in my noodle. In one nod I dreamt I was in a zoo, inside a fence where, down from a steep stone incline, was a green pond filled with alligators. It seemed at one point I was about to be attacked. About ten gators surfaced and headed slowly up the incline, staring directly at me. But just when I seemed pinned against the fence, instead of lunging at me they just opened their huge jaws in slow motion and yelled, "Popcorn." At this point a little zoo keeper shuffled out and tossed huge bags of popcorn onto the water. I ducked out through the hole that suddenly appeared in the fence.

Zonked, but I've been slugging away at orange juice all along, anyway, for vitamin C and dry mouth. I just crawl out of the bed at first; don't even attempt my human posture. Think about my conversation with Brian: "Ever notice how a junkie nodding begins to look like a fetus after a while?" "That's what it's all about, man, back to the womb." I get up and lean on a busted chair. Jimmy Dantone comes running in and grabs me, "Those guys that we sold the phoney acid to the other day are after our asses if they don't get back the bread." "Go tell them I hate them," I tell him. He splits. A wasted peek into the mirror, I'm all thin as a wafer of concentrated rye. I wish I had some now with a little Cheez Whiz on it. I can feel the window light hurting my eyes; it's like shooting pickle juice. What does that mean? Nice June day out today, lots of people probably graduating today. I can see the Cloisters with its million in medieval art out the bedroom window. I got to go in and puke.

Denis Johnson

⚭

Car-Crash While Hitchhiking

A salesman who shared his liquor and steered while sleeping . . . A
Cherokee filled with bourbon . . . A VW no more than a bubble
of hashish fumes, captained by a college student . . .

And a family from Marshalltown who head-onned and killed forever a man driving west out of Bethany, Missouri . . .

. . . I rose up sopping wet from sleeping under the pouring rain,
and something less than conscious, thanks to the first three of the
people I've already named—the salesman and the Indian and the student—all of whom had given me drugs. At the head of the entrance
ramp I waited without hope of a ride. What was the point, even, of
rolling up my sleeping bag when I was too wet to be let into anybody's
car? I draped it around me like a cape. The downpour raked the asphalt and gurgled in the ruts. My thoughts zoomed pitifully. The
traveling salesman had fed me pills that made the linings of my veins
feel scraped out. My jaw ached. I knew every raindrop by its name. I
sensed everything before it happened. I knew a certain Oldsmobile
would stop for me even before it slowed, and by the sweet voices of
the family inside of it I knew we'd have an accident in the storm.

I didn't care. They said they'd take me all the way.

The man and the wife put the little girl up front with them, and left
the baby in back with me and my dripping bedroll. "I'm not taking
you anywhere very fast," the man said. "I've got my wife and babies
here, that's why."

You are the ones, I thought. And I piled my sleeping bag against the left-hand door and slept across it, not caring whether I lived or died. The baby slept free on the seat beside me. He was about nine months old.

. . . But before any of this, that afternoon, the salesman and I had swept down into Kansas City in his luxury car. We'd developed a dangerous cynical camaraderie beginning in Texas, where he'd taken me on. We ate up his bottle of amphetamines, and every so often we pulled off the interstate and bought another pint of Canadian Club and a sack of ice. His car had cylindrical glass-holders attached to either door, and a white, leathery interior. He said he'd take me home to stay overnight with his family, but first he wanted to stop and see a woman he knew.

Under midwestern clouds like great gray brains we left the super highway with a drifting sensation and entered Kansas City's rush hour with a sensation of running aground. As soon as we slowed down, all the magic of travelling together burned away. He went on and on about his girlfriend. "I like this girl, I think I love this girl—but I've got two kids and a wife, and there's certain obligations there. And on top of everything else, I love my wife. I'm gifted with love. I love my kids. I love all my relatives." As he kept on, I felt jilted and sad: "I have a boat, a little sixteen-footer. I have two cars. There's room in the backyard for a swimming pool." He found his girlfriend at work. She ran a furniture store, and I lost him there.

The clouds stayed the same until night. Then, in the dark, I didn't see the storm gathering. The driver of the Volkswagen, a college man, the one who stoked my head with all the hashish, let me out beyond the city limits just as it began to rain. Never mind the speed I'd been taking, I was too overcome to stand up. I lay out in the grass off the exit ramp and woke in the middle of a puddle that had filled up around me.

And later, as I've said, I slept in the back seat while the Oldsmobile—the family from Marshalltown—splashed along through the rain. And yet I dreamed I was looking right through my eyelids, and my pulse marked off the seconds of time. The interstate through western Missouri was, in that era, nothing more than a two-way road, most of it. When a semi-truck came toward us and passed going the other way, we were lost in a blinding spray and a warfare of noises such as you get being towed through an automatic car wash. The wipers stood up and lay down across the windshield without much effect. I was exhausted, and after an hour I slept more deeply.

I'd known all along exactly what was going to happen. But the man and his wife woke me up later, denying it viciously.

"Oh—*no!*"

"NO!"

I was thrown against the back of their seat so hard that it broke. I commenced bouncing back and forth. A liquid which I knew right away was human blood flew around the car and rained down on my head. When it was over I was in the back seat again, just as I had been. I raised up and looked around. Our headlights had gone out. The radiator was hissing steadily. Beyond that, I didn't hear a thing. As far as I could tell, I was the only one conscious. As my eyes adjusted I saw that the baby was lying on its back beside me as if nothing had happened. Its eyes were open and it was feeling its cheeks with its little hands.

In a minute the driver, who'd been slumped over the wheel, sat up and peered over at us. His face was smashed and dark with blood. It made my teeth hurt to look at him—but when he spoke, it didn't sound as if any of his teeth were broken.

"What happened?"

"We had a wreck," he said.

"The baby's okay," I said, although I had no idea how the baby was. He turned to his wife.

"Janice," he said. "Janice, Janice!"

"Is she okay?"

"She's dead!" he said, shaking her angrily.

"No she's not." I was ready to deny everything myself now.

Their little girl was alive, but knocked out. She whimpered in her sleep. But the man went on shaking his wife.

"Janice!" he hollered.

His wife moaned.

"She's not dead," I said, clambering from their car and running away.

"She won't wake up," I heard him say.

I was standing out here in the night, with the baby, for some reason, in my arms. It must have still been raining, but I remember nothing about the weather. We'd collided with another car on what I now perceived was a two-lane bridge. The water beneath us was invisible in the dark.

Moving toward the other car I began to hear rasping, metallic snores. Somebody was flung halfway out the passenger door, which was open, in the posture of one hanging from a trapeze by his ankles. The car had been broadsided, smashed so flat that no room was left inside of it even for this person's legs, to say nothing of a driver or any other passengers. I just walked right on past.

Headlights were coming from far off. I made for the head of the bridge, waving them to stop with one arm, and clutching the baby to my shoulder with the other.

It was a big semi, grinding its gears as it decelerated. The driver rolled down his window and I shouted up at him. "There's a wreck. Go for help."

"I can't turn around here," he said.

He let me and the baby up on the passenger side, and we just sat there in the cab, looking at the wreckage in his headlights.

"Is everybody dead?" he asked.

"I can't tell who is and who isn't," I admitted.

He poured himself a cup of coffee from a thermos and switched off all but his parking lights.

"What time is it?"

"Oh, it's around quarter after three," he said.

By his manner he seemed to endorse the idea of not doing anything about this. I was relieved and tearful. I'd thought something was required of me, but I hadn't wanted to find out what it was.

When another car showed, coming the opposite direction, I thought I should talk to them. "Can you keep the baby?" I asked the truck driver.

"You'd better hang on to him," the driver said. "It's a boy, isn't it?"

"Well, I think so," I said.

The man hanging out of the wrecked car was still alive as I passed, and I stopped, grown a little more used to the idea now of how really badly broken he was, and made sure there was nothing I could do. He was snoring loudly and rudely. His blood bubbled out of his mouth with every breath. He wouldn't be taking many more. I knew that, but he didn't, and therefore I looked down into the great pity of a person's life on this earth. I don't mean that we all end up dead, that's not the great pity. I mean that he couldn't tell me what he was dreaming, and I couldn't tell him what was real.

Before too long there were cars backed up for a ways at either end of the bridge, and headlights giving a night-game atmosphere to the steaming rubble, and ambulances and cop cars nudging through so that the air pulsed with color. I didn't talk to anyone. My secret was that in this short while I had gone from being the president of this tragedy to being a faceless onlooker at a gory wreck. At some point an officer learned that I was one of the passengers, and took my statement. I don't remember any of this, except that he told me, "Put out your cigarette." We paused in our conversation to watch the dying man being loaded into the ambulance. He was still alive, still dreaming obscenely. The blood ran off of him in strings. His knees jerked and his head rattled.

There was nothing wrong with me, and I hadn't seen anything, but the policeman had to question me and take me to the hospital anyway. The word came over his car radio that the man was now dead, just as we came under the awning of the Emergency Room entrance.

I stood in a tiled corridor with my wet sleeping bag bunched against the wall beside me, talking to a man from the local funeral home.

The doctor stopped to tell me I'd better have an X ray.

"No."

"Now would be the time. If something turns up later . . ."

"There's nothing wrong with me."

Down the hall came the wife. She was glorious, burning. She didn't know yet that her husband was dead. We knew. That's what gave her such power over us. The doctor took her into a room with a desk at the end of the hall, and from under the closed door a slab of brilliance radiated as if, by some stupendous process, diamonds were being incinerated in there. What a pair of lungs! She shrieked as I imagined an eagle would shriek. It felt wonderful to be alive to hear it! I've gone looking for that feeling everywhere.

"There's nothing wrong with me"—I'm surprised I let those

words out. But it's always been my tendency to lie to doctors, as if good health consisted only of the ability to fool them.

Some years later, one time when I was admitted to the detox at Seattle General Hospital, I took the same tack.

"Are you hearing unusual sounds or voices?" the doctor asked.

"Help us, oh God, it hurts," the boxes of cotton screamed.

"Not exactly," I said.

"Not exactly," he said. "Now what does that mean?"

"I'm not ready to go into all that," I said. A yellow bird fluttered close to my face, and my muscles grabbed. Now I was flopping like a fish. When I squeezed shut my eyes, hot tears exploded from the sockets. When I opened them, I was on my stomach.

"How did the room get so white?" I asked.

A beautiful nurse was touching my skin. "These are vitamins," she said, and drove the needle in.

It was raining. Gigantic ferns leaned over us. The forest drifted down a hill. I could hear a creek rushing down among rocks. And you, you ridiculous people, you expect me to help you.

WAR

✠

Italo Calvino

※

Last Comes the Raven

The stream was a net of limpid, delicate ripples, with the water running through the mesh. From time to time, like a fluttering of silver wings, the dorsum of a trout flashed on the surface, the fish at once plunging zigzag down into the water.

—Full of trout, one of the men said.

—If we toss a grenade in, they'll all come floating to the top, bellies up, said the other; he detached a grenade from his belt and started to unscrew the baseplate.

Then the boy, who had stood aside looking on, walked over, a mountain youth with an apple-look to his face.—Let me have it, he said, taking the rifle from one of the men.—What does he want to do? the man said, intending to re-claim the rifle. But the boy was levelling it at the water, in search of a target, it seemed. "If you shoot, you'll only scare the fish away," the man started to say, but did not have time. A trout had surfaced, flashing, and the boy had pumped a bullet into it as though having anticipated the fish's exact point of appearance. Now, with its white underside exposed, the trout floated lifeless on the surface. Cripes, the men said. The boy reloaded the rifle and swung it around. The air was crisp and tensed: one could distinguish the pine needles on the opposite bank and the knitted texture of the stream. A ripple broke the surface: another trout. He fired: now it floated dead. The men glanced briefly at the fish, briefly at the boy.— He shoots well, they said.

The boy swung the barrel again, into the air. It was curious, to think of it, that they were encompassed by air, actually cut off from other things by meters of air. But when the boy aimed the rifle, the air then became an invisible straight line stretching from the muzzle to the thing . . . to the hawk, for instance, floating above on wings that seemed scarcely to move. As he pressed the trigger, the air continued crystalline and clear as ever, but at the upper end of the line the kestrel folded its wings, then dropped like a stone. The open breech emitted a fine smell of powder.

He asked for more cartridges. The number of men watching had now swelled behind him on the bank of the stream. The cones at the top of the pine trees on the other bank—why were they visible and withal out of reach? Why that empty span between him and them? Why were the cones, although a part of him, in the chamber of his eye—why were they *there*, so distant? And yet if he aimed the rifle that empty span was clearly a deception: he touched the trigger and at that instant a cone, severed at the stem, fell. The feeling was one of caressive emptiness: the emptiness of the rifle bore which extended off into the air and was occupied by the shot, straight to the pine cone, the squirrel, the white stone, the flowering poppy.—He doesn't miss a one, the men said, and no one had the audacity to laugh.

—Come, come along with us, the leader said.—You give me the rifle then, the boy returned.—All right. Certainly.

So he went.

He left with a haversack filled with apples and two rounds of cheese. His village was a patch of slate, straw, and cattle muck in the valley bottom. And going away was wonderful, for at every turn there was something new to be seen, trees with cones, birds flitting among the branches, lichen-encrusted rocks, everything in the shaft of the false distances, of the distances occupied by gunshot that gulped up the air between. But he wasn't to shoot, they told him: those were places to be passed in silence, and the cartridges were for fighting. But at a certain point a leveret, frightened by the footsteps, scampered across the trail, amid shouts and the bustle of the men. It was just about to vanish into the brake when the boy stopped it with a shot.— A good shot, the leader himself conceded,—but this is not a pleasure hunt. You're not to shoot again, even if you see a pheasant.

But scarcely an hour had elapsed before there were more shots from the column.

—It's the boy again! the leader stormed, going forward to over-take him.

The boy grinned with his rosy and white apple-face.

—Partridges, he said, displaying them. They had burst up from a hedge.

—Partridges, crickets or whatever else, I gave you fair warning. Now let me have the rifle. And if you make me lose my temper once more, back to the village you go.

The boy sulked a little; it was no fun to be hiking without a rifle, but as long as he remained with them he might hope to have it again.

In the night they bedded down in the chalet of herdsmen. The boy awakened immediately the sky grew light, while the others still slept. He took their finest rifle and loaded his haversack with cartridges and went out. The air was timorous and crisp, as one may discover it in the early morning. Not far from the house stood a mulberry tree. It was the hour in which jays were arriving. There, he saw one! He fired, ran to pick it up, and stuffed it into his haversack. Without moving from where the jay had fallen, he looked about for another target. A dormouse! Startled by the first shot, it was scurrying toward safety in the crown of a chestnut tree. Dead, it was simply a large mouse with a grey tail that shed shocks of fur at touch. From beneath the chestnut tree he sighted, in a field off below him, a mushroom, red with white prickles and poisonous. He crumbled it with a shot, then went to see if really he had got it. What fun it was, going from one target to an-other like that: one might in time go all the way round the world! He spied a large snail on a rock; he sighted on its shell, and going over to it noticed nothing but the shattered rock and a spot of iridescent spit-tle. Thus did he wander from the chalet, down through unfamiliar fields.

From the stone he saw a lizard on a wall, from the wall a puddle and a frog, from the puddle a signboard on the zigzagging road, and beneath it: beneath it men in uniform advancing on him with arms at the ready. When the boy came forth with his rifle, smiling, his face rosy and white like an apple, they shouted, raising their guns. But the boy had already seen and fired at one of the gold buttons on the chest of one of them. He heard the man scream and then bullets, in a hail and single shots, whistling over his head: he had already flattened to the ground behind a pile of rocks on the hem of the road, in a dead angle. The rock pile was long and he could move about; and he was able to peep out from unexpected points, see the flash of the soldiers' musketry, the grey and gloss of their uniforms, and fire at a chevron, at an insigne. Then quickly scramble along the ground to fire from a new position.

Then he heard a burst of fire behind him, raking over his head into the ranks of the soldiers: his companions had appeared on the rescue with machine guns.—If the boy hadn't awakened us with his firing . . . they were saying.

Covered by his companions, the boy was better able to see. Suddenly a bullet grazed his cheek. He turned: a soldier had got to the road above him. He threw himself into the drainage ditch, gaining shelter again, at the same time firing; the bullet, though failing to hit the soldier, glanced off his riflestock. Now, from the sounds that he heard, he could tell that his adversary's rifle had jammed; the soldier flung it to the ground. Then the boy rose up. The soldier had taken to his heels and the boy fired at him, popping an epaulette into the air.

The boy gave chase. The soldier dashed into the woods, at first vanishing but presently reappearing within range. The boy burned a crease in the dome of the soldier's helmet, next shot off a belt loop. One after the other, they had meanwhile come into a dale, to which they were both of them strangers, and where the din of the battle was no longer heard. In time, the soldier found himself without any more trees before him, instead a glade overgrown with knotted thicket clumps. And the boy was himself about to come out of the woods.

In the middle of the clearing stood a large rock. The soldier barely made it, jumping behind and doubling up with his head between his knees. There, for the time being, he felt, he was out of danger: he had some grenades with him, and the boy would have to maintain a respectful distance; he could do no more than keep him pinned down with his rifle, insuring that he did not escape. Certainly, had it been possible for him simply to dive into the thickets, he would be safe, able then to slide down the heavily bearded slope. But there was that open tract to cross. How long would the boy wait? And would he continue to keep his rifle trained on him? The soldier decided to try an experiment: he put his helmet on his bayonet and stuck it out from behind the rock. There was a shot and the helmet, pierced through, bowled along the ground.

The soldier kept his wits; doubtless, aiming at the rock and the area around it was quite easy, but the soldier would not get hit if he was nimble enough. Just then a bird raced overhead, a hoopoe perhaps. One shot and it fell. The soldier wiped sweat from around his neck. Another bird, a missel thrush, went over: it fell too. The soldier swallowed. This was very likely a flyway; for other birds continued to go over, all of them different, and as the boy fired, they fell. A thought came to the soldier: "If he's watching birds, then he can't be watching me. Just as he fires I'll jump for the bushes." But it might be well to test his plan first. He picked up his helmet and placed it back on the tip of his bayonet. Two birds flew over this time: snipes. Waiting, the soldier regretted wasting so fine an occasion on the test. The boy fired at one of the snipes; the soldier raised his helmet. A second shot rang out and he saw the helmet leap into the air. The soldier's mouth tasted of lead; he had no sooner noticed this than the second bird fell. He must not lose his head: behind the rock with his grenades, he was safe. And why then, even though hidden, couldn't he try to get the boy with a grenade? He lay on his back and, bewaring not to be seen, stretched back his arm, primed his strength, and pitched the grenade. A good throw; it would go some distance; but describing only half of a parabola, still in mid-air, it was exploded by a rifle blast. The soldier flattened himself against the ground to escape the shrapnel.

When next the soldier raised himself the raven had come.

He saw, circling lazily above him, a bird, a raven perhaps. The boy would certainly shoot it down. But no shot followed. Was the raven perhaps too high? And yet he had brought down higher and swifter birds than that. Finally, he fired: now it would drop. No. Unperturbed, it continued to soar in the sky, slowly, round and round. A pine cone toppled from a near-by tree. Had he taken to shooting at pine cones? One by one, as he hit them, the cones fell, striking with a dry crunch. At each report the soldier glanced up at the raven: was it falling? Not yet. Lower and lower, the black bird continued to circle overhead. Could it be, really, that the boy didn't see it? Or perhaps the raven didn't exist at all, was only a hallucination. But perhaps—perhaps a man near death sees all the birds fly over . . . and when he sees the raven it means that the hour has come. In any case, he must tell the boy, who went on shooting at mere pine cones.

The soldier rose to his feet and pointed up at the black bird:

—There's the raven! he shouted in his own language. The bullet struck him through the heart of the spread eagle embroidered on his jacket.

The raven came down slowly, wheeling.

—translated by Ben Johnson

Paul West

❈

Blind White Fish in Belgium

I

Sister Binche began her duties in a serious manner, taking extra time to unbandage his eyes, which operation felt to him nothing like a turban, but more like someone slowly twirling his head, tapping little messages through the decreasing layer of muslin and tugging him gently this way and that in a horizontal Saint Vitus's dance that did not end when she had finished; his head went on wobbling in the medium called air that you could never see, blind or not. What are you doing now, he would say, and she would always give him the same answer: all that is good for you, in her glaciated, slow English. He did not see the raised bed she made from lint soaked in antiseptic, setting first one eye and then the other in a little rectangle that allowed for the curvature of his upper cheek. From a tiny watering can she poured boracic solution against the puckered, bloody whites, almost cooing to him, and it all felt polar cool, the lint, the liquid, her hands, just the thing he had dreamed about in the heat and sludge of the craters and trenches. Each eye took five minutes and she called it irrigation, carefully directing the spout to all areas of the eye, sometimes pouring for a long time and making a flood, sometimes doing just a quick tip to soothe an area neglected. For the moment at peace, Harry felt he was being christened in an unusual way, though the lotion felt astringent, especially in his left eye, the worse hurt. Other days, she did not use the little pouring can at all, but encouraged him to use an eye cup himself, handing it to him full and then helping him to bring it into place with a sudden tip and plunge, always careful not to jam it hard against whatever was beneath it. Then he held the cup in place and tried to blink, finally removing it with a second tip followed by a groping thrust toward her voice. Sometimes he messed up, spilling boracic on his chest, but mostly he got his eye, grateful that the water used in the solution was tepid. At the moment, this sluicing was the thing he wanted most in life, and he got it every three hours. The hospital staff filled him with eggs and crusty bread, made him strong sweet tea that reminded him of the army, from which he considered himself well and truly severed, stroked his head, combed his hair, cleaned his ears and nostrils, and waited for changes. Strong lights came and went unnoticed as he tried to accustom himself to being a baby, much of the time in bed, but also walked in his wheelchair and escorted on short promenades by Sister Binche, whose protégé he had fast become, partly because he reminded her of her brother, captured in the Somme, partly because she felt for the blind, the deaf, the dumb with a special vicarious gift that argued in her a tremendous capacity to discover how it felt to be somebody else. In Harry she discerned something copiously ascetic, perhaps mistaking the bareness of his early life for girding of the loins, self-denial, the beginning of the *via dolorosa*. She treasured him and taught him some words of French, and after a few weeks they were able to hold private rudimentary conversations about weather, food, the Vickers machine gun, bread dipped in bacon fat, book lovers in his home in Exington, noman's-land, and the man named Blood found on top of him, shattered and dry. For pain, of which he had a great deal, she gripped his fists and almost wrestled him, also letting him bite the heel of her somewhat roughened hand. Older than he, she saw him at the beginning of a career as one of life's victims: not merely a *mutilé de guerre,* a phrase she had candidly taught him (which he said as *matelot de gair*), unless—she did not give him much chance of seeing again, and she would soon have to inform him of the need to learn Braille. But not yet. It was a month since he had been wounded, and not all the right surgeons had been to prod him yet, although he described himself to her as a goner, a useless blighter. There is still Woodbine, the American, she said, who will be here soon. Let *him* see. Harry wanted the issue final, so that he might evolve an absolute attitude and become one thing or another. Having already told Hilly to forget him, to find a stockbroker or an officer, he regarded that piece of business as transacted, and stopped writing, at least until Sister Binche rebuked him and told him not to be so sadistic (a word he did not have). He still did not know her first name, and had not asked it, resolved in some reciprocal maneuver to deny himself things in much the same way as blindness denied him her face, though he had felt at its high cheekbones, the deep compassionate chin, the gray etiolated-looking eyes that sometimes in sunlight seemed not to be there at all, making her eligible for the term *white-eyes* gleaned from the American Indians. She was black haired, she told him, and therefore rather Irish-looking, he thought, with that combination of light and dark, and therefore fair completed too with freckles along her arms but none on her chest. Ari, she called him, or Sergeant Ari, making him feel important and imposing. The double eye patch made him look like a man going out to a firing squad, and she tried to bandage his head down low, screening the eyes just enough, but giving them air, a touch of breeze or her own mouth gently blowing at him to get his attention. She had removed much of the crust from the roots of his lashes and increased with minor coaxing their natural flexure away from the surface of the eye. If this attention soothed him, he never said, accepting it as the due of a blinded man who wondered how terrible he looked.

"Am I a monster?" he asked, hoping never to hear the answer, the white lie.

"Only in your mind, Ari," he heard. "Before you label someone a monster, you must consult his soul, and, if that is in good working order like a chiming clock, then you say the clock is wonderful, like a polar bear in bedroom slippers." Sometimes she went off like that, clinching all with an image that crackled like a firework even while seeming to go off the point. She stroked his arms, his shoulders, tugged on his ears and his toes, and, one night when everyone else was asleep and he was groaning with tiny penetrant pain, she slid her hands beneath the sheets and opened his hospital pajama trousers, exposing himself to himself, hand-galloping the virgin he hardly knew he was, and the headache went away, as well as his memory of what he had considered the happiness of his previous life. "There," she said, "now we've been introduced. You have a beautiful build. I am going to visit you again, Ari, and show you what to do." He knew, but he had hardly had time. His seductions had been toward death, and only young men at that. His orgasms had been those of panic and terror, when the rear end puckered and retched. His only sadness afterward had been his distance from the animating premise of the war: why was it being fought? Fabienne, he said; it doesn't sound like a woman's name at all. At least (he told her), it won't matter if I get any of it in my eye will it? Where it's going, she reassured him in her slowest French, it won't have any chance to get into an eye, *mon trésor*. He was not, he knew, being unfaithful to Hilly because none of this figured in his relationship with her, and probably never would. One day he would tell her about it, much as if confessing a trip to the dentist. Well, perhaps not quite that, but like gambling, shooting pigeons, letting a greased pig loose in a sedate club for foot soldiers. It seemed a great pity to him that this experience in the loins had come to him too late, now that he was a dead man; wouldn't it have been better to have something to compare it with, such as making love with his eyes on the beloved instead of trying to make a difference between dark and dark, between bandage dark and sunshine dark, aghast that, there in the bed as he shoved and stabbed against her, his eyes had only the pawnbroked glory of two bullet holes or, as he invoked one of the oldest soldierly curses, two piss holes in the snow? Better they should bandage his penis to his leg and wait for it to wither, fall off, like the feet of Chinese children. It was no use going home a sexual success but a flop at seeing. Nor was it much use staying here, being felt sorry for by a woman he had never seen. I, he told himself, am only an invitation to blindness; living with me, or even bedding down in the ward in the small hours, is like asking someone else to be blind too. What he had entered was a newly opened wound that she thought was only her normal organ, whereas he had maimed it, set it in a different category altogether, among the sponges, the roots, the fungi, the cuckoo spits. She thought she was still herself, refusing to tell him how many men she had handled, how many had entered her, little knowing that the angel of death had lain with her and irrevocably joined her to the league of the helpless. He was wrong, but his powers of analysis did not take him to the point at which he might realize how she worked: by means of sentimental convection, which meant moving huge areas of feeling around within her, never losing them but frequently combining them in new ways, linking a newly discovered Patagonia (Harry, Ari) to a Latin America already within her possession. *She* lived by comparison, by agglutinating man to man, after a few years without ever thinking herself a nymphomaniac or even promiscuous, creating a piebald lover, a Joseph's coat of satisfactions. Her memory belonged to her much as, sometimes, she belonged to several men in the same phase, or even in the same evening if she could manage it. She was open, she decided, and she should be filled. One day, Ari would be sent to a hospital in London, to be put through further ordeals, and that would be that. If she had unhinged him somewhat, she had no idea of it, choosing rather to think of herself as the angel of satiety, as capable of kissing and licking blind men's eye sockets as their genitals, once you became accustomed, she mused, to the local texture, the topography, the patchwork aromas and the rest. Having risen high in her profession, not least on account of an imperious contralto voice and a way of cowing doctors by raising herself to her full six feet in height, she had become accustomed to the often-vaunted embarrassments of having a body; the soul was a greater obstacle by far, and she wanted to settle herself in the flesh, as it were, to come to terms with all the organedness there was, presuming distantly that, when the Almighty first formed the flesh, He did it out of boredom with abstract ideas. He made the dirty bits to drive his masterpieces crazy.

Amazed he had survived the war while knowing so little of life, Harry caught himself in the middle of the thought and wondered if indeed he had survived. Being alive was one thing, but being alive blind was like being made of gun cotton: one touch and you went sky-high. That just about summed up his days and nights with Fabienne Binche. Diligently she piped chemicals into his eyes while he wished them ever cooler, but she taught him hygiene in other ways too, coming to him, after the lights were dimmed, with a basin of hot water and a rather coarse-feeling facecloth with which she laved his glans after gently peeling the foreskin back. Until only days ago, Harry had not realized the skin retracted, and he now, perhaps alas, linked erection with the act of washing; you never did it when you were soft. Back he lay, humming something Latin from the Gregorians, while Fabienne

Binche worked upon his privates the office of the portable bidet, as-
tounding him with a flick or a finger snap as if she were supervising a
frisky kitten and delighting him later in the performance with cold
cream and eau de cologne until he felt wholly spruced up, for either
the fray or a good night's sleep, depending on her mood and her
hours. It might have been paradise save for his eyes; he certainly felt
ministered to, delighted to have the bulb of his organ aired in this foreign place, sometimes trying to figure out how far this new life of his,
in which ecstasy and pain combined equally, was from the old one, in
which he had neither. If this was France, or Belgium, he wanted to
stay here for ever, blind or not, and he seriously tried to keep his mind
from next month or next year. Aladdin in his own cave, he now knew
that Aladdin's cave had opened because somebody like Fabienne
Binche had greased the hinges of its door with sesame oil. Sometimes
he thought he was flying, the wings of an old biplane between his
teeth, the rigging all screams; sometimes he thought he was underground in one of those tunnels dug under the front, while detona-
tions went on incessantly above them. His conversations with
Fabienne were much the same, day in, day out.

"Who is he," she murmured. "He's an ugly young soldier full of
love." Then she sang, with buoyant nasality: "Will he always be
blind? Will he never see the beauties who attend him?"

To which Harry said nothing, but hummed voluptuous contentment, little realizing how much a novelty—and little else—he was in
her complex and erotic life. Because he could not see, she read aloud
to him the properties of his body, the sexual part, anyway, from the
little steamy fizz she milked from him in the beginning to the splatter
of hot gruel she fostered in him after a week or so, exclaiming in delight as it popped upward in the half-light of the ward; as if an old
clay pipe had given up all its saliva in one go. She taught him names;
said his body was an aviary of flightless parakeets, each wrapped in
fragrant Armenian paper. She taught him how his tongue and hands
might do duty for his benighted eyes, and how his sharp military nose
had lain in abeyance for too long.

Harry began to think of himself as lucky, master-navigator and
master-cocksman in one, at last come into his own, severed from the

prosaic saunter of engagement and marriage so as to become the roué of the ward, a man who almost missed his disgraceful vocation, now fit to be greeted by the male nurse on his morning rounds with hot chocolate: "Good morning, English bums, good morning American bums, *shokolah, shokolah*." Where had he learned such twaddle? Harry wondered about the other patients and tried to estimate how many of them Fabienne had likewise sacrificed to her own imperious mucous membranes. He didn't care if he was the only one or one in twelve; he just knew that he never again wanted to be without this oozing extreme of life that gave the lie to war, blindness, disappointment, lack of hope, loneliness—everything. In a way she was too old for all of them in there, but in another she was the perfect tutor in lubricity, lustful friendliness. She loved what she smelled while tasting. She loved what she tasted while smelling. She loved what she smelled and tasted while touching and listening. She was a waning phantom, already beginning to suffer from varicosity behind her knees, little bouts in which her ankles went sideways, and, she was sure, prey to sudden extra heartbeats that slightly winded her. Well, she was going down in flames, willing to waste nothing so long as she had it.

Here she came, slightly breathless from being big and having to move neatly through the hushed-down ward. Harry felt a little bird heave upward from his chest, and all things begin to twitch and stiffen. Her very approach, in rubber-soled slippers, was aphrodisiac; but Harry, a poor sleeper, was the only one regularly awake, with his organ in his hand, his other hand behind his head, smoothing to a hypnotic and callow rhythm. Here she came, the vestal of the hot-water bottle and the lavender soap, willing to tease him by threatening his penis with a scrubbing brush ("Feel at this, *mon grand*"), but ever disposed to baby him and bring him to climax in the same breath, both cooing and urging to get him ready for a public appearance with his prowess in his pants to begin with and then lofted high in front of the other blind men who to a man cupped their ears for sounds of friction, imminence, bliss and decrescendo. Noncommissioned officers, she found, were reluctant to lie back and be serviced, where everyone from lieutenant upward seemed only too happy not to exert himself, not while the night prowler toiled. It was the strangest orgy she had ever known: muted and impeded. Now she knew what the thought of

death, hemorrhage, or amputation, did to the standing penis, making
it into a fugitive conical toffee busily scurrying for cover in its root. She
was as accustomed to last rites as to first spendings, preferring, with
the one, to weep later in her little garret atop the hospital, with the
other, to let the seepages dry and flake away, as having had a brief tu-
multuous dignity in the arena of the wounded man's groin. Life was
like that, she thought, as she nodded a far from premature yes. Life
spilled, out or over. To die was to go. To come was to die. Those who
had never come much were never at ease with death.

II

One warm sunny Sunday, Fabienne Binche and several other nurses
took the ambulant blind on a little outing, the first of many planned,
although some of the doctors in the Red Cross Hospital had argued
that those who could not walk would feel resentful. In the end, however, it had been decided to send the first group and see what happened. Off they went in two ambulances and, within the hour, were
lining up at the entrance, marching a few steps forward (some, still
military, got it right; Harry shuffled, to show his exclusion from the
war). He reached, he found something bulbous and concrete: the arm
of a mighty statue that blocked his path while, elsewhere in the echoing gallery, other blindfolded men in blue tunics hesitantly made contact with pieces of marble and stone, wondering what they were
feeling. The public were never allowed to touch, but this was a special
occasion: not a guessing game, though it degenerated into one as the
men slowly came to life and a long-lost ribaldry lifted its tactless head.
Those listening pretended not to hear what the men whispered, announced, and shouted: "Goliath's balls, to be sure!" "Jack the
Beanstalk's stalk, lads!" "My old woman's backside, frozen stiff." It
was perhaps the first serious laugh they had had since entering the
hospital. Harry enjoyed the coolness of the various minerals, responding to the muggy weather without the gusto of the others, and
wondering if this laying-on of hands would extend to human bodies
as well. Or were they all, the blind ones, already so sated with Sister
Binche as not to care? He asked, was told that only she, of all the

nurses, made the midnight rounds, and not with everybody either. She played favorites, and had been known to overpower a given soldier for a week, then leave him alone altogether, to wonder what he had done wrong. Nobody else, it seemed, had come in for as many attentions as Harry, for whom she had developed a soft spot banned in the daytime, but allowed to pulse and bulge as soon as the sun had set.

Alas for art and the therapeutic visit, several of the livelier young soldiers had opened their flies and were attempting lewd overtures to what they presumed were appropriate places of the statues in front of them; only a Turkish bath was missing as they pushed and clasped, yelling obscenities about the white cliffs of Dover, blindness from self-abuse, hollow spines from tossing-off, and the big shots of their schooldays who kept enormous stone jars of sperm under their beds, the tribal law being that you must never let any of it get away from you. It had not taken long for the blinded men to revert to adolescent atavism, to fast impromptu exchanges about swishers and danglers, knackers and bollocks, jamrags and horse collars, all of it diffident and amateurish, just the sort of thing they said in the trenches, not to hymn desire but to vent their nerves. Here they had ample reason to open up, quite ignoring the humanitarian motives of Sister Binche's nurses. For a while Harry, more conversant with the peculiar turns of Fabienne Binche's mind, thought there would be naked human beings, women certainly, in between the statues, awaiting only a soldier's touch to erupt into lascivious life. Then he thought that he and his mates were supposed to strip naked, except for their head bandages, and go through the motions that several had attempted—not that he knew—while more or less clad.

In the end he decided this was one of those cultural expeditions he had heard about. Music would be next, followed by a visit to the herbal spice gardens. It was all a way of killing time until the doctors could think of something to do, until each man's future was a certainty. This was a brothel of stone, he decided: if a man's desire was hot enough, the statues would melt, being of wax. He suddenly longed for a Vickers machine gun to lay waste the humanity surrounding him: nurses and soldiers and all. He did not want to see, hear, or any of the rest of it. They had been brought out of the hospital like lunatics from a mental institution, made to look silly and conspicuous, being aired like dogs on an aristocratic whim by people who should know better.

Harry's ruddy skin was pale for all the summer's heat. His hair rose high from the inner perimeter of the bandages and had that slept-on look. His gait had become unsteady; he walked with an invisible tureen of hot liquid balanced on his crown. For all their vulgarities, the blind soldiers conducted themselves with hesitant delicacy, every now and then, among the solid stances of the statues, grooming themselves with one finger raised to the cheek, testing that area for scars or scabs, then another finger or the same (but only ever one) tapping the concavity between chin and bottom lip. They believed that the eyes, once mauled, led the rest of the face downward to extinction too, and they were not going to be thus consecutively wounded without knowing about it. An ark of whirling knives surrounded them. They breathed shrapnel as tiny as grains of sand. Their lips dried so much they made a glow and sometimes caught fire. Blocked with drainage, their nostrils soon clogged up on any outing, and the return journey became mainly a matter of blowing into khaki handkerchiefs, which they then folded back up into the rectangular creases left by the smoothing iron, in effect sticking the little panels together with thumb-flattened blots of blood, which stuck better than anything: one of its main duties, Harry thought. Blood is God's glue. God's in his heaven. All's right with the world. Human skin is blood's best blotter. All nice outings come to an end. I have to keep up my strength for tonight. Odd, you'd think people would find us disgusting, but for some it just sharpens the edge of novelty. They could pull all kinds of faces and we'd never see a thing. They could rent us out to the most twisted sinners in Creation, so many francs a go, and extra to lift up the corner of the bandage and have a peek into the twin glory holes, nothing of the eyes left but two cooked raisins.

On their return, all the men had their eyes bathed. In case we saw anything, Harry thought, they are washing it away. Off. They don't want us to go getting fancy ideas about having a good look at things. Good *shufti*, as the Arabs say. I must say, I don't like having to deal with things on hearsay. Nobody could tell him what Sister Binche looked like. No nurse would. Could she, just perhaps, be blind herself, not a nurse or a sister, but an over-eager blind volunteer for whom night rounds were as natural as graveyards for the dead.

Slowly he was learning to reassemble his body, which meant that his eye wound had unsettled everything else, creating new relationships, new tensions, new alliances. He would never have believed it, but after an hour or two of being put on anew the bandage felt heavy, sagging and cumbersome, pulling his eyebrows down toward his cheeks. As a result, he was constantly shoving it upward, from an imagined droop; up and up it went until the eye sockets came into view and the clandestine light that he no longer revelled in slid over the hurt part of his face, over a barren moon, and the eyes in their nacelles did nothing for him at all. The nurses were always tugging their charges' bandages back into place, wondering if any of them would see again or if this was how it was going to be when they reached twenty and ever thereafter. Harry sensed he was lighter, less bulky, and decided that food you could not see did not nourish you. Nowadays, when he had speared the morsel, he brought his fork close to his nose and inhaled like someone drilled; the aroma was always better than the taste, but that was no doubt because he was accustomed to army fare and this was French food, the best cuisine in the world, at least for those brought up on it. He missed his bread and bacon dip, the bully beef, the mud-encrusted bread, the metallic-tasting tea. Here he got coffee, eggs and ham, soufflés and baguettes: delicious, but in a profound sense alienating: food for a toff, he thought. There was something else wrong with it, he thought; it was peacetime food, and, unless the war had suddenly ended (he envisioned a separate peace signed by France and Belgium while the British went on fighting), inappropriate, as if life was going on as usual while the cream of manhood was mashing itself into fertilizer not twenty miles away. He had thought of refusing such food, and of encouraging his fellow wounded to do likewise; but, what the hell, he thought, we might as well tuck in while we can. No telling when, in the dead of night, with our nightshirts flapping around our rear ends, we'll have to get out of here westward on the run, and only the blind ones know the way.

Behind screens there had been a blinded nurse: a critical demonstration of war's futility. Harry had asked to be led in to her, had spoken and touched her hand, then placed a kiss on her arm, all without so much as a sigh from the Belgian nurse, who had other head wounds too. Today she was not there, Fabienne told him: died during the night without so much as a murmur. A soldier was already in the bed. Harry was still waiting for the American doctor to brave the Atlantic and see him; but Harry was impatient for everything, even for Fabienne to leave—he thought that, so long as she treated him specially, he had not even begun to recover, firm in his conviction that he merited nothing out of the ordinary.

III

One morning, Fabienne Binche seemed in a hurry and her habitually seductive voice, in which matronly languor competed with lascivious bustle, had an edge of pure officiousness. Dr. Woodbine was coming to see Harry and give an opinion, so first they wanted Harry awake and then Harry anesthetized. It would take all day, or so Harry surmised, sniffing as he had learned to, first the noble American at loin level, and discovering from the muted whiff of smegma that Woodbine went uncircumcised in the world and was none too punctilious about washing himself. I'm like a bloody dog, Harry thought. They always come and sniff at you right there. Then he was all shudders and tremors, with the pain slicing clean through his head. The area around his eyes felt like hot soot. His nose oozed blood all the time. His face was being rugged by a puppeteer far away, the lines connected by fishhooks. When it eased, Harry began to recollect the velvet seat of Hilly's music stool, with its lovely fume of lemon furniture polish and combusted groin sweat: not Hilly's only, but of players and crooners and examiners since 1800, all those innocent, unfragrant bottoms sitting it out. Ten minutes after Harry passed out and Dr. Woodbine began in earnest, removing more and more tiny shrapnel, a dapper colonel entered the ward and, with permission from Fabienne Binche, left a decoration in a packet on each man's bed, bestowing on each bandage a kiss before moving on. There was no speech, no music, no fuss. The colonel might have been delivering mail or an advertisement for imported pineapple.

•

What was this decoration? Awarded to officers for gallantry and to non-commissioned officers for professional services, it was the Belgian Order of Leopold I, with swords: plum ribbon, brown metal swords and crown, green leaves upon which sat a white enamel cross and the legend *"L'Union Fait La Force."* Rather than depending from the ribbon, the award was pinned to it. Harry missed his kiss, but his eyes, like those of the other seven NCOs in the ward, had been decorated, and in fine fashion. No one ever queried the Belgian colonel's bona fides, or the fact that he was wearing this same decoration himself. A true Proteus of war, he slipped in and out of uniforms, from one front line to the other, from headquarters to headquarters, taking note with fastidious aversion and, periodically, collecting notes from such of his agents as Sister Fabienne Binche, to whom wounded soldiers talked impetuously.

Beckoned on, Harry allowed his mind to move toward the target of seeing, a literal target with bull, inner, outer, magpie, except that it was no longer one of seeing but of exorbitant pain, almost peaceful in the center but agonizing at the outskirts with a whole spectrum of sensation from tingling and prickling to hot needle and acid drop by drop. Dr. Woodbine had finished, but the legacy of his ministrations went on, converting Harry from casual hedonist to convulsing victim as the anesthetic wore off, and he began clutching, rubbing, trying to thumb both eyes into submission. Woodbine had removed as much shrapnel as he could, and he had also scraped the insides of the lids. Harry wanted to be unconscious again as soon as possible, but no oblivion came to quell the caustic star shells that dominated his vision. Fabienne Binche came and went, almost inured, but feeling dried and pointless, giving him what relief she could while Harry prayed for green water, cold, for warm vinegar, for ice, for raw steak, for a hard ball striking his eye hard enough to knock it out: a hundred-mile-an-hour ball with sharp stitching to slice the eyelids. After the routine euphemism, Harry had relaxed and lain back, believing in the words offered him: discomfort, some pressure, a bit of a push shoving gently against the curvature of each eyeball, then describing slow circles until the rhythm and the rotary slow motion had lulled him almost into a trance that could never have been his until years after. No one was better than Dr. Woodbine, that huge man with snowdrift hair growing in and from his ears, breath that smelled like cinnamon, loins that—or so

Harry thought—needed a scald in a bidet. Never mind, the man had come 3,456 miles, as he put it: no, farther, because he had come to Belgium, beyond Southampton, scheduled for an operation each day. The ward soon filled with writhing, gasping, hissing surgical successes who created, new every morning, an indecorous moan as background for everything else, such as a food spilled or thrown, glasses smashed, sheets torn off the bed and thrown vainly across the new head bandages as if to smother what was blazing underneath.

Each would have fainted, had he been alone there, but none of the blinded soldiers did, each unwilling to put on a bad show in front of the others, who could only hear anyway. Dr. Woodbine sapped them of lechery all right, but ate enormous meals both before and after he operated, devouring fried potatoes and thick grilled ham. From Baltimore, he must have had problems of his own, gastric and cardiac, but he never mentioned them and continued to operate like a dancer, nimble on his feet, sucking in his paunch the instant he approached the patient's head.

Their Belgian decorations hung from the foot of the beds, creamdaubed mistletoe freshly sprouted, and Fabienne made much of them, explaining this or that facet; but no one took much notice, certainly not those in recovery, not even those awaiting Woodbine, who took the trouble to come in and view the decorated beds himself, saying it was swell, all swell. The upshot, she gathered, was that the blinded men weren't Belgians, did not think of themselves as Belgians, were unhappy to be taken for Belgium's allies, did not wish to be in Belgium and couldn't find it on the map. When the dapper colonel returned, complete with ambulance, Sister Fabienne Binche of the erotically adroit hands and the ever-wet zone would take her leave and drive away eastward, her job well done, a Florence Nightingale in wolf's clothing, all hearts broken behind her, and many male virgins converted to what some of them called the old knee-trembler. She considered going off with a souvenir of each man, a hair here, a splash there, but dismissed the idea as coy; she would content herself with a kiss, and collect up the medals before departing—her colonel liked to economize, and his job was far from done.

Except for this. As a nurse genuinely impressed by Woodbine and his Baltimore ways, she handed him a Belgian medal out of something approaching reverence; he took it, but promptly put it back on Harry's bed after she had gone, the purpose of her departure being ostensibly to pick up medical supplies. The other medals went away with her, fireflies of valor, to be temporarily bestowed elsewhere, say a hundred miles farther on. As Woodbine told it, Harry became confused:

"Gave me ya medal, son, she did. These nurses. You got it back. Here, feel."

"What medal?" Harry asked, his mind for some reason on the name of his regiment: the Sherwood Foresters. "Did you say the Binche has gone?"

"She'll be back. You got your medal right here now at the foot of the bed. Funny dame: she took all the others, maybe to get them polished. You got the first one back, I guess. These Belgians, they sure ain't French."

Harry was dreaming of Hilly playing tennis in a wide-brimmed gray hat, from which a mauve bird lifted off, aghast, each time she struck the ball. Harry and Hilly would go for walks again together, newly taken with each other. The ball in the dream was a disk of light from America by sea, a gift from the westering sun of San Francisco, a flash from the heart of things where all medals melted, all bandages came off.

IV

Astounded by the needle's point that fast became a hole made by a knitting needle, then by an awl, Harry felt generous toward the source of light for not having gone away. Painful as it was to do it, he squinted and squinted, half expecting darkness to win out, but nothing went wrong, although the creatures he saw undulated and sagged, billowing and feebly signaling. These were the people who had been alongside him all the time, watching him watch nothing. Where was Fabienne Binche, then? A total apparition? They told him she had been seconded, which sounded vaguely obscene, but it meant she had been sent elsewhere, nobody was quite sure. So he had never seen her, and was unlikely to do so, forever haunted by a lubricious phantom of the everlasting night. But seeing again, never mind how

mottled and unsteady a world, dulled the ache; it was as if he had
been given the world back again, and he knew that the most craven
and craving depravities took place in the dark when heart lost hope
and body shed its pride. He saw a world little changed, except for Dr.
Woodbine's pink cheeks and his huge hands, which had been as intimate with Harry's eyes and their tender sockets as Binche had been
with his genitals. Had he grown up? Who was he to formulate such a
question? Looking at his face in the steel shaving mirror, he saw the
same young, questing Turk, serious but even tempered, more Scottish than Irish, he thought, having a darker tinge, a steadier gaze, a
promise of something stern. It was his father's face minus the waxed
mustache and the sharp points it tapered into. Harry's own mustache,
shaved away by the nurses, had been a sergeant's mustache, allowed
luxuriance to age a boy: that was all, and he was glad to see it gone as
he no longer had men to command, no Vickers, no revolver, no maps,
no bully beef. He was a convalescent, that was all, but he had had an
extraordinary blindness, led into riot by an invisible siren whom he
might just have invented.

When he opened the package, however, he knew she had been
real, for there, stitched elegantly above the famous right-angled Angel
of Albert, manhandled into plunging position lest the Germans use
the top of her erect head for observation purposes, sat his name:
Sergeant Ari Moxon, in red on pale blue, with the dates of his hospitalization: no message, no endearment, but the angel and her tower in
full glorious thread. It was something to treasure, and perhaps something to hate. Each corner formed a half-cross as the two rims of the
frame continued about three inches outward, having intersected. Had
it been rolled up, as for a cardboard tube, certificate-style, Harry
might have squirreled it away under his pillow, or into his kit bag (was
it here? no, but kit bags were easy to come by). Done up in a frame,
however, it was a public object clamoring for a nail to hang on, so as to
announce itself and the feelings it embodied. A nurse had already
hung it, and now, after showing him, she set it back for him to admire
with his newfound eye, which of course meant he had little idea of
how far away it was, and that matched his sense of Fabienne Binche,
whom he now loathed for being gone, for not being there to watch
him take the sampler's measure and delight in its contrasted threads.

Couldn't she have waited? Just a day or two? There was something sneaky about her disappearance, as about the Belgian decoration presented him by the man who spirited his bedmate away. A man with a monocle, obsessed with handing out medals? He could hardly believe it.

He needed to know all about her life, more, actually, than he needed her to make love with, as if she had now discharged her assignment and, becoming more of herself because no longer committed to someone else, more worth knowing—ogling, following, eavesdropping upon. Because she had had relations with other men in the ward, he desired her all the more, but his desire for knowledge was greater than that for her buxom, fluent parts. With his hesitant new eye he wanted to interrogate her, watch her doing all the abominable things she did without him, tasting and fondling other men as if she had no primary sweetheart stuck there in the nest of his blindness. But they were all blind, he told himself, except for Bicester pronounced "Bister," who also had come back from the ravine of blindfold misery. When had she blown out the candle? When removed her underwear? When untrussed her six-footer's breasts? Had she come to him without makeup? How had her face been at moments of acutest pleasure, taking or receiving? What had she been? They showed him her photo, culled from the files, and she was hardly as he had imagined: harelipped, drab as a clock, visibly mustached. Still, why no letter? Why just a sampler, mute as a blind man? That afternoon he took the first of several sedatives for excitement brought on, most supposed, by seeing again. His semijubilant presence upset the other soldiers, so he was moved to a smaller ward, of seeing men who had lost limbs and had a whole series of quite different complaints, none of which he heard. He wanted to see the past, the gone, the irrecoverable, and back he would lunge into the prickly oblivion he had thought would never be his again.

Issue 121, 1991

Primo Levi

❧

from The Art of Fiction CXL

LEVI

My story was an exception. Because they discovered my background as a chemist, I worked in a chemical laboratory. We were three out of ten thousand prisoners. My personal position was extremely exceptional, like the position or situation of every survivor. A normal prisoner died. That was his escape. After passing an examination in chemistry, I expected something more from my bosses. But the only one who had a trace of human comprehension towards me was Dr. Müller, my supervisor at the laboratory. We discussed it after the war in our letters. He was an average man, not a hero and not a barbarian. He had no inkling of our condition. He had been transferred to Auschwitz a few days before. So he was confused. They told him: Yes, in our laboratories, in our factories we employ prisoners. They are fiends, they are adversaries of our government. We put them to work to exploit them, but you are not supposed to talk with them. They are dangerous, they are communists, they are murderers. So put them to work but don't keep in touch with them. This man Müller was a clumsy man, not very clever. He was not a Nazi. He had some traces of humanity. He noticed I was unshaven and asked me why. Look, I told him, we haven't any razor, we haven't even a handkerchief. We are completely naked. Deprived of everything. He gave me a requisition that I must be shaven twice a week, which wasn't really a help, but a sign. Moreover, he noticed I had wooden clogs. Noisy and uncomfortable. He asked me why. I told him our shoes

were taken away the first day. These are our uniform standard. He
made me have leather shoes. This was an advantage because wooden
clogs were a torture. I still have the scars made by the clogs. If you are
not used to them, after a half-mile walking, your feet are bleeding and
encrusted with dirt and so on, and they become infected. To have
leather shoes was an important advantage. So I contracted a sort of
gratefulness to this man. He was not very courageous. He was afraid
of the SS, like me. He was interested in my work being useful, not in
persecuting me. He had nothing against Jews, against prisoners. He
just expected us to be effective workers. This story about him in *The
Periodic Table* is completely real. I never got a chance to meet him after the war. He died a few days before our appointment to meet. He
phoned from a spa in Germany where he was recovering his health.
As far as I know, his death was natural. But I don't know. I purposely
left it undecided in *The Periodic Table* . . . to leave the reader in
doubt, as I was.

Issue 134, 1995

Ezra Pound

⁜

from The Art of Poetry V

INTERVIEWER

The political action of yours that everybody remembers is your broadcasts from Italy during the war. When you gave these talks, were you conscious of breaking the American law?

POUND

No, I was completely surprised. You see I had that promise. I was given the freedom of the microphone twice a week. "He will not be asked to say anything contrary to his conscience or contrary to his duty as an American citizen." I thought that covered it.

INTERVIEWER

Doesn't the law of treason talk about "giving aid and comfort to the enemy," and isn't the enemy the country with whom we are at war?

POUND

I thought I was fighting for a constitutional point. I mean to say, I may have been completely nuts, but I certainly *felt* that it wasn't committing treason.

Wodehouse went on the air and the British asked him not to. Nobody asked me not to. There was no announcement until the collapse that the people who had spoken on the radio would be prosecuted.

Having worked for years to prevent war, and seeing the folly of Italy and America being at war—! I certainly wasn't telling the troops to revolt. I thought I was fighting an internal question of constitutional government. And if any man, any individual man, can say he has had a bad deal from me because of race, creed, or color, let him come out and state it with particulars. The *Guide to Kulchur* was dedicated to Basil Bunting and Louis Zukovsky, a Quaker and a Jew.

I don't know whether you think the Russians ought to be in Berlin or not. I don't know whether I was doing any good or not, whether I was doing any harm. Oh, I was probably offside. But the ruling in Boston was that there is no treason without treasonable intention.

What I was right about was the conversation of individual rights. If when the executive, or any other branch, exceeds its legitimate powers, no one protests, you will lose all your liberties. My method of opposing tyranny was wrong over a thirty-year period; it had nothing to do with the Second World War in particular. If the individual, or heretic, gets hold of some essential truth, or sees some error in the system being practiced, he commits so many marginal errors himself that he is worn out before he can establish his point.

The world in twenty years has piled up hysteria—anxiety over a third war, bureaucratic tyranny, and hysteria from paper forms. The immense and undeniable loss of freedoms, as they were in 1900, is undeniable. We have seen the acceleration in efficiency of the tyrannizing factors. It's enough to keep a man worried. Wars are made to make debt. I suppose there's a possible out in space satellites and other ways of making debt.

Kurt Vonnegut

※

from The Art of Fiction LXIV

VONNEGUT

When the war started, incendiaries were fairly sizeable, about as long as a shoebox. By the time Dresden got it, they were tiny little things. They burnt the whole damn town down. . . .

Our guards were noncoms—a sergeant, a corporal, and four privates—and leaderless. Cityless, too, because they were Dresdenets who'd been shot up on the front and sent home for easy duty. They kept us at attention for a couple of hours. They didn't know what else to do. They'd go over and talk to each other. Finally we trekked across the rubble and they quartered us with some South Africans in a suburb. Every day we walked into the city and dug into basements and shelters to get the corpses out, as a sanitary measure. When we went into them, a typical shelter, an ordinary basement usually, looked like a streetcar full of people who'd simultaneously had heart failure. Just people sitting there in their chairs, all dead. A firestorm is an amazing thing. It doesn't occur in nature. It's fed by the tornadoes that occur in the midst of it and there isn't a damned thing to breathe. We brought the dead out. They were loaded on wagons and taken to parks, large open areas in the city which weren't filled with rubble. The Germans got funeral pyres going, burning the bodies to keep them from stinking and from spreading disease. 130,000 corpses were hidden underground. It was a terribly elaborate Easter egg hunt. We went to work through cordons of German soldiers. Civilians didn't get to see what we were up to. After a few days the city began to smell, and a new technique was invented. Necessity is the mother of invention. We would bust into the shelter, gather up valuables from people's laps without attempting identification, and turn the valuables over to guards. Then soldiers would come in with a flame thrower and stand in the door and cremate the people inside. Get the gold and jewelry out and then burn everybody inside.

Peter Ho Davies

✠

The Ends

Towards the end the GIs at Nuremberg played basketball almost around the clock, it seemed. We couldn't see them from our cells, but the percussive *bap, bap, bap* of the ball on the floor carried to us from the old mess hall where they played. I was interested in the game, as was Göring. What were the rules, we wondered. We wanted like schoolboys to be invited to play (although Göring got short of breath climbing to the dock), or at the very least to watch a game, but when we asked the Colonel refused. Göring persisted. He wanted an exhibition match. He called it a cultural exchange, but the answer was no. "My men aren't here to entertain you, gentlemen," the Colonel said, although as I told Göring when I was in British hands they had let me watch billiard matches between their officers, and even invited me to play on several occasions. Instead, I had Stuckey, the guard, describe basketball to me. I told him it sounded like football—soccer to him—except played with the hands and not the feet, and with a tiny "goal," but he shrugged and said he didn't know soccer. Instead, he showed me how a man "shoots a basket," the ball balanced on the fingers of one hand, the upward pushing motion. He used a ball of socks and my wastebasket, which he set on a shelf.

At first the GIs played early in the evening and then later and later into the night, even after lights out. They were mad for the game, obsessed, it seemed to me. It was as if they had so much energy—guarding us was tedious, I supposed—that they had to expend it in marathon matches. I found myself dreaming of the game, as I imagined it, the men impossibly small, beneath the high basket that hung suspended over them, the rope net swaying, the ball sailing up, missing, falling from a great height.

I asked Stuckey if he played, and he looked confused and shook his head.

Göring eventually complained about the noise. It was keeping him awake, he said. It was like a headache, pounding in his temples. *Bap, bap, bap!* By now the verdicts had come down. I had life; Göring and the others, death. I thought he'd have quite enough time to sleep in the future. But when I told him to let them play, he looked at me steadily and told me to be quiet. "Hess, you fool. That's no game. That's hammering! They're building our gallows in there."

He was right, I suppose. And right to be angry at me, for my stupidity, for having avoided death, that dark rushing beast. But still, at night, I dreamed of fantastic, nail-biting games, ball after ball dropping through swinging baskets.

I never saw a game, and Göring, of course, never saw the scaffold. He took cyanide the night of the executions. What a showman! In the midst of this orchestrated performance, he wrote his own lines. "This'll cost me my star," the Colonel cried, referring to his hoped-for promotion, although at first I took him to mean Göring, his leading man. Who knows where Göring had the cyanide capsule hidden? In the folds of his stomach, some say; up his rectum, others. He may have swallowed it and shat it day after day for months. I have tried to kill myself several times. With a butter knife I ground on an iron bedstead in my cell in Britain; hurdling the banister of a staircase and flinging myself down three flights. Still, I'm not sure I'd swallow anything extracted from Hermann Göring's anus! But then I wasn't condemned to die that night. The end, perhaps, justifies the means.

I heard the others taken out in pairs, until they arrived at von Ribbentrop, the odd man out. He would have hung with Göring and now he was going to die alone. He sounded, as they led him out, more cheated than the Colonel.

I listened, of course, but there was nothing, just the barked (and poorly pronounced) name of each man as he entered the hall, as if he were being announced at a ball. I imagined it strangely like a marriage. These men walking up the aisle together, climbing the scaffold. The hangman waiting to join them. The Frank-Frick execution. The Jodl-Kaltenbrunner function. Seyss-Inquart-Streicher. Rosenberg-Sauckel. Von Ribbentrop. There would be an offer of a blindfold, and I wondered who would accept (Streicher, no doubt) and who would stiffly decline (Keitel, certainly). I wondered what their last words would be. Mostly, though, I listened for the sound of them dying. I expected a noise, a crash, but the gallows were well built, well oiled. Over and over, I strained to hear, half-imagined I did hear, the crack, very like the sound of a basketball on the floor, of each man's neck breaking.

But I could not have. The Americans were in charge of the executions, and I have heard that Americans hang men differently than the British. The British, our fellow Europeans, have a scientific approach to execution, a mathematical formula—the weight of the man, the length of the rope, et cetera—which is intended to ensure that the neck breaks at the end of the drop, and that death comes quickly. The Americans, by contrast, use a standard length of rope, so some have their necks snapped swiftly and some strangle slowly. The ends are the same; the means different. I suppose the standard American length is a measure of equality, of democracy. "Like a lynching," Göring had said. "Like the Wild West. We are going to die like outlaws." He would have preferred the guillotine, he said. Efficient and instantaneous ("One moment here," he said, touching his chin, "the next in a basket") but with a little French flair, and a touch of the aristocrat.

When they took Streicher and Seyss-Inquart the guards didn't return for ten minutes. When they took Jodl and Kaltenbrunner they were gone for almost thirty-five. I remember Speer calling the time out. Trust Speer to be counting. And poor Jodl, so indifferent to dying, had been so fierce in his desire for a firing squad, a soldier's death.

We had all lost weight during our captivity (in part because of our rations, mostly because our appetites failed us) and a lighter man is less likely to have his neck broken by the drop, more likely to die by strangulation. The only one who didn't seem much reduced was Göring. He was twice the size of any of us. His girth seemed to have even swelled during captivity, although this might have been relative to our diminishment. He had never lost his appetite and by this time, when all around him were thin shadows, it looked as if he had swallowed the country. Maybe it was easier to eat knowing he could end it whenever he wanted. He was collected throughout the trial, almost amused. Then again maybe he ate like that to stay regular, to keep the death pill moving through his gut, through and out, around and around. His last meal, at any rate, biting down on that capsule, was his smallest.

The last loose end of Nuremberg, I've come to envy their deaths, all of them, but his most of all. In truth, though, I've never subscribed to the theory that Göring had the pill with him all that time. He was a big man, but he was never a slob. Rather he was that dandyish breed of fat man, vain and a little prim. This was not a man who could swallow his own shit. No, I believe someone gave it to him, the pill. A sympathizer perhaps. There were Germans who came in to clean our cells, although they were always supervised. His lawyer possibly. Maybe even a guard, my own Stuckey perhaps, bribed with riches. Even Göring's poorest possessions would have been a trophy to some, a relic to others. A comb with a few strands of hair, his eyeglasses, his boots, his wristwatch. Any of these might have supplied him the death pill, but I don't think so.

A big man like that, as heavy as Göring, you must understand, would have definitely had his neck broken by the American method— by dint of having his head torn off by the rope. Decapitated. Think of that. Hermann Göring's huge round head, balanced on the rim of the noose, toppling off, falling. Will it bounce? *Bap!* Will it roll?

So I think it was the British—Major Neave, perhaps, who escaped from Colditz and handed us our indictments; Neave who understood the need for escape—the British, then, who saw to it that Göring got the pill, knew when to use it. The British with their bashful sympathy for *our* ends, in respect to the Jews (look at Palestine!); and their fiery contempt for our means. The British with that godlike disdain of theirs for a scene. The *British*!

Frank O'Hara

⚌

Pearl Harbor

I belong here. I was born
here. The palms sift their fingers
and the men shove by in shirts,
shaving in underwear shorts.
They curse and scratch the wet hair
in their armpits, and spit. Whores
spread their delicate little germs
or, indifferently, don't, smiling.
The waves wash in, warm and salty,
leaving your eyebrows white and
the edge of your cheekbone. Your ear
aches. You are lonely. On the
underside of a satin leaf, hot
with shade, a scorpion sleeps. And
one Sunday I will be shot brushing
my teeth. I am a native of this island.

Issue 45, 1968

W.S. Merwin

※

Conquerer

When they start to wear your clothes
do their dreams become more like yours
who do they look like

when they start to use your language
do they say what you say
who are they in your words

when they start to use your money
do they need the same things you need
or do the things change

when they are converted to your gods
do you know who they are praying to
do you know who is praying
for you not to be there

Issue 153, 1999

Harold Pinter

✠

from The Art of Theater III

PINTER

I'll tell you what I really think about politicians. The other night I watched some politicians on television talking about Vietnam. I wanted very much to burst through the screen with a flamethrower and burn their eyes out and their balls off and then inquire from them how they would assess this action from a political point of view.

Issue 39, 1966

Ha Jin

⬖

The Dead Soldier's Talk

*In October 1969, in a shipwreck accident on the Tu-
men River, a young Chinese soldier was drowned saving a plaster statue of Chairman Mao. He was
awarded Merit Citation 2, and was buried at a
mountain foot in Hunchun County, Jilin.*

I'm tired of lying here.
The mountain and the river are not bad.
Sometimes a bear, a boar, or a deer
                  comes to this place
As if we are a group of outcast comrades.
I feel lonely and I miss home.
It is very cold when winter comes.

I saw you coming just now
Like a little cloud wandering over grassland.
I knew it must have been you,
For no other had come for six years.

Why have you brought me wine and meat
            and paper-money again?
I have told you year after year
That I am not superstitious.

Have you the red treasure book with you?
I have forgotten some quotations.

You know I don't have a good memory.
Again, you left it home.
How about the statue I saved?
Is it still in the museum?
Is our Great Leader in good health?
I wish He live ten thousand years!

Last week I dreamed of our mother
Showing my medal to a visitor.
She was still proud of her son
And kept her head up
While going to the fields.
She looked older than last year
And her grey hair troubled my eyes.
I did not see our little sister.
She must be a big girl now.
Has she got a boy friend?

Why are you crying?
Say something to me.
Do you think I cannot hear you?
In the early years
You came and stood before my tomb
Swearing to follow me as a model.
In recent years
You poured tears every time.

Damn you, why don't you open your mouth?
Something must have happened.
What? Why don't you tell me!

Issue 101, 1986

John le Carré

⌗

from The Art of Fiction CXLIX

INTERVIEWER
What is it like to talk to an arms dealer?

LE CARRÉ
I just do my absolute best to be a fly on the wall. The most acute moment of this sort was when I went to Moscow to explore for *Our
Game.* I went with the Chechen and the Ingush groups that were
hanging around in Moscow. All I wanted to do, exactly as when I was
with the Palestinians in south Lebanon, was listen, find out what
made them tick, just listen. But I also wanted to meet a Russian mafia
boss, and through a variety of contacts, mainly ex-KGB people, it was
finally made possible for me at two or three in the morning to meet
Dima. Dima came into the nightclub, which he owned and which was
guarded by young men with Kalashnikovs and grenades strapped to
their belts. He came in wearing Ray-Bans with his hookers and his
men and his people. He looked like the Michelin Man, he was so
blown up with steroids. The music was so loud I had to kneel down
to get close enough to his ear to talk to him, so I seemed to be actually
kneeling in his presence. My interpreter was kneeling beside me.
Dima gave me the whole spiel about how "Russia is anarchic . . . yes,
I've killed people; yes, I've done this and that . . . but actually I've
done nothing against the law; it was all self-defense. Anyway, the law
doesn't work for post-communist Russia." And I said, "Dima, let me
ask you a question. In the United States, great crooks have with time

become serious members of society. They've built museums and hospitals and stadiums. When, Dima, do you think that you might feel it was necessary to take on your responsibility for your grandchildren, your great-grandchildren?" Dima started talking and my interpreter all of a sudden fell into a dark silence. I said, "What is it, Vladimir? What's he saying?" He said, "Mr. David, I am very sorry, but he says fuck off."

Susan Sontag

⚜

from The Art of Fiction CXLIII

INTERVIEWER

We've had to postpone this interview several times because of your frequent trips to Sarajevo which, you've told me, have been one of the most compelling experiences of your life. I was thinking how war recurs in your work and life.

SONTAG

It does. I made two trips to North Vietnam under American bombardment, the first of which I recounted in "Trip to Hanoi," and when the Yom Kippur War started in 1973 I went to Israel to shoot a film, *Promised Lands,* on the front lines. Bosnia is actually my third war.

INTERVIEWER

There's the denunciation of military metaphors in *Illness as Metaphor.* And the narrative climax of *The Volcano Lover,* a horrifying evocation of the viciousness of war. And when I asked you to contribute to a book I was editing, *Transforming Vision: Writers on Art,* the work you chose to write about was Goya's *The Disasters of War.*

SONTAG

I suppose it could seem odd to travel to a war, and not just in one's imagination—even if I do come from a family of travelers. My father, who was a fur trader in northern China, died there during the Japanese invasion: I was five. I remember hearing about "world war" in September 1939, entering elementary school, where my best friend in the class was a Spanish Civil War refugee. I remember panicking on December 7, 1941. And one of the first pieces of language I ever pondered over was "for the duration"—as in "there's no butter for the duration." I recall savoring the oddity, and the optimism, of that phrase.

INTERVIEWER

In "Writing Itself," on Roland Barthes, you express surprise that Barthes, whose father was killed in one of the battles of the First World War (Barthes was an infant) and who, as a young man himself, lived through the Second World War—the Occupation—never once mentions the word *war* in any of his writings. But your work seems haunted by war.

SONTAG

I could answer that a writer is someone who pays attention to the world.

INTERVIEWER

You once wrote of *Promised Lands:* "My subject is war, and anything about any war that does not show the appalling concreteness of destruction and death is a dangerous lie."

SONTAG

That prescriptive voice rather makes me cringe. But . . . yes.

INTERVIEWER

Are you writing about the siege of Sarajevo?

SONTAG

No. I mean, not yet, and probably not for a long time. And almost certainly not in the form of an essay or report. David Rieff, who is my son, and who started going to Sarajevo before I did, has published such an essay-report, a book called *Slaughterhouse*—and one book in the family on the Bosnian genocide is enough. So I'm not spending time in Sarajevo to write about it. For the moment it's enough for me just to be there as much as I can: to witness, to lament, to offer a model of non-complicity, to pitch in. The duties of a human being, one who believes in right action, not of a writer.

Nicholas Christopher

⌖

Terminus

Here is a piece of required reading
at the end of our century
the end of a millenium that began with the crusades

The transcript of an interview
between a Red Cross doctor
and a Muslim girl in Bosnia
twelve years old
who described her rape by men
calling themselves soldiers
different men every night one after the other
six seven eight of them
for a week
while she was chained by the neck
to a bed in her former schoolhouse
where she saw her parents and her brothers
have their throats slit and tongues cut out
where her sister-in-law
nineteen years old and nursing her baby
was also raped night after night
until she dared to beg for water
because her milk had run dry
at which point one of the men

tore the child from her arms
and as if he were "cutting an ear of corn"
(the girl's words)
lopped off the child's head
with a hunting knife
tossed it into the mother's lap
and raped the girl again
slapping her face
smearing it with her nephew's blood
and then shot the mother
who had begun to shriek
with the head wide-eyed in her lap
shoving his gun into her mouth
and firing twice

All of this recounted to the doctor
in a monotone
a near whisper in a tent
beside an icy river
where the girl had turned up frostbitten
wearing only a soiled slip
her hair yanked out
her teeth broken

All the history you've ever read
tells you this is what men do
this is only a sliver of the reflection
of the beast
who is a fixture of human history
and the places you heard of as a boy
that were his latest stalking grounds
Auschwitz Dachau Treblinka
and the names of their dead
and their numberless dead whose names have vanished
each day now find their rolls swelled
with kindred souls

new names new numbers
from towns and villages
that have been scorched from the map

1993 may as well be 1943
and it should be clear now
that the beast in his many guises
the flags and vestments
in which he wraps himself
and the elaborate titles he assumes
can never be outrun

As that girl with the broken teeth
loaded into an ambulance
strapped down on a stretcher
so she wouldn't claw her own face
will never outrun him
no matter where she goes
solitary or lost in a crowd
the line she follows
however straight or crooked
will always lead her back to that room
like the chamber at the bottom
of Hell in the Koran
where the Zaqqum
tree grows
watered by scalding rains
"bearing fruit like devils' heads"

In not giving her name
someone has noted at the end
of the transcript that the girl herself
could not or would not recall it
and then describes her as a survivor

Which of course is from the Latin
meaning to live on
to outlive others

I would not have used that word

Geoffrey Hill

A Prayer to the Sun

i.m. Miguel Hernandez *

(1)
Darkness
above all things
the Sun
makes
rise

(2)
Vultures
salute their meat
at noon
(Hell is
silent)

(3)
Blind Sun
our ravager
bless us
so that
we sleep.

Issue 34, 1964

*Miguel Hernandez, poet of the Spanish Civil War, died in prison in 1942.

WHIMSY

Umberto Eco

✠

How to Travel with a Salmon

According to the newspapers, there are two chief problems that beset the modern world: the invasion of the computer, and the alarming extension of the Third World. The newspapers are right, and I know it.

My recent journey was brief: one day in Stockholm and three in London. In Stockholm, taking advantage of a free hour, I bought a smoked salmon, an enormous one, dirt cheap. It was carefully packaged in plastic, but I was told that, if I was traveling, I would be well-advised to keep it refrigerated. Just try.

Happily, in London, my publisher made me a reservation in a deluxe hotel, a room provided with minibar. But on arriving at the hotel, I have the impression of entering a foreign legation in Peking during the Boxer rebellion.

Whole families are camping out in the lobby; travelers wrapped in blankets are sleeping amid their luggage. I question the staff, all of them Indians, except for a few Malayans, and I am told that just yesterday, in this grand hotel, a computerized system was installed and, before all the kinks could be eliminated, it broke down for two hours. There was no way of telling which rooms were occupied or which were free. I would have to wait.

Towards evening the computer was debugged, and I managed to get into my room. Worried about my salmon, I removed it from the suitcase and looked for the minibar.

As a rule, in normal hotels, the minibar is a small refrigerator containing two beers, some miniature bottles of hard liquor, a few tins of fruit juice and two packets of peanuts. In my hotel, the refrigerator was family size and contained fifty bottles of whisky, gin, Drambuie, Courvoisier, eight large Perriers, two Vitelloises and two Evians, three half-bottles of champagne, various cans of Guinness, Pale Ale, Dutch beer, German beer, bottles of white wine both French and Italian and, besides peanuts, also cocktail crackers, almonds, chocolates and Alka-Seltzer. There was no room for the salmon. I pulled out two roomy drawers of the dresser and emptied the contents of the bar into them, then refrigerated the salmon, and thought no more about it. The next day, when I came back into the room at four in the afternoon, the salmon was on the desk, and the bar was again crammed almost solid with gourmet products. I opened the drawers, only to discover that everything I had hidden there the day before was still in place. I called the desk and told them to inform the chambermaids that if they found the bar empty it wasn't because I had consumed all its contents, but because of the salmon. They replied that the information had to be given to the central computer, but because most of the staff spoke no English, verbal instructions were not accepted. All orders had to be given in BASIC.

I pulled out another two drawers and transferred the new contents of the bar, where I then replaced my salmon. The next day at four P.M., the salmon was back on the desk, and it was already emanating a suspect odor.

The bar was crammed with bottles large and small, and the four drawers of the dresser suggested the back room of a speakeasy at the height of Prohibition. I called the desk again and they told me they were having more trouble with the computer. I rang the bell for room service and tried to explain my situation to a youth with his hair in a bun; he spoke only a dialect that, as an anthropologist colleague explained later, was heard only in Kefiristan at about the time Alexander the Great was wooing Roxana.

The next morning I went down to sign the bill. It was astronomical. It indicated that in two and a half days I had consumed several hectoliters of Veuve Clicquot, ten liters of various whiskies, including some very rare single malts, eight liters of gin, twenty-five liters of mineral water (both Perrier and Evian, plus some bottles of San Pelle-

grino), enough fruit juice to protect from scurvy all the children in
UNICEF's care, enough almonds, walnuts and peanuts to induce vomiting in the attendant on the autopsy of the characters in *La grande
bouffe*. I tried to explain, but the clerk, with a betel-blackened smile,
assured me that this was what the computer said. I asked for a lawyer,
and they brought me an avocado.

Now my publisher is furious and thinks I'm a chronic freeloader.
The salmon is inedible. My children insist I cut down on my drinking.

—translated by William Weaver

Edward Gorey

✠

The Admonitory Hippopotamus:
or, Angelica and Sneezby

One day when she was five Angelica was in the gazebo, playing snap with her brothers.

Suddenly she caught sight of something rising from the ha-ha.

It was a spectral hippopotamus. "Fly at once!" he said. "All is discovered."

She remembered the bread pudding under the carpet.

She ran into the woods, and was not found by the servants until the sun was going down.

Seven years later she sneaked away from St. Torpid's to buy forbidden jujubes.

The hippopotamus attracted her attention from the back of a pantechnicon. "Fly at once!" he said. "All is discovered."

She remembered the novel with yellow covers at the bottom of the laundry bag.

She jumped on a tram, and was noticed only at closing time in a distant cinema.

Ten years came and went, and Angelica was being married for the first time.

The hippopotamus peered out at her from behind the altar. "Fly at once!" he said. "All is discovered."

She remembered the packet of letters up the chimney.

She pedaled off on a stolen bicycle; it was several weeks before she was recognized in a remote seaside lodging.

Another ten years passed; Angelica, at the height of her notoriety, attended a picnic in the Bois de Boulogne.

The hippopotamus showed himself on the top of a rock. "Fly at once!" he said. "All is discovered."

She remembered the emeralds in the cold cream.

She drove off in her host's Panhard-Levassor, and was not seen again until the season had begun in Cagnes-sur-Mer.

Seventeen years went by; on the *Seppuku Maru* in the Indian Ocean, Angelica had an assignation with a Eurasian stoker.

The hippopotamus clambered up the ladder from the second-class deck. "Fly at once!" he said. "All is discovered."

She remembered the screwdriver in the well.

She followed an inflatable raft overboard. It was thirty-eight days before she was picked up.

A quarter of a century afterwards, Angelica, now the Dowager Duchess of Paltry, was perambulating the grounds of Shambles.

The hippopotamus emerged from a grotto made of shells. "Fly at once!" he said. "All is discovered."

She remembered the broiled *champignons veneneux* on toast.

She took the first down train from Much Fidgeting; next morning she was apprehended in the aisles of Listless and Earshot.

In her eighty-sixth year Angelica was sinking rapidly.

The hippopotamus floated in at the window. "Fly at once!" he said. "All is discovered."

But she could not remember what it was he meant.

Her body fell back lifeless on the bed.

Angelica rode away on the back of the hippopotamus.

Eugene Walter

✠

from Milking the Moon

A PARTY AT MOMA

We called ourselves The Apparition Group. It was Jose García Villa, the poet Howard Moss, Robert DeVries, the painter Ruth Hershberger, Josephine Herbst, this wonderful painter Ann Troxel and the actress Marie Donnet. We rehearsed it for a week and timed it, because I wanted some things to happen simultaneously. Nobody else knew what we were doing. We sent little postcards to some well-known artists and writers, saying: The Apparition Group, Sunday at 3:00, August the so-and-so, Museum of Modern Art garden.

I had chosen Edith Zelnicker's birthday. She's my friend from Mobile. I wrote to her and her husband and said, "I'm having a little party for you. You and Edwin come to the Museum of Modern Art and you'll see a little pink crepe-paper flower. That's your table." They thought I was just doing something silly like I always do, that I would come dressed as Santa Claus in August or something like that. They came nervously and sat at the table indicated. They're old Mobile Jewish: conservative and no public display of any kind.

What happened was this: at precisely three o'clock, a very beautiful little boy about ten years old, wearing a rather odd sort of blue hussar jacket and blue short pants, came into the middle of the garden, lifted his toy trumpet and played a fanfare and then ran. That was the only sound we made. So everybody was looking. Then I appeared. I was the Very Sick Poet. My hair was jet black, done with

Kiwi Shoe Polish, and my face was dead white with black eyebrows and shadows under my eyes. I carried a large aspirin bottle and a bouquet of dead white roses. I was dressed in a southern white linen suit with a flowing tie. My jacket pockets were full of diamond flitters—sequin dust. With this I made a little path behind me. Then Jean Garrigue came in as the witch of Christopher Street. She was no longer blond. I had dyed her hair jet black and we added ostrich plumes to her natural curls. She wore black to the floor and this fringed black cape with sequins. She carried a basket of four kittens wearing tiny little ballet skirts and came precisely on my path of sequin dust.

I went to the central table where some tourists were sitting. I put my aspirin down and my dead white roses and in my best Boris Karloff voice, I said, "I'm terribly sorry; this table is taken." They got up and ran. They *ran*. So I sat down and Jean Garrigue came and sat opposite me. She turned the kittens in their ballet skirts loose under the table. We sat and talked in total gibberish. The Filipino boys running the drink booth were so enchanted they brought us drinks on the house right away. The soft-drink people went to the armed guard and said, "They can't do this here. They can't do this here." The delightful German refugee guard who was always there said, "Well they bought their admission tickets . . ."

Suddenly, Garrigue and I stopped our conversation. We raised our champagne glasses, clinked them, and that was the moment when Robert DeVries got up from the table in the corner, hung several globes of colored paper in the trees and started blowing soap bubbles. He was dressed in a proper double-breasted business suit, white shirt and necktie, looking as though he might be a young Wall Street lawyer. When he started blowing bubbles, that was the signal for all our cohorts dressed as ordinary citizens throughout the garden to do the same. Suddenly, there were globes of colored paper in every tree and the whole garden was full of soap bubbles.

Everybody was in silent awe. I looked up and the whole glass wall of the second floor was smashed noses looking into the garden. Then people started sort of coming timidly out of the museum. Nobody was looking at pictures by then.

Jean Garrigue and I sat there and resumed our conversation in an unknown language. People were gathering around staring at us, but we didn't notice anybody. Then this woman in a raincoat with a hood appeared, staring at us. She was very pale with long green hair and a kind of mermaid's costume. This was Ann Troxel. I had copied the Graham Sutherland painting of a chartreuse, red and white beetle. She was carrying it like a baby and rocking it and staring at us. Then the crowd was staring at her. Marie Donnet floated in like a dream figure in a bright red dress of chiffon to the ground and evening makeup, with rhinestone earrings to her knees and a cigarette holder three feet long. At that moment, Jose García Villa was supposed to come in the back door with purple hair, an old-fashioned movie camera, and start filming us and then pull endless yards of tinsel out of the camera and throw it around. But he lost his nerve. Howard Moss was supposed to come in and do something but he lost his nerve and said, "You all are going to be arrested." We said, "No we are not. We bought our tickets. We are not making any noise." The only sound was the initial trumpet and our little nonsense conversation at the table. Everything else was done in silence. The whole idea was silence, except for the little fanfare and our conversation.

By this time the crowd was going mad, trying to talk to us, asking us, "What does it mean? Who are you? What does it mean?" The one guy I remember in the crowd—all the effort was worth it if only for him, this little fat man. He had to have been from somewhere way off. He was climbing onto his table and snapping pictures and shouting, "I just happened to have my camera! I just happened to have my camera!" You could tell he was the guy who sees a train wreck, or a skyscraper collapse, and he's never got his camera when he needs it. He kept saying, "I just happened to have my camera!" For once in his life, he had his camera when he needed it.

At a given moment, we all got up, went through the garden and handed out miniature French playing cards. Everybody got a playing card. People said, "Oh, they are advertising something." Typical American reaction: the meaning is that they are advertising something. But our message was, the moral of the whole thing was: You too can play.

Then we all slowly congregated at the back door as planned; taxis were waiting that had been called in advance. Josephine Herbst gathered up the kittens. Somebody in the museum had called *The New*

York Times and there was a *Times* reporter who was tugging at me, saying, "What is all this? Who are you all?" Again, in my best Boris Karloff voice, I said, "We're The Apparition Group." He said, "What does it mean? What's it all about?" I said, "We are combating dailiness." I got in a taxi and was whisked off. Afterwards, I had a party in my courtyard in the Village. Jose came to apologize. He said, "I really thought we'd get in trouble." I said, "Well, since what we were doing was innocent, what trouble could we have? Seymour Lawrence or New Directions would have bailed us out if we'd been arrested."

New York was full of it for weeks. Nobody quite knew what had happened. Nor did *The New York Times*. We never told them. We never let on.

Issue 159, 2001

Pomework: An Exercise in Occasional Poetry

For a special poetry issue, this year a letter was sent to a number of poets who had previously contributed to the magazine. It said in part, "We thought it would be an interesting exercise (perhaps a welcome relief from serious work) to see what esteemed and established poets would come up with given a specific title from which to work—very much the same sort of task that poet laureates have had to perform . . . any form of verse is urged—no rules."

The editors picked eight titles, drawn from films, classic poems and flights of imagination.

Jaws
The English Are So Nice!
Howl
An Empty Surfboard on a Flat Sea
In the Dark
Lines to Seduce a Stranger an Hour Before the Ship Sails
Upon Julia's Breasts
A Lavatory in a Cathedral
"A Welcome Relief from Serious Work"—George Plimpton

Predictably enough, a few poets sent back return postcards voicing dismay ("frivolous"), others with regret they couldn't comply ("delicious idea but I'm overwhelmed"). David Wagoner wrote that his first reaction was "I don't want to do anything like that. And the next day, I wrote the poem." Charles Wright got carried away, wrote two, but upon working on the third (Upon Julia's Breasts) wrote that "when the first line, 'Whose tits these are I think I know' came tumbling out of my mouth, I reached for the envelope to enclose the two I had already written, deciding judiciously to rest upon my laurels." Seamus Heaney made us feel as if we had actually offered a service: "It so happened," he wrote, "that something floating to the surface found its proper title." We couldn't feel more honored! Perhaps the most enthusiastic entry turned out to be Albert Goldbarth's in which he combined all the titles in one poem. It concludes the pack . . .

JAWS

of cloud dispute
the sky of late afternoon,
the going sun suspended
before it drops behind the horizon
and leaves darkness to debate
whether these predatory shapes
are there still hanging in the black air
as the cold bright stars of Sagittarius
climb glittering and disclose
the prospect of their voyages, an invitation
to a freshly minted moon
to edge its way
towards the galaxy
until it stands mid-sky to show
the place where that unmappable murk
hung below and now not one
of those drifting saurians remains
beneath the high clear chart
stretched between earth and zenith.

—CHARLES TOMLINSON

Bone-ivory thins out to sparkling gauze
as the helices spell out their last revisions,
cascades of microscopic cellular flaws.

Dark quadrants in the X ray of my jaws
mark the retreating toothbed, new excisions,
the ivory thinned out to sparkling gauze.

And the synovial sea that bathed my knee withdraws,
leaving bone nubs to clickings and collisions,
cascades of calcium, microscopic flaws.

What's worse, this age of winters and failed thaws
that should clear my nights for rare auroral visions,
instead blows through my sleep like cradle-gauze

filled with teething rings, plastic tub-baths, straws
that wove about my years of small decisions
a screen against tide of cellular flaws.

Why should the ova and the menses pause
for this salt text of lapses and elisions,
bone-ivory thinning out to sparkling gauze,
cascades of tiny intracellular flaws.

—ANNE WINTERS

JAWS I
Jacqueline—
Alas—
Was
Swallowed . . .

JAWS II
(Jacqueline
Always
Was
Sumptuous.)

JACQUELINE OSHEROW

Having no jaws might be considered
by some to be a handicap, but the scarlet

haw, the cherry and the dogwood trees,
though certainly jawless, yet conduct
themselves with grace and an amazingly
flamboyant intensity of berry and bloom.

And male green midges, despite
lacking jaws, on summer evenings
perform complex aerial dances in swarms
to which females (passionately desired,
though jawless also) are attracted, seized
and gripped in mid-air consummations,
kissless consummations, I suppose.

Possessing only moving mouthparts,
the caddis-fly larvae nevertheless
can creep quite freely over rocks
in rushing river water and spin
silken nets to capture and consume
microscopic creatures having themselves
microscopically missing jaws.

The ogre-faced spider has no chin
and only pitifully diminished jaws
that hold, however, hollow fangs
through which excellent venom
travels to paralyze the punctured
bodies of botflies, wasps and other
hapless prey, thus greatly facilitating
storage and ease in feasting
for the ogre-faced spider.

Although having no jaws renders
singing awkward, jawless hagfishes
proceed in their ancient sea life
without despair over this musical
deprivation, sucking up dead animal

matter to which neither jaws nor singing
will ever be of any concern.

Clams, mussels and cockles could
be said to be composed largely
of one set of jaws, for they can open
and close their hinged, calcareous
shell coverings like jaws to admit
food. But this interpretation
is advanced only by scholars, madmen
and dreamers who are obsessed
with jaws, finding them in every
phenomenon of earth, sky and sea.

Jaws, as we have noted, are not
entirely necessary to the good life.
Jawlessness even imposes a kind
of silence we might envy, encouraging,
as it must, contemplation of the inner
state—the cherry the spiritual dimensions
of its single bronze seed, for example,
the hagfishes the virtues of their primitive
spine, the clams the miracle of their
visceral mass, the ogre-faced spider
the First Cause of venom—wherein
such contemplation lies a sublimity
of pleasure far beyond the reach
of any jaws or teeth.

                                    —PATTIANN ROGERS

Because they live on blood alone, vampires
are the most specialized of the *Phyllostomidae*,

possessing a nasal thermoreceptor, anticlotting
saliva, a tongue that transfers blood to the mouth,

and kidneys that quickly offload plasma after meals.
Early vampires, drawn to the heat of infestations,

fed on eggs of screwworms and muscid flies
that nested in the wounds of large animals. Bats

thus gained incidental access to blood and underwent
a dietary change marked by adaptations for more

efficient feeding: canines that clipped, blade-thin
incisors, teeth that punctured neatly. Sanguinivory

in bats probably arrived coincident with the rise of
unique, Neotropical New World Miocene mammals

that later vanished. For vampires, the subsequent
appearance of domestic stock may have been crucial,

with humans likely intermediates in the transition.

—SIRI VON REIS

Some of our parts
are more amenable to
the mechanical arts
than others; those that
articulate, in particular:
the less gluey, the
more angular, the levers
and pliers more than
the catch basins of juices
or cloud-shaped organs
with vaguer and possibly
higher uses. Yes it is our
mantis parts that extrapolate
best as machinery—our overlaps
with the chitinous or exoskeletal,

the plates and shafts new metals
can mimic—rather than
the murky goings-on between
soft common-walled alembics.
And perhaps of all among the
class of claspers and clampers-down,
(common names given to the Will)
chiefest reigns the jaw
implacable as a nutcracker
and too close to the brain.

—KAY RYAN

Filled to its vaulted roof with flower petals,
it did seem less an aperture for the Lord
and more something of our making,
we who were counted, who had known countless
occasions we might have otherwise been swallowed by.
Being so drawn to what lay across the surfaces,
when we approached we felt ourselves
lit by beauty as wetness is so often lit. We know
what followed as the seed of all belief, and perfected as we were
by shared experience, what else was there to do but see the sea
of Anemones and Trout Lilies at our feet, with
Sea Lavender, Sea Rockets and Virgin's Bower everywhere
to pick, and prop the hinge of our undoing.

—KATHLEEN PEIRCE

Six queens on speed, a high-hatty defrocked priest,
Trainspotters in suede, ex-astronauts, artistes
(—Oh sorry, *contest winners*), eco-sprites,
A boxwallah languidly dissing human rights,
A Page Six mouthpiece, boutonniered old geese,
A rapster moll touting her new release,
Saddle-sore hidalgos in Hilfiger tank tops,
A talk show host and two pumped-up barhops. . . .
It was opening night. The post-performance art
Party on the media mogul's yacht, the *Descartes*,

Has kept the marina hopping til nearly dawn,
So the stars can watch the sun come up. "Like, *yawn!*"
"More urchin roe?" "When can our people meet?"
"Techno sucks, man." "But *my* wasabi's too sweet."
The wit and wisdom of the wee unsteady hours
Is mother's malt to the studio's Higher Powers.
They're all leaning on a starboard rail to sneer
At the sun, rising flush as a racketeer.
Had they lived, the brilliance wanted to blind them,
But something else is opening behind them.

—J.D. McCLATCHY

THE ENGLISH ARE SO NICE!

They like their poetry bumpty-bump,
They like their tea just so,
They like their fucking rump to rump,
They like their horses slow.

They like their speech events rotund,
They like their women thin,
They like to drink till they are stunned,
They like to parse a sin.

They like to think the Yank's a knob.
They like to see him wither,
They like to give his hand a job,
They like to lead him thither.

They like to wank and woof and toss,
They like to get it off,
They like to show you who is boss,
They like at us to scoff.

They like their champers and their gin,
They like their history,

They like to think begat's begin,
They like their sophistry.

The English are so nice, is one,
Another's clear to see,
Mother, father, sister, son,
And him and her and me.

—CHARLES WRIGHT

"I, too, was liege / To rainbows currying" pulsant bones:
So Elizabeth had two hundred Catholics burned
(Bloody Mary had loved the smoke of Protestant bones).

—AGHA SHAHID ALI

The English are so very nice
except of course when they are not.
They'll ply you with a lovely pot
of tea and scones, but then in a trice
kebab you with their rapier wit
and treat you like a piece of shit.
One minute it's a paradise
of tweedy charm, the next a wet
and caste-benighted oubliette.
But the English *are* so very nice!

—BEN DOWNING

HOWL

Startled at first, you think something
    Is being killed. Some poor maimed creature
        Needs help in the night, and all this yelping
Is a last stab before it forgets how
    To make any noise at all. You hear it
        And you want to run out the door into the darkness
With a flashlight and give first aid
    Or the comfort of quick burial,

But before you're out of bed, almost before
You're out of your easy sleep, the coyote raises
   The level of its discourse, the acute angle
     Of its muzzle and lower jaw and pours forth
The beginning of a deeply annoying solo
   Of distress, immediately answered
     And given a skewed dimension by another
From farther out in the prairie, the third and fourth
   Voices flatly and sharply fugal, singing
     We thought we were going to die today
But didn't. And listen: we won't. This is exactly
   How it sounds to die
     But we don't. So isn't it wonderful
To make any kind of music? We're promising
   The best voices and minds of our generation
     Will thrive and make their marks, then howl for the next.
                                —DAVID WAGONER

How'll I learn my lines if there isn't any script?

How'll I find my shoes if I can't find my glasses?

How'll I get to a hundred if I can't get past eleven?

How'll I get to first base if you don't open the ballpark?

How'll I get to Paris unless I review the situation?

How'll I keep the wolf from the car?

How'll I starve the fever if I've got to feed the cold?

How'll I burst Joy's grape?

How'll we make our sun stand still?

How'll we stop without a farmhouse near?

Who'll play with the mice when the cat's away?

Who'll put out the light, and then put out the light?

What'll I do with just a photograph to tell my troubles to?

What'll I do?

How'll I pass through the universities with radiant cool eyes
    hallucinating Arkansas and Blake-light tragedy among the
    scholars of war?

How'll I eat shit without having visions?

How'll I find the party?

How'll I get home?

How'll we end the war in Spain?

How'll I get to heaven?

                                        —LLOYD SCHWARTZ

KARMIC CHUTZPAH

Thousands of readers, *" 'Howl' changed my life in Libertyville
    Illinois"*
*"I saw him read Montclair State Teachers College decided be a
    poet—"*
                        —Allen Ginsberg, "Fame & Death"

Thermal mounting on thermal and voice
on voice on glorifying voice on wings
of quotes uplifting breath after last breath
—death-bound to his bed in New York,
a poet daydreams billowing puffscapes,
crag and dome and tower and crown:
the testimonial-swollen thunderhead
of mourners' throats celebrating now
the swerves he caused, the turns, the turnings-
on-to, the churning . . . making light as if
gravity didn't darken in these
    . . . and bursts in broken flashes and
ruptured vortices and raindrops . . .

—and, swept off its orchis petal perch
in Ulan Bator, a butterfly
like a bright idea,
helplessly cartwheeling out of the sky,
has struck the poet Toghun dead.

—IRVING FELDMAN

PERIODONTAL ABSCESS

When "hyperemia and infiltration of leukocytes
is marked"
and the submaxillary gland (the one along

the jawbone) swells hard
and the pain fills tight,
it's off to the dentist (your own out of town)

if one can be found
not off on Friday or not away on a beep signal
or "not seeing patients this afternoon

because of all the paperwork to catch up on"
for a little curettage, the bright, shiny
instruments blundering in down

along the roots to
"stir things up"
so the pus can drain

(a slow transport by blood ooze)
this followed by a two-minute
Merthiolate soak-pack of cotton pellets:

feels better already:
go home and every four or five hours
rinse, holding the water over the tooth,

with saline
solution (1 tablespoon of salt to
8 oz of water) as hot as you can bear it:

until you've used all the water up:
this old-fashioned stuff beats antibiotics
if it works, but doesn't if it doesn't.

—A.R. AMMONS

AN EMPTY SURFBOAD ON A FLAT SEA

will always gleam in sunlight. There it is,
paint chipped off, still afloat. Now I recall
that day when harsh winds blew into a gale
and lashed a man who climbed a slab like this,

lay prone on green wood, rose up on one knee,
arms flailing, stood and walked high waves to shore.
On land, he stroked his wetsuit, slicked back hair,
kissed the plank for luck, then turned to sea.

As the surfer hauled it, he and the board
were one, a tall cross for a gravestone marker.
I shouted, "Stop!" as though he were no stranger.
He vanished and raced back. I shook in fear

for us who risk the breaker's ride and fall
or skid to firm sand and survive the gale.

—GRACE SCHULMAN

You can hardly call him a flat-earther since the roundness of it
wasn't yet in question. This was back in the wonder days when a
map was a new invention and a man with his mind on stars could
end up in a well. The earth, he said, floated on the air as a leaf
floats on the water.

The next time you begin your descent towards Shannon and see the
island steady as she goes, the next time you cross some estuary
bridge beneath the air socks or see an empty surfboard on the surf,
spare a thought for Aneximenes and his floating world.

—SEAMUS HEANEY

Dewey Weber or Hobie, it doesn't sing to me, this Malibu imagery.
All cocoa buttery, I knew such things, sunburned in bikini strings.
I knew for empty. And empty is bored on an ocean of possibility,
    see?
So bingo, no bitchin' allegory from me as Sandra Dee. No beach
blanket simile. Nothing Gidget cute in a wetsuit. Just this surfer girl's
testimony, who in reality lived the movie (while never feelin' groovy).
Still they can depress me, sand-castle success and Funicello
    fantasy.
So old *Paris Review,* let me hang ten with you and type what's true.
I'll be the muse's slave before I ever catch another wave or submit
    a poem
this depraved. Now go zinc your nose, curl your toes and publish
    prose.

—SUSAN KINSOLVING

    i.
    Today's lecture on absence:
    take the ocean and its glass eye.
    The way waves travel, it's a miracle
    they ever arrive—always late,
    berating each other until
    the front-runner dissipates.

    Take the human and its water eye,
    marrying the sea's interruptions
    into a level surface that dares the peripheral:
    find something else besides me.
    The visionary fan flares, inclusive.
    There is nothing else besides you.

ii.
I will call that wave: mine.
The pleasures of ownership cannot be measured,
though one can paddle out, skim
each saline swell, size up the height
from peak to trough, how long
for the swash to double over,
waiting at the break line—
and as you ride in, finding
the shoulder, the face, the wave
unfolds, forgiving,
even though someone once told you
he didn't know what forgiveness meant.

iii.
Today's lecture on presence:
there is no such thing as a flat sea.
Meet loss's spouse, belonging.

—PATTY SEYBURN

Reminds me once again that good swimmers drown
    & that the will is vexed so easily.
       I paddled beyond the surf, the ripping sea,
The magnesium horizon far withdrawn,

&, napping, saw three dark fish drop like something thrown
    thus in dream three coins falling through the sea
       (I said the will is vexed so easily.
The ripping sea becalmed. Good swimmers drown.)

& I dropped below that spar of glass, the light withdrawn
    Through that bubbled dome & could barely see—
       Swimming upward yet I fell—the emerald sea
& a starling-cloud of brit unfolding on its run,

Which reminded me that good swimmers drown
    & that, like the alchemist of John Aubrey
      Who met *the spirits coming up the stairs like bees,*
The will is vexed so easily.

                    —KEVIN CANTWELL

      I used to live in Laguna Beach,
      In California, don't you know;
      I'd watch the pelicans, each by each,
      Flat-hat the whitecaps, cold as snow.

      Surf's up, surf's down, surf's still as stealth,
      The boys came down to the sea at dawn—
      Surfboards and wet suits bright as delft,
      They'd hit the water and get it on.

      Anita Street was my address,
      Ten steps and a jump from ocean's edge;
      I'd see them armada out and bless
      What gods there were who'd booked my pledge

      That they could hair me, bolt and all,
      Before I'd hang a ten or one,
      Before I'd join *maudits* in thrall
      And to rig-tied riptide run.

      And even when I saw the board,
      Empty on the empty sea,
      Flat as a waffle, flat as a Ford
      Under a bad soprano's C,

      I prayed the x-tide would grab its thong,
      Its ankle noose and pull it back,
      And keep it offshore half as long
      As Coleridge kept his ship intact.

But on it came, inexorably,
On wave pumped up, on wave gone slack,
Until it stalled, and I could see
It had my name across its back

In golden script and golden flake.
But I was nowhere to be seen
Upon it, or upon its wake,
Along the beach or in the dream

I told myself this surely was
Or would become, unless that board,
So lateral, so numinous,
Toute de suite withdrew its gilt untoward

Beyond the clamor of the ocean,
And flatten as it went the wake
Of waves and other sundry motion,
And calm the waters like a lake,

And ease the letters of my name
Under the wing-tipped water's lid,
And let my one ride others blame
A non-occurrence on The Kid,

Mirabile dictu, who's appeared
Out of the sunshine's back-slant lean
sans board, sans suit, sans gloves, sans beard,
Deus dropped down in his machine,

Who paddled westward on it now
Toward Catalina's northmost bend,
The sea flecks golden at its prow,
The sunlight golden on The End.

                    —CHARLES WRIGHT

IN THE DARK

STRANGE LOVE
It was night that made him strange,
not his gold spectacles or the strained
lay of his skin. Always I say love
before it's strange enough, or strange
at all, but this time, Doctor, I love
our silence, the pale gray stain
his eyes leave in my dreams, the strange
burning of his fingers, strangling
in his long kissing, and the straggle
hope burns, a borealis to strafe
my retinas in the dark. A goat strays
through my dreams, Doctor, a crazy dove,
and from Pontormo, a woman struck
blind, her arms raised against the stranger.

—HONOR MOORE

Does *this* hurt? Yes.
Does it hurt now? Yes, yes.
No stains, no strings

that catch, words that parch. No stirrup
slicking in the pivot, Doctor,
no blue-lit whisper

in the vascular canal.
Just circumference
cinched to the center,

of concavity, of rupture,
of torsion, of arc and aim,
fixing the limbs to the digits,

stitch stitch.
Name it ashcan, night-welt,
blister—along, above.

Call it sear-in-the-skull,
heap, hovel.
Philtre; love.

—KAREN VOLKMAN

THE ENGINEER FORMERLY KNOWN AS STRANGELOVE

Mein Führer, they called me Doctor Strangelove
in the 1960s. This now they'd dare not do.
Right and Left then thought in Perverts, like you
but now it's Doctor Preference, Doctor Paralimbic—

I've also left the White race. The ac-
cident of pallor became not worth the flak.
I won't join another. Race is decadent.
Many will hope that this pains you, mein Führer.

In my third sunrise century, Germany
has reconquered Europe on her knees;
this is one of few non-virtual realities
but the flag of the West's now a gourmet tablecloth.

The Cold War is a Dämmerung of dead Götter
but I am still in cutting-edge high tech
in a think-tank up to my neck
I rotate, projecting scenarios.

In one, nearly every birth's a clone
of Elvis, of Guevara, of Marilyn
and hosts more. Few new people get born
then nostalgia for nostalgia collapses.

Of your copies, one's a Trappist, to atone;
the other went through school and never heard of you.
Creased off-register people, fading as they relax?
Those are traveling on the cheap, by 3-D fax.

Marxists will resurge by bringing sexual equality.
Every wallflower will be subject to compulsory
love from the beautiful; deprivation makes Tory.
Evolution likewise, that condones and requires

extinctions will trip the moral wires
of Green thought and become a fascist outlaw.
Darwin will be reread in tooth and claw.
In another projection, most of life is Virtual.

War is in space, in the trenches, in chain armor:
for peace, just doff the Stahlhelm. But some maniac
will purloin a real nuke for his psychodrama—
It's said you would have done the like, mein Führer.

In that model, too, the screen replaces school
and language (alas, English) regains the flavorful
and becomes again inventive, once post-intellectual.
Media story-selection and, in the end, all commentary

will be outlawed as censorship. Like fashion
they will be aspects of the crime Assault.
Direct filming of our underlit dreams will replace them
and poverty, though never called a fault,

will be stamped out by the United World Mafia,
generals and tycoons getting excised like tumors
if they try to impede the conversion to consumers
of all their millionfold peons and garbage sorters.

To forestall migration, all places will be Where the Action is.
People will wear their showers, or dress in light and shade.
Every illness short of duplicity will be cured—
here the Doctor wallowed, and his speech became obscured.

—LES MURRAY

LINES TO SEDUCE A STRANGER AN HOUR BEFORE THE SHIP SAILS

Bilbao, February 14, 2000

A stranger—*Is* it a total stranger?
And what kind of ship?
It's too late for it to be an "angel":
we've changed our chip.

But the "stranger"—If this were an airplane
and if—*iepa!*—I'd kept
my desire to "seduce," acute old angle
inclined to accept,

I'd hereby erase every sign of longing, sadness, anger,
love in the eyes, leaving intact our lips.
If the boat were *itsasontzia,* a seagoing one, and the only ship
in *itsasoa*—the sea—the waves

to the port onomatopoeically making breakers around it
in their selfsame *itsasoa* way,
I might be inclined to—or if, as in the movie, a last train
were leaving a station—to just do it.

If the vessel were merely a museum, it could be arranged,
I suppose, to lose my grip.
But it isn't a stranger at all, for all it's saying
"Zuk nirekiko sentitzen

duzuna—adibidez"—just what a total stranger might say,
or no? I didn't get what it meant
at first, while wanting to know. *Zuk sentitzen duzuna,*
"what you feel," did (since I feel) make sense.

Nire= I got fast, from the one-word "with me," *nirekin*—eighth-
most earth-shaking sound at the time, of thousands.
But =*kiko?* Would someone prefer a more nearly total stranger
to so few clothes? "What you feel for me—for instance,"

if "for" = -*kiko*. Metallic funnels, bellbuoys—what else?—the
airport windsock. Perhaps I adore not taking
in meaning fully? I can remember with bliss the first-time shock
of "*nirekin*." The root of this "for" won't be mistaken.

Who knows what a so-called ship, in an hour, might take
me from? *Nirekiko sentitzen*
duzuna—adibidez. What might even a stranger
have done to warrant a "seduction"?

The remainder—your sweet suffix, our longer ending—is not an
evasion. Only what and how—all but who, where—get silenced:
"What you feel for me" was no product of merely waking imagination,
isn't "about," in the mind, or only just vaguely different.

How do I say, again, what someone I've heard has said? *Hori dela.*
You as a stranger had said *Hori da*—"*That's* it!"
whenever I heard the lyric. Mine *zurekiko*, too: *hori dela.*
Not so strange at all after all. *Hori da*—and not if.

—ELIZABETH MACKLIN

          when you walk your feet   break through and find
                a fallen   and I will save your life
                and mine   we know our need
              the need to pay   attention wavers
              the water to walk on   where glitters

              the wash of sun   on skin
            a recompense   even as gathering
                  damage   warns
          you heeded warnings   in your past
              your little life   still you will
              not move   but feel the light
          particular caress   my hand on your back
            this best hand   takes your right hand and
            we feel the day   descend piece by piece
        a cumulation of catastrophe   some small
            deaths out there   huddled in the light
      your skin exceeds you   I have touched the skin
              as if sudden terror   as if
          your skin were quieter   the trembling
              is of the air   the elemental furor
        neither yours nor mine   this final hour forms
            a skin upon itself   then a body beneath
        when we walk our feet   break through and find
            a fallenness   and we will live this life

                                        —BIN RAMKE

It seems to me everything would depend on the stranger.
And the facts of departure:
is it she or I who is sailing away alone;
or is each of us seeing someone off;
or—best of all—are we leaving together?
If the latter, we'll have the entire voyage—
preferably five days or more—
to enjoy a full-blown affair and then part.
If not, then a half hour in a hastily booked
room overlooking the harbor
will present its own delights,
infinitely sweetened by the pressures of time.
As for the lines employed to effect
the seduction (I am purposely clinical),
no matter if she and I will be together
a week or an hour,

I would try, summoning all my wit,
not to make reference to ships
(especially the kind that pass in the night)
or to insinuate marine metaphors of any sort.
But urgency might overrule novelty,
forcing me to resort to something like:
"In your eyes I see the glittering port
that is my (your) (their) destination—
let us travel there without a ship."
And if I find I am losing her with that one,
there is always the tried-and-true to fall back on,
good, not just for embarkations,
but any occasion:
"How fortunate we are to have
so little time for words . . ."

—NICHOLAS CHRISTOPHER

All but overwhelmed by
your sudden appearance, I

•

Forgive me, it was
only the moon, but now

•

Your shadow has the quality
of substitution I seek

•

A nameless presence
is requested down below

•

My stateroom lies
in wait, my fine-tuned hour

•

The ocean roils,
and later by the bow

•

Jack of hearts, jack of hearts,
where are you leading me now?

—MELANIE REHAK

UPON JULIA'S BREASTS

Who now reads Herrick?
—Allen Tate

Since our proscriptive age cannot abide
the mannish gazing that's objectified
the female shape (both gamine-slim and more
curvaceous in its lineaments), I swore
correctness, chiefly to avoid the din
one risks to laud the callipygian.

So, turning chicken, now I praise your skin
rubbed with fresh herbs; and hungrily begin
to taste the parts you help me to prepare,
so plump, for my delight; and, ravished, dare
to broadcast that your white meat drives me wild,
dear circummortal chef, sweet Julia Child.

—DAVID YEZZI

It is bitter cold tonight at sea,
a thousand miles from any place
you might root your feet and feel at home.

Oh, what I would not give to be,
in these howling hours of wind and ice,
upon Julia's breasts, or even Joan's.

—BILLY COLLINS

How sweetly disappeared the silky distraction
of her clothes, and before that the delicacy
with which she stepped out of her shoes.

Can one ever unlearn what he knows?
Upon Julia's breasts in postcoital calm
I stared at the great world beyond—

all seems aglitter from where I was.
But soon of course the slow surge of dawn
would give way to rush hour and chores.

It would be hard to ignore the ugliness—
the brutal century, the cold, spireless malls.
I had a train to catch. Julia turned to the wall.

—STEPHEN DUNN

A LAVATORY IN A CATHEDRAL

is well concealed. No signs; no arrows. You
have to know where it is, and even then
it's easy to get delayed in the robing room

with its coat tree and waxy candelabra
and book to sign before the ceremony
(what ritual, what calendar, what year?)

and huddled travelers, some long dead. Remember
in the green room all is simultaneous
as to time, fugitive as to space,

which may be why the humble
claims of the body here go begging. Yes,
yes, there's a lavatory—over there,

that way, down the corridor—no, *down*,
farther and darker, scene behind the scenes,
obscure and labyrinthine as a dream.

Choirboys, tourists, poets scuttle past
in their respective costumes—
What men and gods are these?

What mad pursuit? What struggle to escape?—
until the urgent need to pee has vanished.
All this is true of at least one cathedral.

To reinvent the wheel of the rose window
would be a supererogatory chore.
The unacknowledged lavatory's there,

a secret for each one of us to know
and for each other of us to discover,
no sign, no arrow, cued to memory.

—RACHEL HADAS

THE HOLY LOO

for F. W. Grisbie

When, in a church or chapel's hush,
A distant toilet's heard to flush,
And in the nave, above the drone

Of psalm or sermon, all alone,
A child is hiding, a girl of three—
She's hiding in eternity
Already, in these sacred walls,
The child has learned that nature calls
As well as God, at any time,
And any life, as any rhyme,
Is balanced only if, in all,
The sacred and the natural,
Are found together, one for one,
When prayer, oath, creed or day is done.

—ELIZA GRISWOLD

"A WELCOME RELIEF FROM SERIOUS WORK"
—George Plimpton

The English are so nice! One night
during dinner at the captain's table, vicar
Houndstooth-Herringbone accidentally spilled his tea
upon Julia's breasts, and his stuttered apologies
outdid even her uplifted, overspilling delights
in airy profusion. What he didn't know,
that *I* could tell . . . she *liked* it. "If that
was *high* tea," she opined a few hours later,
taking a break in our stateroom bed
from working her jaws around my upper and nether
extremities, "where does his *low* tea get
deposited?" She was *that* kind of lady. Here's
how it happened: I'd been loitering wishfully
about the docks, looking for someone likely upon whom
I could use a few of my surefire
lines to seduce a stranger. "An hour before
the ship sails," she whispered, offering me a scented
card with her stateroom number inscribed in a dainty

lilac hand. We began by playing doctor.
Strange love—that was her specialty:
upside down; all knotted up; in a chicken outfit;
etc. And when the ship left port . . . well,
there I was, her bed toy for the length
of the voyage. At first it was exhilarating,
filling the role of sex stowaway. Sometimes
she was as spotless as a lavatory in a cathedral;
other times, *au contraire,* she was as shameless
as a confessional in a cathouse. But the truth
is, that a steady diet of even various pleasure
numbs the palate. Now, a full week
of our nautical naughtiness later, and the dual howl
of delight is more the grunt of obligation. I believe
we both look forward to our liberation
at voyage's end. Who'd guess the vasty limits
of this vessel, the *Titanic,* would eventually be confining?
And yet they are. She's waiting on the sheets,
an empty surfboard on a flat sea. And
I'll join her for a quick, eventless ride. But first
I simply need to linger at the rail here,
alone a moment, and pondering how
what used to be a passion
has become the merest exercise.

—ALBERT GOLDBARTH

Issue 154, 2001

James Merrill and David Jackson

⬓

from The Plato Club

James Merrill, with the help of David Jackson, used a Ouija board off and on since 1953, when Frederick Buechner gave him one for his birthday. Its most noted manifestation was the book-length trilogy The Changing Light at Sandover.

The idea for the following feature evolved from an interview in which Jackson reported that, using the Ouija board, he and Merrill had contacted Truman Capote in the afterlife, at a place called the Hedge. The Hedge would seem to be a kind of semipermeable screen through which the dead can peer at human life as well as eavesdrop upon the affairs of a higher heaven that only indirectly concern them. Presiding, as hostess and chief of protocol, is Alice B. Toklas. Since everyone wants to talk all at once, she decides—as she did in Gertrude Stein's Parisian salon—who should approach the tea table and in what order. Capote had little to say about his "life" in the other world; heaven was too "black" for him. But he was proud to belong to the Plato Club (founded by its namesake, who periodically looks in) where he and other writers of quality could gossip and worry about their ever-fluctuating reputations on earth. His comments, however few, inspired an editor at the Review, *Antonio Weiss, to write Jackson and Merrill a note suggesting a* Paris Review-*type interview at the Hedge with various writers who had slipped through our fingers over the years.*

To the editors' surprise and delight, Merrill and Jackson agreed. For nine afternoons in a row they sat down at their Ouija board and with

Miss Toklas's flawless instinct to guide them succeeded in capturing quite a pride of literary lions for our pages.

JULY 4, 1991

A brilliant afternoon in Stonington. DJ & JM—Hand and Scribe, as we are known in the other world—at the Ouija board, ready to write down the messages spelt out by the old overturned willowware cup.

ALICE B. TOKLAS
Dear boys I too am poised with pad & pen.

JAMES MERRILL
Did you follow *The Paris Review* interviews in your lifetime?

TOKLAS
I was on the way out when they began. I know them from periodic references up here. Most writers feel that any (good or bad) publication mentioning or printing their work is highly worthwhile.

DAVID JACKSON
Excuse me, I'm trying to light this cigarette.

MERRILL
Alice understands. She gave up smoking at eighty-six.

TOKLAS
And still look on with envy. Shall we get down to work?

MERRILL
You were with Gertrude Stein when she died. Were those really her last words: "In that case, what is the question?"

TOKLAS
Well it nearly was that.

GERTRUDE STEIN

[*Advancing.*] I stammered you see, & darling Alice put it right.

MERRILL

When we last spoke you said that, after your career as Gertrude Stein,
you'd had a brief life as an Argentine gaucho "to straighten out your
gender." May we hear more about that?

STEIN

It was far rougher than one had foreseen. My poor fundament suffered. Sometimes even the horses seemed oversexed. Yet it shed light
upon my buried libido.

MERRILL

Your libido went underground after that early novella, *Things As They
Are*. Its Jamesian donnée of American girls abroad didn't keep it from
being shot through by moments of uncanny frankness. Some critics
wish your later works had carried this further.

STEIN

At that time, dear boy, nobody went (in print) further. In the 20s sex
(seemingly free) still had to be hidden under the guise of metaphors
& other literary devices. We watch & listen with amazement to current political efforts to "clean up" sex.

MERRILL

After that male life on horseback, do you see yourself as an arbiter of
sexual politics, like Tiresias?

STEIN

I feel more like Christopher Columbus. A continent of feminists striv-
ing for equality. Though conservative myself, I agree with some of
their gender agenda. I would remove words such as *spokesman* from
all printed matter & substitute *speaker*.

MERRILL

Do minds change in heaven as they do on earth?

STEIN

Here a sublime opacity reigns, transparent only when focusing on a probable candidate for election to our midst. Not well put. I echo poor Wystan in needing pen & paper. Is that not the answer for writers?

MERRILL

What was the question?

STEIN

O dear.

JACKSON

What is your view of Hemingway now?

STEIN

He now hoes a field in Argentina. We did not find him qualified.

JACKSON

You kicked Papa out of Heaven!

MERRILL

He followed you to Paris, why not to the pampas? Was there a scene? Who is "we"?

STEIN

Much huffing & puffing, but the big bad wolf exited with a most female shriek. In the case of writers "we" are a revolving committee. Currently: Me, Plato, Sophocles, Marianne Moore, Elizabeth Bowen, Cocteau & Henry James.

MERRILL

Who appoints the Committee—Mother Nature?

STEIN

The Mother of us all (blessed be Her name) is quite indifferent to human matters unless, as in the case of the rain forest, they impede natural activity. The next Committee will be chosen by us. Us, do you

hear! Alice often cluck-clucks when we refuse entrance as with Him-
ingway [*sic*]. But I say "Dear girl, heaven is not for the shouters."

MERRILL

Who was on the Committee when you died?

STEIN

Emily Brontë & naturally our most prestigious . . . guess?

MERRILL

Tolstoy? . . . Jack London? . . . George Eliot?

STEIN

Bingo!

MERRILL

Which of your works do you still care for?

STEIN

I think a little-known volume of poetry: *Stanzas in Meditation?*

MERRILL

Oh yes—a favorite of John Ashbery's. I've glanced at it.

STEIN

Naughty Scribe. These speak, as does all poetry worth reading, from
the heart & are regulated by rhythm & form.

SKIP

[*Speaking up.*] How do you feel about the destruction of the traditional center of art in our century? Abstract expressionism was out to
eradicate the center—an impossible task, since the center is an omnis-
cient essence, like a Tibetan mandala, infinite yet constricted, which
isn't to say—

STEIN

Who has been listening?

MERRILL

Let me present our houseguest, a young painter.

STEIN

In art there has never been a center, only a perhaps. If we speak of "centers" I think of the human mind, asleep or awake. In my time we never mentioned "centers." The word suggested genitalia.

SKIP

Like your rose?

STEIN

The rose (a piece I am fearfully bored by) is in effect the mind.

JACKSON

Was *The Autobiography of Alice B. Toklas* written by you or by Alice?

STEIN

By us. She holding the pencil would say "Now let us (us!) take up your food problem." My part was looking at her sweet face bent over writing & thanking whomever for her being. Result: Some pages about A's cooking.

JACKSON

Is there anything you'd like us to ask?

STEIN

"How do you feel, Miss Stein, about the new French prime minister?" Answer: MSerable. She is, as are I must say most Frenchwomen, hopelessly female: not prolesbian (even though vast numbers practice it). Why even Margaret Thatcher allowed her husband to photograph her kissing her cook. It was not a comradely kiss.

MERRILL

What corners of the United States do you keep an eye on?

STEIN

New York, San Francisco . . . I look for signs of human compassion. It delights me to see the homeless cuddled together for warmth.

JACKSON

You're delighted by their plight?

MERRILL

No, no. It's not the homelessness that delights her but—

STEIN

Not so fast, JM. It is a statement, strong & effective, about capitalism. The statement will not be heard for 10 years. Then the politics will change & the world will be much warmer.

JACKSON

She's talking about the greenhouse effect?

STEIN

Yes. We devised it (rather, Mr. Auden devised it) as a warning. [*W.H. Auden, instead of being reincarnated or sitting on committees, bequeathed his poetic energies to the mineral or geological realms. The rise in volcanic activity over the past years is, for example, his doing.*] Not the end of the world. Mr. A. will stop the polar melt in time, & meanwhile the causes dramatically staged will have disappeared.

JACKSON

It's true, you know. I read that volcanic ash in the atmosphere serves as a cooling agent. So God doesn't mean to polish off the earth?

MERRILL

Shouldn't we steer clear of theology?

STEIN

Let Miss Stein summarize! a) God Biology did indeed create our world but his sister, Nature, rules it. b) Their most prized (ahem) creations move upward to heaven. Others are reborn. c) The system of reincarnation is therefore correct. Period.

MERRILL

I only meant that in this interview the spotlight would be trained to better effect on yourself than on the universe.

STEIN

Do admit it reveals a charming microcosm. [*Sweeps out.*]

JACKSON

Is Alice still with us?

TOKLAS

With pencil & pad. Dear Jamey & Mr. Livingstone [*Her name for David Jackson.*] ask her tomorrow about Colette. We like your artist friend. A demain.

UNICE

[*Our unicorn gatekeeper.*] Sirs! I have been eavesdropping & must add that I for one would love Miss Stein on my back, even with a whip!

Issue 122, 1992

HORRORS

Grace Paley

✠

The Little Girl

My old friend Charley that I've known for 20, 25 years stopped me in the street. He said, I've got something to tell you. Now, sit down. Right here. That was the steps of the Café Zipp in the middle of Macdougal Street. He put his hand on my knee. Then he said, now you listen, this is what happened:

Carter stop by the café early. I just done waxing. He said, I believe I'm having company later on. Let me use your place, Charley, hear?

I told him, door is open, go ahead. Man coming for the meter, (why I took the lock off). I told him Angie, my lodger, *could* be home but he strung out most the time. He don't even know when someone practicing the horn in the next room. Carter, you got hours and hours. There ain't no wine there, nothing like it. He said he had some other stuff would keep him on top. That was a joke. Thank you, brother, he said. I told him I believe I *have* tried anything, but to this day, I like whiskey. If you have whiskey, you drunk, but if you pumped up with drugs, you just crazy. Yeah hear that man, he said. Then his eyeballs start walking away.

He went right to the park. Park is full of little soft, yellow-haired baby chicks. They ain't but babies. They far from home and you better believe it, they love them big black cats walking around before lunchtime, jutting their apparatus. They think they gonna leap off that to heaven. Maybe so.

Nowadays, the spades around here got it set out for them. When I was young, *I* put that kettle to cook. *I* stirred it and stirred it, and these dudes just sucking off the gravy.

Next thing: Carter rested himself on the bench. He look this way and that. His pants is tight. His head making pictures. Along comes this child. She just straggling along. Got her big canvas pocket book and she looking around. Carter hollers out, Hey, sit down, he says. By me, here, you pretty thing. She look sideways. Sits, on the edge.

Where you from, baby? he ask her. Hey, relax, you with friends.

Oh thank you. Oh the Midwest, she says. Near Chicago. She want to look good. She ain't from maybe 800 miles.

You left home for a visit, you little dandylion you, your boyfriend let you just go?

Oh, no, she says, getting talky. I just left and for good. My mother don't let me do a thing. I got to do the breakfast dishes when I get home from school and clean and do my two brothers' room and they don't have to do nothing. And I got to be home in my room by 10 P.M. weekdays and 12 P.M. just when the fun starts Saturday and nothing is going on in that town. Nothing! It's dead, a sleeping hollow. *And the prejudice, whew!* She blushes up a little, she don't want to hurt his feelings. It's terrible and then they caught me out with a little bit of a roach I got off of some fellow from New York who was passing through and I couldn't get out at all for a week. They was watching me and watching. They're disgusting and they're so ignorant!

My! Carter says. I don't know how you kids today stand it. The world is changing that's a fact and the old folks ain't heard the news. He ruffle her hair and he lay his cheek on her hair a minute. Testing. And he puts the tip of his tongue along the tip of her ear. He's a fine-looking man, you know, a nice color, medium not too light. Only thing wrong with him is some blood line in his eye.

I don't know when I seen a prettier chick, he says. Just what we call fattening the pussy. Which wouldn't use up no time he could see. She look at him right away, Oh lord, I been trudging around. I am tired. Yawns.

He says, I got a nice place, you could just relax and rest and decide what to do next. Take a shower. Whatever you like. Anyways you do is O.K. My you are sweet. You better'n Miss America. How old you say you was?

Eighteen, she jump right in.

He look at her satisfied, but that was a lie and Carter knew it, I believe. That the Number One I hold against him. Because, why her?
Them little girls just flock, they do. A grown man got to use his sense.

Next thing: They set out for my apartment which is 6, 7 blocks
downtown. Stop for a pizza. 'Mm this is good, she says (she is so simple). She says, they don't make 'em this way back home.

They proceed. I seen Carter courting before. Canvas pocketbook
across his shoulder. They holding hands maybe and hand swinging.

Open the front door of 149, but when they through struggling up
them four flights, she *got* to be disappointed, you know my place,
nothing there. I got my cot. There's a table. There two chairs. Blanket
on the bed. And a pillow. And a old greasy pillow slip. I'm too old
now to give up my grizzly greasy head, but I sure wish I was a young
buck, I would let my Afro flare *out*.

She got to be disappointed.

Wait a minute, he says, goes to the kitchen and brings back ice water, a box of pretzels. Oh thank you, she says. Just what I wanted.
Then he says, rest yourself darling, and she lies down. Down, right in
her coffin.

He shares out a joint with her. Ain't that peaceful, he says. Oh, it
is, she says. It sure is peaceful. People don't know.

Then they finish up. Just adrifting in agreement, and he says, you
like to ball? She says, Man! Do I! Then he put up her dress and take
down her panties and tickle her here and there nibbling away. He
says, you like that baby? Man! I sure do, she says. A colored boy done
that to me once back home, it sure feels good.

Right then he gets off his clothes. Gonna tend to business. Now,
the bad thing there, is, the way Carter told it, and I know it' so, those
little girls come around looking for what they used to, hot dog. And
what they get is knock-wurst. You know we are like that. Matter of
fact, Carter did force her. Had to. She starting to holler, Ow, it hurts,
you killing me, it hurts. But Carter told me, it was her asked for it.
Tried to get away, but he had been stiff as stone since morning when
he stop by the store. He wasn't *about* to let her run.

Did you hit her? I said. Now Carter, I ain't gonna tell anyone. But I
got to know.

I might of hauled off and let her have it once or twice. Stupid little cunt asked for it, didn't she. She was so little, there wasn't enough meat on her thigh bone to feed a sick dog. She could of wriggled by the scoop in my armpit if I had let her. Our black women ain't a bit like that, I told you Charlie. They cook it up, they eat the mess they made. They proud.

I didn't let that ride too long. Carter's head moves quick, but he don't dust me. I ask him, how come when they passing the plate and you *is* presented with the choice, you say like the prettiest dude—a little of that white stuff please man?

I don't! He hollered like I had chopped his neck. And I won't! He grab my shirt front. It was a dirty old workshirt and it tore to bits in his hand. He got solemn. Shit! You right! They are poison! They killing me! That diet gonna send me upstate for nothin' but *bone* diet and I got piles as is.

Joking by the side of the grave trench. That's why I used to like him. He wasn't usual. That's why I like to pass time with Carter in the park in the early evening.

Be cool, I said.

Right on, he said.

He told me he just done shooting them little cotton head darkies into her when Mangie Angie Em poriore lean on the doorway. Girl lying on my bloody cot pulling up a sheet, crying, bleeding out between her legs. Carter had tore her up some. You know Charlie he said, I ain't one of your little Jewboy buddies with half of it cut off. Angie peering and peering. Carter stood up out of his working position. He took a quick look at Angie, hoisted his pants and split. He told me, Man, I couldn't stay there, that dumb cunt sniffling and that blood spreading out around her, she didn't get up to protect herself, she was disgusting and that low white bug your friend, crawled in from under the kitchen sink. Now on you don't live with no white junkie, hear me Charlie, they can't use it.

Where you going now Carter, I ask him. To the pigs he says and jabs his elbow downtown, I hear they looking for me.

That' exactly what he done and he never seen free daylight since.

Not too long that same day they came for me. They know where I am. At the station they said, you sleep somewhere else tonight and tomorrow night. Your place padlocked. You wouldn't want to see it, Charlie. You in the clear. We know your whereabouts to the minute. Sergeant could see I didn't know nothing. Didn't want to tell me neither. I'll explain it. They had put out a warrant for Angel. Didn't want me speaking to him. Telling him anything.

Hector the beat cop over here, can't keep nothing to himself. They are like that. Spanish people. Chatter chatter. What he said: You move Charlie. You don't want to see that place again. Bed smashed in. That little girl broken up in the bottom of the airshaft on top of the garbage and busted glass. She just tossed out that toilet window wide awake alive. They know that. Death occur on ground contact.

The next day I learned worse. Hector found me outside the store. My buffer swiped. Couldn't work. He said: Every bone between her knee and her rib cage broken, splintered. She been brutally assaulted with a blunt instrument or a fist before death.

Worse than that, on her legs high up, inside she been bitten like an animal bit her and bit her and tore her little meat she had on her. I said: All right Hector. Shut up. Don't speak.

They put her picture in the paper every day for five days and when her mother and daddy came on the fifth day, they said: The name of our child is Juniper. She is 14 years old. She been a little rebellious but the kids today all like that.

Then court. I had a small job to say, Yes it was my place, Yes, I told Carter he could use it. Yes, Angie was my roommate and sometimes he lay around there for days. He owed me two months rent. That' the reason I didn't put him out.

In court Carter said, Yes I did force her, but he said he didn't do nothing else.

Angie said, I did smack her when I seen what she done, but I never bit her your honor, I ain't no animal, that black hippie must of.

Nobody said—they couldn't drag out of anyone—they lacking the evidence who it was picked her up like she was nothing, a bag of busted bones and dumped her out the fourth floor window.

But wasn't it a shame, them two studs. Why they take it out on her? After so many fluffy little chicks. They could of played her easy. Why Carter seen it many times hisself. She could of stayed the summer.

We just like the U.N. Every state in the union stop by. She would of got her higher education right on the fourth floor front. September, her mamma and daddy would come for her and they whip her bottom, we know that. We been in this world long enough. We seen lots of the little girls. They go home, then after awhile they get to be grown womens they integrating the swimming pool and picketing the supermarket they blink their eyes and shut their mouth and grin.

But that was my room and my bed so I don't forget it. I don't stop thinking! That child. That child. And it come to me yesterday, I lay down after work: Maybe it wasn't no one. Maybe she pull herself the way she was, crumpled, to that open window. She was tore up, she must of thought she was gutted inside her skin. She must of been in a horror what she got to remember what her folks would see. Her life look to be disgusting like a squashed fish, so what she did: she made up some power somehow and raise herself up that window sill and hook herself onto it and then what I see, she just topple herself out. That' what I think right now.

That is what happened.

Galway Kinnell

※

Lackawanna

Possibly a child is not damaged immediately
but only after some time has passed.
When the parent who sits on the edge
of the bed leans over and moves an elbow
or a forearm or a hand across the place
where the child's torso divides into legs
at last gets up and goes to the door and turns
and says in an ordinary voice, "Good night,"
then in exactly eight minutes a train
in the freight yards on the other side of town
howls, its boxcar loaded up, its doors
rusted shut, its wheels clacking
over the tracks   *lacka   wanna   lacka*.
It may be that the past has the absolute force
of the law that visits parent upon child
unto the third or fourth generation, and the implacability
of vectors, which fix the way a thing
goes reeling according to where it was touched.
What is called spirit may be the exhaust-light
of toil of the kind a person goes through
years later to take any unretractable step
out of that room, even a step no longer
than a platinum-iridium bar in a vault in Paris,
and flesh the need afterwards to find

the nearest brasserie and mark with both elbows
on the zinc bar the start and the finish.
Never mind. The universe is expanding.
Soon they won't know where to look to find you.
There will be even more room when the sun dies.
It will be eight minutes before we know it is dead.
Plenty of time for the ordinary human acts
that will constitute our final mayhem.
In the case of a house there may be less room
when the principal occupants die, especially
if they refuse to leave and keep on growing.
Then in a few years the immaterial bulk
of one of them padding up from the dark
basement can make the stairs shriek
and the sleeper sit up, pivot out of bed, knock
an arm on the dresser, stand there shaking
while the little bones inside the elbow cackle.
The mind can start rippling again at any time
if what was thrown in was large, and thrown in early.
When the frequency of waves increases,
so does the energy. If pressure builds up,
someone could die from it. If they had been
able to talk with him, find out what he was going through,
the children think it would not have been him.
Inquiring into the situation of a thing
may alter the comportment, size, or shape of it.
The female nurse's elbow, for instance,
bumping a penis, could raise it up,
or the male doctor's hand, picking it up
and letting it drop a couple of times for
unexplained medical reasons, could slacken it.
Or vice versa. And the arm passing across it,
like Ockham's razor grabbed off God's chin
eight minutes before the train howls,
could simplify it nearly out of existence.
Is it possible, even, that Werner Heisenberg,
boy genius, hit on his idea in eight minutes?

The train sounds its horn and clickets over
the tracks   *lacka   wanna*   shaking up
a lot of bones trying to lie unnoticed
in the cemeteries. It stops to let off
passengers in a town, as the overturned grail
of copper and tin, lathed and fettled off
to secure its pure minor tierce, booms out
from the sanctus-turret those bulging notes
which, having been heard in childhood,
seem to this day to come from heaven.
So in memory, an elbow, which is without flesh,
touching a penis, which is without bone,
can restart the shock waves of being the one chosen,
even in shame, in a childhood of being left out.
But no one gets off. And a hand
apports in the center of a room suddenly
become empty, which the child has to fill
with something, with anything, with the ether
the Newtonian physicists manufactured
to make good the vacuums in the universe
or the nothing the God of the beginning
suctioned up off the uninhabited earth
and held all this time and now must exhale
back down, making it hard, for some, to breathe.
The hand suspended in the room still has
a look of divinity; every so often
it makes sweet sounds—music can't help it; like maggots
it springs up anywhere. The umbilical string
rubs across the brain, making it
do what it can, sing.

Ian McEwan

⌖

from The Art of Fiction CLXXIII

In 1986 I was at the Adelaide literary festival where I read the scene from *The Child in Time* in which the little girl is stolen from the supermarket. I had finished a first draft the week before and I wanted to try it out. As soon as I was done, Robert Stone got to his feet and delivered a most passionate speech. It really seemed to come from the heart. He said, "Why do we do this? Why do writers do this, and why do readers want it? Why do we reach into ourselves to find the worst thing that can be thought? Literature, especially contemporary literature, keeps reaching for the worst possible case."

I still don't have a clear answer. I fall back on the notion of the test or investigation of character, and of our moral nature. As James famously asked, What is incident but the illustration of character? Perhaps we use these worst cases to gauge our own moral reach. And perhaps we need to play out our fears within the safe confines of the imaginary, as a form of hopeful exorcism.

Issue 162, 2002

Joyce Carol Oates

⚬

Heat

It was midsummer, the heat rippling above the macadam roads. Cicadas screaming out of the trees and the sky like pewter, glaring.

The days were the same day, like the shallow mud-brown river moving always in the same direction but so slow you couldn't see it. Except for Sunday: church in the morning, then the fat Sunday newspaper, the color comics and newsprint on your fingers.

Rhea and Rhoda Kunkel went flying on their rusted old bicycles, down the long hill toward the railroad yard, Whipple's Ice, the scrubby pastureland where dairy cows grazed. They'd stolen six dollars from their own grandmother who loved them. They were eleven years old, they were identical twins, they basked in their power.

Rhea and Rhoda Kunkel: it was always Rhea-and-Rhoda, never Rhoda-and-Rhea, I couldn't say why. You just wouldn't say the names that way. Not even the teachers at school would say them that way.

We went to see them in the funeral parlor where they were waked, we were made to. The twins in twin caskets, white, smooth, gleaming, perfect as plastic, with white satin lining puckered like the inside of a fancy candy box. And the waxy white lilies, and the smell of talcum powder and perfume. The room was crowded, there was only one way in and out.

Rhea and Rhoda were the same girl, they'd wanted it that way.

Only looking from one to the other could you see they were two.

The heat was gauzy, you had to push your way through like swimming. On their bicycles Rhea and Rhoda flew through it hardly noticing, from their grandmother's place on Main Street to the end of South Main where the paved road turned to gravel leaving town. That was the summer before seventh grade, when they died. Death was coming for them but they didn't know.

They thought the same thoughts sometimes at the same moment, had the same dream and went all day trying to remember it, bringing it back like something you'd be hauling out of the water on a tangled line. We watched them, we were jealous. None of us had a twin. Sometimes they were serious and sometimes, remembering, they shrieked and laughed like they were being killed. They stole things out of desks and lockers but if you caught them they'd hand them right back, it was like a game.

There were three floor fans in the funeral parlor that I could see, tall whirring fans with propellor blades turning fast to keep the warm air moving. Strange little gusts came from all directions making your eyes water. By this time Roger Whipple was arrested, taken into police custody. No one had hurt him. He would never stand trial, he was ruled mentally unfit, he would never be released from confinement.

He died there, in the state psychiatric hospital, years later, and was brought back home to be buried, the body of him I mean. His earthly remains.

Rhea and Rhoda Kunkel were buried in the same cemetery, the First Methodist. The cemetery is just a field behind the church.

In the caskets the dead girls did not look like anyone we knew really. They were placed on their backs with their eyes closed, and their mouths, the way you don't always in life when you're sleeping. Their faces were too small. Every eyelash showed, too perfect. Like angels everyone was saying and it was strange it was *so*. I stared and stared.

What had been done to them, the lower parts of them, didn't show in the caskets.

Roger Whipple worked for his father at Whipple's Ice. In the newspaper it stated he was nineteen, he'd gone to DeWitt Clinton until he was sixteen, my mother's friend Sadie taught there and remembered him from the special-education class. A big slow sweet-faced boy with these big hands and feet, thighs like hams. A shy gentle boy with good manners and a hushed voice.

He wasn't simpleminded exactly, like the others in that class. He was watchful, he held back.

Roger Whipple in overalls squatting in the rear of his father's truck, one of his older brothers drove. There would come the sound of the truck in the driveway, the heavy block of ice smelling of cold, ice tongs over his shoulder. He was strong, round shouldered like an older man. Never staggered or grunted. Never dropped anything. Pale washed-looking eyes lifting out of a big face, a soft mouth wanting to smile. We giggled and looked away. They said he'd never been the kind to hurt even an animal, all the Whipples swore.

Sucking ice, the cold goes straight into your jaws and deep into the bone.

People spoke of them as the Kunkel twins. Mostly nobody tried to tell them apart. Homely corkscrew-twisty girls you wouldn't know would turn up so quiet and solemn and almost beautiful, perfect little dolls' faces with the freckles powdered over, touches of rouge on the cheeks and mouths. I was tempted to whisper to them, kneeling by the coffins. Hey Rhea! Hey Rhoda! Wake *up*!

They had loud slip-sliding voices that were the same voice. They weren't shy. They were always first in line. One behind you and one in front of you and you'd better be wary of some trick. Flamey-orange hair and the bleached-out skin that goes with it, freckles like dirty raindrops splashed on their faces. Sharp green eyes they'd bug out until you begged them to stop.

Places meant to be serious, Rhea and Rhoda had a hard time sitting still. In church, in school, a sideways glance between them could do it. Jamming their knuckles into their mouths, choking back giggles. Sometimes laughing escaped through their fingers like steam hissing. Sometimes it came out like snorting and then none of us could hold back. The worst time was in assembly, the principal up there telling us that Miss Flagler had died, we would all miss her. Tears shining in the woman's eyes behind her goggle-glasses and one of the twins gave a breathless little snort, you could feel it like flames running down the whole row of girls, none of us could hold back.

Sometimes the word *tickle* was enough to get us going, just that word.

I never dreamt about Rhea and Rhoda so strange in their caskets sleeping out in the middle of a room where people could stare at them, shed tears and pray over them. I never dream about actual things, only things I don't know. Places I've never been, people I've never seen. Sometimes the person I am in the dream isn't me. Who it is, I don't know.

Rhea and Rhoda bounced up the drive behind Whipple's Ice. They were laughing like crazy and didn't mind the potholes jarring their teeth, or the clouds of dust. If they'd had the same dream the night before, the hot sunlight erased it entirely.

When death comes for you you sometimes know and sometimes don't.

Roger Whipple was by himself in the barn, working. Kids went down there to beg him for ice to suck or throw around or they'd tease him, not out of meanness but for something to do. It was slow, the days not changing in the summer, heat sometimes all night long. He was happy with children that age, he was that age himself in his head, sixth-grade learning abilities as the newspaper stated though he could add and subtract quickly. Other kinds of arithmetic gave him trouble.

People were saying afterward he'd always been strange. Watchful like he was, those thick soft lips. The Whipples did wrong, to let him run loose.

They said he'd always been a good gentle boy, went to Sunday school and sat still there and never gave anybody any trouble. He collected Bible cards, he hid them away under his mattress for safekeeping. Mr. Whipple started in early, disciplining him the way you might discipline a big dog or a horse. Not letting the creature know he has any power to be himself exactly. Not giving him the opportunity to test his will.

Neighbors said the Whipples worked him like a horse in fact. The older brothers were the most merciless. And why they all wore coveralls, heavy denim and long legs on days so hot, nobody knew. The thermometer above the First Midland Bank read 98° F on noon of that day, my mother said.

Nights afterward my mother would hug me before I went to bed. Pressing my face hard against her breasts and whispering things I didn't hear, like praying to Jesus to love and protect *her* little girl and keep *her* from harm but I didn't hear, I shut my eyes tight and endured it. Sometimes we prayed together, all of us or just my mother and me kneeling by my bed. Even then I knew she was a good mother, there was this girl she loved as her daughter that was me and loved more than that girl deserved. There was nothing I could do about it.

Mrs. Kunkel would laugh and roll her eyes over the twins. In that house they were "double trouble"—you'd hear it all the time like a joke on the radio that keeps coming back. I wonder did she pray with them too. I wonder would they let her.

In the long night you forget about the day, it's like the other side of the world. Then the sun is there, and the heat. You forget.

We were running through the field behind school, a place where people dumped things sometimes and there was a dead dog there, a collie with beautiful fur but his eyes were gone from the sockets and the maggots had got him where somebody tried to lift him with her foot and when Rhea and Rhoda saw they screamed a single scream and hid their eyes.

They did nice things—gave their friends candy bars, nail polish, some novelty key chains they'd taken from somewhere, movie stars' pictures framed in plastic. In the movies they'd share a box of popcorn not noticing where one or the other of them left off and a girl who wasn't any sister of theirs sat.

Once they made me strip off my clothes where we'd crawled under the Kunkels' veranda. This was a large hollowed-out space where the earth dropped away at one end, you could sit without bumping your head, it was cool and smelled of dirt and stone. Rhea said all of a sudden, Strip! and Rhoda said at once, Strip!—come *on!* So it happened. They wouldn't let me out unless I took off my clothes, my shirt and shorts, yes and my panties too. Come *on* they said whispering and giggling, they were blocking the way out so I had no choice. I was scared but I was laughing too. This is to show our power over you, they said. But they stripped too just like me.

You have power over others you don't realize until you test it.

Under the Kunkels' veranda we stared at each other but we didn't touch each other. My teeth chattered because what if somebody saw us? Some boy, or Mrs. Kunkel herself? I was scared but I was happy too. Except for our faces, their face and mine, we could all be the same girl.

The Kunkel family lived in one side of a big old clapboard house by the river, you could hear the trucks rattling on the bridge, shifting their noisy gears on the hill. Mrs. Kunkel had eight children, Rhea and Rhoda were the youngest. Our mothers wondered why Mrs. Kunkel had let herself go—she had a moon-shaped pretty face but her hair was frizzed ratty, she must have weighed two hundred pounds, sweated and breathed so hard in the warm weather. They'd known her in school. Mr. Kunkel worked construction for the county. Summer evenings after work he'd be sitting on the veranda drinking beer, flicking cigarette butts out into the yard, you'd be fooled almost thinking they were fireflies. He went bare chested in the heat, his upper body dark like stained wood. Flat little purplish nipples inside his chest hair the girls giggled to see. Mr. Kunkel teased us all, he'd mix Rhea and Rhoda up the way he'd mix the rest of us up like it was too much trouble to keep names straight.

Mr. Kunkel was in police custody, he didn't even come to the wake. Mrs. Kunkel was there in rolls of chin fat that glistened with sweat and tears, the makeup on her face was caked and discolored so you were embarrassed to look. It scared me, the way she grabbed me as soon as my parents and I came in. Hugging me against her big balloon breasts sobbing and all the strength went out of me, I couldn't push away.

The police had Mr. Kunkel, for his own good they said. He'd gone to the Whipples, though the murderer had been taken away, saying he would kill anybody he could get his hands on, the old man, the brothers. They were all responsible he said, his little girls were dead. Tear them apart with his bare hands he said but he had a tire iron.

Did it mean anything special, or was it just an accident, Rhea and Rhoda had taken six dollars from their grandmother an hour before? Because death was coming for them, it had to happen one way or another.

If you believe in God you believe that. And if you don't believe in God it's obvious.

Their grandmother lived upstairs over a shoe store downtown, an apartment looking out on Main Street. They'd bicycle down there for something to do and she'd give them grape juice or lemonade and try to keep them a while, a lonely old lady but she was nice, she was always nice to me, it was kind of nasty of Rhea and Rhoda to steal from her but they were like that. One was in the kitchen talking with her and without any plan or anything the other went to use the bathroom then slipped into her bedroom, got the money out of her purse like it was something she did every day of the week, that easy. On the stairs going down to the street Rhoda whispered to Rhea what did you *do?* knowing Rhea had done something she hadn't ought to have done but not knowing what it was or anyway how much money it was. They started in poking each other, trying to hold the giggles back until they were safe away.

On their bicycles they stood high on the pedals, coasting, going down the hill but not using their brakes. *What did you do! Oh what did you do!*

Rhea and Rhoda always said they could never be apart. If one didn't know exactly where the other was that one could die. Or the other could die. Or both.

Once they'd gotten some money from somewhere, they wouldn't say where, and paid for us all to go to the movies. And ice cream afterward too.

You could read the newspaper articles twice through and still not know what he did. Adults talked about it for a long time but not so we could hear. I thought probably he'd used an ice pick. Or maybe I heard somebody guess that who didn't know any more than me.

We liked it that Rhea and Rhoda had been killed, and all the stuff in the paper, and everybody talking about it, but we didn't like it that they were dead, we missed them.

Later, in tenth grade, the Kaufmann twins moved into our school district. Doris and Diane. But it wasn't the same thing.

Roger Whipple said he didn't remember any of it. Whatever he did, he didn't remember. At first everybody thought he was lying then they had to accept it as true, or true in some way, when doctors from the state hospital examined him. He said over and over he hadn't done anything and he didn't remember the twins there that afternoon but he couldn't explain why their bicycles were where they were at the foot of his stairway and he couldn't explain why he'd taken a bath in the middle of the day. The Whipples admitted that wasn't a practice of Roger's or of any of them, ever, a bath in the middle of the day.

Roger Whipple was a clean boy, though. His hands always scrubbed so you actually noticed, swinging the block of ice off the truck and, inside the kitchen, helping to set it in the icebox. They said he'd go crazy if he got bits of straw under his nails from the icehouse or inside his clothes. He'd been taught to shave and he shaved every morning without fail, they said the sight of the beard growing in, the scratchy feel of it, seemed to scare him.

A few years later his sister Linda told us how Roger was built like a horse. She was our age, a lot younger than him, she made a gesture toward her crotch so we'd know what she meant. She'd happened to see him a few times she said, by accident.

There he was squatting in the dust laughing, his head lowered watching Rhea and Rhoda circle him on their bicycles. It was a rough game where the twins saw how close they could come to hitting him, brushing him with the bike fenders and he'd lunge out not seeming to notice if his fingers hit the spokes, it was all happening so fast you maybe wouldn't feel pain. Out back of the ice house where the yard blended in with the yard of the old railroad depot next door that wasn't used any more. It was burning hot in the sun, dust rose in clouds behind the girls. Pretty soon they got bored with the game though Roger Whipple even in his heavy overalls wanted to keep going. He was red-faced with all the excitement, he was a boy who loved to laugh and didn't have much chance. Rhea said she was thirsty, she wanted some ice, so Roger Whipple scrambled right up and went to get a big bag of ice cubes!—he hadn't any more sense than that.

They sucked on the ice cubes and fooled around with them. He was panting and lolling his tongue pretending to be a dog and Rhea and Rhoda cried, Here doggie! Here doggie-doggie! tossing ice cubes at Roger Whipple he tried to catch in his mouth. That went on for a while. In the end the twins just dumped the rest of the ice onto the dirt then Roger Whipple was saying he had some secret things that belonged to his brother Eamon he could show them. Hidden under his bed mattress, would they like to see what the things were?

He wasn't one who could tell Rhea from Rhoda or Rhoda from

Rhea. There was a way some of us knew, the freckles on Rhea's face were a little darker than Rhoda's, Rhea's eyes were just a little darker than Rhoda's. But you'd have to see the two side by side with no clowning around to know.

Rhea said okay, she'd like to see the secret things. She let her bike fall where she was straddling it.

Roger Whipple said he could only take one of them upstairs to his room at a time, he didn't say why.

Okay said Rhea. Of the Kunkel twins Rhea always had to be first. She'd been born first, she said. Weighed a pound or two more.

Roger Whipple's room was in a strange place—on the second floor of the Whipple house above an unheated storage space that had been added after the main part of the house was built. There was a way of getting to the room from the outside, up a flight of rickety wood stairs. That way Roger could get in and out of his room without going through the rest of the house. People said the Whipples had him live there like some animal, they didn't want him tramping through the house but they denied it. The room had an inside door too.

Roger Whipple weighed about one hundred ninety pounds that day. In the hospital he swelled up like a balloon, people said, bloated from the drugs, his skin was soft and white as bread dough and his hair fell out. He was an old man when he died aged thirty-one.

Exactly why he died, the Whipples never knew. The hospital just told them his heart had stopped in his sleep.

Rhoda shaded her eyes watching her sister running up the stairs with Roger Whipple behind her and felt the first pinch of fear, that something was wrong, or was going to be wrong. She called after them in a whining voice that she wanted to come along too, she didn't want to wait down there all alone, but Rhea just called back to her to be quiet and wait her turn, so Rhoda waited, kicking at the ice cubes melting in the dirt, and after a while she got restless and shouted up to them—the door was shut, the shade on the window was drawn—saying she was going home, damn them she was sick of waiting she said and she was going home. But nobody came to the door or looked out the window, it was like the place was empty. Wasps had built one of those nests that look like mud in layers under the eaves and the only sound was wasps.

Rhoda bicycled toward the road so anybody who was watching would think she was going home, she was thinking she hated Rhea! hated her damn twin sister! wished she was dead and gone, God damn her! She was going home and the first thing she'd tell their mother was that Rhea had stolen six dollars from Grandma: she had it in her pocket right that moment.

The Whipple house was an old farmhouse they'd tried to modernize by putting on red asphalt siding meant to look like brick. Downstairs the rooms were big and drafty, upstairs they were small, some of them unfinished and with bare floorboards, like Roger Whipple's room which people would afterward say based on what the police said was like an animal's pen, nothing in it but a bed shoved into a corner and some furniture and boxes and things Mrs. Whipple stored there.

Of the Whipples—there were seven in the family still living at home—only Mrs. Whipple and her daughter Iris were home that afternoon. They said they hadn't heard a sound except for kids playing in the back, they swore it.

Rhoda was bent on going home and leaving Rhea behind but at the end of the driveway something made her turn her bicycle wheel back . . . so if you were watching you'd think she was just cruising around for something to do, a red-haired girl with whitish skin and freckles, skinny little body, pedaling fast, then slow, then coasting, then fast again, turning and dipping and criss-crossing her path, talking to herself as if she was angry. She hated Rhea! She was furious at Rhea! But feeling sort of scared too and sickish in the pit of her belly knowing that she and Rhea shouldn't be in two places, something might happen to one of them or to both. Some things you know.

So she pedaled back to the house. Laid her bike down in the dirt next to Rhea's. The bikes were old hand-me-downs, the kickstands were broken. But their daddy had put on new Goodyear tires for them at the start of the summer and he'd oiled them too.

You never would see just one of the twins' bicycles anywhere, you always saw both of them laid down on the ground and facing in the same direction with the pedals in about the same position.

Rhoda peered up at the second floor of the house, the shade drawn over the window, the door still closed. She called out Rhea? Hey

Rhea? starting up the stairs making a lot of noise so they'd hear her, pulling on the railing as if to break it the way a boy would. Still she was scared. But making noise like that and feeling so disgusted and mad helped her get stronger, and there was Roger Whipple with the door open staring down at her flush-faced and sweaty as if he was scared too. He seemed to have forgotten her. He was wiping his hands on his overalls. He just stared, a lemony light coming up in his eyes.

Afterward he would say he didn't remember anything—didn't remember anything. Big as a grown man but round shouldered so it was hard to judge how tall he was, or how old. His straw-colored hair falling in his eyes and his fingers twined together as if he was praying or trying with all his strength to keep his hands still. He didn't remember anything about the twins or anything in his room or in the icehouse afterward but he cried a lot, he acted scared and guilty and sorry, they decided he shouldn't be put on trial, there was no point to it.

Mrs. Whipple kept to the house afterward, never went out not even to church or grocery shopping. She died of cancer just before Roger died, she'd loved him she said, she always said none of it had been his fault really, he wasn't the kind of boy even to hurt an animal, he'd loved kittens especially and was a good sweet obedient boy and religious too and whatever happened it must have been because those girls were teasing him, he'd had a lifetime of being teased and taunted by children, his heart broken by all the abuse, and something must have snapped that day, that was all.

The Whipples were the ones, though, who called the police. Mr. Whipple found the girls' bodies back in the icehouse hidden under some straw and canvas.

He found them around nine that night, with a flashlight. He knew, he said. The way Roger was acting, and the fact the Kunkel girls were missing, word had gotten out. He knew but he didn't know what he knew or what he would find. Roger taking a bath like that in the middle of the day and washing his hair too and shaving for the second time and not answering when his mother spoke to him, just sitting there staring at the floor as if he was listening to something no one else could hear. He knew, Mr. Whipple said. The hardest minute of his life was in the icehouse lifting that canvas to see what was under it.

He took it hard too, he never recovered. He hadn't any choice but to think what a lot of people thought—it had been his fault. He was an old-time Methodist, he took all that seriously, but none of it helped him. Believed Jesus Christ was his personal savior and He never stopped loving Roger or turned His face from him and if Roger did truly repent in his heart he would be saved and they would be re-united in Heaven, all the Whipples reunited. He believed, but none of it helped in his life.

The icehouse is still there but boarded up and derelict, the Whipples' ice business ended long ago. Strangers live in the house and the yard is littered with rusting hulks of cars and pickup trucks. Some Whipples live scattered around the county but none in town. The old train depot is still there too.

After I'd been married some years I got involved with this man, I won't say his name, his name is not a name I say, but we would meet back there sometimes, back in that old lot that's all weeds and scrub trees. Wild as kids and on the edge of being drunk. I was crazy for this guy, I mean crazy like I could hardly think of anybody but him or anything but the two of us making love the way we did, with him deep inside me I wanted it never to stop just fuck and fuck and fuck I'd whisper to him and this went on for a long time, two or three years then ended the way these things do and looking back on it I'm not able to recognize that woman as if she was someone not even not-me but a crazy woman I would despise, making so much of such a thing, risking her marriage and her kids finding out and her life being ruined for such a thing, my God. The things people do.

It's like living out a story that has to go its own way.

Behind the icehouse in his car I'd think of Rhea and Rhoda and what happened that day upstairs in Roger Whipple's room. And the funeral parlor with the twins like dolls laid out and their eyes like dolls' eyes too that shut when you tilt them back. One night when I wasn't asleep but wasn't awake either I saw my parents standing in the doorway of my bedroom watching me and I knew their thoughts, how they were thinking of Rhea and Rhoda and of me their daughter wondering how they could keep me from harm and there was no clear answer.

In his car in his arms I'd feel my mind drift. After we'd made love or at least after the first time. And I saw Rhoda Kunkel hesitating on the stairs a few steps down from Roger Whipple. I saw her white-faced and scared but deciding to keep going anyway, pushing by Roger Whipple to get inside the room, to find Rhea, she had to brush against him where he was standing as if he meant to block her but not having the nerve exactly to block her and he was smelling of his body and breathing hard but not in imitation of any dog now, not with his tongue flopping and lolling to make them laugh. Rhoda was asking where was Rhea?—she couldn't see well at first in the dark little cubbyhole of a room because the sunshine had been so bright outside.

Roger Whipple said Rhea had gone home. His voice sounded scratchy as if it hadn't been used in some time. She'd gone home he said and Rhoda said right away that Rhea wouldn't go home without her and Roger Whipple came toward her saying yes she did, yes she *did* as if he was getting angry she wouldn't believe him. Rhoda was calling, Rhea? Where are you? Stumbling against something on the floor tangled with the bedclothes.

Behind her was this big boy saying again and again yes she did, yes she *did*, his voice rising but it would never get loud enough so that anyone would hear and come save her.

I wasn't there, but some things you know.

Rachel Wetzsteon

❧

from Home and Away

I

How different any house looks from outside
and from within. I used to circle mansions
finding out, through guessing and good luck,
what acts of kindness kept the home fires warm
and what was done in dens. Now all unpacked
I feel the leaping flame below the floor,
my dreams consist of madly smoking chimneys
turning into smoking guns. All you
who covet life behind closed doors, look out
for changing views: safe homes can be deceiving
and dusty corners, formerly the mark
of depths unsounded, or of time well spent,
become the cold, gray, fuzzy, woolly monsters
that fill the head before an idea forms.

II

I walked among the gorgeous unturned stones
with rising hopes, a pickax and a plan:
the answers I scraped free would be the bricks
I'd use to build a green and spacious home,
and in this place of knowledge I would glue

wild eyes to lush walls, grateful for the gleams
my mystery, my spur had sent my way.
What I could not predict was that there comes
a time when there are no more stones to scrape
the mossy truth from, that a house composed
of all the answers that I schemed so hard
to get could get so gray. My cellmate and
my stone, who could have known that there was such
a thing as knowing someone else too well?

III

Acting in accordance with your wishes,
let us try a quick experiment:
buy a house and set it down on firm soil
and, completing all the steps required,
fill it to the brim with embryo yous.
When little creatures hang from chandeliers
and steal your treasured hours, ask yourself
the reason for the choice: was it to fill
the wanting world with more endangered lives
like yours? Was it to cauterize old wounds?
Was it to see yourself forever blended
with a beloved other? If the first,
sheer hubris; if the second, lots of luck;
if the third, when water blends with oil.

IV

The oldest story in the book has just
revealed another chapter. There are no
competitors with bedroom eyes who send
encoded notes; no juvenile excuses;
no trio of bored, beautiful delinquents
who flutter past on bicycles, intent
on cigarettes and scandal. In their place
there is a pyramid without a base

on either side of which, the rival lives
of rugged climber, deity of parks
and doomed, descending homeowner, are stationed.
Sometimes they meet in a productive summit
but even then, they cannot miss the sight
of skating eros, red-faced at the bottom.

V

Something, love, is singing in the shower
but it is not me; all the spouts are on
but rather than warm water, I suspect
a flood of doubts comes crashing on my brain.
Wise fools have always said that when you woo,
a breathing world surrounds you; what they save
for later revelations on the stairwell
is how you stand there, listening for clues
leading to the arrest of household objects.
Accessories I use to tame my hair
remind me of the hairpin turns we used
to skirt; cigar butts, fuming in an ashtray,
form just a tiny portion of the troops
gathering daily in this screaming house.

VI

Provocateurs and spies have been among us,
sensitive eyes who knew what we were up to
when we exhaled tornadoes; and when they were
dead to the world or elsewhere, there were portents:
great gusts of rain approved our resolutions,
sunshine meant watch and wait. But in this big house
nobody seems to notice; I could drop hints,
swallow a capsule or a morning toad,
or I could claw the walls until the day came
and there would still be no one there to see it,
no way of telling my heart was not in it

except the banner of decisive action,
the calling of the sharp, impatient helper
that rattles in the cupboard, set on escape.

VII

Before I stab, a moment of polemic:
little fish, aspiring to be big ones,
cannot observe a couple without smirking,
avidly drain the color from our lives
until there is no unrest in our room
except the paper flame that they would put there
to fuel their furnace: we become an excuse.
Great unveilers, chroniclers of the war zone,
certainly talk of the eternal struggle
over the reins, but for our sake remember
there is no background as explosive as its
passionate foreground: get it through your head that
we are not cloth dolls with holes and bulges
but flesh in houses, killing with our own hands.

VIII

We may have our problems, rash explainer,
but at least we are not walking automata,
holding hands to keep a toiler busy,
getting mad to help a tirade along.
The forces of production knock on our door;
I scare them away by the timbre of my voice.
Ghosts barge in and reshuffle the blood on the wall
until it resembles a toolbit or a mother,
but the blood keeps pumping out; I stab and stab
because of a cruel word said the other day,
a gray hair found in the soap scum, a desire
to stop a head from cracking, and most of all
because of the face that flashes past your lashes
and is not mine. I stab at that flinty tempter.

IX

By this I knew I'd never leave my room
to look at cities, parks or art again:
the carnage was a comfort, not a care,
the thing that lay beside me on the bed
improved my mood because it matched the red
around the house, the red that ruled the world.
But even killers singing odes to gore
have lucid intervals. I thought of all
the faces that I never saw because
I was so busy welding them to views:
the bright eyes raised in ecstasy, the head
hung low in grief—for them I carry a torch
that lights the corners of my chamber as
I wait for sirens, as I wait for sleep.

X

Sometimes the flames remind me of your good points;
other times, when I become too bold
and start believing that you might come visit
they leap as if to say, Thus I refute you.
Who knows whether the things I do without you—
making shadow puppets on the walls,
giving private screenings of my crimes—
will cure me of the urge to do it over?
I only know that sometimes when the flames
are cool enough to walk through, I will risk
the shame of being found out by my keeper,
and the worse shame of never being noticed,
by standing at the red-rimmed, steamy window
through which, sometimes, a park bench will appear.

Issue 143, 1997

Charles Tomlinson

❈

The Broom: The New Wife's Tale

I listened hard. I do not believe in ghosts.
   The house was changing. Indeed, I never saw
Such thorough renovation. "You do not know,"
   She said, "how many ghosts there were
Needed to be laid. The dead
   Don't bury their dead: only the living
Can do that for them—they go on breeding.
   In room after room she multiplied herself
And lay in wait. For him, not me.
   Yet one bright day I entered my own kitchen,
Or almost did—inside the door
   The sight of a broom scratched to and fro.
It was the sound—dry, rasping
   Across the quarries, first made me see it,
Stopped me. It was familiar enough, a stark
   Discordant blue I'd never cared for.
I hurried through expecting the cleaning woman.
   Nobody there, of course . . . It was things
She seemed to cling to—a clock, a chair,
   Now this (it was she had bought it)
Left leaning against the wall, but then I saw—
   Whatever it was she'd meant by it—that I
Must sweep the place clean

Of all she was reliving or imagining." Determination
Flawed lines in her young face. I do not believe
In ghosts, except for the one she saw almost.

Vijay Seshadri

❆

Ailanthus

In their distorting internal mirrors,
the battered and in pain
become the dragons mauling them.
Their spirits drain

to their spleens, which manufacture
a substance, viscous, green,
that catalyzes their hearts'
colorless acetylene,

igniting their dragon breath.
Then they breathe and burn.
The ones who did them dirt
are done to a turn.

The ones who stopped to watch
are torched to black pathetic stems
by holographic Greek fire
and ICBMs.

And what happens to
those servants of the state
whose fault it all is is too
painful to relate.

Brothers and sisters to dragons!—
but only in their dreams
the mountain spews,
the fissure steams.

Elsewhere, the tree-of-heaven grows—
in deserted parking lots,
auto graveyards, abandoned
garden plots.

The wind in its leaves
is dry, arrhythmic, and sad.
Everyone, it whispers, has their reasons,
a few of which are bad.

Issue 162, 2002

Paul Auster

In the Country of Last Things

These are the last things, she wrote. One by one they disappear and never come back. I can tell you of the ones I have seen, of the ones that are no more, but I doubt there will be time. It is all happening too fast now, and I cannot keep up.

I don't expect you to understand. You have seen none of this, and even if you tried, you could not imagine it. These are the last things. A house is there one day, and the next day it is gone. A street you walked down yesterday is no longer there today. Even the weather is in constant flux. A day of sun followed by a day of rain, a day of snow followed by a day of fog, warm then cool, wind then stillness, a stretch of bitter cold, and then today, in the middle of winter, an afternoon of fragrant light, warm to the point of merely sweaters. When you live in the city, you learn to take nothing for granted. Close your eyes for a moment, turn around to look at something else, and the thing that was before you is suddenly gone. Nothing lasts, you see, not even the thoughts inside you. And you mustn't waste your time looking for them. Once a thing is gone, that is the end of it.

This is how I live, her letter continued. I don't eat much. Just enough to keep me going from step to step, and no more. At times my weakness is so great, I feel the next step will never come. But I manage. In spite of the lapses, I keep myself going. You should see how well I manage.

The streets of the city are everywhere, and no two streets are the same. I put one foot in front of the other, and then the other foot in front of the first, and then hope I can do it again. Nothing more than that. You must understand how it is with me now. I move. I breathe what air is given me. I eat as little as I can. No matter what anyone says, the only thing that counts is staying on your feet.

You remember what you said to me before I left. William has disappeared, you said, and no matter how hard I looked I would never find him. Those were your words. And then I told you that I didn't care what you said, that I was going to find my brother. And then I got on that terrible boat and left you. How long ago was that? I can't remember anymore. Years and years, I think. But that is only a guess. I make no bones about it. I've lost track, and nothing will ever set it right for me.

This much is certain. If not for my hunger, I wouldn't be able to go on. You must get used to doing with as little as you can. By wanting less, you are content with less, and the less you need, the better off you are. That is what the city does to you. It turns your thoughts inside out. It makes you want to live, and at the same time it tries to take your life away from you. There is no escape from this. Either you do or you don't. And if you do, you can't be sure of doing it the next time. And if you don't, you never will again.

I am not sure why I am writing to you now. To be honest, I have barely thought of you since I got here. But suddenly, after all this time, I feel there is something to say, and if I don't quickly write it down, my head will burst. It doesn't matter if you read it. It doesn't even matter if I send it—assuming that could be done. Perhaps it comes down to this. I am writing to you because you know nothing. Because you are far away from me and know nothing.

There are people so thin, she wrote, they are sometimes blown away. The winds in the city are ferocious, always gusting off the river and singing in your ears, always buffeting you back and forth, always swirling papers and garbage in your path. It's not uncommon to see the thinnest people moving about in twos and threes, sometimes whole families, bound together by ropes and chains, to ballast one another against the blasts. Others give up trying to go out altogether, hugging to the doorways and alcoves, until even the fairest sky seems a threat. Better to wait quietly in their corner, they think, than to be dashed against the stones. It is also possible to become so good at not eating that eventually you can eat nothing at all.

It is even worse for the ones who fight their hunger. Thinking about food too much can only lead to trouble. These are the ones who are obsessed, who refuse to give in to the facts. They prowl the streets at all hours, scavenging for morsels, taking enormous risks for even the smallest crumb. No matter how much they are able to find, it will never be enough. They eat without ever filling themselves, tearing into their food with animal haste, their bony fingers picking, their quivering jaws never shut. Most of it dribbles down their chins and what they manage to swallow, they usually throw up again in a few minutes. It is a slow death, as if food were a fire, a madness, burning them up from within. They think they are eating to stay alive, but in the end they are the ones who are eaten.

As it turns out, food is a complicated business, and unless you learn to accept what is given to you, you will never be at peace with yourself. Shortages are frequent, and a food that has given you pleasure one day will more than likely be gone the next. The municipal markets are probably the safest, most reliable places to shop, but the prices are high and the selections paltry. One day there will be nothing but radishes, another day nothing but stale chocolate cake. To change your diet so often and so drastically can be very hard on the stomach. But the municipal markets have the advantage of being guarded by the police, and at least you know that what you buy there will wind up in your own stomach and not someone else's. Food theft is so common in the streets that it is not even considered a crime anymore. On top of that, the municipal markets are the only legally sanctioned form of food distribution. There are many private food sellers around the city, but their goods can be confiscated at any time. Even those who can afford to pay the police bribes necessary to stay in business still face the constant threat of attack from thieves. Thieves also plague the customers of the private markets, and it has been statistically proven that one out of every two purchases leads to a robbery. It hardly seems worth it, I think, to risk so much for the fleeting joy of an orange or the taste of boiled ham. But the people are insatiable: hunger is a curse that comes every day, and the stomach is a bottomless pit, a hole as big as the world. The private markets, therefore, do a good business, in spite of the obstacles, picking up from one place and going to another, constantly on the move, appearing for an hour or two somewhere and then vanishing out of sight. One word of warning, however. If you must have the foods from the private markets, then be sure to avoid the renegade grocers, for fraud is rampant, and there are many people who will sell anything just to turn a profit: eggs and oranges filled with sawdust, bottles of piss pretending to be beer. No, there is nothing people will not do, and the sooner you learn that, the better off you will be.

When you walk through the streets, she went on, you must remember to take only one step at a time. Otherwise, falling is inevitable. Your eyes must be constantly open, looking up, looking down, looking ahead, looking behind, on watch for other bodies, on your guard against the unforeseeable. To collide with someone can be fatal. Two people collide and then start pounding each other with their fists. Or else, they fall to the ground and do not try to get up. Sooner or later, a moment comes when you do not try to get up anymore. Bodies ache, you see, there's no cure for that. And more terribly here than elsewhere.

The rubble is a special problem. You must learn how to manage the unseen furrows, the sudden clusters of rocks, the shallow ruts, so that you do not stumble or hurt yourself. And then there are the tolls, these worst of all, and you must use cunning to avoid them. Wherever buildings have fallen or garbage has gathered, large mounds stand in the middle of the street, blocking all passage. Men build these barricades whenever the materials are at hand, and then they mount them, with clubs, or rifles, or bricks, and wait on their perches for people to pass by. They are in control of the street. If you want to get through, you must give the guards whatever they demand. Sometimes it is money; sometimes it is food; sometimes it is sex. Beatings are commonplace, and every now and then you hear of a murder.

New tolls go up, the old tolls disappear. You can never know which streets to take and which to avoid. Bit by bit, the city robs you of certainty. There can never be any fixed path, and you can survive only if nothing is necessary to you. Without warning, you must be able to change, to drop what you are doing, to reverse. In the end, there is nothing that is not the case. As a consequence, you must learn how to read the signs. When the eyes falter, the nose will sometimes serve. My sense of smell has become unnaturally keen. In spite of the side effects—the sudden nausea, the dizziness, the fear that comes with the rank air invading my body—it protects me when turning corners, and these can be the most dangerous moments of all. For the tolls have a particular stench that you learn to recognize, even from a great distance. Compounded of stones, of cement, and of wood, the mounds also hold garbage and chips of plaster, and the sun works on this garbage, producing a reek more intense than elsewhere, and the rain works on the plaster, logging it and melting it, so that it too exudes its own smell, and when the one works on the other, interacting in the alternate fits of dry and damp, the odor of the toll begins to blossom. The essential thing is not to become inured. For habits are deadly. Even if it is for the hundredth time, you must encounter each thing as if you have never known it before. No matter how many times, it must always be the first time. This is next to impossible, I realize, but it is an absolute rule.

You would think that sooner or later it would all come to an end. Things fall apart and vanish, and nothing new is made. People die, and babies refuse to be born. In the past year I can't remember seeing a single newborn child. And yet, there are always new people to replace the ones who have vanished. They pour in from the country and the outlying towns, dragging carts piled high with their belongings, sputtering in with broken-down cars, all of them hungry, all of them homeless. Until they have learned the ways of the city, these newcomers are easy victims. Many of them are duped out of their money before the end of the first day. Some people pay for apartments that don't exist, others are lured into giving commissions for jobs that never materialize, still others lay out their savings to buy food that turns out to be painted cardboard. These are only the most ordinary kinds of tricks. I know a man who makes his living by standing in front of the old City Hall and asking for money every time one of the newcomers glances at the tower clock. If there is a dispute, his assistant, who poses as a greenhorn, pretends to go through the ritual of looking at the clock and paying him, so that the stranger will think this is the common practice. The startling thing is not that confidence men exist, but that it is so easy for them to get people to part with their money.

For those who have a place to live, there is always the danger they will lose it. Most buildings are not owned by anyone, and therefore you have no rights as a tenant; no lease, no legal leg to stand on if something goes against you. It's not uncommon for people to be forcibly evicted from their apartments and thrown out onto the street. A group barges in on you with rifles and clubs and tells you to get out, and unless you think you can overcome them, what choice do you have? This practice is known as housebreaking, and there are few people in the city who have not lost their homes in this way at one time or another. But even if you are fortunate enough to escape this particular form of eviction, you never know when you will fall prey to one of the phantom landlords. These are extortionists who terrorize nearly every neighborhood in the city, forcing people to pay protection money just to be able to stay in their apartments. They proclaim themselves owners of a building, bilk the occupants, and are almost never opposed.

For those who do not have a home, however, the situation is beyond reprieve. There is no such thing as a vacancy. But still, the rental agencies carry on a sort of business. Every day they place notices in the newspaper, advertising fraudulent apartments, in order to attract people to their offices and collect a fee from them. No one is fooled by this practice, yet there are many people willing to sink their last penny into these empty promises. They arrive outside the offices early in the morning and patiently wait in line, sometimes for hours, just to be able to sit with an agent for ten minutes and look at photographs of buildings on tree-lined streets, of comfortable rooms, of apartments furnished with carpets and soft leather chairs—peaceful scenes to evoke the smell of coffee wafting in from the kitchen, the steam of a hot bath, the bright colors of potted plants snug on the sill. It doesn't seem to matter to anyone that these pictures were taken more than ten years ago.

So many of us have become like children again. It's not that we make an effort, you understand, or that anyone is really conscious of it. But when hope disappears, when you find that you have given up hoping even for the possibility of hope, you tend to fill the empty spaces with dreams, little childlike thoughts and stories to keep you going. Even the most hardened people have trouble stopping themselves. Without fuss or prelude they break off from what they are doing, sit down, and talk about the desires that have been welling up inside them. Food, of course, is one of the favorite subjects. Often you will overhear a group of people describing a meal in meticulous detail, beginning with the soups and appetizers and slowly working their way to dessert, dwelling on each savor and spice, on all the various aromas and flavors, concentrating now on the method of preparation, now on the effect of the food itself, from the first twinge of taste on the tongue to the gradually expanding sense of peace as the food travels down the throat and arrives in the belly. These conversations sometimes go on for hours, and they have a highly rigorous protocol. You must never laugh, for example, and you must never allow your hunger to get the better of you. No outbursts, no unpremeditated sighs. That would lead to tears, and nothing spoils a food conversation more quickly than tears. For best results, you must allow your mind to leap into the words coming from the mouths of the others. If the words can consume you, you will be able to forget your present hunger and enter what people call the "arena of the sustaining nimbus." There are even those who say there is nutritional value in these food talks—given the proper concentration and an equal desire to believe in the words among those taking part.

All this belongs to the language of ghosts. There are many other possible kinds of talks in this language. Most of them begin when one person says to another: I wish. What they wish for might be anything at all, as long as it is something that cannot happen. I wish the sun would never set. I wish money would grow in my pockets. I wish the city would be like it was in the old days. You get the idea. Absurd and infantile things, with no meaning and no reality. In general, people hold to the belief that however bad things were yesterday, they were better than things are today. What they were like two days ago was even better than yesterday. The farther you go back, the more beautiful and desirable the world becomes. You drag yourself from sleep each morning to face something that is always worse than what you faced the day before, but by talking of the world that existed before

you went to sleep, you can delude yourself into thinking that the present day is simply an apparition, no more or less real than the memories of all the other days you carry around inside you.

I understand why people play this game, but I myself have no taste
for it. I refuse to speak the language of ghosts, and whenever I hear
others speaking it, I walk away or put my hands over my ears. Yes,
things have changed for me. You remember what a playful little girl I
was. You could never get enough of my stories, of the worlds I used
to make up for us to play inside of the Castle of No Return, the Land
of Sadness, the Forest of Forgotten Words. Do you remember them?
How I loved to tell you lies, to trick you into believing my stories, and
to watch your face turn serious as I led you from one outlandish scene
to the next. Then I would tell you it was all made up, and you would
start to cry. I think I loved those tears of yours as much as your smile.
Yes, I was probably a bit wicked, even in those days, wearing the little
frocks my mother used to dress me in, with my skinned and scabby
knees, and my little baby's cunt with no hair. But you loved me, didn't
you? You loved me until you were insane with it.

Now I am all common sense and hard calculation. I don't want to
be like the others. I see what their imaginings do to them, and I will
not let that happen to me. The ghost people always die in their sleep.
For a month or two they walk around with a strange smile on their
face, and a weird glow of otherness hovers around them, as if they've
already begun to disappear. The signs are unmistakable, even the
forewarning hints: the slight flush to the cheeks, the eyes suddenly a
little bigger than usual, the stuporous shuffle, the foul smell from the
lower body. It is probably a happy death, however. I am willing to
grant them that. At times I have almost envied them. But finally, I cannot let myself go. I will not allow it. I am going to hold on for as long
as I can, even if it kills me.

Other deaths are more dramatic. There are the Runners, for example,
a sect of people who run through the streets as fast as they can, flailing their arms wildly about them, punching the air, screaming at the
top of their lungs. Most of the time they travel in groups: six, ten,
even twenty of them charging down the street together, never stopping for anything in their path, running and running until they drop

from exhaustion. The point is to die as quickly as possible, to drive yourself so hard that your heart cannot stand it. The Runners say that no one would have the courage to do this on his own. By running together, each member of the group is swept along by the others, encouraged by the screams, whipped to a frenzy of self-punishing endurance. That is the irony. In order to kill yourself by running, you first have to train yourself to be a good runner. Otherwise, you would not have the strength to push yourself far enough. The Runners, however, go through arduous preparations to meet their fate, and if they happen to fall on their way to that fate, they know how to pick themselves up immediately and continue. I suppose it's a kind of religion. There are several offices throughout the city—one for each of the nine census zones—and in order to join, you must go through a series of difficult initiations: holding your breath under water, fasting, putting your hand in the flame of a candle, not speaking to anyone for seven days. Once you have been accepted, you must submit to the code of the group. This involves six to twelve months of communal living, a strict regimen of exercise and training, and a gradually reduced intake of food. By the time a member is ready to make his death run, he has simultaneously reached a point of ultimate strength and ultimate weakness. He can theoretically run forever, and at the same time his body has used up all its resources. This combination produces the desired result. You set out with your companions on the morning of the appointed day and run until you have escaped your body, running and screaming until you have flown out of yourself. Eventually, your soul wriggles free, your body drops to the ground, and you are dead. The Runners advertise that their method is over ninety percent failure-proof—which means that almost no one ever has to make a second death run.

More common are the solitary deaths. But these, too, have been transformed into a kind of public ritual. People climb to the highest places for no other reason than to jump. The Last Leap, it is called, and I admit there is something stirring about watching one, something that seems to open a whole new world of freedom inside you: to see the body poised at the roof's edge, and then, always, the slight moment of hesitation, as if from a desire to relish those seconds, and the way your own life seems to gather in your throat, and then, unexpectedly (for you can never be sure when it will happen), the body hurls itself through the air and comes flying down to the street. You would be amazed at the enthusiasm of the crowds: to hear their frantic cheering, to see their excitement. It is as if the violence and beauty of the spectacle had wrenched them from themselves, had made them forget the paltriness of their own lives. The Last Leap is something everyone can understand, and it corresponds to everyone's inner longings: to die in a flash, to obliterate yourself in one brief and glorious moment. I sometimes think that death is the one thing we have any feeling for. It is our art form, the only way we can express ourselves.

Still, there are those of us who manage to live. For death, too, has become a source of life. With so many people thinking of how to put an end to things, meditating on the various ways to leave this world, you can imagine the opportunities for turning a profit. A clever person can live quite well off the deaths of others. For not everyone has the courage of the Runners or the Leapers, and many need to be helped along with their decision. The ability to pay for these services is naturally a precondition, and for that reason few but the wealthiest people can afford them. But business is nevertheless quite brisk, especially at the Euthanasia Clinics. These come in several different varieties, depending on how much you are willing to spend. The simplest and cheapest form takes no more than an hour or two, and it is advertised as the Return Voyage. You sign in at the clinic, pay for your ticket at the desk, and then are taken to a small private room with a freshly made bed. An attendant tucks you in and gives you an injection, and then you drift off to sleep and never wake up. Next on the price ladder is the Journey of Marvels, which lasts anywhere from one to three days. This consists of a series of injections, spaced out at regular intervals, which gives the customer a euphoric sense of abandon and happiness, before a last, fatal injection is administered. Then there is the Pleasure Cruise, which can go on for as long as two weeks. The customers are treated to an opulent life, catered to in a manner that rivals the splendor of the old luxury hotels. There are elaborate meals, wines, entertainment, even a brothel, which serves the needs of both men and women. This runs into quite a bit of money, but for some people the chance to live the good life, even for a short while, is an irresistible temptation.

The Euthanasia Clinics are not the only way to buy your own death, however. There are the Assassination Clubs as well, and these have been growing in popularity. A person who wants to die, but who is too afraid to go through with it himself, joins the Assassination Club in his census zone for a relatively modest fee. An assassin is then assigned to him. The customer is told nothing about the arrangements, and everything about his death remains a mystery to him: the date, the place, the method to be used, the identity of his assassin. In some sense, life goes on as it always does. Death remains on the horizon, an absolute certainty, and yet inscrutable as to its specific form. Instead of old age, disease, or accident, a member of an Assassination Club can look forward to a quick and violent death in the not-too-distant future: a bullet in the brain, a knife in the back, a pair of hands around his throat in the middle of the night. The effect of all this, it seems to me, is to make one more vigilant. Death is no longer an abstraction, but a real possibility that haunts each moment of life. Rather than submit passively to the inevitable, those marked for assassination tend to become more alert, more vigorous in their movements, more filled with a sense of life—as though transformed by some new understanding of things. Many of them actually recant and opt for life again. But that is a complicated business. For once you join an Assassination Club, you are not allowed to quit. On the other hand, if you manage to kill your assassin, you can be released from your obligation—and, if you choose, be hired as an assassin yourself. That is the danger of the assassin's job and the reason why it is so well paid. It is rare for an assassin to be killed, for he is necessarily more experienced than his intended victim, but it does sometimes happen. Among the poor, especially poor young men, there are many who save up for months and even years just to be able to join an Assassination Club. The idea is to get hired as an Assassin—and therefore to lift themselves up to a better life. Few ever make it. If I told you the stories of some of these boys, you would not be able to sleep for a week.

All this leads to a great many practical problems. The question of bodies, for example. People don't die here as they did in the old days, quietly expiring in their beds or in the clean sanctuary of a hospital ward—they die wherever they happen to be, and for the most part that means the street. I am not just talking about the Runners, the Leapers, and members of the Assassination Clubs (for they amount to a mere fraction), but to vast segments of the population. Fully half the people are homeless, and they have absolutely nowhere to go. Dead bodies are therefore everywhere you turn—on the sidewalk, in doorways, in the street itself. Don't ask me to give you the details. It's enough for me to say it—even more than enough. No matter what you might think, the real problem is never a lack of pity. Nothing breaks here more readily than the heart.

Most of the bodies are naked. Scavengers roam the streets at all times, and it is never very long before a dead person is stripped of his belongings. First to go are the shoes, for these are in great demand, and very hard to find. The pockets are next to attract attention, but usually it is just everything after that, the clothes and whatever they contain. Last come the men with chisels and pliers, who wrench the gold and silver teeth from the mouth. Because there is no escaping this fact, many families take care of the stripping themselves, not wanting to leave it to strangers. In some cases, it comes from a desire to preserve the dignity of the loved one; in others it is simply a question of selfishness. But that is perhaps too subtle a point. If the gold from your husband's tooth can feed you for a month, who is to say you are wrong to pull it out? This kind of behavior goes against the grain, I know, but if you mean to survive here, then you must be able to give in on matters of principle.

Every morning, the city sends out trucks to collect the corpses. This is the chief function of the government, and more money is spent on it than anything else. All around the edges of the city are the crematoria—called transformation centers—and day and night you can see the smoke rising up into the sky. But with the streets in such bad disrepair now, and with so many of them reduced to rubble, the job becomes increasingly difficult. The men are forced to stop the trucks and go out foraging on foot, and this slows down the work considerably. On top of this, there are the frequent mechanical breakdowns of the trucks and the occasional outbursts from onlookers. Throwing stones at death-truck workers is a common occupation among the homeless. Although the workers are armed and have been known to turn their machine guns on crowds, some of the stone throwers are very deft at hiding themselves, and their hit-and-run tactics can sometimes bring the collection work to a complete halt. There is no coherent motive behind these attacks. They stem from anger, resentment, and boredom, and because the collection workers are the only city officials who ever make an appearance in the neighborhood, they are convenient targets. One could say that the stones represent the people's disgust with a government that does nothing for them until they are dead. But that would be going too far. The stones are an expression of unhappiness, and that is all. For there are no politics in the city as such. The people are too hungry, too distracted, too much at odds with each other for that.

The crossing took ten days, and I was the only passenger. But you know that already. You met the captain and the crew, you saw the cabin, and there's no need to go over that again. I spent my time looking at the water and the sky and hardly opened a book for the whole ten days. We came into the city at night, and it was only then that I began to panic a little. The shore was entirely black, no lights anywhere, and it felt as though we were entering an invisible world, a place where only blind people lived. But I had the address of William's office, and that reassured me somewhat. All I had to do was go there, I thought, and then things would take care of themselves. At the very least, I felt confident that I would be able to pick up William's trail. But I had not realized that the street would be gone. It wasn't that the office was empty or that the building had been abandoned. There was no building, no street, no anything at all: nothing but stones and rubbish for acres around.

This was the third census zone, I later learned, and nearly a year before some kind of epidemic had broken out there. The city government had come in, walled off the area, and burned everything down to the ground. Or so the story went. I have since learned not to take the things I am told too seriously. It's not that people make a point of lying to you, it's just that where the past is concerned, the truth tends to get obscured rather quickly. Legends crop up within a matter of hours, tall tales circulate, and the facts are soon buried under a mountain of outlandish theories. In the city, the best approach is to believe only what your own eyes tell you. But not even that is infallible. For few things are ever what they seem to be, especially here, with so much to absorb at every step, with so many things that defy under-standing. Whatever you see has the potential to wound you, to make you less than you are, as if merely by seeing a thing some part of your-self were taken away from you. Often, you feel it will be dangerous to look, and there is a tendency to avert your eyes, or even to shut them. Because of that, it is easy to get confused, to be unsure that you are really seeing the thing you think you are looking at. It could be that you are imagining it, or mixing it up with something else, or remem-bering something you have seen before—or perhaps even imagined before. You see how complicated it is. It is not enough simply to look and say to yourself. "I am looking at that thing." For it is one thing to do this when the object before your eyes is a pencil, say, or a crust of bread. But what happens when you find yourself looking at a dead child, at a little girl lying in the street without any clothes on, her head crushed and covered with blood? What do you say to yourself then? It is not a simple matter, you see, to state flatly and without equivoca-tion: "I am looking at a dead child." Your mind seems to balk at form-ing the words, you somehow cannot bring yourself to do it. For the thing before your eyes is not something you can very easily separate from yourself. That is what I mean by being wounded: you cannot merely see, for each thing somehow belongs to you, is part of the story unfolding inside you. It would be good, I suppose, to make yourself so hard that nothing could affect you anymore. But then you would be alone, so totally cut off from everyone else that life would become impossible. There are those who manage to do this here, who find the strength to turn themselves into monsters, but you would be surprised to know how few they are. Or, to put it another way: we have all become monsters, but there is almost no one without some remnant inside him of life as it once was.

That is perhaps the greatest problem of all. Life as we know it has ended, and yet no one is able to grasp what has taken its place. Those of us who were brought up somewhere else, or who are old enough to remember a world different from this one, find it an enormous strug-gle just to keep up from one day to the next. I am not talking only of hardships. Faced with the most ordinary occurrence, you no longer know how to act, and because you cannot act, you find yourself unable to think. The brain is in a muddle. All around you one change follows another, each day produces a new upheaval, the old assumptions are so much air and emptiness. That is the dilemma. On the one hand, you want to survive, to adapt, to make the best of things as they are. But, on the other hand, to accomplish this seems to entail killing off all those things that once made you think of yourself as human. Do you see what I am trying to say? In order to live, you must make yourself die. That is why so many people have given up. For no matter how hard they struggle, they know they are bound to lose. And at that point, it is surely a pointless thing to struggle at all.

It tends to blur in my mind now: what happened and did not, the streets for the first time, the days, the nights, the sky above me, the stones stretching beyond. I seem to remember looking up a lot, as if searching the sky for some lack, some surplus, something that made it different from other skies, as if the sky could explain the things I was seeing around me. I could be mistaken, however. Possibly I am transferring the observations of a later period onto those first days. But I doubt that it matters very much, least of all now.

After much careful study, I can safely report that the sky here is the same sky as the one above you. We have the same clouds and the same brightnesses, the same storms and the same calms, the same winds that carry everything along with them. If the effects are somewhat different here, that is strictly because of what happens below. The nights, for example, are never quite what they are at home. There is the same darkness and the same immensity, but with no feeling of stillness, only a constant undertow, a murmur that pulls you downward and thrusts you forward, without respite. And then, during the days, there is a brightness that is sometimes intolerable—a brilliance that stuns you and seems to blanch everything, all the jagged surfaces gleaming, the air itself almost ashimmer. The light forms in such a way that the colors become more and more distorted as you draw close to them. Even the shadows are agitated, with a random, hectic pulsing along the edges. You must be careful in this light not to open your eyes too wide, to squint at just the precise degree that will allow you to keep your balance. Otherwise, you will stumble as you walk,

and I need not enumerate the dangers of falling. If not for the darkness, and the strange nights that descend on us, I sometimes feel the
sky would burn itself out. The days end when they must, at just the
moment when the sun seems to have exhausted the things it shines
on. Nothing could adhere to the brightness anymore. The whole im-
plausible world would melt away, and that would be that.

   Slowly and steadily, the city seems to be consuming itself, even as
it remains. There is no way to explain it. I can only record, I cannot
pretend to understand. Every day in the streets you hear explosions,
as if somewhere far from you a building were falling down or the sidewalk caving in. But you never see it happen. No matter how often you
hear these sounds, their source remains invisible. You would think
that now and then an explosion would take place in your presence.
But the facts fly in the face of probability. You mustn't think that I am
making it up—these noises do not begin in my head. The others hear
them too, even if they don't pay much attention. Sometimes they will
stop to comment on them, but they never seem worried. It's a bit better now, they might say. Or, it seems a little belligerent this afternoon.
I used to ask many questions about these explosions, but I never got
an answer. Nothing more than a dumb stare or a shrug of the shoulders. Eventually, I learned that some things are just not asked, that
even here there are subjects no one is willing to discuss.

For those at the bottom, there are the streets and the parks and the old
subway stations. The streets are the worst, for there you are exposed
to every hazard and inconvenience. The parks are a somewhat more
settled affair, without the problem of traffic and constant passersby,
but unless you are one of the fortunate ones to have a tent or a hut,
you are never free of the weather. Only in the subway stations can you
be sure to escape inclemencies, but there you are also forced to contend with a host of other irritations: the dampness, the crowds, and
the perpetual noise of people shouting, as though mesmerized by the
echoes of their own voices.

   During those first weeks, it was the rain I came to fear more than
anything else. Even the cold is a trifle by comparison. For that, it is
simply a question of a warm coat—which I had—and moving briskly
to keep the blood stimulated. I also learned the benefits to be found

from newspapers, surely the best and cheapest material for insulating your clothing. On cold days, you must get up very early in the morning to be sure of finding a good place in the lines that gather in front of the newsstands. You must gauge the wait judiciously, for there is nothing worse than standing out in the cold morning air too long. If you think you will be there for more than twenty or twenty-five minutes, then the common wisdom is to move on and forget it.

Once you've bought the paper, assuming you've managed to get one, the best thing is to take a sheet, tear it into strips, and then twist them into little bundles. These knots are good for stuffing into the toes of your shoes, for blocking up windy interstices around your ankles, and for threading through holes in your clothing. For the limbs and torso, whole sheets wrapped around a number of loosely floating knots is often the best procedure. For the neck area, it is good to take a dozen or so knots and braid them together into a collar. The whole thing gives you a puffy, padded look, which has the cosmetic advantage of disguising thinness. For those who are concerned about keeping up appearances, the "paper meal," as it is called, serves as a kind of face-saving technique. People literally starving to death, with caved-in stomachs and limbs like sticks, walk around trying to look as though they weigh two or three hundred pounds. No one is ever fooled by the disguise—you can spot one of these people from half a mile off—but perhaps that is not the real point. What they seem to be saying is that they know what has happened to them, and they are ashamed of it. More than anything else, their bulked-up bodies are a badge of consciousness, a sign of bitter self-awareness. They make themselves into grotesque parodies of the prosperous and well-fed, and in this frustrated, half-crazed stab at respectability, they prove that they are just the opposite of what they pretend to be—and that they know it.

The rain, however, is unconquerable. For once you get wet, you go on paying for it hours and even days afterward. There is no greater mistake than getting caught in a downpour. Not only do you run the risk of a cold, but you must suffer through innumerable discomforts: your clothes saturated with dampness, your bones as though frozen, and the ever-present danger of destroying your shoes. If staying on your feet is the single most important task, then imagine the consequences of having less than adequate shoes. And nothing affects shoes more disastrously than a good soaking. This can lead to all kinds of problems: blisters, bunions, corns, ingrown toenails, sores, malformations—and when walking becomes painful, you are as good as lost. One step and then another step and then another: that is the golden rule. If you cannot bring yourself to do even that, then you might as well just lie down right then and there and tell yourself to stop breathing.

But how to avoid the rain if it can strike at any moment? There are times, many times, when you find yourself outdoors, going from one place to another, on your way somewhere with no choice about it, period, and suddenly the sky grows dark, the clouds collide, and there you are, drenched to the skin. And even if you manage to find shelter the moment the rain begins to fall and to spare yourself this once, you still must be extremely careful after the rain stops. For then you must watch for the puddles that form in the hollows of the pavement, the lakes that sometimes emerge from the rifts, and even the mud that oozes up from below, ankle deep and treacherous. With the streets in such poor repair, with so much that is cracked, pitted, pocked, and riven apart, there is no escaping these crises. Sooner or later, you are bound to come to a place where you have no alternative, where you are hemmed in on all sides. And not only are there the surfaces to watch for, the world that touches your feet, there are also the drippings from above, the water that slides down from the eaves, and then, even worse, the strong winds that often follow the rain, the fierce eddies of air, skimming the tops of lakes and puddles and whipping the water back into the atmosphere, driving it along like little pins, darts that prick your face and swirl around you, making it impossible to see anything at all. When the winds blow after a rain, people collide with one another more frequently, more fights break out in the streets, the very air seems charged with menace.

It would be one thing if the weather could be predicted with any degree of accuracy. Then one could make plans, know when to avoid the streets, prepare for changes in advance. But everything happens too fast here, the shifts are too abrupt, what is true one minute is no longer true the next. I have wasted much time looking for signs in the air, trying to study the atmosphere for hints of what is to follow and when: the color and heft of the clouds, the speed and direction of the wind, the smells at any given hour, the texture of the sky at night, the sprawl of the sunsets, the intensity of the dew at dawn. But nothing has ever helped me. To correlate this with that, to make a connection between an afternoon cloud and an evening wind—such things lead only to madness. You spin around in the vortex of your calculations and then, just at the moment you are convinced it will rain, the sun goes on shining for an entire day.

What you must do, then, is be prepared for anything. But opinions vary drastically on the best way to go about this. There is a small minority, for example, that believes that bad weather comes from bad thoughts. This is a rather mystical approach to the question, for it implies that thoughts can be translated directly into events in the physical world. According to them, when you think a dark or pessimistic thought, it produces a cloud in the sky. If enough people are thinking gloomy thoughts at once, then rain will begin to fall. That is the reason for all the startling shifts in the weather, they claim, and the reason why no one has been able to give a scientific explanation of our bizarre climate. Their solution is to maintain a steadfast cheerfulness, no matter how dismal the conditions around them. No frowns, no deep sighs, no tears. These people are known as the Smilers, and no sect in the city is more innocent or childlike. If a majority of the population could be converted to their beliefs, they are convinced the weather would at last begin to stabilize and that life would then improve. They are therefore always proselytizing, continually looking for new adherents, but the mildness of manner they have imposed upon themselves makes them feeble persuaders. They rarely succeed in winning anyone over, and consequently their ideas have never been put to the test—for without a great number of believers, there will not be enough good thoughts to make a difference. But this lack of proof only makes them more stubborn in their faith. I can see you shaking your head, and yes, I agree with you that these people are ridiculous and misguided. But, in the day-to-day context of the city, there is a certain force to their argument—and it is probably no more absurd than any other. As people, the Smilers tend to be refreshing company, for their gentleness and optimism are a welcome antidote to the angry bitterness you find everywhere else.

By contrast, there is another group called the Crawlers. These people believe that conditions will go on worsening until we demonstrate—in an utterly persuasive manner—how ashamed we are of how we lived in the past. Their solution is to prostrate themselves on the ground and refuse to stand up again until some sign is given to them that their penance has been deemed sufficient. What this sign is supposed to be is the subject of long theoretical debates. Some say a month of rain, others say a month of fair weather, and still others say they will not know until it is revealed to them in their hearts. There are two principal factions in this sect—the Dogs and the Snakes. The first contend that crawling on hands and knees shows adequate contrition, whereas the second hold that nothing short of moving on one's belly is good enough. Bloody fights break out often between the two groups—each vying for control of the other—but neither faction has gained much of a following, and by now I believe the sect is on the verge of dying out.

In the end, most people have no fixed opinion about these questions. If I counted up the various groups that have a coherent theory about the weather (the Drummers, the End-of-the-Worlders, the Free Associationists), I doubt they would come to more than a drop in the bucket. What it boils down to mostly, I think, is pure luck. The sky is ruled by chance, by forces so complex and obscure that no one can fully explain it. If you happen to get wet in the rain, you are unlucky, and that's all there is to it. If you happen to stay dry, then so much the better. But it has nothing to do with your attitude or your beliefs. The rain makes no distinctions. At one time or another, it falls on everyone, and when it falls, everyone is equal to everyone else—no one better, no one worse, everyone equal and the same.

Bear with me. I know that I sometimes stray from the point, but unless I write down things as they occur to me, I feel I will lose them for good. My mind is not quite what it used to be. It is slower now, sluggish and less nimble, and to follow even the simplest thought very far exhausts me. This is how it begins, then, in spite of my efforts. The words come only when I think I won't be able to find them anymore, at the moment I despair of ever bringing them out again. Each day brings the same struggle, the same blankness, the same desire to forget and then not to forget. When it begins, it is never anywhere but here, never anywhere but at this limit that the pencil begins to write. The story starts and stops, goes forward and then loses itself, and between each word, what silences, what words escape and vanish, never to be seen again.

For a long time I tried not to remember anything. By confining my thoughts to the present, I was better able to manage, better able to avoid the sulks. Memory is the great trap, you see, and I did my best to hold myself back, to make sure my thoughts did not sneak off to the old days. But lately I have been slipping, a little more each day it seems, and now there are times when I will not let go: of my parents, of William, of you. I was such a wild young thing, wasn't I? I grew up too fast for my own good, and no one could tell me anything I didn't already know. Now I can think only of how I hurt my parents, and how my mother cried when I told her I was leaving. It wasn't enough that they had already lost William, now they were going to lose me as well. Please—if you see my parents, tell them I'm sorry. I need to know that someone will do that for me, and there's no one to count on but you.

Yes, there are many things I'm ashamed of. At times my life seems nothing but a series of regrets, of wrong turnings, of irreversible mistakes. That is the problem when you begin to look back. You see yourself as you were, and you are appalled. But it's too late for apologies now, I realize that. It's too late for anything but getting on with it. These are the words, then. Sooner or later, I will try to say everything, and it makes no difference what comes when, whether the first thing is the second thing or the second thing the last. It all swirls around in my head at once, and merely to hold on to a thing long enough to say it is a victory. If this confuses you, I'm sorry. But I don't have much choice. I have to take it strictly as I can get it.

GOD

Philip Roth

✠

The Conversion of the Jews

You're a real one for opening your mouth in the first place," Itzie said. "What do you open your mouth all the time for?"

"I didn't bring it up, Itz, I didn't," Ozzie said.

"What do you care about Jesus Christ for anyway?"

"I didn't bring up Jesus Christ. He did. I didn't even know what he was talking about. Jesus is historical, he kept saying. Jesus is historical." Ozzie mimicked the monumental voice of Rabbi Binder.

"Jesus was a person that lived like you and me," Ozzie continued. "That's what Binder said—"

"Yeah? . . . So what! What do I give two cents whether he lived or not. And what do you gotta open your mouth!" Itzie Lieberman favored closed-mouthedness, especially when it came to Ozzie Freedman's questions. Mrs. Freedman had to see Rabbi Binder twice before about Ozzie's questions and this Wednesday at four-thirty would be the third time. Itzie preferred to keep *his* mother in the kitchen; he settled for behind-the-back subtleties such as gestures, faces, snarls and other less delicate barnyard noises.

"He was a real person, Jesus, but he wasn't like God, and we don't believe he is God." Slowly, Ozzie was explaining Rabbi Binder's position to Itzie, who had been absent from Hebrew School the previous afternoon.

"The Catholics," Itzie said helpfully, "they believe in Jesus Christ, that he's God." Itzie Lieberman used "the Catholics" in its broadest sense—to include the Protestants.

Ozzie received Itzie's remark with a tiny head bob, as though it were a footnote, and went on. "His mother was Mary, and his father probably was Joseph," Ozzie said. "But the New Testament says his real father was God."

"His *real* father?"

"Yeah," Ozzie said, "that's the big thing, his father's supposed to be God."

"Bull."

"That's what Rabbi Binder says, that it's impossible—"

"Sure it's impossible. That stuff's all bull. To have a baby you gotta get laid," Itzie theologized. "Mary hadda get laid."

"That's what Binder says: 'The only way a woman can have a baby is to have intercourse with a man.'"

"He said *that*, Ozz?" For a moment it appeared that Itzie had put the theological question aside. "He said that, *intercourse?*" A little curled smile shaped itself in the lower half of Itzie's face like a pink mustache. "What you guys do, Ozz, you laugh or something?"

"I raised my hand."

"Yeah? Whatja say?"

"That's when I asked the question."

Itzie's face lit up like a firefly's behind. "Whatja ask about—intercourse?"

"No, I asked the question about God, how if He could create the heaven and earth in six days, and make all the animals and the fish and the light in six days—the light especially, that's what always gets me, that He could make the light. Making fish and animals, that's pretty good—"

"That's damn good." Itzie's appreciation was honest but unimaginative: it was as though God had just pitched a one-hitter.

"But making light . . . I mean when you think about it, it's really something," Ozzie said. "Anyway, I asked Binder if He could make all that in six days, and He could *pick* the six days He wanted right out of nowhere, why couldn't He let a woman have a baby without having intercourse."

"You said *intercourse*, Ozz, to Binder?"

"Yeah."

"Right in class?"

"Yeah."

Itzie smacked the side of his head.

"I mean, no kidding around," Ozzie said, "that'd really be nothing. After all that other stuff, that'd practically be nothing."

Itzie considered a moment. "What'd Binder say?"

"He started all over again explaining how Jesus was historical and
how he lived like you and me but he wasn't God. So I said I under-
stood that. What I wanted to know was different."

What Ozzie wanted to know was always different. The first time he
had wanted to know how Rabbi Binder could call the Jews "The Chosen People" if the Declaration of Independence claimed all men to be
created equal. Rabbi Binder tried to distinguish for him between political equality and spiritual legitimacy, but what Ozzie wanted to
know, he insisted vehemently, was different. That was the first time
his mother had to come.

Then there was the plane crash. Fifty-eight people had been killed
in a plane crash at La Guardia, and in studying a casualty list in the
newspaper his mother had discovered among the list of those dead
eight Jewish names (his grandmother had nine but she counted Miller
as a Jewish name); because of the eight she said the plane crash was "a
tragedy." During free-discussion time on Wednesday Ozzie had
brought to Rabbi Binder's attention this matter of "some of his relations" always picking out the Jewish names. Rabbi Binder had begun
to explain cultural unity and some other things when Ozzie stood up
at his seat and said that what he wanted to know was different. Rabbi
Binder insisted that he sit down and it was then that Ozzie shouted
that he wished all fifty-eight were Jews. That was the second time his
mother came.

"And he kept explaining about Jesus being historical, and so I kept
asking him. No kidding, Itz, he was trying to make me look stupid."

"So what he finally do?"

"Finally he starts screaming that I was deliberately simpleminded
and a wise guy, and that my mother had to come, and this was the last
time. And that I'd never get barmitzvahed if he could help it. Then,
Itz, then he starts talking in that voice like a statue, real slow and deep,

and he says that I better think over what I said about the Lord. He told me to go to his office and think it over." Ozzie leaned his body towards Itzie. "Itz, I thought it over for a solid hour, and now I'm convinced God could do it."

Ozzie had planned to confess his latest transgression to his mother as soon as she came home from work. But it was a Friday night in November and already dark, and when Mrs. Freedman came through the door, she tossed off her coat, kissed Ozzie quickly on the face, and went to the kitchen table to light the three yellow candles, two for the Sabbath and one for Ozzie's father.

When his mother lit candles she would move her arms slowly towards her, dragging them through the air, as though persuading people whose minds were half made up. And her eyes would get glassy with tears. Even when his father was alive Ozzie remembered that her eyes had gotten glassy, so it didn't have anything to do with his dying. It had something to do with lighting the candles.

As she touched the flaming match to the unlit wick of a Sabbath candle, the phone rang, and Ozzie, standing only a foot from it, plucked it off the receiver and held it muffled to his chest. When his mother lit candles Ozzie felt there should be no noise; even breathing, if you could manage it, should be softened. Ozzie pressed the phone to his breast and watched his mother dragging whatever she was dragging, and he felt his own eyes get glassy. His mother was a round, tired, gray-haired penguin of a woman whose gray skin had begun to feel the tug of gravity and the weight of her own history. Even when she was dressed up she didn't look like a chosen person. But when she lit candles she looked like something better; like a woman who knew momentarily that God could do anything.

After a few mysterious minutes she was finished. Ozzie hung up the phone and walked to the kitchen table where she was beginning to lay the two places for the four-course Sabbath meal. He told her that she would have to see Rabbi Binder next Wednesday at four-thirty, and then he told her why. For the first time in their life together she hit Ozzie across the face with her hand.

All through the chopped liver and chicken soup part of the dinner Ozzie cried; he didn't have any appetite for the rest.

•

On Wednesday in the largest of the three basement classrooms of the synagogue, Rabbi Marvin Binder, a tall, handsome, broad-shouldered man of thirty with thick strong-fibered black hair, removed his watch from his pocket and saw that it was four o'clock. At the rear of the room Yakov Blotnik, the seventy-one-year-old custodian, slowly polished the large window, mumbling to himself, unaware that it was four o'clock or six o'clock, Monday or Wednesday. To most of the students Yakov Blotnik's mumbling, along with his brown curly beard, scythe nose, and two heel-trailing black cats, made of him an object of wonder, a foreigner, a relic towards whom they were alternately fearful and disrespectful. To Ozzie the mumbling had always seemed a monotonous, curious prayer; what made it curious was that old Blotnik had been mumbling so steadily for so many years Ozzie suspected he had memorized the prayers and forgotten all about God.

"It is now free-discussion time," Rabbi Binder said. "Feel free to talk about any Jewish matter at all—religion, family, politics, sports—"

There was silence. It was a gusty, clouded November afternoon and it did not seem as though there ever was or could be a thing called baseball. So nobody this week said a word about that hero from the past, Hank Greenberg—which limited free discussion considerably.

And the soul battering Ozzie Freedman had just received from Rabbi Binder had imposed its limitation. When it was Ozzie's turn to read aloud from the Hebrew book the rabbi had asked him petulantly why he didn't read more rapidly. He was showing no progress. Ozzie said he could read faster but that if he did he was sure not to understand what he was reading. Nevertheless, at the rabbi's repeated suggestion Ozzie tried, and showed a great talent, but in the midst of a long passage he stopped short and said he didn't understand a word he was reading, and started in again at a drag-footed pace. Then came the soul battering.

Consequently when free-discussion time rolled around none of the students felt too free. The rabbi's invitation was answered only by the mumbling of feeble old Blotnik.

"Isn't there anything at all you would like to discuss?" Rabbi

Binder asked again, looking at his watch. "No questions or comments?"

There was a small grumble from the third row. The rabbi requested that Ozzie rise and give the rest of the class the advantage of his thought.

Ozzie rose. "I forget it now," he said and sat down in his place.

Rabbi Binder advanced a seat towards Ozzie and poised himself on the edge of the desk. It was Itzie's desk and the rabbi's frame only a dagger's length away from his face snapped him to sitting attention.

"Stand up again, Oscar," Rabbi Binder said calmly, "and try to assemble your thoughts."

Ozzie stood up. All his classmates turned in their seats and watched as he gave an unconvincing scratch to his forehead.

"I can't assemble any," he announced, and plunked himself down.

"Stand up!" Rabbi Binder advanced from Itzie's desk to the one directly in front of Ozzie; when the rabbinical back was turned Itzie gave it five fingers off the tip of his nose, causing a small titter in the room. Rabbi Binder was too absorbed in squelching Ozzie's nonsense once and for all to bother with titters. "Stand up, Oscar. What's your question about?"

Ozzie pulled a word out of the air. It was the handiest word. "Religion."

"Oh, now you remember?"

"Yes."

"What is it?"

Trapped, Ozzie blurted the first thing that came to him. "Why can't He make anything He wants to make!"

As Rabbi Binder prepared an answer, a final answer, Itzie, ten feet behind him, raised one finger on his left hand, gestured it meaningfully towards the rabbi's back, and brought the house down.

Binder twisted quickly to see what had happened and in the midst of the commotion Ozzie shouted into the rabbi's back what he couldn't have shouted to his face. It was a loud, toneless sound that had the timbre of something stored inside for about six days.

"You don't know! You don't know anything about God!"

The rabbi spun back towards Ozzie. "What?"

"You don't know—you don't—"

"Apologize, Oscar, apologize!" It was a threat.

"You don't—"

Like a snake's tongue, Rabbi Binder's hand flicked out at Ozzie's cheek. Perhaps it had only been meant to clamp the boy's mouth shut, but Ozzie ducked and the palm caught him squarely on the nose.

The blood came in a short, red spurt on to Ozzie's shirt front.

The next moment was all confusion. Ozzie screamed, "You bastard, you bastard!" and broke for the classroom door. Rabbi Binder lurched a step backwards, as though his own blood had started flowing, violently in the opposite direction, then gave a clumsy lurch forward and bolted out the door after Ozzie. The class followed after the rabbi's huge blue-suited back, and before old Blotnik could turn from his window, the room was empty and everyone was headed full speed up the three flights leading to the roof.

If one should compare the light of day to the life of man: sunrise to birth; sunset—the dropping down over the edge—to death; then as Ozzie Freedman wiggled through the trapdoor of the synagogue roof—his feet kicking backwards bronco-style at Rabbi Binder's outstretched arms—at that moment the day was fifty years old. As a rule, fifty or fifty-five reflects accurately the age of late afternoons in November, for it is in that month, during those hours, that one's awareness of light seems no longer a matter of seeing, but of hearing: light begins clicking away. In fact, as Ozzie locked shut the trapdoor in the rabbi's face, the sharp click of the bolt into the lock might momentarily have been mistaken for the sound of the vast gray light that had just throbbed through the sky.

With all his weight Ozzie kneeled on the locked door; any instant he was certain that Rabbi Binder's shoulder would fling it open, splintering the wood into shrapnel and catapulting his body into the sky. But the door did not move and below him he heard only the rumble of feet, first loud then dim, like thunder rolling away.

A question shot through his brain, "Can this be *me*?" For a thirteen-year-old who had just labeled his religious leader a bastard, twice, it was not an improper question. Louder and louder the question came to him—"Is it me? It is me?"—until he discovered himself no longer kneeling, but racing crazily towards the edge of the roof, his eyes crying, his throat screaming, and his arms flying every which way as though not his own.

"Is it me? Is it me Me ME ME ME! It has to be me—but is it!"

It is the question a thief must ask himself the night he jimmies open his first window, and it is said to be the question with which bridegrooms quiz themselves before the altar.

In the few wild seconds it took Ozzie's body to propel him to the edge of the roof, his self-examination began to grow fuzzy. Gazing down at the street, he became confused as to the problem beneath the question: was it, is-it-me-who-called-Binder-a-bastard? or, is-it-me-prancing-around-on-the-roof? However, the scene below settled all, for there is an instant in any action when whether it is you or somebody else is academic. The thief crams the money in his pockets and scoots out the window. The bridegroom signs the hotel register for two. And the boy on the roof finds a streetful of people gaping at him, necks stretched backwards, faces up, as though he were the ceiling of the Hayden Planetarium. Suddenly you know it's you.

"Oscar! Oscar Freedman!" A voice rose from the center of the crowd, a voice that, could it have been seen, would have looked like the writing on scroll. "Oscar Freedman, get down from there. Immediately!" Rabbi Binder was pointing one arm stiffly up at him; and at the end of that arm, one finger aimed menacingly. It was the attitude of a dictator, but one—the eyes confessed all—whose personal valet had spit neatly in his face.

Ozzie didn't answer. Only for a blink's length did he look towards Rabbi Binder. Instead his eyes began to fit together the world beneath him, to sort out people from places, friends from enemies, participants from spectators. In little jagged star-like clusters his friends stood around Rabbi Binder, who was still pointing. The topmost point on a star compounded not of angels but of five adolescent boys was Itzie. What a world it was, with those stars below, Rabbi Binder below . . . Ozzie, who a moment earlier hadn't been able to control his own body, started to feel the meaning of the word control: he felt Peace and he felt Power.

"Oscar Freedman, I'll give you three to come down."

Few dictators give their subjects three to do anything; but, as always, Rabbi Binder only looked dictatorial.

"Are you ready, Oscar?"

Ozzie nodded his head yes, although he had no intention in the world—the lower one or the celestial one he'd just entered—of coming down even if Rabbi Binder should give him a million.

"All right then," said Rabbi Binder. He ran a hand through his black Samson hair as though it were the gesture prescribed for uttering the first digit. Then, with his other hand, cutting a circle out of the small piece of sky around him, he spoke. "One!"

There was no thunder. On the contrary, at that moment, as though "one" was the cue for which he had been waiting, the world's least thunderous person appeared on the synagogue steps. He did not so much come out the synagogue door as lean out, onto the darkening air. He clutched at the doorknob with one hand and looked up at the roof.

"Oy!"

Yakov Blotnik's old mind hobbled slowly, as if on crutches, and though he couldn't decide precisely what the boy was doing on the roof, he knew it wasn't good—that is, it wasn't-good-for-the-Jews. For Yakov Blotnik life had fractionated itself simply: things were either good-for-the-Jews or no-good-for-the-Jews.

He smacked his free hand to his in-sucked cheek, gently. "Oy, Gut!" And then quickly as he could he jacked down his head and surveyed the street. There was Rabbi Binder (like a man at an auction with only three dollars in his pocket, he had just delivered a shaky "Two!"); there were the students, and that was all. So far it-wasn't-so-bad-for-the-Jews. But the boy had to come down immediately, before anybody saw. The problem: how to get the boy off the roof?

Anybody who has ever had a cat on the roof knows how to get him down. You call the fire department. Or first you call the operator and you ask her for the fire department. And the next thing there is a great jamming of brakes and clanging of bells and shouting of instructions. And then the cat is off the roof. You do the same thing to get a boy off the roof.

That is, you do the same thing if you are Yakov Blotnik and you once had a cat.

It took a short while for the engines, all four of them, to arrive. As it turned out Rabbi Binder had four times given Ozzie the count of

three; had he not decided to stop, by the time the engines roared up
he would have given him three one hundred and seven times.

The big hook-and-ladder was still swinging around the corner
when one of the firemen leaped from it, plunged headlong towards
the yellow fire hydrant in front of the synagogue, and with a huge
wrench began unscrewing the top nozzle. Rabbi Binder raced over to
him and pulled at his shoulder.

"There's no fire . . ."

The fireman mumbled something sounding like "Screw, buddy,"
back over his shoulder to him and, heatedly, continued working at the
nozzle.

"But there's no fire, there's no fire . . ." Binder shouted. When the
fireman mumbled again, the rabbi grasped his face with both his
hands and pointed it up at the roof.

To Ozzie it looked as though Rabbi Binder was trying to tug the
fireman's head out of his body, like a cork from a bottle. He had to
giggle at the picture they made: it was a family portrait—rabbi in black
skullcap, fireman in red fire-hat, and the little yellow hydrant squatting beside like a kid brother, bareheaded. From the edge of the roof
Ozzie waved at the portrait, a one-handed, flapping, mocking wave;
in doing it his right foot slipped from under him. Rabbi Binder covered his eyes with his hands.

Firemen work fast. Before Ozzie had even regained his balance, a
big, round, yellowed net was being held on the synagogue lawn. The
firemen who held it looked up at Ozzie with stern, feelingless faces.

One of the fireman turned his head towards Rabbi Binder. "What,
is the kid nuts or something?"

Rabbi Binder unpeeled his hands from his eyes, slowly, painfully,
as if they were tape. Then he checked: nothing on the sidewalk, no
dents in the net.

"Is he gonna jump, or what?" the fireman shouted.

In a voice not at all like a statue, Rabbi Binder finally answered.
"Yes, yes, I think so . . . He's been threatening to . . ."

Threatening to? Why, the reason he was on the roof, Ozzie remembered, was to get away; he hadn't even thought about jumping.
He had just run to get away, and the truth was that he hadn't really
headed for the roof as much as he'd been chased there.

"What's his name, the kid?"

"Freedman," Rabbi Binder answered. "Oscar Freedman."

The fireman looked up at Ozzie. "What is it with you, Oscar? You gonna jump, or what?"

Ozzie did not answer. Frankly, the question had just arisen.

"Look, Oscar, if you're gonna jump, jump—and if you're not gonna jump, don't jump. But don't waste our time, willya?"

Ozzie looked at the fireman and then at Rabbi Binder. He wanted to see Rabbi Binder cover his eyes one more time.

"I'm going to jump."

And then he scampered around the edge of the roof to the corner, where there was no net below, and he flapped his arms at his sides, swishing the air and smacking his palms to his trousers on the downbeat; he began screaming like some kind of engine, "Wheeeee . . . wheeeeee," and leaning way out over the edge with the upper half of his body. The firemen whipped around to cover the ground with the net. Rabbi Binder mumbled a few words to Somebody and covered his eyes. Everything happened quickly, jerkily, as in a silent movie. The crowd, which had arrived with the fire engines, gave out a long, Fourth-of-July-fireworks oooh-aahhh. In the excitement no one had paid the crowd much heed, except, of course, Yakov Blotnik, who swung from the doorknob counting heads. "Fier und tsvansik . . . finf und tsvantsik . . . Oy, Gut!" It wasn't like this with the cat.

Rabbi Binder peeked through his fingers, checked the sidewalk and net. Empty. But there was Ozzie racing to the other corner of the roof. The firemen raced with him but were unable to keep up. Whenever Ozzie wanted to he might jump and splatter himself upon the sidewalk, and by the time the firemen scooted to the spot all they could do with their net would be to cover the mess.

"Wheeeee . . . wheeeee . . ."

"Hey, Oscar," the winded fireman yelled, "what the hell is this, a game or something?"

"Wheeeee . . . wheeeee . . ."

"Hey, Oscar—"

But he was off now to the other corner, flapping his wings fiercely. Rabbi Binder couldn't take it any longer—the fire engines from nowhere, the screaming suicidal boy, the net. He fell to his knees exhausted, and with his hands curled together in front of his chest like a little dome, he pleaded, "Oscar, stop it, Oscar. Don't jump, Oscar. Please come down . . . Please don't jump."

And further back in the crowd a single voice, a single young voice, shouted a long word to the boy on the roof.

"Jump!"

It was Itzie. Ozzie momentarily stopped flapping.

"Go ahead, Ozz—jump!" Itzie broke off his point of the star and courageously, with the inspiration not of a wise guy but of a disciple, stood alone. "Jump, Ozz, jump!"

Still on his knees, his hands still curled, Rabbi Binder twisted his body back. He looked at Itzie, then, agonizingly, back up to Ozzie.

"Oscar, DON'T JUMP! PLEASE, DON'T JUMP . . . please please . . ."

"Jump!" This time it wasn't Itzie but another point of the star. By the time Mrs. Freedman arrived to keep her four-thirty appointment with Rabbi Binder, the whole little upside-down heaven was shouting and pleading for Ozzie to jump, and Rabbi Binder no longer was pleading with him not to jump, but was crying into the dome of his hands.

Understandably Mrs. Freedman couldn't figure out what her son was doing on the roof. So she asked.

"Ozzie, my Ozzie, what are you doing? My Ozzie, what is it?"

Ozzie stopped wheeeeeing and slowed his arms down to a cruising flap, the kind birds use in soft winds, but he did not answer. He stood against the low, clouded, darkening sky—light was clicking down more swiftly now, as on a small gear—flapping softly and gazing down at the small bundle of a woman who was his mother.

"What are you doing, Ozzie?" She turned toward the kneeling Rabbi Binder and rushed so close that only a paper-thickness of dusk lay between her stomach and his shoulders.

"What is my baby doing?"

Rabbi Binder gaped up at her but he too was mute. All that moved was the dome of his hands; it shook back and forth like a weak pulse.

"Rabbi, get him down! He'll kill himself. Get him down, my only baby . . ."

"I can't," Rabbi Binder said, "I can't . . ." and he turned his handsome head toward the crowd of boys behind him.

"It's them. Listen to them."

And for the first time Mrs. Freedman saw the crowd of boys and she heard what they were yelling.

"He's doing it for them. He won't listen to me. It's them." Rabbi Binder spoke like one in a trance.

"For them?"

"Yes."

"Why for them?"

"They want him to . . ."

Mrs. Freedman raised her two arms upward as though she were conducting the sky. "For them he's doing it!" And then in a gesture older than pyramids, older than prophets and floods, her arms came slapping down to her sides. "A martyr I have. Look!" She tilted her head to the roof. Ozzie was still flapping softly. "My martyr."

"Oscar, come down, *please*," Rabbi Binder groaned.

In a startlingly even voice Mrs. Freedman called to the boy on the roof. "Ozzie, come down, Ozzie. Don't be a martyr, my baby."

Like a litany, Rabbi Binder repeated her words. "Don't be a martyr, my baby. Don't be a martyr."

"Gawhead, Ozz—*be* a Martin!" It was Itzie. "Be a Martin, be a Martin," and all the voices joined in singing for Martindom. "Be a Martin, be a Martin . . ."

Somehow when you're on a roof the darker it gets the less you can hear. All Ozzie knew was that two groups wanted two new things: his friends were spirited and musical about what they wanted; his mother and the rabbi were even-toned, chanting, about what they didn't want. The rabbi's voice was without tears now and so was his mother's.

The big net stared up at Ozzie like a sightless eye. The big, clouded sky pushed down. From beneath it looked like a gray corrugated board. Suddenly, looking up into that unsympathetic sky, Ozzie realized all the strangeness of what these people, his friends, were asking: they wanted him to jump, to kill himself; they were singing about it now—it made them that happy. And there was an even greater strangeness: Rabbi Binder was on his knees, trembling. If there was a question to be asked now it was not "Is it me?" but rather "Is it us? . . . is it us?"

Being on the roof, it turned out, was a serious thing. If he jumped would the singing become dancing? Would it? What would jumping stop? Yearningly, Ozzie wished he could rip open the sky, plunge his hands through, and pull out the sun; and on the sun, like a coin, would be stamped JUMP or DONT JUMP.

Ozzie's knees rocked and sagged a little under him as though they were setting him for a dive. His arms tightened, stiffened, froze, from shoulders to fingernails. He felt as if each part of his body were going to vote as to whether he should kill himself or not—and each part as though it were independent of *him*.

The light took a long, loud, unexpected click down and the new darkness quickly, like a gag, hushed the friends singing for this and the mother and rabbi chanting for that.

Ozzie stopped counting votes, and in a curiously high voice, like one who wasn't prepared for speech, he spoke.

"Mamma?"

"Yes, Oscar."

"Mamma, get down on your knees, like Rabbi Binder."

"Oscar—"

"Get down on your knees," he said, "or I'll jump."

Ozzie heard a whimper, then a quick rustling, and when he looked down where his mother had stood he saw the top of a head and beneath that a circle of dress. She was kneeling beside Rabbi Binder.

He spoke again. "Everybody kneel." There was the sound of everybody kneeling.

Ozzie looked around. With one hand he pointed toward the synagogue entrance. "Make *him* kneel."

There was a noise, not of kneeling, but of body-and-cloth stretching. Ozzie could hear Rabbi Binder saying in a gruff whisper, ". . . or he'll *kill* himself," and when next he looked there was Yakov Blotnik off the doorknob and for the first time in his life upon his knees in the Gentile posture of prayer.

As for the firemen—it is not as difficult as one might imagine to hold a net taut while you are kneeling.

Ozzie looked around again; and then, still in the voice high as a young girl's, he called to Rabbi Binder.

"Rabbi?"

"Yes, Oscar."

"Rabbi Binder, do you believe in God?"

"Yes."

"Do you believe God can do Anything?" Ozzie leaned his head out into the darkness. "Anything?"

"Oscar, I think—"

"Tell me you believe God can do Anything."

There was a second's hesitation. Then:

"God can do Anything."

"Tell me you believe God can make a child without intercourse."

"He can."

"Tell me!"

"God," Rabbi Binder admitted, "can make a child without intercourse."

"Mamma, you tell me."

"God can make a child without intercourse," his mother said.

"Make *him* tell me." There was no doubt who *him* was.

In a few moments Ozzie heard an old comical voice say something to the increasing darkness about God.

Next, Ozzie made everybody say it. And then he made them all say they believed in Jesus Christ—first one at a time, then all together.

When the catechizing was through it was the beginning of evening. From the street it sounded as if someone on the roof might have sighed.

"Ozzie?" A woman's voice dared to speak. "You'll come down now?"

There was no answer, but the woman waited, and when a voice finally did speak it was thin and crying, and exhausted as that of an old man who has just finished pulling the bells.

"Mamma, don't you see—you shouldn't hit me. He shouldn't hit me. You shouldn't hit me about God, Mamma. You should never hit anybody about God—"

"Ozzie, please come down now."

"Promise me, Mamma, promise me you'll never hit anybody about God."

He had asked only his mother, but for some reason everyone kneeling in the street promised he would never hit anybody about God.

Once again there was silence.

"I can come down now, Mamma," the boy on the roof finally said. He turned his head both ways as though checking the traffic lights. "Now I can come down . . ."

And he did, right into the center of the yellow net that glowed in the evening's edge like an overgrown halo.

Pattiann Rogers

The Fallacy of Thinking
Flesh Is Flesh

Some part of every living creature
is always trembling, a curious
constancy in the wavering rims
of the cup coral, the tasseling
of fringe fish, in the polyrippling
of the polyclad flatworm even under the black
bottom water at midnight when nothing
in particular notices.

The single topknot, head feather,
of the horned screamer or the tufted
quail can never, in all its tethered
barbs and furs, be totally still.
And notice the plural flickers
of the puss moth's powdery antennae.
Not even the puss moth knows how
to stop them.

Maybe it's the pattern of the shattering
sea-moon so inherent to each body
that makes each more than merely body.
Maybe it's the way the blood possesses
the pitch and fall of blooming grasses
in a wind that makes the prairie

of the heart greater than its boundaries.
Maybe it's god's breath swelling
in the breast and limbs, like a sky
at dawn, that gives bright bone
the holiness of a rising sun.
There's more to flesh than flesh.
The steady flex and draw of the digger
wasp's blue-bulbed abdomen—I know
there's a fact beyond presence
in all that fidgeting.

Even as it sleeps, watch the body
perplex its definition—the slight shift
of the spine, the inevitable lash shiver,
signal pulse knocking. See, there,
that simple shimmer of the smallest
toe again, just to prove it.

Issue 133, 1994

Larry Brown

✠

A Roadside Resurrection

Story opens, Mr. Redding is coughing in a cafe by the Yocona River, really whamming it out between his knees. He's got on penny loafers with pennies in them, yellow socks, madras shorts, a reversible hat and a shirt that's faded from being washed too many times. His wife, Flenco, or Flenc, as he calls her, is slapping him on the back and alternately sucking her chocolate milk shake through a straw and looking around to see who's watching. She's got a big fat face, rollers in her hair, and she's wearing what may well be her nightgown and robe. Fingernails: bright red.

"Damn!" Mr. Redding coughs. "Godamighty . . . damn!"

Flenco hits him on the back and winces at his language, sucking hard on her straw and glancing around. Mr. Redding goes into a bad fit of coughing, kneels down on the floor heaving, tongue out and curled, veins distended on his skinny forearms, hacking, strangling, and the children of the diners are starting to look around in disgust.

"Oh," he coughs. "Oh shit. Oh damn."

Mr. Redding crawls back up in the booth and reaches into his shirt pocket for a Pall Mall 100, lights it, takes one suck, then repeats the entire scenario above. This goes on three times in thirty minutes.

Customers go in and out and people order beers and drink them at the counter on stools, but Mr. Redding lies back in the booth while his wife mops his feverish forehead with wetted paper towels brought by a waitress from the kitchen, along with another milk shake just like the last one. The hair on Mr. Redding's forearms is dark and scattered like hair on a mangy dog just recovering, and his sideburns sticking out from under the reversible cap are gray. Twenty years ago he could do a pretty good imitation of Elvis. Now he's washed up.

"Oh crap," he says. "Oh shit. Oh hell."

Flenco mops him and sops up his sweat and sucks her big round mouth around the straw and looks at people and pats him on the back. Truckers come in with their names on their belts and eat eggs and ham and wash down pills with coffee and put their cigarettes out in their plates, stagger back outside and climb up into their sleepers. Flenco looks down the road and wonders what road she'll be on before long.

"Oh shit," Mr. Redding wheezes.

Miles away down the road a legendary young healer is ready to raise the roof on a tent gathering. Sawdust is on the floor and the lights are bright and a crippled boy in a wheelchair has been brought forward to feel his healing hands. The boy lies in his chair drooling up at the lights, hands trembling, the crowd watching on all sides, spectators all piled up along the back and sides and others peeking in the opened opening, some lying on the ground with their heads stuck up between the tent pegs. The crippled child waits, the mother trembling also, nearby, hands clasped breastwise to the Holy Father Sweet Mary Mother of Saints heal my child who was wrong from the womb Amen. The lights flicker. The healer is imbued with the Spirit of God which has come down at the edge of this cotton field and put into his fingers the strength of His love and healing fire. Outside bright blades of lightning arch and thunderclouds rumble in the turbulent sky as the healer goes into his trance. His fine dark hair is sleek on the sides of his head and he cries out: "Heeeeeal! Heal this boy, Lord! Heal him! Dear sweet merciful God if You ever felt it in Your heart to heal somebody heal this boy! This boy! This one right here, Lord! I know there's a bunch of 'em over there in darkest Africa need healing too Lord but they ain't down on their knees to You right now like we are!"

The healer sinks to his knees with these words, hands locked and upflung before him. Ushers are moving slowly through the crowd with their plates out, but nobody's putting much into the plates yet because they haven't seen the boy get up and walk.

"Lord what about Gethsemane? Lord what about Calvary's cross? Lord what about Your merciful love that we're here to lay on this child? There's his mama, Lord. I guess his daddy's in here, too. Maybe all his brothers and sisters."

"He's a only child," the mama whispers, but nobody seems to notice. The rain has started and everybody's trying to crowd inside.

"Neighbors? I don't believe there's much faith in this house tonight. I believe we've done run into a bunch of doubting Thomases, folks who want to play before they pay. Maybe they think this ain't nothing but a sideshow. Maybe they think this boy works for me. Because I don't believe they're putting in any money to further our work."

The ushers make another pass through the crowd and collect six dollars and fifty-two cents. The boy lies in the wheelchair, legs dangling. This child has never walked before. The mother has told the healer his history. He was born with spinal meningitis, his heart outside his body, and she said God only gave him one kidney. She said on the day she goes to her grave she will still owe hospital bills on him. The healer can see that the congregation thinks nothing is going to happen. He can almost read their faces, can almost read in their countenances the unsaid accusations: *Ha! Unclean! Prove yourself! Make him walk!*

The healer comes down from the podium. The fire of God is still in him. The wheels of the wheelchair are mired in the sawdust. The mother has already begun to feel what has come inside the tent. She faints, falls over, shrieks gently. An uncle stands up. The healer lays his hands on.

"Now I said *heal*! I don't give a damn! About what's happening over there in Saudi Arabia! I don't care what else You got on Your mind! You got to heal this boy! Either heal him or take him right now! Heal him! Or take him! We don't care! He's with You either way!"

The child wobbles in the wheelchair. The healer digs his fingers down deep into the flesh. More people stand up to see. The mother wakes up, moans and faints again. The lightning cracks overhead and the lights go out and then come back on dim. The ushers are moving more quickly through the crowd. An aura of Presence moves inside the tent to where everybody feels it. The child grips the armrests of his chair. His feet dig for purchase in the sawdust. He cries out with eyes closed in a racked and silent scream.

"Yeah!" the healer shouts. "Didn't believe! Look at him! Watch him walk!"

The boy struggles up out of the chair. People have come to his mother's side with wet handkerchiefs and they revive her in time to witness him make his stand. He rises up on his wasted legs, the healer's hands octopused on his head.

"Heal! Heal! Heal! Heal! Heal! Heal! Heal!"

The boy shoves the hands away. The mother looks up at her son from the dirt. He takes a step. His spine is straight. He takes another step. People are falling to their knees in the sawdust. They are reaching for their purses and wallets.

Mr. Redding has to be taken outside because he is bothering the other customers. Flenco lets him lie on the seat of the truck for a while and fans him with a Merle Haggard album.

"Oh shit," Mr. Redding says. "Oh arrrrgh."

"It's gonna be all right, baby," Flenco says.

Mr. Redding is almost beyond talking, but he gasps out: "What do . . . you mean . . . it's . . . gonna . . . be . . . all right?"

"Oh, baby, I heard he'd be through here by nine o'clock. And they say he can really heal."

"I don't . . . believe . . . none of that . . . *bull*shit!"

Mr. Redding says that, and goes into great whoops of coughing.

A lot of money in the plates tonight. The mission can go on. But some helpers have wives back home, trailer payments have to be met, others want satellite dishes. The healer requires nothing but a meal that will last him until the next meal. He gives them all the money except for the price of steak and eggs at a Waffle House and heads for the car. The road is mud. The tent is being taken down in the storm. The memory of the woman is on him and he doesn't feel very close to God.

"Oh shit," Mr. Redding says. "Oh damn oh hell oh shit."

"Baby?" Flenco says. "Don't you think you ought not be cussing so bad when you're like this?"

"Li . . . iii . . . iiike what?" Mr. Redding spews out.

"When you're coughing so bad and all. I bet if you'd quit smoking them cigarettes you wouldn't cough so bad."

She pats him on the back like she saw the respiratory therapist do and feels she knows a little about medicine.

"Oh crap," Mr. Redding says. "Oh *shit!*"

Flenco mops his sweaty head and fans hot air with her hand. She has heard that the healer drives a long black Caddy. They say he refuses to appear on network television and will not endorse products. They say he comes speeding out of the dusty fields in his dusty black car and they say the wind his machine brings whips the trousers of the state troopers before they can get into their cruisers and take pursuit. They say he lives only to heal and that he stops on the roadsides where crippled children have been set up and where their mothers stand behind them holding up cardboard placards painstakingly printed HEALER HEAL MY CHILD. They say that if the state troopers catch up with him while he is performing some miracle of mercy on one of God's bent lambs, the people pull their cars out into the road and block the highway, taking the keys out of the ignitions, locking the doors. It's said that in Georgia last year a blockade of the faithful ran interference for him through a web of parked police cars outside Waycross and allowed him to pass unmolested, such is the strength of his fame. Flenco hasn't a placard. She has rented a billboard beside the cafe, letters six feet tall proclaiming HEALER HEAL MY HUSBAND. Telephone reports from her sister-in-law in Bruce confirm the rumor that he has left Water Valley and is heading their way. Flenco imagines him coming down out of the hilly country, barreling down the secondary roads and blasting toward the very spot where she sits fanning Mr. Redding's feverish frame.

"Oh shit," Mr. Redding says. "Oh God . . . dang!"

"Just rest easy now, honey," Flenco says. "You want me to go get you some Co-Coler?"

"Hell naw, I don't want no goddamn Co-Coler," Mr. Redding says. "I want some . . . want some goddamn . . . I want some . . . shit! Just carry me . . . back home and . . . goddamn . . . let me die. I'm . . . goddamn . . . burning up out here."

Flenco hugs his skinny body tight and feels one of his emaciated wrists. Hands that used to hold a silver microphone hang limply from his cadaverous arms, all speckled with liver spots. She wants him to hold on a little longer because she doesn't know if the healer has worked his way up to raising the dead yet. She knows a little of his scanty history. Born to Christian Seminoles and submerged for thirty-seven minutes in the frigid waters of Lake Huron at the age of fourteen, he was found by divers and revived with little hope of ultimate survival by fire fighters on a snow-covered bank. He allegedly lay at death's door in a coma for nine weeks, then suddenly got out of his bed, ripping the IV tubes out, muttering without cursing, and walked down the hall to the intensive care unit where a family of four held a death vigil over their ninety-year-old grandmother fatally afflicted with a ruptured duodenum and laid his hands on her. The legend goes that within two minutes the old lady was sitting up in the bed demanding fudge ripple on a sugar cone and a pack of Lucky Strikes. Fame soon followed and the boy's yard became littered with the sick and the crippled, and the knees of his jeans became permanently grass-stained from kneeling. The walking canes piled up in a corner of the yard as a testament to his powers. A man brought a truck once a week to collect the empty wheelchairs. He made the blind see, the mute speak. A worldwide team of doctors watched him cure a case of wet leprosy. The president had him summoned to the White House, but he could not go; the street in front of his house was blocked solid with the bodies of the needing-to-be-healed. People clamored after him, and women for his seed. The supermarket tabloids proclaim that he will not break the vow he gave to God in the last few frantic moments before sinking below the waters of Lake Huron: if God would bring him back from a watery death he would remain pure and virginal in order to do His work. And now he has come south like a hunted animal to seek out the legions of believers with their sad and twisted limbs.

"Flenc," Mr. Redding coughs out, "How many goddamn times I told you . . . oh shit . . . not to . . . aw hell, ahhhhh."

The tent is down, the rain has ceased. The footsteps of many are printed in the mud. He's had to sign autographs this time, and fighting the women off is never easy. They are convinced the child they'd bear would be an Albert Einstein, an Arnold Schwarzenegger, a Tom Selleck with the brain of Renoir. Some tell him they only want him for a few moments to look at something in the back seat of their car, but he knows they are offering their legs and their breasts and their mouths. He can't resist them any more. He's thinking about getting out of the business. The promise has already been broken anyway, and the first time was the hardest.

His bodyguards and henchmen push with arms spread against the surging crowd and his feet suck in the mud as he picks his way to his Caddy. All around sit cars and pickup trucks parked or stuck spinning in the mud as the weak sun tries to smile down between the parting clouds.

He gets into the car and inserts the ignition key and the engine barks instantly into life with the merest flick of the key. The engine is as finely tuned as a Swiss watchmaker's watch and it hums with a low and throaty purring that emanates from glass-pack mufflers topped off with six feet of chrome. He tromps on the gas pedal and the motor rumbles, cammed up so high it will barely take off.

He hits the gas harder and the Caddy squats in the mud, fishtailing like an injured snake through the quagmire of goop. The crowd rushes the bodyguards, pushing their burly bodies back and down and trampling them underfoot, stepping on their fingers, surging forward to lay their once withered hands on the dusty flanks of the healer's automobile. Faces gather around the windows outside and the healer steers his machine through the swampy mess of the pasture and over to a faint trail of gravel that leads to the highway. Many hands push and when he guns the big car mud balls thwack hollowly and flatten on the pants and shirts of the faithful left gawking after him in his wake. They wave, beat their chests to see him go. Liberated children turn handsprings in the mud and perform impromptu fencing matches with their useless crutches and these images recede quickly through the back window as the car lurches toward the road.

The healer looks both ways before pulling out on the highway. Cars are lined on both sides all the way to the curves that lie in the distance. Horns blare behind him and he turns the car north and smashes the gas pedal flat against the floorboard. The big vehicle takes the road under its wheels and rockets past the lines of automobiles. Small hands wave from the back seats as he accelerates rapidly past them.

The needle on the speedometer rises quickly. He eyes the gas gauge's red wedge of metal edged toward FULL. He finds K.D. Lang on the radio and fishes beneath the seat for the flask of vodka his bodyguards have secreted there. The prearranged destination is Marion, Arkansas, where droves of the helpless are rumored to be gathered in a field outside the town.

He takes one hit, two hits, three hits of vodka and pops the top on a hot Coke while reaching for his smokes. His shoes are slathered with mud and his shirt is dirty, but fresh clothes await him somewhere up ahead. Everything is provided. Every bathroom in the South is open to him. The Fuzzbuster on the dash ticks and he hits the brakes just in time to cruise by a cruiser hidden in a nest of honeysuckle. At fifty-seven mph.

He feels weak and ashamed for breaking his vow, but the women won't let him alone. They seem to know the weakness of his flesh. A new issue of *Penthouse* is under the seat. He reaches over and takes his eyes off the road for a moment, pulls the magazine out. He flips it open and the pictures are there, with nothing left to the imagination, the long legs, the tawny hair, the full and pouting lips. With a sharp stab of guilt he closes it up and shoves it back under the seat. He can't go on like this. A decision has to be made. There are too many who believe in him and he is the vessel of their faith. He knows he's unworthy of that trust now. It's going to be embarrassing if God decides to let him down one night in front of a hundred and fifty people. The crowd might even turn ugly and lynch him if he's suddenly unable to heal. They've come to expect it. They have every right to expect it. But they don't know about his needs. They don't know what it's like to be denied the one thing that everybody else can have: the intimate touch of another.

He lights the cigarette and cracks the vent as a smattering of raindrops splatters across the windshield. He turns the wipers on and passes through a curtain of rain as perpendicular as a wall, crosses over onto a shiny darkened highway with tiny white explosions of water pinging up on its surface. He tromps on the gas pedal and the

Caddy's tires sing their high-speeded whine. Small heads on front porches turn like tennis spectators as a black flash shoots down the road. He waves.

Mr. Redding lies near comatose under the shade tree Flenco has dragged him to, and people coming out of the cafe now are giving him queasy looks. Flenco knows that some good citizen might have an ambulance called.

"Just hold on now, baby," Flenco says. "I feel it in my heart he's coming any minute now."

"I don't give a . . . give a good . . . a good . . . a good god-damn . . . I don't give a shit who's coming," Mr. Redding hacks out. His lips are slimy with a splotching of pink foam and his breath rattles in his chest like dry peas in a pod. He quivers and shakes and licks his lips and groans. Flenco cradles his graying head in her ample lap and rubs the top of his hat with her tremendous sagging breasts. Her rose-tipped nipples miss the passion that used to be in Mr. Redding's tongue. Flenco deeply feels this loss of sexual desire and sighs in her sleep at night on the couch while Mr. Redding hacks and coughs and curses in the bedroom and gets up to read detective magazines or rolls all over the bed. She's ashamed of her blatant overtures and attempts at enticement, the parted robe, the naked toweling off beside the open bathroom door, the changing of her underwear in the middle of the day. Mr. Redding appears not to notice, only lights one Pall Mall after another and swears.

She has sent a wide-eyed little boy inside for another chocolate milk shake and he brings it out to her under the tree where she holds the gasping wheezebag who used to belt out one Elvis song after another in his white jumpsuit with the silver zippers. He'd been nabbed for bad checks in Texas, was on the run from a Mann Act in Alabama, but Flenco fell in love with his roguey smile and twinkling eyes the first time she saw him do "You Ain't Nothing but a Hound Dog" at the junior-senior prom. His battered travel trailer had a cubbyhole with a stained mattress that held the scented remnants of other nights of lust. But Flenco, pressed hard against the striped ticking with her head in a corner, found in his wild and enthusiastic gymnastics a kind of secret delight. Shunned by her schoolmates, sent to the office for passing explicit notes to boys, downtrodden by the depression caused by her steady eating, Flenco was hopelessly smitten in the first few minutes with his hunk of "Burning Love."

Now her lover lies wasted in her lap, his true age finally showing, his wrinkled neck corded with skin like an old lizard's as he sags against her and drools. She's not asking for immortality; she's not asking for the Fountain of Youth; she's only asking for a little more time. The hope that burns in her heart is a candle lit to the memory of physical love. She wipes his hot face tenderly with a wadded napkin soaked in the cold sweat from the milk-shake cup. Mr. Redding turns and digs his head deeper into her belly. People at the tables in the cafe are staring openly through the windows now and Flenco knows it's only a matter of time before somebody calls the lawdogs.

"Can I do anything for you, baby?" she says.

Mr. Redding turns his eyes up to her and the pain buried in them is like a dying fire.

"Hell yeah you can . . . do . . . something . . . goddamn . . . do something . . . oh shit . . . for me. You can . . . goddamn . . . oh shit . . . you can . . . just . . . hell . . . by God . . . shoot me."

"Oh baby, don't talk like that," Flenco says. Her eyes mist up and she covers his face with her breasts until he reaches up with both hands and tries to push the weighty mass of her mammary monsters up out of the way.

"Goddamn, what you . . . what you trying to . . . trying to . . . I didn't say . . . smother me," Mr. Redding says.

Flenco doesn't answer. She closes her eyes and feels the former flicks of his tongue across her breastworks in a memory as real as their truck.

The road is straight, the cotton young and strong, and the Caddy is a speeding bullet across the flat highway. The needle is buried to the hilt at 120 and the car is floating at the very limit of adhesion, weightless, almost, drifting slightly side to side like a ship lightly tacking on the ocean in the stiff edges of a breeze. The blue pulses of light winking far behind him in the sun are like annoying toys, no more. The healer dips handful after handful of roofing tacks out of the sack beside him and flings them out the open window, scattering them like ever the healer is tempted to burn rubber and leave them smelling his getaway fumes, leave behind him unheard the story of their huge drooling son, prisoner of the basement, chained in the garage at the family reunions. But the faces of these two parents are lit like rays of sunshine with the knowledge that a modern messiah has chosen the road that borders their alfalfa patch to receive His divine instructions.

The woman runs up to the side of the car and lays her hands on the fender as if she'd hold it to keep the car from leaving. Her beady eyes and panting breath and hopeless, eternal, hope-filled face tell the healer this woman has a task of such insurmountable proportions she's scarce shared the secret of her problem with minister or preacher or parson, that this one's so bad he can't quit now. Holy cow. What pining cripple on his bed of moldy quilts with his palsied arms shaking lies waiting nearly forever for his release? What afflicted lamb has lain behind a curtain to be hidden from company all these years? Here, he sees, are the mother and the father, the suffering parents, here with their pain and their hope and their alfalfa patch and cows and fish ponds, their world struck askew by the birth or the affliction or the accident that befell their fallen one, with neither hope of redemption or cure available for what might be eating mothballs or masturbating in old dirty underwear and hiding it under his mother's mattress to be discovered when the springs need turning, might be roaming the pastures by night creeping stealthily upon the female livestock.

"Healer," the woman asks. "Will you heal my child?"

He's not coming, Flenco suddenly decides. In a burst of thought process too deep for her to understand, a mere scab on the broad scar of telepathy which man's mind forgot to remember eons ago, she knows somehow that another emergency has detained him. She knows, too, that they must therefore go find him. She gets up and catches Mr. Redding under the armpits and drags him through the dust toward the truck, where now in large numbers on the other side of the cafe windows people stand gathered to track the proceedings and place wagers on the estimated time of arrival of Mr. Redding's demise.

"Oh hope, there's hope," she chants and pants. His heels make two trails of dust through the parking lot but his loafers stay on like a bad seeds. The blue lights fade, are gone, left far behind. Others oi like bent are waiting probably somewhere ahead but he'll deal with them when the time comes.

Fruit and vegetable stands flash by the open windows of the car, junk peddlers, mobile homes, stacked firewood corded up on the sides of the road for sale, waving people, fans. It is these people he heals, these people crushed and maimed by the falling trees, by the falling house trailers, by the falling cars and junk. These innocents carving a life out of the wilderness with their hands, these with so much faith that he is merely an instrument, a transmitter to funnel the energy required to make them stand up and throw away their braces. He thinks of the promise he made going down reaching for the surface of Lake Huron. He gets another drink of the vodka and lights another cigarette and shakes his head as the hubcaps glitter in the sun.

"Lord God I wouldn't have touched her if I was the Pope!" he suddenly screams out into the car, beating his fist on the seat. He turns his head and shouts out the open window: "Why didn't you let me die and then bring me back as the Pope? Huh? You want to answer that one, Lord?"

He takes another quick suck of the hot vodka. His shoulders shiver, and he caps it.

"I cain't cure everbody in the whole world!"

He slows down and rolls to about fifteen mph and shouts to a God maybe lurking behind a dilapidated cotton pen and guarded by a pink Edsel with the hood on the roof.

"You ought not made it so tough on me! I ain't like Jesus, I'm human! I can't do it no more, they's too many of 'em! They's too many women! I take back my promise, I quit!"

The long low surprised face of a farmer in a 1953 Chevrolet pickup with a goat in the back passes by him in slow motion, his head hanging out the window, a woman looking over his shoulder, seeing, figuring the black car and the haranguing finger poking out at a telephone pole, gathering her wits, her thoughts, her breath, to point back, inhale, scream: "It's HIM! PRAISE WONDERFUL GOD IT'S HIIIIIIM!"

The healer looks. He sees the old black pickup grind to a halt, the one brake light coming on, the woman hopping out the door, arms waving, the farmer leaning out the window waving. For the first time miracle or a magic trick. Flenco gets him next to the running board and stoops to release the precious burden of him, opens the door, gives a hefty grunt and hauls him up into the seat. Mr. Redding falls over against the horn of the truck and it begins to blow as Flenco shuts the door and runs around to the other side. She yanks open the door and pushes him erect in the seat and reaches across him and locks the door so he won't fall out and hurt himself any worse. Those cigarettes have a hold on him that keeps him from eating, from gaining weight, from not wheezing in the early morning hours when she awakens beside him and lies in the dark staring at his face and twirling the tufts of gray hair on his chest around her fingers. But maybe the healer can even cure him of his addiction, drive the blackness from his lungs, the platelets from his aorta, flush the tiny capillaries in their encrusted fingers of flesh. She belts him in.

Mr. Redding sits in a perfect and abject state of apathy, his head keened back on his neck and his closed eyes seeing nothing. Not even coughing.

"Hold on, baby," Flenco says, and cranks the truck. Truckers and patrons stand gawking at the rooster tail of dust and gravel kicked up by the spinning wheel of the truck, then it slews badly, hits the road sliding and is gone in a final suck of sound.

With stabbing motions of her arm and hand, index finger extended, the mother directs the healer into the yard. A white picket fence with blooming daffodils belies the nature of the thing inside.

"Please, he's a baby, harmless really, come, in here, behind, I just know you, please, my mother she, my brother too they," she gasps.

The healer turns in and sees the black pickup coming behind him, the goat peeking around the cab as if directing its movement, this Nubian. Before he can fully stop the car, the woman is tugging on his arm, saying, "In here, you, oh, my husband, like a child, really."

He opens the door and starts out as the truck slides to a stop beside him, dust rising to drift over them. The healer waves his hand and coughs and the woman pulls on his arm. The farmer jogs around the hood on his gimpy leg and they each take an arm and lead him up the steps, across the porch, both of them talking in either ear a mix of latent complaints, untold griefs and shared blames for the years this child born wrong and then injured in the brain has visited on this house. The healer is dragged into a living room with white doilies under lamps and a flowerful rug spread over polished wood and a potbellied stove in one corner where a dead squirrel sits eating a varnished walnut.

"Back here, in here, he," the woman rants.

"You know, he, by golly, our field," the farmer raves.

The healer is afraid they're going to smell his breath and he turns his face from side to side as he's dragged with feet sliding to the back room, inside the closet, down hidden stairs revealed by a trapdoor. The farmer unlocks a door in the dark, hits a switch. A light comes on. Gray walls of drabness lie sweating faintly deep in the earth's damp and they're hung with old mattresses brown with spots. The furniture in the room is soft with rot, green with mold. A large, naked, drooling hairy man sits playing with a ball of his own shit in the center of the room, his splayed feet and fuzzy toes black with dirt and his sloped forehead furrowed in concentration. He says, "Huuuuuuuuurrrrrnnn . . ."

The healer recoils. The hairy man sits happily in the center of the floor amongst plates of old food and the little pies he has made, but looks up and eyes his parents and the paling youth between them and instantly his piglike eyes darken with total ignorance or, like the darkest of animals, an unveiled hostile threat.

"Hurrrrr," he says, and swivels on his buttocks to face them.

"Sweet Lord Jesus Christ," the healer whispers. "Get me out of here."

"Not so fast, young fella," the farmer says, and unlimbers from a back pocket a hogleg of Dirty Harry proportions, backs to the door behind him, locks it, pockets the key deep in his overalls.

It doesn't smell nice at all in this dungeon and the thing before him begins to try to get up on its knees and make sounds of wet rumbling wanting deep in its throat. The eyebrows knit up and down and together and apart and the healer draws back with his hands up because the man is sniffing now, trying like a blind calf to scent his mother, maybe remembering milk.

Mr. Redding lies back in the seat not even harrumphing but merely jackknifed into the position his wife has seated him in like a form set in concrete while the truck roars down the road. Flenco slurps the sediment of her shake through the straw and flings the used container out the window into a passing mass of sunflowers' bright yellow faces. Her right hand is clenched upon the wheel and her foot is pressed hard on the gas.

"Hold on, baby," she says. "I don't know where he's at but we're going to find him." Her mouth is grim.

Mr. Redding doesn't answer. He sits mute and unmoving with his head canted back and lolling limply on his neck, the squashed knot of his reversible fishing hat pulled down over his ears. He seems uninterested in the green countryside flashing by, the happy farms of cows grazing contentedly on the lush pasture grass, the wooded creeks and planted fields within the industry of American agriculture thriving peacefully beside the road.

Flenco reaches over and gets one of his cigarettes from his pocket and grabs a box of matches off the dash. She doesn't usually smoke but the situation is making her nervous. Afraid that his rancid lips might never again maul her fallow flesh, she scratches the match on the box and touches the whipping flame to the tip of the Pall Mall 100. Deluged with the desperation of despair, she draws the smoke deep and then worries her forehead with the cigarette held between her fingers. Her eyes scan the fertile fields and unpainted barns for a gathering of cripples miraculously assembled somewhere to seek out the ultimate truth. Somewhere between the borders of three counties a black Caddy runs speeding to another destination and she must intercept it or find its location. The rotting fruit of her romance lies hanging in the balance. The sad wreck of her lover must be rejuvenated. All is lost if not.

Flenco remembers the early years with Mr. Redding. Through him the ghost of Elvis not only lived but sang and whirled his pumping hips to dirges engraved on the brains of fans like grooves in records. He could get down on one knee and bring five or six of them screaming to their feet and rushing to the edge of the stage, the nostalgic, the overweight, the faded dyed ever faithful. Now this sad wasted figure lays his head back on the seat with his lips slightly parted, his tongue drying.

Flenco smokes the cigarette furiously, stabs the scenery with her eyes, roars down the left fork of a road where a sign says HILLTOP 10 MILES. Dust hurtles up behind the pickup as it barrels down the hill. Flenco has the blind faith of love but she panics when she thinks that she might not find the healer, that he might be out of reach already, that he might have taken an alternate road and be somewhere else in the county, doing his work, healing the minions who seek him out, laying his hands on other unfortunates whose despair has eclipsed hers. But as long as there is gas in the truck, as long as Mr. Redding draws breath, she will drive until the wheels fall off the truck, until the cows come home, until they piss on the fire and call the dogs. Until hope, however much is left, is smashed, kicked around, stomped on or gone. Until Mr. Redding is dead.

Flenco eyes him and feels uneasy over his stillness. She's never known him to be this quiet before. She mashes harder on the gas and her beloved sways in the curves.

"Hold on, baby," she whispers.

The healer stands unmoving with the hard round mouth of the pistol in his back. The man on the floor is growling low and grinding his tartared teeth. His hairy arms are encrusted with a nasty crap.

"Aaaarrrrr," he says.

"Yes, darling," the mother coos. "The nice man has come to help us. You like the nice man, don't you, dear?"

"He likes to play," the farmer says. "He plays down here all the time, don't you, son?" the farmer says. "We just keep him down here so he won't scare people," he explains.

The parents see no need to recite the list of stray dogs and hapless cats caught and torn limb from limb, dripping joints of furred meat thrust mouthward without mayonnaise. The six-year-old girl still missing from last year is best not spoken of. The farmer now makes use of a pneumatic tranquilizer gun before laying on the chains and padlocks at night. Delivered at home beside his stillborn twin like Elvis, the hairy one has a headstone over his undug grave.

The warped and wavy line of his dented skull is thick with a rancid growth where small insect life traverses the stalks of his matted hair. He sways and utters his guttural verbs and fixes the healer's face with his bated malevolence and grunts his soft equations into the dusty air.

"He wants to play," the mother says. "Ain't that cute."

"Cute as a bug," the farmer says, without loosening his grip on the pistol.

"I can't heal him," the healer says.

"What did you say?" the farmer says.

"Did he say what I think he said?" the mother says.

"I think you better say that again," the farmer says.

"I can't heal him. I can't heal anything like this."

"What are you saying?" the mother says.

"You heard what he said," the farmer says. "Says he can't heal him."

"Can't?" the mother says.

"I can't," the healer says, as the man on the floor drools a rope of drool and moans a secret rhyme and moves his shoulders to and fro and never takes his eyes off the healer's face.

"I bet you'd like to know what happened to him," the mother says.

"Horse kicked him," the farmer says.

"Right in the head," the mother says.

"Turned him ass over teakettle," the farmer says. "Kicked him clean over a fence."

"Like to kicked half his head off," the mother says. "But you've cured worse than this. That little girl over in Alabama last year with that arm growed out of her stomach and that old man in the Delta who had two and a half eyes. You can heal him. Now heal him."

"We done read all about you," the farmer says. "We been trying to find you for months."

"And then he just come driving right by the place," the mother says. "Will wonders never cease."

The man on the floor is trying to form the rude impulses necessary to gather his legs beneath himself and put his feet flat on the floor. He wants to stand and will stand in a moment and the farmer reaches quickly behind him for the coiled whip on a nail.

"Easy now, son," he says.

A low uneasy moaning begins at sight of the bullwhip and the bared teeth alternate with that in a singsong incantation as he totters up onto his knees and rests his folded knuckles flat on the floor. The hair is long on his back and arms and legs. His face is transfixed with an ignorance as old as time, yet a small light burns in his eyes, and he has a little tail six inches in length extending from the coccyx bone with a tufted tip of bristles. He slides forward a few inches closer to the healer. Old bones lie piled in corners for safekeeping with their scraps of blackened flesh.

"You might as well go on and heal him," the farmer says. "We ain't letting you out of here till you do."

"He's been like this a long time," the mother says.

"You don't understand," the healer says. "I've never dealt with anything like this."

"You cured cancer," the farmer says.

"Raised the dead, I've heard," the mother says.

"No ma'am. Ain't nobody ever raised the dead but Jesus Himself," the healer says, as the thing begins to look as if it would like to grab his leg. He tries to retreat, but the gun is in his back like a hard finger.

"What you think, mama?" the farmer says.

"I think he's trying to pull our leg," she says.

"You think he's a false prophet?"

"Might be. Or maybe he's used up all his power?"

"What about it, young feller? You used up all your power?"

"I known it was him when I seen that black car," she says.

"Lots of people have black cars," the healer says dully, unable to take his own eyes off those dully glinting ones before him. What lies inside there will not do to look at, it won't be altered by human hands, probably should have been drowned when it was little. "Don't let him hurt me," he says.

"Hurt you? Why he ain't going to hurt you," the mother says. "He just wants to play with you a little bit. We come down here and play with him all the time, don't we, daddy."

"That's right," the farmer says. "Hopfrog and leap-scotch and like that. Go on and lay your hands on him. He won't bite or nothing, I promise."

"He's real good most of the time," she says. "We just keep him penned up so he won't hurt hisself."

"I can't . . . I can't . . ." the healer begins.

"Can't what?" the farmer says.

"Can't what?" the mother says.

"*Touch* him," the healer breathes.

"Uh oh," says the farmer. "I's afraid of that, mama."

"You people have got to let me out of here," the healer says. "I'm on my way to Arkansas."

"Wrong answer, mister," the farmer says.

"Definitely the wrong answer," the mother says.

Their boy moves closer and his snarling mouth seems to smile.

Flenco stands in her nightgown and robe and curlers, pumping gas into the neck of the fuel tank located in the left rear quarter panel of the truck. Years ago Mr. Redding took a hammer and screwdriver to it so that it would readily accept a leaded gasoline nozzle. Flenco pumps five dollars worth into it and hands the money to the attendant who wiped no windshield and checked no oil but stood gawking at the rigid figure of Mr. Redding displayed in the seat like a large sack of potatoes. The attendant takes the five and looks thoughtfully at Flenco, then opens his mouth to ask:

"Lady, is this guy all right?"

Flenco starts to go around and get behind the wheel and then, when she sees the beer signs hung in the windows of the gas station, thinks of the twenty-dollar bill wadded in the pocket of her robe like used facial tissue.

"Well he's been sick," she says, hurrying toward the door of the building.

"I don't believe he's feeling real good right now," he says to her disappearing back. When she goes inside, he watches her heading for the beer coolers at the back of the store and steps closer to the open window of the truck. He studies Mr. Redding from a vantage point of ten inches and notices that his lips are blue and his face is devoid of any color, sort of like, a *lot* like, an uncle of his who was laid out in a coffin in the comfort of his own home some two weeks before.

"Mister," he says. "Hey, mister!"

Mr. Redding has nothing to say. Flenco comes rushing back out the door with three quart bottles of cold Busch in a big grocery sack and a small package of cups for whenever Mr. Redding feels like waking up and partaking of a cool refreshing drink. She eyes the attendant suspiciously and gets in the truck and sets the beer on the seat between them, pausing first to open one bottle and set it between her massive thighs. She leans up and cranks the truck and looks at the attendant who steps back and holds up one hand and says, "Don't mind me, lady, it's a free country." Then she pulls it down into D and roars out onto the road.

Flenco gooses it up to about sixty and reaches over briefly to touch Mr. Redding's hand. The hand is cool and limp and she's glad the fever has passed. He'll feel better now that he's had a nap, maybe, not be so irritable. Maybe she can talk to him reasonably. His temper's never been good even when he was sober which hasn't been much these last twenty years. Flenco wonders where all those years went to and then realizes that one day just built onto another one like with a mason stacking bricks. All those nights in all those beer joints with all that singing and stomping and screaming and women shouting out declarations of desire for the frenzied figure that was him just past his prime blend together in her mind and spin like carousel horses in a fun-house ride. They billed him as Uncle Elvis, and he's told Flenco a little about his one trip up the river and how they'd hit you in the head with something if you didn't act right, but those days are long gone and what does it matter now since the cars he stole were transient things and even now probably lie stripped and rusted out in some junkyard bog, a hulking garden of flowers adorning their machine-gunned sides?

Flenco feels guilty for feeling her faith sag a little when she thinks of all the miles of roads the healer could be on and how easy it will be to miss him. She wonders if it was smart to abandon her big billboard sign by the side of the road and take off like this, but she was feeling the grip of a helpless sudden hopeless inertia and there was nothing to do but put some road under her wheels.

Flenco glances at Mr. Redding who is still oblivious to everything with the wind sailing up his nostrils. She takes a hefty slug of the beer between her legs. She nudges him.

"You want some of this beer, baby? You still asleep? Well you just go on and take you a nap, get rested. Maybe you'll feel better when you wake up."

Flenco hopes that's so. She hopes for a clue, a sign somehow, maybe that gathering of the crippled in a field like she's heard happens sometimes. If she can find him, she'll deliver Mr. Redding into the healer's healing hands herself. But if she can't, she doesn't know what she's going to do. She feels like the eleventh hour is fast approaching, and her beloved sits on the seat beside her in stony silence, his mouth open, his head canted back, the wind gently riffling his thin gray hair now that his reversible cap has blown off.

"I think maybe they need a little time to get to know one another, mama, what do you think?" the farmer says.

"That might be a good idear," the mother says. "Leave 'em alone together a while and maybe they can play."

The healer looks for a place to run but there are no windows in the airless chamber of what his good work has brought him to and no door but the one the farmer guards with the point of a gun.

"You can't leave me down here with him," the healer says, and he searches for some shred of sanity in the seamed faces of the farmer and his wife. His playmate edges closer.

"You could even eat supper with us if you wanted to after you heal him," the mother says. "Be right nice if we could all set down at the table together."

"He makes too big a mess for him to eat with us very much," the farmer says, a little apologetically, gesturing with the gun. "Thows his food everwhere and what not."

The farmer turns with the key in his pocket and fumbles down deep in there for it. He takes the key out and has to almost turn his back on the healer to get it in the lock, but he says, "I wouldn't try nothing funny if I was you."

"If you're scared of him biting you we'll hold him and not let him bite you," the mother says.

The key clicks in the lock and the farmer says, "I just don't believe he's much of a mind to heal him, mama. We can go up here and take us a nap and when we come back down they liable to be discussing philosophy or something, you cain't never tell."

"You people don't understand," the healer says. "He's beyond help. There's nothing I can do for him. I don't deal with the mind. I deal with the body."

"Ain't nothing wrong with his body," the mother says. "We just had to slow him down a little."

"His body's in good shape," the farmer says. "He's strong as a ox. Why I've seen him pull cows out of mud holes before. I don't believe he knows how strong he is."

"We'll be back after a while," the mother says, and out the door she goes. "Come on, daddy," she says back. The farmer backs out the door holding the gun on the healer and then the door closes. There are sounds of the other lock being affixed on the other side. The healer backs hard into the corner and eyes the mumbling being in front of him.

"Jesus would heal him if He was here!" the farmer hollers through the thick door. "I done read all about what He done in the Bible! What They've done, They've done laid this burden on us to test our faith! Ain't that right, mama!"

"That's right, daddy!" the mother shouts through the door.

"We been tested!" the farmer screams. "We been tested hard and we ain't been found wanting! Have we, mama!"

"You got that right, daddy! Lot of folks couldn't put up with what we've put up with!"

"Just don't make him mad!" the farmer shrieks. "Don't try to take nothing away from him if he's playing with it! He don't like that! He's a little spoiled!"

"He likes to rassle but don't get in a rasslin' match with him 'cause he gets mad sometimes! Don't get him mad! We'll be back in about a hour! Talk to him! He likes that!"

A rapid clump of footsteps climbing up the stairs fades away to a slammed door above. The healer flattens himself in the corner with his arms bracing up the walls.

"Don't touch me, please," he says, then adds: "I'm not going to hurt you."

The prisoner has made himself a bed of soiled quilts and assorted bedding and he pillows his head with a discarded tire. His nest is knotted with hairs and his lair is infested with lice. The farmer has snipped his hamstrings and Achilles tendon on alternate legs and cauterized the severed sinews while the mother kept the head restrained and the howling muffled with towels rolled and stuffed over his mouth one midnight scene years ago. He moves toward the healer slowly, hard. The healer watches the painful stance, the shifting feet, the arms outspread for balance, and he walks like a man on a tightrope as he makes his way across. Perhaps to kiss? His dangling thangling is large and hairy, swaying there like a big brown anesthetized mole.

The healer watches him come. On the edges of the wasted fields of the South and stuck back in the roadless reaches of timber where people have trails like animals, the unseen faceless sum of mankind's lesser genes quietly disassemble cars and squat underneath trees talking, and back of them lie small dwellings of rotted wood and sagging floors where strange children sit rapt for hours on end slavering mutely and uttering no words from their stunned mouths. Pictures of porches full of them all shy and embarrassed or smiling in delight turn up now and again here and there, but no visitor but the documenter of the far less fortunate comes to visit again. It is not that they are not God's children, but that mankind shuns them, bad reminders of rotted teeth and mismatched eyes, uncontrollable sexual desire turned loose in the woods to procreate a new race of the drooling mindless eating where they shit. He is like them, but even they would not accept him. An old midwife who knew anything would not allow the question. In the first few desperate moments the hand would smother the mouth, pinch the nostrils, still the heaving chest trying to draw in the first tiny breath. The brother and sister above know this. They have known it for years.

The thing comes closer and the healer looks into its depthless eyes, eyes like a fish that lives so deep in the dark black of the ocean and has no need to see. He thinks of the woman's legs in the back seat of the car parked behind a Walgreen's in Sumter and the strength of the promise to God. He thinks not of retribution or outrage, and not even fear anymore. He thinks of mercy, and lambs, and he brings his hands out from his sides to suffer to him this outcast. His fingers reach and they touch and he clamps them down hard over the ears. Dust motes turn in the air. They stand in stillness, hardly breathing, locked by the touch of another hand. Their eyes close. The healer fills his chest with air. He prepares to command him to heal.

Flenco sits sobbing beside the road in a grove of trees with a cool breeze wafting through, gently moving the hair on Mr. Redding's head. It's a nice afternoon for a nap, but Flenco has no thoughts of sleep. The search is over and he is cold like a slice of bologna, an egg from the refrigerator. The state troopers cluster behind her and slap their ticket books along their legs, heads shaking in utter solemnity or undisguised amazement. The ambulance crew waits, their equipment useless, their ambu bags and cardiopulmonary cases still scattered over the gravelly grass. The sun is going down and the legendary speeder has not appeared, and the roadblock will soon be broken up, the blue and white cruisers sent out to other destinations like prowling animals simply to prowl the roads.

But an interesting phenomenon has briefly materialized to break the boredom of an otherwise routine afternoon, a fat woman drunk and hauling the dead corpse of her husband down the road at ninety, sobbing and screaming and yelling out loud to God, and they wait now only for the coroner to place his seal of approval so that the body can be moved. One trooper leans against a tree chewing a stem of grass and remarks to nobody in particular: "I been to three county fairs, two goat-ropin's and one horse-fuckin', and I ain't never seen nothing like that."

Some chuckle, others shake their heads, as if to allow that the world is a strange place and in it lie things of another nature, a bent order, and beyond a certain point there are no rules to make man mind.

A wrecker is moving slowly with its red light down the road. Doves cry in the trees. And down the road in a field stand three giant wooden crosses, their colors rising in the falling sunlight, yellow, and blue, and tan.

Issue 120, 1991

Robert Bly

✠

The Breath

a translation from Kabir

Are you looking for me? I am in the next seat!
My shoulder is against yours.
You will not find me in stupas, nor in Indian shrine rooms,
   nor in the synagogues, nor in cathedrals:
not in masses, nor kirtans, not in legs winding around
   neck, nor in eating nothing but vegetables.
When you really look for me, you will see me instantly—
you will find me in the tiniest house of time.
Kabir says, "Student, tell me, what is God?
He is the breath inside the breath."

Issue 63, 1975

Gabriel García Márquez

❇

The Saint

I saw Margarito Duarte, after twenty-two years, on one of the narrow
secret streets in Trastevere, and at first I had trouble recognizing
him because he spoke halting Spanish and had the appearance of an
old Roman. His hair was white and thin, and there was nothing left of
the Andean intellectual's solemn manner and funereal clothes with
which he had first come to Rome, but in the course of our conversation I began, little by little, to recover him from the treachery of his
years and see him again as he had been: secretive, unpredictable and
as tenacious as a stonecutter. Before the second cup of coffee in one
of our bars from the old days, I dared to ask the question that was
gnawing inside me.

"What happened with the Saint?"

"The Saint is there," he answered. "Waiting."

Only the tenor Rafael Ribero Silva and I could understand the
enormous weight of his reply. We knew his drama so well that for
years I thought Margarito Duarte was the character in search of an
author we novelists wait for all our lives, and if I never allowed him to
find me it was because the end of his story seemed unimaginable.

He had come to Rome during that radiant spring when Pius XII
suffered from an attack of hiccups that neither the good nor evil arts
of physicians and wizards could cure. It was his first time away from
Tolima, his village high in the Colombian Andes, a fact that was obvious even in the way he slept. He presented himself one morning at
our consulate carrying the polished pine box that was the shape and

size of a cello case, and he explained the surprising reason for his trip to the consul, who then telephoned his countryman, the tenor Rafael Ribero Silva, asking that he find him a room at the pensione where we both lived. That is how I met him.

Margarito Duarte had not gone beyond primary school, but his vocation for letters had permitted him a broader education through the impassioned reading of everything in print he could lay his hands on. At the age of eighteen, when he was the village clerk, he married a beautiful girl who died not long afterward when she gave birth to their first child, a daughter. Even more beautiful than her mother, she died of essential fever at the age of seven. But the real story of Margarito Duarte began six months before his arrival in Rome, when the construction of a dam required that the cemetery in his village be moved. Margarito, like all the other residents in the region, disinterred the bones of his dead to carry them to the new cemetery. His wife was dust. But in the grave next to hers, the girl was still intact after eleven years. In fact, when they pried the lid off the coffin, they could smell the scent of the fresh cut roses with which she had been buried. Most astonishing of all, however, was that her body had no weight.

Hundreds of the curious, attracted by the resounding news of the miracle, poured into the village. There was no doubt about it. The incorruptibility of the body was an unequivocal sign of sainthood, and even the bishop of the diocese agreed that such a prodigy should be submitted to the judgment of the Vatican. And therefore they took up a public collection so that Margarito Duarte could travel to Rome to do battle for the cause that was no longer his alone or limited to the narrow confines of his village, but had become a national issue.

As he told us his story in the pensione in the peaceful Parioli district, Margarito Duarte removed the padlock and raised the lid of the beautiful trunk. That was how the tenor Ribero Silva and I participated in the miracle. She did not look like the kind of withered mummy seen in so many museums of the world, but like a little girl dressed as a bride who was still sleeping after a long stay underground. Her skin was smooth and warm, and her open eyes were clear and created the unbearable impression that they were looking at us from death. The satin and artificial orange blossoms of her crown had not withstood the rigors of time as well as her skin, but the roses that had been placed in her hands were still alive. And it was in fact true that the weight of the pine case did not change when we removed the body.

Margarito Duarte began his negotiations the day following his arrival, at first with diplomatic assistance that was more compassionate than efficient, and then with every strategy he could think of to circumvent the countless barriers set up by the Vatican. He was always very reserved about the measures he was taking, but we knew they were numerous and to no avail. He communicated with all the religious congregations and humanitarian foundations he could find, and they listened to him with attention but no surprise and promised immediate steps that were never taken. The truth is that it was not the most propitious time. Everything having to do with the Holy See had been postponed until the Pope overcame the attack of hiccuping that proved resistant not only to the most refined techniques of academic medicine, but to every kind of magic remedy sent to him from all over the world.

At last, in the month of July, Pius XII recovered and left for his summer vacation in Castel Gandolfo. Margarito took the Saint to the first weekly audience, hoping he could show her to the Pope, who appeared in the inner courtyard on a balcony so low that Margarito could see his burnished nails and smell his lavender scent. He did not circulate among the tourists who came from around the world to see him, as Margarito had anticipated, but repeated the same statement in six languages and concluded with a general blessing.

After so many delays, Margarito decided to take matters into his own hands, and he delivered a handwritten letter almost sixty pages long to the Secretariat of State but received no reply. He had foreseen this, for the functionary who accepted it with all due formality did not deign to give more than an official glance at the dead girl, and the clerks passing by looked at her with no interest at all. One of them told him that in the previous year they had received more than eight hundred letters requesting sainthood for intact corpses in various places around the world. At last Margarito requested that the weightlessness of the body be verified. The functionary verified it but refused to admit it.

"It must be a case of collective suggestion," he said.

In his few free hours, and on the dry Sundays of summer, Margarito remained in his room, devouring any book that seemed relevant to his cause. At the end of each month, on his own initiative, he wrote a detailed calculation of his expenses in a composition book, using the exquisite calligraphy of a senior clerk to provide the contributors from his village with strict and up-to-date accounts. Before the year was out he knew the Roman labyrinths as if he had been born there, spoke fluent Italian with as few words as in his Andean Spanish and knew as much as anyone about the process of canonization. But much more time passed before he changed his funereal dress, the vest and magistrate's hat, which in the Rome of that time were typical of certain secret societies with unconfessable aims. He went out very early with the case that held the Saint, and sometimes it was late at night when he returned, exhausted and sad but always with a spark of light that filled him with new courage for the next day.

"Saints live in their own time," he would say.

It was my first visit to Rome, where I was studying at the Experimental Film Center, and I lived his calvary with unforgettable intensity. Our pensione was in reality a modern apartment a few steps from the Villa Borghese. The owner occupied two rooms and rented the other four to foreign students. We called her Bella Maria, and in the ripeness of her autumn she was good-looking and temperamental and always faithful to the sacred rule that each man is absolute king of his own room. The one who really bore the burden of daily life was her older sister, Aunt Antonietta, an angel without wings who worked for her hour after hour during the day, moving through the apartment with her pail and brush, polishing the marble floor beyond the realm of the possible. It was she who taught us to eat the little songbirds that her husband Bartolino caught—a bad habit left over from the war—and who, in the end, took Margarito to live in her house when he could no longer afford Bella Maria's prices.

Nothing was less suited to Margarito's nature than that house without law. Each hour had some surprise in store, even the early hours of the morning, when we were awakened by the fearsome roar of the lion in the zoo at the Villa Borghese. The tenor Ribero Silva had earned this privilege: Romans did not resent his early practicing.

He would get up at six, take his medicinal bath of icy water, arrange his Mephistophelian beard and eyebrows, and only when he was ready, wearing his Scotch-plaid bathrobe, Chinese silk scarf and personal cologne, give himself over, body and soul, to his vocal exercises. He would throw open the window in his room, even when the wintry stars were still in the sky, and begin to warm up with progressive phrasings of great love arias until he was singing at full voice. The daily expectation was that when he sang his *do* at top volume, the Villa Borghese lion would answer him with an earthshaking roar.

"You are the reincarnation of Saint Mark, *figlio mio,*" Aunt Antonietta would exclaim in true amazement. "Only he could talk to lions."

One morning it was not the lion who replied. The tenor began the love duet from *Otello: "Già nelle notte densa s'estingue ogni clamor,"* and from the bottom of the courtyard we heard the answer in a beautiful soprano voice. The tenor continued, and the two voices sang the complete selection to the delight of all the neighbors, who opened the windows to sanctify their houses with the torrent of that irresistible love. The tenor almost fainted when he learned that his invisible Desdemona was no less a personage than the great Maria Caniglia.

I have the impression that this was the episode that gave Margarito Duarte a valid reason for joining in the life of the house. From that time on he sat with the rest of us at the common table and not, as he had done at first, in the kitchen, where Aunt Antonietta indulged him almost every day with her masterful songbird stew. When the meal was over, Bella Maria would read us the daily newspapers to teach us Italian phonetics and comment on the news with an arbitrariness and wit that brought joy to our lives. One day, with regard to the Saint, she told us that in the city of Palermo there was an enormous museum that held the incorruptible corpses of men, women and children, and even several bishops, who had all been disinterred from the same Capuchin cemetery. The news so disturbed Margarito that he did not have a moment's peace until we went to Palermo. But a passing glance at the oppressive galleries of inglorious mummies was all he needed to make a consolatory judgment.

"These are not the same," he said. "You can tell right away they're dead."

After lunch Rome would succumb to its August stupor. The afternoon sun remained immobile in the middle of the sky, and in the two o'clock silence one heard nothing but water, which is the natural voice of Rome. But at about seven the windows were thrown open to summon the cool air that began to circulate, and a jubilant crowd took to the streets with no other purpose than to live, in the midst of backfiring motorcycles, the shouts of melon sellers, and love songs among the flowers on the terraces.

The tenor and I did not take a siesta. We would ride on his Vespa, he driving and I sitting behind, and bring ices and chocolates to the little summer whores who fluttered under the centuries-old laurels in the Villa Borghese and watched for sleepless tourists in the bright sun. They were beautiful, poor and affectionate, like most Italian women in those days, and they dressed in blue organdy, pink poplin, green linen, and protected themselves from the sun with parasols damaged by storms of bullets during the recent war. It was a human pleasure to be with them, because they ignored the rules of their trade and allowed themselves the luxury of losing a good client in order to have coffee and conversation with us in the bar on the corner, or ride in the carriages for hire along the paths in the park, or fill us with pity for the deposed monarchs and their tragic mistresses who went horseback riding at dusk along the *galoppatoio*. More than once we served as their interpreters with some foreigner gone astray.

They were not the reason we took Margarito Duarte to the Villa Borghese: we wanted him to see the lion. He lived uncaged on a small desert island in the middle of a deep moat, and as soon as he caught sight of us on the far shore he began to roar with an agitation that astonished his keeper. The visitors to the park gathered round in surprise. The tenor tried to identify himself with his full-voiced morning *do,* but the lion paid him no attention. He seemed to roar at all of us without distinction, but the keeper knew right away that he roared only for Margarito. It was true: wherever he moved the lion moved, and as soon as he was out of sight, the lion stopped roaring. The keeper, who held a doctorate in classical literature from the University of Siena, thought that Margarito had been with other lions that day and was carrying their scent. Aside from that reasoning, which was invalid, he could think of no other explanation.

"In any event," he said, "they're roars of compassion, not battle."

And yet, what most affected the tenor Ribero Silva was not that supernatural episode, but Margarito's confusion when they stopped to talk with the girls in the park. He remarked on it at the table, and we all agreed—some in order to make mischief, and others because they were sympathetic—that it would be a good idea to help Margarito resolve his loneliness. Moved by our tender hearts, Bella Maria pressed her hands, covered by rings with imitation stones, against her bosom worthy of a doting biblical matriarch.

"I would do it for charity's sake," she said, "except that I never could abide men who wear vests."

That was how the tenor rode his Vespa to the Villa Borghese at two o'clock in the afternoon and returned with the little butterfly he thought best able to give Margarito Duarte an hour of good company. He had her undress in his bedroom, bathed her with scented soap, dried her, perfumed her with his personal cologne, and dusted her entire body with his camphorated after-shave talc. And then he paid her for the time they had already spent plus another hour and told her step by step what she had to do.

The naked beauty tiptoed through the shadowy house like a siesta dream and gave two gentle little taps at the rear bedroom. Margarito Duarte, barefoot and shirtless, opened the door.

"*Buona sera giovanotto*," she said, with the voice and manners of a schoolgirl. "*Mi manda il tenore.*"

Margarito absorbed the shock with great dignity. He opened the door wide to let her in, and she lay down on the bed while he rushed to put on his shirt and shoes to receive her with all due respect. Then he sat beside her on a chair and began the conversation. The bewildered girl told him to hurry because they only had an hour. He did not seem to understand.

The girl said later that in any event she would have spent all the time he wanted and not charged him a cent because there could not be a better behaved man in the world. Not knowing what to do in the meantime, she glanced around the room and saw the wooden case on the mantle. She asked if it was a saxophone. Margarito did not answer, but opened the blind to let in a little light, carried the case to the bed and raised the lid. The girl tried to say something, but her jaw

was hanging open. Or as she told us later: "*Mi se gelò il culo*." She fled
in utter terror but lost her way in the hall and ran into Aunt Antonietta
who was going to put a new bulb in the lamp in my room. They were
both so frightened that the girl did not dare leave the tenor's room until very late that night.

Aunt Antonietta never learned what happened. She came into my
room in such fear that she could not turn the light bulb in the lamp because her hands were shaking. I asked her what was wrong. "There
are ghosts in this house," she said. "And now in broad daylight." She
told me with great conviction that during the war a German officer
had cut the throat of his mistress in the room occupied by the tenor.
As she had gone about her work, Aunt Antonietta often saw the ghost
of the beautiful victim making her way along the corridors.

"I've just seen her walking naked down the hall," she said. "She
was identical."

The city returned to its autumn routine. The flowering terraces of
summer closed down with the first winds, and the tenor and I returned to our old haunts in Trastevere where we ate supper with the
vocal students of Count Carlo Calcagni and with some of my classmates from film school, among whom the most faithful was Lakis, an
intelligent, amiable Greek whose soporific discourses on social injustice were his only fault. It was our good fortune that the tenors and so-
pranos almost always drowned him out with opera selections that
they sang at full volume, but which did not bother anyone even after
midnight. On the contrary, some late night passersby would join in
the chorus, and the neighbors opened their windows to applaud.

One night, while we were singing, Margarito walked in on tiptoe
in order not to interrupt us. He was carrying the pine case that he
had not had time to leave at the pensione after showing the Saint to
the parish priest at San Giovanni in Laterano, whose influence with the
Holy Congregation of the Rite was common knowledge. From the
corner of my eye I caught a glimpse of him putting it under the isolated table where he sat until we finished singing. As always, just after
midnight, when the trattoria began to empty, we would push several
tables together and sit in one group—those who sang, those of us
who talked about movies, and all our friends. And among them Margarito Duarte, who was already known there as the silent, melancholy

Colombian no one knew anything about. Lakis, intrigued, asked him if he played the cello. I was caught off guard by what seemed to me an indiscretion that was difficult to handle. The tenor, as uncomfortable as I, could not save the situation. Margarito was the only one who responded to the question with absolute naturalness.

"It's not a cello," he said. "It's the Saint."

He placed the case on the table, opened the padlock and raised the lid. A gust of stupefaction shook the restaurant. The other customers, the waiters, even the people in the kitchen with their blood-stained aprons, gathered in astonishment to see the miracle. Some crossed themselves. One of the cooks, overcome by a feverish trembling, fell to her knees with clasped hands and prayed in silence.

And yet, when the initial commotion was over, we became involved in a shouting argument about the lack of saintliness in our day. Lakis, of course, was the most radical. All that was clear at the end of it was his idea of making a critical movie about the Saint.

"I'm sure," he said, "that old Cesare would never let this subject get away."

He was referring to Cesare Zavattini who taught us plotting and screenwriting. He was one of the great figures in the history of film and the only one who maintained a personal relationship with us outside class. He tried not only to teach us the craft but a different way of looking at life. He was a machine for inventing plots. They poured out of him, almost against his will, and with so much speed that he always needed someone to help him catch them in midflight as he thought them up aloud. His enthusiasm would flag only when he had completed them. "Too bad they have to be filmed," he would say. For he thought that on the screen they would lose much of their original magic. He kept his ideas on cards arranged by subject and pinned to the walls, and he had so many they filled an entire room in his house.

The following Saturday we went to see him with Margarito Duarte. He was so greedy for life that we found him at the door of his house on Angela Merici Street, burning with interest in the idea we had described to him on the telephone. He did not even greet us with his customary amiability but led Margarito to a table he had prepared and opened the case himself. Then something happened that we never could have imagined. Instead of going wild, as we expected, he suffered a kind of mental paralysis.

"*Ammazza!*" he whispered in fear.

He looked at the Saint in silence for two or three minutes, closed the case himself and, without saying a word, led Margarito to the door as if he were a child taking his first steps. He said good-bye with a few pats on his shoulder. "Thank you, my son, thank you very much," he said. "And may God be with you in your struggle." When he closed the door he turned toward us and gave his verdict.

"It's no good for the movies," he said. "Nobody would believe it."

That surprising lesson rode with us in the streetcar we took home. If he said it, it had to be true: the story was no good. Yet Bella Maria met us with the urgent message that Zavattini was expecting us that same night, but without Margarito.

We found him in one of his stellar moments. Lakis had brought along two or three classmates, but he did not even seem to see them when he opened the door.

"I have it," he shouted. "The picture will be a sensation if Margarito performs a miracle and resurrects the girl."

"In the picture or in life?" I asked.

He suppressed his annoyance. "Don't be stupid," he said. But then we saw in his eyes the flash of an irresistible idea. "What if he could resurrect her in real life?" he mused, and added in all seriousness:

"He ought to try."

It was no more than a passing temptation, and then he took up the thread again. He began to pace every room, like a happy madman, waving his hands and reciting the film in great shouts. We listened to him, dazzled, and it seemed we could see the images, like flocks of phosphorescent birds that he set loose in a mad flight through the house.

"One night," he said, "after something like twenty Popes who refused to receive him have died, Margarito goes into his house, tired and old, and he opens the case, caresses the face of the little dead girl and says with all the tenderness in the world: 'For love of your father, my child, arise and walk.'"

He looked at all of us and finished with a triumphant gesture:

"And she does!"

He was waiting for something from us. But we were so befuddled we could not think of a thing to say. Except Lakis the Greek, who raised his hand, as if he were in school, to ask permission to speak.

"My problem is that I don't believe it," he said, and to our surprise he was speaking to Zavattini: "Excuse me, Maestro, but I don't believe it."

Then it was Zavattini's turn to be astonished.

"And why not?"

"How do I know?" said Lakis in anguish. "But it's impossible."

"*Ammazza!*" the maestro thundered in a voice that must have been heard throughout the entire neighborhood. "That's what I can't stand about Stalinists: they don't believe in reality."

For the next fifteen years, as he himself told me, Margarito carried the Saint to Castel Gandolfo in the event an occasion arose for displaying her. At an audience for some two hundred pilgrims from Latin America, he managed to tell his story, amid shoves and pokes, to the benevolent John XXIII. But he could not show him the girl because, as a precaution against assassination attempts, he had been obliged to leave her at the entrance along with the knapsacks of the other pilgrims. The Pope listened with as much attention as he could in the crowd and gave him an encouraging pat on the cheek.

"*Bravo, figlio mio,*" he said. "God will reward your perseverance."

But it was during the fleeting reign of the smiling Albino Luciani that he really felt on the verge of fulfilling his dream. One of the Pope's relatives, impressed by Margarito's story, promised to intervene. No one paid him much attention. But two days later, as they were having lunch, someone telephoned the pensione with a rapid, simple message for Margarito: he should not leave Rome, because some time before Thursday he would be summoned to the Vatican for a private audience.

No one ever found out if it was a joke. Margarito did not think so, and he stayed on the alert. He did not leave the house. If he had to go to the bathroom he announced it: "I'm going to the bathroom." Bella Maria, still witty in the dawn of her old age, laughed her free woman's laugh.

"We know, Margarito," she shouted, "just in case the Pope calls."

The following week, two days before the date specified in the message, Margarito almost collapsed when he saw the headline in the newspaper slipped under the door: *Morto il Papa*. For a moment he was sustained by the illusion that it was an old paper delivered by mistake, for it was not easy to believe that a Pope would die every month. But it was true: the smiling Albino Luciani, elected thirty-three days earlier, had died in his sleep.

I returned to Rome twenty-two years after I met Margarito Duarte, and perhaps I would not have thought about him if we had not met by accident. I was too depressed by the ruinous weather to think about anybody. An imbecilic drizzle like warm soup never stopped falling, the diamond light of another time had turned muddy, and the places that had once been mine and sustained my memories were strange to me now. The house where the pensione was located was still the same, but nobody knew anything about Bella Maria. No one answered at the six different telephone numbers that the tenor Ribero Silva had sent me over the years. At lunch with the new movie people, I evoked the memory of my teacher, and a sudden silence fluttered over the table for a moment until someone dared to say:

"*Zavattini? Mai sentito.*"

That was true: no one had heard of him. The trees in the Villa Borghese were disheveled in the rain, the *galoppatoio* of the sorrowful princesses had been devoured by weeds with no flowers, and the beautiful girls of long ago had been replaced by athletic androgynes cross-dressed in flashy clothes. The only survivor among all the extinct fauna was the old lion, who suffered from mange and a head cold on his island surrounded by dried waters. No one sang or died of love in the plastic trattorias on the Piazza di Spagna. For the Rome of our memory was by now another ancient Rome within the ancient Rome of the Caesars. Then, a voice that might have come from the beyond stopped me cold on a narrow street in Trastevere:

"Hello, Poet."

It was he, old and tired. Four popes had died, eternal Rome was showing the first signs of decrepitude, and still he waited. "I've waited so long it can't be much longer now," he told me as he said good-bye after almost four hours of nostalgia. "It may be a matter of months." He shuffled down the middle of the street wearing the combat boots and faded cap of an old Roman, ignoring the puddles of rain where the light was beginning to decay. Then I had no doubt, if I ever had any at all, that the Saint was Margarito. Without realizing it, by means of his daughter's incorruptible body, and while he was still alive, he had spent twenty-two years fighting for the legitimate cause of his own canonization.

—translated by Edith Grossman

Yusef Komunyakaa

※

Memory Cave

A tallow worked into a knot
of rawhide, with a ball of waxy light
tied to a stick, the boy
scooted through a secret mouth
of the cave, pulled by the flambeau
in his hand. He could see
the gaze of agate eyes
& wished for the forbidden
plains of bison & wolf, years
from the fermented honey
& musty air. In the dried
slag of bear & bat guano,
the initiate stood with sleeping
gods at his feet, lost
in the great cloud of their one
breath. Their muzzles craved
touch. How did they learn
to close eyes, to see into
the future? Before the Before:
mammon was unnamed & mist
hugged ravines & hillocks.
The elders would test him
beyond doubt & blood. Mica
lit the false skies where

stalactite dripped perfection
into granite. He fingered
icons sunlight & anatase
never touched. Ibex carved
on a throwing stick, reindeer
worried into an ivory amulet,
& a bear's head. Outside,
the men waited two days
for him, with condor & bovid,
& not in a thousand years
would he have dreamt a woman
standing here beside a man,
saying, "This is as good
as the stag at Salon Noir
& the polka-dotted horses."
The man scribbles *Leo loves*
Angela below the boy's last bear
drawn with manganese dioxide
& animal fat. This is where
sunrise opened a door in stone
when he was summoned to drink
honey wine & embrace a woman
beneath a five-pointed star.
Lying there beside the gods
hefty & silent as boulders,
he could almost remember
before he was born, could see
the cliff from which he'd fall.

Issue 144, 1997

Susan Power

⁜

Snakes

Father La Frambois was anxious to baptize me in the Missouri River, to change my name from *Čuwignaka Duta,* or Red Dress, to the holier appellation Esther. He was an energetic old man and vivid in color; his cheeks so brightly red they looked slapped, and his eyes a dark blue like the night sky, although sometimes dimming to black in moments of anger. I would not be coaxed into the Missouri, not even to repay him for the hours he spent teaching me to read, to write, to recite, to form my thoughts into plain, desolate English until I could speak in terms more lovely than the priest. He bribed me with stories of heaven and eternal life, told me it was within my power to transform my soul from a black crusted thing into a white snow goose with silken wings. When that failed, he bribed me with sugar and silver crosses for me to wear dangling from my earlobes. I wore the crosses to test their potency, expected Christ to whisper his message directly into my ears. And when he was silent, I knew that the silver crosses were really symbols of the morning star, the same image we painted on our buckskin clothes. But I did not tell Father La Frambois, because it isn't polite to point out to an elder person that he is mistaken.

The missionary priest traveled alone throughout Dakota Territory, perched on a tall American horse that routinely charged our ponies and had to be led through the village with a blanket covering its head. The priest arrived year after year in the fall, noticed first by *Šunka Gleška,* Spotted Dog, who would race in circles around my father's lodge, occasionally pausing to howl. This clever companion was a pumpkin-colored dog with wiry fur and white speckles on his muzzle. He could respond to commands made in either Dakota or English, which greatly impressed my father. Once alerted by Spotted Dog, the village would turn out to welcome Father La Frambois, moving towards him like an errant wave from the river. We became accustomed to his annual arrival at our winter camp, familiar with the heavy black dress he wore falling awkwardly from his crooked shoulders; he resembled a turkey vulture with broken wings. He would remain with us until spring, drill me in my lessons and study my careful penmanship. He taught me to write the name Esther so that I would be ready to claim it once I had saved my soul, and although I refused the name, I liked to draw it; managing the ink so that it would flow gracefully without bleeding, and fashioning the "E" with dramatic flourishes, curved into the shape of a lush bear heavy with winter fat.

Perhaps I should have told the Jesuit directly: "I will never be the convert you desire. I am Red Dress, beloved of snakes." I know he would have found that statement foolish. He had no patience for spirits, dreams or animal totems, despite his self-confessed ability to transform wine into blood and a crisp wafer of bread into living flesh. That is why, although I listened quietly to his stories and studied Scriptures, translated his teachings into the Dakota language so that my curious father, Bear Soldier, and his seven subchiefs could decide for themselves the merit of Father's words, I never told the priest my own legend.

My mother was Black Moon, the lady whose long features threatened to slip off her face until she smiled, beautifully, lifting them back into place. In her care I came to know myself, and her memories of me became my own. I recalled being set out to play on a vast buffalo hide, then, made drowsy by the sun, tipping over and sliding into sleep. My mother was visiting with friends a short distance away, her hands busy with quillwork. She didn't notice the two rattlesnakes gliding onto my infant's shadow, where they coiled together, joining me in a nap. I remember their chalky smell and graceful movements, the feel of their cool glossy skin. As I slept I clutched a serpent by the tail and shook it like a

baby's toy. The rattler never struck, was patient with me even when my
mother and her friends hovered, horrified, above his twisting head.

"Don't move," the women whispered to each other. They pulled my
mother back and made her sit on the ground. "Look at how they are
claiming her," one woman said. Eventually my grasping fist released
the viper, and he and his companion left the buffalo hide. I think I cried
for them to return, but my mother crushed me into her arms, and I
grabbed her braids, thinking they were black snakes.

"That one charms the snakes," people have whispered all my life, but
they have it wrong. The snakes charmed me.

The final winter of my friendship with the priest was 1864 by his
reckoning. Father La Frambois was determined to impress, to introduce us to that deity he called the True God. He told me to inform
the village crier that he would be saying mass on the prairies.

"The vaulting sky is my cathedral," he fairly shouted at me. His
arm swept the horizon. "Everyone must attend. Everyone must be
given this opportunity to hear the word of God and discover the life
everlasting."

His skin was slick with the heat of his emotion; I thought of melting tallow. Pity pricked my heart, and when I opened my mouth to tell
the crier what Father had said, scheming words emerged. "Tomorrow Father La Frambois will dance for us on the grass." It was a minor
deception I felt would bring the people rushing, curious, to the level
floodplain Father had selected for his impromptu church. Even the
older warriors—dispassionate, believing they had seen everything
worth noticing in the world—would surely turn out for such a spectacle.

"You will be my voice," Father said that evening, ignorant of my
treason. "You will be the instrument of your people's salvation." His
bright cheeks were flames; he looked ready to burn.

I had often wondered why the priest chose me for his pupil, an unwilling acolyte. Why not my younger brother or little sister? Why not
a patient child whose mind was untroubled, so rarely did she question
what she heard? I asked him now, "Father, why am I your voice?"

I received the answer that is no answer: "It is God's will."

The next afternoon four hundred people assembled on the level plain to witness Father's dance. He received everyone—even the crawling infants—with a handshake, and made the people stand in straight rows. "These are pews," he said. When everyone was settled, he faced the orderly group and began to speak: "Welcome to your grass church. The Lord is all around you—let Him into your heart. You have been a stubborn people, a great challenge to me. I have come this year, and in past years, because I care about you, and your souls are in jeopardy."

Father paused, waiting for me to translate. I told my tribesmen: "Welcome, friends. The past winters we spent together have been very pleasant. I've learned a great deal from these visits and I have respect for you. You are a strong people."

The warriors nodded, breathing, "*Oha(n),*" and several of the women trilled their tongues to make the *wičağalata* cry of approval. "They say you are making sense," I told the priest. He spoke for an hour about the necessity of cleansing our spirits until I began to think of the soul as a garment I could rinse in the river and then spread on a smooth rock to dry in the sun. Mind you, when I translated inaccurately it was not out of carelessness or spite. Father was tactless but he had been a friend to me. It was loyalty that led me to overlook his indelicate remarks and speak in a voice of my own.

All during Father's sermon the rows held. No one faltered in the chill air or stamped his feet. None of the children squawked. Afterwards, Father removed his ornate thurible from a velvet-lined casket and lit the incense. He paraded in front of the patient families, swinging the thurible up and back, and then in a full dramatic circle. The cloying scent of burning incense blew into their faces. He marched past the people, behind them, surrounding them with smoke. Spotted Dog trailed after him, imitating the priest's dignified pace and inspecting his tracks with something like suspicion. I moved to signal the dog but never completed the gesture. A tall figure lunged into the neat lines Father referred to as pews. The intruder clapped his hands and doubled over, his shoulders shaking with laughter.

"*Šunka Wakan Wanaği,*" people murmured. They were whispering his name, Ghost Horse. The community pulled back and watched as he rolled on the ground like a mad colt; he brayed with laughter and tore the grass with his white teeth. Father La Frambois moved to stand over Ghost Horse, the thurible still rocking in his hands.

"The poor boy is deranged," Father said.

"No, he is *heyo'ka*. He dreamed of the thunderbirds," I tried to explain.

"Stop there, stop there!" Smoke coiled from the thurible like pale ribbon snakes dancing on their tails. I couldn't see Father's face but I could hear his tongue clicking sharply in his mouth. "I thought we were progressing. I believed you were beyond all this."

Father La Frambois trudged back to his guest lodge, his shoulders collapsed in defeat. Spotted Dog trotted behind him, snapping at the threads of smoke and coughing whenever he swallowed the rich vapor.

The people quickly dispersed, disappointed with the program, until only Ghost Horse remained, thrashing at my feet. He quieted, sat up and dusted his graceful arms. White streaks of lightning painted his arms and legs, and his face was striped with vertical lines in black and white. A bunch of switchgrass was tied to his forelock, hiding eyes I knew were clear and black as polished buffalo horns. A cold wind was blowing from the northwest, the place winter came from, but Ghost Horse didn't shiver. He fanned his face and complained of the scorching heat.

After dreaming of the giant thunderbirds who could shoot lightning from their glimmering eyes, Ghost Horse had become *heyo'ka*, a sacred clown. His behavior was perverse: he wept at social dances, laughed at solemn events, shivered in the hot summer sun and sweltered in frigid temperatures. He rushed into battle ahead of other warriors, treating war as play, and he always said the opposite of what he meant. I sensed he was lonely, burdened by his powerful dream, which obligated him to appease the thunder-beings through public humiliation.

Ghost Horse stood and shook his limbs as if to rouse himself. I stared at the ground, polite, demure, my legs shaking beneath my dress. "I disappointed the priest," I finally said. "He doesn't understand the way we do things."

Ghost Horse was silent a long moment. Then he told me: "That man understands everything."

That winter, as in years past, Father La Frambois failed to secure a single convert. "I've made headway with other bands. Why are you people so obstinately, willfully blind?" he asked me.

I shall say here what I couldn't tell Father La Frambois: his stories did not make sense to us. Bear Soldier, head-chief of our band and my own father, was a logician whose counsel was solicited by other leaders. He listened to the anecdotes I dutifully translated for the priest—Cain slaying Abel, Abraham's willingness to sacrifice Isaac, Joseph delivered into slavery by his jealous brothers—and shook his head. My father wanted to know, "Why are his people so determined to kill their relatives?"

So I asked Father, "Why did Cain murder his brother?"

Father pointed at me and shook his finger. "Because he didn't have faith."

I told my father, "When the priest's people don't believe in the higher spirits they go crazy."

"Then we'll pray for them," he said.

My father had seen other bands trade with white people, succumb to diseases and grow dependent upon their superior goods. He decided that we would only trade with our traditional sources: other bands and friendly tribes. Our arrows were tipped with filed bone not metal; we used the stomach lining of a buffalo to cook our meals rather than shiny kettles; we passed over mirrors, flour, coffee, and used quills and paint to decorate our clothing rather than the colorful beads from Europe. I felt it would be rude to tell the priest his teachings were just another import for us to resist. Instead I told him, "We will not be degraded."

Father's mouth fell open and his tongue flicked out and then back in, like an alert frog's. He swallowed the words he was about to deliver. I quickly apprehended. In Father La Frambois's view of the world we were already a degraded people that he intended to elevate, single-handedly, into the radiant realm of civilization.

I dream of that place where the North Platte River crosses the Laramie, a place of soldiers, treaties and immigrant trains. I've never been there in waking life, but I still recognize Fort Laramie. I've heard that in springtime this area is a green blanket of lush buffalo grass, but in my dream the ground is dead white. I am walking through a field of—what? My legs push through tall stalks of limp parchment paper, shredded, tattered, a grim harvest sprouting from chalky soil. Death crackles beneath my moccasins. The grass is gone, and the wildflowers and delicate lacewings, the plump grasshoppers, cottonwood trees, the lively killdeer. As far as I can see—squinting in every direction— the paper spreads, licking across the land like a prairie fire out of control. I want to leave this nightmare. I look at my feet and notice that each step I take leaves a stunted patch of pale dry grass, struggling to grow.

I am here for a reason, I tell the wind, and it whips the paper, threatens to tear it from the white plains. *I am the uneasy voice of the grass.*

Like Ghost Horse, my life was altered by a dream. It was decided that I would travel to Fort Laramie after the spring thaw. No one knew what would happen once I arrived—assuming I completed the treach- erous journey—least of all myself. Father La Frambois had said the Lord called him into service, and this is how I felt; directed by the spirits. All winter I suppressed a nervous euphoria, vacillating be- tween fear and anticipation.

My brother Long Chase was two years younger than I, sixteen, but had already brought down buffalo bulls and accompanied war parties on raids against the Arikara. Long Chase told me: "*Tanke,*" older sis- ter, "I am coming with you. You can tell me not to, but I'll just follow anyway. Get used to it."

Father La Frambois left before I did to visit more promising bands: Indians who pressed their lips to the large crucifix dangling from his belt, who could chant prayers in Latin. When he departed, his horse seemed aware that the village was watching, and it minced across the prairie, lifting its stocky legs higher than was necessary.

I had written the priest a formal farewell message to show off my elegant script and signed it *Esther* as a final act of kindness. But nowhere in the missive did I mention Fort Laramie or the dream or my coming trip. For years I thought I was shielding Father La Frambois from information I felt he would never understand, would, in fact, find disturbing. It was only as I watched his bent figure diminish to a speck, that I realized my motives were suspect. I had been protecting myself, refusing to speak aloud the legends and ideas I thought would sound absurd in bare English. I nurtured secrecy to avoid derision. Perhaps this was why the dream came to me. A rare opportunity for redemption.

The day before my journey was to begin I climbed the flat top of Angry Butte to pray. I added my prayer—a heavy flat rock—to all the others. They formed a neat pile that rose to my waist. I was careful not to brush my fingers across the other invocations, this place was so powerful I thought I could hear the stones speak. My foot slipped on a round pebble and I fell on my back with such force the wind left my body. I looked for the pebble with angry intentions. I found it touching a second stone, its duplicate, and scooped them into my hand. The stones were perfectly round and unblemished. I lifted one to my cheek, it was impossibly smooth.

"They are twin sisters," my mother told me when I showed them to her. "You were meant to find them." I painted them red, the color of life, and wrapped them in soft buckskin.

The stones move with a purpose, I told Father La Frambois in my thoughts, though the purpose was a mystery to me.

The next is hard to say, the picture is so vivid. Bear Soldier and Black Moon stood in front of their lodge, their hands fastened on my sister's frail shoulders. Walks Visibly winced in pain. She anchored them there, too young to follow me as Long Chase would. No one cried, it would be disrespectful to the spirits who had planned this course of action, but the family must have feared it would never see me or my brother again.

This is what we looked like as we slipped into the unknown. One pony carried our household goods, our water, fire horn, pemmican and jerky. The other carried a small lodge, the smoked hides lashed onto the poles. Long Chase carried a compact short bow and would ride ahead. We had both packed moccasins stolen from enemy tribes—Crow and Arikara—to wear in their territory so our tracks wouldn't give us away.

Spotted Dog shivered with excitement and sat down only to jump up again, running between the ponies' legs. "You'll get kicked in the head," my brother warned him. "Settle down." The dog sighed and crouched impatiently.

The last face I saw was partially hidden by a clump of switchgrass. Ghost Horse moved quickly past everyone else, his arms and legs flashing, a lightning storm in our midst. He chuckled as he handed me a smoked shield of tough buffalo bull hide. I turned it over to inspect its face. It pictured a woman in a red dress clutching an arrow of lightning in her hand. She seemed fierce, unfamiliar. Twenty-one rattlesnake rattles dangled from the bottom edge of the shield, so with each step I sounded like a den of restless snakes.

Ghost Horse grinned at me, baring his perfect teeth, but the one eye I could see beneath cords of grass was so red he could have been weeping blood. I clutched the shield as I mounted my pony, tried to still my shaking hands. Ghost Horse seized the bridle and for one moment tossed the grass from his forehead.

"I will never miss you," he said.

That day there was a white sky. Clouds choked the horizon and crowded the sun. The sky was so low we were in the sky, we were air, we were something other than what we had been before.

"*Tanke,*" I heard my brother whisper. "The spirits are all around us."

We traveled southwest on the heels of Spotted Dog, who glanced over his shoulder every few steps to be certain he was heading in the right direction.

"You're not fooling us," my brother called to him. "You're not in charge."

The pale sky sapped my spirits. I was glad when the sun burned through the clouds, and searing light peeled back layers of mist. We rode into a valley of trembling flowers, the lacy petals fluttered in the wind.

"Butterflies," Long Chase breathed. Indeed, the flowers were actually swallowtail butterflies, their creamy wings edged in blue. I had never seen so many in one place. There were enough of them to bend stems of grass, they dripped from the stalks.

"The ancestors are watching us," I said. "Look at how many we have."

The butterflies lifted then in a rippling cloud and took over the sky. My brother stopped his pony to watch what looked like a snowstorm in reverse, the drifts banking heaven. "This is an odd day," he finally said.

Father La Frambois was frequently in my thoughts. How would he have explained what happened next? I would have told him: *Father, we stepped into a dream, into a world governed by the spirits. Father, for two weeks we never saw another person; no tribesmen, no enemies, only passing herds of elk and antelope.* My brother carried his short bow, and I held my shield, and Spotted Dog pretended to lead the way, his tail straight as a flag, and we marched across the territory as if we were the only creatures in the land. We covered the distance in two weeks and camped within sight of the fort, dazed and exhausted. Even Spotted Dog collapsed in a careless sprawl.

"What happens next?" Long Chase asked me.

"Tomorrow we visit the fort. One thing at a time."

He looked at me, and I saw the boy in his face, the deep pucker of dimples on either side of his mouth he tried so hard to smooth. The edge of one thick braid was clamped between his teeth, rolled back and forth to produce a wet squeak. He caught himself and spat the braid from his mouth. He trusted that I understood what had brought us here. I didn't. But as the older sister I flashed a smile and told him: "Tomorrow will be an adventure. Your friends would be jealous."

That night I noticed that Spotted Dog crept beside Long Chase and slept with his forepaws against my brother's chest. All night their hearts beat together.

Upstream from the fort was a village I would later hear the soldiers refer to as Squaw Town. This was the place we visited first. The people who lived there were our cousins—a different band of the same tribe. Their leader was a man with a name I have forgotten because I thought of him as Death Shirt, and when my brother and I spoke of him, that was the name we used. His cloth shirt was decorated with tiny metal snuffboxes—sinister as coffins—pierced and sewn so closely together he jangled. He wore a soldier's forage cap squashed low on his head and ragged moccasins shedding beads. He blinked at me and then at Long Chase. We were wearing our ceremonial clothes,

our finest buckskins. My dress was painted red and decorated with
elk teeth, and my brother's shirt dyed blue and stitched with quilled
stars—he was a piece of the sky.

Death Shirt shuffled his feet. He asked us: "Are you the ghosts of
our ancestors?"

"No," I said. "Where we come from we still dress the old way."

He passed his hand across his eyes, and I noticed three parallel
scars on his chin. "Come with me," he said.

We were led through the village and several times I heard Long
Chase draw breath too quickly. He stepped close to me and whispered in my ear, "*Unšika*." Pitiful. The children were barefoot, chewing their fingers, and their mothers stood with long hair unbraided,
tangling in the wind. Many of them wore fabric clothes that were
coming apart at the seams.

"These ones come from a long time ago," Death Shirt told the village, gesturing at the two of us.

Some of the women were crying, but silently, tears running quick
as water. Gifts were pressed into our hands: pebbles, berries, a handful of earth beans and another of parched corn. "We give what we
can," an older woman said. She lifted her arm like a hunter wielding a
lance and trilled her tongue in thunderous rolls, she could have had a
thousand tongues. My brother and I shook hands with our cousins
and packed the gifts in parfleche containers strapped to our ponies.
We handed out presents of our own: moccasins, jerky and our last
cake of pemmican. The women continued to praise us with their
voices, even after we rode away. By the time we reached Fort Laramie
the noise was a sad drone, like bees singing in our ears.

Fort Laramie was little more than a hodgepodge of buildings scattered across a flat plain. Mismatched structures of white-washed
adobe and blond wood cluttered the area, framed by Laramie Peak
some fifty miles to the west. The soldiers smelled of rancid butter and
looked uncomfortably warm in their uniforms. When I introduced
myself as Esther and Long Chase as Joseph, and tilted my head so the
silver crosses I wore fell forward, we were told that the Post Chaplain,
a Reverend Pyke, would be most eager to meet us.

"He's convinced the Sioux will never be real Christians," the private said.

We were led beyond the parade grounds to a cluster of cotton-wood trees hunched together like old men. I saw the giant's back and smelled his malodorous top hat of poorly tanned beaver hide from several yards away. He was shooting at a tree, I thought, until we were close enough to see that he had nailed a dozen bull snakes to the trunk and was methodically firing at their heads. They were still moving, rippling against the wood. I had to look at the ground. My brother touched my arm to comfort me. His fingers felt like five smooth serpents wrapped around my wrist.

Reverend Pyke turned, and I looked into his eyes. They were a remarkable color, somewhere between green and black, charred, like burnt grass. A broad forehead dominated his features and his brown beard wasn't on his chin but below it, like a thick strip of bear fur stuck to his throat. His red skin was peeling in several places, and he fingered the patches as he stared at me. He didn't seem to notice my brother.

The first words he spoke were: "*Mine enemies are lively and they are strong, and they that hate me wrongfully are multiplied.*" In unison we continued: "*They also that render evil for good are mine adversaries, because I follow the thing that good is.*"

Pyke thrust his fingers in his beard and scratched the hidden flesh. "Do you follow the thing that good is?" he asked me.

"I would if I knew what that was," I replied.

He nodded his great head, substantial as a cannonball. "You are of upright conversation," he said.

As easily as that I attached myself to the fort, becoming a kind of personal secretary to Reverend Pyke. "I want to know what my left hand is doing," he bellowed on that first day. He called me Esther Left Hand. I passed myself off as the Christian Father La Frambois had tried so long to create. I relished the irony and would have been rather smug were it not for the fact that each day was a step into the void. I was no closer to understanding the purpose of my mission.

My brother and I camped between the fort and the village of our cousins, and went in opposite directions for most of the day. Long Chase had befriended several young warriors and together they trekked north to find game. "You're a good influence on them," I told him one evening. "You're already so capable." He scowled to hide his pleasure.

Long Chase had instructed Spotted Dog to watch over me, so

every morning the dog led me to the fort and settled in a corner of the patched windowless lean-to Pyke referred to as his study. A vast mirror hung above his desk, its gilt frame a horror of twisted vines and sharp leaves; angry-looking foliage. I thought of it as Eden Lost. The first time I was alone in that room I stepped to the looking glass and touched my reflection with a finger. It was the only time I'd seen myself in a proper mirror, but the glass was so wavy it was like staring into water. I was struck by how my mouth tipped downwards in a child's pout, and I hadn't realized that I watched the world through my eyelashes. I didn't observe myself for very long. My eyes were the same shape as my mother's, curved like wings, watching them made me lonesome.

I transcribed Pyke's sermons, my hand dipping into ink like a bird pecking at water and then sweeping across the page to keep pace with the rapid language. I knew the Bible well enough to catch when Pyke departed from his own words to quote Scripture. One passage he returned to again and again, while his fingers wandered over the silver revolver he kept on his blotter, *"The wicked have drawn out the sword and bent their bow, to cast down the poor and needy, to slay such as be of upright conversation. Their sword shall enter their own heart, and their bows shall be broken."*

Pyke often raged in the study, his lecture becoming personal, perhaps more revelatory than he intended. "I'm a child of the wilderness," he told me. "God's child. I sprouted from the earth like a bean. No mother, no father, no strangling ties to come between me and the Lord."

Pyke was never without his smelly top hat and on the windiest days managed to keep it glued to his enormous head. His fingers were strangely flat and pale as grubs, except for the rim of dirt under the nails. I observed that while his flesh was none too clean, and I believe his clothes had never been scrubbed, he was fastidious about his space. His cherry-wood desk was so well polished it looked as if crimson flames burned beneath the surface, his books were regularly dusted and arranged in terms of size so that the shortest books led to the tallest, and the planks forming the study floor—though gapping and uneven—were soaped and buffed to reveal the wood's golden heart. Insect life wasn't safe in his presence, he crushed what he could, and Pyke said there was nothing natural about the natural world; it was an evil disorder requiring the cleansing hand of God. When he came across a spider's sac of eggs nestled in the folds of his heavy jacket, he squashed it with his fingers and licked them clean.

"I've swallowed the spit of Satan," he announced.

He watched me while I worked. I kept my eyes on the papers before me but I could feel him staring and I could smell the sharp decay of his hat. I marveled that his fingers never grabbed me by the braids, tearing me from the earth so that I too was no longer part of the natural world but his creature, a lifeless polished trophy like the preserved prairie dog mounted on a block of wood and serving as a doorstop. Instead he fingered the beard at his throat or the silver revolver, and I labored to set down Pyke's vision of America: a place where animals were bred for food behind neat fences, mountains were leveled, valleys filled, rivers straightened and grass trained with a ruler.

"Man is the organizer," he said. "Adam named the creatures, mastered the elements and answered to no one but the Lord. This is the legacy we must claim for ourselves."

I scratched the words onto stiff paper but had the sudden urge to yank the land from beneath Pyke's feet like a slippery rug.

On Sundays I sat in the back of the low-ceilinged hall Reverend Pyke borrowed for his services and tried not to envy Long Chase his freedom. Pyke's voice didn't have anywhere to go in the small space, even the thick wool uniforms couldn't absorb the fierce syllables, so his commotion penetrated my ears like a great clanging bell. I watched the congregation through my eyelashes, practiced stillness and control of my heart, which I thought of as a fist-sized Indian pony, all kicking legs and snapping tail. I slowed its gallop to a walk and measured each step it took. *I run my own body,* I thought.

The handful of officers' wives sat together towards the front, surrounded by their husbands. I couldn't tell if the women were fenced in or the men shut out. I was fascinated by their pallor, a white so pale it was tinted blue, like thin milk. Their clothes squeezed the breath from them and rendered their bodies tight as bow strings. I longed to reach out and pluck them, play their one quavering note. The laundresses from Soapsuds Row and the housekeepers sat behind them, decidedly healthier in complexion. These ladies had tired feet that looked to be planted for eternity, and darting eyes. I don't know how many of Pyke's words they digested, they seemed intent on soaking up the subterranean sounds of people trapped together: the rustles, coughs, whispers, sighs.

One lady, like myself, was without a group and sat to the far right of the congregation, so diminutive her feet didn't touch the ground. Pyke had said she was a recent widow and it seemed so, her black dress was still crisp and tidy, unlike those of other widows who turned them inside-out after a time to get more wear. The color pinched her even tighter than her corset and in profile she nearly vanished like the flat of a sword, except for her breasts, tiny and round as ground cherries. I soon noticed that while this lady always wore black she also managed a spot of color, perhaps a folding fan, a ribbon pinned beneath her brooch, a nodding sunflower threaded into her bonnet. I thought of these items as her intentions speaking through.

One morning at dress parade I found myself standing beside the widow. She interested me more than the mechanical movements of the soldiers who stretched across the horizon, their white gloves gleaming like teeth.

"Oh, look at the guidons," she murmured. One open hand covered her pulsing throat and the other dabbed at her upper lip with a square of delicate lace. The flags streamed behind the soldiers, pulled taut by the wind. The sky was pasted with the company colors. Sweeping gusts took most of the sounds—the orders being called, the jingling of spurs and harnesses, the indignant snorts of cavalry horses—so the parade became an eerie drama of tremendous silent activity. I was unimpressed with the display, it struck me as the kind of thing Pyke would have dreamed up in his hankering for artificial order, simulated grace. But I said something appreciative to the widow, to make out I was enjoying the spectacle as much as she did.

When the soldiers were given orders to retire and began leaving the field, the widow turned to me. Her eyes were light brown and unusually bright, they reminded me of the nuggets of fool's gold Father La Frambois carried in his pocket. "I'm Fanny Brindle," she said. "You've been watching me."

I must have started because she touched my arm with one finger. "That's not a complaint, it's an observation."

Fanny Brindle removed her hat. Her dark blond hair was pinned up but seemed to strain against the combs, several wisps rolled across the slopes of her head like miniature tumbleweeds. She had a tight little face and sharp nose that pointed downwards, steady as a compass.

"Are you a woman alone?" she asked me.

"No," I shook my head. "I have my brother Joseph, and my dog, and—" Here I should have said something about the Lord to continue my pose as a Christian Sioux, but I forgot myself. "And my ancestors are looking out for me," I said.

Fanny didn't notice. "I am alone," she said. "My husband was Sergeant Guy Brindle, but he died three months ago from scarlet fever. I dosed him with potassium chlorate and ordered him not to leave, but you see the good it did me." She wrenched a tall sunflower from the ground and tucked it into her belt. "Not to worry, though. It wasn't a love match. I came here as a governess, and he offered me an easier life than that. I think it's the reason polite company won't breathe in my direction. I used to enter their rooms by the back door."

"We should be friends," Fanny told me. She laughed and nudged the dirt with her toe. "I can't get any lower."

Fanny's artlessness—some would have said thoughtlessness—was part of her charm. I began to think of her as a sunflower, all open face and spitting seeds. She liked to stroll from one end of the fort to the other, her slender twig of an arm hooked through mine. She was eager to share the latest gossip gleaned from Bailey Roe, the enlisted man who had worked for her husband as striker and still offered some occasional assistance.

"He is a man of remarkable hearing and recall," she confided. "His word is gospel."

It was early October, *Čanwapekasna Wi,* the moon when the leaves rustle. The buffalo grass was a drab brown and winter's breath swirled across the plain. Pyke was working on a treatise titled "Laramie, the Lord's Outpost," and didn't release me or the watchful Spotted Dog until the sun was well into its downward arc. On these days Fanny met me at the door of Pyke's study, quickly taking my arm and heading in the direction of the river. Fanny wasn't one to stifle her curiosity. She came right out and asked me: "Does he pay you for the work you do?"

"I don't think he makes much more than the enlisted men," I said. "But he takes me to the sutler's store every now and then for supplies."

"Well, he should," Fanny sniffed.

I had a habit of addressing Fanny and Pyke and the others at the fort in silence, speaking in my head. The truth had to let itself out some way or I would have confused myself. What I said in the secrecy of my thoughts was: *Fanny*, mazaska—*the white iron you call money— is useless to me. Even the goods I take from the sutler's store, the flour, coffee, sugar and tobacco, the knives and blankets, are things I do not want. I give them to my cousins who live upriver.*

Fanny squeezed my arm impatiently—perhaps she saw these ideas moving across my forehead—and said: "Do you know what they're saying about you? That you're a princess." I didn't react but she nodded her head in affirmation. "Yes, a Sioux princess with the light of the world in your heart, and a devotion to Jesus Christ that is so pure your soul is white as cream. I think it's because of your remarkable English," she mused to herself. "They can't conceive of it as anything but a miracle, and it is, you know. It is."

I smiled at Fanny, assured her that I wasn't a princess and thanked her for complimenting my speech. But what I really said to Fanny was, "Kola, *friend, look at this sullen brown grass, dispirited because winter is coming to punish it. This, to me, is English. It is little pebbles on my tongue, gravel, the kind of thing you chew but cannot swallow. Dakota is the lush spring grass that moves like water and tastes sweet.*"

By November, *Waniyetu Wi*, the month of the winter moon, Fanny could not be persuaded to go on long walks but remained in her room, wrapped in a heavy shawl. I visited her there though it shamed her to have company, even mine, in such a place. After her husband died a new lieutenant had claimed his apartments as a superior officer was entitled to do, so Fanny had been ranked out of her home and into a narrow hallway of the same quarters. The young lieutenant was sensitive enough to her plight to avoid using the hallway; he left and entered his rooms via the window.

An overstuffed divan pushed against one wall served as her couch and bed, and she told me that she washed and dressed in the huge walnut wardrobe which took up so much of the hallway one could barely squeeze past it. Sergeant Brindle's photograph dominated a mother-of-pearl-inlaid table, and while he may have looked bright and hopeful if you saw the picture alone, the drumming clock placed beside it cast a shadow across his face so that he looked wistful, aware of the coming fever.

"He wasn't very handsome, was he?" Fanny said. It had been decided, so I knew better than to respond. "But he wasn't cruel or petty, you can see the kindness, there, in his moustache." Fanny pointed to meager wisps of hair sprouting above a plump lip.

I ventured a question of my own. "Do you think you'll marry again?"

"I hope to," she said, without a breath or any pause. "Oh, it would be a shame to be here, so outnumbered by men they're thick as fleas, and not claim another. I work on it a little." Her face flushed then, becoming a red mask, "I go to all the hops, and dance and dance until I lose my feet, forget my toes were ever there. I just float in the officers' arms and turn into a cloud." She laughed. "A rather black cloud. Well, they have fair warning then!" Fanny looked at her little feet, tapped her heels together and grinned so broadly her eyes squeezed shut.

Fanny's mention of fleas proved prescient. The fort suffered a terrible infestation of the pests, flourishing despite the cold weather. The enlisted men blamed a recent shipment of blankets, though the sutler blanched and swore whenever this possibility was mentioned. I washed my skin and Spotted Dog's fur with buffalo grease and ashes, so we didn't suffer, but Pyke, the soldiers, and even the fine ladies were patched with welts and scabs from zealous scratching.

Fanny decided to organize a theatrical to take everyone's mind off the plague.

"I want to be distracted, don't you?" she asked. When I didn't answer quickly enough she said, "Oh, you. You aren't bothered in the slightest. I can see it. They don't like that Indian blood, do they?" No, I had to admit they didn't.

The next day she tacked up a neat sign on the porch of Old Bedlam—the unmarried officers' quarters—announcing the staging of *Macbeth*.

"You have to help me with this," she pleaded, so I became her assistant.

I had read the play aloud under the tutelage of Father La Frambois and was curious to see what Fanny and the soldiers would make of it. I thought Reverend Pyke might disapprove of the scheme, but he supported it and in fact landed a role, three roles to be precise, since he would play all three of the witches.

"Measured fun is a holy pleasure," Pyke blasted that Sunday to a chorus of nodding heads.

A stage only slightly larger than an oven range was erected in the front parlor of Old Bedlam, and auditions were held in the evening between stable call and Retreat. Pyke was cast as the three witches because there simply wasn't room for more of them onstage. Many of the roles were combined and speeches cut. Fanny insisted we would get to the meat of the story and trim the rest, and by the time the officers in the company had their say, the scenes were mostly swordplay, complete with uncorked sabres and plumed hats. One of my jobs was to prompt the actors in their lines, what lines remained, and the text became as familiar to me as Scriptures until I began to confuse the two, and would quote Shakespeare as readily as passages from Ecclesiastes.

Long Chase was curious about my activities and asked me what I was doing. There was no term in Dakota for "Assistant Director," so I said I was helping the *wašičuns* tell stories. Then I told him about the fleas and leapt on my pony to imitate the soldiers' odd canter, how they leaned forward in the saddle to scratch their ankles. Long Chase collapsed on the ground, clutching his ribs and rolling with laughter. Spotted Dog jumped over him, barked, thrust his wet nose into Long Chase's face.

"That was a good one," my brother said when he could finally speak.

During the two-week rehearsal period I became acquainted with several of the officers I'd previously thought of as faceless.

The three I came to know best were those with the largest roles, needing the most prompting from my corner. It was my opinion that Fanny had miscast them, each woefully unsuited to the part. Lieutenant Royal Bourke, who would play Macbeth, had sky eyes and blond hair like moist honey dripping to his shoulders. He was polished, without being insincere, and had the smoothest voice, really it was like the bolt of silk I'd seen in the sutler's store. He never failed to notice the lurking Spotted Dog and spoke to him so gently the dog came forward and bowed his head, then, in perfect Dakota etiquette, lifted one pumpkin-colored paw to shake hands. And this man would play the irresolute tyrant? I would have chosen Captain Philander Merritt, the handsomest of the three and the most inscrutable. His pale skin glimmered against hair that was thick and black as my own, eyes brown as acorns. His long eyelashes fluttered before he spoke and white teeth perched prettily on his bottom lip when he smiled, but there was tension in his face and shoulders, lines in his young forehead that made me question his friendliness. His body was compact but dense, and as the betrayed Banquo who returns as a ghost to haunt Macbeth, ineffective; he was too solidly in the world for me to ever imagine dead.

Finally, the bold, heroic Macduff who so capably vanquishes Macbeth would be portrayed by Lieutenant Lemon Van Horn, youngest of the officers and the one whose questions frequently went unanswered because no one heard him. I could tell that his uniform had been altered to hide a wispy figure, but his face was round, plumped out by soft jowls too smooth for whiskers. His face was fairly red with freckles and his hair red-gold, though lusterless, like his spirits. People seemed to either confuse or tire him, and when he mocked Macbeth during the play's climax, charging, "*Turn, hellhound, turn!*" it was with great drawn-out sighs.

Lady Macbeth proved to be the most difficult part to cast since the ladies felt it would be undignified to participate, and Fanny couldn't cast herself. At the last minute she convinced a recent arrival to the fort, the young wife of a non-commissioned officer, Melody Kendall, to step into the role. The young woman could recite well enough but had to be dissuaded from wearing hoops and the latest gown from Boston, decorated with fabric roses large as cabbages. "Ringlets will never do," Fanny scolded gently. She pointed to the tight clusters springing above Melody's ears.

The night of the performance Fanny was in a generous mood. She

ushered me to a seat near the front, just behind the commanding officers and their carefully coiffed wives who surreptitiously, or so they
thought, scratched beneath smooth waves of hair, behind spread fans.

"You've made a hit," she whispered loudly in my ear. "Just look at
you. Old Bedlam will never be the same."

"What do you mean?"

"Oh, you. Everyone's half mad with love, or maybe lust." Here she
pinched my forearm so enthusiastically it hurt.

"No, no," I demurred, quite honestly.

Fanny sat down beside me, and her small forehead worked itself
into a web of lines. "Don't you know you're beautiful?" she asked. I
felt Spotted Dog shift against my leg. Fanny picked up one of my
hands as casually as she would a teacup. "Look at this, look at these
long delicate bones, nails glossy as porcelain. I can't stand it." She
dropped my hand and fell back into the chair in one motion. "I think
it's that curl of a smile that finally does them in, partway between a
sneer and a laugh. Makes them work to impress you.

"I thought you knew," she concluded. "I thought it was a manipulation."

I could only shake my head at Fanny, my friend who was surely
carried away by the night's festivities and her own complicated flirta-
tions.

A brocade curtain rigged up by Fanny's striker, Bailey, lifted to enthusiastic applause and so much squirming I thought I could see a fog
of fleas rise up and redistribute themselves. Pyke's witches were in
good voice, he thundered spells while energetically stirring soapy water in one of the laundress's borrowed tubs. When he came to the familiar chorus—"Double, double toil and trouble; fire burn and
cauldron bubble"—there emerged a dozen witches as soldiers in the
audience shouted the lines with him.

Too often actors absentmindedly raked fingernails through beards
or across their flesh to discourage the biting fleas, but since the spectators were similarly afflicted it was overlooked. Lady Macbeth, as it
turned out, was determined to be fashionable, and her hoops took up
the entire stage, causing anyone sharing her scenes to stand on the
floor and gaze up at her. Her ringlets bounced with passion, eliciting
titters from the crowd, and one man snickered loudly when she

scratched rather than rubbed the imagined spot of blood on her hand, all the while wearing elbow-length kidskin gloves and twirling an open parasol.

The final battle was vigorously performed, an exchange of blows that went on for nearly half an hour, but when the curtain plunged to the ground we clapped at the effort, and the parlor was filled with a happy buzz. The ladies produced eggnog, and I was about to leave, when Lemon Van Horn—Macbeth's cloth head still tucked under one arm—handed me a glass of the creamy liquid.

"You aren't leaving?" he said in his weary voice.

Surrounded by Lemon, Royal, a handful of other officers and even the wary Merritt, I saw truth in Fanny's observations. I felt stifled by attention and sought comfort in Spotted Dog, resting at my feet. I spread my fingers through his coarse fur and felt the regular rhythm of his heart pulsing beneath my fingertips. He occasionally rolled his eyes to meet mine and wouldn't look away until I smiled.

What can they possibly want from me? I wondered. A midnight rendezvous in Squaw Town? Something furtive and shameful, to be quickly forgotten? The eggnog left a sour taste; I ran my tongue across my teeth and nearly gagged. I sat as straight as I could and smiled, or sneered, however they chose to read my expression. I was careful not to look into their eyes so there would be no message.

The men chattered, told anecdotes and in the telling staggered or waved their arms, jumped onto chairs, pounded their comrades on the back, punched shoulders. It became a blur of sound and movement I associated with the smell of curdled cream. Somewhere during the mayhem I slipped my hand into the quilled pouch dangling from my waist. My fingers searched for a sliver of the bitter muskrat root which would quickly change the taste in my mouth. I touched something else. Two smooth stones clicking together, released from buckskin wrapping. I cupped one in my palm to be certain of the object. Earlier that evening when I left the lodge I shared with my brother, these stones had been buried in a shallow hole beneath my pallet. Some hidden force had pushed them through the ground, propelled them through the air, and tucked them into my bag where they nested like crimson eggs.

The stones move with a purpose, I told the officers. But in my private way, which was no warning.

•

I am leaving Old Bedlam, which has lived up to its name on this occasion. Men watch me as I travel lightly down the steps. Now I am a dark figure, a shadow moving across the yard. I bend smoothly to place the stones beneath a clump of weeds, not knowing I would do it. Every step, every gesture is natural, spontaneous. I am inevitable as light or darkness, steady as rain. I push out my breath to match the wind and soar in the direction of my brother's sleep. Spotted Dog is ahead of me, grinning to himself as he leads the way.

I'm coming, I sing to him. *I'm coming.* But now I think I'm telling the ancestor-spirits who have waited so long for me to move, as I am moving now.

Upon arriving I don't enter the lodge, but sit outside, my arms and legs carefully folded. Spotted Dog leans into my side, lets his weight fall against me. For once I am the alert one, impervious to chill winds and tired feet, to hunger and thirst. "You rest," I tell him.

Later I will find myself standing beside the river, drawn to the battered cottonwood tree blasted by a revolver. I am utterly alone. I will hear the man before I see him. He is not so graceful, his stumbling feet churn the dry grass. Whiss. Whiss. He is the sleepy one with red hair and freckles, the one whose voice is easily lost. He walks to me without hesitation and doesn't flinch when I reach for his hand. The stones are there, clenched in the fist I peel open one finger at a time. I return the stones to my pouch and pluck a strand of hair from my head. I lean into the man as I wind the thread of hair around a brass button on his jacket; the slow circles enchant us both. He wears the rope across his chest like a cartridge belt. I tell him what to do. I look into his eyes for the first time and see only myself. I have forgotten their color. I leave him to his work, turning my back on the man and the tree.

I will return to Long Chase and Spotted Dog, sidestepping their dreams as I make my way to the buffalo hide I use to cover myself. I will not see how the man, so recently a boy, climbs the tree and coils the rope as tenderly as I wound hair around the button beneath his heart. He will be graceful as he steps into black air, the night space, flying for a long moment. And when he is forced to land, I will not see the color of his face. The sudden emptiness.

It was Pyke, prowling the fort's perimeter on his early morning reconnaissance with the Lord, who came across Lemon Van Horn hanging from a cottonwood tree. His boots were only a few inches from the ground, so for a moment it must have looked to Pyke as if Lemon were just standing in front of the tree.

"He has thrown his soul to the dogs," Pyke growled that day. "He will languish in purgatory for what he has done. Quick, Esther, take this down. I will address the subject on Sunday."

I had noticed before that any mention of the loss of human life filled Pyke with a peculiar dread. I don't mean the inevitable sorrow, or the rage one feels when a loved one dies, but a terrible fear penetrating his thoughts, drilling his bones.

"Man is close to almighty, he should not be cut down. And to tear himself out of the world—this is an abomination!" Pyke stamped across the study floor, his arms flung open and fingers trembling. "I am unsettled," he said. His candor took me by surprise. He tore at the strip of fur beneath his chin and strode past me. He left the study and didn't think to shut the door.

I observed Pyke closely to escape my own feelings which were heavy as a hundred stones. *I am at war,* I told myself, knowing it was more complicated than that. I was also at war with myself.

I do not know who the stones will claim next. They are like red eyes that can see everything. Moonlight washes over me like a graceful blessing. This man is silent as he approaches the river, carrying a coiled lasso of rope. I can't hear his steps or the rope slapping against his thigh, but I can feel the force of his will. His black hair fades into the night, so the fair skin beneath that dark crest is like a torch. This man's body shudders with a dense quivering, his mind attempting to surface. The shaking stops him in his tracks. I move forward gently as a pulse of air and take the stones from his hand.

He is gasping as I wind a strand of my hair around his jacket button. This I do more tightly than before, longing to be finished so I can release him. His eyes are burning at the core, the pin of light at the center of his black pupil. He would like to kill me, but he cannot will his hands to do it.

"You are another one we won't have to fight," I tell him, but it isn't enough. I am forced to watch this time. The tree is hard to climb, several times he slides down the trunk. His movements are slow, reluctant. But the rope nearly twists itself.

A week before Christmas Fanny Brindle organized a skating party. "This will lift our spirits," she declared. Most of the officers and their families turned out, grateful for the distraction, though Pyke was conspicuously absent.

After Philander Merritt was found dangling from the same tree where Lemon had cast his rope, Pyke took an axe to it and not only felled the tree but chopped it into kindling. He said it would produce an evil smoke, so he tossed the chunks of wood into the river, watching grimly as they swirled away. I knew he was probably brooding in his study as we gathered beside the now frozen river, studiously avoiding the forlorn cottonwood stump.

"I am lost in a mysterious world," he had told me just the day before. He even grabbed my hand as I made ready to leave, kneading it with his flat paws. "Death is chaos," he said.

I was happy to be on the river where the cold wind drew tears from my eyes and whipped my mind clean. Several of the soldiers had crude blades strapped onto their boots and were moving across the ice like delicate insects skimming water. Their weight shifted from side to side in an elegant rhythm, hypnotizing me as I stood wrapped in a small buffalo calf robe.

The ladies without skates were being pushed in wooden chairs, whirled quickly on the ice, evoking cries of pleasure. Fanny was there, her skirt tucked around her legs and her hands inside a muff of beaver hide. She waved to me, then nearly lost the muff as she grabbed for the chair's back. Her face spun away.

Royal Bourke approached, his sky eyes wide with happiness and shoulders sparkling with snow. "Why are you standing here?" he asked me. "Why aren't you laughing?"

I avoided his blue gaze by counting his brass buttons. "I like to watch," I said.

"That isn't good enough." He extended his arm, and I took it as lightly as I could. He settled me in a sturdy ladder-back chair and then pressed me forward into currents of bright air; a place without breath or sound. The sky became a wheel as I twirled on the ice, the clouds streaming together and the sun becoming a long string of suns. I smiled, I bent over to laugh into my hands. The chair stopped.

"What's wrong?" Royal asked. He knelt on the ice. I shook my head and laughed a little more. "Oh, good. I thought you were dizzy," he chuckled.

"I was. But it was nice," I told him.

When I thought Royal must surely be tired of the game—though he protested he could push me straight to Canada—I joined Fanny beside a table set with steaming mugs of cider.

"Wasn't it wonderful?" she asked. "It breaks my heart to go back to my hallway. I tell you, I wake up with frost on my eyebrows, hugging nothing friendlier than a can of yeast. To keep it warm, you know, or it would freeze like my potatoes. They're hard as rocks." Fanny sipped cider so tenderly it was almost like a kiss. "How do you make out in nothing better than a tent?"

I told her how Long Chase and I had built a willow stockade around our tipi, with a small runway for the ponies to protect them from night drafts. I worked the smoke flaps so we could build a fire in the lodge, the flames keeping us warm all night. "And Spotted Dog warms my feet," I said. His ears flicked forward at the mention of his name.

Later that night I told Long Chase about my dizzy ride.

"I wish I'd seen that. You must have looked funny," he teased. "We were playing too," he continued. "I made those kids a sled out of buffalo ribs, and we took it up there," he pointed to a distant coulee.

"That was a good thing," I said. I was proud of my generous brother who spent so many hours with the children of our cousins, teaching them things the old people in their village only talked about. But it was not our way to fuss over one another, my terse praise was enough.

I looked forward to sleep that night, having exhausted myself the way children do. I checked beneath my pallet, as I did every night, for the sacred stones I collected from Angry Butte and transported to this place of dying grass. My fingers anticipated their sleek texture, stretched eagerly to graze their faces. I marvelled at the warmth they emanated, even packed in frozen ground. I scratched the dirt, eventually turning my hands into claws that raked the earth. But it was useless, the stones were gone.

The sentries are sleepy by the time I reach the fort's perimeter. One dreams with his eyes open, and the other is crushing the snow with his boots to make animal figures. I brush past them, first one and then the other, mad with potent energy, determined to be invisible. I take chances because I think I am the wind. The tree is gone and although there are others, I know better than to head in that direction. I move towards Old Bedlam and mount the stairs leading to its second story porch. I sway at the top, flinging my head back to count the stars. *I will give them officers' names,* I think. *I will send them soldiers.*

I hear footsteps and reach out to grasp the railing. He steps onto the porch and carefully closes the door behind him. He is not drowsy and he doesn't resist. I think if I told him to fly he would spread his arms and leap at the moon. He hands me the stones before I look for them and lifts the rope in his hands. It is a coarse snake wound between us.

"Give me your hair," he whispers, complice to this act. I wrap the button, but only once or twice. The thread floats free, and I don't snatch another from my open braid. He moves to the railing, his steps like a dance, and ties the rope in ugly ways. He slips his head in the loop, and I put out my hand for him to catch. There is a twitch of a smile on my lips because I have called him back. But he is suddenly a golden bird risen from the deck. He flies away.

Fort Laramie was a place of death—I had seen that in my dream—but now it was a place of ghosts, some of them living. Pyke retreated like a turtle, reading tracts for most of the day, the reading material in one hand and revolver in the other.

"You can't help me," he said when I knocked on his study door.

Rope was confiscated, placed under guard, and more soldiers assigned watch duty. Royal Bourke had sky eyes, but now he was buried in a shallow grave laboriously chipped out of the frozen earth. People walked with their heads down, moving briskly to get somewhere. Even Fanny was reclusive, seldom in sight. So I took it upon myself to pay her a visit, bringing her a piece of salt pork Long Chase had received from our cousins.

I rapped on her door but there was no answer. I opened it a crack so I could slip the package inside, and was stunned by what I saw. Fanny Brindle was no longer a woman alone. She lay on the divan, pressed into it by the weight of her striker, Bailey Roe. They seemed to have sprouted additional arms and legs, and were flailing them about. They resembled tangled crabs.

I chucked the salt pork into a corner and fled the room before the two could find their voices. I nearly stepped on Spotted Dog in my haste, for he lingered at the door. I was short with him. "Move it," I growled. We walked slowly away from the fort, Spotted Dog beside me rather than loping ahead. Perhaps he noticed the drag of my feet. My limbs were heavy and cut deep tracks through the snow. Loneliness swept across me until I thought my heart would disintegrate like powder. Fanny Brindle was a woman from the other world, but I would miss her. And I had understood, from the moment we latched eyes, that Fanny would never forgive me what I had seen.

Long Chase's warrior friends told him that a small buffalo herd had been spotted thirty miles to the north.

"*Tanke,* we're going to bring some back for your soup so you'll have something to talk to the corn," he said. He rubbed the lodge's skin wall, the smoked hide so worn it was becoming transparent. "We could use some new walls too. We're like a lantern at night."

Long Chase set off the next morning wearing his buffalo-hide shirt with the coarse hair against his skin. I knew that before he turned his pony into the fleet stream of buffalos, he would shed the garment. My brother could ride like that, his flesh exposed to temperatures that would have claimed a soldier's fingers and toes with frostbite, inured to the cold through careful childhood training. He washed in the snow each morning, joined by Spotted Dog who thought it was a romp. I had seen them dive headlong into the powder as if it were the river back home.

Now I clasped my brother's hand and looked up at him settled on his horse. I didn't tell him to be careful. I didn't tell him anything at all because the child was missing that morning, replaced by a smiling man. He squeezed my hand and gave it back to me. I watched him ride away. I knelt on the ground beside Spotted Dog, my arms wrapped around his neck. The dog looked forlorn, upset to be left behind. He knew where Long Chase was headed after hearing "*Tatanka*," the term for buffalo.

"You don't want to leave me all by myself," I scolded him. And for a moment he lifted his eyes from my brother's receding back to look at me. His tongue rolled out, the sure sign of forgiveness, so I left him there and moved to tidy our camp.

I was visited that night by a bear. Not *mato*, our fierce brother whose claws are greatly prized, but a human bear bundled in furs. Reverend Pyke entered my lodge without a greeting, looking like a man of snow.

"Good evening," I said, polite though his abrupt entrance was rude. I gestured towards the caller's space to the left of my sputtering fire. "Make yourself comfortable," I told him.

Pyke's legs were stiff as tree trunks, his head grazed the wall. "I am not calling," he said to me. "I am not here." I looked at Spotted Dog as if he had an explanation. "But the Lord is here," Pyke continued. "The Lord suffuses my soul and expunges the wickedness he finds there with a flick of his tongue."

I was motionless before the raving giant, my senses assailed by his reeking hat and rumbling voice.

"The Lord told me that I was blessed," he continued. "He bade me *replenish the earth and subdue it, and have dominion over the fish of the sea, and over the fowl of the air, and over every living thing that moveth upon the earth.* You will not work your ways on me," Pyke thundered. "I made you and fostered your demon intelligence. I will unmake you." And the one I had not spelled or visited with sacred stones brought his flat hand out of the fur wrappings strapped to his body. He raised his silver revolver, aiming it at my heart. The gun's barrel was a black eye, and when it exploded, a streak of bright color rose to meet the bullet. Spotted Dog fell at my feet. I knelt beside him and stroked his back. I rubbed the loose skin behind his ears.

"You are a brave dog," I murmured in Dakota, speaking the language I told myself he preferred. His blood spilled across my hands and it was while I struggled to catch each precious drop that the tent exploded a second time.

I had turned my back on the giant, he loomed somewhere above me. "*Mičeȟpi,*" I called, but not to him. "*Mičeȟpi.*" My flesh.

I fell into a river of liquid as smooth as the cream *wašičuns* favored, and in that warm bath drawing me through *Ina's*—the mother's— heart, I was unperturbed by my own death. The recent events were banished from my mind, and I was free to indulge my sensibilities in ways forbidden me in life. I was raised to believe that discipline and self-control were signs of maturity, necessitating the suppression of individual desires. My feelings swept over me now, I was in a womb of my affections. Music penetrated the fluid and my wandering soul; a piercing sweetness from our Dakota courting flute. It was a tune composed by Ghost Horse, the thunder dreamer, a melody he played when I carried water from the river or collected wood for kindling. This was in the days before our dreams—so devastating in retrospect— set us upon divergent courses. My spirit throbbed in anger. I was like an old woman weeping for her children. Ghost Horse and I were victims of utter faith, I realized. We were Job, lonely and afflicted. Chosen. Only the music could stir me from my sudden brooding. I let it move through me until it became the words I couldn't speak and the tears I could not cry.

You will think that I was borne away but in fact I was a witness to what followed. I tracked Reverend Pyke in the snow as capably as a coyote. He hadn't gone far from the lodge; the ancestor-spirits had trapped him in the drifts and he was half-buried in snow. My sight was sharper than before so I could see into his deep pockets where twin sisters with red faces clacked together. The sacred stones had moved for the last time. Pyke's revolver had loosed a final shot, taking him by surprise, I think, for he looked puzzled and his left hand was latched onto his right wrist as if there'd been a struggle.

My brother Long Chase returned hours later with enough buffalo meat, tallow and winter hides to last us through the winter. He sang for me and for Spotted Dog, gashed his arms and legs to wear his grief and let it pour out of him. He removed the note Reverend Pyke had pinned to my dress. My brother couldn't read the words, but knew it was some work of spite. I read the lines, curious as I had ever been: *"Upon thy belly shalt thou go, and dust shalt thou eat all the days of thy life."*

I shook my fists and smiled to hear them rattle. Was it madness, I wondered, or a crystal sanity that led him to write these words?

Long Chase quickly discovered Pyke after I nudged him in that direction. I didn't want him seeking vengeance. *You see, it's already done,* I told my brother. And then I whispered, *Go home.*

The return trip was a trek of heartbreak, exhaustion and hunger. Long Chase trudged through the snow and rarely looked ahead of him, so defeated, our enemies were the least of his concerns. I scouted for him, and the few times I spotted distant trouble my spirit made a nuisance of itself, torturing my brother's adversaries with flung rocks and snowy twisters until they changed direction.

Grass was beginning to poke through melting snow when Long Chase reached our winter camp. He emerged from a cloud of horses and was met by Father La Frambois, out for a stroll. My brother walked past him, numbly discourteous, and when the priest moved towards the body the ponies dragged behind them on a bed of furs, Long Chase caught his arm. No words passed between them but Father La Frambois soon gathered that he was shut out of the proceedings. He would not be allowed to handle my body or baptize me posthumously. His blessings and masses were politely refused. He never learned that in death, I finally became a bride.

Ghost Horse brought my father three sturdy ponies he'd captured from the Crows. "I have fulfilled my obligations as *heyo'ka,*" he told my parents. "And I am free to take a wife. Your daughter never watched me, sent me messages, or stepped away from herself, but she is in here anyway." He tapped his chest. "I have these feelings that are only pitiful grains, but they are planted in my blood and growing." He held out his arms and stared at the veins as if he expected to find bold spikes of grass.

"I request the honor of marrying your daughter's spirit, mourning her as a devoted husband would grieve."

Ghost Horse did not bury me in the ground or build a scaffold, but placed me near the crown of a majestic bur oak tree. I was cradled by its spreading branches, rocked in its stout arms. My husband stood beside me in the tree and looked in every direction.

"You will see the world," he said. He ate the fruit of a dried plum and when its meat was gone, he very gently placed the pit in my mouth. It was the most intimate gesture that ever passed between us.

Before he left, my husband lifted the shield he had given me just a year earlier. "I want you to see what I've done," he told me. He pointed to fresh tracks of blue paint drawn across the tough bull hide. "I recorded your accomplishments," Ghost Horse continued. "You are a warrior and this is your shield."

I peered at the blue marks, my spirit slow to recognize the figures. Comprehension came in a rush, and when my hands flew to cover my eyes, I stirred a powerful wind. My husband nearly fell from the tree. I shrank from the paint, from the woman in a red dress wielding lightning. The jagged bolt was sharp at its tip, and three blue figures—men in uniform—were impaled by it, collected like beads strung on a needle.

Ghost Horse turned the shield to face this fierce woman. "We honor you," he said. He threaded his arm through the handles to wear the shield and rolled his arm in quick circles, making the rattlesnake gourds hiss. My spirit was tangled in the tree, dismayed and bewildered. *Who is this woman?* I wondered, and didn't want the answer to come to me. But the rattlesnake gourds produced a soothing sound, and my heart lifted when I saw the creatures emerge from their dens and hiding places. Serpents flowed toward the tree, forming creeks and rivers of writhing motion. They washed over one another, rising and then falling; they became a single unit of grace.

The snakes are dancing, I murmured. And when they surrounded the tree my spirit fell into their midst, prostrate. We danced together.

Ghost Horse kept my spirit for one year; the most onerous form of grief. His younger brother, Wind Soldier, agreed to help him, and together they prepared my spirit lodge and collected goods to be distributed at the culminating feast. But when the year had passed, and the village assembled for my spirit release ceremony, it was unsuccessful. Ghost Horse did what was expected of him, said the words and gave away his last possession, but he did not loose me from this earth. His heart was a stone room without doors.

My husband sought death on the battlefield, and it wasn't long before a bold Arikara complied. I did my best to deflect the arrows, pushed the air with both hands to send them swerving harmlessly away. But the Ree's horse wouldn't stumble when I leapt for its legs. It carried him so close to my husband, the Ree's shot was deadly, and by the time I reached Ghost Horse he was on the ground.

I thought he might see me now that his eyes were focused on the next world. I held his head in my arms and spread his long hair across my thighs. *Old man,* I teased, *are you ready for this old lady?* But he was silent, and his polished eyes were stones.

I didn't see him leave though it was like him to accept another adventure instantly. He moved on to the place our ancestors inhabit; there was no one living to capture his spirit as mine had been.

"You went without me!" I cried. I shook him by the shoulders. My spirit stubbornly clutched his body which made it hard for his uncles to lift him. "We go together!" I shrieked in their ears. I finally departed when Ghost Horse's pony spooked and almost flung his body back to the ground. The uncles were horrified and scolded the horse, but I understood its terror. It didn't want me on its back.

At least a hundred years have passed, and the plum pit in my mouth has become a grove of trees. I can smell the fruit when it ripens, and my breath makes the leaves rustle.

I am hitched to the living, still moved by their concerns. My spirit never abandons the Dakota people, though sometimes all it can do is watch. I was there when the army confiscated our horses to cut off our legs. I stood behind the Ghost Dancers and when they fainted in desperate, useless ecstasy, I blew a refreshing wind into their faces. There have been too many soldiers and too many graves. Too many children packed into trains and sent to the other side of the country. Many times I ran alongside those tracks and waved at the bleak copper faces. *You are Dakota,* I called to them. *You are Dakota.* One time I stood in front of a chuffing engine and tried to keep it from moving forward, but it blasted through me. I saw the language shrivel, and though I held out my hands to catch the words, so many of them slipped away, beyond recall. I am a talker now and chatter in my people's ears until I grow weary of my own voice. *I am memory,* I tell them when they're sleeping.

I prefer to watch the present unravel moment by moment, than to look close behind me or far ahead. Time extends from me, flowing in many directions, meeting the horizon and then moving beyond to follow the curve of the earth. But I will not track its course with my eyes. It is too painful. I can bear witness to only a single moment of loss at a time. Still, hope flutters in my heart; a delicate pulse. I straddle the world and pray to *Wakan Tanka* that somewhere ahead of me He has planted an instant of joy.

DEATH

✠

Allen Ginsberg

✠

City Midnight Junk Strains

for Frank O'Hara

Switch on lights yellow as the sun
                              in the bedroom . . .
The gaudy poet dead   Frank O'Hara's bones
                                        under squares of grass
An emptiness at 8 PM in the Cedar Bar
          Throngs of drunken
                    guys talking about paint
          & lofts, and Pennsylvania youth.
                    Klein attacked by his heart
& chattering Frank
          stopped forever—
     Faithful drunken adorers, mourn.
                    The busfare's a nickel more
          past his old apartment on 9th Street by the park.
Delicate Peter loved his praise,
          I wait for the things he says
                              about me—
          Did he think me an Angel
          as angel I am still talking into earth's microphone
                              willy nilly
          —to come back as words ghostly hued
                    by early death

  but written so bodied
     mature in another decade.
Chatty prophet
     of yr own loves, personal
     memory feeling fellow
    Poet of building-glass
I see you walking as you said with your tie
flopped over your shoulder in the wind down 5th Avenue
     under the handsome breasted workmen
       on their scaffolds ascending Time
        & washing the windows of Life
—off to a date with Martinis & a blond
      beloved poet far from home
       —with thee and Thy sacred Metropolis
    in the enormous bliss of a long afternoon
    where death is the shadow
       cast by Rockefeller Center
         over your intimate street.
Who were you, black suited, hurrying to meet,
    Unsatisfied one?
      Unmistakable,
        Darling date
for the charming solitary/ young poet with a big cock
      who could fuck you all night long
        till you never came,
    trying your torture on his/ obliging fond body
    eager to satisfy god's whim that made you
      Innocent, as you are.
I tried/ your boys and found them ready
    sweet and amiable
      collected gentlemen
       with large sofa apartments
lonesome to please for pure language;
and you mixed with money
      because you knew language enough to be rich
       If you wanted your walls to be empty—

deep philosophical terms   for Edwin Denby   serious as Herbert
    Read
with silvery hair   announcing   your dead gift
to the crowd   whose greatest op art   frisson
was the new sculpture   your big blue wounded body
        made in the Universe
     when you went away   to Fire Island for the weekend
tipsy with a crowd of decade-olden friends
Peter stares out the window   at the robbers
     distracted   in Amphetamine
and I stare into my head & look for your/ broken roman nose
        your wet mouth-smell of martinis
          & a big artistic tipsy kiss.
40's only half a life   to have filled
      with so many fine parties and evenings'
      interesting drinks together with one
         faded friend or new
         understanding social cat
I want to be there in your garden party in the clouds
       all of us naked
strumming our harps and reading each other   new poetry
     in the boring celestial
       friendship Committee Museum.
You're in a bad mood?
     Take an Asprin.
      In the dumps?
       I'm falling asleep
          safe in your thoughtful arms.
Someone uncontrolled by History would have to own Heaven,
        on earth as it is.
I hope you satisfied your childhood love
Your puberty fantasy   your sailor punishment on your knees
         your mouth-suck
Elegant insistency
       on the honking self-prophetic Personal
       as Curator of funny emotions to the mob,

Trembling one, whenever possible.   I see New York thru your eyes
and hear of one funeral a year nowadays
From Billie Holliday's time
appreciated more and more
a common ear
for our deep gossip.

July 29, 1966

Jeffrey Eugenides

❧

The Virgin Suicides

O n the morning the last Lisbon daughter took her turn at suicide—it was Mary this time, and sleeping pills, like Therese—the two paramedics arrived at the house knowing exactly where the knife drawer was, and the gas oven, and the beam in the basement from which it was possible to tie a rope. They got out of the EMS truck, as usual moving much too slowly in our opinion, and the fat one said under his breath, "This ain't TV, folks, this is how fast we go." He was carrying the heavy respirator and cardiac unit past the bushes that had grown monstrous and over the erupting lawn, tame and immaculate eleven months earlier when the trouble began.

Cecelia, the youngest, only thirteen, had gone first, slitting her wrists like Cato while taking a bath, and when they found her, afloat in her pink pool, with her yellow eyes of someone possessed and her small body giving off the odor of a mature woman, the paramedics had been so frightened by her tranquility that they had stood mesmerized. But then Mrs. Lisbon lunged in, screaming, and the reality of the room reasserted itself: blood on the bathmat; Mr. Lisbon's razor sunk in the toilet bowl, marbling the water. The paramedics fetched Cecelia out of the warm water because it quickens the bleeding and put a tourniquet on her arm. Her wet hair hung down her back and already her extremities were blue. She didn't say a word, but when they parted her hands they found the laminated picture of the Virgin Mary she held against her budding chest.

That was in June, fish fly season, when each year our town is covered by the flotsam of those ephemeral insects. Rising in clouds from the algae in the polluted lake, they blacken windows, coat cars and streetlamps, plaster the municipal docks and festoon the rigging of sailboats, always in the same brown ubiquity of flying scum. Mrs. Scheer, who lives down the street, told us she saw Cecelia the day before she attempted suicide. The girl was standing in the street, wearing the antique wedding dress with the shorn hem she always wore, looking at a Thunderbird encased in fish flies. "You better get a broom, honey," Mrs. Scheer advised. But Cecelia fixed her with her spiritualist's gaze. "They're dead," she said, "they only live twenty-four hours. They hatch, they reproduce, and then they croak. They don't even get to eat." And with that she stuck her hand into the foamy layer of bugs and cleared her initials—C.L.

We've tried to arrange the photographs chronologically. A few are fuzzy but nonetheless revealing. Plate #1 shows the Lisbon house shortly before Cecelia's suicide attempt. It was taken by a real estate agent, Ms. Carmina D'Angelo, whom Mr. Lisbon had hired to sell the house his large family was outgrowing. As the snapshot shows, the slate roof had not yet begun to shed its shingles, the porch was still visible above the grass, and the windows were not yet held together with strips of masking tape. A comfortable suburban home. The upper right second story window contains a blur that Mrs. Lisbon identified as Mary Lisbon. "She used to tease her hair because she thought it was limp," she said, recalling how her daughter had looked for her brief time on earth. In the photograph Mary is caught in the act of blow-drying her hair. Her head appears to be on fire but that is only a trick of the light. It was June third, eighty-three degrees out, under sunny skies.

When the paramedics were satisfied they had reduced the bleeding to a trickle, they put Cecelia on a stretcher and carried her out of the house. She looked like a tiny Cleopatra on a palanquin. We saw the gangly paramedic with the Wyatt Earp mustache come out first—the one we'd call "Sheriff" when we got to know him better through these domestic tragedies—and then the fat one appeared, carrying the back end of the stretcher and stepping daintily across the lawn, peering at his police-issue shoes as though looking out for dog shit, though later, when we were better acquainted with the machinery, we knew he was checking the blood pressure gauge. Sweating and fumbling, burdened with reality, they moved toward the shuddering, blinking truck. The fat one tripped on a lone croquet wicket. In revenge he kicked it; the wicket sprang loose, plucking up a spray of dirt, and fell with a ping on the driveway. Meanwhile, Mrs. Lisbon burst onto the porch, trailing Cecelia's flannel nightgown. She let out a long wail which stopped time. Under the molting trees and above the blazing overexposed grass those four figures paused in tableau—the two slaves offering the victim to the altar (lifting the stretcher into the truck), the priestess brandishing the torch (waving the flannel nightgown) and the virgin, drugged, or dumb, rising up on her elbows, with an otherworldly smile on her pale lips.

Mrs. Lisbon rode in the back of the EMS truck, but Mr. Lisbon followed in the station wagon, observing the speed limit. Two of the Lisbon daughters were away from home. Therese was in Pittsburgh at a science convention, and Bonnie was at music camp, trying to learn the flute after giving up the piano (her fingers were too short), the violin (her chin hurt), the guitar (her fingers hurt) and the trumpet (she didn't want to get one of those big lips). Mary and Lux, hearing the siren, had run home from their voice lesson down the street with Mr. Jessup. Barging into that crowded bathroom, they registered the same shock as their parents at the sight of Cecelia with her spattered forearms and pagan nudity. Outside they hugged on a patch of uncut grass that Butch, the brawny boy who mowed it on Saturdays, had missed. Across the street, a truckful of men from the Parks Division attended to some of our dying elms. The EMS siren shrieked, going away. The botanist and his crew withdrew their insecticide pumps and watched the truck. When it was gone, they began spraying again. The stately elm tree, also visible in the foreground of Plate #1, has since succumbed to the Dutch elm beetles and has been cut down.

The paramedics took Cecelia to Bon Secours Hospital on Kercheval and Maumee. In the emergency room Cecelia watched the attempt to save her life with an eerie detachment. Her yellow eyes did not blink, nor did she flinch when they stuck a needle in her arm. Dr. Armonson stitched up her wrist wounds. Within five minutes of the transfusion he declared her out of danger. Chucking her under the chin, he said, "What are you doing here, honey? You're not even old enough to know how bad life gets."

And it was then Cecelia gave orally what was to be her only form of suicide note, and a useless one at that, because she was going to live: "Obviously, doctor," she said, "you've never been a thirteen-year-old girl."

The Lisbon girls were thirteen (Cecelia), and fourteen (Lux), and fifteen (Bonnie), and sixteen (Mary), and seventeen (Therese). They were short, round-buttocked in denim, with roundish cheeks that recalled the same dorsal softness. Whenever we got a glimpse, their faces looked indecently revealed, as though we were used to seeing women in veils. No one could understand how Mr. and Mrs. Lisbon had produced such beautiful children. Mr. Lisbon taught high school math. He was thin, boyish, stunned by his own gray hair. He had a high voice, and when Lux Lisbon told us how he had cried on the day he learned that Bonnie was pregnant with Joe the Retard's kid, we could easily imagine the sound of his girlish weeping.

Whenever we saw Mrs. Lisbon we looked in vain for some sign of the beauty that must have once been hers. But the plump arms, the brutally cut steel-wool hair, the church choir dresses and the librarian's glasses foiled us every time. We saw her only rarely, in the morning, fully dressed though the sun hadn't come up, stepping out to snatch up the dewy milk bottles, or on Sundays when the family drove in their panelled station wagon to St. Paul's Catholic Church on the Lake. On those mornings Mrs. Lisbon assumed a queenly iciness. Clutching her good purse, she checked each daughter for signs of make-up before allowing her to get in the car, and it was not unusual for her to send Lux back inside to put on a less revealing top. None of us went to church so we had a lot of time to watch them, the two parents leeched of color, like photographic negatives, and then the five glittering daughters in their homemade dresses, all lace and ruffle, bursting with their fructifying flesh.

Only one boy had ever been allowed in the house. Peter Sissen had helped Mr. Lisbon install a working model of the solar system in his classroom at school, and in return Mr. Lisbon had invited him for dinner. He told us the girls had kicked him continually under the table, from every direction so that he couldn't tell who was doing it. They gazed at him with their blue, febrile eyes and smiled, showing their crowded teeth, the only feature of the Lisbon girls we could ever find fault with. Bonnie was the only one who didn't give Peter Sissen a secret look or kick. She only said grace and ate her food silently, lost in the piety of a fifteen-year-old. After the meal Peter Sissen asked to go to the bathroom, and because Cecelia and Mary were both in the downstairs one, giggling and whispering, he had to use the upstairs. He came back to us with stories of bedrooms filled with crumpled panties, of stuffed animals torn to shreds by the passion of the girls, of a crucifix draped with a brassiere, of gauzy chambers of canopied beds, and of the effluvia of so many young girls becoming women together in the same cramped space. In the bathroom, running the faucet to cloak the sounds of his search, Peter Sissen found Mary Lisbon's secret cache of cosmetics tied up in a sock under the sink. Tubes of red lipstick and the second skin of blush and base, and the depilatory wax that informed us she had a mustache we had never seen. In fact, we didn't know whose make-up Peter Sissen had found until we saw Mary Lisbon two weeks later on the pier with a crimson mouth that matched the shade of his descriptions.

He inventoried the deodorants and the perfumes and the scouring pads for rubbing away dead skin, and we were surprised to learn that there were no douches anywhere because we had thought girls douched every night like brushing their teeth. But our disappointment was forgotten in the next second when Peter Sissen told us of a discovery that went beyond our wildest imaginings. In the trashcan was one Tampax, spotted, still fresh from the insides of one of the Lisbon girls. Peter Sissen had said that he wanted to bring it to us, that it wasn't gross but a beautiful thing, you had to see it, like a modern painting or something, and then he told us he had counted twelve boxes of Tampax in the cupboard. It was only then that Lux knocked on the door, asking if he had died in there, and he sprang to open it. Her hair, up in a barrette at dinner, was down, and fell over her shoulders. She didn't move into the bathroom but stared into his eyes. Then, laughing her hyena's laugh, she pushed past him, saying, "You done hogging the bathroom? I need something." She walked to the cupboard, then stopped and folded her hands behind her. "It's private. Do you mind?" she said, and Peter Sissen sped down the stairs, blushing, and after thanking Mr. and Mrs. Lisbon he hurried off to tell us that Lux Lisbon was bleeding between the legs that very instant, while the fish flies made the sky filthy and the streetlamps came on.

When Paul Borado heard Peter Sissen's story, he swore that he would get inside the Lisbons' house and see things even more unthinkable than Sissen had. "I'm going to watch those girls taking their showers," he vowed. Already at the age of fourteen Paul Borado had the gangster gut and hit-man face of his father, Black Bill Borado, and of all of the men who entered and exited the big Borado house with the two lions carved in stone on the front steps. He moved with the sluggish swagger of urban predators who smelled of cologne and had manicured nails. We were frightened of him, and of his imposing, doughy cousins, Rico Manollo and Vince Lametta, and not only because his house appeared in the paper every so often, not because of the bulletproof black limousines that glided up the circular drive ringed with laurel trees imported from Italy, but because of the dark circles under his eyes and his mammoth hips and his brightly polished black shoes which he wore even when playing baseball. He had also snuck into other forbidden places in the past, and though the information he brought back was not always reliable, we were still impressed with the bravery of his reconnaissance. In sixth grade, when they took the girls into the auditorium to show them a special film, it was Paul Borado who had infiltrated the room, hiding in the old voting booth, to tell us what it was about. Out on the playground we kicked gravel and waited for him, and when he finally appeared, chewing a toothpick and playing with the gold ring on his finger, we were breathless with anticipation.

"I saw the movie," he said. "I know what it's about. Listen to this. When girls get to be about twelve or so," he leaned toward us, "their tits bleed."

Despite the fact that we now knew better, Paul Borado still commanded our fear and respect. His rhino's hips were even larger by then and the circles under his eyes had deepened to a cigar-ash-and-mud color that made him look acquainted with death. This was about the time the rumors began about the escape tunnel. A few years earlier, behind the spiked Borado fence patrolled by two identical white

German shepherds, a group of workmen had appeared one morning. They hung tarpaulins over ladders to obscure what they did, and after three days, when they whisked the tarps away, there, in the middle of the lawn, stood an artificial tree trunk. It was made of cement, painted to look like bark, the size of a redwood, complete with fake knothole and two lopped limbs pointing at the sky with the fervor of amputee stubs. In the middle of the tree, a chainsawed wedge contained a metal grill.

Paul Borado said it was a barbecue and we believed him. But, as time passed, we noticed that no one ever used it. The papers said the barbecue had cost $50,000 to install, but not one hamburger nor hot dog was grilled upon it. Soon the rumor began to circulate that the tree trunk was an escape tunnel, that it led to a hideaway along the river where Black Bill Borado kept a speedboat, and that the workers had hung tarps to conceal the digging. Then, a few months after the rumors began, Paul Borado began emerging in people's basements, through the sewer pipes. He came up in Miles Blunt's house, covered with a gray dust that smelled like friendly shit; and then he came up in Danny Zinn's house, this time with a flashlight, baseball bat, and a bag containing two dead rats; and finally he ended up on the other side of Tom Nihem's boiler which he clanged three times.

He always explained to us that he had been exploring the sewer system underneath his own house and had gotten lost, but we began to suspect that he was playing in his father's escape tunnel. When he boasted that he would see the Lisbon girls taking their showers, we all believed he was going to enter the Lisbon house in the same way he had entered the others. We never learned exactly what happened, though the police interrogated Paul Borado for over an hour. He told them only what he told us. He said he had crawled in the sewer duct underneath his own basement and had started walking, a few feet at a time. He described the cramped pipes, the coffee cups and cigarette butts left by workmen, and the charcoal drawings of naked women that resembled cave paintings. He told how he had chosen tunnels at random, and how as he passed under people's houses he could smell what they were cooking. Finally, he had come up through the sewer grate in the Lisbon's basement. After brushing himself off, he went looking for someone on the first floor, but no one was home. He called out again and again, moving through the rooms. He climbed the stairs to the second floor. Down the hall, he heard water running. He approached the bathroom door. He insisted that he knocked. And then Paul Borado told how he had stepped into the bathroom and found Cecelia, naked, her wrists oozing blood, and how after overcoming his shock he had run downstairs to call the police first thing, because that was what his father had always taught him to do.

The paramedics found the laminated picture first, of course, and in the crisis the fat one put it in his pocket. Only at the hospital did he think to give it to Mr. and Mrs. Lisbon. Cecelia was out of danger by that point, and her parents were sitting in the waiting room, relieved but confused. Mr. Lisbon thanked the paramedic for saving his daughter's life. Then he turned the picture over and saw the message printed on the back: *The Virgin Mary has been appearing in our city, bringing her message of peace to a crumbling world. As in Lourdes and Fatima, Our Lady has granted her presence to people just like you. For information call* 1-800-555-MARY.

Mr. Lisbon read the words three times. Then he said in a defeated voice: "We baptized her, we confirmed her, and now she believes this crap."

It was his only blasphemy during the entire ordeal. Mrs. Lisbon reacted by taking the picture and crumpling it in her fist. (It survived; we have a photocopy here.)

Our local newspaper neglected to run an article on the suicide attempt, because the editor, Mr. Baubee, felt such depressing information wouldn't fit between the front-page article on the Junior League Flower Show and the back-page photographs of the grinning brides. The only newsworthy article in that day's edition concerned the cemetery workers strike (bodies piling up, no agreement in sight), but that was on page four beneath the Little League scores.

After they returned home, Mr. and Mrs. Lisbon shut themselves and the girls in the house, and didn't mention a word about what had happened. Only when pressed by Mrs. Scheer did Mrs. Lisbon refer to "Cecelia's accident," acting as though she had cut herself in a fall. With precision and objectivity, however, already bored by blood,

Paul Borado described to us what he had seen, and left no doubt that
Cecelia had done violence to herself.

Mrs. Buck found it odd that the razor ended up in the toilet. "If
you were cutting your wrists in the tub," she said, "wouldn't you just
lay the razor on the side?" This led to the question as to whether Cecelia had cut her wrists while already in the bathwater, or while standing on the bath mat, which was bloodstained. Paul Borado had no
doubts: "She did it on the john," he said. "Then she got into the tub.
She sprayed the place, man."

Cecelia was kept under observation for a week. The hospital records show that the artery in her right wrist was completely severed,
because she was lefthanded, but the gash in her left wrist didn't go as
deep, leaving the underside of the artery intact. Both arteries were
closed with dissolving sutures. She received twelve stitches in each
wrist.

She came back still wearing the wedding dress. Mrs. Patz, whose
sister was a nurse at Bon Secours, said that Cecelia had refused to put
on a hospital gown, demanding that her wedding dress be brought to
her, and Dr. Hornicker, the staff psychologist, thought it best to humor her. She returned home during a thunderstorm. We were in Joe
Larson's house, right across the street, when the first clap of thunder
hit. Downstairs Joe's mother shouted to close all the windows, and we
ran to ours. Outside a deep vacuum stilled the air. A gust of wind
stirred a paper bag which lifted, rolling, into the lower branches of the
trees. Then the vacuum broke with the downpour, the sky grew black,
and the Lisbons' station wagon tried to sneak by in the darkness.

We called Joe's mother to come see. In a few seconds we heard her
quick feet on the carpeted stairs and she joined us by the window. It
was Tuesday and she smelled of furniture polish. Together we
watched Mrs. Lisbon push open her car door with one foot, and then
roll out, holding her purse over her head to keep dry. Crouching and
frowning, she opened the rear door. Rain fell. Mrs. Lisbon's hair fell
into her face. At last, Cecelia's small head came into view, hazy in the
rain, swimming up with odd thrusting movements because of the
double slings that impeded her arms. It took her a while to get up
enough steam to roll to her feet. When she finally tumbled out she

lifted both slings like canvas wings and Mrs. Lisbon took hold of her left elbow and led her into the house. By that time the rain found total release and we couldn't see across the street.

In the following days we saw Cecelia a lot. She would sit on the front steps of her house, picking red berries off the bushes and eating them, or staining her palms with the juice. She was always wearing the wedding dress and her bare feet were dirty. In the afternoons, when sun lit the front yard, she would watch ants swarming in sidewalk cracks or lie on her back in fertilized grass staring up at clouds. One of her sisters always accompanied her. Therese brought science books onto the front steps, studying photographs of deep space and looking up whenever Cecelia strayed to the edge of the yard. Lux spread towels in the backyard and lay suntanning while Cecelia scratched Arabic designs on her leg with a stick. At other times Cecelia would accost her guard, hugging her neck and whispering in her ear.

Everyone had a theory as to why she had tried to kill herself. Mrs. Blunt said the parents were to blame. "That girl didn't want to die," she told us. "She just wanted out of that house." Mrs. Scheer added, "She wanted out of that decorating scheme." On the day Cecelia returned from the hospital, those two women brought over a Bundt cake in sympathy, but Mrs. Lisbon refused to acknowledge any calamity.

We found Mrs. Blunt much aged and hugely fat, still sleeping in a separate bedroom from her husband, the Christian Scientist. Propped up in bed she still wore pearled cat's-eye sunglasses during the daytime, and still rattled ice cubes in the tall glass she claimed contained only water, but there was a new odor of afternoon indolence to her, a soap-opera smell. "As soon as Lily and I took over that Bundt cake, that woman told the girls to go upstairs. We said, 'It's still warm, let's all have a piece,' but she took the cake and put it in the refrigerator. Right in front of us."

Mrs. Scheer remembered it differently. "I hate to say it, but Joan's been potted for years. The truth is, Mrs. Lisbon thanked us quite graciously. Nothing seemed wrong at all. I started to wonder if maybe it was true that the girl had only slipped and cut herself. Mrs. Lisbon invited us out to the sunroom and we each had a piece of cake. Joan disappeared at one point. Maybe she went back to her house to have another belt. It wouldn't surprise me."

We found Mr. Blunt down the hall from his wife, in a separate bedroom with a sporting theme. On the shelf stood a photograph of his first wife, whom he had loved ever since divorcing her, and when he rose from his desk to greet us, he was still stooped from the shoulder injury faith had never quite healed. "It was like anything else in this sad society," he told us. "They didn't have a relationship with God." When we reminded him about the laminated picture of the Virgin Mary, he said, "Jesus is the one she should have had a picture of." Mr. Blunt had been a pilot in the Second World War. Shot down over Burma, he led his men on a two-hundred-mile hike through the jungle to safety. He never accepted any kind of medicine after that, not even aspirin. One winter he broke his shoulder skiing, and could only be convinced to get an X ray, nothing more. From that time on he would wince when we tried to tackle him, and raked leaves one-handed, and no longer flipped daredevil pancakes on Sunday morning. Otherwise he persevered, and always gently corrected us when we took the Lord's name in vain. In his bedroom, so many years later, the shoulder had fused into a graceful humpback. "It's sad to think about those girls," he said. "What a waste of life."

The most popular theory at the time held Buzz Palazollo to blame. Buzz was the immigrant kid staying with relatives until his family got settled in New Mexico. He was the first boy in our neighborhood to wear sunglasses, and within a week of arriving, he had fallen in love. The object of his desire wasn't Cecelia but Diana Porter, a girl with chestnut hair and a horsey though pretty face who lived in an ivy-covered house on the lake. Unfortunately, she didn't notice Buzz peering through the fence as she played her fierce tennis on the clay court, nor as she lay, sweating nectar, on the poolside recliner. On our corner, in our group, Buzz Palazollo didn't join in conversations about baseball or busing because he could only speak a few words of English, but every now and then, he would tilt his head back so that the lenses of his sunglasses reflected the sky, and would say: "I love her." Every time he said it he seemed delivered of a profundity that amazed him, as though he had coughed up a pearl. When, at the beginning of June, Diana Porter left on vacation to Switzerland, Buzz Palazollo was stricken. "Fuck the Holy Mother," he said, despondent, "Fuck God." And to show his desperation and the validity of his love, he climbed onto the roof of his relatives' house and jumped off.

We watched him. We watched Cecelia Lisbon watching from her front yard. Buzz Palazollo, with his tight pants, his dingo boots, his pompadour, went into the house; we saw him passing the plate glass picture windows downstairs; and then he appeared at an upstairs window, with a silk handkerchief around his neck. Climbing onto the ledge, he swung himself up to the flat roof. Aloft, he looked frail, diseased, and temperamental, as we expected a European to look. He toed the roof's edge like a high diver, and whispered, "I love her," to himself as he dropped past the windows and into the yard's calculated shrubbery.

He didn't hurt himself. He stood up after the fall, having proved his love, and down the block, some maintained, Cecelia Lisbon developed her own. Amy Schraff, who knew Cecelia in school, said that Buzz had been all she could talk about for the final weeks before commencement. Instead of studying for exams, she spent study halls looking up ITALY in the encyclopedia. She started saying "Ciao," and began slipping into St. Paul's to sprinkle her forehead with holy water. In the cafeteria, even on hot days when the place was thick with the fumes of institutional food, Cecelia always chose the spaghetti con carne, as though by eating the same food as Buzz Palazollo she could be closer to him. At the height of her crush she purchased the crucifix Peter Sissen had seen decorated with the brassiere.

The supporters of this theory always pointed to one central fact: the week before Cecelia's suicide attempt, Buzz Palazollo's family had called him to New Mexico. He went telling God to fuck Himself all over again because New Mexico was even further from Switzerland where Diana Porter was strolling under summer trees, moving unstoppably away from the world he was going to inherit as the owner of a carpet cleaning service. Cecelia had unleashed her blood in the bath, Amy Schraff said, because the ancient Romans had done that when life became unbearable, and she thought when Buzz heard about it, on the highway amid the cactus, he would realize that it was she who loved him.

The psychologist's report takes up most of the hospital record. After talking with Cecelia, Dr. Hornicker made the diagnosis that her suicide was an act of aggression inspired by the repression of adolescent libidinal urges. For three wildly different ink blots, she had responded, "a banana." She also saw "prison bars," "a swamp," "an afro," and "the earth after an atomic bomb." When asked why she had tried to kill herself, she said only, "It was a mistake," and clammed up when Dr. Hornicker persisted. "Despite the severity of her wounds," he wrote, "I do not think the patient truly meant to end her life. Her act was a cry for help." He met with Mr. and Mrs. Lisbon and recommended that they relax their rules: He thought Cecelia would benefit by "having a social outlet, outside the codification of school, where she can interact with males of her own age. At thirteen, Cecelia should be allowed to wear the sort of make-up popular among girls her age, in order to bond with them. The apeing of shared customs is an indispensable step in the process of individuation."

From that time on, the Lisbon house began to change. Almost every day, and even when she wasn't keeping an eye on Cecelia, Lux would suntan on her towel, wearing the swimsuit that caused the knife-sharpener to give her a fifteen-minute demonstration for nothing. The front door was always left open, because one of the girls was always running through it. Once, outside Jeff Maldrum's house, while we were playing catch, we saw a group of girls dancing to rock and roll in his living room. They were very serious about learning the right ways to move, and we were amazed to learn that girls danced together for fun, while Jeff Maldrum rapped the glass and made kissing noises until they pulled down the shade. Before they disappeared we saw Mary Lisbon in the back near the bookcase. She was wearing bell-bottomed blue jeans with a heart embroidered on the seat.

There were other miraculous changes. Butch, who cut the Lisbon grass, was now allowed inside for a glass of water, no longer having to drink from the outside faucet. Sweaty, shirtless, and tattooed, he walked right into the kitchen where the Lisbon girls lived and breathed, but we never asked him what he saw because we were scared of his muscles and his poverty.

We assumed Mr. and Mrs. Lisbon were in agreement about the new leniency, but when we met with Mr. Lisbon years later, he told us his wife had never agreed with the psychologist. "She just gave in for a while," he said. Divorced from her by this time, he lived alone in an efficiency apartment, the floor of which was covered with shavings from his wood carvings. Whittled birds and frogs crowded the shelves. According to Mr. Lisbon, he had long harbored doubts about his wife's strictness, knowing in his heart that girls who were never allowed to dance would only attract husbands with bad complexions and sunken chests. Also, the odor of all those cooped-up girls had begun to annoy him. He felt at times as though he were living in the bird house at the zoo. Everywhere he looked he found hairpins and fuzzy combs, and because so many females roamed the house they forgot he was a male and discussed their menstruation openly in front of him. Cecelia had just gotten her period, on the same day of the month as the other girls who were all synchronized in their lunar rhythms. Those five days of each month were the worst for Mr. Lisbon, who had to dispense aspirin as though feeding the ducks and comfort crying jags that arose because a dog was killed on TV. He said the girls also displayed a dramatic womanliness during their menarche. They were more languorous, descended stairs in an actressy way, and kept saying with a wink, "Cousin Herbie's come for a visit." On some nights they would send him out to buy more Tampax, not just one box but four or five, and the young storeclerks with their thin mustaches would smirk. He loved his daughters, they were precious to him, but he longed for the presence of a few boys.

That was why, a week after Cecelia returned home, Mr. Lisbon persuaded his wife to allow the girls to throw the first of the innumerable parties they would have over the next year. We all received invitations, made by hand from construction paper, with balloons containing our names drawn in Magic Marker. Our amazement at being formally invited to a house where we had only gone in our bathroom fantasies was so great that we had to compare one another's invitations before we believed it. It was thrilling to know that the Lisbon girls knew our names, that their delicate vocal cords had pronounced their syllables, and that our names meant something in their lives. They had had to labor over the proper spellings and to check our addresses in the phone book or by the metal numbers nailed to the trees.

As the night of the party approached, we watched the house for signs of decorating or other preparations, but saw none. The yellow bricks retained their look of a church-run orphanage and the silence of the lawn was absolute. The curtains did not rustle and no delivery trucks arrived with six-foot submarine sandwiches or drums of potato chips.

Then the night arrived. In blue blazers, with khaki trousers and clip-on neckties, we walked along the sidewalk in front of the Lisbon house as we had so many times before, but this time we turned up the walk, and came up the front steps between the pots of red geraniums, and rang the doorbell. Peter Sissen acted as our leader, and even looked slightly bored, saying again and again, "Wait'll you see this." The door opened. Above us the face of Mrs. Lisbon took form in the dimness. She told us to come in, we bumped against each other getting through the doorway, and as soon as we set foot on the hooked rug in the foyer we knew that Peter Sissen's descriptions of the house had been all wrong. Instead of a heady atmosphere of feminine chaos, we found the house to be a tidy dry-looking place that smelled faintly of stale popcorn. A piece of needlepoint saying "Bless This Home" was framed over the arch, and to the right, on a shelf above the radiator, five pairs of bronzed baby shoes retained for all time the unstimulating stage of the Lisbon daughters' infancy. The dining room was full of stark colonial furniture. On one wall hung a painting of Pilgrims plucking a turkey. The living room revealed orange carpeting and a brown vinyl sofa. Mr. Lisbon's La-Z-Boy flanked a small table on which sat the partially completed model of a sailing ship, without rigging and with the busty mermaid on the prow painted over.

We were directed downstairs to the rec room. The steps were metal-tipped and steep, and as we descended, the light at the bottom grew brighter and brighter, as though we were approaching the molten core of the earth. By the time we reached the last step it was blinding. In addition to overhead strips of fluorescent lights, table lamps stood everywhere. Green and red squares of linoleum flamed beneath our buckled shoes. On a card table, the punch bowl erupted lava. The panelled walls gleamed, and for the first few seconds the Lisbon girls were only a patch of glare like a congregation of angels. Then, however, our eyes got used to the light and informed us of something we had never realized: the Lisbon girls were all different people. Instead of five replicas with the same blonde hair and puffy cheeks we saw that they were distinct beings, that their personalities were beginning to transform their faces and reroute their expressions. We saw at once that Bonnie, who introduced herself now as Bonaventure, had the bloodless cheeks and sharp nose of a nun. Her eyes watered and she was a foot taller than any of her sisters, mostly because of the length of her neck which would one day hang from the end of a rope. Therese Lisbon had a heavier face, the cheeks and eyes of a cow, and she came forward to greet us on two left feet. Mary Lisbon's hair was darker; she had a widow's peak and fuzz above her upper lip which suggested that her mother had found her depilatory wax. Lux Lisbon was the only one who accorded with our image of the Lisbon girls. She radiated health and mischief. Her dress fit tightly and when she came forward to shake our hands, she secretly moved one finger to tickle our palms, giving off at the same time a strange gruff laugh. Cecelia was wearing, as usual, the wedding dress with the shorn hem. The dress was vintage 1920s. It had sequins on the bust she didn't fill out, and someone, either Cecelia herself or the owner of the used clothing store, had cut off the bottom of the dress with a jagged stroke so that it ended above Cecelia's chafed knees. She sat on a bar stool, staring into her punch glass, and the shapeless bag of a dress fell over her. She had colored her lips with red crayon, which gave her face a deranged harlot look, but she acted as though no one was there.

We knew to stay away from her. The bandages had been removed, but she was wearing a collection of bracelets to hide the scars. None of the other girls had any bracelets on, and we assumed they'd given Cecelia all they had. Scotch Tape attached the undersides of the bracelets to Cecelia's skin, so they wouldn't slide. The wedding dress bore spots of hospital food, stewed carrots and beets. We got our punch and stood on one side of the room while the Lisbon girls stood on the other.

We had never been to a chaperoned party. We were used to parties when our parents went out of town, to dark rooms vibrating with heaps of bodies, musical vomiting, beer kegs beached on ice in the bathtub, riots in the hallways and the destruction of coffee table art. This was all different. Mrs. Lisbon ladled out more glasses of punch while we watched Therese and Mary play dominoes, and across the room Mr. Lisbon opened his tool kit. He showed us his ratchets, spinning them in his hand so that they whirred, and he showed us a long sharp tube he called his router, and another covered with putty he called his scraper, and one more with a pronged end he said was his gouger. His voice was hushed as he spoke about these implements, but he never looked at us, only at the tools themselves, running his fingers over their lengths or testing their sharpness with the tender whitened bulb of his thumb. A single vertical crease deepened in his forehead, and in the middle of his dry Nordic face his lips grew moist.

Through all this Cecelia remained on her stool.

We were happy when Joe the Retard showed up. He arrived on his mother's arm, wearing his baggy bermuda shorts and his blue baseball cap, and as usual he was grinning with the face he shared with every other mongoloid. He had his invitation tied with a red ribbon around his wrist, which meant that the Lisbon girls had spelled out his name along with our own, and he came murmuring with his oversize jaw and loose lips, his tiny Japanese eyes, his smooth cheeks shaved by his brothers. Nobody knew exactly how old Joe the Retard was, but as long as we could remember he had had whiskers. His brothers used to take him onto the porch with a bucket to shave him, yelling to keep still, saying if they slit his throat it wouldn't be their fault, while Joe turned white and became as still as a lizard. We also knew that retards didn't live long and aged faster than other people, which explained the gray hairs peeking out from under Joe's baseball cap. As children we had expected that Joe the Retard would be dead by the time we became adolescents, but now we were adolescents and Joe the Retard was still a child.

Now that he had arrived we were able to show the Lisbon girls all the things we knew about him, how his ears wiggled if you scratched his chin, how he could only say, "Heads," when you flipped a coin, never "Tails," because that was too complicated, even if we said, "Joe, try tails," he would say, "Heads!" thinking he won every time

because we let him. We had him sing the song he always sang, the one
Mr. Pappas taught him. He sang "Oh, the monkeys have no tails in
Sambo Wango, oh, the monkeys have no tails in Sambo Wango, oh
the monkeys have no tails, they were bitten off by whales," and we
clapped, and the Lisbon girls clapped, Bonnie clapped, and pressed
against Joe the Retard who we thought was too dense to appreciate it.

The party was just beginning to get fun when Cecelia slipped off her
stool and made her way to her mother. Playing with the bracelets on her
left wrist, she asked if she could be excused. It was the only time we
ever heard her speak, and we were surprised by the maturity of her
voice. More than anything she sounded old and tired. She kept pulling
on the bandage, until Mrs. Lisbon said, "If that's what you want, Cecelia. But we've gone to all this trouble to have a party for you."

Cecelia tugged the bracelets until the tape came unstuck. Then she
froze. Mrs. Lisbon said, "All right. Go up then. We'll have fun without you." As soon as she had permission, Cecelia made for the stairs.
She kept her face to the floor, moving in her personal oblivion, her
sunflower eyes fixed on the predicament of her life we would never
understand. She climbed the steps, closed the door behind her, and
proceeded along the upstairs hallway. We could hear her feet right
above us. Halfway up the staircase to the second floor her steps made
no more noise, but it was only thirty seconds later that we heard the
wet sound of her body falling on the fence that ran alongside the
house. First came the sound of wind, a rushing we decided later must
have been caused by her wedding dress filling with air. This was
brief. A human body falls fast. The main thing was just that: the fact
of a person taking on completely physical properties, falling at the
speed of a rock. It didn't matter whether her brain continued to flash
on the way down, or if she regretted what she'd done, or if she had
time to focus on the fence spikes shooting toward her. Her mind no
longer existed in any way that mattered. The wind sound huffed,
once, and then the moist thud jolted us, the sound of a watermelon
breaking open, and for that moment everyone remained still and composed, as though listening to an orchestra, heads tilted to allow the
ears to work and no belief coming in yet. Then Mrs. Lisbon, as
though she were alone, said, "Oh my God."

Mr. Lisbon ran upstairs. Mrs. Lisbon ran to the top and stood holding the banister. In the stairwell we could see her silhouette, the thick legs, the great sloping back, the big head stilled with panic, the eyeglasses jutting into space and filled with light. She took up most of the stairs and we were hesitant to go around her until the Lisbon girls did. Then we squeezed by. We reached the first floor. Through a window in the side of the house we could see Mr. Lisbon's lower half bending into the shrubbery. When we came out the front door we saw that he was holding Cecelia, one hand under her neck and the other under her knees. He was trying to lift her off the spike which had punctured her left breast, travelled through her inexplicable heart, separated two vertebrae without shattering either, and come out her back, ripping the dress and finding the air again. The spike had gone through so fast there was no blood on it. It was perfectly clean. There was no blood at all that we could see and Cecelia merely seemed balanced on the pole like a gymnast. The fluttering wedding dress added to this circusy effect. Mr. Lisbon kept trying to lift her off, gently, but even in our ignorance we knew it was hopeless and that despite Cecelia's open eyes and the way her mouth kept contracting like that of a fish on a stringer it was just nerves and she had succeeded, on the second try, in hurling herself out of the world.

Billy Collins

❊

Picnic, Lightning

My very photogenic mother died in a freak accident
(picnic, lightning) when I was three . . .

—Lolita

It is possible to be struck by a meteor
or a single-engine plane
while reading in a chair at home.
Pedestrians are flattened by safes
falling from rooftops
mostly within the panels of the comics,
but still, we know it is possible,
as well as the flash of summer lightning,
the thermos toppling over,
spilling out on the grass.

And we know the message
can be delivered from within.
The heart, no valentine,
decides to quit after lunch,
the power shut off like a switch,
or a tiny dark ship is unmoored
into the flow of the body's rivers,
the brain a monastery,
defenseless on the shore.

This is what I think about
when I shovel compost
into a wheelbarrow,
and when I fill the long flower boxes,
then press into rows
the limp roots of red impatiens—
the instant hand of Death
always ready to burst forth
from the sleeve of his voluminous cloak.

Then the soil is full of marvels,
bits of leaf like flakes off a fresco,
red-brown pine needles, a beetle quick
to burrow back under the loam.
Then the wheelbarrow is a wilder blue,
the clouds a brighter white,

and all I hear is the rasp of the steel edge
against a round stone,
the small plants singing
with lifted faces, and the click
of the sundial
as one hour sweeps into the next.

Issue 145, 1997

Seamus Heaney

✣

from The Art of Poetry LXXV

INTERVIEWER

Do you think losing both your parents affected your work? In a way, in "Squarings," there is an obliteration of the past, which is what comes with the death of one's parents.

HEANEY

I was at each deathbed, in the room with my siblings. Moments of completion. Both of them died peacefully—"got away easy," as they might have said themselves. There wasn't much turmoil or physical distress. My father died of cancer; of course, there was a period of deterioration, but at the end the actual hour-by-hour decline was relatively predictable and relatively untroubled. My mother died from a stroke much more quickly, inside three days. Again, we all had time to assemble. There was a sense of an almost formal completion. But also a recognition that nothing can be learned, that to be in the presence of a death is to be in the presence of something utterly simple and utterly mysterious. In my case, the experience restored the right to use words like *soul* and *spirit*, words I had become unduly shy of, a literary shyness, I suppose, deriving from a misplaced obedience to proscriptions of the abstract, but also a shyness derived from a complicated relationship with my own Catholic past. In many ways I love it and have never quite left it, and in other ways I suspect it for having given me such ready access to a compensatory supernatural vocabulary. But experiencing my parents' deaths restored some of the verity to that vocabulary. These words, I realized, aren't obfuscation. They have to do with the spirit of life that is within us.

A.S. Byatt

※

from The Djinn in the Nightingale's Eye

At a nightclub in Istanbul once, Gillian had been shocked, without quite knowing why, to find one of those vacant, sweetly pink and blue church Virgins, life-size, standing as part of the decorations, part hat-stand, part dumb-waitress, as you might find a many-handed Hindu deity or a plaster Venus in an equivalent occidental club. Now suddenly, she saw a real bewildered old woman, a woman with a shriveled womb and empty eyes, a woman whose son had been cruelly and very slowly slaughtered before her eyes, shuffling through the streets of Ephesus, waiting quietly for death until it came. And then, afterwards, this old woman, this real dead old woman had in part become the mother goddess, the Syria Dea, the crowned Queen. She was suddenly aware of every inch of her own slack and dying skin. She thought of the stone eyes of the goddess, of her dangerous dignity, of her ambiguous plump breasts, dead balls, intact eggs, wreathed round her in triumph and understood that real-unreal was not the point, that the goddess was still, and always had been, and in the foreseeable future would be more alive, more energetic, infinitely more powerful than she herself, Gillian Perholt, that she would stand here before her children, and Orhan's children, and their children's children and smile, when they themselves were scattered atomies.

And when she thought this, standing amongst a group of smiling friends in the centre of the theatre at Ephesus, she experienced again the strange stoppage of her own life that had come with the vision of Patient Griselda. She put out a hand to Orhan and could move no more; and it seemed that she was in a huge buzzing dark cloud, sparking with flashes of fire, and she could smell flowers, and her own blood, and she could hear rushing and humming in her veins, but she could not move a nerve or a muscle. And after a moment, a kind of liquid sob rose in her throat, and Orhan saw the state she was in, and put an arm round her shoulder, and steadied her, until she came to herself.

Priscilla Becker

Letter After an Estrangement

I forgot to tell you my husband
died. He was in Spain and something
strange happened with alcohol or water. He loved them
both so much. Which reminds me, do you want
to be cremated or buried? The difference,
if you do not know, is the ghost
or the body; heaven or sex.

Also I am planning a trip. No place special
just somewhere God has been.
Do you have any ideas? From there I will bring back
vials of ambergris. Did I mention I am carrying
his baby. I am in the tenth month and still
he does not show. The house hates me
and breaks everything I touch.

I myself prefer to be left
face up in a ditch and for someone to go
to jail because of what he's done to me.
That way I can watch the stars
as they move toward the end of the sky
and he can plan his last
meal or some other consolation.

Issue 155, 2000

Maile Meloy

Aqua Boulevard

Each day I walk to the Polo Club while my wife is at work and my children at school. I have my lunch at the club, a little wine, and I walk home. I don't work anymore; I worked long enough, and very hard. I could have a horse at the club, well groomed and cared for. I would not get any better, at my age, but I could ride. But I like only to ride in the country—going somewhere—not in a hall in the middle of Paris, going in circles. I would rather walk. So I walk to my lunch, I watch the horses, I walk back.

Last week at the Polo I saw a woman I knew. She would not have been allowed before: she is a black woman from Martinique. But the club now lets many people in, and she was an actress in films for some years. I knew her when she was young; her husband and I were like brothers. It was strange to see her that day at the club because she had not changed in thirty years. She was still beautiful, still sexy. A bright girl, with energy. I remember her always laughing, swinging her legs on the dock at Cap-Ferrat, or sitting on a boat or in a café, but always laughing, showing the gap between her front teeth. She was not laughing so much this time, but when she did it was the same laugh, the same gap. She had the good skin of black women, the face and hands still young. She called herself Mia. We watched her grand-daughter do vaultige; the girl stood on the back of the horse at a *petit galop* around the ring. Eleven years old, a little older than my daughter, with light brown skin and brown curls flying out behind her. There were other children trying to stand on their horses, but none

was so accomplished as this granddaughter. She turned upside down
and stood on her head.

It was thirty years ago that I knew Mia, the grandmother, and we
were not so careful about what we said thirty years ago; Mia had three
bambini, all with a German father, and we used to say they were not
black or white, they were gray. They were green, we said. We called
them *les petits verts*. But you see—the eldest of *les petits verts* grew up
to be a film actress like her mother, and had this daughter who can
stand on her head on a horse in the Polo Club in Paris. The little girl
came from the horses and kissed me hello, on the left and right, with
a shining face and blue eyes. Life is long, when you live a long time—
that seems a simple fact, but you don't know it until you have a lunch
like this one.

Mia's husband—my dear friend, my brother—was called Renard. I
played guitar then, and I was young. You have to be young to play the
guitar, unless you are very great. It took me ten years to discover I had
no ear, and five years more to discover I had no head to remember the
words. My fingers, my technique, they were above the rest, but I was
not gifted. Renard was gifted. He played the piano more beautifully
than you have ever heard, with no music, all by ear. He could play
anything. He used to help me, writing down the music, working out
the harmonies, teaching me songs. We played at parties—not for
money, because that was not our aim, but people asked us to come,
and we had a trumpet and bass and clarinet and the whole thing.

Renard had some money, and he was raised with a rich life. Because of the music he met a girl, Elsa, who was a little blonde op-
erettiche singer, with a little voice. Elsa had a daughter, and she and
the child were always with Renard. After some years, Renard said, "I
have to marry this girl. I can't *not* marry this girl." We all said, "Why?
Keep on like you are." But he had to marry her, for his soul maybe, I
don't know. He adopted the child and I became godfather, and then
Elsa became jealous of Renard's ability, of his success and his
friends, and she started to drink.

At this time I married my first wife, and I could not impose Renard
and his family on my wife. I loved Renard, and the child was my god-
daughter, but Elsa was too much. When this happens, you grow apart,
and I did not see him for some years. Eventually he divorced her.

We were close again, when he divorced, and we had the same friends at the Travellers' Club and in the south. When he met Mia, the actress from Martinique, we all understood. She was so sexy, and he loved her, and she was fun. But she had the not-black, not-white bambini from the German, and this was Paris, and Paris was not so generous. It was not so well accepted then, to have these children. They all moved south to a big white house in Cap-Ferrat, and Renard had some money still, but he was gambling it away. My wife would not go to visit there, but I went. It was like a colony. The girl Mia and the green bambini were only the beginning. There were also the girl's two sisters, with bambini of their own. Kids all over the house, you did not know whose. They always had guests, because they had poker games in the house, and the guests came to take Renard's money. When he was out of money he would sit at the piano, and they shouted out what to play.

Finally Renard said he was going to marry the girl Mia. Just like the first time, with Elsa, he said he couldn't *not* marry her. We didn't understand, but we went to the wedding and drove in a parade down to the sea at Cap-Ferrat. Everyone felt a little embarrassed, with the family not approving, and all the fatherless bambini in wedding clothes, and the drunken blonde first wife in the memory. But Renard acted very happy, and chartered a yacht for his honeymoon, and flew everyone to Miami to take his new wife and his friends to Martinique. I didn't go on the yacht, of course, but some did.

They went to La Dominique, with the moving sands. There is a big sign there that says DANGEROUS BEACH. The water is very shallow and the sand is loose and deep, like quicksand. It sucks you down in the water, and the currents pull you out into the sea. The laughing girl, home again, swung her legs on the deck of the boat. The beach is not authorized, but Renard went swimming. With his debts and his adopted children and his family and his gambling, he went in at the unauthorized beach. He was a strong swimmer, but a strong swimmer is not what you need at La Dominique. What you need is to stop fighting, to let the arms and legs go limp. If you let go, and don't fight, the water sucks you down, but then it takes you back to the surface. Spits you out. If you fight and try to swim, you die. They didn't find Renard's body. His friends on the boat looked a long time. I went to the beach myself when I heard, and walked up and down, as close to the water as possible without slipping into the sands. I stayed there two days, looking at the water and thinking about my friend, then I flew back to Paris where I was getting a divorce and had a job. They found a jawbone a month later—the drowned body all eaten by sharks or whatever was there.

Mia and I did not talk of Renard's death when I saw her last week at the Polo, old but still the same, but we were both thinking of it. It was why she did not laugh so much, I know. She might have laughed more with another, but I brought the memory of Renard to her. It was not the thing to talk about. When I left the club, Mia said to me, "My life has been a good life, and Renard would be happy with that."

I had nowhere to be at that moment, so I walked back along the rue de Babylone, where I lived when I was young. I used to walk to work from there, and brought girls home to the apartment with the purple bathtub sunk low into the tile. Each job and each girl, at that time, was the most important thing in the world and demanded everything. I was still young enough to play guitar not so well.

My second wife is young, the age of my first son, who played guitar too long and has made nothing of his life. She is beautiful, and sparkles like jewels when she is wearing none: skin like gold, white teeth and clear blue eyes. We have two small children. The more I see other children, the more I think mine are the most attractive. Since I realized I was too old for guitar and married, I have had two good lives, with two good wives. I am a lucky man. When I ride in the country, not in circles but moving forward, all alone, I think what could happen to leave behind a widow. Nothing much would have to happen; my brother is younger than I, and already dead. But sometimes I think I will fall from the horse, hit my head or break my spine, with no one to help. I would leave the widow that much sooner, and she would marry again and have two lives, too, with two husbands. She is young enough for that, the way she shines. And then sometimes I think I can outlive them all.

When I reached home, and walked into the courtyard below our apartment, I could hear my son screaming at his sister from the windows above. The elevator is tiny and slow, and when the children race it on the stairs, they win. I took the stairs, too many at a time, and reached the third floor with my heart in my ears and a dizziness across my eyes. I opened the apartment door and climbed the last steps past the umbrellas. The keys fell from my hand at the top. My son Gaétan looked up and slid to a halt in his socks, surprised to see me standing there. Gaétan is seven, the age of reason, the age of charm.

"What is going on here?" I demanded, waiting for the dizzy feeling to go. "What is the purpose of this noise that shakes the building?"

His sister Alix ran out from her room and there came an absolute chaos, both arguing at once, and the dog barking. Tati the Filipina came from the kitchen and started, too. Three voices, like angry bells, plus the dog. "*Aqua Boulevard . . . Gaétan ne veut pas . . . Oliver . . . la merde . . . Maman . . . comme les autres—*"

"Stop!" I said.

I could see straight now, and I made them go slow. Gaétan first, then his sister, then Tati. To have some order. A child was giving a birthday party at Aqua Boulevard, with the waterslides, and the pool that makes waves like an ocean. Alix wanted to go. Gaétan said the brother of the girl with the birthday was a jerk. They know this American word. *C'est un jerk.* My wife was not home and Tati is only one person, so Alix could not go to the party without Gaétan. Oliver, my wife's dog, the dog she bought to make the children fight not so much, had done a shit on the rug. Tati had been all afternoon cleaning it up.

Gaétan is impatient. I started with him. I bent down on my stiff knees so he could see my eyes. "This is a lesson for you," I said. "You don't play with the jerk. There are other children. It's easy, yes?"

Gaétan frowned.

"Alix, you get your bathing suit," I said. She went wild, kissing me, hugging me, then she ran to her room. Gaétan made a terrible noise.

I said, "Tati, you want to go to Aqua Boulevard?"

Tati smiled. She was tired of dog shit, and she could sit with the other nannies by the pool with the waves.

"Gaétan," I said, taking his shoulders in my hands, "you go on the biggest waterslide, without your sister. I want to hear you did that today."

Sometimes my son has a face like a storm, and then it clears, and again he is the most attractive child I have ever seen. He ran to his bedroom for his bathing suit. I gave Tati the money for a birthday present for the sister of the jerk.

"I'm going to take Oliver for a walk," I said. "I will teach him discipline."

Tati gave me the leash, a long orange strap, and the children kissed Oliver good-bye and went out the door. I had told my wife I was going to order a leather leash from Hermès, and it was a joke, but maybe I would. With Oliver's initials. Oliver danced at my feet, his toenails scraping on the wood floor. On the rug was a white towel where Tati had cleaned.

My wife studied for the dog like when you buy a house, and finally she bought a Border terrier, a small dog, but not as small as the ridiculous dogs you see in the streets of Paris. Small enough for an apartment but not a dog to make you a fool. Oliver and I went down the elevator, out through the courtyard, and toward the Luxembourg. He ran ahead of me on the orange strap. He was excited about everything, still a puppy. He didn't know not to sniff at women's shoes, like he didn't know not to shit on the carpet. I smiled at the women in the shoes and they smiled back. I had not wanted a dog, but the children loved him. It was true they did not fight so much now. The day my wife brought him home, my daughter held the dog in her arms and said, "This is the happiest day of my life." Children are whores. They will say anything. But I thought it could be true.

I had never trained a dog. I had not even taken this dog for a walk, because I could not take him for lunch at the Polo. When I was still working for the Greeks, with the shipping, we were given a beautiful Arabian horse, a king's horse. We had no use for it, but to slaughter it would offend the king, so it must be kept like a king's horse, and that was left to me. I found a stable and thought I would ride in the Bois de Boulogne, but the horse would not cross the road. We reached the road each time, and then it stopped. The most elegant horse you have ever seen, afraid of roads. I tried a long time to make the horse cross, and then paid an old cavalry officer to train the horse in the cavalry style. Make the horse obey. Be the commander. He came back to me in six weeks and said the horse did not want to cross the road. So maybe Oliver did not want to shit outside. This would be a problem.

We were at the street corner, almost to the jardin, and I was thinking how the dog would like to see the trees and the grass, and then Oliver ran on his long orange strap into the road. A Mercedes taxi hit him square with the tire.

Oliver did not move. There was no blood. I held him against my shirt and I could feel his small breaths. His eyes were half open but looked at nothing. The taxi was gone, and no one for me to shout at. I stood on the corner looking at the Jardin du Luxembourg across the street with its green grass, then turned to look at the shops, trying to think where was an animal doctor. I thought of going back to the Polo, where they would have a horse doctor. The beautiful Mia could still be there, and she knew death and would know what to do. But it was a foolish thought, and I began to walk down the street, looking at the names on the buildings for a doctor. The orange strap hit my ankles at each step. Then I remembered taxis as a help and I waved to one, holding the dog tightly in one arm. The taxi stopped, but by the time I was in, the breathing and the heartbeat were gone.

I let the taxi drive me home, though it was a short way, because I didn't think I could stand to walk. In the car my thoughts were mixed up between the dog, and the taxi's tire, and Mia swinging her legs, and my friend drowning under the waves, and then I felt my lungs like ice and told the driver to take me to Aqua Boulevard. I had to see my children in front of me. I had sent them with only Tati to that ridiculous pool.

The taxi let me out at Aqua Boulevard with the dog in my arms. They would not let me take a dead dog, but I walked past the security smiling, holding Oliver's head up. Women carry their dogs in their arms all the time, and the gendarme looked at my face strangely but said nothing. Past the security there is a glass wall to watch the slides and the pool, and I stood there with the dog. The room is enormous, full of people in bathing suits, fat ones and thin ones, all colors but all greenish through the water-spotted window, with the plastic tubes snaking around overhead and a glass roof to let in the sun. The horn blew that says the waves will start, and all the people ran into the water. I looked for my children, and didn't see them there. I wanted to run in and find them, but I had no bathing suit and could not let them see their dog.

The waves rolled in to the concrete beach painted the color of sand. Small children rode the water to the shore, and there among the heads was Gaétan. My son's face, wide-eyed and afraid. The water pushed him to where he could touch the bottom and he stood, laughing. He raised his fists in the air and shouted, like a man who wins a boxing match, tired and happy. He ran back into the waves. I breathed again. There was still the feeling in my lungs, stopping the air to my chest, but it was melting.

The dog had grown stiff in my arms. I looked for my daughter and saw her run across the painted beach into the water, her young body in a black bathing suit shining with wet. I leaned my head against the green glass, the warm dog still against my chest. I said thank you for my children and listened to the rushing of the waves that did not stop but came and came again.

Robert Pinsky

✠

The Saving

Though the sky still was partly light
Over the campsite clearing
Where some men and boys sat eating
Gathered near their fire,
It was full dark in the trees,
With somewhere a night-hunter
Up and out already to pad
Unhurried after a spoor,
Pausing maybe to sniff
At the strange, lifeless aura
Of a dropped knife or a coin
Buried in the spongy duff.

Willful, hungry and impatient,
Nose damp in the sudden chill,
One of the smaller, scrawnier boys
Roasting a chunk of meat
Pulled it half-raw from the coals,
Bolted it whole from the skewer
Rubbery gristle and all,
And started to choke and strangle—
Gaping his helpless mouth,
Struggling to retch or to swallow

As he gestured, blacking out,
And felt his father lift him

And turning him upside down
Shake him and shake him by the heels,
Like a woman shaking a jar—
And the black world upside-down,
The upside-down fire and sky,
Vomited back his life,
And the wet little plug of flesh
Lay under him in the ashes.
Set back on his feet again
In the ring of faces and voices,
He drank the dark air in,
Snuffling and feeling foolish

In the fresh luxury of breath
And the brusque, flattering comfort
Of the communal laughter. Later,
Falling asleep under the stars,
He watched a gray wreath of smoke
Unfurling into the blackness;
And he thought of it as the shape
Of a newborn ghost, the benign
Ghost of his death, that had nearly
Happened: it coiled, as the wind rustled,
And he thought of it as a power,
His luck or his secret name.

Issue 80, 1981

Thom Gunn

❈

Sacred Heart

For one who watches with too little rest
A body rousing fitfully to its pain
—The nerves like dull burns where the sheet has pressed—
Subsiding to dementia yet again;
For one who snatches what repose he can,
Exhausted by the fretful reflexes
Jerked from the torpor of a dying man,
Sleep is a fear, invaded as it is
By coil on coil of ominous narrative
In which specific isolated streaks,
Bright as tattoos, of inks that seem to live,
Shift through elusive patterns. Once in those weeks
You dreamt your dying friend hung crucified
In his front room, against the mantelpiece;
Yet it was Christmas, when you went outside
The shoppers bustled, bells rang without cease,
You smelt a sharp excitement on the air,
Crude itch of evergreen. But you returned
To find him still nailed up, mute sufferer
Lost in a trance of pain, toward whom you yearned.
When you woke up, you could not reconcile
The two conflicting scenes, indoors and out.
But it was Christmas. And parochial school
Accounted for the Dying God no doubt.

Now since his death you've lost the wish for sleep,
In which you might mislay the wound of feeling:
Drugged you drag grief from room to room and weep,
Preserving it from closure, from a healing
Into the novelty of glazed pink flesh.
We hear you stumble vision-ward above,
Keeping the edges open, bloody, fresh
Wound, no—the heart, His Heart, broken with love.

An unfamiliar ticking makes you look
Down your left side where, suddenly apparent
Like a bright plate from an anatomy book
—In its snug housing, under the transparent
Planes of swept muscle and the barrelled bone—
The heart glows, and you feel the holy heat:
The heart of hearts transplanted to your own
Losing rich purple drops with every beat.
Yet even as it does your vision alters,
The hallucination lighted through the skin
Begins to deaden (though still bleeding), falters,
And hardens to its evident origin
—A red heart from a cheap religious card,
Too smooth, too glossy, too securely cased!

Stopped in a crouch, you wearily regard
Each drop dilute into the waiting waste.

Issue 106, 1988

John Montague

Return

From the bedroom you can see
straight to the fringe of the woods
with a cross-staved gate to re-
enter childhood's world:

                        the pines
wait, dripping.

                     Crumbling black-
berries, seized from a rack
of rusty leaves, maroon tents
of mushroom, pillars uprooting
with a dusty snap;

                 as the bucket
fills, a bird strikes from the bushes
and the cleats of your rubber boot crush
a yellow snail's shell to a smear
on the grass

                   (while the wind starts
the carrion smell of the dead fox
staked as warning).

                Seeing your former
self saunter up the garden path

afterwards, would you flinch,
acknowledging
                              that sensuality,
that innocence?

Norman Mailer

✠

from A Work in Progress

Author's Note: The ancient Egyptians believed there were seven parts to the soul which all behaved in different fashion after one's death, some departing quickly, others resting within the body to emerge at the appropriate hour. The Ka, or Double, of the dead man, for example, did not usually present himself until the mummy was resting in his tomb some seventy days and more after death.

These seven lights and forces, souls and spirits of the Soul, can be characterized as the Ren (one's secret name), the Sekhem (one's vital energy), the Khu (one's guardian angel), the Ba (one's heart), the Ka (one's double), the Khaibit (one's shadow, that is, one's memory), and the Sekhu (the remains), which is to say the residue of the man or woman's life that rests in the body while it is being embalmed, a much muted version of the self analogous to pools of water on a sand flat after the tide has receded.

The description that follows is told by the Sekhu of a dead man. It is his remains who speak:

A hook went into my nose, battered through the gate at the roof of the nostril, and plunged into my brain. Pieces, gobbets, and whole parts of the dead flesh of my mind were now brought out through one aperture of my nose, then the other.

Yet for all it hurt, I could have been made of small rocks and roots. I ached no more than the earth when a weed is pulled and comes up with its hairs tearing away from the clods of the soil. Pain is present, but as the small cry of the uprooted plant. So did the hooks, narrow in their curve, go up the nose, enter the head, and poke like blind fingers in a burrow to catch stuffs of the brain and pull them away. Now I felt like a rock wall at the base of which rakes are ripping, and was warm curiously as though sunlight were baking, but it was only the breath of the first embalmer, hot with wine and figs—how clear was the sense of smell!

Still, an enigma remained. How could my mind continue to think while they pulled my brain apart? They were certainly scooping chunks of material as lively as dry sponge through the dry tunnels of my nose, and I realized—for there was a flash in my cranium when the hook first entered—that one of my lights in the Land of the Dead had certainly stirred. Was it the Ba, the Khaibit or the Ka that was now helping me to think? And I gagged as a particularly caustic drug, some wretched mixture of lime and ash, was poured in by the embalmers to dissolve whatever might still be stuck to the inside of my skull.

How long they worked I do not know, how long they allowed that liquid to dwell in the vault of my emptied head is but one more question. From time to time they lifted my feet, held me upside down, then set me back. Once they even turned me on my stomach to slosh the fluids, and let the caustic eat out my eyes. Two flowers could have been plucked when those eyes were gone.

At night my body would go cold; by midday it was close to warm. Of course I could not see, but I could smell, and got to know the embalmers. One wore perfume yet his body always carried the unmistakable pungency of a cat in heat; the other was a heavy fellow with a heavy odor not altogether bad—he was the one with breath of wine and figs. He smelled as well of fields and mud, and rich food was usually in him—a meat-eater, his sweat was strong yet not unpleasant—something loyal came out of the gravies of his flesh. Because I could smell them as they approached, I knew it was daylight so soon as the embalmers arrived, and I could count the hours. (Their scent altered with the heat of the air in this place.) From midday to three, every redolence, good and bad, of the hot banks of the Nile was also near. After a time I came to realize I must be in a tent. There was often the crack of sailcloth flapping overhead, and gusts would clap at my hair, a sensation as definite in impression as a hoof stepping on grass. My hearing had begun to return but by a curious route. For I had no interest in what was said. I was aware of the voices of others, but felt no desire to comprehend the words. They were not even like the cry of animals so much as the lolling of surf or the skittering of wind. Yet my mind felt capable of surpassing clarity.

Once I think Hathfertiti came to visit, or since it is likely the tent was on family grounds, it is possible she strolled through the gardens and stopped to look in. Certainly I caught her scent. It was Hathfertiti, certain enough; she gave one sob, as if belief in the mortal end of her son had finally come, and left immediately.

Somewhere in those first few days they made an incision in the side of my belly with a sharp flint knife—I know how sharp for even with the few senses my Remains could still employ, a sense of sharpness went through me like a plow breaking ground, but sharper, as if I were a snake cut in two by a chariot wheel, and then began the most detailed searching. It is hard to describe, for it did not hurt, but I was ready in those hours to think of the inside of my torso as common to a forest in a grove, and one by one trees were removed, their roots disturbing veins of rock, their leaves murmuring. I had dreams of cities drifting down the Nile like floating islands. Yet when the work was done, I felt larger, as if my senses now lived in a larger space. Was it that my heart and lungs had been placed in one jar, and my stomach and small intestines in another? Leave it that my organs were spread out in different places, floating in different fluids and spices, yet still existing about me, a village. Eventually, their allegiance would be lost. Wrapped and placed in the Canopic jars, what they knew of my life would then be offered to their own God.

How I brooded over what those Gods would know of me once my organs were in Their jars. Qebhsenuf would dwell in my liver and know of all the days when my liver's juices had been brave; as well would Qebhsenuf know of the hours when the liver, like me, lived in the fog of a long fear. A simple example, the liver, but more agreeable to contemplate than my lungs. For, with all they knew of my passions would they still be loyal once they moved into the jar of the jackal Tuamutef, and lived in the domain of that scavenger? I did not know. So long, at least, as my organs remained unwrapped, and therefore in a manner still belonged to me, I could understand how once em- balmed, and in their jar, I would lose them. No matter how scattered my parts might be over all the tables of this tent, there still remained the sense of family among us—the vessel of my empty corpse com- fortably surrounded by old fleshly islands of endeavor, these lungs, liver, stomach and big and little guts all attached to the same memo- ries of my life (if with their own separate and fiercely prejudiced view—how different, after all, had my life seemed to my liver and to my heart). So, not at all, therefore, was this embalming tent as I had expected, no, no bloody abattoir like a butcher's stall, more like an herb kitchen. Certainly the odors encouraged the same long flights of fancy you could find in a spice shop. Merely figure the vertigos of my nose when the empty cavity of my body (so much emptier than the belly of a woman who has just given birth) was now washed, soothed and stimulated, cleansed, peppered, herbified, and left with a reso- nance through which no hint of the body's corruption could breathe. They scoured the bloody inside with palm wine, and left the memo- ries of my flesh in ferment. They pounded in spices and peppers, and rare sage from the limestone foundations to the West; then came leaves of thyme and the honey of bees who had fed on thyme, the oil of orange was rubbed into the cavity of the ribs, and the oil of lemon blamed the inside of my lower back to free it of the stubborn redo- lence of the viscera. Cedar chips, essence of jasmine, and branchlets of myrrh were crushed—I could hear the cries of the plants being broken more clearly than the sound of human voices. The myrrh even made its clarion call. A powerful aromatic (as powerful in the kingdom of herbs as the Pharaoh's voice) was the myrrh laid into the open shell of my body. Next came cinnamon leaves, stem, and cinna- mon bark to sweeten the myrrh. Like rare powders added to the sweetmeats in the stuffing of a pigeon, were these bewildering atmo- spheres they laid into me. Dizzy was I with their beauty. When done, they sewed up the long cut in the side of my body, and I seemed to rise through high vales of fever while something of memory, intoxi- cated by these tendrils of the earth, began to dance and the oldest of my friends was young while the children of my mistresses grew old. I was like a royal barge lifted into the air under the ministrations of a rare vizier.

Cleaned, stuffed, and trussed, I was deposited in a bath of natron— that salt which dries the meat to stone—and there I lay with weights to keep me down. Slowly, over the endless days that followed, as the waters of my own body were given up the thirst of the salt (which drank at my flesh like caravans arriving at an oasis) so all moisture, with its insatiable desire to liquefy my meats, had to leave my limbs. Bathed in natron, I became hard as the wood of a hull, then hard as the rock of the earth, and felt the last of me depart to join my Ka, my Ba, and my fearsome Khaibit. And the shell of my body entered the stone of ten thousand years. If there was nothing I could smell any longer (no more than a stone can be aware of a scent), still the hardened flesh of my body became like one of those spiraled chambers of the sea that are thrown up on the beach, yet contain the roar of waters when you hold them to your ear. I became not unlike the roar of waters, for I was close to hearing old voices that passed across the sands—if now I could not smell, I could certainly hear—and like the dolphin whose ears are reputed able to pick up echoes from the other end of the sea, so I sank into the bath of natron, and my body passed farther and farther away. Like a stone washed by fog, baked by sun, and given the flavor of the water on the bank, I was entering that universe of the dumb where it was part of our gift to hear the story told by every wind to every stone.

Issue 86, 1982

DINNER

✠

Daniel S. Libman

⚏

In the Belly of the Cat

The same day that he canceled all his newspaper and magazine
subscriptions, Mr. Christopher deveined a pound of jumbo
shrimp by hand. He had never done this before, and used nearly a
whole roll of paper towels wiping the snotty black entrails off his fingers one by one. He also grated a package of cheddar cheese with a
previously unused grater that he uncovered in his silverware drawer,
kneaded a loaf of oatmeal raisin bread, then called the escort service
and arranged for a girl. "I want Carlotta; she's a Latina, right?"

He had called the *Tribune* earlier that morning. "Stop my subscription. The relationship is over; deliver it no longer. The advice
columns just rehash the same situations—alcoholism, smoking,
infidelity—although sometimes those columns are titillating, which I
appreciate. The comic strips are contrived, and the punch lines aren't
ever that good. That cranky columnist on page three ought to have his
head examined; I think he's finally lost it, and your media critic is always biased towards the TV stations you own. But what I object to
mostly, the reason I'm canceling, is because it comes too often: once a
day, and anyway what good is it? I don't have that much time left and
do you know how much I've wasted over the years slogging through,
reading and cringing, hands and fingers covered in the ink, hauling
paper-bloated garbage bags stuffed with Sports and Food sections,
which I never even touch, down three flights of stairs every week?"

Mr. Christopher was hurt by the cavalier way the man at the *Trib*
took care of the cancellation. After so much loyal readership he felt

that they should have put up some sort of struggle, a little token of respect: "But Mr. Christopher, please think about it; you want to throw away sixty years just like that?" Not that it would have gotten them anywhere. His mind was made up.

He had been a widower now for a year and a half, retired, down to only two thirds of what he weighed at forty, dentures, a toupee he no longer wore but kept hanging off his hall tree, an artificial hip; and a brother a couple of states to the east whom he didn't like with a mouthy know-it-all wife. This had come to him one evening earlier in the week, a cold-cut sandwich and a pickle on a plate in front of him, eyeing the pile of papers; he had had enough of them.

Mr. Christopher canceled all the magazines too: *The East Coast Arbiter, Harbingers', The New Statesman,* even *The Convenience Store Merchandiser,* a holdover from work that they sent him for free.

He was bundling up the last week of *Tribs* he would ever receive, when his hands landed on a Food section. "Special Dishes to Commemorate Any Event," the headline said. I'll give you an event, he thought, How's finally ending sixty years of crap sound to you, Mr. Tribune.

Mr. Christopher decided to open up the Food section for the first time and cook those commemorative dishes. He mapped out what he needed to do in his head: buy fresh fruit, two pounds of shrimp; he'd need to take a bus to that specialty food store for some of it. . . . He even scanned the tips on what makes a good party: fancy utensils, music and special friends.

He was cubing the honeydew for the fruit slaw when she buzzed. He gave a start and walked to the intercom and thought how odd it sounded. No one had buzzed him for . . . weeks? months? decades? He leaned down to the grill, painted the same off-white as the rest of the apartment, and pressed.

Talk: Yes?

Listen: You call for me?

Talk: Who is it?

Listen: This is Monique. You call for me?

Talk: No. I called for Carlotta.

Listen: I'm Carlotta. Buzz me in.

Talk: Who are you?

Listen: Carlotta. You want me, baby?

He touched DOOR and heard the faraway buzzing. She was in the building now; his heart raced. It would take a minute or two to climb the three flights, and then she would have to decide which direction to walk; that would take a few seconds. He was in 3A, towards the front of the building so she would have to look at 3B first, because it was right across from the stairs, and then make a choice, and she might choose right, which would take her to 3C—and in all this time he could back out, decide not to go ahead with this. He slid the security chain across the door.

But he had already gone to so much trouble. He had found the escort service in another part of the *Tribune* never before looked at, the match ads. At the very end were listings for adult services; these included descriptions of women, measurements and height and weight, and he wasn't born yesterday.

Mr. Christopher heard her footsteps and a knock. She had gotten to his door very quickly. Nervously, he touched his front pocket where he had put the money. It was a lot of cash to have at one time, the most he had carried in years. He looked down, considering himself, his paunch and his house slippers; he saw that the end of his belt was loose. He tucked it behind the proper loop in his corduroys, and she was knocking again, harder and faster.

"Yes, yes," he said quickly. "Hello."

"It's me," she answered, as if it might really be someone he knew. He was suddenly grateful that she hadn't said, "The whore you called for," or something equally provocative that might arouse suspicion, and he quickly undid the chain and opened the door.

She was about a foot taller, starchy white, with large fleshy legs that dropped out of a tiny skirt. Her midriff was showing, and her shoulders were bare, too. It was a lot of flesh for Mr. Christopher to mentally process, and he sputtered once before speaking.

"No," he said. "You are not a Carlotta. Not petite and not a coed."

"Carlotta sent me. I'm her friend, Monique."

She pushed past him, Mr. Christopher squinted against her redolent perfume as she breezed confidently into his living room. She had a small purse and tossed it onto his reading chair as if she had been in the apartment many times before.

His apartment building had once been a three-flat, but it had been sectioned off into nine uneasy units. His living room was long, but narrow; a wall had been added to make a bedroom where the other half of the living room had been. Knowing that the other three units on the floor had once been part of his apartment made him curious to know what the other units looked like. On those rare occasions when a neighbor left the door open—like if they were getting ready to go out or trying to get a better breeze in the summer—and Mr. Christopher happened to be walking by, he would linger, just a little bit, craning his neck slightly to get a peek. He always wanted to know how the units fit together, and it vaguely irritated him that two-thirds of his apartment were being lived in by other people.

"Smells good," she said.

"You're smelling the onions and green peppers that I will be using to stuff the pork chops, our main course."

"Having a fancy party?" she asked, turning slowly and eyeing the elaborately set table for the first time. Although Mr. Christopher usually ate on his couch with his plate and a magazine on the ottoman, tonight he had set out the best plates he had, the good silverware and had even put two candles right in the center.

"No no, it's just us," he said, taking a step to his cassette player.

"I already ate."

"No no. I told the man on the phone this was for dinner and . . . that it would be for dinner as well as the other stuff."

A tinny version of Benny Goodman's clarinet came out of the box.

"No one told me," she said. "I don't have that much time."

"I need you here for at least three hours. I told the man that; I told him. I can't get all the food prepared in an hour, let alone eat it. We're going to have salad and soup and appetizers and bread—the bread's not even completely baked yet."

"You have an hour from when I got out of the car, and that was a couple of minutes ago. If I don't get back to Mickey by then—"

"Who's Mickey?"

"Look out your window. Across the street."

The blinds were shut, but he shuffled between the table and the window and lowered a couple of slats with his hand.

In the no-parking zone, an enormous man sat on the hood of a town car, feet spread-eagle on the pavement, reading a newspaper. Even though it was a large and bulky car, it dipped under the weight of the man's bottom.

"What's he doing?" Mr. Christopher asked.

"Wasting time, now. But I'm telling you, if I don't get down in . . . fifty-three minutes, he'll come tearing up here. You've never seen anything like it. You won't be able to reason with him, you won't be able to stop him. He'll come up those steps, bust down your door, and he'll clean your clock."

Mr. Christopher pulled his hands off the blinds and looked towards his kitchen. "Okay," he said. "We'll do it first, what you came here for, and that will give time for the bread to rise and also for the sugar—this is part of the dessert—to caramelize so that I can pour it, drizzle it, onto the flan. I need forty-five minutes for dinner. That gives me fifteen minutes for the rest of it. Can we do that in fifteen minutes, not even fifteen, but now it's already just twelve or eleven as you pointed out. Can it be done that fast?"

"Normally I have a routine I do, dancing and a rub down, and tickling on the genitalia to arouse you. If you want to skip all that, go right to it . . . Well, it's your money."

"I wasn't picturing dancing or a rub down, but now that I hear about it, it does sound like fun. This is my first time, Monique, so you'll have to guide me."

"Your first time, a guy of your age?"

"First time with a call girl. Okay, we're wasting time. I need to finish sautéing the onions. We better do this in the kitchen."

The kitchen had once been the hallway that connected Mr. Christopher's third of the apartment to the rest of the building. It was narrow and ended abruptly in a Sheetrock wall. The floor changed from hard wood to linoleum about a foot away from the wall, giving the impression that it might have led to a bathroom or a utility closet at one time. One side of the corridor was a narrow countertop, now covered in fruit peelings, shrimp shells and other food debris. Across the corridor was the sink, mini-refrigerator and a two-burner stove that was already covered with large pots. Another small countertop separated the two appliances.

He found the Food section and brushed some cheese shavings off the page and put his finger on the right passage. He took a sniff of her perfume and knew she was behind him. "Clear and soft . . . I'm going to add the green peppers and the cumin and then cook that . . . Then I have to slice the fat off the chops and carve little pockets—" He put a wooden spoon into his sautéing onions and turned his neck slightly so he could see her bare shoulder.

She reached around him unceremoniously and unbuckled his belt and lowered his pants. His legs were hairy with thick blue veins, but his underwear was shockingly white. When she pulled it down to his knees she reached under and grabbed his limp penis. Her hand was so cold and dry that he jumped, but didn't scream. He reached over to the small counter without moving his feet and began to scoop the melon pieces into a large blue bowl.

"I can't get around you here," she told him from the floor. "Can I open one of these cabinets by your knees, so that I can move my head closer, and I'll be able to reach you while you're working?"

He said, "Hang on a second, I'll be able to turn around in a second. Do you think . . . ," he took a pair of black food scissors and slowly began snipping away at the tips of a large artichoke. "Do you think you could take off some clothing too, maybe just your top. Otherwise I'd feel too self-conscious to enjoy it."

She pulled her tank top over her head, and when he turned around she was kneeling in front of him with her hands folded in her lap. Her shirt was lying next to her, and he allowed himself to stare at her breasts. They were the largest he had ever seen, which made him feel a flash of pride, as if he had gotten a surprisingly good return on a shaky investment. Her nipples were oval, straining to keep their shapes on top of such large breasts.

Monique looked right at him and took his balls in her hand. Uncomfortable at the strangely clinical turn this had taken, he cleared his throat once. "My, eh, testicles . . . They're much larger than they should be for the size of my . . ."

She waved the comment away, which did make him feel better. She surely had seen all sorts of genitalia; and she leaned down and put him in her mouth.

The tail on his kitty-cat clock swung back and forth with each second, matching the absurd ping-pong eyes in the cat's head. The clock, painted into the torso of the cat, showed that he had only six minutes left for this part of the night if he was going to have the minimum amount of time he needed to serve the meal. A burning spit of grease from the onions hit him on the back of the neck.

Concentration was difficult for Mr. Christopher and, without moving from his spot, he picked up the big wooden spoon and pushed his onions around in the oil. When he felt his legs getting wobbly, he put the spoon down and held the countertop.

He was losing time now, it was going by quicker than usual; the kitty-cat's eyes and tail had been sped up by some strange force. But he had to admit that it felt good, what she was doing. His legs shook and he was afraid he might fall. He dug in with the heels of his house slippers and gripped tightly to the countertop, his hips involuntarily moved closer to the heat of her face. He wheezed from the back of his throat and felt her breasts against his legs, and he let himself go.

"Okay," he said. "You can spit that out in the sink."

She waved that comment away too, and put her shirt back on.

"Don't spoil your appetite," he said, as he did the top button on his pants and pulled his belt snug against his waist.

"I told you I ate already."

"Look," he told her. "I've got you for another thirty-three minutes. Go take a seat at the table."

She left, and he turned around and scooped the last melon pieces from the counter and used his hands to mix it all up in the bowl. He felt tired for a second, useless. He steadied himself against the counter and realized he just wanted to sleep—to pull the blanket up to his chest and open a magazine and relax. But the pot on the far burner began to bubble, and he remembered the magazines weren't coming anymore, although he couldn't remember why exactly. Mr. Christopher put the artichoke into the water and watched it simmer for a second before covering it.

She was already sitting when he walked back into the living room. He used a book of matches and lit the candles.

"You're going all out for this dinner, huh?" she asked.

Mr. Christopher wanted to smile, but he felt the pressure from the kitty-cat. The soup was done, and he went back into the kitchen, aware of the pathetic way his hip made him look when he was in a hurry. He ladled out two bowls, making sure each serving had the same number of shrimp and pineapple chunks.

"Lemongrass soup," he said, walking slowly out with the bowls. He placed them on the table and sat across from her.

"What is that smell?" she asked, cocking an eye at him.

"That's the lemongrass," he told her. "It's spicy, and I hope you like it."

"Should we say grace?"

Mr. Christopher had dipped his spoon in and was stirring his portion. "No time," he said, and slurped a loud mouthful. "Mmmm," he said, dabbing his lips with his napkin. "Okay, you keep eating, and I have to finish the fruit."

When he returned three minutes later, carrying four small bowls, he was breathing hard. Beads of sweat glistened on his forehead.

She looked up from her bowl and said excitedly, "You know, this is really good. Much better than it smells."

"I'm glad."

"You know what? The pineapple was even better than the shrimp. Pineapple in soup!" she said, and shook her head.

"This is fruit slaw, and this is a cheese and pea salad." He put both bowls in front of her and took her soup bowl. Her hand clenched momentarily, as if she might yank the soup bowl back and this pleased Mr. Christopher, but he didn't have time to think about it.

"Oh God, the wine," he said. He went towards the kitchen but turned around after a few steps and took the soup bowls with him. On the way, he limped to the cassette player and flipped the tape, which had stopped at some point.

The music was back on, and Mr. Christopher poured two glasses of wine. The song was one that he really liked—one of his favorites—Benny Goodman's "Belly of the Cat," and he suddenly felt self-conscious listening to it while pouring a woman wine. He quickly asked, "So, how do you like the salad?"

"It's okay," she said. "The soup was exotic, and this is sort of everyday type of food, so it's a strange menu."

"The Food section said the salad is best served in a glass bowl. That way you can see the layers, the mayonnaise on the bottom, then the peas, then more mayonnaise, then the cheddar cheese, which I shredded myself. It's too bad I don't have a glass bowl."

"Why don't you sit down for a second?" she asked.

He twisted the blinds so he could see out the window. Mickey had put the newspaper away and was leaning against the car now, facing Mr. Christopher's doorway. He was dressed in a bow tie and a sporty tuxedo coat, like a bouncer at a banquet hall or a limo driver on prom night.

"I guess I'll sit down for a second," Mr. Christopher said, lowering himself uneasily into the chair. "And rest. I had planned on a nice conversation with you." He dabbed his forehead with the napkin, but he still felt sweaty. "So," he said, "how many people will you visit tonight?"

"I usually try to get five or six customers a night," she told him. "At least four, but six is a good night. Eight is the most I would do."

"When I worked retail, it was the same. Just like you, get to as many people as possible. So that's something we have in common, me and you," Mr. Christopher nodded once to himself. "But about you, eight times in one night? That's a lot. Good for business, I guess. Right?"

"That would be real good," she said. "Yes. It's not that tough. How many times do you do it a night?"

"Usually, none," he told her.

"But what's the most?"

He made a face.

"Come on, for a conversation. What's the most you've ever done it in a night."

"If I've ever done it twice in a night, then two. But I can't remember. I usually get tired and there isn't enough time in a single night to rest up entirely. So we're different, that's why it's so nice to spend time with someone you don't know, to share different experiences. . . ." These sentences that he had prepared and even rehearsed a few times now sounded stilted and ridiculous in his mouth; although she was nodding in apparent agreement with him. Who was he trying to kid anyway? He looked at his watch to cover his embarrassment. "Okay," he said. "Time for the main course. Let's go, let's go."

He took her bowls away and returned a few minutes later with a platter. "We're going to eat dessert now, but save enough room for the pork chops. They're still a little pink and if we wait for them we might not have time for dessert. So we'll go out of turn."

She put her hand on her bare stomach. "That's fine with me anyway, because I'm not especially hungry. I told you that, that I had eaten already. I don't even know if I could eat another bite."

He brought four helpings of flan, each perfectly shaped like a large quivering eyeball. He had hoped she would want more than one helping, but he knew that wasn't going to happen, so he said, "I think it's time to make a toast."

She picked up her glass of wine, which was still full.

"To a lovely night," he said. "A lovely woman, a lovely meal and a lovely time."

He tipped his glass towards her slightly and she did the same in imitation, and they both drank.

"Okay," he said. "Now dessert."

He looked at his watch for a second and saw that he had nine minutes left. When he checked the window, he was surprised to see Mickey was walking back and forth. His legs and arms were thick, like sausages. Mickey checked his watch and looked up to the third floor of the building.

"It's time for the pork chops," he mumbled.

"Are you sure there's time? You don't want him—Mickey, coming up here. It's better that I should leave a few minutes early than he get mad—come up those stairs and start banging on your door."

"I have eight more minutes of your time," Mr. Christopher answered icily, and he walked into the kitchen.

When he returned a few minutes later, he was carrying a plate with two sickly pink and gray slabs of meat. Corn and onions had been stuffed into slits along the sides of the chops, but they oozed like puddles of sewage. Mr. Christopher skewered the largest one and tried to get it off the tray, but every time he lifted the fork, the chop slid off. Finally he pushed it with the prongs onto her plate and slid the other one onto his plate. He put the serving platter on the floor.

"Bon appetit, my sweet."

"Are you sure these are done?" She said, poking her chop with a knife. "You've really got to cook meat, pork especially; and I thought I saw these out on your counter, raw, when I was in the kitchen."

"That's right," he told her. He cut off a slice. It was dull pink on the inside and she looked away before he put it in his mouth. "But I turned the oven up as high as it would go and had them in since we began eating. Mmmm. Anyway, I don't have any more time." His lips were glistening and he sliced off another piece and waited for her to begin.

"It smells good," she stood up. "But I ate before I got here, and the custard and the soup, and that's it. I couldn't eat another bite. Thank you for the night. That'll be a hundred and forty bones, and that's not including a tip."

"Take a bite of the dinner. The bread isn't done yet and we'll forget about the liqueur; I haven't even begun to make the garlic butter sauce for the artichoke appetizer. So we'll forget all the rest, but I want you to at least try the pork chop. It's stuffed with corn and sautéed onions. You know, festively."

He wolfed down another bite, swallowing it as quickly as possible to show how good it was.

"My money," she said putting her palm out.

"My time," he said into his plate. "This is all I wanted, for you to come here and have a nice meal and a nice time. It's my special day and this was all I wanted."

"Listen, old man. You didn't cook it long enough; I'm going to retch just from the smell and I'm already nauseous from the spicy soup and the bowl of mayonnaise."

He forced himself to take another piece of the pork chop. When it reached his tongue his stomach lurched, and the meat fell apart unnaturally. He put his napkin up to his mouth and spit it up. When he was done gagging and had wiped his lips hard onto the napkin, he said, "The money is in my front pants pocket. Seven twenty-dollar bills." He covered his head with his hands and rested his elbows on the table.

"Give it to me," she said.

"It's too late," he told her. "Check the window."

The door lurched in its frame and then popped open. Monique put her arm around Mr. Christopher's shoulders. "It's okay, Mickey," she yelled. "It's okay, I'm all right."

Mr. Christopher closed his eyes as a hand grabbed his shoulder and pulled him up off the chair. He opened them and saw Mickey's teeth, a row of little rat triangles.

"You see that door, buddy," Mickey snarled. "I suggest you hand over the money right this instant, or that's what's going to happen to your head."

"The money's in my pocket, sir," Mr. Christopher said, dropping back in the chair.

"The money's in my pocket," he repeated. He stood up and took a step back. "Here." He put the wad of folded bills onto the table.

"And hold on you two. Hold on a minute." He put up a finger towards Mickey and Monique and ambled into his kitchen. The pot with the artichoke was boiling over and Mr. Christopher turned off the burners and shut off the stove. A stack of old newspapers were piled under the counter, waiting to be taken to the trash.

"I know your time is valuable," Mr. Christopher called out. "And I know I've wasted some of it. I'm sorry about that . . ." Brightening up, he slipped on an oven-mitt and took the platter of pork chops from the oven. "And six customers is a lot, and I know you've got to be going . . . Believe me, I respect the need for speed. So maybe this will help, with dinner . . ." As he spoke, he wrapped in newspaper three of the juiciest chops he had. He pulled the artichoke out of the water with tongs and put it into a large Ziploc baggie. When that was done, he dumped the rest of the fruit slaw into another baggy, and the cheese and pea salad into a third. "I appreciate you coming over, Monique, and you too, Mickey! I appreciate the time you spent with me . . ." Mr. Christopher pulled a brown shopping bag out of the garbage and put the moist newspaper packages and all the baggies into it.

The soup was hot, but he found a square tupperware in a cabinet and poured it in, burped the lid and put it in the brown bag with the rest of it. The flan was more delicate, but Mr. Christopher emptied an egg carton and filled the cups with the lumpy brown custard.

"I remember on Thanksgiving," Mr. Christopher called while

skittering around his kitchen, "or any food holiday like that, Christmas and the Fourth of July—barbecues on the Fourth—and at the end the host always would ask what you wanted to . . . take home with you, leftovers . . ."

He had no plastic forks or spoons, but now wasn't the time to worry about his stuff. It would be a long time before he ever had guests over for such an occasion, if ever, so he put his nice silverware into the bag. Two of everything: two salad forks, two regular forks, two sets of each spoon—fruit, dessert, soup—two sets of steak knives and two butter knives. He pulled the bread loaf out of the oven, slapped the bottom of the pan with his mitted fist, and the oatmeal raisin mass fell solidly into the bag.

"That's when you know you've had a good time—didn't waste your time—when you walked out with an armload of food for the next couple of days . . ." He folded the top over twice, put his hand on his hip and walked into the living room.

The room was empty. Mr. Christopher held the warm shopping bag to his chest and looked at his door. It was only attached at the top hinge and looked like it might fall, and he could see past it, into the empty hallway, all the way to his neighbor's closed door.

Gary Snyder

✠

Oysters

First   Samish Bay
      then all morning, hunting oysters

A huge feed on white
wood State Park slab-plank bench-
      and table
         "at" Birch Bay
      where we picked up rocks
    for presents.

And ate oysters, fried—raw—cookt in milk
    rolled in crumbs—
all we wanted.
      ALL WE WANTED

& got back in our wagon,
drove away.

Issue 37, 1966

Anthony Burgess

⌘

from The Art of Fiction XLVIII

INTERVIEWER

What are "hot pot" and "lobscowse"?

BURGESS

Hot pot, or Lancashire hot pot, is made in this way. An earthenware dish, a layer of trimmed lamb chops, a layer of sliced onions, a layer of sliced potatoes, then continue the layers till you reach the top. Add seasoned stock. On top put mushrooms or more potato slices to brown. Add oysters or kidneys as well if you wish. Bake in a moderate oven for a long time. Eat with pickled cabbage. Lobscowse is a sailor's dish from Liverpool (Liverpudlians are called "scousers" or "scowsers") and is very simple. Dice potatoes and onions and cook in a pan of seasoned water. When they're nearly done get rid of excess liquid and add a can or two of cubed (or diced) corned beef. Heat gently. Eat with mixed pickles. I love cooking these dishes and, once known, everybody loves them. They're honest and simple. Lancashire has a great cuisine, including a notable shop cuisine—meaning you can buy great delicacies in shops. Lancashire women traditionally work in the cotton mills and cook dinner only at weekends. Hence the things you can get in cooked-food shops—fish and chips, Bury puddings, Eccles cakes, tripe, cowheel, meat pies (hot, with gravy poured into a hole from a jug), and so on. Fish and chips is now, I think, internationally accepted. Meat and potato pie is perhaps the greatest of the Lancashire dishes—a "drier" hot pot with a fine flaky crust.

Marie Ponsot

Non-Vegetarian

It haunts us, the misappropriated flesh,
be it Pelops' shoulder after Demeter's feast
or Adam's rib supporting Eve's new breasts,
or the nameless root of Gilgamesh.

Who am I that a given beast must die
to stake the smolder of my blood or eyes?
Were only milk, fruit, honey to supply
my table, I would not starve but thrive.

But then the richer goods I misappropriate
(time wasted, help withheld, mean words for great)
would blaze forth and nag me to repudiate
the habitual greed of my normal state.

My guts delight twice in the death I dine on,
once for hunger, once for what meat distracts me from.

Issue 153, 1999

Jim Crace

✠

from The Devil's Larder

ROOM SERVICE

Here, after midnight on the seventh floor, room service is provided by a refugee. Her name—unlikely consonants, and then
too many vowels—is printed on an apron tag. Her face is fiery, peppered by the many sweets she sucks from "late till six" as she sits on
her hard chair at what the waiters call the Bus Station. It is her job to
collect the ordered trays of food and drink from the service hatch and
take them down the corridors—now reeking of cigars, cheap scent
and cannabis, and far from silent with the clatterings of one-night
stands and thoughtless television sets and arguments—to restless,
needy men who ought to be in bed asleep. A man, awake beyond midnight, is unpredictable.

The refugee—let's not attempt to say her name—is only meant to
place the tray outside the room, knock lightly on the door and disappear. Those are the rules. Wise rules. A dark hotel is ruinous. No
close contact between the busgirls and the guests is tolerated. No
touting for gratuities. No entry to the rooms. No extra services. They
have to come and go unseen, discreet and tedious as nuns. Before the
rules were imposed, a girl had been attacked, and many had been
bribed or groped or compromised. One girl, on the second floor, had
been a part-time prostitute. She'd tucked her business card into the
napkin on each tray and done quite nicely for herself. Another one
had sold thin reefers to the regulars. A third, invited into rooms for

God knows what, had stolen watches, wallets, credit cards. A fourth, just for the hell of it, had helped herself to shoes and dropped them down the lift shaft for rats to eat and ghosts to wear.

Sometimes, of course, the busgirl on the seventh floor cannot avoid the guests. They have to pass her as they come and go. Or else she finds them waiting at an open door. And then she says *good morning,* and *good night, excuse me, thank you, please, good-bye*—but that is almost all she says or understands. She has, however, learned the menu words for those occasions when the men don't use their telephones but come along the corridor and try to order food through her. *Club sandwich* comes out almost perfectly. The choice of coffees, beers and snacks are quickly recognized. *Champagne. Fish chowder. House burger and a side of fries. Rice salad with a pork brochette.* She can recite a list of fourteen whiskies. She's tasted all of them.

But ask her anything about herself and she will turn a deep and helpless red. She will not understand, she cannot say, she cannot tell her story, what has happened to her home, her village and her family. She shakes her damaged face at these late men, but nothing tumbles out. There are no words inside the pepper pot except the words for hotel food.

So then, how can she tell the man who occupies Suite 17 on Tuesday nights that she's in love with him, that she has fallen for the suppers on his service tray and is seduced by what he wants to eat? He always orders open sandwiches, sweet salad and the sort of hinting, aromatic tea that, normally, a woman drinks.

How can she tell the gentleman how much she hates the corridors? She doesn't have the vowels or consonants.

In the closing hours of the night, when it is quiet, she has to tour the seventh floor collecting trays and crockery and anything that's left outside the rooms. There's always bread for her to eat and untouched vegetables, sometimes a piece of meat or cheese, some fries, some long-cold soup. She puts the almost empty bottles to her mouth. She licks the liqueur glasses clean. Once in a while, if she's in luck, she's drunk by dawn on other people's dregs. And then—her shift fast coming to an end—she snoozes at the Bus Station and dreams, rehearsing what she'll need to say to change, to resurrect her life. Despite wise rules, the day must come when she'll have the opportunity to go through doors. All of the doors that have been shut on her. A corridor of locked and bolted doors. The door to Suite 17. The door to all those hazards and gratuities.

And if she ever dares to knock and wait until the door is opened, when it swings, when all the light from outside is let in, then she will not be lost for words, not in her dreams. She will not turn a deep and helpless red. She'll see herself reflected in the bathroom's steamy mirrors, wrapped in the hotel's thick white towels, feet up before the television set. She'll see herself propped up by cushions on the bed. Beyond the perfume and the smoke, the man is waiting on her with a tray.

Her new life seems a long way off. Ten thousand trays away. Meanwhile, she mutters to herself and practices vocabulary with all the items she can name: dressed prawns, Jack Daniel's, chowder, salt, a single glass of dry white wine, champagne. *Club sandwich* comes out almost perfectly again. She orders for herself—another dream— the sort of hinting, aromatic tea that, normally, a woman drinks. She says *good morning* to the places she has lost. And *good night,* too. *Excuse me. Thank you. Please. Good-bye.*

PASTA

My daughter asked me, "Do you think that pasta tastes the same in other people's mouths?" Let's try, I said. You first.

I picked a pasta shell from the bowl, dropped it, red with sauce, onto my tongue and closed my mouth. My lips were pursed as if I were waiting to be kissed. I sat down on the kitchen chair and spread my knees. Come on, I said, trying not to laugh or swallow, be sensible. She'd started giggling but struggled to compose herself. She pushed against my stretched skirts and reached my face with hers. It was a kiss of sorts. She had to turn her head like lovers do, invade my lips and hunt the pasta with her tongue. She pushed the shell about inside my mouth and then stepped back, a little shocked by what she'd done, at what I'd let her do.

What do you think? "Tomato, onion, pesto paste," she said, remembering the sauce we'd made. "And lipstick, too. A sort of cherry flavor. Except for that, it tastes exactly the same as it does in my mouth. Your go."

She picked a piece of pasta for herself and put it on her tongue. Again she came between my legs. Again we kissed. My tongue got snagged on her loose tooth. Our lips and noses rubbed, we breathed into each other's lungs, our hair was tangled at our chins. I tasted sauce and toothpaste, I tasted sleep and giggling, I tasted disbelief and love that knows no fear. My daughter tasted just the same as me. We held each other by the elbows while I hunted for the pasta in her mouth.

BASEBALL

Jim Shepard

⌖

Batting Against Castro

In 1951 you couldn't get us to talk politics. Ball players then would just as soon talk bed wetting as talk politics. Tweener Jordan brought up the H-bomb one seventh inning, sitting there tarring up his useless Louisville Slugger at the end of a Bataan Death March of a road trip when it was 104° on the field and about nine of us in a row had just been tied in knots by Maglie and it looked like we weren't going to get anyone on base in the next five weeks except for those hit by pitches, at which point someone down the end of the bench told Tweener to put a lid on it, and he did, and that was the end of the H-bomb as far as the Philadelphia Phillies was concerned.

I was one or two frosties shy of outweighing my bat and wasn't exactly known as Mr. Heavy Hitter; in fact me and Charley Caddell, another Pinemaster from the Phabulous Phillies, were known far and wide as such banjo hitters that they called us—right to our faces, right during a game, like confidence or bucking up a teammate was for noolies and nosedroops—Flatt and Scruggs. Pick us a tune, boys, they'd say, our own teammates, when it came time for the eighth and ninth spots in the order to save the day. And Charlie and I would grab our lumber and shoot each other looks like we were the Splinter himself, misunderstood by everybody, and up we'd go to the plate against your basic Newcombe or Erskine cannon volleys. Less knowledgeable fans would cheer. The organist would pump through the motions and the twenty-seven thousand who did show up (PHILS WHACKED IN TWINIGHTER; SLUMP CONTINUES; LOCALS SEEK TO SALVAGE

LAST GAME OF HOME STAND) wouldn't say boo. Our runners aboard would stand there like they were watching furniture movers. One guy in our dugout would clap. A pigeon would set down in right field and gook around. Newcombe or Erskine would look in at us like litter was blowing across their line of sight. They'd paint the corners with a few unhittable ones just to let us know what a mismatch this was. Then Charley would dink one to second. It wouldn't make a sound in the glove. I'd strike out. And the fans would cuff their kids or scratch their rears and cheer. It was like they were celebrating just how bad we could be.

I'd always come off the field looking at my bat, trademark up, like I couldn't figure out what happened. You'd think by that point I would've. I tended to be hitting about .143.

Whenever we were way down, in the 12–2 range, Charley played them up, our sixth- or seventh-, or worse, ninth-inning Waterloos— tipped his cap and did some minor posing—and for his trouble got showered with whatever the box seats didn't feel like finishing: peanuts, beer, the occasional hot-dog roll. On what was the last straw before this whole Cuba thing, after we'd gone down one-two and killed a bases-loaded rally for the second time that day, the boxes around the dugout got so bad that Charley went back out and took a curtain call, like he'd clubbed a round-tripper. The fans howled for parts of his body. The Dodgers across the way laughed and pointed. In the time it took Charley to lift his cap and wave someone caught him in the mouth with a metal whistle from a Cracker Jack box and chipped a tooth.

"You stay on the pine," Skip said to him while he sat there trying to wiggle the ivory in question. "I'm tired of your antics." Skip was our third-year manager who'd been through it all, seen it all and lost most of the games along the way.

"What's the hoo-ha?" Charley wanted to know. "We're down eleven-nothing."

Skip said that Charley reminded him of Dummy Hoy, the deaf-mute who played for Cincinnati all those years ago. Skip was always saying things like that. The first time he saw me shagging flies he said I was the picture of Skeeter Scalzi.

"Dummy Hoy batted .287 lifetime," Charley said. "I'll take that anytime."

The thing was, we were both good glove men. And this was the Phillies. If you could do anything right, you were worth at least a spot on the pine. After Robin Roberts, our big gun on the mound, it was Katie bar the door.

"We're twenty-three games back," Skip said. "This isn't the time for bush-league stunts."

It was late in the season, and Charley was still holding that tooth and in no mood for a gospel from Skip. He let fly with something in the abusive range, and I, I'm ashamed to say, became a disruptive influence on the bench and backed him up.

Quicker than you could say Wally Pipp, we were on our way to Allentown for some Double A discipline.

Our ride out there was not what you'd call high-spirited. The Allentown bus ground gears and did ten, tops. It really worked over those switchbacks on the hills, to maximize the dust coming through the windows. Or you could shut the windows and bake muffins.

Charley was across the aisle, sorting through the paper. He'd looked homicidal from the bus station on.

"We work on our hitting, he's got to bring us back," I said. "Who else has he got?" Philadelphia's major-league franchise was at that point in pretty bad shape, with a lot of kids filling gaps left by the hospital patients.

Charley mentioned an activity involving Skip's mother. It colored the ears of the woman sitting in front of us.

It was then I suggested the winter leagues, Mexico or Cuba.

"How about Guam?" Charley said. "How about the Yukon?" He hawkered out the window.

Here was my thinking: the season was almost over in Allentown, which was also, by the way, in the cellar. We probably weren't going back up afterwards. That meant that starting October we either cooled our heels playing pepper in Pennsylvania, or we played winter ball. I was for Door Number Two.

Charley and me, we had to do something about our self-esteem. It got so I'd wince just to see my name in the sports pages—before I

knew what it was about, just to see my name. Charley's full name was
Charles Owen Caddell, and he carried a handsome suitcase around
the National League that had his initials, C.O.C., in big letters near
the handle. When asked what they stood for, he always said, "Can o'
Corn."

Skip we didn't go to for fatherly support. Skip tended to be hard
on the non-regulars, who he referred to as "you egg-sucking noodle-
hanging gutter trash."

Older ballplayers talked about what it was like to lose it: the way
your teammates would start giving you the look, the way you could
see in their eyes, Three years ago he'd make that play, or He's lost a
step going to the hole; the quickness isn't there. The difference was,
Charley and me, we'd seen that look since we were twelve.

So Cuba seemed like the savvy move: a little seasoning, a little time
in the sun, some señoritas, drinks with hats, maybe a curve ball
Charley *could* hit, a heater I could do more than foul off.

Charley took some convincing. He'd sit there in the Allentown
dugout, riding the pine even in Allentown, whistling air through his
chipped tooth and making faces at me. This Cuba thing was stupid,
he'd say. He knew a guy played for the Athletics went down to Mexico or someplace, drank a cup of water with bugs in it that would've
turned Dr. Salk's face white and went belly-up between games of a
doubleheader. "Shipped home in a box they had to *seal*," Charley
said. He'd tell that story, and his tooth would whistle for emphasis.

But really what other choice did we have? Between us we had the
money to get down there, and I knew a guy on the Pirates who was
able to swing the connections. I finished the year batting .143 in the
bigs and .167 in Allentown. Charley hit his weight and pulled off
three errors in an inning his last game. When we left, our Allentown
manager said. "Boys, I hope you hit the bigs again. Because we sure
can't use you around here."

So down we went on the train and then the slow boat, accompanied the whole way by a catcher from the Yankee system, a big bird
from Minnesota named Ericksson. Ericksson was out of Triple A and
apparently had a fan club there because he was so fat. I guess it had
gotten so he couldn't field bunts. He said the Yankee brass was paying
for this. They thought of it as a fat farm.

"The thing is, I'm not fat," he said. We were pulling out of some skeeter-and-water stop in central Florida. One guy sat on the train platform with his chin on his chest, asleep or dead. "That's the thing. What I am is big boned." He held up an arm and squeezed it the way you'd test a melon.

"I like having you in the window seat," Charley said, his Allentown hat down over his eyes. "Makes the whole trip shady."

Ericksson went on to talk about feet. This shortened the feel of the trip considerably. Ericksson speculated that the smallest feet in the history of the major leagues belonged to Art Herring, who wore a size three. Myril Hoag, apparently, wore one size four and one size four and a half.

We'd signed a deal with the Cienfuegos club: seven hundred a month and two-fifty for expenses. We also got a place on the beach, supposedly, and a woman to do the cleaning, though we had to pay her bus fare back and forth. It sounded a lot better than the Mexican League, which had teams with names like Coatzacoalcos. Forget the Mexican League, Charley'd said when I brought it up. Once I guess he'd heard some retreads from that circuit talking about the Scorpions, and he'd said, "They have a team with that name?" and they'd said no.

When Ericksson finished with feet he wanted to talk politics. Not only the whole Korean thing—truce negotiations, we're on a thirty-one-hour train ride with a Swedish glom who wants to talk truce negotiations—but this whole thing with Cuba and other Latin American countries and Kremlin expansionism. Ericksson could get going on Kremlin expansionism.

"Charley's not much on politics," I said, trying to turn off the spigot.

"You can talk politics if you want," Charley said from under his hat. "Talk politics. I got a degree. I can keep up. I got a B.S. from Schenectady." The B.S. stood for Boots and Shoes, meaning he worked in a factory.

So there we were in Cuba. Standing on the dock, peering into the sun, dragging our big duffel bags like dogs that wouldn't cooperate.

We're standing there sweating on our bags and wondering where the team rep who's supposed to meet us is, and meanwhile a riot breaks out about a block and a half away. We thought it was a block party at first. This skinny guy in a pleated white shirt and one of those cigar-ad pointed beards was racketing away at the crowd, which was yelling and carrying on. He was over six feet. He looked strong, wiry, but in terms of heft somewhere between flyweight and poster child. He was scoring big with some points he was making holding up a bolt of cloth. He said something that got them all going and up he went onto somebody's shoulders, and they paraded him around past the storefronts, everybody shouting, "*Castro! Castro! Castro!*" which Charley and me figured was the guy's name. We were still sitting there in the sun like idiots. They circled around past us and stopped. They got quiet, and we looked at each other. The man of the hour was giving us his fearsome bandito look. He was tall. He was skinny. He was just a kid. He didn't look at all happy to see us.

He looked about ready to say something that was not any kind of welcome when the *policia* waded in, swinging clubs like they were getting paid by the concussion. Which is when the riot started. The team rep showed up. We got hustled out of there.

We got there, it turned out, a few weeks into the season. Cienfuegos was a game down in the loss column to its big rival, Marianao. Charley called it Marianne.

Cuba took more than a little getting used to. There was the heat: one team we played had a stadium that sat in a kind of natural bowl that held in the sun and dust. The dust floated around you like a golden fog. It glittered. Water streamed down your face and back. Your glove dripped. One of our guys had trouble finding the plate, and while I stood there creeping in on the infield dirt sweat actually puddled around my feet.

There were the fans: one night they pelted each other and the field with live snakes.

There were the pranks: as the outsiders, Charley and me expected the standards—the shaving-cream-in-the-shoe, the multiple hotfoot— but even so never got tired of the bird-spider-in-the-cap, or the crushed-chiles-in-the-water-fountain. Many's the time, after such good-natured ribbing from our Latino teammates, we'd still be holding our ribs, toying with our bats and wishing we could identify the particular jokester in question.

There was the travel: the bus trips to the other side of the island that seemed to take short careers. I figured Cuba, when I figured it at all, like something about the size of Long Island, but I was not close. During one of those trips Ericksson, the only guy still in a good mood, leaned over his seat back and gave me the bad news: if you laid Cuba over the eastern United States, he said, it'd stretch from New York to Chicago. Or something like that.

And from New York to Chicago the neighborhood would go right down the toilet, Charley said, next to me.

Sometimes we'd leave right after a game, I mean without showering, and that meant no matter how many open windows you were able to manage you smelled bad feet and armpit all the way there and all the way back. On the mountain roads and switchbacks we counted roadside crosses and smashed guardrails on the hairpin turns. One time Charley, his head out the window to get any kind of air, looked way down into an arroyo and kept looking. I asked him what he could see down there. He said a glove and some bats.

And finally there was what Ericksson called A Real Lack of Perspective. He was talking, of course, about that famous South of the Border hotheadness we'd all seen even in the bigs. In our first series against Marianao after Charley and I joined the team (the two of us went two for twenty-six, and we got swept; so much for gringos to the rescue) an argument at home plate—not about whether the guy was out, but about whether the tag had been too hard—brought out both managers, both benches, one or two retirees from both teams, a blind batboy who kept feeling around everyone's legs for the discarded lumber, a drunk who'd been sleeping under the stands, reporters, a photographer, a couple of would-be beauty queens, the radio announcers and a large number of interested spectators. I forget how it came out.

After we dropped a doubleheader in Havana our manager had a pot broken over his head. It turned out the pot held a plant, which he kept and replanted. After a win at home our starting third baseman was shot in the foot. We asked our manager, mostly through sign language, why. He said he didn't know why they picked the foot.

But it was more than that, too: on days off we'd sit in our hammocks and look out our floor-to-ceiling windows and our screened

patios and smell our garden with its flowers with the colors from Mars
and the breeze with the sea in it, and we'd feel like DiMaggio in his
penthouse, as big league as big league could get. We'd fish on the
coral reefs for yellowtail and mackerel, for shrimp and rock lobster.
We'd cook it ourselves. Ericksson started eating over, and he did great
things with coconut and lime and beer.

And our hitting began to improve.

One for five, one for four, two for five, two for five with two doubles: the box scores were looking up and up, Spanish or not. One
night we went to an American restaurant in Havana, and on the place
on the check for comments I wrote, *I went 3 for 5 today.*

Cienfuegos went on a little streak: nine wins in a row, fourteen out
of fifteen. We caught and passed Marianao. Even Ericksson was
slimming down. He pounced on bunts and stomped around home
plate like a man killing bees before gunning runners out. We were on
a winner.

Which is why politics, like it always does, had to stick its nose in.
The president of our tropical paradise, who reminded Charley more
of Akim Tamiroff than Harry Truman, was a guy named Batista who
was not well-liked. This we could tell because when we said his name
even in our cracked Spanish our teammates would repeat it and then
spit on the ground or our feet. We decided to go easy on the political
side of things and keep mostly mum on the subject of our opinions,
which we mostly didn't have. Ericksson threatened periodically to get
us all into trouble or, worse, a discussion, except his Spanish was
even more terrible than ours, and the first time he tried to talk politics
everyone agreed absolutely with what he was saying and then brought
him a bedpan.

Neither of us, as I said before, were much for the front of the
newspaper, but you didn't have to be Mr. News to see that Cuba was
about as bad as it got in terms of who was running what: the payoffs
got to the point where we figured that guys getting sworn in for public
office put their hands out instead of up. We paid off local mailmen to
get our mail. We paid off traffic cops to get through intersections. It
didn't seem like the kind of thing that could go on forever, especially
since most of the Cubans on the island didn't get expense money.

So this Batista—"Akim" to Charley—wasn't doing a good job, and it looked like your run-of-the-mill Cuban was hot about that. He kept most of the money for himself and his pals. If you were on the outs and needed food or medicine it was pretty much your hard luck. And according to some of our teammates, when you went to jail—for whatever, for spitting on the sidewalk—bad things happened to you. Relatives wrote you off.

So there were a lot of protests, *demonstraciones,* that winter, and driving around town in cabs we always seemed to run into them, which meant trips out to eat or to pick up the paper might run half the day. It was the only non-fineable excuse for showing up late to the ballpark.

But then the demonstrations started at the games, in the stands. And guess who'd usually be leading them, in his little pleated shirt and a Marianao cap? We'd be two or three innings in, and the crowd out along the third-base line would suddenly get up like the chorus in a Busby Berkeley musical and start singing and swaying back and forth, their arms in the air. The first time it happened Batista himself was in the stands watching the game, surrounded by like forty bodyguards. He had his arms crossed and was staring over at Castro, who had *his* arms crossed and was staring back. Charley was at the plate, and I was on deck.

Charley walked over to me, bat still on his shoulder. I'm not sure anybody had called time. The pitcher was watching the crowd, too. "Now what is this?" Charley wanted to know.

I told him it could have been a religious thing, or somebody's birthday. He looked at me. "I mean like a national hero's, or something," I said.

He was still peering over at Castro's side of the crowd, swinging his bat to keep limber, experimenting with that chipped-tooth whistle. "What're they saying?" he asked.

"It's in Spanish," I said.

Charley shook his head and then shot a look over to Batista on the first-base side. "Akim's gonna love this," he said. But Batista sat there like this happened all the time. The umpire straightened every inch of clothing behind his chest protector and then had enough and started signaling play to resume, so Charley got back into the batter's box, dug in, set himself, and unloaded big time on the next pitch and put it on a line without meaning to into the crowd on the third-base side. A whole side of the stands ducked, and a couple people flailed and went down like they were shot. You could see people standing over them.

Castro in the meantime stood in the middle of this with his arms still folded, like Peary at the Pole, or Admiral Whoever taking grapeshot across the bow. You had to give him credit.

Charley stepped out of the box and surveyed the damage, cringing a little. Behind him I could see Batista, his hands together over his head, shaking them in congratulation.

"Wouldn't you know it," Charley said, still a little rueful. "I finally get a hold of one and zing it foul."

"I hope nobody's dead over there," I said. I could see somebody holding up a hat and looking down, like that was all that was left. Castro was still staring out over the field.

"Wouldn't that be our luck," Charley said, but he did look worried.

Charley ended up doubling, which the third-base side booed, and then stealing third, which they booed even more. While he stood on the bag brushing himself off and feeling quite the pepperpot, Castro stood up and caught him flush on the back of the head with what looked like an entire burrito of some sort. Mashed beans flew.

The crowd loved it. Castro sat back down, accepting congratulations all around. Charley, when he recovered, made a move like he was going into the stands, but no one in the entire stadium went for the bluff. So he just stood there with his hands on his hips, the splattered third baseman pointing him out to the crowd and laughing. He stood there on third and waited for me to bring him home so he could spike the catcher to death. He had onions and probably some ground meat on his cap.

That particular Cold War crisis ended with my lining out, a rocket, to short.

In the dugout afterwards I told Charley it had been that same guy, Castro, from our first day on the dock. He said that that figured and that he wanted to work on his bat control so he could kill the guy with a line drive if he ever saw him in the stands again.

This Castro came up a lot. There was a guy on the team, a light-hitting left fielder named Rafa, who used to lecture us in Spanish, very worked up. Big supporter of Castro's. You could see he was up-set about something. Ericksson and I would nod, like we'd given what he was on about some serious thought, and were just about to weigh in on that very subject. I'd usually end the meetings by giving him a thumbs-up and heading out onto the field. Ericksson knew it was about politics so he was interested. Charley had no patience for it on good days and hearing this guy bring up Castro didn't help. Every so often he'd say across our lockers, "He wants to know if you want to meet his sister."

Finally Rafa took to bringing an interpreter, and he'd find us at dinners, waiting for buses, taking warm-ups, and up would come the two of them, Rafa and his interpreter, like this was sports day at the U.N. Rafa would rattle on while we went about our business, and then his interpreter would take over. His interpreter said things like, "This is not your tropical playground." He said things like, "The govern-ment of the United States will come to understand the Cuban peo-ple's right to self-determination." He said things like, "The people will rise up and crush the octopus of the North."

"He means the Yankees, Ericksson," Charley said.

Ericksson meanwhile had that big Nordic brow all furrowed, ready to talk politics.

You could see Rafa thought he was getting through. He went off on a real rip, and when he finished the interpreter said only, "The poverty of the people in our Cuba is very bad."

Ericksson hunkered down and said, "And the people think Batista's the problem?"

"Lack of money's the problem," Charley said. The interpreter gave him the kind of look the hotel porter gives you when you show up with seventeen bags. Charley made a face back at him as if to say, Am I right or wrong?

"The poverty of the people is very bad," the interpreter said again. He was stubborn. He didn't have to tell us: on one road trip we saw a town, like a used car lot, of whole families, big families, living in abandoned cars. Somebody had a cradle thing worked out for a baby in an overturned fender.

"What do you want from us?" Charley asked.

"You are supporting the corrupt system," the interpreter said. Rafa hadn't spoken and started talking excitedly, probably asking what'd just been said.

Charley took some cuts and snorted. "Guy's probably been changing everything Rafa wanted to say," he said.

We started joking that poor Rafa'd only been trying to talk about how to hit a curve. They both gave up on us, and walked off. Ericksson followed them.

"Dag Hammarskjöld," Charley said, watching him go. When he saw my face he said, "I read the papers."

But this Castro guy set the tone for the other ballparks. The demonstrations continued more or less the same way (without the burrito) for the last two weeks of the season, and with three games left we found ourselves with a two-game lead on Marianao, and we finished the season guess where against guess who.

This was a big deal to the fans because Marianao had no imports, no Americans, on their team. Even though they had about seven guys with big league talent, to the Cubans this was David and Goliath stuff. Big America vs. Little Cuba, and our poor Rafa found himself playing for Big America.

So we lost the first two games, by ridiculous scores, scores like 18–5 and 16–1. The kind of scores where you're playing out the string after the third inning. Marianao was charged up and we weren't. Most of the Cuban guys on our team, as you'd figure, were a little confused. They were all trying—money was involved here—but the focus wasn't exactly there. In the first game we came unraveled after Rafa dropped a pop-up that went about seven thousand feet up into the sun, and in the second we were just wiped out by a fat forty-five-year-old pitcher that people said when he had his control and some sleep the night before, was unbeatable.

Castro and Batista were at both games. During the seventh-inning stretch of the second game, with Marianao now tied for first place, Castro led the third-base side in a Spanish version of "Take Me Out to the Ball Game."

They jeered us—Ericksson, Charley and me—every time we came up. And the more we let it get to us, the worse we did. Ericksson was pressing, I was pressing, Charley was pressing. So we let each other down. But what made it worse was with every roar after one of our strikeouts, with every stadium-shaking celebration after a ball went through our legs, we felt like we were letting America down, like some poor guy on an infantry charge who can't even hold up the flag, dragging it along the ground. It got to us.

When Charley was up, I could hear him talking to himself: "The kid can still hit. Ball was in on him, but he got that bat head out in front."

When I was up, I could hear the chatter from Charley: "Gotta have this one. This is where we need you, big guy."

On Friday Charley made the last out. On Saturday I did. On Saturday night we went to the local bar that seemed the safest and got paralyzed. Ericksson stayed home, resting up for the rubber match.

Our Cuban skipper had a clubhouse meeting before the last game. It was hard to have a clear-the-air meeting when some of the teammates didn't understand the language, and were half-paralyzed with hangovers besides, but they went on with it anyway, pointing at us every so often. I got the feeling the suggestion was that the Americans be benched for the sake of morale.

To our Cuban skipper's credit, and because he was more contrary than anything else, he penciled us in.

Just to stick it in Marianao's ear, he penciled us in the 1–2–3 spots in the order.

The game started around three in the afternoon. It was one of the worst hangovers I'd ever had. I walked out into the Cuban sun, the first to carry the hopes of Cienfuegos and America to the plate, and decided that as a punishment I'd been struck blind. I struck out, though I have only the umpire's say-so on that.

Charley struck out too. Back on the bench he squinted like someone looking into car headlights. "It was a good pitch," he said. "I mean it sounded like a good pitch. I didn't see it."

But Ericksson, champion of clean living, stroked one out. It put the lid on some of the celebrating in the stands. We were a little too hungover to go real crazy when he got back to the dugout, but I think he understood.

Everybody, in fact, was hitting but us. A couple guys behind Ericksson including Rafa put together some doubles, and we had a 3–0 lead which stood up all the way to the bottom of the inning, when

Marianao batted around and through its lineup and our starter and went into the top of the second leading 6–3.

Our guys kept hitting, and so did their guys. At the end of seven we'd gone through four pitchers and Marianao five, Charley and I were regaining use of our limbs, and the score was Cuba 11, Land of the Free 9. We got another run on a passed ball. In the ninth we came up one run down with the sun setting in our eyes over the centerfield fence and yours truly leading off. The crowd was howling like something I'd never heard before. Castro had everybody up and pointing at me on the third-base side. Their arms went up and down together like they were working some kind of hex. Marianao's pitcher—by now their sixth—was the forty-five-year-old fat guy who'd worked the day before. The bags under his eyes were bigger than mine. He snapped off three nasty curves, and I beat one into the ground and ran down the first-base line with the jeering following me the whole way.

He broke one off on Charley, too, and Charley grounded to first. The noise was solid, a wall. Everyone was waving Cuban flags.

I leaned close to Charley's ear in the dugout. "You gotta lay off those," I said.

He shook his head. "I never noticed anything wrong with my ability to pull the ball on an outside pitch," he said.

"Then you're the only one in Cuba who hasn't," I said.

But in the middle of this local party with two strikes on him Ericksson hit his second dinger, probably the first time he'd had two in a game since Pony League. He took his time on his home-run trot, all slimmed-down two hundred sixty pounds of him, and at the end he did a somersault and landed on home plate with both feet.

For the Marianao crowd it was like the Marines had landed. When the ball left his bat the crowd noise got higher and higher pitched and then just stopped and strangled. You could hear Ericksson breathing hard as he came back to the bench. You could hear the pop of the umpire's new ball in the pitcher's glove.

That sent us into extra innings, a lot of extra innings. It got dark. Nobody scored. Charley struck out with the bases loaded in the sixteenth, and when he came back to the bench someone had poured a beer onto the dugout roof and it was dripping through onto his head. He sat there under it. He said, "I deserve it," and I said, "Yes, you do."

The Marianao skipper overmanaged and ran out of pitchers. He had an outfielder come in and fling a few, and the poor guy walked our eighth and ninth hitters with pitches in the dirt, off the backstop, into the seats. I was up. There was a conference on the mound that included some fans and a vendor. Then there was a roar, and we stretched forward out of the dugout and saw Castro up and moving through the seats to the field. Someone threw him a glove.

He crossed to the mound, and the Marianao skipper watched him come and then handed him the ball when he got there like his relief ace had just come in from the pen. Castro took the outfielder's hat for himself, but that was about it for uniform. The tails of his pleated shirt hung out. His pants looked like Rudolph Valentino's. He was wearing dress shoes.

I turned to the ump. "Is this an exhibition at this point?" I said. He said something in Spanish that I assumed was, "You're in a world of trouble now."

The crowd, which had screamed itself out hours ago, got its second wind. Hurricanes, dust devils, sandstorms in the Sahara—I don't know what the sound was like. When you opened your mouth it came and took your words away.

I looked over at Batista, who was sitting on his hands. How long was this guy going to last if he couldn't even police the national pastime?

Castro toed the rubber, worked the ball in his hand, and stared in at me like he hated everyone I'd ever been associated with.

He was right-handed. He fussed with his cap. He had a windmill delivery. I figured, let him have his fun, and he wound up and cut loose with a fastball behind my head.

The crowd reacted like he'd struck me out. I got out of the dirt and did the pro brush-off, taking time with all parts of my uniform. Then I stood in again, and he broke a pretty fair curve in by my knees, and down I went again.

What was I supposed to do? Take one for the team? Take one for the country? Get a hit, and never leave the stadium alive? He came back with his fastball high, and I thought, enough of this, and tomahawked it foul. We glared at each other. He came back with a changeup—had this guy pitched somewhere, for somebody?—again way inside, and I thought, forget it, and took it on the hip. The umpire waved me to first, and the crowd screamed about it like we were cheating.

I stood on first. The bases were now loaded for Charley. You could see the Marianao skipper wanted Castro off the mound, but what could he do?

Charley steps to the plate, and it's like the fans had been holding back on the real noisemaking up to this point. There are trumpets, cowbells, police whistles, sirens and the god-awful noise of someone by the foul pole banging two frying pans together. The attention seems to unnerve Charley. I'm trying to give him the old thumbs-up from first, but he's locked in on Castro, frozen in his stance. The end of his bat's making little circles in the air. Castro gave it the old windmill and whipped a curve past his chin. Charley bailed out and stood in again. The next pitch was a curve, too, which fooled him completely. He'd been waiting on the fastball. He started to swing, realized it was a curve breaking in on him, and ducked away to save his life. The ball hit his bat anyway. It dribbled out toward Castro. Charley gaped at it and then took off for first. I took off for second. The crowd shrieked. Ten thousand people, one shriek. All Castro had to do was gun it to first and they were out of the inning. He threw it into right field.

Pandemonium. Our eighth and ninth hitters scored. The ball skipped away from the right fielder. I kept running. The catcher'd gone down to first to back up the throw. I rounded third like Man o' War, Charley not far behind me, the fans spilling out onto the field and coming at us like a wave we were beating to shore. One kid's face was a flash of spite under a Yankee hat, a woman with long scars on her neck was grabbing for my arm. And there was Castro blocking the plate, dress shoes wide apart, Valentino pants crouched and ready, his face scared and full of hate like I was the entire North American continent bearing down on him.

Issue 127, 1993

Anne Waldman

✠

Curt Flood

Spring 1971

a box   a camera with a one-track mind

behind it

    can't see too good

        Running Man

all opening up in the dream of throaty Janis swaggering
I had last night
she's a cowboy

    a fixed star

        shining & singing

    far inside the windy city

far inside the windy country too

        you're swift & your name really turns me on,
        Mr. Flood

Curt Flood   Curt Flood   Curt Flood   Curt Flood

we're watching

& drinking beer & fretting & rooting for you!

arms & legs go so fast
I wonder why we're built
this way

big & religious

& shaky too

the wind that gives my baby chill shaky too

Money

The Big (Mental) Diamond Monkey

Energy:

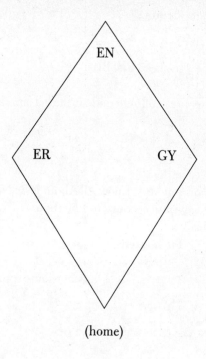

(home)

ho hum

I wonder why this game
stays the same
year after year

taut

not too easy   not too sleepy

just enough
—Balance—

(wire)

Curt Flood

stops short
        then go ahead Full Blast

suddenly break off into mid-air the bat smacks & the ball
                                                    sails

(curt)

a flood of You Must Know All About It By Now
from the hysterical crowd of 250 thou

        I'm hooked

                        in tribute sound . . .

Donald Hall

✠

The Third Inning

1. Alexander, first over the wall,
collapsed battered by stones. Instantly
the Macedonian companions
gathered their shields over his body
and these athletes of honor and brawn
withstood repeated iron assault—
to defend, to survive, to triumph.
When the King's wound healed, he divided
the known world among his companions.

2. At the center of a baseball is
five pounds of cat intestines, pressured
into a tiny marble-sized sphere.
While I write "Baseball," Ada the cat
rubs at my ankles to inform me
that nothing whatever bothers her.
Jennifer and I make love at night;
afterwards, something good continues,
as if the radio, turned on low at

3. Three A.M., told about a baseball
game all night long in Japanese or
Spanish, with the crowd noises intact.
The next morning, as Jennifer stands

at the kitchen sink staring out the
window, I gaze measuring her ass.
Then she squeezes an orange: Its bright
gelatinous membranes rupture to
fill her blue cup with sunny ichor.

4. The ship made twenty-five knots into
a fifty-knot wind over hot Gulf
water. I climbed to the topmost deck,
tilting my weight into the hot wind,
poising my heavy body into
the wind's weight, pulling myself along
rails with both hands to push against wind
that scudded black clouds into blackness
with the moon down and few stars showing.

5. Wind flattened my beard and my nostrils.
Wind gathered my shout and shuffled it.
All night the kitten walked back and forth
on our bodies biting and poking.
Meantime the old cat sniffed, hissed, and sighed
to lifelist many disloyalties;
as when the Dodgers left Ebbets Field.
It is ecstasy beyond pleasure
to watch Jennifer squeeze orange juice.

6. So the new dog's pet is the kitten.
All day she hurls herself at his huge
muzzle, bigger than she is, her mouth
wide open and her claws stretched. He snaps
without biting, love-bites; she pauses
in her fury to lick his jaws clean.
Then she hides—to leap from her secret
place onto the great boa of his
wagging magnificent golden tail.

7. All winter now aged ballplayers
rehearse their young manhood, running and
throwing under Florida's sunshine;
but remain old. In my sixtieth
year I wake fretting over some new
failure. Meeting an old friend's new wife,
I panicked and was rude. Or I ache
mildly feeling some careless anger
with my son I cannot turn away.

8. The bodies of major league baseball
players are young. We age past the field
so quickly; we diminish, watching
over decades, applauding the young
who come and go. The old cat hisses
at the kitten and pokes the new dog.
Her life is ruined and she will sink
bitter into death. At night she purrs
briefly, lying restored on our bed.

9. The leg is the dancer and the mouth
the sculptor. The tongue models vowels
or chisels consonants. Pause, pitch, pace,
and volume patina a surface
of smooth shapes the mouth closes over.
Behind our listening lips, working
the throat's silent machine, one muscle
shuts on/off/on/off: the motionless
foot and thigh of the word's world-leaper.

Issue 120, 1991

T. Coraghessan Boyle

The Hector Quesadilla Story

He was no Joltin' Joe, no Sultan of Swat, no Iron Man. For one thing, his feet hurt. And God knows no legendary immortal ever suffered so prosaic a complaint. He had shinsplints too, and corns and ingrown toenails and hemorrhoids. Demons drove burning spikes into his tailbone each time he bent to loosen his shoelaces, his limbs were skewed so awkwardly his elbows and knees might have been transposed and the once-proud knot of his frijole-fed belly had fallen like an avalanche. Worse: he was old. Old, old, old, the graybeard hobbling down the rough-hewn steps of the Senate building, the Ancient Mariner chewing on his whiskers and stumbling in his socks. Though they listed his birthdate as 1942 in the program, there were those who knew better: it was way back in '54, during his rookie year for San Buitre, that he had taken Asunción to the altar, and even in those distant days, even in Mexico, twelve-year-olds didn't marry.

When he was younger—really young, nineteen, twenty, tearing up the Mexican League like a saint of the stick—his ears were so sensitive he could hear the soft rasping friction of the pitcher's fingers as he massaged the ball and dug in for a slider, fastball, or changeup. Now he could barely hear the umpire bawling the count in his ear. And his legs. How they ached, how they groaned and creaked and chattered, how they'd gone to fat! He ate too much, that was the problem. Ate prodigiously, ate mightily, ate as if there were a hidden thing inside him, a creature all of jaws with an infinite trailing ribbon of gut. Huevos con chorizo with beans, tortillas, camarones in red sauce and a twelve-ounce steak for breakfast, the chicken in mole to steady him before afternoon games, a sea of beer to wash away the tension of the game and prepare his digestive machinery for the flaming machaca and pepper salad Asunción prepared for him in the blessed evenings of the home stand.

Five foot seven, one hundred eighty-nine and three quarters pounds. Hector Hernán Jesus y María Quesadilla. Little Cheese, they called him. Cheese, Cheese, Cheesus, went up the cry as he stepped in to pinch-hit in some late-inning crisis, Cheese, Cheese, Cheesus, building to a roar until Chavez Ravine resounded as if with the holy name of the Savior Himself when he stroked one of the clean line-drive singles that were his signature or laid down a bunt that stuck like a finger in jelly. When he fanned, when the bat went loose in the fat brown hands and he went down on one knee for support, they hissed and called him *Viejo*.

One more season, he tells himself, though he hasn't played regularly for nearly ten years and can barely trot to first after drawing a walk, One more. He tells Asunción too: One more, One more, as they sit in the gleaming kitchen of their house in Boyle Heights, he with his Carta Blanca, she with her mortar and pestle for grinding the golden petrified kernels of maize into flour for the tortillas he eats like peanuts. *Una más,* she mocks. What do you want, the Hall of Fame? Hang up your spikes, Hector.

He stares off into space, his mother's Indian features flattening his own as if the legend were true, as if she really had taken a spatula to him in the cradle, and then, dropping his thick lids as he takes a long slow swallow from the neck of the bottle, he says: Just the other day driving home from the park I saw a car on the freeway, a Mercedes with only two seats, a girl in it, her hair out back like a cloud, and you know what the license plate said? His eyes are open now, black as pitted olives. Do you? She doesn't. Cheese, he says. It said Cheese.

Then she reminds him that Hector Jr. will be twenty-nine next month and that Reina has four children of her own and another on the way. You're a grandfather, Hector—almost a great-grandfather if your son ever settled down. A moment slides by, filled with the light of the sad waning sun and the harsh Yucatano dialect of the radio announcer. *Hombres* on first and third, one down. *Abuelo,* she hisses, grinding stone against stone until it makes his teeth ache. Hang up your spikes, *abuelo*.

But he doesn't. He can't. He won't. He's no grandpa with hair the color of cigarette stains and a blanket over his knees, he's no toothless old gasser sunning himself in the park—he's a big leaguer, proud wearer of the Dodger blue, wielder of stick and glove. How can he get old? The grass is always green, the lights always shining, no clocks or periods or halves or quarters, no punch-in and punch-out: This is the game that never ends. When the heavy hitters have fanned and the pitchers' arms gone sore, when there's no joy in Mudville, taxes are killing everybody and the Russians are raising hell in Guatemala, when the manager paces the dugout like an attack dog, mind racing, searching high and low for the canny veteran to go in and do single combat, there he'll be—always, always, eternal as a monument—Hector Quesadilla, utility infielder, with the .296 lifetime batting average and service with the Reds, Phils, Cubs, Royals, and L.A. Dodgers.

So he waits. Hangs on. Trots his aching legs round the outfield grass before the game, touches his toes ten agonizing times each morning, takes extra batting practice with the rookies and slumping millionaires. Sits. Watches. Massages his feet. Waits through the scourging road trips in the Midwest and along the East Coast, down to muggy Atlanta, across to stormy Wrigley and up to frigid Candlestick, his gut clenched round an indigestible cud of meatloaf and instant potatoes and wax beans, through the terrible nightgames with the alien lights in his eyes, waits at the end of the bench for a word from the manager, for a pat on the ass, a roar, a hiss, a chorus of cheers and catcalls, the marimba pulse of bat striking ball and the sweet looping arc of the clean base hit.

And then comes a day, late in the season, the homeboys battling for the pennant with the big-stick Braves and the sneaking Jints, when he wakes from honeyed dreams in his own bed that's like an old friend with the sheets that smell of starch and soap and flowers, and feels the pain stripped from his body as if at the touch of a healer's fingertips. Usually he dreams nothing, the night a blank, an erasure, and opens his eyes on the agonies of the martyr strapped to a bed of nails. Then he limps to the toilet, makes a poor discolored water, rinses the dead taste from his mouth and staggers to the kitchen table where food, only food, can revive in him the interest in drawing another breath. He butters tortillas and folds them into his mouth, spoons up egg and melted jack cheese and frijoles refritos with the green salsa, lashes into his steak as if it were cut from the thigh of Kerensky, the Atlanta relief ace who'd twice that season caught him looking at a full-count fastball with men in scoring position. But not today. Today is different, a sainted day, a day on which sunshine sits in the windows like a gift of the Magi and the chatter of the starlings in the crapped-over palms across the street is a thing that approaches the divine music of the spheres. What can it be?

In the kitchen it hits him: pozole in a pot on the stove, carnitas in the saucepan, the table spread with sweetcakes, buñuelos and the little marzipan *dulces* he could kill for. *Feliz cumpleaños,* Asunción pipes as he steps through the doorway. Her face is lit with the smile of her mother, her mother's mother, the line of gift-givers descendant to the happy conquistadors and joyous Aztecs. A kiss, a *dulce* and then a knock at the door and Reina, fat with life, throwing her arms around him while her children gobble up the table, the room, their grandfather, with eyes that swallow their faces. Happy birthday, Daddy, Reina says, and Franklin, her youngest, is handing him the gift.

And Hector Jr.?

But he doesn't have to fret about Hector Jr., his firstborn, the boy with these same great sad eyes who'd sat in the dugout in his Reds uniform when they lived in Cincy and worshiped the pudgy icon of his father until the parish priest had to straighten him out on his hagiography, Hector Jr. who studies English at USC and day and night writes his thesis on a poet his father has never heard of, because here he is, walking in the front door with his mother's smile and a store-wrapped gift—a book, of course. Then Reina's children line up to kiss the *abuelo*—they'll be sitting in the box seats this afternoon—and suddenly he knows so much: He will play today, he will hit, oh yes, can there be a doubt? He sees it already. Kerensky, the son of a whore. Extra innings. Koerner or Manfredonia or Brooksie on third.

The ball like an orange, a mango, a muskmelon, the clean swipe of the bat, the delirium of the crowd, and the gimpy *abuelo*, a big leaguer still, doffing his cap and taking a tour of the bases in a stately trot, Sultan for a day.

Could things ever be so simple?

In the bottom of the ninth, with the score tied at five and Reina's kids full of Coke, hotdogs, peanuts, and ice cream and getting restless, with Asunción clutching her rosary as if she were drowning and Hector Jr.'s nose stuck in some book, Dupuy taps him to hit for the pitcher with two down and Fast Freddie Phelan on second. The eighth man in the lineup, Spider Martinez from Muchas Vacas, D.R., has just whiffed on three straight pitches and Corcoran, the Braves' left-handed relief man, is all of a sudden pouring it on. Throughout the stadium a hush has fallen over the crowd, the torpor of suppertime, the game poised at apogee. Shadows are lengthening in the outfield, swallows flitting across the face of the scoreboard, here a fan drops into his beer, there a big mama gathers up her purse, her knitting, her shopping bags and parasol and thinks of dinner. Hector sees it all. This is the moment of catharsis, the moment to take it out.

As Martinez slumps toward the dugout, Dupuy, a laconic, embittered man who keeps his suffering inside and drinks Gelusil like water, takes hold of Hector's arm. His eyes are red-rimmed and paunchy, doleful as a basset hound's. Bring the runner in, Champ, he rasps. First pitch fake a bunt, then hit away. Watch Booger at third. Uh-huh, Hector mumbles, snapping his gum. Then he slides his bat from the rack—white ash, tape-wrapped grip, personally blessed by the Archbishop of Guadalajara and his twenty-seven acolytes—and starts for the dugout steps, knowing the course of the next three minutes as surely as his blood knows the course of his veins. The familiar cry will go up—Cheese, Cheese, Cheesus—and he'll amble up to the batter's box, knocking imaginary dirt from his spikes, adjusting the straps of his golf gloves, tugging at his underwear and fiddling with his batting helmet. His face will be impenetrable. Corcoran will work the ball in his glove, maybe tip back his cap for a little hair grease and then give him a look of psychopathic hatred. Hector has seen it before. Me against you. My record, my career, my house, my family, my life, my mutual funds and beer distributorship against yours. He's been hit in the elbow, the knee, the groin, the head. Nothing fazes him. Nothing. Murmuring a prayer to Santa Griselda, patroness of the sun-blasted Sonoran village where he was born like a heat blister on his mother's womb, Hector Hernán Jesus y María Quesadilla will step into the batter's box, ready for anything.

But it's a game of infinite surprises.

Before Hector can set foot on the playing field, Corcoran suddenly doubles up in pain, Phelan goes slack at second and the catcher and shortstop are hustling out to the mound, tailed an instant later by trainer and pitching coach. First thing Hector thinks is a groin pull, then appendicitis, and finally, as Corcoran goes down on one knee, poison. He'd once seen a man shot in the gut at Obregon City, but the report had been loud as a thunderclap and he hears nothing now but the enveloping hum of the crowd. Corcoran is rising shakily, the trainer and pitching coach supporting him while the catcher kicks meditatively in the dirt, and now Mueller, the Atlanta *cabeza*, is striding big-bellied out of the dugout, head down as if to be sure his feet are following orders. Halfway to the mound, Mueller flicks his right hand across his ear quick as a horse flicking its tail, and it's all she wrote for Corcoran.

Poised on the dugout steps like a bird dog, Hector waits, his eyes riveted on the bullpen. Please, he whispers, praying for the intercession of the Niño and pledging a hundred votary candles—at least, at least. Can it be? Yes, milk of my Mother, yes—Kerensky himself strutting out onto the field like a fighting cock. Kerensky!

Come to the birthday boy, Kerensky, he murmurs, so certain he's going to put it in the stands he could point like the immeasurable Bambino. His tired old legs shuffle with impatience as Kerensky stalks across the field, and then he's turning to pick Asunción out of the crowd. She's on her feet now, Reina too, the kids come alive beside her. And Hector Jr., the book forgotten, his face transfigured with the look of rapture he used to get when he was a boy sitting on the steps of the dugout. Hector can't help himself: He grins and gives them the thumbs-up sign.

Then, as Kerensky fires his warm-up smoke, the loudspeaker crackles and Hector emerges from the shadow of the dugout into the tapering golden shafts of the late-afternoon sun. That pitch, I want that one, he mutters, carrying his bat like a javelin and shooting a glare at Kerensky, but something's wrong here, the announcer's got it screwed up: BATTING FOR RARITAN, NUMBER THIRTY-NINE, DAVE TOOL. What the—? And now somebody's tugging at his sleeve and he's turning to gape with incomprehension at the freckle-faced batboy, Dave Tool striding out of the dugout with his big forty-two-ounce stick, Dupuy's face locked up like a vault and the crowd, on its feet, chanting Tool, Tool, Tool! For a moment he just stands there, frozen with disbelief. Then Tool is brushing by him and the idiot of a batboy is leading him toward the dugout as if he were an old blind fisherman poised on the edge of the dock.

He feels as if his legs have been cut from under him. Tool! Dupuy is yanking him for Tool? For what? So he can play the lefty-righty percentages like some chess head or something? Tool, of all people. Tool, with his thirty-five home runs a season and lifetime B.A. of .234, Tool who's worn so many uniforms they had to expand the league to make room for him, what's he going to do? Raging, Hector flings down his bat and comes at Dupuy like a cat tossed in a bay. You crazy, you jerk, he sputters. I woulda hit him, I woulda won the game. I dreamed it. And then, his voice breaking: It's my birthday for Christ's sake!

But Dupuy can't answer him, because on the first pitch Tool slams a real worm burner to short and the game is going into extra innings.

By seven o'clock, half the fans have given up and gone home. In the top of the fourteenth, when the visitors came up with a pair of runs on a two-out pinch-hit home run, there was a real exodus, but then the Dodgers struck back for two to knot it up again. Then it was three up and three down, regular as clockwork. Now, at the end of the nineteenth, with the score deadlocked at seven all and the players dragging themselves around the field like gutshot horses, Hector is beginning to think he may get a second chance after all. Especially the way Dupuy's been using up players like some crazy general on the western front, yanking pitchers, juggling his defense, throwing in pinch runners and pinch hitters until he's just about gone through the

entire roster. Asunción is still there among the faithful, the foolish,
and the self-deluded, fumbling with her rosary and mouthing prayers
for Jesus Christ Our Lord, the Madonna, Hector, the home team, and
her departed mother, in that order. Reina too, looking like the survivor of some disaster, Franklin and Alfredo asleep in their seats, the
niñitas gone off somewhere—for Coke and dogs, maybe. And Hector
Jr. looks like he's going to stick it out too, though he should be back in
his closet writing about the mystical so-and-so and the way he illus-
trates his poems with gods and men and serpents. Watching him,
Hector can feel his heart turn over.

In the bottom of the twentieth, with one down and Gilley on first—
he's a starting pitcher but Dupuy sent him in to run for Manfredonia
after Manfredonia jammed his ankle like a turkey and had to be
helped off the field—Hector pushes himself up from the bench and
ambles down to where Dupuy sits in the corner, contemplatively spitting a gout of tobacco juice and saliva into the drain at his feet. Let me
hit, Bernard, come on, Hector says, easing down beside him.

Can't, comes the reply, and Dupuy never even raises his head.
Can't risk it, Champ. Look around you—and here the manager's
voice quavers with uncertainty, with fear and despair and the dull
edge of hopelessness—I got nobody left. I hit you, I got to play you.

No, no, you don't understand—I'm going to win it, I swear.

And then the two of them, like old bankrupts on a bench in Miami
Beach, look up to watch Phelan hit into a double play.

A buzz runs through the crowd when the Dodgers take the field for
the top of the twenty-second. Though Phelan is limping, Thorkelsson's asleep on his feet and Dorfman, fresh on the mound, is the only
pitcher left on the roster, the moment is electric. One more inning
and they tie the record set by the Mets and Giants back in '64, and
then they're making history. Drunk, sober, and then drunk again, saturated with fats and nitrates and sugar, the crowd begins to come to
life. Go Dodgers! Eat shit! Yo Mama! Phelan's a bum!

Hector can feel it too. The rage and frustration that had consumed
him back in the ninth are gone, replaced by a dawning sense of
wonder—he could have won it then, yes, and against his nemesis

Kerensky too—but the Niño and Santa Griselda have been saving him for something greater. He sees it now, knows it in his bones: He's going to be the hero of the longest game in history.

As if to bear him out, Dorfman, the kid from Albuquerque, puts in a good inning, cutting the bushed Braves down in order. In the dugout, Doc Pusser, the team physician, is handing out the little green pills that keep your eyes open and Dupuy is blowing into a cup of coffee and staring morosely out at the playing field. Hector watches as Tool, who'd stayed in the game at first base, fans on three straight pitches, then he shoves in beside Dorfman and tells the kid he's looking good out there. With his big cornhusker's ears and nose like a tweezer, Dorfman could be a caricature of the green rookie. He says nothing. Hey, don't let it get to you, kid—I'm going to win this one for you. Next inning or maybe the inning after. Then he tells him how he saw it in a vision and how it's his birthday and the kid's going to get the victory, one of the biggest of all time. Twenty-four, twenty-five innings maybe.

Hector had heard of a game once in the Mexican League that took three days to play and went seventy-three innings, did Dorfman know that? It was down in Culiacán. Chito Martí, the converted bullfighter, had finally ended it by dropping down dead of exhaustion in center-field, allowing Sexto Silvestro, who'd broken his leg rounding third, to crawl home with the winning run. But Hector doesn't think this game will go that long. Dorfman sighs and extracts a bit of wax from his ear as Pantaleo, the third-string catcher, hits back to the pitcher to end the inning. I hope not, he says, uncoiling himself from the bench, my arm'd fall off.

Ten o'clock comes and goes. Dorfman's still in there, throwing breaking stuff and a little smoke at the Braves, who look as if they just stepped out of *Night of the Living Dead*. The home team isn't doing much better. Dupuy's run through the whole team but for Hector, and three or four of the guys have been in there since two in the afternoon; the rest are a bunch of ginks and gimps who can barely stand up. Out in the stands, the fans look grim. The vendors ran out of beer an hour back, and they haven't had dogs or kraut or Coke or anything since eight-thirty.

In the bottom of the twenty-seventh Phelan goes berserk in the dugout and Dupuy has to pin him to the floor while Doc Pusser shoves something up his nose to calm him. Next inning the balls-and-strikes ump passes out cold and Dorfman, who's beginning to look a little fagged, walks the first two batters but manages to weasel his way out of the inning without giving up the go-ahead run. Meanwhile, Thorkelsson has been dropping ice cubes down his trousers to keep awake, Martinez is smoking something suspicious in the can and Ferenc Fortnoi, the third baseman, has begun talking to himself in a tortured Slovene dialect. For his part, Hector feels stronger and more alert as the game goes on. Though he hasn't had a bite since breakfast he feels impervious to the pangs of hunger, as if he were preparing himself, mortifying his flesh like a saint in the desert.

And then, in the top of the thirty-first, with half the fans asleep and the other half staring into nothingness like the inmates of the asylum of Our Lady of Guadeloupe where Hector had once visited his halfwit uncle when he was a boy, Pluto Morales cracks one down the first base line and Tool flubs it. Right away it looks like trouble, because Chester Bubo is running around right field looking up at the sky like a birdwatcher while the ball snakes through the grass, caroms off his left foot and coasts like silk to the edge of the warning track. Morales meanwhile is rounding second and coming on for third, running in slow motion, flat-footed and humpbacked, his face drained of color, arms flapping like the undersized wings of some big flightless bird. It's not even close. By the time Bubo can locate the ball, Morales is ten feet from the plate, pitching into a face-first slide that's at least three parts collapse and that's it, the Braves are up by one. It looks black for the home team. But Dorfman, though his arm has begun to swell like a sausage, shows some grit, bears down and retires the side to end the historic top of the unprecedented thirty-first inning.

Now, at long last, the hour has come. It'll be Bubo, Dorfman, and Tool for the Dodgers in their half of the inning, which means that Hector will hit for Dorfman. I been saving you, Champ, Dupuy rasps, the empty Gelusil bottle clenched in his fist like a hand grenade. Go on in there, he murmurs and his voice fades away to nothing as Bubo pops the first pitch up in back of the plate. Go on in there and do your stuff.

Sucking in his gut, Hector strides out onto the brightly lit field like a nineteen-year-old, the familiar cry in his ears, the haggard fans on their feet, a sickle moon sketched in overhead as if in some cartoon strip featuring drunken husbands and the milkman. Asunción looks as if she's been nailed to the cross, Reina wakes with a start and shakes the little ones into consciousness and Hector Jr. staggers to his feet like a battered middleweight coming out for the fifteenth round. They're all watching him. The fans whose lives are like empty sacks, the wife who wants him home in front of the TV, his divorced daughter with the four kids and another on the way, his son, pride of his life, who reads for the doctor of philosophy while his crazy *padrecito* puts on a pair of long stockings and chases around after a little white ball like a case of arrested development. He'll show them. He'll show them some *cojones,* some true grit and desire: The game's not over yet.

On the mound for the Braves is Bo Brannerman, a big mustachioed machine of a man, normally a starter but pressed into desperate relief service tonight. A fine pitcher—Hector would be the first to admit it— but he just pitched two nights ago and he's worn thin as wire. Hector steps up to the plate, feeling legendary. He glances over at Tool in the on-deck circle, and then down at Booger, the third-base coach. All systems go. He cuts at the air twice and then watches Brannerman rear back and release the ball: Strike one. Hector smiles. Why rush things? Give them a thrill. He watches a low outside slider that just about bounces to even the count, and then stands there like a statue as Brannerman slices the corner of the plate for strike two. From the stands, a chant of *Viejo, Viejo,* and Asunción's piercing soprano, Hit him, Hector!

Hector has no worries, the moment eternal, replayed through games uncountable, with pitchers who were over the hill when he was a rookie with San Buitre, with pups like Brannerman, with big lea-guers and Hall of Famers. Here it comes, Hector, ninety-two m.p.h., the big *gringo* trying to throw it by you, the matchless wrists, the flaw-less swing, one terrific moment of suspended animation—and all of a sudden you're starring in your own movie.

How does it go? The ball cutting through the night sky like a comet, arching high over the centerfielder's hapless scrambling form to slam off the wall while your legs churn up the base paths, rounding first in a gallop, taking second and heading for third . . . but wait, you spill hot coffee on your hand and you can't feel it, the demons apply the live wire to your tailbone, the legs give out and they cut you down at third while the stadium erupts in howls of execration and abuse and the *niñitos* break down, faces flooded with tears of humiliation, Hector Jr. turning his back in disgust, and Asunción raging like harpie, *Abuelo! Abuelo! Abuelo!*

Stunned, shrunken, humiliated, you stagger back to the dugout in a maelstrom of abuse, paper cups, flying spittle, your life a waste, the game a cheat, and then, crowning irony, that bum Tool, worthless all the way back to his washerwoman grandmother and the drunken muttering whey-faced tribe that gave him suck, stands tall like a giant and sends the first pitch out of the park to tie it. Oh, the pain. Flat feet, fire in your legs, your poor tired old heart skipping a beat in mortification. And now Dupuy, red in the face, shouting: The game could be over but for you, you crazy gimpy old beaner washout! You want to hide in your locker, bury yourself under the shower room floor, but you have to watch as the next two men reach base and you pray with fervor that they'll score and put an end to your debasement. But no, Thorkelsson whiffs and the new inning dawns as inevitably as the new minute, the new hour, the new day, endless, implacable, world without end.

But wait, wait: Who's going to pitch? Dorfman's out, there's nobody left, the astonishing thirty-second inning is marching across the scoreboard like an invading army and suddenly Dupuy is standing over you—no, no, he's down on one knee, begging. Hector, he's saying, didn't you use to pitch down in Mexico when you were a kid, didn't I hear that someplace? Yes, you're saying, yes, but that was—

And then you're out on the mound, in command once again, elevated like some half-mad old king in a play, and throwing smoke. The first two batters go down on strikes and the fans are rabid with excitement, Asunción will raise a shrine, Hector Jr. worships you more than all the poets that ever lived, but can it be? You walk the next three and then give up the grand slam to little Tommy Oshimisi! Mother of God, will it never cease? But wait, wait, wait: Here comes the bottom of the thirty-second and Brannerman's wild. He walks a couple, gets a couple out, somebody reaches on an infield single and the bases are loaded for you, Hector Quesadilla, stepping up to the plate now like the Iron Man himself. The wind-up, the delivery, the ball hanging there like a *piñata,* like a birthday gift, and then the stick flashes in your hands like an archangel's sword, and the game goes on forever.

Issue 93, 1984

TRAVELS

Jack Kerouac

※

The Mexican Girl

I had bought my ticket and was waiting for the L.A. bus when all of a sudden I saw the cutest little Mexican girl in slacks come cutting across my sight. She was in one of the buses that had just pulled in with a big sigh of airbrakes and was discharging passengers for a rest stop. Her breasts stuck out straight; her little thighs looked delicious; her hair was long and lustrous black; and her eyes were great blue windows with timidities inside. I wished I was on her bus. A pain stabbed my heart, as it did every time I saw a girl I loved who was going the opposite direction in this too big world. "Los Angeles coach now loading in door two," says the announcer and I get on. I saw her sitting alone. I dropped right opposite her on the other window and began scheming right off. I was so lonely, so sad, so tired, so quivering, so broken, so beat that I got up my courage, the courage necessary to approach a strange girl, and acted. Even then I had to spend five minutes beating my thighs in the dark as the bus rolled down the road. "You gotta, you gotta or you'll die! Damn fool talk to her! What's wrong with you? Aren't you tired enough of yourself by now?" And before I knew what I was doing I leaned across the aisle to her (she was trying to sleep on the seat) "Miss, would you like to use my raincoat for a pillow?" She looked up with a smile and said "No, thank you very much." I sat back trembling; I lit a butt. I waited till she looked at me, with a sad little sidelook of love, and I got right up and leaned over her. "May I sit with you, Miss?"

"If you wish."

And this I did. "Where going?"

"L.A." I loved the way she said L.A.; I love the way everybody says L.A. on the Coast, it's their one and only golden town when all is said and done.

"That's where I'm going too!" I cried. "I'm very glad you let me sit with you, I was very lonely and I've been traveling a hell of a long time." And we settled down to telling our stories. Her story was this; she had a husband and child. The husband beat her so she left him, back at Sabinal south of Fresno, and was going to L.A. to live with her sister awhile. She left her little son with her family, who were grape pickers and lived in a shack in the vineyards. She had nothing to do but brood and get mad. I felt like putting my arms around her right away. We talked and talked. She said she loved to talk with me. Pretty soon she was saying she wished she could go to New York too. "Maybe we could!" I laughed. The bus groaned up Grapevine Pass and then we were coming down into the great sprawls of light. Without coming to any particular agreement we began holding hands, and in the same way it was mutely and beautifully and purely decided that when I got my hotel room in L.A. she would be beside me. I ached all over for her; I leaned my face in her beautiful hair. Her little shoulders drove me mad, I hugged her and hugged her. And she loved it.

"I love love," she said closing her eyes. I promised her beautiful love. I gloated over her. Our stories were told, we subsided into silence and sweet anticipatory thoughts. It was as simple as that. You could have all your Peaches and Vi's and Ruth Glenarms and Marylous and Eleanors and Carmens in this world, this was my girl and my kind of girlsoul, and I told her that. She confessed she saw me watching from the bus station bench. "I thought you was a nice college boy."

"Oh I'm a college boy!" I assured her. The bus arrived in Hollywood. In the gray dirty dawn, like the dawn Joel McCrea met Veronica Lake in the diner in the picture *Sullivan's Travels,* she slept in my lap. I looked greedily out the window; stucco houses and palms and Drive-ins, the whole mad thing, the ragged promised land, the fantastic end of America. We got off the bus at Main Street which was no different than where you get off a bus in Kansas City or Chicago or

Boston, redbrick, dirty, characters drifting by, trolleys grating in the hopeless dawn, the whorey smell of a big city.

And here my mind went haywire, I don't know why. I began getting foolish paranoiac visions that Teresa, or Terry, her name, was a common little hustler who worked the buses for a guy's bucks by making regular appointments like ours in L.A. where she brought the sucker first to a breakfast place, where her boy waited, and then to a certain hotel to which he had access with his gun or his whatever. I never confessed this to her. We ate breakfast and a pimp kept watching us; I fancied Terry was making secret eyes at him. I was tired and felt strange and lost in a faraway, disgusting place. The goof of terror took over my thoughts and made me act petty and cheap. "Do you know that guy?" I said.

"What guy you mean, ho-ney?" I let it drop. She was slow and hungup in everything she did; it took her a long time to eat, she chewed slowly and stared into space, and smoked a cigarette slowly, and kept talking, and I was like a haggard ghost suspicioning every move she made, thinking she was stalling for time. This was all a fit of sickness. I was sweating as we went down the street hand in hand. Fellows kept turning and looking at us. The first hotel we hit had a vacant room and before I knew it I was locking the door behind me and she was sitting on the bed taking off her shoes. I kissed her meekly. Better she'd never know. To relax our nerves I knew we needed whiskey, especially me. I ran out and fiddled all over for twelve blocks hurrying till I found a pint of whiskey for sale at a newsstand. I ran back all energy. Terry was in the bathroom fixing her face. I poured one big drink in a waterglass and we had slugs. Oh it was sweet and delicious and worth my whole life and lugubrious voyage. I stood behind her at the mirror and we danced in the bathroom that way. I began talking about my friends back east. I said "You oughta meet a great girl I know called Dorie. She's a sixfoot redhead. If you came to New York she'd show you where to get work."

"Who is this sixfoot redhead?" she demanded suspiciously. "Why do you tell me about her?" In her simple soul she couldn't fathom my kind of glad nervous talk. I let it drop. She began to get drunk in the bathroom.

"Come on to bed!" I kept saying.

"Sixfoot redhead, hey? And I thought you was a nice college boy, I saw you in your nice sweater and I said to myself 'Hmm ain't he nice'—No! And no! And no! You have to be a goddam pimp like all of them!"

"What in the hell are you talking about?"

"Don't stand there and tell me that sixfoot redhead ain't a madam, 'cause I know a madam when I hear about one, and you, you're just a pimp like all the rest of 'em I meet, everybody's a pimp."

"Listen Terry, I am not a pimp. I swear to you on the Bible I am not a pimp. Why should I be a pimp. My only interest is you."

"All the time I thought I met a nice boy. I was so glad, I hugged myself and said 'Hmm a real nice boy instead of a damn pimp'!"

"Terry," I pleaded with all my soul, "please listen to me and understand. I'm not a pimp, I'm just Sal Paradise, look at my wallet." And an hour ago I thought *she* was a hustler. How sad it was. Our minds with their store of madness had diverged. O gruesome life how I moaned and pleaded and then I got mad and realized I was pleading with a dumb little Mexican wench and I told her so; and before I knew it I picked up her red pumps and threw them at the bathroom door and told her to get out. "Go on, beat it!" I'd sleep and forget it; I had my own life; my own sad and ragged life forever. There was a dead silence in the bathroom. I took my clothes off and went to bed. Terry came out with tears of sorriness in her eyes. In her simple and funny little mind had been decided the fact that a pimp does not throw a woman's shoes against the door and does not tell her to get out. In reverent and sweet silence she took her things off and slipped her tiny body into the sheets with me. It was brown as grapes. Her hips were so narrow she couldn't bear a child without getting gashed open; a Caesarian scar crossed her poor belly. Her legs were like little sticks. She was only four foot ten. I made love to her in the sweetness of the weary morning. Then, two tired angels of some kind, hung up forlornly in an L.A. shelf, having found the closest and most delicious thing in life together, we fell asleep and slept till late afternoon.

For the next fifteen days we were together for better or worse. We decided to hitchhike to New York together; she was going to be my girl in town. I envisioned wild complexities, a season, a new season.

First we had to work and earn enough money for the trip. Terry was all for starting at once with my twenty dollars. I didn't like it. And like a damnfool I considered the problem for two days reading the want ads of wild new L.A. papers I'd never seen before in my life, in cafeterias and bars, until my twenty'd dwindled to twelve. The situation was growing. We were happy as kids in our little hotel room. In the middle of the night I got up because I couldn't sleep, pulled the cover over baby's bare brown shoulder, and examined the L.A. night. What brutal, hot, siren-whining nights they are! Right across the street there was trouble. An old rickety rundown roominghouse was the scene of some kind of tragedy. The cruiser was pulled up below and the cops were questioning an old man with gray hair. Sobbings came from within. I could hear everything, together with the hum of my hotel neon. I never felt sadder in my life. L.A. is the loneliest and most brutal of American cities; New York gets godawful cold in the winter but there's a feeling of whacky comradeship somewhere in some streets. L.A. is a jungle.

South Main Street, where Terry and I took strolls with hotdogs, was a fantastic carnival of lights and wildness. Booted cops frisked people on practically every corner. The beatest characters in the country swarmed on the sidewalks—all of it under those soft Southern California stars that are lost in the brown halo of the huge desert encampment L.A. really is. You could smell tea, weed, I mean marijuana floating in the air, together with the chili beans and beer. That grand wild sound of bop floated from beerparlor jukes, Dizzy and Bird and Bags and early Miles; it mixed medleys with every-kind of cowboy and boogiewoogie in the American night. Everybody looked like Hunkey. Wild negroes with bop caps and goatees came laughing by; then longhaired brokendown hipsters straight off Route 66 from New York, then old desert rats carrying packs and heading for a park bench at the Plaza, then Methodist ministers with ravelled sleeves, and an occasional Nature Boy saint in beard and sandals. I wanted to meet them all, talk to everybody, but Terry hurried along, we were busy trying to get a buck together, like everybody else.

We went to Hollywood to try to work in the drugstore at Sunset and Vine. The questions that were asked of us in upstairs offices to determine our fitness for the slime of the sodafountain greaseracks were so sinister that I had to laugh. It turned my gut. Sunset and Vine!—what a corner! Now there's a corner! Great families off jalopies from the hinterlands stood around the sidewalk gaping for sight of some movie star and the movie star never showed up. When a limousine passed they rushed eagerly to the curb and ducked to look: some character in dark glasses sat inside with a bejewelled blonde. "Don Ameche! Don Ameche!" "No George Murphy! George Murphy!" They milled around looking at one another. Luscious little girls by the thousands rushed around with Drive-in trays; they'd come to Hollywood to be movie stars and instead got all involved in everybody's garbage including Darryl Zanuck's. Handsome queer boys who had come to Hollywood to be cowboys walked around wetting their eyebrows with hincty fingertip. Those beautiful little gone gals cut by in slacks in a continuous unbelievable stream; you thought you were in heaven but it was only Purgatory and everybody was about to be pardoned, paroled, powdered and put down; the girls came to be starlets; they up-ended in Drive-ins with pouts and goosepimples on their bare legs. Terry and I tried to find work at the Drive-ins. It was no soap anywhere, thank God. Hollywood Boulevard was a great screaming frenzy of cars; there were minor accidents at least once a minute; everybody was rushing off towards the furthest palm . . . and beyond that was the desert and nothingness. So they thought. You don't expect everybody to know that you can find water in a kopash cactus, or sweet taffy in your old mesquite. Hollywood Sams stood in front of swank restaurants arguing exactly, loudly and showoff the same way Broadway Sams argue on Jacobs Beach sidewalks New York, only here they wore lightweight suits and their talk was even more dreary and unutterably cornier. Tall cadaverous preachers shuddered by. Seventy-year-old World Rosicrucian ladies with tiaras in their hair stood under palms signifying nothing. Fat screaming women ran across the Boulevard to get in line for the quiz shows. I saw Jerry Colona buying a car at Buick Motors; he was inside the vast plateglass window fingering his mustachio, incredible, real, like seeing the Three Stooges seriously ashen-faced in a real room. Terry and I ate in a cafeteria downtown which was decorated to look like a grotto, with metal tits spurting everywhere and great impersonal stone buttoxes belonging to deities of fish and soapy Neptune. People

ate lugubrious meals around the waterfalls, their faces green with marine sorrow. All the cops in L.A. looked like handsome gigolos; obviously, they'd come to L.A. to make the movies. Everybody had come
to make the movies, even me. Terry and I were finally reduced to trying to get jobs on South Main Street among the beat countermen and
dishgirls who made no bones about their beatness and even there it
was no go. We still had twelve dollars.

"Man, I'm going to get my clothes from Sis and we'll hitchhike to
New York," said Terry. "Come on man. Let's do it. If you can't boogie I know I'll show you how." That last part was a song of hers she
kept singing, after a famous record. We hurried to her sister's house
in the sliverous Mexican shacks somewhere beyond Alameda Avenue. I waited in a dark alley behind Mexican kitchens because her
sister wasn't supposed to see me and like it. Dogs ran by. There were
little lamps illuminating the little rat alleys. I stood there swigging
from the bottle of wine and eyeing the stars and digging the sounds of
the neighborhood. I could hear Terry and her sister arguing in the
soft warm night. I was ready for anything. Terry came out and led me
by the hand to Central Avenue, which is the colored main drag of
L.A. And what a wild place it is, with chickenshacks barely big
enough to house a jukebox and the jukebox blowing nothing but
blues, bop and jump. We went up dirty tenement stairs and came to
the room of Terry's friend, Margarina, a colored girl apparently
named by her loving mother after the spelling on an oleo wrapper.
Margarina, a lovely mulatto, owed Terry a skirt and a pair of shoes;
her husband was black as spades and kindly. He went right out and
bought a pint of whiskey to host me proper. I tried to pay part of it
but he said no. They had two little children. The kids bounced on the
bed, it was their play-place. They put their arms around me and
looked at me with wonder. The wild humming night of Central Avenue, the night of Hamp's *Central Avenue Breakdown,* howled and
boomed along outside. They were singing in the halls, singing from
their windows, just hell be damned and lookout. Terry got her
clothes and we said goodbye. We went down to a chickenshack and
played records on the jukebox. Yakking with our beer we decided
what to do: we decided to hitch to New York with our remaining
monies. She had five dollars coming from her sister, we rushed back

to the shacks. So before the daily room rent was due again we packed up and took off on a red car to Arcadia, California, where Santa Anita racetrack is located under snowcapped mountains as I well knew from boyhood pastings of horserace pictures in sad old notebooks showing Azucar winning in 1935 the great $100,000 'Cap and you see dim snows heaped over the backstretch mountains. Route 66. It was night. We were pointed towards that enormity which is the American continent. Holding hands we walked several miles down the dark road to get out of the populated district. It was a Saturday night. We stood under a roadlamp thumbing when suddenly cars full of young kids roared by with streamers flying. "Yaah! yaah! we won! we won!" they all shouted. Then they yoo-hooed us and got great glee out of seeing a guy and a girl on the road. Dozens of them passed in successive jalopies, young faces and "throaty young voices" as the saying goes. I hated every one of them. Who did they think were yaahing at somebody on the road because they were little high school punks and their parents carved the roast beef on Sunday afternoons. Nor did we get a ride. We had to walk back to town and worse of all we needed coffee and had the misfortune of going into the same gaudy wood-laced place with old soda johns with beerfountain mustaches out front. The same kids were there but we were still minding our own business. Terry and I sipped our coffee and cocoa. We had battered bags and all the world before us . . . all that ground out there, that desert dirt and rat tat tat. We looked like a couple of sullen Indians in a Navajo Springs sodafountain, black bent heads at a table. The schoolkids saw now that Terry was a Mexican, a Pachuco wildcat; and that her boy was worse than that. With her pretty nose in the air she cut out of there and we wandered together in the dark up along the ditches of highways. I carried the bags and wanted to carry more. We made tracks and cut along and were breathing fogs in the cold night air. I didn't want to go on another minute without a warm night's rest in a warm sack together. Morning be damned, let's hide from the world another night. I wanted to fold her up in my system of limbs under no light but stars in the window. We went to a motel court and asked if they had a cabin. Yes. We bought a comfortable little suite for four dollars. I was spending my money anyhow. Shower, bath towels, wall radio and all, just for one more night. We held each other tight. We had long serious talks and took baths and discussed things on the pillow with light on and then with light out. Something was being proved, I was convincing her of something, which she accepted, and we concluded the pact in the dark, breathless. Then pleased, like little lambs.

In the morning we boldly struck out on our new plan. Terry wore her dark glasses with authority. Her pretty little, severe face beneath, with the noble nose, almost hawk-like Indian nose but with upswerved cute hollow cheekbones to make an oval and a prettywoman blush, with red ruby full lips and Aunt Jemima Skirt teeth, mud nowhere on her but was imprinted in the pigment of the Mongol skin. We were going to take a bus to Bakersfield with the last eight dollars and work picking grapes. "See instead of going to New York now we're all set to work awhile and get what we need, then we'll go, in a bus, we won't have to hitchhike, you see how no good it is . . ."

We arrived in Bakersfield in late afternoon, with our plan to hit every fruit wholesaler in town. Terry said we could live in tents on the job. The thought of me lying there in a tent, and picking grapes in the cool California mornings after nights of guitar music and wine with dipped grapes, hit me right. "Don't worry about a thing."

But there were no jobs to be had and much confusion with everybody giving confused Indian information and innumerable tips ("Go out to County Road you'll find Sacano") and no job materialized. So we went to a Chinese restaurant and had a dollar's worth of chow mein among the sad Saturday afternoon families, digging them, and set out with reinforced bodies. We went across the Southern Pacific tracks to Mexican town. Terry jabbered with her brethren asking for jobs. It was night now, we had a few dollars left, and the little Mextown street was one blazing bulb of lights: movie marquees, fruit stands, penny arcades, Five and Tens and hundreds of rickety trucks and mudspattered jalopies parked all over. Whole Mexican fruitpicking families wandered around eating popcorn. Terry talked to everybody. I was beginning to despair. What I needed, what Terry needed too was a drink so we bought a quart of California port wine for 35 cents and went to the railyards to drink. We found a place where hoboes had drawn up crates to sit over fires. We sat there and drank the wine. On our left were the freight cars, sad and sooty red beneath the moon; straight ahead the lights and airport pokers of Bakersfield proper; to our right a tremendous aluminum Quonset warehouse. I remembered it later in passing. Ah it was a fine night, a warm night, a wine-drinking night, a moony night, and a night to hug your girl and talk and spit and be heavengoing. This we did. She was a drinking little fool and kept up with me and passed me and went right on talking till midnight. We never moved from those crates. Occasionally bums passed, Mexican mothers passed with children, and the prowl car came by and the cop got out to leak but most of the time we were alone and mixing up our souls more and ever more till it would be terribly hard to say goodbye. At midnight we got up and goofed towards the highway.

Terry had a new idea. We would hitch to Sabinal, her hometown up the San Joaquin valley, and live in her brother's garage. Anything was all right to me, especially a nice garage. On the road I made Terry sit down on my bag to make her look like a woman in distress and right off a truck stopped and we ran for it all glee-giggles. The man was a good man, his truck was poor. He roared and crawled on up the Valley. We got to Sabinal in the wee hours of the morning not until after that tired sleepy beau' pushed his old rattle rig from Indian Ponce de Leon Springs of down-valley up the screaming cricket fields of grape and lemon four hours, to let us off, with a cheerful "So long pard," and here we were with the wine finished (I, while she slept in the truck). Now I'm stoned. The sky is grey in the east. "Wake, for morning in the bowl of night . . . ." There was a quiet leafy square, we walked around it, past sleeping sodafountains and barber shops, looking for some garage. There was no garage. Ghostly white houses. A whistle stop on the S.P. A California town of old goldbottle times. She couldn't find her brother's garage but now we were going to find her brother's buddy who would know. Nobody home. It all went on in rickety alleys of little Mextown Sabinal, wrong side of the tracks. As dawn began to break I lay flat on my back in the lawn of the town square, and I'd done that once before when they thought I was drowned in an eastern resort, and I kept saying over and over, "You won't tell what he done up in Weed will you? What'd he do up in Weed? You won't tell will you? What'd he do up in Weed?" This was from the picture *Of Mice and Men* with Burgess Meredith talking to the big foreman of the ranch; I thought we were near Weed. Terry giggled. Anything I did was all right with her. I could lay there and go on saying "What'd he do up in Weed?" till the ladies come out for church and she wouldn't care.

Because her brother was in these parts I figured we'd be all set soon and I took her to an old hotel by the tracks and we went to bed comfortably. Five dollars left. It was all smelling of fresh paint in there, and old mahogany mirrors and creaky. In the bright sunny morning Terry got up early and went to find her brother. I slept till noon; when I looked out the window I suddenly saw an S.P. freight going by with hundreds of hoboes reclining on the flatcars and in gons and rolling merrily along with packs for pillows and funny papers before their noses and some munching on good California grapes picked up by the watertank. "Damn!" I yelled. "Hooee! It is the promised land." They were all coming from Frisco; in a week they'd all be going back in the same grand style.

Terry arrived with her brother, his buddy, and her child. Her brother was a wildbuck Mexican hotcat with a hunger for booze, a great good kid. His buddy was a big flabby Mexican who spoke English without much accent and was anxious to please and overconcerned to prove something. I could see he had always had eyes for Terry. Her little boy was Raymond, seven years old, darkeyed and sweet. Well there we were, and another wild day began.

Her brother's name was Freddy. He had a '38 Chevy. We piled into that and took off to parts unknown. "Where we going?" I asked. The buddy did the explaining, Ponzo, that's what everybody called him. He stank. I found out why. His business was selling manure to farmers, he had a truck. We were going to check on that. Freddy always had three or four dollars in his pocket and was happygolucky about things. He always said "That's right man, there you go—dah you go, dah you go!" And he went. He drove 70 miles an hour in the old heap and we went to Madera beyond Fresno, throwing dust back our tires, and saw farmers about manure. Their voices drawled to us from the hot sun open. Freddy had a bottle. "Today we drink, tomorrow we work. Dah you go man—take a shot." Terry sat in back with her baby; I looked back at her and saw a flush of homecoming joy on her face. She'd been driving around like this for years. The beautiful

green countryside of October in California reeled by madly. I was
guts and juice again and ready to go.

"Where do we go now man?"

"We go find a farmer with some manure layin around—tomorrow
we drive back in the truck and pick up. Man we'll make a lot of
money. Don't worry about nothing."

"We're all in this together!" yelled Ponzo who wouldn't have got
the manure by himself. I saw this was so—everywhere I went everybody was in it together. We raced through the crazy streets of Fresno
and on up the Valley to some farmers in certain backroads. Ponzo got
out of the car and conducted confused conversations with old Mexicans; nothing of course came of it.

"What we need is a drink!" yelled Freddy and off we went to a
crossroads saloon. Americans are always drinking in crossroads saloons on Sunday afternoon; they bring their kids; there are piles of
manure outside the screendoor; they gabble and brawl over brews
and grow haggly baggly and you hear harsh laughter rising from routs
and song, nobody's really having any fun but faces get redder and
time flies fading faster. But everything's fine. Come nightfall the kids
come crying and the parents are drunk. Around the jukebox they go
weaving back to the house. Everywhere in America I've been in crossroads saloons drinking with whole families. The kids eat popcorn
and chips and play in back or sneak stale beers for all I know. Freddy
and I and Ponzo and Terry sat there drinking and shouting. Vociferous types. The sun got red. Nothing had been accomplished. What
was there to accomplish? "Mañana," said Freddy, "mañana man we
make it; have another beer, man, dah you go, DAH YOU GO!" We staggered out and got in the car; off we went to a highway bar. This one
had blue neons and pink lights. Ponzo was a big loud vociferous type
who knew everybody in San Joaquin Valley apparently from the way
every time we clomped into a joint he'd let out loud Ho-Yo's. Now I
had a few bucks left and ruefully counted them. Festooned all over my
brain were the ideas of going back home to New York at once with
this handful of change, hitching as I'd been doing at Bakersfield that
night, leave Terry with her wild brothers and mad Mexican manure
piles and mañanas of crazy beer. But I was having a hell of a time.
From the highway bar I went with Ponzo alone in the car to find some

certain farmer; instead we wound up in Madera Mextown digging the girls and trying to pick up a few for him and Freddy; and then, as purple ·dusk descended over the grape country, I found myself sitting dumbly in the car as he argued with some old farmer at the kitchen door about the price of a watermelon the old man grew in the backyard. We had a watermelon, ate it on the spot and threw the rinds on the old Mexican's dirt sidewalk. All kinds of pretty little girls were cutting down the darkening street. I said "Where the hell are we?"

"Don't worry man" said big Ponzo "tomorrow we make a lot of money, tonight we don't worry." We went back and picked up Terry and the others and wailed to Fresno in the highway lights of night. We were all raving hungry. We bounced over the railroad tracks and hit the wild streets of Fresno Mextown. Strange Chinamen hung out of windows digging the Sunday night streets; groups of Mex chicks swaggered around in slacks; mambo blasted from jukeboxes; the lights were festooned around like Halloween. We went into a restaurant and had tacos and mashed pinto beans rolled in tortillas; it was delicious. I whipped out my last shining four dollars and change which stood between me and the Atlantic shore and paid for the lot. Now I had three bucks. Terry and I looked at each other. "Where we going to sleep tonight baby?"

"I don't know." Freddy was drunk; now all he was saying was: "Dah you go man—dah you go man" in a tender and tired voice. It had been a long day. None of us knew what was going on, or what the Good Lord appointed. Poor little Raymond fell asleep against my arm. We drove back to Sabinal. On the way we pulled up sharp at a roadhouse on the highway, 99, because Freddy wanted one last beer. In back were trailers and tents and a few rickety motel-style rooms. I inquired about the price and it was two bucks for a cabin. I asked Terry how about that and she said great, because we had the kid on our hands now and had to make him comfortable. So after a few beers in the saloon, where sullen Okies reeled to the music of a cowboy band and sprawled drawling at sticky tables where they'd been swigling brew since one o'clock in the afternoon and here it was twelve hours later and all the stars out and long sleepy, Terry and I and Raymond went into a cabin and got ready to hit the sack. Ponzo kept hanging around, talking to us in the starry door; he had no place to sleep. Freddy slept at his father's house in the vineyard shack. "Where do you live, Ponzo?" I asked.

"Nowhere, man. I'm supposed to live with Big Rosey but she threw me out last night. I'm goin to get my truck and sleep in it to-night." Guitars tinkled. Terry and I gazed at the stars together from the tiny bathroom window and took a shower and dried each other.

"Mañana," she said, "everything'll be all right tomorrow, don't you think so sal-honey man?"

"Sure baby, mañana." It was always mañana. For the next week that was all I heard, Mañana, a lovely word and one that probably means heaven. Little Raymond jumped in bed, clothes and all and went to sleep; sand spilled out of his shoes, Madera sand. Terry and I had to get up in the middle of the night and brush it off the sheets. In the morning I got up, washed and took a walk around the place. Sweet dew was making me breathe that human fog. We were five miles out of Sabinal in the cotton fields and grape vineyards along Highway 99. I asked the big fat woman who owned the camp if any field tents were vacant. The cheapest one, a dollar a day, was vacant. I fished up that last dollar and moved into it. There was a bed, a stove and a cracked mirror hanging from a pole; it was delightful. I had to stoop to get in, and when I did there was my baby and my baby-boy. We waited for Freddy and Ponzo to arrive with the truck. They ar-rived with beer and started to get drunk in the tent. "Great tent!"

"How about the manure?"

"Too late today—tomorrow man we make a lot of money, today we have a few beers. What do you say, beer?" I didn't have to be prod-ded. "Dah you go—DAH YOU GO!" yelled Freddy. I began to see that our plans for making money with the manure truck would never ma-terialize. The truck was parked outside the tent. It smelled like Ponzo. That night Terry and I went to sleep in the sweet night air beneath our dewy and made sweet old love. I was just getting ready go to sleep when she said "You want to love me now?"

I said, "What about Raymond."

"He don't mind. He's asleep." But Raymond wasn't asleep and he said nothing.

The boys came back the next day with the manure truck and drove off to find whiskey; they came back and had a big time in the tent.

Talking about the great old times when they were kids here and when they were kids in Calexico and their eccentric old uncles from Old Mexico and the fabulous characters out of the past I missed. "You tink I'm crazy!" yelled Freddy wildeyed, his hair over his eyes. That night Ponzo said it was too cold and slept on the ground in our tent wrapped in a big tarpaulin smelling of cowflaps. Terry hated him; she said he hung around her brother just to be close to her. He was probably in love with her. I didn't blame him.

Nothing was going to happen except starvation for Terry and me, I had a dime left, so in the morning I walked around the countryside asking for cottonpicking work. Everybody told me to go to a farm across the highway from the camp. I went; the farmer was in the kitchen with his women. He came out, listened to my story, and warned me he was only paying so much per hundred pound of picked cotton, three dollars. I pictured myself picking at least three hundred pounds a day and took the job. He fished out some old long canvas bags from the barn and told me the picking started at dawn. I rushed back to Terry all glee. On the way a grapetruck went over a bump in the road and threw off great bunches of grape on the hot tar. I picked it up and took it home. Terry was glad. "Raymond and me'll come with you and help."

"Pshaw!" I said "No such thing!"

"You see, you see, it's very hard picking cotton. If you can't boogie I know I show you how." We ate the grapes and in the evening Freddy showed up with a loaf of bread and a pound of hamburg and we had a picnic. In a larger tent next to ours lived a whole family of Okie cottonpickers; the grandfather sat in a chair all day long, he was too old to work; the son and daughter, and their children, filed every dawn across the highway to my farmer's field and went to work. At dawn the next day I went with them. They said the cotton was heavier at dawn because of the dew and you could make more money than in the afternoon. Nevertheless they worked all day from dawn to sundown. The grandfather had come from Nebraska during the great plague of the Thirties, that old selfsame dustcloud, with the entire family in a jalopy truck. They had been in California ever since. They loved to work. In the ten years the old man's son had increased his children to the number of four, some of whom were old enough now to pick cotton. And in that time they had progressed from ragged poverty in Simon Legree fields to a kind of smiling respectability in better tents, and that was all. They were extremely proud of their tent. "Ever going back to Nebraska?"

"Pshaw, there's nothing back there. What we want to do is buy a trailer." We bent down and began picking cotton. It was beautiful. Across the field were the tents, and beyond them the sere brown cottonfields that stretched out of sight, and over that the brown arroyo foothills and then as in a dream the snowcapped Sierras in the blue morning air. This was so much better than washing dishes on South Main Street. But I knew nothing about cottonpicking. I spent too much time disengaging the white ball from its crackly bed; the others did it in one flick. Moreover my fingertips began to bleed; I needed gloves, or more experience. There was an old Negro couple in the field with us. They picked cotton with the same Godblessed patience their grandfathers had practised in prewar Alabama: they moved right along their rows, bent and blue, and their bags increased. My back began to ache. But it was beautiful kneeling and hiding in that earth; if I felt like resting I just lay down with my face on the pillow of brown moist earth. Birds sang an accompaniment. I thought I had found my life's work. Terry and Raymond came waving at me across the field in the hot lullal noon and pitched in with me. Damn if he wasn't faster than I was!!—a child. And of course Terry was twice as fast. They worked ahead of me and left me piles of clean cotton to add to my bag, my long lugubrious nightmare bag that dragged after me like some serpent or some bedraggled buttoned dragon in a Kafkean dream and worse. My mouth drops just to think of that deep bag. Terry left workmanlike piles, Raymond little childly piles. I stuck them in with sorrow. What kind of an old man was I that I couldn't support my own can let alone theirs. They spent all afternoon with me; the earth is an Indian thing. When the sun got red we trudged back together. At the end of the field I unloaded my burden on a scale, to my surprise it weighed a pound and half only, and I got a buck fifty. Then I borrowed one of the Okie boys' bicycles and rode down 99 to a crossroads grocery where I bought cans of spaghetti and meatballs, bread, butter, coffee and five cent cakes, and came back with the bag on the handlebars. L.A.-bound traffic zoomed by;

Fresno-bound harrassed my tail. I swore and swore. I looked up at the dark sky and prayed to God for a better break in life and a better chance to do something for the little people I loved. Nobody was paying any attention to me up there. I should have known better. It was Terry who brought my soul back; on the tent stove she warmed up the food and it was one of the greatest meals of my life I was so hungry and tired. Sighing like an old Negro cottonpicker, I reclined on the bed and smoked a cigarette. Dogs barked in the cool night. Freddy and Ponzo had given up calling in the evenings. I was satisfied with that. Terry curled up beside me, Raymond sat on my chest, and they drew pictures of animals in my notebook. The light of our tent burned on the frightful plain. The cowboy music twanged in the roadhouse and carried across the fields all sadness. It was all right with me. I kissed my baby and we put out the lights.

In the morning the dew made the tent sag; I got up with my towel and toothbrush and went to the general motel toilet to wash; then I came back, put on my pants which were all torn from kneeling in the earth and had been sewed by Terry in the evening; put on my ragged strawhat which had originally been Raymond's toy hat; and went across the highway with my canvas cottonbag. The cotton was wet and heavy. The sun was red on moist earth.

Every day I earned approximately a dollar and a half. It was just enough to buy groceries in the evening on the bicycle. The days rolled by. I forgot all about the East and the ravings of the bloody road. Raymond and I played all the time: he liked me to throw him up in the air and down on the bed. Terry sat mending clothes. I was a man of the earth precisely as I had dreamed I would be in New York. There was talk that Terry's husband was back in Sabinal and out for me; I was ready for him. One night the Okies went beserk in the roadhouse and tied a man to a tree and beat him with two-by-fours. I was asleep at the time and only heard about it. From then on I carried a big stick with me in the tent in case they got the idea we Mexicans were fouling up their trailer camp. They thought I was a Mexican, of course; and I am.

But now it was getting on in October and getting much colder in the nights. The Okie family had a woodstove and planned to stay for the winter. We had no stove, and besides the rent for the tent was due.

Terry and I bitterly decided we'd have to leave and try something else. "Go back to your family," I gnashed. "For God's sake you can't be batting around tents with a baby like Raymond; the poor little tyke is cold." Terry cried because I was criticizing her motherly instincts; I meant no such thing. When Ponzo came in the truck one gray afternoon we decided to see her family about the situation. But I mustn't be seen and would have to hide in the vineyard. "Tell your mother you'll get a job and help with the groceries. Anything's better than this."

"But you're going, I can hear you talk."

"Well I got to go *some* time—"

"What do you mean, some time. You said we'd stick together and go to New York together. Freddy wants to go to New York too! Now! We'll all go."

"I dunno, Terry, goddamit I dunno—"

We got in the truck and Ponzo started for Sabinal; the truck broke down in some backroad and simultaneously it started to rain wildly. We sat in the old truck cursing. Ponzo got out and toiled in the rain in his torn white shirt. He was a good old guy after all. We promised each other one big more bat. Off we went to a rickety bar in Sabinal Mextown and spent an hour sopping up the cerveza as the rain drove past the door and the jukebox boomed those brokenhearted campo lovesongs from old Mexico, sad, incredibly sad like clouds going over the horizon like dogs on their hind legs, the singer breaking out his wild Ya Ya Henna like the sound of a coyote crying, broken, half laughter, half tears. I was through with my chores in the cottonfield, I could feel it as the beer ran through me like wildfire. We screamed happily our insane conversations. We'd do it, we'd do everything! I could feel the pull of my own whole life calling me back. I needed fifty dollars to get back to New York. While Terry and Ponzo drank I ran in the rain to the postoffice and scrawled a penny postcard request for $50 and sent it to my aunt; she'd do it. I was as good as saved; lazy butt was saved again. It was a secret from Terry.

The rain stopped and we drove to Terry's family shack. It was situated on an old road that ran between the vineyards. It was dark when we got there finally. They let me off a quarter-mile up the road and drove to the door. Light poured out of the door, Terry's six other brothers were playing their guitars and singing all together like a professional recording and beautiful. ". . . si tu corazon . . ." The old man was drinking wine. I heard shouts and arguments above the singing. They called her a whore because she'd left her no good husband and gone to L.A. and left Raymond with them. At intervals the brothers stopped singing to regroup their choruses. The old man was yelling. But the sad fat brown mother prevailed, as she always does among the great Fellaheen peoples of the world, and Terry was allowed to come back home. The brothers began to sing gay songs, fast. I huddled in the cold rainy wind and watched everything across the sad vineyards of October in the valley. My mind was filled with that great song "Lover Man" as Billy Holiday sings it: I had my own concert in the bushes. "Someday we'll meet, and you'll dry all my tears, and whisper sweet, little words in my ear, hugging and akissing, Oh what we've been missing, Lover Man Oh where can you be . . ." It's not the words so much as the great harmonic tune and the way Billy sings it, like a woman stroking her man's hair in soft lamplight. The winds howled. I got cold. Terry and Ponzo came back and we rattled off in the old truck to meet Freddy, who was now living with Ponzo's woman Big Rosey; we tooted the horn for him in woodfence alleys. Big Rosey threw him out, we heard yelling and saw Freddy running out with his head ducking. Everything was collapsing. Everybody was laughing. That night Terry held me tight, of course, and told me not to leave. She said she'd work picking grapes and make enough money for both of us; meanwhile I could live in Farmer Heffelfinger's barn down the road from her family. I'd have nothing to do but sit in the grass all day and eat grapes. "You like that?"

I rubbed my jaw. In the morning her cousins came to the tent to get us in the truck. These were also singers. I suddenly realized thousands of Mexicans all over the countryside knew about Terry and I and that it must have been a juicy romantic topic for them. The cousins were very polite and in fact charming. I stood on the truck platform with them as we rattlebanged into town, hanging onto the rail and smiling pleasantries, talking about where we were in the war and what the pitch was. There were five cousins in all and every one of them was nice. They seemed to belong to the side of Terry's family that didn't act up like her brother Freddy. But I loved that wild

Freddy. He swore he was coming to New York and join me. I pictured
him in New York putting off everything till mañana. He was drunk in
a field someplace today.

I got off the truck at the crossroads and the cousins drove Terry
and Raymond home. They gave me the high-sign from the front of
the house: the father and mother weren't home. So I had the run of
the house for the afternoon, digging it and Terry's three giggling fat
sisters and the crazy children sitting in the middle of the road with
tortillas in their hands. It was a four-room shack; I couldn't imagine
how the whole family managed to live in there, find room. Flies flew
over the sink. There were no screens, just like in the song: "The window she is broken and the rain she's coming in . . ." Terry was at
home now and puttering around pots. The sisters giggled over True
Love Magazines in Spanish showing daguerrotype brown covers of
lovers in great, somehow darker more passionate throes, with long
sideburns and huge worries and burning secret eyes. The little children screamed in the road, roosters ran around. When the sun came
out red through the clouds of my last valley afternoon Terry led me to
Farmer Heffelfinger's barn. Farmer Heffelfinger had a prosperous
farm up the road. We put crates together, she brought blankets from
the house, and I was all set except for a great hairy tarantula that
lurked at the pinpoint top of the barnroof. Terry said it wouldn't
harm me if I didn't bother it. I lay on my back and stared at it. I went
out to the cemetery and climbed a tree. In the tree I sang "Blue
Skies." Terry and Raymond sat in the grass; we had grapes. In California you chew the juice out of the grapes and spit the skin and pits
away, the gist of the grape is always wine. Nightfall came. Terry went
home for supper and came to the barn at nine o'clock with my secret
supper of delicious tortillas and mashed beans. I lit a woodfire on the
cement floor of the barn to make light. We made love on the crates.
Terry got up and cut right back to the shack. Her father was yelling at
her, I could hear him from the barn. "Where have you been? What
you doing running around at night in the fields?" Words to that effect.
She'd left me a cape to keep warm, some old Spanish garment, I
threw it over my shoulder and skulked through the moonlit vineyard
to see what was going on. I crept to the end of a row and kneeled in
the warm dirt. Her five brothers were singing melodious songs in

Spanish. The stars bent over the little roof; smoke poked from the stovepipe chimney. I smelled mashed beans and chili. The old man growled. The brothers kept right on singing. The mother was silent. Raymond and the kids were giggling on one vast bed in the bedroom. A California home, I hid in the grapevines digging it all. I felt like a million dollars; I was adventuring in the crazy American night. Terry came out slamming the door behind her. I accosted her on the dark road. "What's the matter?"

"Oh we fight all the time. He wants me to go to work tomorrow. He says he don't want me fooling around with boys. Sallie-boy I want to go to New York with you."

"But how?"

"I don't know honey. I'll miss you. I love you."

"But I can't stay here."

"You say what you like, I know what you mean. Yes yes, we lay down one more time then you leave." We went back to the barn; I made love to her under the tarantula. What was the tarantula doing? We slept awhile on the crates as the fire died. She went back at midnight; her father was drunk; I could hear him roaring; then there was silence as he fell asleep. The stars folded over the sleeping countryside.

In the morning Farmer Heffelfinger stuck his head through the horse gate and said "How you doing young fella?"

"Fine. I hope it's all right my staying here."

"Sure. You going with that little Mexican floozie?"

"She's a very nice girl."

"Pretty too. S'got blue eyes. I think the bull jumped the fence there . . ." We talked about his farm.

Terry brought my breakfast. I had my handbag all packed and ready to go back east, as soon as I picked up my money in Sabinal. I knew it was waiting there for me. I told Terry I was leaving. She had been thinking about it all night and was resigned to it. Emotionlessly she kissed me in the vineyards and walked off down the row. We turned at a dozen paces, for love is a duel, and looked at each for the last time. "See you in New York Terry," I said. She was supposed to drive to New York in a month with her brother. But we both knew she wouldn't make it somehow. At a hundred feet I turned to look at her.

She just walked on back to the shack, carrying my breakfast plate in one hand. I bowed my head and watched her. Well lackadaddy, I was on the road again. I walked down the highway to Sabinal eating black walnuts from the walnut tree then on the railroad track balancing on the rail.

Issue 11, 1955

Robyn Selman

⌖

Exodus

Open your eyes, O beloved homeland, and behold your son, Sancho Panza, returning to you. If he does not come back very rich, he comes well flogged. Open your arms and receive also your other son, Don Quixote, who returns vanquished by the arm of another but a victor over himself and this, so I have been told, is the greatest victory that could be desired.

—Cervantes

I

And so I went forth, exhilarated
in uniform: worn-through jeans, muscle tees,
stripped of bras and ancestral history.
Since I had nothing real to take along,

I took along a fig-shaped stone,
a bag of gold buds, a resin-stained bong,
hash oil, in which papers were coated,
and two tabs of four-way blotter acid;

lactose-laced cocaine, cut to average,
a fifth of scotch, which was a parting gift,

a poncho, a guitar, feminist sheet music
and *Court and Spark,* which I'd tape-recorded.

With all this I'd find someone of my own.
An ill-equipped bride-to-be, I left home.

II

The old man waves to me through iron bars
on his window, and I wave back at him.
Ten years back, at a spring semester end,
I went to Greece with three other women.

Joanne, whom I called Joey, my lover then,
was the only woman I knew who'd speak
the word proudly. She worked and was older
and didn't do drugs like I did, or bars.

She even looked what I thought was the part:
hair close-cropped, the top in a boyish mop.
We met in a club called The Other Side,
then fell in side by side later that night

on a futon with psychedelic sheets
that lay in an attic under beamed eaves.

III

An ill-equipped bride-to-be, I left home.
The coke I'd flown with in my underwear
had melted into a yellowish loam.
Cheryl, who'd once caused a fire somewhere

drying her wet shirt in a microwave,
suggested that we lay the gluey high

on the warm radiator to try to save
what stash we could, and I agreed to try.

Moments later, the flakes began to fly
down to the floor like mocking stalactites.
My new roommate looked on, removed, dry-eyed.
She was a grad architecture student

with pre-fab plans for life in blueprints.
I befriended Mike with the good hash pipe.

IV

We lay in an attic under beamed eaves,
then headed to New York from Washington.
My new lover, whom I didn't discover
for weeks was depressed and addicted,

for real, to caffeine and cigarettes,
piloted a Buick big as a hearse.
And when the speed she was sipping kicked in
the car did ninety. I waited for sirens.

We were rushing to a conference on women:
Millet, Morgan, Griffin, Rich, and Steinem.
I asked a woman who wasn't Millet
for her autograph. Mistaken, somewhat

humbler, I returned to Joey in the stands.
They called the next panel, "New Lesbians."

V

I befriended Mike with the good hash pipe
and a constant yen for bourbon on ice.

I stayed straight. A consequence of having
no clue how I'd get that other kind of date.

I wore lavender tops, ankhs, stopped shaving,
carried code books face out though my arms ached,
hoped *she'd* recognize *Lesbian Nation,*
Millet's *Flying,* poems by Susan Griffin.

As I grew needy, the book chimney grew.
Finally, I turned back to what I knew:
the last of the coke, the dope, me and Mike,
moved in together with the good hash pipe.

He was pretty, but he wasn't a girl.
Next came Bob, but before him I had Phil.

VI

They called the next panel, "New Lesbians."
I spent the day in the bleachers transfixed.
Joey had to walk off her nicotine fit.
We went to the ladies' (women's) room and kissed.

We were in love, we weren't saying we were.
I wasn't saying that the words I'd heard
were having a drug-like effect: *gay pride*
shot through me, some other blood mixed with mine.

The women I'd known didn't call themselves
lesbians, but winked across tennis courts
in short shorts, and gave slaps in locker rooms
that took the place (psychically) of bedrooms.

Was that sex or athletics? One panelist
asked, "Is sex as much fun with politics?"

VII

Next came Bob, but before him I had Phil
who wore overalls with an unlatched bib
and an army sweater worn at the wrists.
He liked Schumann, Mao, Marx and Joplin's *Pearl*.

He rarely shaved, he washed infrequently
and spoke with a strong uncorrected lisp
which made him seem younger than twenty-six.
I didn't move in. He broke up with me.

Bob was a prize my mom couldn't resist:
six foot, an accountant-to-be, Jewish,
a hard worker, he'd make love then make coffee.
He took me home on the big holidays.

On weekends, with his parents, we saw plays.
We saw everything except that we were gay.

VIII

"What did sex have to do with politics?"
Susan, my first, wrestled me to the floor
after her two-set win: six/one, six/four.
She was privileged, both pretty and rich.

Though I wasn't in love with her riches,
the idea that she passed was seductive.
We escaped the closeted coaches' judgment.
She was younger, but had already had

stacks of lovers: boys, girls, even a divorced
mother. Both she and her sister lost their
virginity to their older brother.
She said, "*It* had nothing to do with *it*."

I didn't know what *it* she meant, or
pretended I didn't, as I licked and kissed.

IX

We saw everything except that we were gay.
Or, I saw everything except the way
around being gay. So I took to bars,
Donna Summer and Gloria Gaynor.

But I liked the stone butch I met better,
who by day flipped hamburgers and at night
was a chest-taped male impersonator.
Nothing ever happened with her, but I

paid the cover charge again and again
though I didn't speak to any new lesbians.
For cover, I'd take my closeted friends.
We danced shackled together like prisoners.

Eleanor, R., Nat, Virginia, or me—
One of us had to be the first to lead.

X

I licked and kissed her in a bathroom stall
as a line of sisters wound down the hall,
Joey's eyes shut against the light green walls.
I drank the warm juices in, swallowing

sips of her like heroin, swallowing
her pride, still unable to summon
any of mine. Months after that kiss
she'd scold me in the Acropolis

for something I'd never heard of that she
loudly termed my *goddamambivalence*.

I snapped back that she was too serious
and imagined leaving her for good right there.

I didn't. I was too in love and scared—
thousands of years up in the chalky air.

XI

One of us had to be the first to lead:
Eleanor R., Natalie B., Virginia
Woolf, Elizabeth R., Elizabeth B.,
Hedda and Alla Nazimova,

Debbie Reynolds, Gertrude Stein, Amelia,
Willa Cather, Cheryl, Whitney Houston,
Sylvia Beach, Billie Jean, Martina,
Jodie Foster, Marion Dickerman,

Lisa, Elizabeth Cady Stanton,
Lesley Gore and Susan B. Anthony,
Bessie, Babe Dietrichson, Val, Anne Murray,
Barbara Jordan and life-long companion,

Yourcenar, Colette, Marlene, H.D.—
the minds I admired, the strong-bodied.

XII

Thousands of cheers filled the chalky air
in the hot Dalton School gymnasium.
Joey sipped cola and chewed Aspergum.
The speaker railed against the oppression

of gay/straight/black/white/Latino women.
They called a break. We hit the streets, like a gang, in
our "Sisterhood Is Powerful" buttons.
I was firmly a not-quite believer,

while Joey's button seemed to protect her.
At Sixtieth and Lex, I doubled over.
Outside things were different. I could see
that people could see. But that didn't seem

to bother Joey, whose hand lay on my knee,
a gesture I thought was only about me.

XIII

The minds I admired, the strong-bodied,
the women who had started my fire,
all in the impregnable closet with me,
shackled together, caged by the same wire.

I was, at the time, just turning twenty
and lacked the mettle to try to unbend
thousands of years of history of women.
And so, like many women before me,

I let other women come out before me.
It wasn't that I had a wicked itch,
for I had long before gladly scratched *it,*
but I was still afraid of the language.

It was in the closet that the words took form
and with them I went forth in uniform.

XIV

I thought the gesture was only about me.
We made our way through Greek islands by boat:
Joey in a chair; I, cross-legged and tortured
as Crane, reading his poems on a heap of rope.

I don't remember the other two women
except they were straight and Canadian.

That night after dinner and too much wine
I went to one (with blue eyes?) with the hope

of blurring the line between her kind and mine.
I found Joey walking with a cup of coffee.
I still hear the metronome of her steps,
that morning quiet as our empty bed.

The old man waves to me through iron bars
on his window and I wave back at him.

XV

And so I went forth in uniform.
Through iron bars, the old man waved to me.
I left home, an ill-equipped bride-to-be
and lay in an attic under beamed eaves.

I befriended Mike with the good hash pipe.
They called the next panel, "New Lesbians."
Then came Bob, but before him was Phil.
What does sex have to do with politics?

We saw everything except that we were gay,
or pretended we didn't, as we licked and kissed.
One of us had to be the first to lead,
thousands of years up in the chalky air.

The minds I admired, the strong-bodied—
I thought the gesture was only about me.

Issue 128, 1993

Joel Brouwer

⌖

Rostropovich at Checkpoint Charlie, November 11, 1989

The maestro, in his Paris hotel, clicks
the television on. A girl with a purple mohawk
chops at the Wall with a hatchet, blasting

chunks of concrete and a cloud of gray dust
into the floodlit air. Beside her, a man in a tuxedo
jimmies his crowbar into a chink, hands his jacket

to someone in the crowd and drives the bar down
with all his weight. Cracks spider up
through the motley graffiti. The mob roars.

Someone shouts "Mehr Licht!" and a hundred drunk
Berliners run for flashlights. The maestro checks
his watch, lifts the phone. Six hours later he steps from a taxi

onto Friedrichstrasse, just as dawn is staining
the sky. He buys coffee from a vendor and together
they survey the street's disaster: splintered

splits of champagne, heaps of broken stone tentacled
with steel, a woman's shoe, fast-food wrappers,
and the half-smashed Wall as a backdrop: dilapidated

curtain in an abandoned theater. "Today all Berlin
will have a hangover," says the vendor. "There are worse
afflictions," Rostropovich replies. He has lived in exile

for sixteen years. "It's fine by me," shrugs the vendor.
"The hungover buy coffee by the bucketful."
The maestro asks for a chair. The man finds a rusty one

and unfolds it with a creak. The maestro sits
in the shadow of the Wall, lifts his cello from its case, then
lunges, stabs the bow across the strings,

and instantly the street is possessed: Bach's Suite #5.
The chords circle low, wary as a flock of crows, then vault
into melody, retreat, begin again: threnody, aubade,

threnody, aubade, like a man who wakes up
on the morning he's longed for and finds he can think of nothing
but the night just ended and the night to come.

Issue 147, 1998

Anne Carson

⌘

TV Men: Antigone (Scripts 1 and 2)

Antigone likes walking behind Oedipus
to brake the wind.
As he is blind he often does not agree to this.
March sky cold as a hare's paw.
Antigone and Oedipus eat lunch on the lip of a crater.
Trunks of hundred-year-old trees forced
down
by wind
crawl on the gravel. One green centimeter of twig
still vertical—
catches her eye. She leads his hand to it.
Lightly
he made sure
what it was.
Lightly left it there.

[Antigone felt a sting against her cheek. She motions the soundman
out of the way and taking the microphone begins to speak.]

There is nowhere to keep anything, the way we live.
This I find hard. Other things I like—a burnish
along the butt end of days
that people inside houses never see.
Projects, yes I have projects.

I want to make a lot of money. Just kidding. Next
question. No I do not lament.
God's will is not some sort of physics, is it.
Today we are light, tomorrow shadow, says the song.

> Ironic? Not really. My father is the ironic one.
> I have my own ideas about it.
> At our backs is a big anarchy.
> If you are strong you can twist a bit off
> and pound on it—your freedom!

Now Oedipus has risen, Antigone rises. He begins to move off,
into the wind,
immersed in precious memory.
Thinking *Too much memory* Antigone comes after.
Both of them are gold all along the sunset side.
Last bell, he knew.
Among all fleshbags you will not find
one who if God
baits
does not bite.

[For sound bite purposes we had to cut Antigone's script from 42
seconds to 7: substantial changes of wording were involved but we
felt we got her "take" right.]

> Other things I like: a lot of money!
> The way we live, light and shadow are ironic.
> Projects? yes: physics. Anarchy. My father.
> Here, twist a bit off.
> Freedom is next.

Issue 142, 1997

Agha Shahid Ali

✠

A History of Paisley

for Anuradha Dingwaney

Their footsteps formed the paisley when Parvati, angry after a quarrel, ran away from Shiva. He eventually caught up with her. To commemorate their reunion, he carved the Jhelum river, as it moves through the Vale of Kashmir, in the shape of the paisley.

You who will find the dark fossils of paisleys
one afternoon on the peaks of Zabarvan—
Trader from an ancient market of the future,
alibi of chronology, that vain
collaborator of time—won't know that these

are her footprints from the day the world began
when land rushed, from the ocean, toward Kashmir.
And above the rising Himalayas? The air
chainstitched itself till the sky hung its bluest
tapestry. But already—as she ran

away—refugee from her Lord—the ruins
of the sea froze, in glaciers, cast in amber.
And there, in the valley below, the river
beguiled its banks into petrified longing:
(O see, it is still the day the world begins:

and the city rises, holding its remains,
its wooden beams already their own fire's prophets.)
And you, now touching sky, deaf to her anklets
still echoing in the valley, deaf to men
fleeing from soldiers into dead-end lanes

(Look! Their feet bleed; they leave footprints on the street
which will give up its fabric, at dusk, a carpet)—
you have found—you'll think—the first teardrop, gem
that was enticed for a Mughal diadem
into design. For you, blind to all defeat

up there in pure sunlight, your gauze of cloud thrown
off your shoulders over the Vale, do not hear
bullets drowning out the bells of her anklets.
This is her relic, but for you the first tear,
drop that you hold as you descend past flowstone,

past dried springs, on the first day of the world.
The street is rolled up, ready for southern ports.
Your ships wait there. What other cargo is yours?
What cables have you sent to tomorrow's bazaars?
What does that past await: the future unfurled

like flags? news from the last day of the world?
You descend quickly, to a garden-café:
At a table by a bed of tzigane
Roses three men are discussing, between
Sips of tea, undiscovered routes on emerald

Seas, ships with almonds, with shawls bound for Egypt.
It is dusk. The gauze is torn. A weaver kneels,
gathers falling threads. Soon he will stitch the air.
But what has made you turn? Do you hear her bells?
O alibi of chronology, in what script

in your ledger will this narrative be lost?
In that café, where they discuss the promise
of the world, her cry returns from its abyss
where it hides, by the river. They don't hear it.
The city burns; the dusk has darkened to rust

by the roses. They don't see it. O Trader,
what news will you bring to your ancient market?
I saw her. A city was razed. In its debris
her bells echoed. I turned. They didn't see me
turn to see her—on the peaks—in rapid flight forever.

Issue 131, 1995

Barry Lopez

⌗

The Interior of North Dakota

The Bergdorf Hills rise unobtrusively in south-central North Dakota east of the badlands and were not fully described until 1923, in a book by the youngest son of a prominent New York family, Meyer Bergdorf, who went west at the age of twenty, exasperated by the wealth and insouciance of his parents.

Bergdorf disembarked the Great Northern Railroad at Bismarck in May, 1918. He took three disheveled Lakota into his employ, outfitted them and rode south into the basin of the Heart River. He told the Indians he only wanted to look into that country, that he wasn't searching for anything specific. Indeed, he had intended to get off the train in Fargo, but gazing from the train door at Fargo's streets and stores he'd been so put off by the town's earnestness he'd returned to his seat.

The Lakota Bergdorf elected to travel with—the whole party drew smirks of bemusement from the stable men and shop clerks who fitted them out—took Bergdorf initially for an impulsive and presumptuous man, common features to them of white culture. But they were intrigued by the diversion he offered. When they saw that he could ride and, once they were clear of Bismarck, that Bergdorf rode alertly, studying the ground as if gleaning it; when they found he wasn't an incessant talker, they were pulled in by his determination. The alcoholic daze in which he'd found them began to fall away, like rotten and sour clothing.

At dusk on the first day they camped in country vaguely familiar to

the Lakota. By the second day, moving always at Bergdorf's scrutinizing pace, they'd crossed to the south bank of the Heart and followed
the river into a landscape none of them knew. Bergdorf studied the
woody draws and stared at the grassy swales with their clusters of
wild roses. The trail sign in the short grama grass showed nothing of
the passage of horses or cattle. It was now only that of wild creatures.
The eldest Indian, a man in his fifties called Weasel Confused by
Sparrows, said they should cleanse themselves before they went any
farther. They should build a sweat lodge the next morning.

Weasel Confused and the others, a man about forty named Five
Handed Horse and a younger man called Wind That Comes at
Night, remained aloof with Bergdorf but each had come to a similar
conclusion—that the young man was possessed. They thought he was
headed to a specific place. Five Handed, heavyset and with short
hair, remembered a story he'd heard when he was young, about some
low hills that now lay to the south of them. It was a holy place, like the
Black Hills where he and the other two had grown up. But, he told
Bergdorf, these were very much smaller and treeless hills. And they
were sacred to the Crow. (The Crow, the three Indians reflected privately, had once been their traditional enemies. Now, with all that
shattered, it almost made no difference. If that was where this white
man was headed, they would go.)

The next morning they built a sweat lodge close to the river; a willow frame covered tightly with wool blankets. Weasel Confused said
he couldn't remember all the proper prayers or what their sequence
was. But he assured Bergdorf that the purification would put life into
them, no matter. When Bergdorf asked how well he knew the rite,
Weasel Confused said, "I am using all the knowledge I have."

Bergdorf appreciated the rising sense of gravity in his companions and the emergence of their enthusiasm. He had asked them to
accompany him—he'd found them sleeping in the city's park—partly
as a show of contempt for the burghers of Bismarck but also because
he wasn't entirely confident of his own skills. He assumed these three
swarthy men—Night Wind wearing rimless dark glasses and a fedora, all of them dressed in rumpled trousers and mismatched suit
coats—knew the country. They knew it, he found out later, no better

than he did. They had arrived only two days before, on the train from Dickinson.

Late in the afternoon, after they'd sweated, Five Handed Horse approached Bergdorf and extended his hand wordlessly. Bergdorf, slicing bacon for dinner, knew instantly what he wanted. He handed Five Handed the Colt .38/40 and three cartridges. A few hours later he and Night Wind came back with a mule deer, a small doe.

The next morning, Bergdorf records, the four of them worked quietly at personal chores in the warming light. Bergdorf, whose nearly chronic disaffection had begun to abate, wrote and drew in a pasteboard journal. Five Handed, having restitched the split uppers of his two-toned wing-tip shoes, was helping Weasel Confused cut and dry the deer's flesh. Night Wind, a heavily pockmarked man with delicate hands, was painting his horse's face, a row of yellow bars down the muzzle and white circles around the eyes.

They left long before noon and rode the rest of the day south before they entered the low hills which Five Handed could remember no name for. Bergdorf, then and there, named them the Four Man Hills; but in a journal entry a few days later he says that naming them at all was a mistake. He meant to follow Weasel Confused's advice and inquire among the Crow as to their name.

The four of them spent a week there. The Lakota, in Bergdorf's estimation, rose visibly to a level of splendid awareness, of hawklike and wolverinelike behavior, economical and deliberate in their activities. Bergdorf, wandering the hills, sometimes astride his Appaloosa mare, sometimes on foot, focused his obvious pleasure on flowers. Though he knew almost nothing of botany, he examined several dozen species closely enough to draw them in their entirety. The drawings are clumsy, with no variation in the thickness of his line or the pressure of his pencil, but they are evocative and charming—a young man's self-conscious act of respect.

Just as they had not discussed the hills as a destination, so they did not later discuss their departure, but only rose one morning after a week and left. (In reading Bergdorf's journal, one is compelled by the short, enigmatic entry of his fifth day in the hills to believe that something unusual took place here, a kind of epiphany for Bergdorf, certainly, but of a sort he could not at first imagine, or which he didn't care to try to explain. Perhaps it wasn't obvious to him. But some realization of self-worth, an infusion of joy, seems to have reached him. The entries that follow on the return trail to Bismarck, where the journal abruptly ends, are marked by an attitude of profound courtesy and a prepossessing tone not present in the earlier entries.)

The riders, ranging far out to both sides of their original trail, returned to Bismarck in three days. Bergdorf alone no longer determined their route. They rode easily together, following each other by turns, a rhythm determined by the roll of the land and their combined idiosyncrasies. A day out of town, Bergdorf took certain of his possessions—a heavy overcoat, some packaged food, an extra pair of trousers—and set them in a neat pile on the gray white trunk of a fallen cottonwood. Night Wind lay his rimless dark glasses alongside.

In Bismarck, Bergdorf sold the horses back to their original owner. He gave each of his three companions twenty dollars and some store-bought items—shoes, a small traveling bag for each one, a saddle blanket for each man. He got them rooms in the Centennial Hotel and treated them to dinner in the dining room. Bergdorf had by now the same dark patina of the trail the other three had had when they'd met. People glared at them while they ate. One or two, Bergdorf writes, murmured in disgust.

Bergdorf could not sleep that night. He dressed and went down to the livery stable where their horses were corralled—his Appaloosa, Weasel Confused's strawberry roan, the sorrel gelding that Five Handed had ridden and the two paints, Night Wind's and the pack animal. They nickered at his presence and then bore off slowly into the far dimness of the corral.

The Lakota were gone in the morning. They took the night train to Dickinson, the station agent told him.

Bergdorf boarded the train east that morning. A week later he enlisted in the American army. On August 1, 1918, he was shot dead north of the Marne River in the Meunière Wood. His eldest sister, Isabel, succeeded in having his journal published by a small press in Connecticut in 1923. In a brief introduction she writes that her brother returned to New York from North Dakota burning with a sense of purpose and "marvelously poised." (It was she who petitioned the United States Board on Geographic Names to call the Bergdorf Hills after her brother.)

During the American depression of the 1930s, much of the settled land to the south and west of Bismarck was deserted. Ranching operations established along the Heart River as recently as the twenties went out of business, large sections of Morton and northern Grant counties were acquired by banks in Bismarck, Fargo and Minneapolis in default of loans. After the Second World War, most of these several hundred square miles of abandoned land were absorbed in the already huge holdings of ranches and farms on the surrounding shortgrass prairie. With so many documents involved, however, some parcels were unintentionally deeded to two different owners, some foreclosed land was assigned but never deeded and some parcels were deliberately sold twice, by itinerant land operators.

In May 1958, a records clerk in the state archives in Bismarck began to sort through this confusion and legerdemain—a private preoccupation. Partway through she realized that a section of nearly twenty square miles in the drainage of the Heart River, including the Bergdorf Hills, was mostly without clear title and also unoccupied. The counties involved had not taken any notice because the taxes on the undeeded land had always been paid—since 1937 the aggregate of land had been apportioned in the tax parcels of twelve different ranching families. The ranches in question had not put stock on the sections because their fence lines followed the boundary lines described in their original deeds.

The clerk, a divorced woman without children named Lenore Crandall, traveled on her own, bit by bit, all across the undeeded land. She finally determined that the Bergdorf Hills themselves, about ten square miles, had never been occupied, and that little of even the deeded land along the south bank of the Heart River was being ranched. In 1963 Crandall bought a house near the Bergdorf Hills and moved there, fifty miles from Bismarck. She continued to work for the state. She explored widely around her home and in later years she painted, mostly images from her childhood in Chicago, though in her last years she began to paint the landscape of the Bergdorf Hills. Her journals of exploration are painstaking in their detail and striking in the range of subjects that held her attention, from the germination of grasses to the hunting behavior of swift foxes.

In the spring of 1977 I met Lenore Crandall while looking for work around Bismarck. I'd heard that a man was hiring in Almont, a small town to the east, and had gone there but found no one hiring and no work. I'd started out along the road south away from Almont with the idea of finding work in Rapid City, but also because the country in that direction, at that time of year, was beautiful. I am a decent-looking man, dress neatly and am not alarming or offensive in my manner, so do not anticipate trouble in getting rides. It was Lenore Crandall who stopped for me.

She lived about ten miles south of Almont, on the Heart River. In those few miles we had an amiable conversation, the sort of conversation you can have when no one has any pressing plan of action, no clear object of desire. She asked me if I would like to stay for dinner and overnight. It was not the last time I was to be startled by her. I said yes. I remember most acutely, I think, her integrity with a stranger. And her generosity. In the morning I went on my way, promising to write when I settled somewhere for the winter.

I kept up my correspondence, and before she passed away in 1983, at the age of seventy, I managed to visit her twice at her home. Her attraction for me lay in that peculiar tension some people are able to affect by maintaining intimacy in their conversation while actually revealing little of their private lives. The last time I saw her, I brought her a present, a copy of Meyer Bergdorf's book, which I'd found in Salt Lake City. I picked it up initially out of curiosity, but finished it excited by a sense of coincidence. Lenore read it through that same night. The following morning she seemed both pensive and ebullient. She told me, then, for the first time, about the Bergdorf Hills, about their disposition and how she'd discovered them.

I had never heard such a story, and as much as I respected her I was skeptical. There was always a part of Lenore that was slightly out of reach. It wasn't that she was unapproachable but that part of her was unattainable, as when a person doesn't have words or experience enough to grasp a particular frame of mind. She read to me all that morning from her journals. As I listened to her descriptions I saw that unattainable part of her more clearly than I ever had before. She described how she reached the Bergdorf Hills by following a path, hidden from the road, down the Heart River, before turning south at a certain spot. It wasn't until she said this that I realized I had never seen the Bergdorf Hills. They were not visible from her home. You could barely make them out from the road.

Lenore's gratitude for a copy of Bergdorf's book was extreme. I thought, after all that had passed between us that morning, the significance of what she had revealed, that she would invite me to walk with her into the hills. But she did not.

I learned of her passing several months after she died. A letter from probate court reached me in Omaha and I came back up to North Dakota. She'd left me a small amount of money and, to my surprise, the house with its few acres on the Heart River. I slowly realized that Lenore had made me aware of a certain aspect of my own isolation, and I was very grateful to her.

One morning, feeling somewhat apprehensive and also a little doubtful, I walked east along the Heart, down to the spot that Lenore had described. I then headed south toward the Bergdorf Hills. I'd not gone very far before I felt I could go no farther. The character of the land had changed distinctly in less than a mile. It had risen up gleaming, like a painting stripped of grime, the prairie colors richer, the air more prismatic. The smell of sun-warmed grasses and brush had become dense and fresh. I was still eager to go on, but in the face of this intensification I felt like an interloper. What was here, the undisturbed brilliance, belonged, it seemed, to Meyer Bergdorf and his Lakota friends and to the unheard-from Crow, and to Lenore.

That afternoon I withdrew because it was so obvious to me that I was unprepared. I was also afraid. The vividness of the land was intimidating. It had in every detail the penetrating aura, the immediacy, the insistence of a creature viewed through ground glass. The intertwining of wild rose thickets, the wind rushing the broad leaves of summer cottonwoods and the calls of meadowlarks, a sound like running water, held me up. I turned on my trail and walked back to the river. I knew that I would return, but it would be with a desire clearer and deeper than what I then possessed. I had little doubt now that these hills would open out on a landscape of "unreasonable extent," as Lenore had indicated, and that if I were patient I might come to see aspects of the hills that were also bewildering and terrifying.

That night I sat at Lenore's dining table reading her journals, all that was left of her personal effects. The Chicago paintings had been sold. The canvases she'd painted in the Bergdorf Hills, which I'd seen and now knew were full of disguise, had been taken from their frames and destroyed. She had asked that I read and destroy her journals. I considered her request wrongheaded, an act of selfishness. I understood, though she had not been explicit, that she wanted me to care for the Bergdorf Hills after she was gone. It might be years before they were entered, but she thought it would probably not be long before computers discovered the patchwork of deeds, the errant tax structure. Legal ownership of the hills would be settled on someone. By that very act, she believed, parceled and possessed, their vividness would pale, their pungency and resonance fade. They would become another, almost indistinguishable part of the prairie. Against that eventuality, or at least until then, she had suggested to me—always indirectly, but with a passion that in other women is sexual—that I stay on.

So my plans are very simple. I'll finish reading her journals. I'll try to imagine as I read, though it runs against her wishes, whether there might not be some way to preserve the ecstatic and wondrous tone of her work. The reverie with which she writes of the Bergdorf Hills; whether by calling the hills by some other name, by giving them a different geography, I can't see to the publication of the journals. For she wrote not only of the charm and beauty of the land but of its darkness, about the panic of being lost in it, its resolute indifference, of how lean and hard it had made her, of how profound an order had come to her core through all her foot travel, her night sleeps, in these inconspicuous hills.

I will finish the journals then and think on that. And then, one day, I will walk off into that country to see it for myself. I'll imagine the Crow there, and their traditional enemies the Lakota. I will travel, I am certain now, with a companion, another person with whom it will be possible to speak and to imagine. Then if the hills should indeed disappear, if they should be realized in some other way, there will, at least, be our stories to preserve the memory of travel there.

I will step off into that country with the possibility of fathoming, perhaps, what made Lenore, on that last night that I saw her, rise and wander off into the dusky light along the Heart River like an anguished bear. And I will know, perhaps, what Bergdorf meant when he wrote, "In all my travels I have never known a country so sweet, so redolent with the earth's perfume, nor air so full of light. When I think on my companions, different from me and whom I barely know, I sense the same resolve in them to strip away the horror of what we have accepted. I look on these hills, writing by the light of the full moon this evening, and know that, though this land is not mine nor ever could be, that for what I have found here I would die. These hills, their deer and badgers, their calling coyotes, the azure, red and yellow species of birds, have lifted me out of myself. My anger is diminished, my loneliness gone."

James Baldwin

✠

from The Art of Fiction LXXVIII

Would you tell us how you came to leave the States?

I was broke. I got to Paris with forty dollars in my pocket, but I had to get out of New York. My reflexes were tormented by the plight of other people. Reading had taken me away for long periods at a time, yet I still had to deal with the streets and the authorities and the cold. I knew what it meant to be white and I knew what it meant to a nigger, and I knew what was going to happen to me. My luck was running out. I was going to go to jail, I was going to kill somebody or be killed. My best friend had committed suicide two years earlier, jumping off the George Washington Bridge.

When I arrived in Paris in 1948 I didn't know a word of French. I didn't know anyone and I didn't want to know anyone. Later, when I'd encountered other Americans, I began to avoid them because they had more money than I did and I didn't want to feel like a freeloader. The forty dollars I came with, I recall, lasted me two or three days. Borrowing money whenever I could—often at the last minute—I moved from one hotel to another, not knowing what was going to happen to me. Then I got sick. To my surprise I wasn't thrown out of the hotel. This Corsican family, for reasons I'll never understand, took care of me. An old, old lady, a great old matriarch, nursed me back to health after three months; she used old folk remedies. And she had to climb five flights of stairs every morning to make sure I was kept alive. I went through this period where I was very much alone, and wanted to be. I wasn't part of any community until I later became the Angry Young Man in New York.

INTERVIEWER

Why did you choose France?

BALDWIN

It wasn't so much a matter of choosing France—it was a matter of getting out of America. I didn't know what was going to happen to me in France but I knew what was going to happen to me in New York. If I had stayed there, I would have gone under, like my friend on the George Washington Bridge.

INTERVIEWER

You say the city beat him to death. You mean that metaphorically.

BALDWIN

Not so metaphorically. Looking for a place to live. Looking for a job. You begin to doubt your judgment, you begin to doubt everything. You become imprecise. And that's when you're beginning to go under. You've been beaten, and it's been deliberate. The whole society has decided to make you *nothing*. And they don't even know they're doing it.

INTERVIEWER

Has writing been a type of salvation?

BALDWIN

I'm not so sure! I'm not sure I've escaped anything. One still lives with it, in many ways. It's happening all around us, every day. It's not happening to me in the same way, because I'm James Baldwin; I'm not riding the subways and I'm not looking for a place to live. But it's still happening. So salvation is a difficult word to use in such a context. I've been compelled in some ways by describing my circumstances to learn to live with them. It's not the same thing as accepting them.

Issue 91, 1984

Philip Larkin

✠

from The Art of Poetry XXX

INTERVIEWER

You haven't been to America, have you?

LARKIN

Oh no, I've never been to America, nor to anywhere else, for that matter. Does that sound very snubbing? It isn't meant to. I suppose I'm pretty unadventurous by nature, partly that isn't the way I earn my living—reading and lecturing and taking classes and so on. I should hate it.

And of course I'm so deaf now that I shouldn't dare. Someone would say, What about Ashbery, and I'd say, I'd prefer strawberry, that kind of thing. I suppose everyone has his own dream of America. A writer once said to me, If you ever go to America, go either to the East Coast or the West Coast: the rest is a desert full of bigots. That's what I think I'd like: where if you help a girl trim the Christmas tree you're regarded as engaged, and her brothers start oiling their shotguns if you don't call on the minister. A version of pastoral.

V.S. Naipaul

from The Art of Fiction CLIV

INTERVIEWER

You left Trinidad in 1950 to study at Oxford—setting out across the seas to an alien land in pursuit of ambition. What were you looking for?

NAIPAUL

I wanted to be very famous. I also wanted to be a writer: to be famous for writing. The absurdity about the ambition was that, at the time, I had no idea what I was going to write about. The ambition came long before the material. The filmmaker Shyam Benegal once told me that he knew he wanted to make films from the age of six. I wasn't as precocious as he: I wanted to be a writer by the age of ten.

I went to Oxford on a colonial government scholarship, which guaranteed to see you through any profession you wanted. I could have become a doctor or an engineer, but I simply wanted to do English at Oxford—not because it was English and not because it was Oxford, but only because it was away from Trinidad. I thought that I would learn about myself in the three or four years I was going to be away. I thought that I would find out my material and miraculously become a writer. Instead of learning a profession, I chose this banality of English—a worthless degree, it has no value at all.

But I wanted to escape Trinidad. I was oppressed by the pettiness of colonial life and by (this relates more particularly to my Indian-Hindu family background) the intense family disputes in which peo-

ple were judged and condemned on moral grounds. It was not a generous society—neither the colonial world nor the Hindu world. I had
a vision that, in the larger world, people would be appreciated for
what they were—people would be found interesting for what they
were.

INTERVIEWER

You have been to so many places—India, Iran, West Africa, the American Deep South. Are you still drawn to travel?

NAIPAUL

It gets harder, you know. The trouble is that I can't go places without
writing about them. I feel I've missed the experience. I once went to
Brazil for ten days and didn't write anything. Well, I wrote something
about Argentina and the Falklands, but I didn't possess the experience—I didn't work at it. It just flowed through me. It was a waste of
my life. I'm not a holiday taker.

Charles D'Ambrosio

⚏

Her Real Name

for P.L.A.

I

The girl's scalp looked as though it had been singed by fire—strands of thatchy red hair snaked away from her face, then settled against her skin, pasted there by sweat and sunscreen and the blown grit and dust of travel. For a while her thin hair had remained as light and clean as the down of a newborn chick, but it was getting hotter as they drove west, heading into a summerlong drought that scorched the landscape, that withered the grass and melted the black tar between expansion joints in the road and bloated like balloons the bodies of raccoon and deer and dog and made everything on the highway ahead ripple like a mirage through waves of rising heat. Since leaving Fargo, it had been too hot to wear the wig, and it now lay on the seat between them, still holding within its webbing the shape of her head. Next to it, a bag of orange candy—*smiles*, she called them—spilled across the vinyl. Sugar crystals ran into the dirty stitching and stuck to her thigh. Gum wrappers and greasy white bags littered the floor, and on the dash, amid a flotsam of plastic cups, pennies and matchbooks, a bumper sticker curled in the heat. EXPECT A MIRACLE, it read.

The girl cradled a black Bible in her lap, the leather covers as worn and ragged as old tennis shoes. The inner leaf contained a family tree dating back to 1827, names tightly scrawled in black against yellowing parchment, a genealogy as ponderous as those kept in Genesis, the book of the generations of Adam. The list of ancestors on the in-

ner leaf was meaningless ancient history to the man, whose name was
Jones, but the girl said her family had carried that same Bible with
them wherever they went, for one hundred and fifty years, and that
she wanted it with her too. "That's me," the girl had said, showing
Jones her name, the newest of all, penned in generous loops of Bic
blue. She'd written it in herself along the margin of the page. *b.
1960—*. The girl read different passages aloud as they drove, invoking a mix of epic beauty and bad memories, of Exodus and the
leather belt her stepfather used to beat her when she broke a com-
mandment—one of the original ten or one of his additions. Jones
wasn't sure what faith she placed in the austere Christianity of her
forefathers, but reading aloud seemed to cast a spell over her. She had
a beautiful church-trained voice that lifted each verse into a soothing
melody, a song whose tune of succor rose and fell somewhere beyond
the harsh demands of faith. Only minutes before she'd read herself to
sleep with a passage from Jeremiah.

Now, as if she felt Jones staring, the girl stirred.

"You were looking at me," she said. "You were thinking something."

Her face was shapeless, soft and pale as warm putty.

"I could feel it," she said. "Where are we?"

They hadn't gone more than a mile since she'd dozed off. She
reached for the candy on the seat.

"You hungry? You want a smile, Jones?"

"No, none for me," Jones said.

"A Life Saver?" She held the unraveled package out.

"Nothing, thanks."

"Me eating candy, and my teeth falling out." The girl licked the
sugar off a smile and asked, "How far to Las Vegas?"

Jones jammed a tape in the eight-track. He was driving a 1967
Belvedere he'd bought for seven hundred dollars cash in Newport
News, and it had come with a bulky eight-track, like an atavistic organ, bolted beneath the glove box. He'd found two tapes in the trunk,
and now, after fifteen thousand miles, he was fairly sick of both Tom
Jones and Steppenwolf. But he preferred the low-fidelity noise of either tape to the sound of himself lying.

"Why don't you come with me little girl," he sang along, in a high, mocking falsetto, "on a magic-carpet ride."

"How far?" the girl asked.

Jones adjusted his grip on the steering wheel. "Another day, maybe."

She seemed to fall asleep again, her dry-lidded eyes shut like a lizard's, her parched, flaking lips parted, her frail body given over to the car's gentle rocking. Jones turned his attention back to the road, a hypnotic black line snaking through waves of yellow grass. It seemed to Jones that they'd been traveling through eastern Montana forever, that the same two or three trees, the same two or three farmhouses and grain silos were rushing past like scenery in an old movie, only suggesting movement. Endless fields, afire in the bright sun, were occasionally broken by stands of dark cottonwood or the gutted chassis of a rusting car. Collapsing barns leaned over in the grass, giving in to the hot wind and the insistent flatness, as if passively accepting the laws of a world whose only landmark, as far as Jones could see, was the level horizon.

"He's out there," the girl said. "I can feel him out there when I close my eyes. He knows where we are."

"I doubt that very much," Jones said.

The girl struggled to turn, gripping the headrest. She looked through the rear window at the warp of the road as it narrowed to a pinprick on the pale edge of the world they'd left behind: it was out of the vanishing point that her father would come.

"I expect he'll be caught up soon," she said. "He's got a sense. One time he predicted an earthquake."

"It's a big country," Jones said. "We could've gone a million other ways. Maybe if you think real hard about Florida that'll foul up his super-duper predicting equipment."

"Prayer," the girl said. "He prays. Nothing fancy. We're like Jonah sneaking on that boat in Tarshish; they found him out."

The girl closed her eyes; she splashed water on her face and chest.

"It's so hot," she said. "Tell me some more about the Eskimos."

"I'm running out of things to say about Eskimos," Jones said. "I only read that one book."

"Say old stuff, I don't care."

He searched his memory for what he remembered of Knud Rasmussen.

"Nothing's wasted," Jones said. "They use everything. The Inuit can make a sled out of a slain dog. They kill the dog and skin it, then cut the hide into two strips."

"I'm burning alive," the girl said.

"They roll up the hide and freeze the strips in water to make the runners. Then they join the runners together with the dog's rib bones." Jones nibbled the corner of an orange smile. "One minute the dog's pulling the sled, the next minute he is the sled." He saw that the girl was asleep. "That's irony," he said and then repeated the word. "Irony." It sounded weak, inadequate; it described nothing; he drove silently on. Out through the windshield he saw a landscape too wide for the eye to measure—the crushing breadth of the burnt fields and the thin black thread of road vanishing into a vast blue sky as if the clouds massed on the horizon were distant cities, and they were going to them.

She'd been working the pumps and the register at a crossroads station in southern Illinois, a rail-thin girl with stiff red hair the color of rust, worried, chipped nails and green eyes without luster. She wore gray coveralls that ballooned over her body like a clown's outfit, the long legs and sleeves rolled into thick cuffs. "I've never seen the ocean," she'd said, pointing to the remains of a peeling bumper sticker on Jones's car. . . . BE SAILING, it read. She stood on the pump island while Jones filled his tank. The hooded blue lights above them pulsed in sync to the hovering sound of cicadas, and both were a comforting close presence in the black land spreading out around the station. Jones wanted to tell the girl to look around her, right now: this flat patch of nothing was as good as an ocean. Instead, making conversation, Jones said, "I just got out of the navy."

"You from around here?" she asked.

"Nope," Jones said.

He topped off his tank and reached into the car where he kept his money clipped to the sun visor.

"I knew that," she said. "I seen your plates."

Jones handed her a twenty from his roll of muster pay. The money represented for him his final six months in the navy, half a year in which he hadn't once set foot on land. Tired of the sea, knowing he'd never make a career out of it, on his last tour Jones had refused the temptations of shore leave, hoping to hit land with enough of a stake to last him a year. Now, as he looked at the dwindling roll, he was torn between exhaustion and a renewed desire to move on before he went broke.

"Where in Virginia you from?"

"I'm not," Jones said. "I bought the car in Newport News. Those are just old plates."

"That's too bad," the girl said. "I like the name. Virginia. Don't you?"

"I guess it's not special to me one way or the other," Jones said.

The girl folded the twenty in half and ran her thin fingers back and forth over the crease. That she worked in a gas station in the middle of nowhere struck Jones as sexy, and now he looked at her closely, trying to decide whether or not he wanted to stop a night or two in Carbondale. Except for the strange texture and tint of her red hair, he thought she looked good, and the huge coveralls, rippling in the breeze, made her seem sweet and lost, somehow innocent and alone in a way that gave Jones the sudden confidence that he could pick her up without much trouble.

"You gonna break that?" Jones asked, nodding at the bill.

Her arm vanished entirely as she reached into the deep pocket of her coveralls and pulled out a roll of bills stained black with grease and oil. Jones took the change, then looked off, around the station. In the east a dome of light rose above Carbondale, a pale yellow pressing out against the night sky. The road running in front of the station was empty except for a spotlight that shone on a green dinosaur and a Sinclair sign that spun on a pole above it.

"Don't get scared, working out here?" he asked.

"Nah," she said. "Hardly anyone comes out this way, 'less they're like you, 'less they're going somewhere. Had a man from Vernal gas here the other night. That's in Utah."

"Still—"

"Some nights I wouldn't care if I got robbed."

Jones took his toilet kit—a plastic sack that contained a thin,

curved bone-like bar of soap, a dull razor and a balding toothbrush—
out of the glove box. "You mind if I wash up?"

"Washroom's around back," she said. "By the propane tanks."

In the bathroom, he took off his T-shirt and washed himself with
a wetted towel, watching his reflection in the mirror above the sink as
though it were someone else, someone from his past. Gray eyes, a
sharp sculpted jaw, ears that jutted absurdly from his close-cropped
head: a navy face. Six months of shipboard isolation had left him with
little sense of himself outside of his duties as an officer. In that time,
held in the chrysalis of his berth, he'd forgotten not only what he
looked like, but what other people might see when they looked at
him. Now he was a civilian. He decided to shave, lathering up with
the bar of soap. The mustache came off in four or five painful strokes.

For a moment the warm breeze was bracing against his cleanly
shaven face. He stood in the lot, a little stiff, at attention, and when the
girl waved to him from the cashier's widow, Jones saluted.

"See you later," he said.

"Okay," she said.

Jones drove away, stopping at a convenience store about a mile
down the road. He grabbed two six-packs, a cheap Styrofoam cooler
and a bag of ice and wandered down the aisle where the toys were
kept. He selected a pink gun that fired rubber suction darts. He returned to the station and parked his car in the shadow of the dinosaur. He waited. The girl sat in the glass booth behind a rack of
road atlases, suddenly the sweetheart of every town he'd traveled
through in the last few months. To be with someone who knew his
name, to hear another voice would be enough for tonight. Jones
twisted open a beer and loaded the dart gun. He licked the suction
tip, took aim and fired.

"Hey," the girl shouted.

"Wanna go somewhere?" Jones asked.

They'd crossed the Mississippi three weeks ago and driven north
through Iowa, staying in motels and eating in diners, enjoying high
times until his money began to run out. Then they started sleeping in
the car, parked at rest stops or in empty lots, arms and legs braided together in the backseat of the Belvedere. One morning Jones had gone

to a bakeshop and bought a loaf of day-old sourdough bread for thirty-five cents. It was the cool blue hour before dawn, but already, as he crossed the parking lot, the sky was growing pale, and the patches of tar were softening beneath his shoes, and in the sultry air the last weak light of the streetlamps threw off dull coronas of yellow and pink. Only one other car was parked in the empty lot, and its windows had been smashed out, a spray of glass scattered like seeds across the asphalt. As Jones approached the Belvedere, he saw the girl slowly lift the hair away from her head. It was as if he were witness to some miracle of revelation set in reverse, as if the rising sun and the new day had not bestowed but instead stripped the world of vision, exposed and left it bare. Her skull was blue, a hidden thing not meant for the light. Jones opened her door. She held the wig of curly red hair in her lap.

"Damn," he said. He paced off a small circle in the parking lot.

The girl combed her fingers calmly through the hair on her lap. She'd understood when she removed the wig that revealing herself to Jones would tip fate irrevocably. She felt that in this moment she would know Jones and know him forever. She waited for Jones to spend his shock and anger, afraid that when he cooled down she might be on her way back to Carbondale, to the gas station and her stepfather and the church and the prayers for miraculous intercession. When Jones asked what was wrong with her, and she told him, he punted the loaf of sourdough across the empty lot.

"Why haven't you said anything?"

"What was I supposed to say, Jones?"

"The truth might've made a good start."

"Seems to me you've been having yourself a fine time without it," she said. "Hasn't been all that crucial so far."

"Jesus Christ."

"Besides, I wouldn't be here now if I'd told you. You'd have been long gone."

Jones denied it. "You don't know me from Adam," he said.

"Maybe not," she said. She set the wig on her head. "I'll keep it on if you think I'm ugly." The girl swung her legs out of the car and walked across the lot. She picked up the bread and brought it back. "These things drag out," she said.

She brushed pebbles and dirt and splinters of grass from the crust and then cracked the loaf in half.

"You didn't get any orange juice, did you?" she asked. "This old bread needs orange juice."

She reached inside and tore a hunk of clean white bread from the core and passed the loaf to Jones. He ate a piece and calmed down.

"Who knows how long I've got?" she said.

When they headed out again that morning, going west seemed inevitable—driving into the sun was too much to bear, and having it at their backs in the quiet and vacant dawn gave them the feeling, however brief, that they could outrace it. It was 1977, it was August, it was the season when the rolling fields were feverish with sunflowers turning on withered stalks to reach the light, facing them in the east as they drove off at dawn, gazing after them in the west as the sun set, and they searched the highway ahead for the softly glowing neon strip, for the revolving signs and lighted windows and the melancholy trickle of small-town traffic that would bloom brightly on the horizon and mean food and a place to stop for the night. If Jones wasn't too tired, he pushed on, preferring the solitude of night driving, when actual distances collapsed unseen, and the car seemed to float unmoored through limitless space, the reassuring hum of tires rolling beneath him, the lights of towns hovering across the darkened land like constellations in a warm universe. By day, he stopped only when the girl wanted to see a natural wonder, a landmark, a point of historical interest. Early this morning they'd visited the valley of The Little Bighorn. Silence held sway over the sight, a silence that touched the history of a century ago and then reached beyond it, running back to the burnt ridges and bluffs and to a time when the flat golden plain in the West had not yet felt the weight of footprints. Jones watched the girl search among the huddled white markers, looking for the blackened stone where Custer fell. She'd climbed over the wrought-iron fence to stand beside the stone, and a bull snake cooling in the shadow slithered off through the yellow grass. She seemed okay, not really sick, only a little odd and alien when she took off the wig. Now and then Jones would look at the girl and think, *you're dying,* but the unvarying heat hammered the days into a dull sameness, and driving induced a kind of amnesia, and for the most part Jones had shoved the idea out of his mind until this morning when they'd discussed their next move.

"We could drive to Nevada," she'd said. "Seems we're headed that direction, anyhow."

"Maybe," Jones had said.

"It only takes an hour to get married," the girl said, "and they rent you the works. A veil, flowers. We'll gamble. I've never done that. Have you? Roulette—what do you think, Jones?"

"I said maybe."

"Jones," she said. "I'm not into maybe."

"I don't know," Jones said. "I haven't thought it out."

"What's to think?" the girl said. "You'd be a widower in no time."

Jones squeezed the girl's knee, knobby and hard like a foal's. "Jesus," he said.

"It's not a big commitment I'm asking for."

"Okay, all right," Jones had said. "Don't get morbid."

Night fell, and the highway rose into the mountains. With the continental divide coming up, Jones couldn't decide whether or not to wake the girl. She didn't like to miss a landmark or border or any attraction advertised on a billboard. They'd stopped for the Parade of Presidents, AMERICA'S HERITAGE IN WAX, and to see alligators and prairie dogs and an ostrich and the bleached white bones of dinosaurs, and by now the back of the car was covered with bumper stickers and decals, and the trunk was full of souvenirs she'd bought, snow-filled baubles, bolo ties, beaded Indian belts, engraved bracelets, pennants. Wall Drug, Mt. Rushmore, The Little Bighorn and a bare rutted patch of dirt in the sweet grass that, according to a bullet-riddled placard, was the Lewis and Clark Trail—she'd stocked up on hokey junk and sentimental trinkets, and the stuff now commemorated a wandering path across state lines, over rivers, up mountains, into empty fields where battles had been fought and decided and down the streets of dirty, forgotten towns where once, long ago, something important had happened.

Jones gave her a shake and said, "Now all the rivers flow west."

"Jones?" She was disoriented, a child spooked on waking in unfamiliar surroundings. "I'm not feeling too good."

"You want to lie down?"

"I could use a beer," the girl said. "Something to kill this."

Jones eased the car over the breakdown line. The mountains cut a crown of darkness out of the night sky, and a row of telephone poles, silhouetted in the starlight, seemed like crosses planted along the highway. He arranged the backseat, shoving his duffle to the floor and unrolling the sleeping bag. The car shook as a semi passed, spraying a phalanx of gravel in its wake.

"Let's get there soon," the girl said.

"Get in back," Jones said.

"I'm praying," she said.

"That's good," he said. Jones ran his hand over the girl's head. Wispy strands of hair pulled loose and stuck to his palm. "We'll stop in the next town."

Back on the road, the wind dried his T-shirt, and the sweat-soaked cotton turned stiff as cardboard. Beneath him the worn tires rolled over the warm asphalt like the murmur of a river. On the move once more, he felt only relief, a sense of his body freed from its strict place in time, drifting through the huddled blue lights of towns named after Indians and cavalrymen and battles, after blind expectations and the comforts of the known past, after the sustaining beliefs and fears of pioneers. Outlook, Savage, Plentywood. Going west, names changed, became deposits of utopian history, places named Hope and Endwell, Wisdom and Independence and Loveland. Whenever the road signs flashed by, luminous for an instant, Jones felt as though he were journeying through a forgotten allegory.

The girl asked, "When do you think we'll be there?"

"We're not going to Las Vegas," Jones said. He had not known his decision until he spoke and heard the words aloud.

"Why not?"

"I'm taking you to a hospital."

"They'll send me home," the girl said.

"They might."

"Dad'll say you abducted me."

"You know that's not the deal."

"Don't matter," the girl said. "He'll say you're working for Satan and his demonic forces, even if you don't know it. He says just about everybody is."

"Well, I'm not," Jones said.

"You might be without you knowing it," the girl said.

They were crossing the Bitterroot. Jones lost radio reception, and so he listened to the girl's prayers, words coming to him in fragments, *Jesus* and *savior* and *amen*, the music of her voice carried away by the wind, choked off whenever she dry-heaved in the seat behind him. Somewhere in western Idaho she fell asleep, and for the next few hours Jones listened to the car tires sing. Outside Spokane, on an illuminated billboard set back in a wheat field, a figure of Jesus walked on water, holding a staff. Jones considered the odd concession to realism: a man walking on water would hardly need to support himself with a crutch. The thought was gone as soon as the billboard vanished behind him. No others took its place. Bored, he searched the radio dial for voices but for long empty stretches pulled in nothing but the sizzle of static, a strange surging cackle filling the car as if suddenly he'd lost contact with earth.

A red neon vacancy sign sputtered ambiguously, the NO weakly charged and half-lit. Behind the motel and across the railroad tracks, the Columbia River snaked through Wenatchee, flowing wide and quiet, a serene blue vein dividing the town from the apple orchards. The low brown hills were splotched with squares of green, patches of garden carved out of burnt land, and beyond them to the west, rising up, etched into the blue sky, a snowcapped mountain range rimmed the horizon like teeth set in some huge jaw.

"We're here," Jones said.

"Where?"

"Wen-a-tchee," he said.

"Wena-tchee," he tried again.

"Just a place," he said, finally. "Let's get upstairs."

In their room, Jones set the girl on the bed. He spritzed the sheets with tap water, cooling them, and opened the window. A hot breeze pushed the brown burlap curtains into the room. The gray, dusty leaves of an apple tree spread outside the window, and beneath the tree the unnatural blue of a swimming pool shimmered without revealing any depth in the morning sun. A slight breeze rippled the water, and an inflated lifesaver floated aimlessly across the surface.

The girl was kneeling at the foot of the bed, her hands folded and her head bowed in prayer. She was naked, her body a dull, white votary candle, the snuffed flame of her hair a dying red ember.

"Kneel here with me," she said.

"You go ahead," Jones said. He sat on the edge of the bed and pulled off his boots.

"It wouldn't hurt you," she said, "to get on your knees."

"We had this discussion before," he said.

"I believe it was a miracle," the girl said. She was referring to the remission of her cancer, the answered prayers. Her stepfather belonged to an evangelical sect that believed the literal rapture of Judgment Day was near at hand. Several dates he'd predicted for the end of time had already come and gone. Two months ago, he'd taken her out of medical treatment, refusing science in favor of prayer. Her illness bloomed with metaphoric possibilities and large portents for the congregation of the Church of the Redeemer in Carbondale and was used as a kind of augury, variously read as a sign of God's covenant, or as proof of Man's fallenness, his wickedness and sin. For a while she'd been in remission, and news of her cure had brought a host of desperate seekers to the church.

At a display in South Dakota, against the evidence of bones before them, the girl had said dinosaurs didn't die sixty million years ago. "It was about ten thousand years ago," she had insisted. Her stepfather believed they'd been on the boat with Noah.

"Some big ass boat," Jones had said. Jones no longer had any interest in arguing. But he said, "And now that you're sick again, what's that?"

"It's what the Lord wants."

"There's no talking to you," Jones said.

"We're all just here to bear witness," she said.

"Have your prayers ever been answered?"

"The night you came by the station, I asked for that. I prayed, and you came."

"I was hungry. I wanted a candy bar."

"That's what you think," the girl said. "But you don't know. You don't really know why you stopped, or what the plan is or anything. Who made you hungry? Huh? Think about that."

The rush of words seemed to exhaust her. She wrapped a corner of the sheet around her finger and repeated, "Who made you hungry?"

"So you prayed for me, and I came," Jones said. "Me, in particular? Or just someone, anyone?" He stripped off his shirt, wadded it up and wiped the sweat from his armpits. "Your illness doesn't mean anything. You're just sick, that's all."

Jones cranked the hot water and stayed in the shower, his first in days, until it scalded his skin a splotchy pink. Finished, he toweled off, standing over the girl. She was choking down cries.

"Why don't you take a shower?" Jones said.

"Maybe I should go back home."

"Maybe you should just stand out there on the road and let your old dad's radar find you." Then Jones said, "If that's what you want, I'll get you a bus ticket. You can be on your way tomorrow."

The girl shook her head. "It's no-place to me," she said.

"The Eskimos don't have homes, either," Jones said. "They don't have a word for it. They can't even ask each other, Hey, where do you live?"

II

Dr. McKillop sat on an apple crate and pulled a flask from his coat pocket. The afternoon heat was bad, but the harsh light was worse; he squinted uphill, vaguely wishing he were sober. It was too late, though, and with a sense of anticipation, of happy fatality, he drank, and the sun-warmed scotch bit hard at the back of his throat. McKillop felt the alcoholic's secret pleasure at submitting to something greater than himself, a realignment with destiny: he took another drink. Swimming in the reflection of the silver flask, he noticed a young white man. He was tall and thin, his cheekbones sharp and high, and in the glare his deep eye sockets seemed empty, pools of cool blue shadow. When the man finally approached, McKillop offered him the flask.

"I was told in town I could find you here," Jones said.

McKillop nodded. "You must be desperate."

The doctor wiped dust and sweat from his neck with a sun-bleached bandana. One of the day pickers had fallen from a tree and broken his arm, and McKillop had been called to reset it. He was no longer a doctor, not legally, not since six months ago when he'd been caught prescribing cocaine to himself. The probationary status of his medical license didn't matter to the migrants who worked the apple orchards, and McKillop was glad for the work. It kept trouble at a distance.

"Let me guess," McKillop said. "You don't have any money? Or you're looking for pharmaceuticals?"

"The bartender at Yakima Suzie's gave me your name," Jones said.

"You can get drunk, you can smoke cigars and gamble in a bar. You can find plenty in a bar. I know I have." McKillop pressed a dry brown apple blossom between his fingers, then sniffed beneath his nails. "But a doctor, a doctor you probably shouldn't find in a bar." He looked up at Jones and said, "I've been defrocked."

"I'm not looking for a priest," Jones said. The doctor's stentorian voice and overblown statements were starting to annoy him. The doctor wore huaraches with tire-tread soles, and his toes were caked with dirt, and the long curled nails looked yellow and unhealthy. He knotted his long raggedy hair in a ponytail.

Jones remained silent while a flatbed full of migrants rumbled by, jouncing over a worn two-track of gray dust and chuckholes. The green of the garden, of the orchards he'd seen from the valley, was an illusion; the trail of rising dust blew through the trees and settled and bleached the branches and leaves bone gray. A grasshopper spit brown juice on Jones's hand; he flicked it away and said, "I've got a girl in pain."

"Well, a girl in pain." McKillop capped his flask and wiped his forehead again. He spat in the dust, a dry glob rolling up thick and hard at his feet. He crushed it away with the rubber heel of his sandal. He looked up into the lattice of leaves, the sun filtered through; many of the apples with a western exposure were still green on the branch. McKillop stood and plucked one of the unripe apples and put it in his pocket. "For later," he said.

The room smelled like rotting mayonnaise. Her body glistened with a yellow liquid. She'd vomited on herself, on the pillows, on the floor. Face down, she clutched the sheets and tore them from the bed. She rolled over on her back, kicking the mattress and arching herself off the bed, lifting her body, twisting as though she were a wrestler attempting to escape a hold.

Jones pinned her arms against the bed while she bucked, trying to free herself. Her teeth were clenched, then she gasped, gulping for air. Her upper lip held a delicate dew of sweat in a mustache of faint blonde hair. She made fists of her thin, skeletal hands, and then opened them, clawing Jones with her yellowed nails.

McKillop drew morphine from a glass vial and found a blue vein running in the girl's arm. A drop of blood beaded where the needle punctured her skin. McKillop dabbed the blood away with the bed-sheet and pressed a Band-Aid over the spot.

The girl's body relaxed, as if she were suddenly without skeleton.

Windblown dust clouded the window. Jones slid it open along runners clogged with dirt and desiccated flies and looked down into the motel pool. Lit by underwater lights, it glowed like a jewel. A lawn chair lay on its side near the bottom, gently wavering in an invisible current.

"She needs a doctor," McKillop said.

"That's you," Jones said. "You're the doctor."

McKillop shook his head.

"Don't leave," the girl said. Only her index finger flickered, lifting slightly off the bed, as if all her struggle had been reduced to a tiny spasm.

"Wait outside," Jones said to the doctor.

When he'd gone, Jones turned on the television, a broken color set that bathed the room in a blue glow; he searched for a clear channel, but the screen remained a sea of pulsing static behind which vague figures swam in surreal distortion, auras without source. He stripped the bed and wetted a thin, rough towel with warm water and began to wipe the vomit off the girl's face, off her hard, shallow chest, off her stomach as it rose and fell with each breath. "Feels good," she said. Jones rinsed the towel and continued the ablution, working down her stick-thin legs and then turning her on to her stomach, massaging the tepid towel over her back and buttocks, along her thighs. The curtains fluttered, parting like wings and rising into the room. It was early, but the sun was setting in the valley, the brown rim of hills holding a halo of bright light, an emphatic, contoured seam of gold and different sounds—the screeching of tires, the jangling of keys, a dog barking—began to carry clearly, sounds so ordinary and near they seemed to have a source, not within the room, not out in the world, but in memory.

When the girl sank into sleep, Jones slipped out into the hallway.

"Your wife?" McKillop asked.

"Just a girl I picked up."

"Jesus, man." With forced jocularity, the doctor slapped Jones on the back. "You know how to pick them."

Out on the street dusk settled, a moment of suspension. The sky was still deep blue with a weak edge of white draining away in the west. An Indian crouched on the curb outside the motel, his face brown and puckered like a windfall apple in autumn.

Jones and McKillop entered a bar next door.

"I'm taking her to a hospital," Jones said.

"There's precious little a hospital can do," the doctor said. "Let's have a drink here," he called out. "They'll start a morphine drip. It'll keep her euphoric until she dies."

"Then I'll send her home," Jones said. In the navy he'd learned one thing, and for Jones it amounted to a philosophy: there was no real reason to go forward, but enormous penalties were paid by those who refused. He'd learned this lesson rubbing Brasso into his belt buckle and spit shining his boots for inspections that never came. "I could leave right now," he said. "I could drive away."

"Why don't you," the doctor said. "Turn tail, that's what I'd do." He ordered boilermakers and drank his by dumping the shot of bourbon into the schooner of beer. He polished off his first drink and called for another round.

"Deep down," McKillop said, "I'm really shallow."

Jones said, "I had this feeling if I kept driving everything would be okay."

"The healing, recuperative powers of the West," the doctor said. "Teddy Roosevelt and all that. The West was a necessary invention of the Civil War, a place of harmony and union. From the body politic to the body—"

Jones only half-listened. He found himself resisting the doctor's glib reductions.

"I'd like to hit the road," McKillop was saying. The phrase had an antiquated sound. Even in the cool of the bar, McKillop was sweating. He pressed a fat finger down on a bread crumb, then flicked it away.

"You looked bad when you saw her," Jones said.

"I'll be all right," McKillop said. He downed his drink. "I'm feeling better now. You'll need help, but I'm not your doctor."

McKillop bought a roll of quarters and made a few sloppy calls to friends in Seattle, waking them, demanding favors for the sake of old times, invoking old obligations, twice being told to fuck off and finally getting through to an old resident friend at Mercy Hospital, who said he'd look at the girl if nothing else could be done.

"We'll take care of her," McKillop said to Jones. They walked down to the section of windowless warehouses and blank-faced cold-storage buildings, walked along cobbled streets softly pearled with blue lamplight, apple crates stacked up twenty, thirty feet high against the brick. Beyond the train tracks, the Columbia flowed quietly; a path of cold moonlight stretched across the water like a bridge in a dream, the first step always there, at Jones's feet. Through crate slats Jones saw eyes staring, men slumped in the boxes for the night, out of the wind, behind a chinking of newspaper, cardboard, fluttering plastic. Jones stopped. A canvas awning above a loading dock snapped in the breeze like a doused jib sail.

"Don't you worry, Jonesy boy," the doctor said. "We'll get her squared away. Tomorrow, in Seattle." He reached into his bag and handed Jones a vial and a syringe. "If it gets too much, the pain, you know, give her this. Only half, four or five milligrams. You can do it, right? Just find a vein."

A fire burned on the banks of the river. A circle of light breathed out and the shadows of stone-still men danced hilariously. A woman walked through the grass outside the circle; her legs were shackled by her own pants, blue jeans dropped down around her ankles; she stumbled, stood, stumbled, struggled. "I know what you want," she shouted back at the circle of men. "I know what you want." She fell, laughing hideously.

The doctor was clutching Jones's hand, squeezing and shaking it, and Jones got the idea that the doctor might never let go.

Outside the motel, the same wrecked Indian stood and approached Jones. His left cowboy boot was so worn down around the heel that the bare shoe tacks gave a sharp metallic click on the cement with each crippled step. He blinked and thrust a hand at Jones.

"My eyes hurt when I open 'em," he said. "And they hurt when I close 'em. All night I don't know what to do. I keep opening and closing my eyes."

Jones reached into his pocket and pulled a rumpled dollar loose from his wad of muster pay.

"I swear," the Indian said. "Somebody's making my eyes go black."

Jones gave him the bone. He tried to see in the man the facial lines of an Eskimo, but his skin was weathered, the lines eroded.

"SoHappy," he said.

"Me too," Jones said.

"No," the Indian said, thumping his chest. "SoHappy. Johnny So-Happy, that's me. Fucking me."

He blinked and backed away, wandering off alone, shoe tacks roughly clawing the sidewalk.

•

The girl was awake, shrouded in white sheets, staring at the ceiling, her breathing shallow but regular. Jones lay in the bed beside her, suffering a mild case of the spins. The walls turned, soft and summery, like the last revolution of a carousel wobbling to a stop. He looked out the window. Under the moonlight each leaf on the apple tree was a spoonful of milk.

Jones felt the girl's dry, thin fingers wrap around his wrist like a bird clutching at a perch.

"I love you," she whispered. Her voice was hoarse and frightening.

Jones shut his eyes against the spinning room. The movement crept beneath his closed lids, and Jones opened his eyes, to no effect. The room continued to spin.

"How about you Jones? You could just say it, I wouldn't care if it wasn't the truth. Not anymore."

Jones pressed her hand lightly.

"Where are we, Jones?" she asked. "I mean, really. What's the name of this place?"

They were a long way from Carbondale, from the home he'd seen the night they left. An oak tree hiding the collapsing remains of a childhood fort, a frayed rope with knotted footholds dangling from the hatch, a sprinkler turning slowly over the grass, a lounge chair beneath a sun shade, a paper plate weighted against the wind by an empty cocktail glass.

"I'm hot," she said.

Jones lifted her out of bed. She was hot, but she wasn't sweating. Against his fingers, her skin felt dry and powdery, friable, as if the next breeze might blow it all away, and he'd be left holding a skeleton. He wrapped her in a white sheet. She hooked her arms around his neck, and Jones carried her, airy as balsa, into the aqueous green light of the hallway and down the steps.

"Where we going?" she asked.

The surface of the pool shimmered, smooth as a turquoise stone. Jones unwrapped the sheet and let it fall. The girl was naked underneath.

"Hold on," Jones said.

He walked down the steps at the shallow end, the water washing up around his ankles, his knees, his waist, and then he gently lowered the girl until her back floated on the surface.

"Don't let go," she said, flinching as she touched water. In panic, she gasped for air.

"I won't," Jones said. "Just relax."

Her skin seemed to soak in water, drink it up like a dehydrated sponge, and she felt heavier, more substantial. Her arms and legs grew supple, rising and falling in rhythm to the water. He steered her around the shallow end.

"Except in songs on the radio," she said, "nobody's ever said they love me."

Her eyes were wide and vacant, staring up through the leaves of the apple tree, out past them into the night sky, the moon, the vault of stars.

"You think anybody's watching us?" the girl asked.

Jones looked up at the rows of darkened rooms surrounding the pool. Here and there a night-light glowed. Air conditioners droned.

"I doubt it," he said.

She let her arms spread wide and float on the surface as Jones eased her toward the edge of the pool. He lifted her out and set her down on the sheet. At the deep end of the pool, below the diving board, he saw the lounge chair, its yellow webbing and chrome arms shining in the beams of underwater light. He took a deep breath and dove in. The water was as warm as the air, easing the descent from one element to the next. Jones crept along the bottom until he found the chair. Pressure rang in his ears, and a dizziness spread through him as he dragged it along the length of the pool. For a moment he wanted to stop, to stay on the bottom and let everything go black; he held himself until every cell in his blood screamed and the involuntary instincts of his body craving air drove him back up and he surfaced, his last breath exploding out of him. He set the chair against the apple tree.

They sat beneath the tree while Jones caught his breath. A hot wind dried their skin.

"I liked Little Bighorn the best," the girl said.

"It was okay." Jones watched a leaf float across the pool. "You really think he's looking for you?"

"I know he is," she said. "He's got all his buddies on the police force that are saved—you know, born again."

"You want to go back there?"

The girl was quiet, then she said, "Weekends Dad and them hunt around under bridges by rivers, looking for graffiti with satanic messages. For devil worship you need the four elements. You need earth, wind, fire and water. That's what he says. So they look by rivers, and maybe they see some graffiti, or they find an old chicken bone, and they think they really got themselves something."

It seemed an answer, wired through biblical circuitry.

"Tomorrow you're going to a hospital," Jones said. "The doctor arranged it. Everything's set."

He carried the girl upstairs and placed her on the bed. In five weeks she'd gone from a girl he'd picked up in the heartland to an old woman, her body retreating from the world, shrunken and curled and lighter by the hour, it seemed. Her hair had never grown back, and the ulcerations from early chemo treatments had so weakened her gums that a tooth had come loose, falling out, leaving a black gap in a smile that should have been seductive to the young boys back in Carbondale. The whites of her eyes had turned scarlet red. Her limbs were skeletal, fleshless and starved. She'd said she was eighteen, but now she could have passed for eighty.

"You think I'll go to hell?"

"Probably."

"Jones—"

"Well, why do you talk like that?"

"I don't know." She clutched the sheet around her neck. "When I open my mouth these things just come out. They're the only words I have."

"One of my tours," Jones said, "we were on maneuvers in the Mediterranean." A boiler exploded, he said, and a man caught fire in a pool of burning oil. Crazed, aflame, engulfed, the man ran in erratic circles on the deck, a bright, whirling light in the darkness, shooting back and forth like an errant Roman candle, while other men chased him, half-afraid to tackle the man and catch fire themselves. Finally, beyond all hope, out of his mind, the man jumped over the deck railing, into the sea. "You could hear the flames whipping in the wind as he fell," Jones said. "Then he was gone. It was the sorriest thing I ever witnessed." Afterwards, he'd helped extinguish the fire, and for doing his duty he'd been awarded a dime-sized decoration for heroism.

"Everywhere we go," she said, and there was a long pause as her breath gurgled up through lungs full of fluid, "there's never any air-conditioning."

Jones held her hand, a bone. He thought she coughed this time, but again she was only trying to breathe. Suddenly he did not want to be in bed beside her. But he couldn't move.

"The Eskimos live in ice huts," he said.

"Sounds nice right now."

"It's very cold," Jones continued.

"I wish we were going there."

The girl coughed, and then curled into a fetal ball. "It's like hot knives stabbing me from inside," she said.

Jones lifted himself from the bed. He turned on the bedside lamp and took the morphine and the syringe from his shirt pocket. "The first explorers thought Eskimos roamed from place to place because they were poor," he said. "They thought the Eskimos were bums." He ripped the cellophane wrapper from the syringe and pushed the needle into the vial, slowly drawing the plunger back until half the clear liquid had been sucked into the barrel. "They were always on the move," he said. The girl bit into the pillow until her gums bled and left an imprint of her mouth on the case. Her body had an alertness, a tension that Jones sensed in the tortured angles she held her arms at, the faint weak flex of her atrophied muscles. She raised her head and opened her mouth wide, her startled red eyes searching the room as if to see where all the air had gone. "But when you think about it, you understand that it's efficient." Jones pushed the air bubbles out of the syringe until a drop of morphine beaded like dew at the tip of the needle. "Movement is the only way for them to survive in the cold. Even their morality is based on the cold, on movement." Jones now continued speaking only to dispel the silence and the lone sound of the girl's labored breathing. He unclenched her hand from the sheets and bent her arm back, flat against the bed. "They don't have police," he said, "and they don't have lawyers or judges. The worst punishment for an Eskimo is to be left behind, to be left in the cold." Inspecting her arm, he found the widest vein possible and imagined it flowing all the way to her heart and drove the needle in.

McKillop had taken the girl's purse and dumped the contents on the bed. He rummaged through it, and found a blue gumball, safety pins, pennies, a shopping list and several pamphlets from which he read. "Listen," he said. " 'For centuries lovers of God and of righteousness have been praying: Let your kingdom come. But what is that kingdom that Jesus Christ taught us to pray for? Use your Bible to learn the who, what, when, why and where of the Kingdom.'" He laughed. "Ironic, huh?"

"We don't know, do we?" Jones said.

"Oh come on," the doctor said. He took up a scrap of notepaper. "Blush. Lipstick—Toffee, Ruby Red. Two pair white cotton socks. Call Carolyn."

"Stay out of her stuff," Jones said.

"I was looking for ID," he said. "What's her name?"

Jones thought for a moment and then said, "It's better that you don't know."

"You didn't OD her, did you?"

"No," Jones said. Once last night he'd woken to the sound of the girl's voice, calling out. She spoke to someone who was not in the room and began to pick invisible things out of the air. Watching her struggle with these phantoms had made Jones feel horribly alone. Delirious, she ended by singing the refrain of a hymn. He said to the doctor, "I thought about it though."

"You could tell the truth. It's rather unsavory, but it's always an option."

Jones looked at the doctor. "It's too late," he said.

"I've tried the truth myself, and it doesn't work that well anyway. Half the time, maybe, but no more. What good is that? The world's a broke-dick operation. The big question is, who's going to care?"

"Her family," Jones said. "Born-again Christians."

"I was raised a Catholic." McKillop pulled a silver chain from around his neck and showed Jones a tarnished cross. "It was my mother's religion. I don't believe, but it still spooks me."

"This is against the law."

"If you sent her home, there'd be questions."

"There'll be questions anyway," Jones said. "Her stepdad's a fanatic. He'll be looking for me. He believes in what he's doing, you know?"

"I vaguely remember believing—"

"Not everything has to do with you," Jones said. He felt the sadness of language, the solitude of it. The doctor had no faith beyond a system of small ironies: it was like trying to keep the rain off by calling to mind the memory of an umbrella.

The doctor had dispensed with the nicety of a flask and now drank straight from the bottle.

"Never made it home last night," McKillop said.

"You look it," Jones said.

"I got lucky," McKillop said. "Sort of." He wiped his lips and said, "I wish I had a doughnut." He pulled a green apple from his pocket, buffing it on the lapel of his wrinkled jacket. He offered the bottle to Jones. Jones shook his head. "I'd watched this woman for a long time, desired her from afar, and then suddenly there I was, in bed with her, touching her, smelling her, tasting her. But I couldn't get it up."

"Maybe you should stop drinking."

"I like drinking."

"It's not practical," Jones said.

"Quitting's a drastic measure," McKillop said. He took a bite of the apple. "For a man who gets lucky as little as I do."

"I'll see you," Jones said.

III

By afternoon he had crossed the bridge at Deception Pass and driven south and caught a ferry to Port Townsend. He drove west along 101 and then veered north, hugging the shoreline of the Strait of Juan de Fuca, passing through Pysht and Sekiu, driving until he hit Neah Bay and the Makah Reservation, when finally there was no more road. It had remained hot all the way west, and now a wildfire burned across the crown of a mountain rising against the western verge of the reservation. The sky turned yellow under a pall of black smoke. Flecks of ash sifted like snow through the air. White shacks lined either side of the street, staggering forward on legs of leaning cinder block, and a few barefoot children played in the dirt yards, chasing dust devils. Several girls in dresses as sheer and delicate as cobwebs stood shielding their eyes and staring at the fire. Sunlight spread through the thin fabric, skirts flickering in the wind, so that each of the young girls seemed to be going up in flames.

Jones moved slowly through town, raising a trail of white dust, which mingled with the black ash and settled over the children, the shacks, a scattering of wrecked cars, and then along the foot of the mountain he followed an eroded logging road until it too vanished. A yellow mobile home sat on a bluff, and behind it, hidden by a brake of wind-crippled cedar, was the ocean. Jones heard the surf and caught the smell of rough-churned sea. A man in overalls came out of the mobile home—to Jones, he looked like an Eskimo. Jones switched off the ignition. The car rocked dead, but for a moment he felt the pressure of the entire country he'd crossed at his back, the vibration of the road still working up through the steering column, into his hands and along his arms, becoming an ache in his shoulders, a numbness traveling down his spine. Then the vibrations stopped, and he felt his body settle into the present.

Jones got out of the car. The man hooked a thumb in his breast pocket, the ghost habit of a smoker. Behind cracked lips, his teeth were rotten. He watched a retrofit bomber sweep out over the ocean, bank high and round and circle back over the hill, spraying clouds of retardant. The chemicals fell away in a rust red curtain that closed over the line of fire.

"How'd it start?" Jones asked.

"Tiny bit of broken bottle will start a fire, sun hits it right." The man lit a cigarette. "Been a dry summer. They logged that hill off mostly, and don't nobody burn the slash. Where you headed?"

Jones said he was just driving.

"Used to be a love colony down there," the man said. He pointed vaguely toward the ocean. "You get the hippies coming back now and again, looking for the old path down. But the trails all growed over." The man ran his tongue over the black gum between missing front teeth. "I thought maybe you was one of them."

"No," Jones said. "Never been here before."

"You can park, you want," he said. "There's a game trail runs partways down."

"Thanks."

"You'll see the old Zellerbach mill."

He found the abandoned mill in ruin, a twisted heap of metal. He sat on a rusted flume and pulled a patch of burnt weeds from the foundation. With a stick he chipped at the hard, dry ground and dug out three scoops of loose dirt, wrapping them in one of the girl's shirts. When he finished, he sat against a stump, counting the growth rings with his finger until near heartwood he'd numbered 200 years.

A clam-shell chime chattered like cold teeth beneath the awning of a bait shop. Inside the breakwater, boats pulled at their moorings. Jones walked up and down the docks of the marina until he found a Livingston slung by davits to the deck of a cabin cruiser. The windows of the cruiser were all dark, canvas had been stretched across the wheelhouse, and the home port stenciled across the stern was Akutan. He lowered the lifeboat into the water, pushed off and let himself drift quietly away from the marina.

When he'd rowed out into the shipping lane, Jones pull-started the twenty-horse Evinrude, and followed a flashing red beacon out around the tip of Cape Flattery to the ocean. He kept just outside the line of breaking waves, hugging the shore, the boat tossed high enough at times along the crest of a swell to see a beach wracked with bone-gray driftwood. Jones pulled the motor and rode the surf until the hull scraped sand. He loaded the girl into the boat, up front for ballast.

He poled himself off the sand with the oar and then rowed. Each incoming wave rejected his effort, angling the bow high and pushing the boat back in a froth of crushed white foam. Finally he managed to cradle the boat in the trough between breaking waves. The motor kicked out of the water with a high-rev whine, and Jones steered for open sea, heading due west. Beyond the edge of the shelf, the rough surface chop gave way to rolling swells, and Jones knew he was in deep water. He'd forgotten how black a night at sea was, how even the coldest, dying star seemed near and bright in the dark. He became afraid and drew the world in like a timid child, trembling with unreasonable fears—the terrible life below him, the girl's stepfather and his fanatic pursuit, his own fugitive life in flight from this moment. If it became history he would be judged and found guilty. Spindrift raked over the bow, splashing his face. The sea heaved in a sleepy rhythm. He crossed the black stern of a container ship at anchor, four or five stories of high wall, and when he throttled back to a dead drift he heard voices from the deck top, human voices speaking in a language he did not understand.

He ran another mile and cut the engine. The round world was seamless with the night sky, undivided, the horizon liquid and invisible except for a spray of stars that flashed like phosphorescence, rising out of the water. A cool breeze whispered over the surface. August was over. He'd piled the sleeping bag with beach rocks, and then he'd cleaned the car of evidence, collected the souvenirs, the trinkets, the orange smiles, the wig, and stuffed them down into the foot of the bag, knotting it shut with nylon rope. He'd taken the Bible, opened it to the genealogy, and scratched the month and year into the margins. Jones considered the possibility, as he rocked in the trough of a swell, that all this would one day break free from its deep hold in the sea, wash to the surface, the bumper stickers from Indian battles and decals commemorating the footpaths and wagon trails of explorers and pioneers, the resting places of men and women who'd left their names to towns and maps. And then the girl herself, identified by her remains, a story told by teeth and bones, interpreted.

Jones looped a rope tether around the handle of his flashlight and tied the other end to the sleeping bag. He checked the beam, which shone solidly in the darkness, a wide swath of white light carved out of the air. He unpackaged the soil he'd collected from the collapsed mill and sprinkled it across the sleeping bag, spreading earth from head to foot. It seemed a paltry ritual—the dirt, the light—but he was determined to observe ceremony. With his tongue he licked away a coating of salt from the rim of his lips. His hands were growing cold and stiff. He hoisted the head end of the bag over the port side and then pivoted the girl's feet around until the whole bag pitched overboard. Jones held it up a final instant, clutching the flashlight, allowing the air bubbles to escape, and then let go. Down she swirled, a trail of light spinning through a sea that showed green in the weakening beam and then went black. In silence Jones let himself drift until, borne away by the current, he could no longer know for certain where she'd gone down.

Back within the breakwater, Jones tied the lifeboat with a slack line to a wooden cleat. The mountain had vanished from view, swallowed by darkness, but a prevailing westerly had blown the wildfire across its crown, and a flare of red-yellow flame swept into the sky. An old Makah trudged up the road, dragging a stick through the dust, leaning on it when he stopped to watch the hieroglyphic write itself in fire on the edge of the reservation. Jones sat on the dock, dangling his legs. Flakes of feathery black ash drifted through the air and fanned lightly against his face. Spume crusted and stung his lips, and he was thirsty. He listened to the rhythm of the water as it played an icy cool music in the cadenced clinking of ropes and pulleys and bell buoys. Out beyond the breakwater the red and green running lights of a sailboat appeared, straggling into port. The wind lifted the voices of the sailors and carried them across the water like a song. One of the sailors shouted, "There it is." He stood on the foredeck and pointed toward the banner of flames rising in the sky.

Issue 126, 1993

THE ART OF WRITING

John Ashbery

✠

Musica Reservata

Then I reached the field and I thought
this is not a joke not a book
but a poem about something—but what?
Poems are such odd little jiggers.
This one scratches himself, gets up, then goes off to pee
in a corner of the room. Later looking quite
stylish in white jodhpurs against the winter
snow, and in his reluctance to talk to the utterly
discursive: "I will belove less than feared . . ."

He trotted up, he trotted down, he trotted all around the town
Were his relatives jealous of him?
Still the tock-tock machinery lies half-embedded in sand.
Someone comes to the window, the wave is a gesture proving
nothing,
and that nothing has receded. One gets caught
in servants like these and must lose the green leaves,
one by one, as an orchard is pilfered, and then, with luck,
nuggets do shine, the baited trap slides open.
We are here with our welfare intact.

Oh but another time, on the resistant edge of night
one thinks of the pranks things are.
What led the road that sped underfoot

to oases of disaster, or at least the unknown?
We are born, buried for a while, then spring up just as
everything is closing. Our desires are extremely simple:
a glass of purple milk, for example, or a dream
of being in a restaurant. Waiters encourage us, and squirrels.
There's no telling how much of us will get used.

My friend devises the cabbage horoscope
that points daily to sufficiency. He and all those others go home.
The walls of this room are like Mykonos, and sure enough,
green plumes toss in the breeze outside
that underscores the stillness of this place
we never quite have, or want. Yet it's wonderful, this
being; to point to a tree and say don't I know you from somewhere?
Sure, now I remember, it was in some landscape somewhere,
and we can all take off our hats.

At night when it's too cold
what does the rodent say to the glass shard?
What are any of us doing up? Oh but there's
a party, but it too was a dream. A group of boys
was singing my poetry, the music was an anonymous
fifteenth-century Burgundian anthem, it went something like this:

"This is not what you should hear,
but we are awake, and days
with donkey ears and packs negotiate
the narrow canyon trail that is
as white and silent as a dream,
that is, something *you* dreamed.
And resources slip away, or are pinned
under a ladder too heavy to lift.
Which is why you are here, but the mnemonics
of the ride are stirring."

That, at least, is my hope.

J.D. McClatchy

❈

At a Reading

Anthony Hecht's

And what if now I told you this, let's say,
By telephone. Would you imagine me
Talking to myself in an empty room,
Watching myself in the window talking,
My lips moving silently, birdlike,
On the glass, or because superimposed
On it, among the branches of the tree ·
Inside my head? As if what I had to say
To you were in these miniatures of the day,
When it is last night's shadow shadows
Have made bright.
⠀⠀⠀⠀⠀⠀⠀⠀⠀Between us at the reading—
You up by that child's coffin of a podium,
The new poem, your "Transparent Man," to try,
And my seat halfway back in the dimmed house—
That couple conspicuous in the front row
You must have thought the worst audience:
He talked all the while you read, she hung
On *his* every word, not one of yours.
The others, rapt fan or narcolept,
Paid their own kind of attention, but not
Those two, calm in disregard, themselves

A commentary running from the point.
Into put-down? you must have wondered,
Your poem turned into an example, the example
Held up, if not to scorn, to a glaring
Spot of misunderstanding, some parody
Of the original idea, its clear-obscure
Of passageways and the mirrory reaches
Of beatitude where the dead select
Their patience and love discloses itself
Once and for all.
                    But you kept going.
I saw you never once look down at them,
As if by speaking *through* her you might
Save the girl for yourself and lead her back
To *your* poem, *your* words to lose herself in,
Who sat there as if at a bedside, watching,
In her shift of loud, clenched roses, her hands
Balled under her chin, a heart in her throat
And gone out in her gaze to the friend
Beside her. How clearly she stood out
Against everything going on in front of us.

It was then I realized that she was deaf
And the bearded boy, a line behind you,
Translating the poem for her into silence,
Helping it out of its disguise of words,
A story spilled expressionless from the lip
Of his mimed exaggerations, like last words
Unuttered but mouthed in the mind and formed
By what, through the closed eyelid's archway,
Has been newly seen, those words she saw
And seeing heard—or not heard but let sink in,
Into a darkness past anyone's telling,
There between us.
                What she next said,

The bald childless woman in your fable,
She said, head turned, out the window
Of her hospital room to trees across the way,
The leaflorn beech and the sycamores
That stood like enlargements of the vascular
System of the brain, minds meditating on
The hill, the weather, the storm of leukemia
In the woman's bloodstream, the whole lot
Of it "a riddle beyond the eye's solution,"
These systems, anarchies, ends not our own.

The girl had turned her back to you by then,
Her eyes intent on the thickness of particulars,
The wintery emphasis of that woman's dying,
Like facing a glass-bright, amplified stage,
Too painful not to follow back to a source
In the self. And like the girl, I found myself
Looking at the boy, your voice suddenly
Thrown into him, as he echoed the woman's
Final rendering, a voice that drove upward
Onto the lampblack twigs just beyond her view
To look back on her body there, on its page
Of monologue. The words, as they came—
Came from you, from the woman, from the voice
In the trees—were his then, the poem come
From someone else's lips, as it can.

Issue 97, 1985

John Hollander

⁜

Making It

a poem to something longer

Once, but once, did I fail my Muse, who, lying
(Golden-shadowed shape) by the flaring candle,
Urged me upward. But there was more to dying
      Than I could handle.

Girl of gold, you worked such a leaden vengeance
On my poor pen three weeks ago: I tried to
Raise it. No. Despite your presumed attentions
      All I could ride to

Was the jangling creak of a bedspring, failing
Sounds not even mine, that were made to shake it
On some record, behind a swish youth's wailing.
      Help me to make it!

How the candle guttered and died! Its throbbing
Flame had dripped a sadness of wax that crowned us
Both with hot, red drops of its final sobbing:
      Heavens around us

Seemed just then to flicker a stormy warning.
Was it that? Or was it the candle's trembling,
Making instant shiftings from night to morning,
      Never dissembling

Really, but immersed in imaginations?
Fireworks sprouting visions aloft, and breaking
Up the mindless night with illuminations,
          Feigning, not faking,

Never can quite vanish completely for us,
After-images will outlast the hissing
Violence of rocketing lights, the chorus,
          Sighing and kissing.

Come then, let us celebrate all this fire:
Not to do it now would be to deny it.
Mirror, bed and discarded clothes conspire,
          Beg us to try it.

Help me now, dear girl; neither pot nor liquor
Turns the poem on, helps us to get connected.
All our golden cities are growing sicker.
          Am I infected?

Are you down with something? I'm feeling seedy,
As I grope through blankets of silence. Bend, O
Unforgiving presence! But no: *Perdidi*
          Musam tacendo

(Help me!) *nee me Apollo respicit* (as A-
Nonymous once whispered, a played-out Roman);
I, laid-up New Yorker, feel that it has a
          Touch of the omen,

This half-buried failure of mine to make it,
One July night, tangled up with the legs of
Her who was my Muse once. We both must take it.
          Using the dregs of

Sour wines of embarrassment, and refusing
Drinks from untipped cups of delight, my shaking

Hand must mix some cocktail of your own choosing,
    And of my making;

Drink; then do and die. If I've been too clever
This should make me stop, for my stomach's queasy:
Making something up out of nothing's never
    Happy or easy.

Issue 31, 1964

Elizabeth Bishop and May Swenson

❈

Correspondence

For years I have enjoyed teaching May Swenson's subtle poem "Dear Elizabeth," an intricate meditation on sexuality and exoticism, though I have found my classes startled when I claimed it constituted a kind of causerie between the two lesbian poets about their situation as lesbians, as poets. Through the good offices of Judith Hemschemeyer and Zan Knudson, I have culled an illustrative bouquet (it is what anthology *means in Greek) from the letters between Bishop and Swenson (part of their extended correspondence now in the Olin Library at Washington University, Saint Louis) which concern "Dear Elizabeth" and other literary matters of interest to both poets at the time (1963–1965).*

A reference in Swenson's letter of November 6, 1965, compels comment; she regrets Bishop's omission of the poem "Exchanging Hats" from Questions of Travel *(Swenson herself had performed the poem at a reading in New York in 1962, reporting to its author that the audience responded with "respectful hilarity"). Indeed "Exchanging Hats" is one of only four poems that Bishop published (in* New World Writing, *1956) and decided not to collect. One biographer suggests that the poem seemed "to appropriate distorted versions of real people in a way Elizabeth always hated," but most critics note that the poem is much franker about the powers of transvestite perspective—and its implicit criticism of gender stereotypes—than Bishop was willing to acknowledge. Swenson's question ("Why didn't you include it?") is perhaps answered in the course of her own poem, presented here, with its interesting*

citations from Bishop herself that constitute a sort of descant on the
likelihood of "song without husbands."

—Richard Howard

RIO, AUGUST 27, 1963

Dear May,

I gave Betty Theorides the samba record for you, and put a note in
it . . . you'll be hearing from her on the telephone around the 20th of
September, I think—whenever the SS *Brazil* gets into New York . . .
The trouble is that now I can't remember what I've written you and
what I haven't! I think I did write you about Lota's having been in the
hospital, etc.—and the note with the record wasn't news, just information about the samba . . .

Oh—I have three new birds—Betty T. had about 20 and gave them
all away except one lonely little yellow and green creature she handed
to me at the last minute. It turns out to be a female wild canary and I
think I'll have to get it a husband. Then I couldn't resist a pair of Bica
Lacquas (lacquer beaks, or maybe sealing-wax beaks—the word's the
same)—I wish I could send you a pair and I wonder if they import
them. They're the most adorable bird I know—about 3" long, including the tail—extremely delicate; bright red bills and narrow bright red
masks. The male has a sort of mandarin drooping moustache—one
black line—otherwise they're just alike. They're tiny but plump—and
the feathers are incredibly beautiful, shading from brown and gray on
top to pale beige, white, and a rose-red spot on the belly—but all this
in almost invisible ripples of color blending with white—wave-
ripples, just like sand ripples on a sand flat after the tide has gone
out—all so fine I have to put on my reading-glasses to appreciate it
properly. They're almost as affectionate as lovebirds, and they have a
nest—smaller than a fist—with a doorway in the side, that they both
get in to sleep. The egg is about as big as a baked bean—rarely hatches
in captivity—but I'm hoping. From the front they look like a pair of
half-ripe strawberries. You'd like them! But now I have two unwed female canaries—must find them husbands in order to have a little song
around here. We're all silent together for the present.

Much love, Elizabeth

NEW YORK, SEPTEMBER 25, 1963

Dear Elizabeth:

The Samba record came today—just before I left for work. I only had time to play "love isn't like that"—very exciting rhythm, very pure. I'll give you my complete reactions to all of them—Pearl and I both will—when we've had a chance to enjoy them properly. . . . We couldn't have imagined a nicer present—and it's something *nobody* else will have around here. (Like the Brazilian birds record that we still startle people with—but the samba is danceable—and how!) . . .

Elizabeth, I've written a poem about those *Bica Lacquas* that you described in a recent letter—I've used *your words* almost exactly, because the way you expressed their appearance and habits, etc. is so charming—and, by chance, without your knowing it, you made some rhymes. I've put quotes around most of what you wrote—which is a good portion of the poem. It's written like a letter—but of course I don't actually *mean* for you to send me the *Bica Lacquas* (as I ask you to do in the poem). Soon as I make it presentable I'll send it to you. Have the wild canaries got husbands yet? . . .

SEPTEMBER 26

I worked on the poem some more, so I'm sending it. Although it's probably not done. Too wordy, and too cute, maybe. What do you think? The only good parts are yours . . . Thanks again for the record . . . I'll write you about it in detail next letter.

Love to you, and to Lota. From Pearl, too.

*Dear Elizabeth**

Yes, I'd like a pair of *Bicos de Lacre*—
meaning beaks of "lacquer" or "sealing wax"?
(the words are the same in Portuguese)
". . . about 3 inches long including the tail,
red bills and narrow bright red masks . . ."
You say the male has a sort of "drooping
mandarin-mustache—one black stripe"—

*A reply to Elizabeth Bishop in Brazil.

otherwise the sexes are alike. "Tiny but
plump, shading from brown and gray on top
to pale beige, white, and a rose red spot
on the belly"—their feathers, you tell
me, incredibly beautiful "alternating
lights and darks like nearly invisible
wave-marks on a sandflat at low tide,

and with a pattern so fine one must put on
reading glasses to appreciate it properly."
Well, do they sing? If so, I expect their
note is extreme. Not something one hears,
but must watch the cat's ears to detect.
And their nest, that's "smaller than a fist,
with a doorway in the side just wide enough

for each to get into to sleep." They must
be very delicate, not easy to keep. Still,
on the back porch on Perry St., here, I'd
build them a little Brazil. I'd save every
shred and splinter of New York sunshine
and work through the winter to weave them
a bed. A double, exactly their size,

with a roof like the Ark. I'd make sure to
leave an entrance in the side. I'd set it
in among the morning-glories where the
gold-headed flies, small as needles' eyes,
are plentiful. Although "their egg is apt
to be barely as big as a baked bean . . ."
It rarely hatches in captivity, you mean—

but we could hope! In today's letter you
write, "The *Bicos de Lacre* are adorable as
ever—so tiny, neat, and taking baths
constantly in this heat, in about ¼ inch
of water—then returning to their *filthy*

little nest to lay another egg—which
never hatches." But here it might! And it

doesn't matter that "their voice is weak,
they have no song." I can see them as I
write—on their perch on my porch. "From
the front they look like a pair of half-
ripe strawberries"—except for that stripe.
"At night the cage looks empty" just as
you say. I have "a moment's fright"—

then see the straw nest moving softly.
Yes, dear Elizabeth, if you would be so
kind, I'd like a pair of *Bicos de Lacre*—
especially as in your P.S. you confess,
"I already have two unwed female wild
canaries, for which I must find husbands
in order to have a little song around here."

—May Swenson

SAMAMBAIA, OCTOBER 3, 1963

Dear May:

. . . I am glad you got the record safely—how did Betty get it to
you—and I shall expect you to be samba-ing next time I see you. That
record *sounds* like Carnival—there are many more beautiful old sam-
bas and *marchinhas*—but it's hard to get good recordings—they insist on jazzing them up, or making them pretty—and the words are
the best part anyway . . .

Now our bird poem: Oh dear I had the name partly wrong, I see—It's
Bico Lacre—I had the *lacre* wrong because I went by the way the man in
the shop and our maid say it—and the "lower orders" often leave out
"r"s—sort of baby-talk. Also, I'm afraid they come from Africa . . . You
can probably see them among the finches in the Radio City subway pet
shop. Joanna swore they had them up in her northern state and described them most poetically, but a boy I know, a zoologist, was here yesterday and said they're either Australian or African. So you can go see

them and check on my accuracy. There's no real "spot"—just a faintly deeper rose color on the belly. The egg is—well, I think I said "jelly bean" but maybe it's smaller: a *Boston* baked bean would be right—not a N.Y. one. *I* must put on my reading-glasses—not *tudo o mundo*. I'm just getting more & more far-sighted with age. There's no "stripe," just the male's black pencil-line moustache. I think you should have a pair, too. Here I paid what—with inflation—came to 22 cents each for them . . . The brute of a woman in the pet shop said "if you cut their claws they'll get tame"! if you cut their claws they'll die of heart attacks, more like it.

The name might be different in English—but you should recognize them after writing a poem about them. I think the poem might work out rather well . . . Someone told me he'd seen a poem dedicated to me in the last Donald Hall paperback anthology—I have no idea whose it is—but thought it might be yours about the owl. The someone is actually a nice young American couple—he's here from Rutgers on a Fulbright, teaching Am. Lit.—the first really nice U.S. academics I've met here and I wish I could see more of them—but with 3 children and no telephone it is hard. But it is fun to discuss Mark Twain again, or *Moby-Dick* . . . except I am so much harder on novelists than the young seem to be—I rarely like them . . . Now I've just read *The Group*—felt I had to. Mary was a year ahead of me so I was not in her "group" (thank heavens) although we were friends. My oldest friend, with whom I went to school, camp, *and* college, is "Helena"— if you read it. Mary lets her off lightly! but doesn't bring her to life. I recognize "Helena" and her mother and Mary's 1st husband, and pieces of Mary herself, and Eunice Jessup, and bits of the others— but its too much like trying to remember a dream for me to judge it at all—I imagine it's very uneven—almost as if she really hadn't finished it—I admire her *gall*. I dislike the age we live in that makes that kind of writing seem necessary, though. We're all brutes . . .

John Cheever

from On the Literary Life

My father had a black Remington portable. He hit the keys so ardently
that he wore their letters off. He'd sit at that machine and smoke cigarettes and drink coffee and make the most ferocious sound, not like a
typewriter at all, more like a machine gun.

He wrote novels, letters and, of course, stories. He also kept a journal. This was typed on lined paper and collected in miniature loose-
leaf notebooks. There were twenty-eight of these notebooks when he died.

No, he didn't write in his journals with the idea that they would be
read by anybody else. We weren't even supposed to peek. But yes, ultimately he wanted them published, although he didn't make that decision until quite late in life. These were workbooks, a place to take notes,
to practice and to fume.

The entries were not dated. Nor was there any attempt to bring order. He'd take up a lined page, type on it until he was done, and then
he'd put it aside. Add to this the fact that my father was a fiction machine. Give him a screwdriver, have him walk across the room, and
he'd be holding a hammer. Often, in the course of a paragraph, he'd
jump from fact to fiction and back to fact.

Line up these obstacles, and you see what a miracle Robert Gottlieb
performed in excerpting a sort of memoir from the mass of words. This
was published by Knopf in 1991.

The magnificent thing about the journals is that they present the
writer at his most candid, nasty and depressed. For those of us who perform our wretched lives against the glowing and imaginary world that

advertisers, TV producers, and—to a lesser extent—movie directors throw up at us, it can be a relief to see such unhappiness in a man of some stature.

The trouble with the journals is that they present one strand of a relatively complex piece of tapestry. They give the impression that my father spent his entire life sitting around feeling worthless. Of course he did spend a lot of time sitting around feeling worthless. But that time was recorded disproportionately in his journals, which probably took him about fifteen minutes a day to write.

The Paris Review went back to the original notebooks and unearthed a good deal of fascinating and previously unpublished material on writing and other writers. It makes a great read. But the distortion is even more pronounced. He's not just sitting around feeling worthless, now he's sitting around feeling worthless and fretting about his place in the literary sweeps. Please remember that this is just one piece of the man. An interesting piece, I think: diverting, instructive, candid and intimate. But not the whole guy.

So read it, but remember also the stories, the novels, and the man whom friends and neighbors were always so happy to see. I liked to hear the rattle of that old Remington. He was working, and it was hard, it was deadly work. But that wasn't all of it. I could be wrong, of course, but it seemed to me, to his son, that John Cheever was also having the time of his life.

—Benjamin Cheever

I think today of a burning glass; these clear green trees standing in the deep grass, covered with white flowers, from some happier time. And I wonder if these wild excursions into self-discovery might not damage my interest in fictions and contrivances; but this cannot be so since I believe that writing is an account of the powers of extrication. And I must say this in "West Farm."

Again; this is what I want to do; to write something that describes the growth of a personality. For Coverly this process of growth would be so painful that he might be tempted. He seemed to be changing his form; to be putting off an old skin. His apprehensions about the success of this metamorphosis; his excitement at the happiness it promised, and the mental and physical anguish of reforming so many

deeply rooted habits seemed to tax his strength. He found himself torn
by the generation of nearly unbearable tensions. And mingled with this
triumph was a bitter sense of loss. He would remember coming back
from a trout stream in the northern woods late in the day, following
tiredly with his eyes the path that would take him back to where his boat
was moored and where he would cross the lake to the camp where there
would be dry fire-wood and a bed to sleep in. He had stayed at the
stream too late; the woods were getting dark. Just before dark the path
he had followed with so much good cheer and confidence dwindled
into a narrow animal track—a thread—and vanished in a bed of ferns.
He was lost. Coverly drank nearly a pint of whiskey before lunch.

I would like a more muscular vocabulary. And I must be careful about
my cultivated accent. When this gets into my prose my prose is at its
worst.

First I want a landscape that corresponds to the landscapes of our
dreams. It can be anything—frame houses, palaces, farms, fishing
shacks but it must have the fitness of those houses we walk through,
those beaches we swim on while we sleep. And I would like a narrative pace that has the quality of storytelling, that lost art.

The foolish hours I spend sitting in my library. I think that a writer,
my kind of writer, shouldn't have too much impedimenta and what
do I mean by this: chairs and tables, carpets and views of Rome. I
mean either this, or that since the possibilities of luck and disaster are
always vivid for my kind of writer, it may be that it takes me longer to
accustom myself to an environment. All of this will change; so will
everything else, but now I like to think of the house and its contents as
belonging to M. and the children, I like to feel that this bare room
with its chair and table is all I possess. Anxiety, from which I am suffering, strikes directly at my scrotum.

I think I can mail this chapter today; so it will be today or tomorrow.
If it turns out to be rubbish I would not be crushed. Nothing of any
importance, really. I must remember not, like a drunk, to exploit
these highs.

Praise be to thee Oh Lord. Of Thine own have we given Thee. I say this often and often feel it. I am a medium; and I mean to avoid the agony of Prometheus, Orpheus and Marsyas by closing my song with a pratfall. I think this is correct. I can discourse on my method or lack of method or what I know of my method but I do not do anything so scientific as play by ear. I merely strum. I think of Mrs. Trask with her numerous, white upright pianos being moved into whatever room she wished to fill with music. She must have been a great pianist, I said. Oh no, said Mr. Paul. All she could do was strum. By which I guess he meant that she would fumble for chords and resolutions that pleased her uneducated and I guess vulgar ear. This is very like me. I seem to have a little perspective on the affectation of prodigality, but not much. The piece in hand seems, at this moment, to be the heart of the book. But I'm not sure what the book is. I cannot state it in a sentence. So I would like to play by ear, to strum for another hundred pages. So today is a holiday. Do the tires, spade the garden.

I had a dream that a brilliant reviewer pointed out that there was an excess of lamentation in my work. I had, fleetingly, this morning, a sense of the world, one's life, one's friends and lovers as a given. Here it all is, comprehensible, lovely, a sort of paradise. That this will be taken quite as swiftly as it has been given is difficult to remember.

Ian McEwan

※

from The Art of Fiction CLXXIII

MCEWAN

The joy is in the surprise. It can be as small as a felicitous coupling of noun and adjective. Or a whole new scene, or the sudden emergence of an unplanned character who simply grows out of a phrase. Literary criticism, which is bound to pursue meaning, can never really encompass the fact that some things are on the page because they gave the writer pleasure. A writer whose morning is going well, whose sentences are forming well, is experiencing a calm and private joy. This joy itself then liberates a richness of thought that can prompt new surprises. Writers crave these moments, these sessions. If I may quote the second page of *Atonement,* this is the project's highest point of fulfillment. Nothing else—cheerful launch party, packed readings, positive reviews—will come near it for satisfaction.

Gabriel García Márquez

✠

from The Art of Fiction LXIX

GARCÍA MÁRQUEZ

One night [at college] a friend lent me a book of short stories by
Franz Kafka. I went back to the pension where I was staying and began to read *The Metamorphosis*. The first line almost knocked me off
the bed, I was so surprised. The first line reads, "As Gregor Samsa
awoke that morning from uneasy dreams, he found himself transformed in his bed into a gigantic insect. . . ." When I read the line I
thought to myself that I didn't know anyone was allowed to write
things like that. If I had known, I would have started writing a long
time ago. So I immediately started writing short stories.

Issue 82, 1981

Mario Vargas Llosa

✠

from The Art of Fiction CXX

VARGAS LLOSA

In the beginning there's something very nebulous, a state of alert, a wariness, a curiosity. Something I perceive in the fog and vagueness which arouses my interest, curiosity, and excitement and then translates itself into work, note cards, the summary of the plot. Then when I have the outline and start to put things in order, something very diffuse, very nebulous still persists. The "illumination" only occurs during the work. It's the hard work that, at any given time, can unleash that . . . heightened perception, that excitement capable of bringing about revelation, solution, and light. When I reach the heart of a story I've been working on for some time, then, yes, something does happen. The story ceases to be cold, unrelated to me. On the contrary, it becomes so alive, so important that everything I experience exists only in relation to what I'm writing. Everything I hear, see, read seems in one way or another to help my work. I become a kind of cannibal of reality. But to reach this state, I have to go through the catharsis of work. I live a kind of permanent double life.

Tennessee Williams

※

from The Art of Theater V

WILLIAMS

The process by which the idea for a play comes to me has always been something I really couldn't pinpoint. A play just seems to materialize, like an apparition it gets clearer and clearer and clearer. It's very vague at first, as in the case of *Streetcar,* which came after *Menagerie.* I simply had the vision of a woman in her late youth. She was sitting in a chair all alone by a window with the moonlight streaming in on her desolate face, and she'd been stood up by the man she planned to marry.

I believe I was thinking of my sister because she was madly in love with some young man at the International Shoe Company who paid her court. He was extremely handsome, and she was profoundly in love with him. Whenever the phone would ring, she'd nearly faint. She'd think it was he calling for a date, you know? They saw each other every other night, and then one time he just didn't call anymore. That was when Rose first began to go into a mental decline. From that vision *Streetcar* evolved. I called it, at the time, *Blanche's Chair in the Moon*, which is a very bad title. But it was from that image, you know, of a woman sitting by a window that *Streetcar* came to me.

Gertrude Stein

※

from A Radio Interview

STEIN

I was walking in the gardens of the Luxembourg in Paris it was the
end of summer the grass was yellow I was sorry that it was the end of
summer and I saw the big fat pigeons in the yellow grass and I said to
myself, pigeons on the yellow grass alas, and I kept on writing pigeons on the grass, alas, short longer grass short longer longer shorter
yellow grass pigeons large pigeons on the shorter longer yellow grass,
alas pigeons on the grass, and I kept on writing until I had emptied
myself of the emotion.

Issue 116, 1990

Octavio Paz

❄

from The Art of Poetry XLII

PAZ

Each poem is different. Often the first line is a gift, I don't know if from the gods or from that mysterious faculty called inspiration. Let me use *Sun Stone* as an example: I wrote the first thirty verses as if someone were silently dictating them to me. I was surprised at the fluidity with which those hendecasyllabic lines appeared one after another. They came from far off and from nearby, from within my own chest. Suddenly the current stopped flowing. I read what I'd written: I didn't have to change a thing. But it was only a beginning, and I had no idea where those lines were going. A few days later, I tried to get started again, not in a passive way but trying to orient and direct the flow of verses. I wrote another thirty or forty lines. I stopped. I went back to it a few days later and, little by little, I began to discover the theme of the poem and where it was all heading. It was a kind of a review of my life, a resurrection of my experiences, my concerns, my failures, my obsessions. I realized I was living the end of my youth and that the poem was simultaneously an end and a new beginning.

Issue 119, 1991

E.L. Doctorow

⚏

from The Art of Fiction XCIV

DOCTOROW

What you call the poem [from *Loon Lake*] was the very first writing I did on that book. I never thought of it as a poem, I thought of it as lines that just didn't happen to go all the way across the page. I broke the lines according to the rhythm in which they could be read aloud. I didn't know it at the time, but I was writing something to be read aloud—I think because I liked the sound of the two words together— *loon lake*. I had these opening images of a private railroad train on a single track at night going up through the Adirondacks with a bunch of gangsters on board, and a beautiful girl standing, naked, holding a white dress up in front of a mirror to see if she should put it on. I didn't know where these gangsters came from. I knew where they were going—to this rich man's camp. Many years ago the very wealthy discovered the wilderness in the American eastern mountains. They built these extraordinary camps—C.W. Post, Harriman, Morgan— they made the wilderness their personal luxury. So I imagined a camp like this, with these gangsters, these lowdown people going up there on a private railroad train. That's what got me started. I published this material in the *Kenyon Review,* but I wasn't through. I kept think- ing about the images and wondering where they'd come from. The time was in the 1930s, really the last era a man would have had his own railroad car, as some people today have their own jetliners. There was a depression then, so the person to see this amazing train was obviously a hobo, a tramp. So then I had my character, Joe, out there in this chill, this darkness, seeing the headlamp of the engine coming round the bend and blinding him, and then as the train goes by seeing these people at green baize tables being served drinks and this girl standing in a bedroom compartment holding the dress. And at dawn he follows the track in the direction the train has gone. And he's off and running and so am I.

Joseph Heller

✠

from The Art of Fiction LI

HELLER

I was lying in bed in my four-room apartment on the West Side when suddenly this line [the first line of *Catch-22*] came to me: "It was love at first sight. The first time he saw the chaplain, Someone fell madly in love with him." I didn't have the name Yossarian. The chaplain wasn't necessarily an army chaplain—he could have been a *prison* chaplain. But as soon as the opening sentence was available, the book began to evolve clearly in my mind—even most of the particulars . . . the tone, the form, many of the characters, including some I eventually couldn't use. All of this took place within an hour and a half. It got me so excited that I did what the cliché says you're supposed to do: I jumped out of bed and paced the floor. That morning I went to my job at the advertising agency and wrote out the first chapter in longhand. Before the end of the week I had typed it out and sent it to Candida Donadio, my agent. One year later, after much planning, I began chapter two.

Issue 60, 1974

Italo Calvino

⌘

from The Art of Fiction CXXX

CALVINO
I'm very slow getting started. If I have an idea for a novel, I find every conceivable pretext to not work on it. If I'm doing a book of stories, short texts, each one has its own starting time. Even with articles, I'm a slow starter. Even with articles for newspapers, every time I have the same trouble getting under way. Once I have started, then I can be quite fast. In other words, I write fast, but I have huge blank periods. It's a bit like the story of the great Chinese artist: the Emperor asked him to draw a crab, and the artist answered, "I need ten years, a great house, and twenty servants." The ten years went by, and the Emperor asked him for the drawing of the crab. "I need another two years," he said. Then he asked for a further week. And finally he picked up his pen and drew the crab in a moment, with a single, rapid gesture.

Chinua Achebe

from The Art of Fiction CXXXIX

INTERVIEWER
Is writing easy for you? Or do you find it difficult?

ACHEBE
The honest answer is, it's difficult. But the word *difficult* doesn't really express what I mean. It is like wrestling; you are wrestling with ideas and with the story. There is a lot of energy required. At the same time, it is exciting. So it is both difficult and easy. What you must accept is that your life is not going to be the same while you are writing. I have said in the kind of exaggerated manner of writers and prophets that writing, for me, is like receiving a term of imprisonment: you know that's what you're in for, for whatever time it takes. So it is both pleasurable and difficult.

Paul Bowles

※

from The Art of Fiction LXVII

BOWLES

I don't feel that I wrote these books. I feel as though they had been written by my arm, by my brain, my organism, but that they're not necessarily mine. The difficulty is that I've never thought anything belonged to me. At one time, I bought an island off Ceylon and I thought that when I had my two feet planted on it I'd be able to say: "This island is mine." I couldn't; it was meaningless. I felt nothing at all, so I sold it.

Issue 81, 1981

John Updike

❈

from The Art of Fiction XLIII

UPDIKE

When I write, I aim in my mind not toward New York but toward a vague spot a little to the east of Kansas. I think of the books on library shelves, without their jackets, years old, and a countryish teenaged boy finding them, and having them speak to him. The reviews, the stacks in Brentano's are just hurdles to get over, to place the books on that shelf.

John Mortimer

✠

from The Art of Fiction CVI

MORTIMER

I found writing novels rather a lonely business. You very rarely actually catch anyone reading them. I've heard of a novelist who got onto the tube at Piccadilly Circus for the purpose of getting out at Green Park, a distance of one stop. And as he got onto the tube he found himself sitting next to a girl who was in fact reading one of his novels. And he knew that two hundred pages further on there was a joke. So he sat on till Cockfosters, the end of the line, in the faint hope of hearing a laugh which never came.

Issue 109, 1988

Robert Creeley

from The Art of Poetry X

CREELEY

One time, again some years ago, Franz Kline was being questioned—not with hostility but with intensity, by another friend—and finally he said, "Well, look, if I paint what *you* know, then that will simply bore you, the repetition from me to you. If I paint what *I* know, it will be boring to myself. Therefore I paint what I don't know." Well, I believe that. I write what I don't know.

Thornton Wilder

❖

from The Art of Fiction XVI

WILDER

I think I write in order to discover on my shelf a new book which I would enjoy reading, or to see a new play that would engross me. That is why the first months of work on a new project are so delightful: you see the book already bound, or the play already produced, and you have the illusion that you will read or see it as though it were a work by another that will give you pleasure.

Issue 15, 1957

Wendy Wasserstein

⚎

from The Art of Theater XII

WASSERSTEIN

Sitting in the garage in a nightgown with a typewriter—it might be the only time I'm calm. It's an ageless sort of happiness. It's what made me happy when I was twenty-seven and writing *Uncommon Women,* and what made me feel happy last summer. I'm a pretty nervous gal. So there is always the anxiety of writing, which is awful, but at those moments I do feel at one.

Issue 142, 1992

Ernest Hemingway

✠

from The Art of Fiction XXI

HEMINGWAY

The stories you mention I wrote in one day in Madrid on May 16 when it snowed out the San Isidro bullfights. First I wrote *The Killers* which I'd tried to write before and failed. Then after lunch I got in bed to keep warm and wrote *Today Is Friday*. I had so much juice I thought maybe I was going crazy and I had about six other stories to write. So I got dressed and walked to Fornos, the old bull fighter's café, and drank coffee and then came back and wrote *Ten Indians*. This made me very sad and I drank some brandy and went to sleep. I'd forgotten to eat and one of the waiters brought me up some Bacalao and a small steak and fried potatoes and a bottle of valdepeñas.

The woman who ran the pension was always worried that I did not eat enough and she had sent the waiter. I remember sitting up in bed and eating, and drinking the Valdepeñas. The waiter said he would bring up another bottle. He said the señora wanted to know if I was going to write all night. I said no, I thought I would lay off for a while. Why don't you try to write just one more, the waiter asked. I'm only supposed to write one, I said. Nonsense, he said. You could write six. I'll try tomorrow, I said. Try it tonight, he said. What do you think the old woman sent the food up for?

I'm tired, I told him. Nonsense, he said (the word was not *nonsense*). You tired after three miserable little stories. Translate me one.

Leave me alone, I said. How am I going to write it if you don't leave me alone. So I sat up in bed and drank the Valdepeñas and thought what a hell of a writer I was if the first story was as good as I'd hoped.

Issue 18, 1958

James Salter

✠

from The Art of Fiction CXXXIII

SALTER

What is the ultimate impulse to write? Because all this is going to vanish. The only thing left will be the prose and poems, the books, what is written down. Man was very fortunate to have invented the book. Without it the past would completely vanish, and we would be left with nothing, we would be naked on earth.

Don DeLillo

✠

from The Art of Fiction CXXXV

DELILLO

Writing is a concentrated form of thinking. I don't know what I think about certain subjects, even today, until I sit down and try to write about them. Maybe I wanted to find more rigorous ways of thinking. We're talking now about the earliest writing I did and about the power of language to counteract the wallow of late adolescence, to define things, define muddled experience in economical ways: Let's not forget that writing is convenient. It requires the simplest tools. A young writer sees that with words and sentences on a piece of paper that costs less than a penny he can place himself more clearly in the world. Words on a page, that's all it takes to help him separate himself from the forces around him, streets and people and pressures and feelings. He learns to think about these things, to ride his own sentences into new perceptions.

Issue 128, 1993

Henry Miller

✠

from The Art of Fiction XXVIII

MILLER
Each man has his own way. After all, most writing is done away from the typewriter, away from the desk. I'd say it occurs in the quiet, silent moments, while you're walking or shaving or playing a game or whatever, or even talking to someone you're not vitally interested in. You're working, your mind is working, on this problem in the back of your head. So, when you get to the machine it's a mere matter of transfer.

•

What is an artist? He's a man who has antennae, who knows how to hook up to the currents which are in the atmosphere, in the cosmos; he merely has the facility for hooking on, as it were. Who is original? Everything that we are doing, everything that we think, exists already, and we are only intermediaries, that's all, who make use of what is in the air. Why do ideas, why do great scientific discoveries often occur in different parts of the world at the same time? The same is true of the elements that go to make up a poem or a great novel or any work of art. They are already in the air, they have not been given voice, that's all. They need *the* man, *the* interpreter, to bring them forth.

Issue 28, 1962

William Faulkner

✠

from The Art of Fiction XII

FAULKNER

Always dream and shoot higher than you know you can do. Don't bother just to be better than your contemporaries or predecessors. Try to be better than yourself. An artist is a creature driven by demons. He don't know why they choose him and he's usually too busy to wonder why. He is completely amoral in that he will rob, borrow, beg, or steal from anybody and everybody to get the work done.

●

The writer's only responsibility is to his art. He will be completely ruthless if he is a good one. He has a dream. It anguishes him so much he must get rid of it. He has no peace until then. Everything goes by the board: honor, pride, decency, security, happiness, all, to get the book written. If a writer has to rob his mother, he will not hesitate; the "Ode on a Grecian Urn" is worth any number of old ladies.

Issue 12, 1956

Elizabeth Hardwick

⌖

from The Art of Fiction LXXXVII

HARDWICK

As I have grown older I see myself as fortunate in many ways. It is fortunate to have had all my life this passion for studying and enjoying literature and for trying to add a bit to it as interestingly as I can. This passion has given me much joy, it has given me friends who care for the same things, it has given me employment, escape from boredom, everything. The greatest gift is the passion for reading. It is cheap, it consoles, it distracts, it excites, it gives you knowledge of the world and experience of a wide kind. It is a moral illumination.

The Contributors

Chinua Achebe is the author of several novels, including *Things Fall Apart* and, most recently, *Home and Exile*. He was interviewed by **Jerome Brooks.**

Agha Shahid Ali (1949–2001) wrote several volumes of poetry, including *The Country Without a Post Office*, in which "A History of Paisley" appears, and *Rooms Are Never Finished: Poems.*

A.R. Ammons (1926–2001) received the National Book Award in Poetry in 1973 for *Collected Poems, 1951–1973* and in 1993 for *Garbage.*

John Ashbery won both the Pulitzer Prize and the National Book Award in 1976 for *Self-Portrait in a Convex Mirror*. His most recent volume of poetry is *As Umbrellas Follow Rain.*

Margaret Atwood received the Governer General's Award in 1966 for her collection of poetry *The Circle Game* and in 1986 for her novel *The Handmaid's Tale*. Her most recent novel is *The Blind Assassin*. She was interviewed by **Mary Morris.**

Paul Auster's novels include *In the Country of Last Things,* of which the story in this anthology was an excerpt, and, most recently, *The Book of Illusions.*

James Baldwin (1924–1987) wrote many novels and works of nonfiction, including *Go Tell It on the Mountain* and *Nobody Knows My Name: More Notes of a Native Son*. He was interviewed by **Jordan Elgrably.**

Donald Barthelme (1931–1989) wrote many novels and collections of short stories, including *Snow White* and *Sixty Stories,* in which the story in this anthology appears.

Priscilla Becker received *The Paris Review* Prize in Poetry in 2000 for her first collection of poems, *Internal West.*

Louis Begley has written several novels, including *About Schmidt* and, most recently, *Schmidt Delivered*. He was interviewed by **James Atlas**.

Elizabeth Bishop (1911–1979) received the Pulitzer Prize in Poetry in 1956 for *Poems: North and South* and the National Book Critics' Circle Award for Poetry in 1976 for *Geography III*.

Robert Bly won the National Book Award in 1968 for *The Light Around the Body*. His most recent book is *Snowbanks North of the House*.

Jorge Louis Borges (1899–1986) shared the International Congress of Publishers' Prix Formentor with Samuel Beckett in 1961. Among his many collections of short stories is *Ficciones,* in which "Funes the Memorious" appears.

Paul Bowles (1910–1999) wrote several novels, including *The Sheltering Sky,* and many collections of short stories, including *The Delicate Prey and Other Stories* and *The Stories of Paul Bowles*. He was interviewed by **Jeffrey Bailey**.

Joel Brouwer is the author of *This Just In* and, most recently, *Exactly What Happened*.

T. Coraghessan Boyle is the author of many novels and collections of short stories, including *Greasy Lake and Other Stories,* in which "The Hector Quesadilla Story" appeared. His most recent collection is *After the Plague*.

Joseph Brodsky (1940–1996) received the Nobel Prize in Literature in 1987. His volumes of poetry include *Elegy to John Donne and Other Poems* and *To Urania: Selected Poems, 1965–1985*.

Larry Brown has written several novels and collections of short stories, including, most recently, *Fay*.

Anthony Burgess (1917–1993) wrote many novels and works of nonfiction, including *A Clockwork Orange* and *Joysprick: An Introduction to the Language of James Joyce*. He was interviewed by **John Cullinan**.

William Burroughs (1914–1997) wrote several novels, including *Junkie* and *Naked Lunch*. He was interviewed by **Conrad Knickerbocker**.

A.S. Byatt's novels include *Possession: A Romance,* for which she was awarded the Booker Prize in 1990, and, most recently, *A Whistling Woman*.

Italo Calvino (1923–1985) wrote several novels and collections of short stories, including *If on a Winter's Night a Traveler* and *Invisible Cities*. He was interviewed by **William Weaver**.

Kevin Cantwell's first collection of poems, *Something Black in the Green Part of Your Eye,* was published in 2002.

Truman Capote (1924–1984) wrote many books, including *Breakfast at Tiffany's: A Novel and Three Stories* and *In Cold Blood: A True Account* *of a Multiple Murder and Its Consequences*. He was interviewed by **Pati Hill**.

John le Carre's novels include *The Tailor of Panama* and, most recently, *The Constant Gardener*. He was interviewed by **George Plimpton**.

Jim Carroll's books include *The Basketball Diaries*, in which the piece in this anthology appears, and, most recently, *Void of Course: Poems 1994–1997*.

Anne Carson's books include *Plainwater: Essays and Poetry* and, most recently, *The Beauty of the Husband: A Fictional Essay in Twenty-nine Tangoes*.

Raymond Carver (1938–1988) wrote two volumes of poetry and many collections of short stories, among them *Will You Please Be Quiet, Please?* and *Where I'm Calling From: Selected Stories*, in which the story in this anthology appears.

John Cheever (1912–1982) wrote several novels and many collections of short stories, including *The Wapshot Chronicle* and *The Stories of John Cheever*.

Nicholas Christopher's most recent publications include a novel, *Atomic: Two Poems and A Trip to the Stars*.

Lucille Clifton has written many collections of poetry, including *An Ordinary Woman* and, most recently, *Blessing the Boats: New and Selected Poems 1988–2000*.

Billy Collins is the eleventh U.S. Poet Laureate. His works include *Picnic, Lightning*, in which the poem in this anthology appears, and, most recently, *Nine Horses: Poems*.

Bernard Cooper is the author of a collection of autobiographical poems and essays, *Maps to Anywhere*, and a collection of short stories, *Guess Again*.

Jim Crace received the National Book Critics' Circle Award for Fiction in 2001 for *Being Dead*. The piece in this anthology appears in his most recent collection of short stories, *The Devil's Larder*.

Robert Creeley's many books of poetry include *For Love: Poems 1950–1960* and, most recently, *Just in Time: Poems 1984–1994*. He was interviewed by **Linda Wagner-Martin** and **Lewis MacAdams, Jr.**

Michael Cunningham received the Pulitzer Prize for Fiction in 1999 for his most recent novel, *The Hours*.

Charles D'Ambrosio received *The Paris Review*'s Aga Khan Prize for Fiction in 1993 for "Her Real Name," which also appeared in his first collection of short stories, *The Point*.

Peter Ho Davies is the author of two collections of short stories, *The Ugliest House in the World* and *Equal Love*.

Don DeLillo's novels include *White Noise,* for which he won the National Book Award in 1985, and, most recently, *The Body Artist: A Novel.* He was interviewed by **Adam Begley**.

E.L. Doctorow is a novelist and playwright whose works include *Ragtime, Loon Lake,* and, most recently, *City of God.* He was interviewed by **George Plimpton**.

Ben Downing is the managing editor of *Parnassus: Poetry in Review.*

Stephen Dunn received the Pulitzer Prize for Poetry in 2001 for his most recent volume of poetry, *Different Hours.*

Umberto Eco's many books include *The Name of the Rose* and, most recently, *Baudolino.*

Stanley Elkin (1930–1995) received the National Book Critics' Circle Award for Fiction in 1982 for *George Mills* and in 1995 for *Mrs. Ted Bliss.*

Louise Erdrich received the National Book Critics' Circle Award for Fiction in 1984 for *Love Medicine.* Her most recent novel is *The Last Report on the Miracles at Little No Horse.*

Jeffrey Eugenides's most recent novel is *Middlesex.* The story in this anthology received *The Paris Review*'s Aga Khan Prize in 1991 and became the first chapter of his first novel, *The Virgin Suicides.*

William Faulkner (1897–1962) wrote many collections of poetry and short stories, as well as novels, among them *As I Lay Dying* and *A Fable,* for which he was awarded the Pulitzer Prize and the National Book Award in 1955. He was interviewed by **Jean Stein**.

Irving Feldman is the author of many collections of poems, among them *Leaping Clear* and, most recently, *Beautiful False Things.*

Zelda Fitzgerald (1900–1948) was married to F. Scott Fitzgerald. She also painted and wrote plays and novels, among them *Scandalabra* and *Save Me the Waltz.*

Jonathan Franzen's most recent book is *How to Be Alone.* The story in this anthology is an early draft of the first chapter of his novel *The Corrections.*

Jonathan Galassi is the author of *Morning Run* and, most recently, *North Street.*

Allen Ginsberg (1926–1997) wrote many books of poetry, among them *Howl, New Year Blues,* and *Death and Fame: Poems, 1993–1997.*

Albert Goldbarth received the National Book Critics' Circle Award in 2002 for *Saving Lives: Poems.* He also has written numerous essay collections, most recently, *Many Circles: New and Selected Essays.*

Edward Gorey (1925–2000) illustrated many books, including *The Dong with a Luminous Nose* by Edward Lear and *The Old Possum's Book of*

Practical Cats by T.S. Eliot. He also wrote and self-illustrated several books, including *The Wuggly Ump* and *The Beastly Baby*.

Eliza Griswold is a contributing editor of *The Paris Review*.

Thom Gunn (1925–2004) is the author of many collections of poetry, including *Selected Poems 1950–1975* and, most recently, *Boss Cupid*.

Beth Gylys is the author of *Balloon Heart* and, most recently, *Bodies that Hum*.

Marilyn Hacker's many collections of poetry include *Assumptions* and, most recently, *Squares and Courtyards*.

Rachel Hadas has written many books of poetry, essays, and translations, including *Living in Time* and, most recently, *The Double Legacy*.

Donald Hall was the poetry editor of *The Paris Review* from 1953 to 1961. His recent books include *Principal Products of Portugal: Prose Pieces* and *Donald Hall in Conversation with Ian Hamilton*.

Barbara Hamby's collections of poems include *The Alphabet of Desire* and, most recently, *Delirium*.

Elizabeth Hardwick is the author of several novels, collections of short stories, and works of nonfiction. Her most recent book is a biography, *Herman Melville*. She was interviewed by **Darryl Pinckney**.

Seamus Heaney received the Nobel Prize for Literature in 1995. His most recent collection of poems is *Electric Light*. He was interviewed by **Henri Cole.**

Anthony Hecht received the Pulitzer Prize in 1968 for *The Hard Hours*. His most recent book is *The Darkness and the Light*.

Joseph Heller (1923–1999) wrote several novels, including *Catch-22* and *God Knows*. He was interviewed by **George Plimpton**.

Ernest Hemingway (1899–1961) received the Pulitzer Prize in 1953 for *The Old Man and the Sea* and the Nobel Prize for Literature in 1954. He was interviewed by **George Plimpton**.

Geoffrey Hill received the Whitbread Award in 1971 for *Mercian Hymns*. His most recent collection of poems is *The Orchards of Syon*.

John Hollander's many collections of poetry include *In Time and Place* and, most recently, *War Poems*.

Richard Howard is the poetry editor of *The Paris Review*. He received the Pulitzer Prize in 1970 for *Untitled Subjects*. His most recent collection of poetry is *If I Dream I Have You, I Have You: Poems*.

Ted Hughes (1930–1998) was the British Poet Laureate from 1984 until his death. His publications include *Animal Poems* and *The Birthday Letters*. He was interviewed by **Drue Heinz**.

John Irving is the author of many novels, including *The World According to Garp*, which received the American Book Award in 1980, and *The*

Cider House Rules. His most recent book is an autobiography, *The Imaginary Girlfriend.* He was interviewed by **Ron Hansen**.

David Jackson's stories have appeared in the O. Henry Prize volumes. He collaborated with James Merrill at the Ouija board for over thirty-five years.

Ha Jin received the National Book Award in 1999 for *Waiting.* His most recent book is a collection of short stories, *The Crazed.*

Denis Johnson is the author of several novels, among them *Jesus' Son,* in which the story in this anthology appears, and, most recently, *Shopping: Two Plays.*

Jack Kerouac (1922–1969) wrote many novels and collections of poetry. The story in this anthology is part of his first novel, *On the Road.*

Galway Kinnell received the Pulitzer Prize in 1983 for *Selected Poems.* His most recent collection is *A New Selected Poems.*

Susan Kinsolving's collections of poetry include *Among Flowers* and, most recently, *Dailies and Rushes.*

Kenneth Koch (1925–2002) wrote many collections of poetry, including *When the Sun Tries to Go On* and *New Address,* for which he was awarded the National Book Award in 2000.

Yusef Komunyakaa's works include *I Apologize for the Eyes in My Head* and, most recently, *Pleasure Dome: New and Collected Poems.*

Philip Larkin (1922–1985) wrote many collections of poetry, including *The North Ship* and *High Windows.* He was interviewed by **Robert Phillips**.

Jonathan Lethem received the National Book Critics' Circle Award in 1999 for *Motherless Brooklyn,* from which the story in this anthology was excerpted. His most recent novel is *This Shape We're In.*

Primo Levi (1919–1987) wrote many novels and volumes of poetry, including *The Periodic Table* and *The Mirror Maker.* He was interviewed by **Gabriel Motola.**

Daniel S. Libman received *The Paris Review*'s Discovery Prize in 1999 for "In the Belly of the Cat."

Mario Vargas Llosa received the National Book Critics' Circle Award for Criticism for *Making Waves.* His most recent novel is *The Feast of the Goat.* The interview was conducted by **Ricardo Setti** and translated by **Susannah Hunnewell.**

Barry Lopez's books include *Desert Notes: Reflections in the Eye of a Raven* and, most recently, *Light Action in the Caribbean.*

Malcolm Lowry (1909–1957) wrote several novels, including *Under the Volcano,* and a novella, *Lunar Caustic,* from which the story in this anthology was excerpted.

Elizabeth Macklin is the author of *A Woman Kneeling in the Big City* and, most recently, *You've Just Been Told.*

Norman Mailer received a Pulitzer Prize in 1969 for *Armies of the Night* and in 1979 for *The Executioner's Song.* His most recent novel is *The Gospel According to the Son.*

Gabriel García Márquez was awarded the Nobel Prize for Literature in 1982. His most recent novel is *Of Love and Other Demons.* He was interviewed by **Peter H. Stone.**

Bobbie Ann Mason's books include *Shiloh and Other Stories* and, most recently, *Zigzagging Down a Wild Trail.*

Mary McCarthy (1912–1989) wrote novels, including *The Group* and *Cannibals and Missionaries,* essays, and literary criticism. She was awarded the National Medal for Literature in 1984. She was interviewed by **Elisabeth Sifton.**

J.D. McClatchy is the editor of *The Yale Review.* His most recent book of poems is *Twenty Questions.*

Ian McEwan received the Booker Prize in 1998 for his novel *Amsterdam.* His most recent novel is *Atonement.* He was interviewed by **Adam Begley.**

Heather McHugh is the author of several books of poetry, including *Hinge and Sign: Poems 1968–1993* and *The Father of the Predicaments.* Her most recent book is a translation, *Euripides: Cyclops.*

Jay McInerney's books include *Bright Lights, Big City,* from which the story in this anthology was taken, and, most recently, *Bacchus & Me: Adventures in the Wine Cellar.*

Maile Meloy received *The Paris Review*'s Aga Khan Prize for Fiction in 2001 for "Aqua Boulevard," which appeared in her first collection of short stories, *Half in Love.*

James Merrill (1926–1995) was awarded the Pulitzer Prize in 1976 for *Divine Comedies* and the National Book Critics' Circle Award for Fiction in 1989 for *The Changing Light at Sandover.*

W.S. Merwin received the Pulitzer Prize in 1971 for *The Carrier of Ladders.* His most recent book of poetry is *The Pupil.*

Henry Miller's (1891–1980) books include *Tropic of Cancer* and *Black Spring.* He was interviewed by **George Wickes.**

Susan Mitchell's collections of poetry include *Rapture* and, most recently, *Erotikon.*

John Montague is the author of many collections of poetry, including *Collected Poems* and, most recently, *Smashing the Piano.*

Rick Moody's most recent books are the story collection *Demonology* and *The Black Veil: A Memoir with Digressions.* "The Ring of Brightest Angels Around Heaven" was awarded *The Paris Review*'s Aga Khan Prize for Fiction in 1994.

Lorrie Moore's books include *Who Will Run the Frog Hospital?* and *Birds of America,* in which the story in this anthology appears.

Honor Moore's books include a play, *Mourning Pictures,* and, most recently, a volume of poetry, *Darling.*

Toni Morrison received the Pulitzer Prize in 1988 for *Beloved* and the Nobel Prize for Literature in 1993. She was interviewed by **Claudia Brodsky Lacour** and **Elissa Schappell.**

John Mortimer has written many novels, including *Rumpole of the Bailey* and, most recently, *Rumpole Rests His Case.* He was interviewed by **Rosemary Herbert.**

Alice Munro received the National Book Critics' Circle Award for Fiction in 1998 for *The Love of a Good Woman.* Her most recent collection of short stories is *Hateship, Friendship, Courtship, Loveship, Marriage: Stories.*

Les Murray's many collections of poetry include *The Weatherboard Cathedral* and, most recently, *Learning Human: Selected Poems.*

Vladimir Nabokov (1899–1977) was awarded the National Medal for Literature in 1973. Among his novels are *Lolita* and *Speak, Memory.* He was interviewed by **Herbert Gold.**

V.S. Naipaul was awarded the Nobel Prize for Literature in 2001. His novels include *A House for Mr. Biswas* and *Half a Life.* His most recent book is *The Writer and the World.* He was interviewed by **Jonathan Rosen.**

Joyce Carol Oates's many books include the novel *them,* for which she won the National Book Award in 1970, *Heat and Other Stories,* in which the story in this anthology appears, and, most recently, *Beasts.*

Frank O'Hara's (1926–1966) many collections of poetry include *A City Winter and Other Poems,* and *The Collected Poems of Frank O'Hara,* which was awarded the National Book Award in 1972.

Jacqueline Osherow's collections of poetry include *Conversations with Survivors* and, most recently, *Dead Men's Praise.*

Grace Paley has written many collections of short stories, including *The Little Disturbances of Man: Stories of Women and Men at Love* and *The Collected Stories.* Her most recent book is *Begin Again: Collected Poems.*

Octavio Paz (1914–1998) wrote many collections of poetry, including *Selected Poems of Octavio Paz* and *Delta de cinco brazos.* He was awarded the Nobel Prize for Literature in 1990. He was interviewed by **Alfred Mac Adam.**

Kathleen Peirce's collections of poetry include *Mercy* and, most recently, *The Oval Hour: Poems.*

Robert Pinsky served as the tenth U.S. Poet Laureate from 1997 to 2000. His most recent volume of poetry is *Jersey Rain.*

Harold Pinter's many plays include *The Caretaker: A Play in Three Acts* and *The Homecoming: A Play in Two Acts.* He was interviewed by **Larry M. Bensky.**

Marie Ponsot received the National Book Critics' Circle Award in 1998 for her most recent collection of poetry, *The Bird Catcher.*

Ezra Pound (1885–1972) wrote many collections of poetry, including *The Cantos (1–109).* He was interviewed by **Donald Hall.**

Susan Power is the author of *The Grass Dancer* and *Strong Heart Society.*

Bin Ramke has written several books of poetry, including *The Difference Between Night and Day* and, most recently, *Airs, Waters, Places: Poems.*

Melanie Rehak's poems have appeared in *Salmagundi, Partisan Review,* and *The New Republic.*

Siri von Reis has written several books on ethnobiology and a volume of poetry, *The Love-Suicides at Sonezaki.*

Adrienne Rich received the National Book Award in 1974 for *Diving into the Wreck: Poems 1971–1972.* Her most recent book is *Fox: Poems 1998–2000.*

Mordecai Richler (1931–2001) received *The Paris Review*'s John Train Humor Prize in 1967 for "A Liberal Education" and the Governor-General's Literary Award in 1968 for the novel from which this story was taken, *Cocksure and Hunting Tigers Under Glass.*

Pattiann Rogers's many volumes of poetry include *The Expectations of Light* and, most recently, *Song of the World Becoming: Poems, New and Collected, 1981–2001.*

S.X. Rosenstock is the author of *United Artists: Poems.*

Philip Roth received *The Paris Review*'s Aga Khan Prize for Fiction in 1958 and the National Book Award in 1960 for *Goodbye, Columbus.* His most recent novel is *The Dying Animal.*

Kay Ryan's collections of poetry include *Flamingo Watching* and, most recently, *Say Uncle: Poems.*

James Salter's works include *The Hunters, Dusk and Other Stories,* and, most recently, a memoir, *Burning the Days: Recollections.* He was interviewed by **Edward Hirsch.**

Grace Schulman has written several collections of poetry, including *Hemispheres* and, most recently, *Days of Wonder: New and Selected Poems.*

Lloyd Schwartz received the Pulitzer Prize for Criticism in 1994. His most recent volume of poetry is *Cairo Traffic.*

Joanna Scott's books include the story collection *Various Antidotes,* in which the story in this anthology appears, and, most recently, the novel *Tourmaline.*

Robyn Selman is the author of *Directions to My House.*

Patty Seyburn's volumes of poetry include *Diasporadic: Poems* and, most recently, *Mechanical Cluster.*

Vijay Seshadri is the author of *Wild Kingdoms.*

Jim Shepard's books include *Batting Against Castro,* in which the story in this anthology appeared, and, most recently, *Nosferatu.*

Charles Simic received the Pulitzer Prize in 1990 for *The World Doesn't End.* His most recent collection of poems is *Night Picnic.*

Charlie Smith's recent publications include a novel, *Cheap Ticket to Heaven,* and a collection of poems, *Heroin and Other Poems.*

Gary Snyder received the Pulitzer Prize in 1975 for *Turtle Island.* His most recent book is *Mountains and Rivers Without End.*

Susan Sontag received the National Book Award in 2000 for *In America.* Her most recent book is a collection of essays, *Where the Stress Falls.* She was interviewed by **Edward Hirsch**.

Gertrude Stein (1874–1946) wrote many works of fiction and nonfiction, including *Things as They Are: A Novel in Three Parts* and *The Autobiography of Alice B. Toklas.*

Robert Stone received the National Book Award in 1975 for *Dog Soldiers* and the National Book Critics' Circle Award for Fiction in 1982 for *A Flag for Sunrise.* "The Ascent of Mount Carmel" is an excerpt from *Children of Light.* His most recent novel is *Damascus Gate.*

William Styron's many novels include *Sophie's Choice* and *The Confessions of Nat Turner,* for which he received the Pulitzer Prize in 1968.

May Swenson (1919–1989) wrote many collections of poetry, among them *Iconographs* and *May Out West.*

Hunter S. Thompson's many books include *Fear and Loathing in Las Vegas* and, most recently, *Fear and Loathing in America: Brutal Odyssey of an Outlaw Journalist.* He was interviewed by **George Plimpton** and **Terry McDonell.**

Charles Tomlinson is the author of many volumes of poetry, including *The Necklace* and, most recently, *Selected Poems, 1955–1997.*

John Updike's most recent novel is *Seek My Face.* He was interviewed by **Charles Thomas Samuels.**

Karen Volkman is the author of *Crash's Law: Poems* and *Spar: Poems.*

William T. Vollmann's books include *The Rainbow Stories* and, most recently, *Argall.* He was interviewed by **Madison Smartt Bell.**

Kurt Vonnegut's many novels include *Slaughterhouse-Five* and, most recently, *Timequake.* He was interviewed by **Richard L. Rhodes, George Plimpton, David Michaelis,** and **David Hayman.**

David Wagoner is the editor of *Poetry Northwest*. His most recent books include *Traveling Light: Collected and New Poems* and *Walt Whitman Bathing*.

Anne Waldman's collections of poetry include *On the Wing, Shaman,* and *Kin*.

David Foster Wallace is the author of several novels, including *Infinite Jest* and, most recently, *Brief Interviews with Hideous Men*.

Eugene Walter (1927–1998) was the author of *Monkey Poems* and *Milking the Moon: A Southerner's Story of Life on This Planet*.

Rosanna Warren is the author of several volumes of poetry, including *Snow Day* and *Stained Glass*.

Wendy Wasserstein's plays include *The Heidi Chronicles, The Sisters Rosenzweig,* and, most recently, *An American Daughter*. She was interviewed by **Laurie Winer**.

Paul West has written poetry, criticism, essays, novels, and short stories. His recent fiction publications include *Terrestrials: A Novel of Aviation* and *Life with Swan*.

Rachel Wetzsteon is the author of *The Other Stars* and *Home and Away*.

Edmund White received the National Book Critics' Circle Award for Biography in 1994 for *Genet: A Biography*. He has written several novels, including, most recently, *The Married Man*. He was interviewed by **Jordan Elgrably**.

Thornton Wilder (1897–1975) received the Pulitzer Prize in 1928 for *The Bridge of San Luis Rey*, in 1938 for *Our Town*, and in 1943 for *The Skin of Our Teeth*. He was interviewed by **Richard H. Goldstone**.

Tennessee Williams (1911–1983) wrote many plays, including *The Glass Menagerie*, for which he was awarded the New York Drama Critics' Circle Award in 1945, and *Cat on a Hot Tin Roof*, for which he received the Pulitzer Prize in 1955. He was interviewed by **Dotson Raider**.

Anne Winters received the National Book Critics' Circle Award for Poetry in 1986 for *The Key to the City*. Her most recent book is *Collegial Damage*.

Jeanette Winterson has written several novels, among them *Oranges Are Not the Only Fruit* and, most recently, *The Powerbook*. She was interviewed by **Audrey Bilger**.

Charles Wright was awarded the National Book Award in Poetry for *Country Music: Selected Early Poems*. His most recent book is *Negative Blue: Selected Later Poems*.

David Yezzi is the director of the Unterberg Poetry Center at the 92nd Street Y in New York City and the author of a chapbook, *Sad Is Eros*.

Acknowledgments

The editors and readers who selected the material for this anthology include: Oceana Baity, Oliver Broudy, Charles U. Buice, David Eustace, Elizabeth Gaffney, Tara Gallagher, Benjamin Ryder Howe, Brigid Hughes, Fiona Maazel, Thomas Moffett, and Justine Post.

Allen Ginsberg, "City Midnight Junk Strains," copyright © 1968 by the Estate of Allen Ginsberg

Edward Gorey, "The Admonitory Hippopotamus: or, Angelica and Sneezby," copyright © 2002 by the Estate of Edward Gorey

Thom Gunn, "The Sacred Heart," copyright © 1988 by Thom Gunn

Beth Gylys, "Marriage Song," copyright © 1998 by Beth Gylys

Marilyn Hacker, "Migraine Sonnets," copyright © 2001 by Marilyn Hacker

Donald Hall, "The Third Inning," copyright © 1991 by Donald Hall

Barbara Hamby, "Delirium," copyright © 1995 by Barbara Hamby

Anthony Hecht, "Le Jet d'Eau," copyright © 1998 by Anthony Hecht

Ernest Hemingway, "The Art of Fiction 21: Ernest Hemingway," as it appeared in *The Paris Review*, #18 (Spring 1958), copyright © 1958 by The Paris Review, Inc. Copyright renewed © 1986. Reprinted with permission of Scribner, an imprint of Simon & Schuster Adult Publishing Group, and the Hemingway Foreign Rights Trust.

Geoffrey Hill, "A Prayer to the Sun," from *New and Collected Poems, 1952–1982*, copyright © 1994 by Geoffrey Hill. Reprinted by permission of Houghton Mifflin Company. All rights reserved.

John Hollander, "Making It," copyright © 1964 by John Hollander

Richard Howard, "With a Potpourri from Down Under," copyright © 1981 by Richard Howard

Ted Hughes, "The Art of Poetry LXXI," copyright © 1995 by the Estate of Ted Hughes

Ha Jin, "The Dead Soldier's Talk," copyright © 1986 by Ha Jin

Denis Johnson, "Car-Crash While Hitchhiking," copyright © 1989 by Denis Johnson

Jack Kerouac, "The Mexican Girl," copyright © 1955 by Jack Kerouac

Galway Kinnell, "Lackawanna," copyright © 1994 by Galway Kinnell

Kenneth Koch, "To the French Language," copyright © 2001 by Kenneth Koch

Yusef Komunyakaa, "Memory Cave," copyright © 1997 by Yusef Komunyakaa

Jonathan Lethem, "Tugboat Syndrome," copyright © 1991 by Jonathan Lethem

Daniel S. Libman, "The Belly of the Cat," copyright © 1999 by Daniel S. Libman

Barry Lopez, "The Interior of North Dakota," copyright © 1992 by Barry Lopez

Malcolm Lowry, *from* "Lunar Caustic," copyright © 1963, 1991 by the Estate of Malcolm Lowry

Pattiann Rogers, "The Fallacy of Thinking Flesh is Flesh," copyright © 1994 by Pattiann Rogers

S. X. Rosenstock, "Rimininny!", copyright © 1996 by S. X. Rosenstock

Philip Roth, "Conversion of the Jews," copyright © 1958 by Philip Roth

Joanna Scott, "You Must Relax," copyright © 1993 by Joanna Scott

Robyn Selman, "Exodus," from *Directions to My House*, copyright © 1995 by Robyn Selman. Reprinted by permission of the University of Pittsburgh Press.

Vijay Seshadri, "Ailanthus," copyright © 2002 by Vijay Seshadri

Jim Shepard, "Batting Against Castro," copyright © 1993 by Jim Shepard

Charles Simic, "Against Winter," copyright © 1995 by Charles Simic

Charlie Smith, "Los Dos Rancheros," copyright © 2000 by Charlie Smith

Gary Snyder, "Oysters," copyright © 1966 by Gary Snyder

Susan Sontag, "The Art of Fiction CXLIII," copyright © 1995 by Susan Sontag. Reprinted by permission of The Wylie Agency, Inc.

Gertrude Stein, "Radio Interview," copyright © 1990 by the Estate of Gertrude Stein

Robert Stone, "The Ascent of Mount Carmel," copyright © 1985 by Robert Stone

Charles Tomlinson, "The Broom: The New Wife's Tale," copyright © 1991 by Charles Tomlinson

John Updike, "Two Cunts in Paris," copyright © 1997 by John Updike

Anne Waldman, "Curt Flood," copyright © 1971 by Anne Waldman

David Foster Wallace, "Little Expressionless Animals," copyright © 1988 by David Foster Wallace

Eugene Walter and Katherine Clark, *from* "Milking the Moon" copyright © 2001 by Katherine Clark and the Estate of Eugene Walter. Used by permission of Crown Publishers, a division of Random House, Inc.

Rosanna Warren, "Cyprian," copyright © 2000 by Rosanna Warren

Paul West, "Blind White Fish in Belgium," copyright © 1991 by Paul West

Rachel Wetzsteon, *from* "Home and Away," copyright © 1997 by Rachel Wetzsteon

Tennessee Williams, "The Art of Theater V," copyright © 1981. Reprinted by permission of the University of the South, Sewanee, Tennessee.

Join Us for the Next Fifty Years:
SUBSCRIBE to *The Paris Review*

☐ $40 for one year (four issues)
☐ $76 for two years (eight issues)

To order a subscription (Visa, MasterCard, checks accepted):
1. Call 760.291.1553.
2. Visit The Paris Review online at *www.theparisreview.com*
3. Send a check (made out to The Paris Review Foundation) to:
   The Paris Review
   P.O. Box 469052
   Escondido, CA 92046

"*The Paris Review* is one of the few truly essential literary magazines of the twentieth century—and now of the twenty-first. Frequently weird, always wondrous."

—MARGARET ATWOOD